World War I Songs

World War I Songs

A History and Dictionary of
Popular American Patriotic Tunes,
with Over 300 Complete Lyrics

by FREDERICK G. VOGEL

McFarland & Company, Inc., Publishers
Jefferson, North Carolina, and London

British Library Cataloguing-in-Publication data are available

Library of Congress Cataloguing-in-Publication Data

World War I songs : a history and dictionary of popular American patriotic tunes, with over 300 complete lyrics / by Frederick G. Vogel.
    p. cm.
Includes bibliographical references (p.) and index.
ISBN 0-89950-952-5 (lib. bdg. : 50# alk. paper) ∞
1. War songs—United States—History and criticism. 2. War songs—United States—Bibliography. 3. War songs—United States—Texts. 4. World War, 1914–1918—Songs and music—History and criticism. 5. World War, 1914–1918—Songs and music—Bibliography. 6. World War, 1914–1918—Songs and music—Texts. I. Title.
ML3561.W3V64   1995
782.42'1599'09041—dc20   95-10420
                                                            CIP
                                                            MN

Manufactured in the United States of America

McFarland & Company, Inc., Publishers
  Box 611, Jefferson, North Carolina 28640

As always,
To Mary with Love

Table of Contents

Preface

With the exception of World War II, no episode in American history has stimulated the nation's songwriters into action more than World War I, the "Great War," the "war to end all wars" that eventually engulfed the United States 32 months after it broke out in Europe. Many of the patriotic and war songs published in America between late 1914 and mid–1919 served admirably as brief, often wildly popular, commentaries on the national nervousness caused by Austria-Hungary's declaration of war on Serbia, and, later, on the determination, and eventual success, of the American public and troops to win the war for the stalemated Allies, preserve democracy, and return peace to the Western world.

Scarcely a major American songwriter neglected to chronicle the fear and fury unleased by that tremendously savage conflict. Some, like Al Piantadosi, Al Bryan, Gus Edwards, James V. Monaco, the Von Tilzer brothers, and Charles K. Harris, were established composers and lyricists. Others—Arthur Freed, Lew Brown, Peter DeRose, Harry Ruby, and James McHugh, for example—were then on the threshold of their careers. Together with hundreds of rank amateurs whose names would never appear on the sheet music cover of a hit song, on a marquee, or in a theatrical program, these writers copyrighted more than 35,000 World War I–related marches,

patriotic anthems, and ballads, in effect creating an extended series of musical documentaries covering one of America's, and Western Europe's, most tumultuous periods.

The overwhelming majority of the minor writers' songs were never published; those that were, with a few notable exceptions, rarely retained whatever initial popularity they achieved for more than several weeks. Quickly replacing them were new tunes reechoing the derring-do and valor of Americans in battle or comforting parents and sweethearts with another promise of the swift, triumphal return of their men from No Man's Land.

In this discussion of the songs of World War I, the author sought to link their messages to specific events during America's war-preparedness years (1915–1916) and finally to its actual military participation in the gory conflict (1917–1918). The events of both periods gripped the nation to an elevated degree, initiating and then sustaining the gigantic outpouring of songs advocating a resurgence of patriotism among the citizens of an as yet uncommitted nation and, after the spring of 1917, proclaiming the certainty of the Allies' victory over the Central Powers.

Most of the song titles, of course, will not strike a chord of recognition among descendants of the World War I generation. Nevertheless, at least a minuscule number of them, including several imported from Great Britain, should be familiar to a respectable percentage of adults in the 1990s, regardless of the songwriters' tendency to indulge in pollyannish morale-building and excursions into unrestrained sentimentality. Adding to the songs' fall from fashion shortly after war's end was their strict adherence to outdated structure, which typically consisted of a wordy title followed by the mandatory two verses and single chorus, and frequent reliance on vaudeville-based humor to ridicule the enemy.

The second part of this book is a listing of *all* American World War I songs verified as published, immediately preceded by a description of the research tools used to extract the information from long-neglected archives. Each entry includes title, lyricist, composer, and year of publication. Of particular interest to American popular music historians and the growing ranks of sheet music collectors, the song list should prove of value to students of American culture during the World War I years.

The third part of the book is a compilation of the complete lyrics to more than 300 representative songs, arranged alphabetically by title. Many of the songs are illustrated with their original sheet music covers, some of which featured artwork that makes them highly prized these many decades later. Commonly reflected in the titles and lyrics are such themes as mother love, nostalgia for the war-free past, and idealistic love, all of which pervaded most of the popular non-war songs of the 1914–1919 era as well. The war-song titles are also indicative of the vital role that the marches played in stirring a reluctant nation into accepting its obligation to participate in a crusade that would forever alter the lives of its citizens after President Wilson's declaration of war on Germany on April 6, 1917.

For the most part, the songwriters performed their duty well, sympathizing with families whose sons were sent overseas to fight, cheering the troops onward

from battle to battle, and finally saluting their heroism upon their return to the States. They exceeded their creativity fourfold during the Second World War, when they copyrighted about 127,000 war and patriotic songs. Again, as with World War I, that estimated song total is based largely on the copyrighted titles of the thousands upon thousands of unknown and unavailable tunes.

Although it is not the intent of this book to cover the music of World War II in any detail, it is revealing to view the World War I songs in light of the parallel songs that emerged from World War II. Thus brief references are made to the major war songs published between late 1939 and December 7, 1941, when the Japanese attacked Pearl Harbor. The remarkable similarities between the outbreak and the early conduct of both wars—and between the songs written to describe their terrors and triumphs—are indeed noteworthy, and deserve at least brief recognition. In certain ways, a fuller picture of the World War I songs is built by such a comparison.

On January 15, 1993, with the death of Sammy Cahn, the popular music world lost one of its most gifted lyricists. The author of this book also lost a dear friend and constant helpmate. Sammy not only enthusiastically supported this history and compendium of war songs, but as one of their chief writers in World War II ("Vict'ry Polka," "I'll Walk Alone," "The Fighting 86th! The Fighting 86th! [The Fighting Men of the 86th!]," "It's Been a Long, Long Time"), he had contributed greatly to uplifting American spirits during that conflict. Although he did not live to see the book in print, I respectfully remember him with deep appreciation for his assistance and many kindnesses.

Also sharing generously in my gratitude are longtime friends Stewart and Leslie Siegel and John and Dorrie Pagones, ever available to offer wise insights into the preparation and execution of this project, to which their individual knowledge of twentieth-century history proved to be invaluable in the fact-verification process. Similar thanks for similar reasons are due Richard Fehr, my collaborator on an earlier book on popular songs from Hollywood films and discerning commentator on this one. To my patient, exacting wife, Mary, and George Porcella, I extend my heartiest praise for computerizing my handwritten material in order to present the publisher with a professionally tailored manuscript.

To Beverly A. Hamer and Catherine Fredette, of East Derry, New Hampshire, and Sandy Marrone, of Cinnaminson, New Jersey, I extend my special appreciation for their splendid cooperation in digging up numerous difficult-to-find original sheet music pieces that were absent from my own war-song collection. Mrs. Ann Pfeiffer Latella was extremely helpful in supplying me with valuable first-hand information on her grandfather, the famous sheet music illustrator Edward H. Pfeiffer, and I am in her debt for doing so with admirable promptness and thoroughness.

Thanks are also happily given to the staffs of the New York Public Library, especially its Lincoln Center Library of the Performing Arts, in New York City, and of the Library of Congress in Washington, D.C., for their assistance in evaluating and then directing me to the authoritative source materials needed to collect the names of the songs, authors, and publishers of the various musical works, and other factual data included in the book. My thanks also to several persons who permitted me to quote directly from various post–1919 popular songs that were still under copyright: Jack Rosner, vice president for special projects at Warner/Chappell Music, and Carl Michaelson, manager of the Copyright & Royalty Department of the highly esteemed Carl Fischer, Inc., which began publishing songs in New York City almost 125 years ago. Extremely helpful in gaining access to essential reference materials was L. Ward Zilliox, Sr., whose gifts of books and other materials on American songwriters of the 1900–1940 period were invaluable.

Obviously, the persons deserving the greatest tribute are the men and women who served so nobly in the war. Many never returned from the battlefield, and still others carried their combat wounds into their postwar lives without bitterness, without complaint. Heroes all, they defeated those who would extinguish the lamp of liberty and kept the home fires burning throughout the long and perilous years of one of the most horrible international conflicts in human history.

So bless 'em all—the long and the short and the tall—those patriotic, ever-dependable young Americans whose heroism and sacrifices freed an entire world from tyranny, and in whose debt succeeding generations will forever remain.

FREDERICK G. VOGEL
Maplewood, New Jersey
December 1994

Introduction: Songs of Heroism and Sacrifice

When you go home
Tell them of us, and say—
For your tomorrow
We gave our today.

Inscription on the War Memorial to the
2nd British Division, Kohima, Assam, India

Music, to Martin Luther, was "one of the fairest and most glorious gifts of God," uniquely able to lift the "weight of sorrow" from the afflicted. According to Shakespeare, "Music with her silver sound, / With speedy help doth lend redress" to the pains that wound the heart and oppress the mind. Alexander Pope wrote that music "the fiercest grief can charm, / And fate's severest rage disarm."

Certainly, the blood-soaked twentieth century has immersed humanity in enough sorrow, pain, oppression, grief, and rage to test the validity of these lofty sentiments on the healing power of what Longfellow called the "language spoken by angels." Two catastrophic world wars and an almost continuous series of smaller-scale conflicts have produced a surfeit of victims of the anxiety and despair born of battlefield slaughter.

The most rewarding music may be conducive to reverie. Childhood is revisited briefly with the chance hearing of a kindergarten class singing a nursery rhyme. A long-forgotten ballad can evoke pleasurable recollections of a once-upon-a-time prom, a romance, or a friend that had been consigned to the dimmest recesses of memory over the intervening years.

So, too, do songs written in a martial tempo direct the attention to earlier times, unwelcome as the reminders may be, when the survival of America's troops and indeed its way of life was imperiled. Throughout U.S. involvement in World Wars I and II, songs promoting patriotism tapped vast and highly receptive markets, and the best of them, few as they are, have retained such popularity that they still rank among the most familiar melodies in all of American music. Some of these hardy perennials accented the quick-step cadence of servicemen and women on the march. Others, in particular the sentimental ballads, were aimed at the aggrieved they had left behind, encouraging those on the

1

home front to carry on and muddle through while promising that the individual and collective valor of their absent loved ones would be enshrined in history.

Like the upbeat melodies and lyrics that honeycombed the film musicals of the Great Depression, a generous supply of 1914–1918 songs, as well as of those published between 1939 and 1945, sought to build confidence in the future, regardless of how dismal the present happened to be. Written by innumerable tunesmiths, amateur and professional alike, the songs dispensed cheer and comfort, assuring eventual victory and the subsequent reuniting of families and sweethearts in a peaceful world.

Remembrances of Things Past

On September 3, 1989, people everywhere observed the fiftieth anniversary of one of the darkest days of the twentieth century. For it was on September 3, 1939, that Great Britain and France went to war with Germany over Adolf Hitler's incursion into Poland, as brutal a military campaign as has ever been waged.

The German "Barbarossa" invasion of the Soviet Union on June 22, 1941, and the Japanese attack at Pearl Harbor on December 7 passed their half-century marks in 1991. The great naval battles of the Coral Sea and Midway Island, the land battles on Bataan, Corregidor, and Guadalcanal, and the "Operation Torch" invasion of North Africa passed theirs in 1992. Revived in 1993 were 50-year-old memories of the battles in and around Anzio, Salerno, and Monte Cassino, the overthrowing of Benito Mussolini, and the unconditional surrender of Italy, the first partner to desert the Axis alliance.

In mid–1994 millions of people observed the half-century anniversary of the D-Day (or "Overlord," as Winston Churchill dubbed it) invasion of continental Europe. On August 26, the French paid homage to Charles de Gaulle's triumphal march along the Champs Élysées the

day after the German Army that had gripped Paris for more than four years surrendered; in December the Von Rundstedt Offensive, or the "Battle of the Bulge," claimed the world's attention. Still to be celebrated at this writing are the horrendous final battles of World War II on Iwo Jima and Okinawa; V-E Day; the dropping of atomic bombs on Hiroshima and Nagasaki; and finally V-J Day, which, on August 15, 1945, brought the most awesome war in history to an end, almost six years to the day after it began.

So vivid are these and other World War II milestones that people may be excused for failing to celebrate with appropriate enthusiasm another epochal date in history—November 11, 1993, the seventy-fifth anniversary of the signing of the Armistice that concluded the First World War. That the political and economic errors committed by the victorious Allies and the German Weimar government itself from 1919 to 1932 led directly to Hitler's appointment as chancellor of Germany, and subsequently to World War II, should not have obscured the significance of that occasion.

Official acknowledgments of the impact of the Armistice on postwar America, however, were unsurprisingly perfunctory. A lapse of three quarters of a century was too long a time for most people to refresh memories of an unpopular war that was reviled from the start. Even before what once was known as "Armistice Day" in the United States was subsumed into the more generic "Veterans Day," many people were regarding it as a minor holiday to be given over to relaxation or mall shopping. In their November 12, 1993, coverages of various Veterans Day parades, typically attended by skimpy crowds of onlookers, newspaper and television reporters rarely discussed even the most basic terms of the Armistice.

Karl E. Meyer, writing under the headline "Almost Forgotten on Veterans Day" in the November 12, 1993, edition of the *New York Times*, adequately summarized the almost universal disregard of that war-ending document in a single sentence: "That so little has been made of the anniversary reflected the heartbreaking letdown that clings to the memory of World War I."

Left unsaid was the equally depressing fact that by overlooking the importance of that war, Americans were making a mockery of the songwriters' contention in "Our Own American Boy" and other pre– and post–Armistice songs that the deeds of the heroic servicemen would "never be forgotten / In our own land of liberty"; that General Pershing's name would live forever in honor in all nations; that the world will never forget the debt it owes to "you sonless mothers of France."

Few survivors of World War I, soldier or civilian, were alive at the end of 1994, most having been scythed down by the passage of seven and one-half decades. For the most part, the names of the field commanders and government officials are familiar only to teachers and students of history. With the exception of Woodrow Wilson, such once-publicized names and battles as John J. Pershing, Ferdinand Foch, Kaiser Wilhelm II, Gallipoli, the Argonne, and Verdun now pose recognition problems.

On the other hand, over the past five decades the cast of bigger-than-life personalities who dominated the World War II years have been memorialized — or damned — in an abundant assortment of books, plays, and films that attained spectacular popularity throughout the world. Roosevelt, Churchill, Hitler, Stalin, Mussolini, Hirohito, de Gaulle, Erwin Rommel, Douglas MacArthur, Dwight D. Eisenhower, Bernard Montgomery, George S. Patton, Jr.,* Hideki Tojo, Chiang Kaishek, Pearl Harbor, Leningrad, and D-Day and V-J Day are still identifiable to a significant number of adults. So cataclysmic were the causes and effects of World

War II that they have been woven permanently into the collective memory of battlefield and homefront witnesses and, from them, passed on to the consciousness of the generations that followed.

Already, at the tail end of 1994, the U.S. Postal Service had announced plans to issue an unprecedented ten more commemorative World War II stamps in September 1995, bringing to 50 the total number of stamps marking milestones of that war made available since 1991. Scrapped immediately was a proposed pictorial reminder of the atomic bombing of Hiroshima and Nagasaki bearing the caption, "Atomic bombs hasten war's end, August 1945." Protests by the Japanese government, coupled with President Bill Clinton's stated preference for an alternative, resulted in another stamp, this one showing President Harry S Truman, who had ordered the dropping of the bombs, preparing to announce Japan's surrender.

The Second World War has often been described as the "Good War," surely a contradiction in terms, but nonetheless apt, since that *bellum justum* did draw seemingly the clearest Manichean line of demarcation between the forces of good and those of evil. Its other popular nickname as the "Big One" refers to its vast scope, the number of nations enmeshed in battle, its unparalleled ferocity, and the humongous toll on civilians as well as combatants. The war is also notable in the annals of popular music for inspiring thousands of songs commending the bravery of American fighting forces overseas and sending messages of solace and hope to their loved ones at home.

Thanks particularly to the radio and talking pictures, both absent from the First Great War, these songs were heard by fighting forces on duty and on leave in cities and villages on six continents. Certainly, the World War II songs, like those

---

*General Patton's poem "God of Battles" was set to music twice during World War II. The first version (1943) was by Peter ("Deep Purple") DeRose, the second in 1945 by Patrick Andrew Crorkin, who also rewrote a few of Patton's lines. Patton earned his first Distinguished Service Cross as commander of a World War I tank brigade in the Meuse-Argonne offensive.

of the earlier conflict, did absolutely nothing to abate the raw ferocity of combat. But they did achieve their sole purpose of putting a song in the hearts of listeners, perhaps even ameliorating their cares, if only sporadically.

Calls to Arms

The popularity of the best patriotic and war songs is not difficult to fathom. Songwriters of many nationalities have been remarkably successful in intensifying nationalism and inciting people to action, whether it be to rebel against a conqueror, overthrow their own government, invade another country perceived as a potential adversary, or defend against across-the-border aggression. As actual combat superseded warnings to prepare for it, mushrooming legions of songwriters proceeded to propagandize their countrymen into blind acceptance of their leaders' cause as righteous. The enemy was typically branded an international felon that had to be crushed regardless of the cost in life and treasury. Agreement on the absolute necessity of waging war became a litmus test for patriotism.

Besides carrying messages that vilified the opposing armies and governments, the war tunes typically chronicled events in terms of battles won (and sometimes lost), extolled the bravery of specific branches of the various military services, and reminded listeners that ultimate victory was essential to the preservation of humanity itself.

Dramatists and novelists have excelled at probing the underlying reasons for hostilities, typically after the fact. Painters and sculptors have visualized the harrowing consequences of wartime violence on both warriors and innocents. Poets have catalogued the nobility of purpose that automatically converts commanders into heroes, issuing brave, aphoristic phrases to accompany their troops into even such a disaster as the ill-conceived 1854 British cavalry charge into a "valley of death."

Only songwriters have combined im-mediacy and a rallying call to arms that affect the illiterate recruit as strongly as the professional soldier. The marching masterpiece "La Marseillaise" was composed by Claude Joseph Rouget de Lisle, an army captain, on April 24, 1792, four days after France went to war with Austria. It has been the national anthem of France since July 14, 1795. Similarly created in wartime were "The Star-Spangled Banner," written toward the end of the War of 1812, and "Remember Pearl Harbor," which became a bestseller within one month after the United States entered World War II. Because of these songs' timely publication, listeners experienced little difficulty relating their lyrics to the conflicts they commemorated.

The first song, with a lyric by Francis Scott Key (1780–1843), a lawyer, was written on September 14, 1814, the day after the British shelling of Fort McHenry, near Baltimore. Prestige was added to renown when it was officially designated as the American national anthem during World War I. Ironically, the melody was an adaptation of an earlier air by a British composer and organist, John Stafford Smith, who entitled it "To Anacreon in Heaven," a convivial song of the Anacreonic Society of London. It was published in 1771. Once falsely attributed to composer Samuel Arnold, the "Anacreon" music was well known in America during Revolutionary War days. Various texts were sung to it, including "Adams and Liberty," written by Robert Treat Paine.

The second song, "Remember Pearl Harbor," by Don Reid and bandleader Sammy Kaye (of "Swing and Sway" fame), quickly became the best known of the 27 late–1941 and early–1942 tunes using the same or similar titles to recount the notorious Japanese attack on that American military installation on Oahu, Hawaii. It remained a resounding piece of bellicose sloganeering from its publication date of December 29, 1941, right up to the formal surrender of the Japanese aboard "Mighty Mo," otherwise known as the U.S. battle ship *Missouri*, in Tokyo Bay, on September 2, 1945.

Several of John Philip Sousa's 136 marches are still very much alive, but cannot be classified as war songs. The absence of words detracts from their pertinency to specific battles or even wars, forcing the instrumentals of "March King" Sousa to share the same fate with those of "Waltz King" Johann Strauss. It is often challenging to identify by title either composer's most famous works, although hearing one inevitably summons up recognition of the melody.

Such Sousa favorites as "Semper Fidelis" (1888), "Washington Post March" (1889), "The Liberty Bell" (1893), "El Capitan" (1896), and "Stars and Stripes Forever" (1897) are as spirited as any country could hope to get for the purpose of adding sparkle to a patriotic holiday celebration or escorting troops past a reviewing stand on a parade ground. The fourteenth leader of the U.S. Marine Band from 1880 to 1892, Sousa served the Wilson Administration in World War I as adviser on military music, a position for which he was undeniably qualified. He continued to contribute marches and other kinds of patriotic music during the war, among the last of them "We Are Coming (Marching-Song of America)" and "In Flanders Fields the Poppies Grow," both with lyrics and composed in 1918.

At his death at age 77 on March 6, 1932, the *New York Herald-Tribune* justifiably termed Sousa the "pied piper of patriotism" in its obituary. Twenty years later, in 1952, one-time Broadway musical comedy dancer Clifton Webb portrayed Sousa in the 20th Century–Fox film *Stars and Stripes Forever*.

Wartime Love

The songwriters of both world wars were adept at taming the thunderous drumbeat of Mars to permit the gentle rhythms of Venus to seep through. Besides touching tenderly on the enforced separation of lovers caused by circumstances beyond their control, the love songs were often not only pleasurable to listen to, but danceable as well. The result was their scaling the heights of popularity quickly and, in some instances, retaining familiarity into succeeding decades.

Some of the war-based ballads of the First Great War were introduced in stage musicals and by vaudeville and nightclub headliners. Thousands appeared on sheet music, many also finding their way onto phonograph records and piano rolls. Persons lacking the wherewithal to view the live entertainment or buy the recordings or music sheets were invited to request free hearings at local department stores, the largest of which employed pianists to plug the latest songs in their sheet music sections. In the Second World War, the movies and radio joined with the stage and nightspots in promoting a fresh new ballad series to dance to at USO centers throughout the world, and in the Stage Door Canteen in New York City and Hollywood Canteen in Los Angeles.*

A few of the best World War I songs had only marginal relevance to the conflict in Europe, but they expressed sympathy for people bereft of their lovers so poignantly, in both words and music, that they immediately caught the fancy of huge publics on both sides of the ocean. To cite one example, John L. Golden and Raymond Hubbell's lyrical "Poor Butterfly," a song written for the 1916 Broadway production *The Big Show*, prompted images of luckless wartime romances, particularly in the lines describing the misfortunes that struck a Japanese girl.

Taking a cue from Puccini's *Madame Butterfly*, she falls in love with an American seaman who is subsequently called to duty but vows to return. He fails to reappear, however, leaving "Miss Butterfly"

Among the dozens of writers of songs honoring the United Service Organizations as a powerful additive to building morale was Prescott S. Bush, then the USO's national campaign chairman. He was one of the three

alone and anticipating her own death of a broken heart. Even in neutral America the lyric was interpreted as an elegy to a young man most likely killed in the war.

Golden, a charter member of the American Society of Authors, Composers and Publishers, was a producer as well as a songwriter. A theater on West 45th Street is named after him, a tribute befitting the man chiefly responsible for bringing such dramas as *Lightnin'*, which in 1918 set a Broadway record with a run of 1,291 consecutive performances; *Seventh Heaven*, *Counsellor-at-Law*; *Susan and God*; and *Claudia* to Times Square theatergoers. Hubbell was one of the nine founders of ASCAP. "Poor Butterfly" is his sole masterpiece, but he contributed many other stage songs, including several for the Ziegfeld Follies between 1911 and 1914.

The enthusiasm the song generated in the United States was surpassed by the reception accorded it by Europeans, many of whom shared a bereavement similar to Miss Butterfly's. To reinforce its recognition by the succeeding generation, "Poor Butterfly" was inserted into the 1938 film remake of *The Dawn Patrol*, with Errol Flynn and David Niven playing fighter pilots in the Royal Flying Corps, renamed the Royal Air Force on April 1, 1918. Hearing it inevitably reminded both men and their comrades, in the finest tradition of the conventional war film, of earlier years before their lives were wrenched from their moorings by warfare.

During World War II, the songwriting team of lyricist Mack Gordon and composer Harry Warren won the Academy Award for Best Song with the lovely "You'll Never Know," a hit romantic ballad that assured an absent sweetheart that the love flame still burned and would continue to do so until he returned to the safe haven of home and hearth. No war had separated the couple, but as sung by Alice Faye to John Payne in the 1943 costume

musical *Hello Frisco, Hello*, the lines "You went away and my heart went with you, / I speak your name in my every prayer" perfectly reflected the prevailing sentiment that although the missing are out of sight, they are never out of mind. Echoing one of the major themes of the thousands of World War I and II goodbye songs, this tender lyric implied that true love has a way of transcending all obstacles, even those associated with life-and-death struggles on the battlefield.

The popular songs of both eras did contribute mildly to the war effort. The marches confidently predicted victory—not to be achieved by a few rubs of a genie's lamp, surely, but inevitable nonetheless. Similarly, the ballads helped to soften the fears of a vulnerable population burdened with open-ended loneliness, ever wary of the appearance of a Western Union messenger bearing tragic news at the front door.

The writers of both wars publicly acknowledged these families' grief and even shared in it, as did the artists who performed the songs. Their message was a consistent and simple one: Our hearts go out to you, but try to remember in your pain that the sacrifices being made by you and your loved ones are necessary to cleanse a world lately gone demented of evils that, if unchecked, will plunge it into even greater misery.

The number of World War I songs copyrighted in America is astonishing. Although the war lasted 52 months, the United States was an official combatant for only 19 of them. From the outset of the Great War in the summer of 1914 to the return of the last troops by mid-1919, American writers copyrighted about 35,600 patriotic and war songs. (Even this number pales when compared to the 127,000 copyrighted during the 75 months of World War II.)

In addition, hundreds of other World

[continued]   collaborators on "The Spirit of the U.S.O.," published in 1942. In later life he would become a U.S. senator from Connecticut. His war-hero son and future president, George H.W. Bush, flew 58 missions as a Navy fighter pilot in World War II.

War I ballads, marches, and fight songs were exported to America by the British, Canadians, French, Belgians, Italians and even the Germans. Add these titles to the American songs and one arrives at the obvious conclusion that never before 1914 had the country been exposed to so many musical commentaries on any single event in its history.

Trite and transitory as most of the American World War I songs were, as a whole they exceeded the originality and quality of even the finest hits produced in World War II. In fact, the vast majority of the published songs of each war came and went as randomly as waves upon a beach, leaving behind only the vaguest of imprints. But like history book references to misery in No Man's Land, knitting societies, Liberty Bond promotions, victory gardens, defense-factory production lines, and scarcities of consumer goods, the lyrics of most World War I songs described with uncanny clarity the day-to-day personal crises confronting Americans both at home and abroad.

Part I
Songs of the War and Their Cultural Context

1. Outbreak of Hostilities

The United States must be neutral in fact as well as in name.... We must be impartial in thought as well as in action, must put a curb upon our sentiments as well as upon every transaction that might be construed as a preference of one party to the struggle before another.

President Woodrow Wilson, August 19, 1914

The Congress of Berlin in 1878 placed the predominantly Turkish nation of Bosnia and Herzegovina under the occupation and administration of the German-oriented Austro-Hungarian Empire. In 1908, the empire formally annexed the little Balkan country, fomenting bitter resentment in neighboring Serbia against the emperor's clamping down on the freedom of the Slavic peoples residing in Bosnia and Herzegovina. Serbia's hatred of Austria, the archenemy of the Slavs, led it into undertaking a protracted propaganda campaign aimed at liberating its kinsmen from Austro-Hungarian rule.

In the Balkan Wars of 1912–1913 the Serbs, along with Bulgars, Greeks, and Rumanians, expelled the Turks from most of the remnants of their European possessions beyond the city of Constantinople, but then fought among themselves over the spoils. Scant attention was paid by the leading world powers, including the United States, to the intervention of Austria-Hungary to prevent Serbia from using its victory to secure a much-desired port on the Adriatic Sea. The action, how-ever, added still more fuel to Serbian hatred of the Austro-Hungarian Empire.

On June 28, 1914, Archduke Francis Ferdinand, heir to the dual thrones of Austria and Hungary, was shot to death by the uncompromising nationalist Gavrilo Princip, a Bosnian Serbian student, during his official visit to Sarajevo, Bosnia and Herzegovina's capital city. Also killed in the gunfire was Ferdinand's wife Sophie, duchess of Hohenberg.

On July 23, some 25 days after the assassinations, a shocked Austria-Hungary presented Serbia with a 48-hour ultimatum that, in effect, would have practically eliminated the sovereignty of the tiny kingdom. When Serbia rejected several of the terms, Austria-Hungary retaliated on July 28 with a declaration of war against Serbia, marking the opening of World War I.

Germany supported Austria-Hungary by declaring war on Russia, which had been acting as quasi-guardian of Slavic independence in the Balkans, on August 1. Two days later Germany also went to war with France, which had refused to give assurance of its neutrality in the burgeoning conflict; then, on August 4, Germany declared war on Belgium for denying passage to its armies en route to France.

That same day, Great Britain declared war on Germany, ostensibly as a joint guarantor of Belgian neutrality, but more realistically because of its unwillingness to acquiesce in the domination of western Europe by Britain's most dangerous Continental rival. Within the next few weeks, Turkey and Bulgaria entered the war on the German side, while Italy, Rumania, and Japan joined up as allies of the British and French.

Eventually 32 nations, including 4 British dominions and India, became participants in a savage, stubbornly stalemated war that claimed the lives of at least 10 million soldiers on both sides and wounded an estimated 21 million. Included in the toll were the 116,500 deaths and 204,000 wounded inflicted on U.S. forces. France lost 1,358,000 lives, the British Empire 908,000, Germany 1,774,000, and Austria-Hungary about 1,200,000.

During the Battle of the Somme, the British army suffered almost 58,000 casualties on a single day, July 1, 1916, roughly equalling the total number of Americans killed in the Vietnam War. World War I was indeed a most appropriate prelude to its even more destructive successor of 1939–1945.*

Informed Americans had been aware of the growing tensions in Europe, but the actual outbreak of war took the public and government totally by surprise. The Sarajevo assassinations made newspaper headlines for a day but were largely dismissed, then forgotten over the next three weeks, when newspapers produced few hints that serious trouble was brewing. The world talked of peace, but Europe was preparing for war.

President Wilson's confidential friend and adviser, Colonel Edward M. House,

correctly sensed in mid–1914 that European tension had reached an alarming pitch. He visited Berlin and other European capitals in May, June, and July 1914 in hopes of insuring peace. House received some encouragement, but on June 28, while he was in London, Ferdinand and his wife were shot to death. House sailed for home on July 21. Two days later, Austria-Hungary presented its ultimatum to Serbia.

President Wilson issued a formal proclamation of neutrality on August 4, 1914, but the war almost immediately adversely affected the economy. American exports were cut off from German markets by the British Navy, plunging the United States into a severe economic downturn. Soon, however, relief came in the form of large munitions orders from the Allies, and by the closing months of 1915, the United States was enjoying a war-born prosperity.

These sales raised questions of American neutrality. German sympathizers complained that the sales, being made exclusively to the Allied side, were "unneutral." There was, however, no doubt that the American position was correct in both law and precedent. Selling munitions of war to the combatants was not a breach of neutrality. The fact that only one set of belligerents could buy American goods was the result of Britain's mastery of the seas, not of United States policy. The sales continued at a rapidly climbing rate, jumping from about $6 million in 1914 to $467 million in 1916.

More than anything else, it was supplying arms to the Allies that brought the United States into direct confrontation with the German government. Another important factor was American acquiescence, however reluctant, in Britain's virtual blockade of ports in neutral Holland and Denmark, an act that further inhibited exports of non-war goods into Germany, in-

---

*The bloodiest single day's fighting in American military annals was September 17, 1862, during the Battle of Antietam in Maryland. Some 23,000 men were killed or wounded, about evenly divided between Union and Confederate troops.

cluding food, cotton, and many other essential commodities. In 1915, Germany announced that henceforth the waters around the British Isles were to be considered a "war zone," and that it no longer could guarantee the safety of any neutral vessels that ventured into that area. The warning was regarded by many American officials as a challenge to the traditional right of U.S. vessels to travel freely on the high seas. The world waited to see how Wilson would answer it.

Churchill, Montgomery, MacArthur, de Gaulle, Mussolini, Patton, Rommel, and Georgi Zhukov all saw service, much of it distinguished, in World War I. But of all the names that tied both world wars together none was more pivotal than that of Adolf Hitler. On August 3, 1914, less than one week after the outbreak of the war, the 25-year-old Hitler, an Austrian citizen, petitioned King Ludwig III of Bavaria for permission to join a Bavarian regiment of the German army.

The future Führer detested Austria, especially Vienna, where he had lived for the five years between 1908 and 1913, and he refused to serve in that country's army, filled as it was with Slavs and Jews, then as later Hitler's favorite scapegoats. The lance corporal turned out to be a brave German soldier, winning several medals, including the Iron Cross (First Class), an honor rarely bestowed on a common infantry soldier.

Not until 1932, when he ran for president of Germany, did Hitler decide, out of political necessity, to become a German citizen. Appointment to an official post in any German state carried with it citizenship in that state. In turn, Reich citizenship was automatically conferred on any citizen of any German state. Before the election, the Nazi-controlled government of the State of Brunswick hurriedly named Hitler to the largely ceremonial post of councilor to the Reichsrat, the lesser house of the Berlin parliament, and Hitler duly swore an oath to uphold the German constitution.

Now qualified to run in the 1932 election, Citizen Hitler lost twice to the World War I general Paul von Hindenburg, first in the general election, then in the runoff. But he had severed his last tie to his native Austria, and in 1938 the gifted demagogue annexed it to Germany, having suspended the constitution to which six years earlier he had sworn allegiance.

Disenchantment and Isolationism

Hardly had the First Great War begun when American songwriters settled down to the serious business of providing the public with musical chronicles bearing on the new European conflict. Practically all of their songs with lyrics were meditative rather than bellicose. Frequently set to music were the words of the national hymn, "America" (or "My Country, 'Tis of Thee"), written in 1831 by Samuel Francis Smith while a 23-year-old student at Andover Theological Seminary in Massachusetts. None of the latter-day American composers, however, was able to separate the poem from its original melody, which is the same as that of the dignified English national anthem, "God Save the King," published in 1744. All 12 "revisions" quickly faded into oblivion.

Undoubtedly, some of the 1914–1916 anthems to peace and patriotism were inspired by U.S. incursions into Mexico, but very few of the titles referred to Mexico by name. Most did wrestle with the worrisome problem of whether the United States might become militarily involved sooner or later in the war that was ravaging France. Either nervous or otherwise reluctant to create songs dealing directly with that combat, however, the Americans largely deferred to foreign tunesmiths in directly badgering the Central Powers from August of 1914 to April of 1917. Especially throughout 1916, when U.S. neutrality was being increasingly threatened, American songwriters varied their war themes, dividing them almost equally between isolationism and preparedness.

Foremost among the songwriters who feared that the war would expand into other countries, possibly including America, was Charles K. Harris, whose lyrical "When Angels Weep," copyrighted November 19, 1914, became the first overt musical recognition of the uneasiness pervading the American populace from East to West Coast. To Harris, World War I should be halted forthwith. Subtitled "Waltz of Peace," his hymn sought divine intervention, through an "Angel of Love," to sweep the battlefields free from clashing armies. The lyric asks that the Heavenly Host "hear our prayers ascending above," "bless all the nations on earth," and promptly restore "good will to men." The concluding lines were far the most emotional and persuasive of all the earliest American entreaties to God to withdraw the warring factions and end the bloodshed:

> Grant us sweet peace,
> Oh, Angel of Love,
> We all are pleading
> This war to cease,
> Let us dwell in love and peace.

It was not that Americans at the time were unfamiliar with warfare. Vying for attention—and not at all successfully—with the scattershots of early World War I patriotic songs was the occasional fight-on march glorifying the valor of American troops who had been sent across the Rio Grande on punitive expeditions against two of the rivals for the office of president of Mexico. In the spring of 1914, only a few months before the incident at Sarajevo, President Wilson went to war with the dictatorial Victoriano Huerta, who in 1913 had overthrown strongman Francisco Madero, who himself had ousted strongman Porfirio Díaz in 1911 in the opening round of what became known as the "Mexican Revolution."

Like his predecessor, William Howard Taft, Wilson refused to recognize Huerta as fit to lead the Mexican government. The already strained relations between the two countries worsened when a Mexican official arrested and briefly detained a few American sailors stationed aboard ships anchored off Tampico, near the Gulf of Mexico. On April 21, 1914, U.S. forces were sent to Vera Cruz, Mexico, where they defeated enemy forces in a brief skirmish. Huerta promptly broke off diplomatic relations with the United States. Shortly afterward, Huerta was forced by his own Mexican rivals to resign and flee the country. He was succeeded by Venustiano Carranza, whose regime was granted American recognition.

Angered that Wilson had not helped him instead of Carranza to power, Francisco (better known as "Pancho") Villa retaliated on March 9, 1916, by raiding the small border town of Columbus, New Mexico, killing a number of American citizens. Wilson's response was to dispatch General John J. Pershing into Mexico to capture Villa, a one-time bandit who had risen to the rank of general under Madero. Pershing's cavalry units, however, were unable to capture their elusive prey. The two major battles they fought were not against Villa, but against the Mexican army under President Carranza, who fiercely resented the invasion.

Wilson withdrew Pershing's punitive expedition in early February 1917. Two months later the president went to war with Germany. Embroiled in its own immensely complicated and bloody revolution until 1920, when Álvaro Obregón overthrew Carranza, Mexico never entered World War I.

Regardless of the dangers it posed for American soldiers actually under fire, Pershing's incursion produced only a slight case of war fever north of the border. None of the scores of published American songs relating specifically to Mexico stimulated patriotism very much. A generous share of the songs actually consisted of older marches and fight songs carried over from the Spanish-American War of almost two decades earlier. Arthur J. Lamb and Charles Bown's typical farewell song, "I'll Take Your Heart to Mexico and Leave My Heart Behind," was briefly popular in 1916, as was E. Magnus's march, "When They Get Down to Mexico." But none of the songs, old or new, overshadowed those that referred to the much more catastrophic hostilities under way on the other side of the Atlantic. In fact, several of the patriotic "Mexican Revolution" songs were later redirected toward the European conflict, typically those that had omitted "Mexico" and "Rio Grande" from their titles and lyrics.

The Awakening

In the months immediately following the outbreak of World War I in July of 1914, the few farewell and fight songs published by Americans naturally reflected conditions in the United Kingdom rather than in the United States. It was British troops who were bidding goodbye at docks to families and sweethearts; it was they who were receiving their countrymen's pats on the back and wishes of good luck on their desperate exodus from homeland to "No Man's Land"—the territory lying between opposing armies and over which no control had been established.

Such early wartime American songs as "Bring Back My Soldier Boy to Me," "Daddy, Please Don't Let Them Shoot You," "Don't Take My Darling Boy Away," "Freedom Forever," "Give Us Peace Again," "Goodbye, My Soldier Boy," "March On to Victory," "Meet Me When I Come Back Home," "Soldier Boy," and "When the Boys Come Home" referred either to British soldiers or, in several instances, to members of Pershing's cavalry. Even Charles K. Harris's "When Did You Write to Mother Last?" was universally interpreted as the first in what would become a prolonged series of songs encouraging Allied and American doughboys to mail letters of love and cheer to the home folks on a regular basis.

It made no difference to singers or listeners that this song had been copyrighted May 12, 1914, ten weeks before the war erupted, or that Harris's appeal was a generic admonition to young civilian adults to keep in touch with their mothers after leaving home to strike out on their own. An identical apropos reception was awarded to the prewar "When You're a Long, Long Way from Home," Sam M. Lewis and George W. Meyer's miss-you song that was reinterpreted as a tale of melancholy British and French soldiers in the trenches, not the intended one of homesick Americans alone in strange towns. So appropriate to wartime was the message that the song enjoyed a brief revival in the early years of World War II as well.

Few American songwriters expressed overt support for the Allies or pride in the overseas defenders of democracy, although the writers were certainly not pro–German. Antiwar sentiment was powerful in the United States, particularly among the millions of immigrants who had fled Europe in part to escape the intermittent armed clashes that had pitted neighbor against neighbor, class against class, and one ethnic group against another. Nevertheless, America's eventual participation was inevitable. The nation had reached a turning point in its history with the Spanish-American War in 1898, when it shed its isolationism and walked onto the world stage. Indeed, after that war was over, the United States had assembled a tiny empire of its own. Never again would it be possible for Americans to divest themselves entirely of concern over wars on other continents.

In the fall of 1914, Blanche Merrill gained a high degree of grass-roots support when she praised the president for keeping the country out of the war in her bellwether anti-involvement song "We Take Our Hats Off to You, Mr. Wilson." Copyrighted seven weeks into the war on September 23, it was popularized mainly by two stars of the entertainment field, Nora Bayes and Fanny Brice. The song had not been intended to dishonor the president by suggesting that he shrug off his responsibility for steering the ship of state through a perilous course, nor was it designed as an affront to Americans who sympathized with democratic movements in countries that had traditionally suppressed them. It was simply the first in a string of songs to protest active U.S. participation in any struggle to save Europe from itself.

Later in the year, Duncan J. Muir's ultra-patriotic "Take Off Your Hat, It's a Grand Old Flag," written originally as a 1914 Memorial Day anthem, was embraced by interventionists as one means to counter Miss Merrill's and her fellow songwriters' anti-involvement stance. It would allegedly do so by reminding people of the nation's proud role as the champion of democracy. Muir's prewar lyric, which of course omitted any direct appeal for sending troops abroad to preserve freedom in countries where it existed or press for its introduction where the disenfranchised were ruled by royal decree, remained untouched. The time for fighting on behalf of the European democracies might very well come, but Muir's tribute to Old Glory was not designed to accelerate any American call to arms.

Another remembrance song, this one effectively revived by isolationists, was "Cover with Flowers Each Hero's Deep Bed." Also written as a 1914 Memorial Day prayer to fallen soldiers in all American wars from the Revolution to the Spanish-American War, the W.N. Hull–H.C. Varner song began serving later in the year as a dirge for Allied soldiers being killed in France, as well as an implied warning that additional graves would be filled with Americans if the goal of supporters of the Allied cause were achieved.

These were only two of the mildly contentious songs written between 1914 and 1917 to express opposing points of view on what America's role in the war should be. Disinterest in the matter was definitely not greeted warmly; one was expected to stand either for or against entering the war. Chief among the spokespersons taking sides in the controversy were newspaper editors and politicians, who forcefully espoused in print and speech what some songwriters were subtly promulgating in the lyrics of their songs.

Their efforts clearly foreshadowed those undertaken by partisans of such opposing organizations as the America First Committee and the Committee to Defend America by Aiding the Allies in the early years of World War II.

Get Ready, Uncle Sam!

A clear majority of the World War I songwriters favored non-participation in "Europe's war." Preferring not to antagonize, they created such basically inoffensive antiwar pieces as "Oh, God! Let My Dream [of Peace] Come True," with words by Blanche Merrill; "If They'd Only Fight the War with Wooden Soldiers"; "No Matter What Flag He Fought Under (He Was Some Mother's Boy After All)"; and "We Stand for Peace While Others War." In their songs, the writers were content to let each faction's adherents debate with proper vigor and venom which of the two philosophies better served the interests of the United States. The writers wanted merely to focus attention on either isolationism and interventionism, appealing directly to a public they felt would depend more on reason than emotion to decide for themselves which alternative to favor.

One of the better and more popular of the isolationist songs, Darl MacBoyle and S. Roughsedge's "(Whether Friend or Foe, They're Brothers) When They're Dreaming of Home Sweet Home," attracted listeners by concentrating on the anti-humanistic destructiveness of warfare. All day behind the guns on the killing fields the soldiers keep thundering "songs of hate to fellow men," the writers declared. Men of all nationalities, after all, do share instinctive loathing of their enemies. But no matter for whom they fight, they are also united in universal brotherhood by the same virtues, joys, and fears:

> The soldier boys dream not of glory
> That will be theirs in the battles won,
> Nor do they care if song or story

Will tell the world how it was done.
Back to their sweethearts, wives, and
    mothers,
That's where their mem'ries always
    roam;
And whether friend or foe they're
    brothers
When they're dreaming of home sweet
    home.

Also siding with Wilson's proclamation of neutrality were "Mr. Wilson, We're All with You," "Hurrah! For President Wilson," "I'm Glad My Sweetheart's Not a Soldier," "Let Us Have Peace," "Let Peace Go Marching On," "Join the Army for Peace Instead of War," and the proudly defiant "If They Want to Fight, All Right, but Neutral Is My Middle Name." All these songs upheld pacifism without being strident, a strategy that deflected harsh criticism from the interventionist camp. But their mild tone also failed to generate enough enthusiasm to convert very many opponents into disciples.

The musical anti-isolation forces meanwhile produced their own series of patriotic verses. Also devoid of invective, they preached preparedness, sometimes as a means of insuring peace in the United States, more often as the necessary first step in a potential rescue of the Allies. "The Home of Liberty," "My Country Right or Wrong," "The Red, White and Blue Is Calling You," "Fight for the American Flag," "Wake Up, Uncle Sam," and "Let's Be Ready, That's the Spirit of '76" were among the most popular of the interventionist anthems. In mid–1916 a pair of increasingly worried songwriters, W.H. Pease and O.E. Hermann, Jr., came closer to desperation than any of their artistic compatriots, crying out that "I Want Uncle Sam to Build a Navy That Can Lick All Creation." Their thesis was that with such a formidable armada at its disposal, America would quickly make short shrift of any enemy foolhardy enough to launch an attack.

Of more than minor significance was "Wake Up, America," if only because it was written by John Philip Sousa and automatically commanded respect. "Wake up, America," Sousa wrote; "If we are called to war, / Are we prepared to give our lives / For our sweethearts and our wives? / Are our mothers and our homes worth fighting for? / Let us pray, God, for peace with honor, / But let's get ready to answer duty's call."

Among the best of the "preparedness" songs, it was introduced Sunday evening, March 5, 1916, at New York City's Hippodrome by singer Roy LaPearl before an enthusiastic audience. Sousa himself conducted the pit orchestra. In a preperformance interview with the *New York American*, he was quoted as offering the following defense of the activist philosophy he meant his song to impart: "I do not believe anymore this country wants war. Certainly, the soldiers themselves do not. But they realize the necessity of adequate preparedness for defense as the best means of preserving peace."

Sousa added, "Ninety-five percent of the people of this country want peace and not war. The people are waking up already and they will demand that the politicians stop wrangling and appropriate sufficient money for defense. Men don't clutch their pocketbooks so tightly when their hearts are touched, and that is another reason why such a song as 'Wake Up, America' will do much good. In fact, it will not be a bad idea to sing it to Congress!"

Praising other songwriters who shared his buildup viewpoint, Sousa ended by commenting on the influence that patriotic music can wield: "Lecture me, write editorials at me, and I may be convinced that preparedness is necessary, but sing me a song that contains your message and I WILL BE won over at once!"

The Rise of Pacifism

A frequently recurring theme of many other American war-song lyrics throughout the 1914–1916 period was that the war was a significant tragedy, a conviction that the majority of Americans shared regardless of philosophical persuasion. It would be a huge one, a bloody one, and would last far longer than all but a few Allied leaders anticipated. Most likely an entire generation of young men would be butchered before quiet was restored to the western front.

Thanks to isolationist lyrics preaching tolerance of one's adversaries and to such a firm as Breitkopf & Härtel, based in Leipzig, Germany's publishing capital, a few German and Austrian patriotic songs were recopyrighted and published in America early in the war without arousing provocation. Hans See's "Germany Forever" and Karl Pätzold-Fritz Lubrich's "*Heil, Kaiser, Dir,*" were two examples of pro–German musical sentiments given brief uncontroversial airings in the United States between 1914 and 1916. Similarly, Karl Hiess' "Hindenburg March," published in 1915 by Adolph Robitschek, Vienna, peaceably made the rounds of the American marketplace, along with such other pro–German tunes as "*Hurra, Germania!*", "*Unser Kaiser,*" "*Deutschland Mein Heimat,*" and "*Gott Erhalte Unsre Kaiser.*"

Obviously, the major victims of the mechanized carnage would be the soldiers doing their duty on Continental battlefields. The relatively small number of American songs supporting the British and French praised their valor and cried out for their eventual triumph in battle. But lyric writers did not forget the very old and the mothers, sweethearts, and children of servicemen, since they too bore the pain of their own particular suffering.

Inherent in many of these songs was the warning that American families would be confronted with the same ordeals, should the United States become involved. Rather than quibble over the relative merits of the contrasting isolationist and interventionist messages, the writers dispensed with references to either group's doctrine. What they wanted was a total ban on war as an instrument of foreign policy everywhere in the world.

Abetting the growing pacifist move-ment — and casting additional somberness over the earliest World War I songs — was the widespread doubt that Europe, with its Victorian Age trappings still in large part intact, would ever be able to revert to its prewar status. The war would change everything, most likely for the worse, and imperil the very fabric of Western civilization. Songwriters E. J. Pourmon, Joseph Woodruff, and Henry Andrieu shadowed the future with unrelenting pessimism. With "After the War Is Over (Will There Be Any 'Home Sweet Home')" they offered one of the gloomier assessments of life in postwar Europe.

> After the war is over and the world's
> at peace,
> Many a heart will be aching after the
> war has ceased.
> Many a home will be vacant,
> Many a child alone;
> But I hope they'll all be happy
> In a place called "Home Sweet Home."

Meanwhile, pacifist George Bernard Shaw's play *Heartbreak House* in 1917 superbly demonstrated the validity of the war generation's gnawing fear of a permanent decline in social values. An identical theme coursed through Jean Renoir's French motion picture classic *Le Grande Illusion/Grand Illusion* 20 years later. According to both play and film, the antiwar crusaders had been correct: the barbarism unleashed by World War I had succeeded only in shattering Victorian codes of conduct and the civility once fostered by traditional family rituals.

Many American songwriters sensed what politicians and pundits already knew, and what the average citizen was learning: the war was the means of last resort to settle great-power rivalries over colonies, especially in North Africa, and domination in the Balkan peninsula. Tying the various competing nations together had been a labyrinth of alliances and treaties and ententes, many of which contradicted others and some of which threatened to unsheathe the saber if certain provisions were breached.

None of the American anti-interventionist or pacifist songs came close, however, to matching the virulent denunciation of war expressed by the British poet Siegfried Sassoon, who enlisted in 1914 and survived the Armistice by more than 50 years. Nor did they challenge the antiwar bittersweetness that attracted large audiences to the poems of Wilfred Owen and Rupert Brooke, both of whom, like Sassoon, served valiantly in the war. Their unfettered vilification of warfare has survived into present-day America. Jimmy Carter, a graduate of the U.S. Naval Academy, for example, has expressed similar outrage at the folly of war in a series of poems, several of which are included in *Always a Reckoning*, a 1994 book of the ex-president's verses.

Owen was only 25 when he was killed in France one week before the Armistice, and before he was able to complete a book of poetry that, in the preface, he explained was to be on "war and the pity of war." Earlier he had excoriated armed combat in a series of brilliantly provocative battlefield images in his "Anthem for Doomed Youth." An elegy for fighting men, the poem laments "these who die as cattle" under the "monstrous anger of guns," the "stuttering rifles' rapid rattle," and the "shrill, demented choirs of wailing shells."

Brooke obtained a commission in the Hood Battalion of the Royal Naval Division on September 14, 1914, and was ordered to the disastrous but heroic expedition to Antwerp. The next year, after sailing with the British Expeditionary Force, he died of blood poisoning at age 28 aboard a French hospital ship anchored at Skyros, off central Greece.

Among the newspaper eulogies lamenting his death was one written by "W.S.C.," who described Brooke as "all that one would wish England's noblest sons to be in days when no sacrifice but the most precious is acceptable, and the most precious is that which is most freely proffered." The initials stood for (the Right Honorable) Winston Spencer Churchill, then First Lord of the Admiralty and a personal friend and warm admirer of the poet.

It is in Brooke's eloquent sonnet sequence *1914* that one finds his most plaintive reference to the war and himself:

> If I should die, think only this of me:
> That there's some corner of a foreign field
> That is forever England. There shall be
> In that rich earth a richer dust concealed;
> A dust whom England bore, shaped, made aware,
> Gave, once, her flowers to love, her ways to roam,
> A body of England's breathing, breathing English air,
> Washed by the rivers, blest by suns of home.

In late 1917 the poem was set to music as a baritone solo by Britisher Sydney H. Nicholson, who about the same time musicalized a few other of Brooke's antiwar verses.

Less known but equally savage in poetizing the misery of trench warfare was Isaac Rosenberg. A writer of great promise, he was killed in battle in 1918 at age 28. America, too, lost a poet in the person of Joyce Kilmer, whose "Trees" (1913) brought him popularity at home if not international acclaim. He joined the New York Seventh Regiment two weeks after Wilson's war declaration in 1917, although he was exempt from the draft as the father of four children. He later transferred to Douglas MacArthur's National Guard regiment that became the famous "Rainbow" (A.E.F. 42nd) Division. A renowned unit of the division was New York's 69th Regiment, renamed the 165th U.S. Infantry, A.E.F., but far better known as the "Fighting 69th." Kilmer was 31 when he was killed in 1918 during the battle at the Bois Colas, about 70 miles from Paris. He died instantly from a bullet to the head at the side of his commander, Lieutenant Colonel William J. Donovan, who would later become the first director of the Office of Strategic Services (OSS), the forerunner of the Central Intelligence Agency (CIA). Former President Theodore Roosevelt's son Quentin was killed in the same battle. Among Kilmer's war poems, less known than "Trees" but superior to it, were "Rouge Bouquet," "Prayer of a Soldier," and "When the Sixty-Ninth Comes Back," which was set to music by Victor Herbert in 1919. Unfortunately for Kilmer, he was not alive to sail with his comrades back to their homes.

Another famous member of the "Fighting 69th" was Father Francis P. Duffy, chaplain of the 165th Infantry and recipient of the Legion of Honor, Distinguished Service Cross, Distinguished Ser-

vice Medal, Conspicuous Service Cross, and Croix de Guerre. Promoted up the military ranks to lieutenant colonel, Father Duffy had also served in the Spanish-American War. Sightseers at New York City's Times Square might notice his statue, standing a few yards behind George M. Cohan's in the busy "vest-pocket" park that separates Broadway and Seventh Avenue from West 46th to West 47th Street. Few, however, know that the surrounding area is known as "Duffy Square" or that the statue is only a few blocks northeast of Father Duffy's pastoral church, the Church of the Holy Ghost, on West 42nd Street near Eighth Avenue.

2. Mothers
of America, Unite

The British poets' closest songwriting rival in debunking the glory that some persons associated with warfare was lyricist Al(fred) Bryan, a sturdy pacifist whose "When Our Mothers Rule the World" declared that the ladies' first order of business would be to outlaw war. Similarly, his words to composer Al Piantadosi's "I Didn't Raise My Boy to Be a Soldier," the finest of all the mother songs written during the war, imparted a chilling noninvolvement message dispensing equal rations of protest and hope.

The melody had been copyrighted by Piantadosi as early as December 19, 1914; after Bryan contributed the words, the song was recopyrighted on January 13, 1915. As befit his message, Bryan subtitled the song "A Mother's Plea for Peace" and "respectfully dedicated" it to "every mother — everywhere."

In the song, Bryan refused to dampen his own intense feeling while expressing the anger of one American mother at the prospect of the federal government's snatching her son, wrapping him in a uniform and the flag, and shipping him abroad. Already, ten million soldiers from other countries had been called to duty, she points out. Even more tragic is the certainty that many will never return from it.

"Who dares to place a musket on his shoulder / To shoot some other mother's darling boy?" she demands, referring to her own son.

Then, in one of the strongest antiwar statements in popular music, she warns that other American mothers' hearts will be broken, too, if the United States enters the war and calls on its young men to augment the Allied forces. Even victory would be unable to assuage motherly sorrow:

> What victory can cheer a mother's heart
> When she looks at her blighted home?
> What victory can bring her back
> All she cared to call her own?
> Let each mother answer
> In the years to be,
> "Remember that my boy belongs to
>   me!"

Rather than fight, the mother suggests, forecasting the dream of President Wilson for an international agency to insure peace, "Let nations arbitrate their future troubles, / It's time to lay the sword and gun away." Had Europe's mothers stood together against their civilian and military leaders in 1914, as she hopes their American counterparts will, the massacre could have been prevented. "There'd be no war today," she asserts, "If mothers all would say, / I didn't raise my boy to be a soldier."

President Wilson, in a speech delivered in January 1917, three months before the United States entered the war, did call for peace without victory and foresaw a time when armies and navies would become a "power for order merely, not an instrument of aggression or of selfish violence." He then proposed the establishment of a "League to Enforce Peace" under which the nations of the world would join together to prevent future wars.

So powerful and so deftly attuned to American antiwar sentiment was the Bryan-Piantadosi song that few voices were available throughout early 1915 to contest what amounted to outspoken advocation of passive resistance to enforced military service.

Persons who agreed with Bryan's position actively solicited additional support for it, even to the extent of preaching his message in classrooms. Unsurprisingly, the controversial song soon fell under attack by militarists.

"There is an antiwar song war now raging in Brooklyn," reported the *New York Tribune* of May 7, 1915. "It all started because Alexander Fichandler, principal of Public School 165, teaches the children to sing 'I Didn't Raise My Boy to Be a Soldier.'" The news article continued:

When Major Sydney Grant, of the 13th Coast Artillery, of Brooklyn, visited the school and heard the children's voices blended in the above peace anthem, he was very indignant. When he saw a picture in the hall depicting a little girl looking up at a soldier in full uniform and asking, "Papa, are you going to kill some other girl's papa?", the major left in dismay and sent a complaint to the Board of Education. It was a formal protest against anti-military propaganda in the schools.

Major Grant asserts the principal is violating the state constitution and injuring the national guard. Mr. Fichandler says he will not stop the objectionable song. He says he is doing all in his power

to breed in the schools a wholesome horror of war.

National guardsmen are the more incensed because they are about to begin a recruiting campaign for the 13th and fear Mr. Fichandler's anti-military influence will tend to discredit soldiers, sailors, and guardsmen.

Downsizing the Mother's Plea

Also taking a bold stand against the song was James V. Monaco, a successful composer whose "You Made Me Love You" was almost as big a hit in 1915 as it had been when he composed it in 1912. Blending patriotism and pride in the nation's past, his and lyricist Grant Clarke's interventionist "What If George Washington's Mother Had Said, 'I Didn't Raise My Boy to Be a Soldier'?" was copyrighted April 30, 1915, about three and one-half months after publication of the mother's lament.

Implying that the outcome of the Revolutionary War might have been catastrophically different if the "Father of Our Country" had not made his services available to the colonists, Clarke's lyric argued that there are times when the risks associated with sending young men to the battlefield are justified. Such a time was now and Americans must respond accordingly.

The song's appeal for preparing for a war that undoubtedly would require U.S. participation to bring about a successful conclusion was no match for the Bryan-Piantadosi song it hoped to displace. Few people took it seriously; even fewer bought a copy. But even "I Didn't Raise My Boy to Be a Soldier," which publisher Leo Feist boasted had sold more than 700,000 copies in the first eight weeks, suffered a similar fate. Sheet music and record sales fell dramatically shortly afterward, and any impact the authors had hoped to exert on policymakers was minimal and short-lived.

Even worse, from Bryan and Piantadosi's viewpoint, was the subsequent 1915–

1917 publication of approximately 20 tunes that appropriated the title of their song to bitterly denounce or mock the mother's fear. Few songs written in America have prompted so many musical responses from writers holding an opposing view. In America, Charles Bayha sided with Clarke and Monaco by retaliating with his own "I'd Be Proud to Be the Mother of a Soldier." Frank Huston's "I Tried to Raise My Boy to Be a Hero" expressed even stronger resentment toward parents who failed to make certain that their sons were prepared to do their utmost in a national emergency. In warring England, J.E. McManus retained Piantadosi's melody while revising Bryan's lyric for his rebuttal entitled "I'm Glad My Boy Grew Up to Be a Soldier."

On the comic front, Charles R. McCarron and Herman Paley's "I Didn't Raise My Dog to Be a Sausage" (alluding to the growing meat shortage) submerged the sentiment of the original song in ridicule. So, too, did the colloquial "Ah Didn't Raise Mah Boy to Be a Slacker," and the more directly patriotic threesome, "I'm Going to Raise My Boy to Be a Soldier and a Credit to the U.S.A.," "I'm Raising My Boy to Be a Soldier to Fight for the U.S.A.," and "I'm Sure I Wasn't Raised to Be a Soldier (But I'll Fight for Dear Old Red, White and Blue)."

Jack Frost's "I Didn't Raise My Ford to Be a Jitney" referred laconically to one motorist's objection to converting the family car into an early version of the stretch limousine in order to conserve gasoline by transporting as many passengers as the automobile could comfortably hold.* Exercising what the World War I era regarded as correct grammar—one "raises" an animal but "rears" children—was Bernarr Macfadden, the eccentric physical culturist who replied to Bryan with "I May Not Have Reared My Boy to Be a Soldier." Even if the lad never faces the enemy, the rewards of keeping fit, as

taught in boot camp, would be bound to contribute significantly to his health and longevity, explained the writer, who decades later parachuted out of an airplane at the age of 83 and lived to tell of it.

In the 1920s Macfadden added *Liberty*, *True Story*, *True Romances*, and other magazines to his publishing stable, along with the New York City tabloid *The Evening Graphic*. So graphic was it, especially in covering juicy scandals, that wags renamed it "The Pornographic." The paper was the journalistic jumping-off platform for Ed Sullivan, who wrote on sports, and Walter Winchell, whose slang-laden columns became the model for later purveyors of gossip involving the wealthy and Broadway and Hollywood stars. Like his employer, Winchell also wrote one World War I song.

When war came to America in 1917, military bands and marches, government-sponsored propaganda, and rally-round-the-flag speeches drowned out American mothers' tears, as millions of their sons volunteered for duty or answered the draft call without protest. In the 1917 war song "It's Time for Every Boy to Be a Soldier," even pacifist Bryan modified his ideology—though he never abandoned it—by supporting Wilson's revised foreign policy. Monaco, too, collaborated with lyricist Al Dubin on a song pertaining to the revised international situation with "The Dream of a Soldier Boy." Peace is indeed preferable to war, but his soldier spokesman sadly admits that only by vanquishing the enemy will its return be assured.

"I Haven't Got Time for Anyone Else Till John Gets Home" and "There'll Be Sunshine for You and for Someone You Are Waiting For" were two of Monaco's other lackluster, therapeutic songs. Nonetheless the composer, like a number of his contemporaries, refined his songwriting skill on the proving ground of World War I, emerging from it as a first-class professional. Twenty years later, he would

---

*Jitney was slang for a nickel, which was the price of a ride in the shiny blue and white motor carts, also known as jitneys, that traveled up and down Pacific Avenue on the Boardwalks in Atlantic City.

compose such hit Bing Crosby film songs as "I've Got a Pocketful of Dreams," "East Side of Heaven," and the Academy Award–nominated "Only Forever." Monaco also teamed in 1940 with lyricist Johnny Burke for the hit "Too Romantic," crooned by Crosby in the first of Paramount Pictures' "Road" films—*The Road to Singapore*—which co-starred Bob Hope and Dorothy Lamour.

One Girl Named Lilli, the Other Marleen

While U.S. songwriters and public were choosing sides in the debate over Wilsonian neutrality in 1915, a German soldier wrote a poem that 24 years later would be transformed into one of the loveliest—and briefest—war songs of the 20th century. Entitled "My Lilli of the Lamp-post," it was the work of the Hamburg poet Hans Leip, then on his way to the Russian front. Written in praise of his two girlfriends, one named Lilli, the other Marleen—later merged into one girl and Anglicized as Lili Marlene—the poem was reprinted in a book of poetry, *The Little Harbour Organ*, in 1937 and set to music two years later by Norbert Schultze. The song was published in Berlin by Apollo–Verlag Paul Lincke in 1940, when Germany, Great Britain, and France were again the chief protagonists in a new world war.

Much of the credit for the celebrity of "Lili Marlene" in World War II was due to another Marlene—Marie Magdalene Dietrich, better known as Marlene, who had lost her soldier father in World War I. Among the best loved of all the wartime traveling entertainers, she carried the song with her on morale-building tours of Allied military camps throughout Western Europe and North Africa. For her tireless efforts, Dietrich was awarded the Medal of Freedom, America's highest civilian honor. France made her a Chevalier of the Legion of Honor, and Belgium appointed her a Knight of the Òrder of Leopold.

Affected by the gravitational pull of "Lili Marlene," the actress continued to sing it frequently during nightclub and stage appearances throughout much of her post–World War II career. By 1950, it was rivaling her *Blue Angel* movie solo, "Falling in Love Again," as her official theme-song. One of the great glamour stars of the cinema, the lady whom Ernest Hemingway fondly dubbed "The Kraut" died in 1991 and was buried in Berlin, the city of her birth.

Several different sets of lyrics were added to the original Leip-Schultze song between 1941 and 1944, and it became known by a variety of titles, including "The Sentry Serenade" and "The Lamppost Serenade." Among the new versions were one with words and music by Phil Park, "adapted for American audiences" by Mack Davis, and another with a revised lyric and new arrangement by Al Stillman.

The German version was first sung in a Berlin cafe in the late 1930s but failed to make a lasting impression. In early 1941, the German cabaret singer Lale Andersen made a gramophone record of it under the title "Lilli Marleen." That summer the recording was played over Belgrade, the German soldiers' radio station that was beamed to all war fronts. The song's reception was tremendous, resulting in a deluge of letters from German soldiers stationed in France and Norway, as well as in such distant points as Crete and the Ukraine, asking for reprises of the "song with something about a lamp-post in it," as one writer phrased his request. The radio station responded by playing the song every evening for months at exactly 10 P.M. In her subsequent personal appearances, Lale Andersen sang it at least twice during every performance.

It was while "Lilli Marleen" was being broadcast to "Desert Fox" Rommel's Afrika Korps in 1941-42 that the British Eighth Army, its members enamored of the melody, appropriated the song as its own. The story of how the British "captured" the song was the subject of the 1944 British film *The True Story of the Song*

"Lili Marlene," produced by the Crown Film Unit and distributed by Pathé Pictures, Ltd. Popular as the melody was with British soldiers, its impact on the public was stunted by the lack of a truly romantic lyric in English. Marius Goring remedied the situation by writing one for the Pathé picture. Retaining the Schultze melody, the song is sung to Lili by a young German soldier, following in the tracks of poet Leib himself in World War I, before he leaves for duty on the Eastern Front.

A second English lyric, a potent blend of sadness and outrage, was written by actress Lucie Mannheim. It was she who sang it in the film in the form of a letter from Lili to her absent lover. Her heart is sad and weary, the Mannheim lyric opens, since her soldier love marched away. Compounding her loneliness with fear is the premonition that the young man is destined to die in the Russian snow. He has been sent to that cruel country by the Führer, who, the song maintains, cares little whether or not he, or any of the other troops, survives the cold and Soviet artillery.

The third and final chorus contains the most bitter condemnation of Hitler to be found in any song of the period. He is sarcastically thanked for turning Germany into a nation of widows and orphans, and the final lines propose that the Great Dictator himself be strung up from a lantern post for his evil deeds.

It was in the second 1944 film, *Lilli Marlene*, this one from Monarch Productions, that Lisa Daniely sang Tommy Connor's words, the best known of all the "Lili Marlene" lyrics, in which a soldier recalls how Lili used to wait to meet briefly with him near the barracks gate. Suddenly called to duty, he is unable to say goodbye to her before he departs for the battlefield. His conviction that he will never again see his lover dramatized a fear recognizable to people everywhere in 1944, in the same manner that the poem struck a chord in 1915. Subtitled "My Lili of the Lamplight," the World War I–inspired song rose above its national origin to reign as one of the most popular of the century's war ballads throughout America and Western Europe, regardless of whether the individual country was leagued with the Allies or the Axis or neutral.

3. Wistful Reminders of Peacetime

Since England had been at war long before the United States, it was natural that the British would introduce the first songs dealing with battlefield and home-front agony. The best of the songs were theirs; only a sparse few were written by foreigners, including Americans, with several of the most popular ones rearranged by the British into wartime marches.

The majority of the earliest British war songs, like those written in America, were designed specifically to play upon the heartstrings and raise spirits rather than abuse the Kaiser and proclaim the Allies' invincibility in battle. The songs created a wellspring of sympathy in the United States, resembling the pioneering World War II British songs exported to America from mid–1940 to the end of 1941, when Great Britain stood as the sole bulwark against the conquering Nazis.

Most of the English World War I songs that made their way into the American market came from such mammoth London publishers as Ascherberg, Hopwood & Crew, Inc., Chappell & Co., Ltd., Boosey & Co., B. Feldman & Co., Francis, Day & Hunter, Hermann Dareweski Music Publishing Co., Keith Prowse & Co., Ltd., Star Music Publishing Co., Ltd., and Novello & Co., Ltd. The Italo-American Music Publishing Co. in Philadelphia introduced Italian war songs, as did G. Ricordi & Co. from its offices in New York City as well as in London and Milan. French and Belgian songs were fed to the United States by such Paris-based music publishing houses as Durand et Cie and Enoch & Co.

One of the first and finest of the emotionally charged war anthems from London was "Keep the Home-Fires Burning (Till the Boys Come Home)," a 1914 collaboration by lyricist Lena Guilbert Ford and Ivor Novello. Only 21 when he composed the melody, Novello later became an actor in British, French, and American silent and sound pictures, as well as a playwright and screenwriter.

Among the loveliest of all World War I songs, "Keep the Home-Fires Burning" was also the most plaintive in predicting a long war. Addressed to families back home, it issued a plea from a soldier that his loved ones remember him as the years go by. Yet, true to the British convention of maintaining a stiff upper lip in crises, he also asks that his countrymen do not add to the recruits' "hardship" by shedding tears as they march to the transport ships awaiting their presence. The soldiers' duty is the honorable one of helping France defeat the tyrannical Kaiser and preserve European democracy. Such a goal should arouse pride, not pity, the soldier counsels:

> Overseas there came a pleading,
> "Help a nation in distress!"
> And we gave our glorious laddies,
> Honour bade us do no less;
> For no gallant sons of freedom
> To a tyrant's yoke should bend,
> And a noble heart must answer
> To the sacred call of "Friend."

In 1915, J. Ord Hume enhanced the song's popularity by making a march arrangement of it under the title "Till the Boys Come Home."

An excellent, if unprolific, melodist, Novello in 1945 would write the equally tender "We'll Gather Lilacs" for the London stage production *Perchance to Dream*, again musicalizing the hopes of another soldier in the later war. Like its predecessor, this song dwelled on the vow of one young man to rejoin his beloved and resume their prewar pleasures, including pursuing and sharing the dreams (lilacs) that bonded them together.

A second pensive gem that took England and much of Western Europe by storm early in the war was "There's a Long, Long Trail (A-Winding)." This American song had been written by two recent Yale graduates, composer Zo (Alonzo) Elliott and lyricist Stoddard King, in 1913. Combining a solemn, almost elegiac, melody and a poignant lyric, the ballad enjoyed immediate popularity on both sides of the Atlantic, though it was modest compared with the acclaim it generated after British troops left for the Continent.

Accounting for the song's spectacular revival in Britain was its counseling lovers on the importance of keeping dreams alive regardless of the difficulties impeding their realization. The lyric's relevance to World War I had to be inferred, something the British accomplished with ease, since its evocative message so adequately complemented that of the contemporaneous

"Keep the Home-Fires Burning." Again, the lovers will be kept apart for an unusually long period by the intervention of a tragedy they had no hand in creating. In a rare switch of format, the words are appropriate to either the soldier abroad or his sweetheart back home. What the singer longs to do is travel to the land of his or her dreams, where the couple will be together once more, where nightingales sing and the moon sheds white beams over a peaceful landscape:

> Nights are growing very lonely,
> Days are very long;
> I'm a-growing weary only list'ning for
>   your song;
> Old remembrances are thronging
>   through my memory,
> Till it seems the world is full of dreams
> Just to call you back to me.

But before they can begin their trip, both must contend with a "long, long night of waiting" that will cloud their vision of happiness regained with doubt. Accepting the cruel night as a metaphor for the war was not difficult for Allied audiences, becoming increasingly inured after months of fierce combat to revised predictions that it would be many years before Europe would be at peace again. Enthusiastically received by prewar civilians, the song became a particular favorite with British soldiers after the publisher, M. Witmark & Sons, added a military flavor to it with a followup 1915 second edition in march tempo.

With 1916 came the beautiful and still-familiar "Roses of Picardy," an exemplary combination of a simple melody wedded to a deft poetic lyric, by Fred E. Weatherly and Haydn Wood. Picardy, an ancient and frequently invaded region of northern France, was the site of some of World War I's bitterest clashes. The red of the soldiers' blood is carried through the title into the lyric, particularly in the references to roses, which doubled as a metaphor for youth struck down in full flower. The "little song of love" is sung from the perspective of the sweetheart, who in her sorrow is determined that at least her dead soldier shall never lie forgotten under French soil. Her profound love insures that he will be the one rose that will live forever:

"Roses are shining in Picardy
In the hush of the silver dew,
Roses are flow'ring in Picardy,
But there's never a rose like you.
And the roses will die with the
     summertime.
And our roads may be far apart;
But there's one rose that dies not in
     Picardy,
'Tis the rose that I keep in my heart."

The Industrious Sister Susie

The tension the war exported to America naturally called out for humor to counteract, or at least counterbalance, its debilitating effects. As always in times of national nervousness, the entertainment industry provided a dose of levity in just the right amount needed to stimulate emotional release.

In late 1914, stage star Al Jolson broke the ice by introducing America to the first witty commentary on the war in Europe. Producing pieces of clothing for the troops, by hand or on a Singer sewing machine, had long been a noble avocation with women in wartime. So it was again. But Jolson's heroine, as presented in "Sister Susie's Sewing Shirts for Soldiers," was simply too disoriented and inept to succeed. Clearly, if Britain could adopt "There's a Long, Long Trail" as a battle march, the United States could return the favor by Americanizing one of England's best-known comic love songs.

The writers of the Susie song, R.P. Weston and Hermann E. Dareweski (sometimes spelled Herman E. Darewski), ranked among the best and most prolific of Great Britain's World War I collaborators. Jolson took kindly to their young lady, and the saga of her travail was the dynamic entertainer's biggest non-production hit in·the earliest months of the

war. Its popularity encouraged the American songwriter Jack Norworth to further repay the British by turning the novelty song into a march with the help of arranger J. Ord Hume.

Unquestionably, Susie was motivated by a sincere desire to help the British war effort, but the task far exceeded her reach. She disrupted her family from her kitchen headquarters by overflowing the whole house with miles and miles of flannel and cotton. Her father frequently suffered wounds by sitting on the needles she left on chairs. As for Susie's beneficiaries, the neglected sailors were comforted to find that her nightshirts went only to soldiers. Not that the doughboys were all that thrilled with parcels containing samples of Susie's handiwork. "Some soldiers send epistles," Jolson sang at his alliterative best, "Say they'd sooner sleep in thistles / Than the saucy, soft, short shirts for soldiers sister Susie sews."

Despite her inadequacy as a seamstress, Susie nevertheless was fated to find happiness, as fictional heroines of the time usually did, in the summer of 1915. Ignoring the fact that she was described as married, and pregnant as well, in the obscure third verse of "Sister Susie's Sewing Shirts for Soldiers," Weston and Dareweski announced her impending marriage in their followup song, "Sister Susie's Marrying Tommy Atkins Today." She had fallen in love with a British soldier, and he with her, the songwriters noted in reporting the forthcoming nuptials. Tommy apparently appreciated sleeping in her nightshirts, flaws and all, and presumably would live with her in domestic harmony forever after.

Another comical song, this one American-written and directly involving men under fire, was "Down in the U-17," advertised in 1915 by Chicago publisher F.J. Forster as "A Musical Torpedo Launched by Roger Lewis and Ernie Erdman." It was one of the few songs from either world war to concentrate on a submarine crew. Despite Forster's reference to that most fearsome underwater weapon, then plaguing British shipping, this early "gang" song presented the fun-loving Anglo crew members as basically "jolly old sports" addicted to bellying up to the nearest bar while ashore. When not engaged in a sea fight, they would lock up the hatches and get down to the serious business of harmonizing, nautical-style. The jovial lyric, however, does fairly indicate the tricky maneuvering of a British or German submarine in battle. According to the musical sailors, they "glide like a fish" and "rock like a bear." They "wobble like a jelly fish and crawl like a snail"; then they "reel and then twist like an eel." Little wonder, in the final stanza of the song, they boast that "on the seas, we're a wonder."

Overall, few attempts were made in neutral America to gloss over the tragedies being acted out in Europe through laughter or by reassuring the Allies that they were capable of bringing them to a quick end. The major exception was Edgar Leslie and Archie Gottler's excellent 1915 march, "America, I Love You." Adroitly incorporating elements of both sweetheart and mammy song lyrics, this exercise in patriotic solidarity was designed specifically as a serenade to a nation the writers described as truly deserving of her people's unstinting respect and devotion. It also served satisfactorily as a tap on the shoulder, reminding Americans that they were connected to something much bigger than themselves and the trappings of their insular lives. Reinforcing pride in the country for its democratic ideals and for welcoming people of all nationalities and creeds, the lyric implied that America's greatness, if ever challenged, would be well worth the struggle to defend. And that defense would assume powerful proportions, the song obliquely warns in the final line, a patriotic crescendo that united the entire population under the banner of defiance toward any enemy:

> "America, I love you,
> You're like a sweetheart of mine;
> From ocean to ocean,

> For you my devotion
> Is touching each bound'ry line;
> Just like a little baby
> Climbing its mother's knee,
> America, I love you,
> And there's a hundred million others
>   like me!"

Notes of Cheerfulness

In the morale-building category was "It's a Long, Long Way to Tipperary," actually written in 1912 as a recruiting song for the British military by Jack Judge and Harry Williams. Like many of the other songs in both world wars, this one achieved popularity by joining an animated melody to a robust lyric, written in peacetime, that nonetheless addressed contemporary fears and longings.

As originally written, the words expressed the wish of a "Tommy Atkins," the nickname given to privates in the British Army, to say goodbye once and for all to Piccadilly and Leicester Square and, above all, to military service, and return home "to the sweetest girl I know." Although the song naturally omits any reference to World War I, it served, as the publisher proudly proclaimed on the sheet music cover of later editions, as both a "marching anthem on the battlefields of Europe" and a tribute to all soldiers' determination to recapture past joys, now all the more precious because of the intervening months of combat.

Aimed at Irishmen in the service of King George V, but applicable to all nationalities simply by substituting the name of another city in another country, "It's a Long, Long Way to Tipperary," like "There's a Long, Long Trail," surpassed its prewar popularity to become one of the best remembered of all World War I songs. Despite the peppy rhythm, however, the words conveyed an undercurrent of sorrow in their new wartime context.

Tipperary, Ireland, after all, was simply not that far from France. What would make the return trip difficult, then, was not distance but delay. Tommy Atkins in 1912 had only to await the expiration of his enlistment to hurry back to his home land. Soldiers in the Great War had no idea how long the struggle to crush the Central Powers would take; as history would prove, the war's 52-month duration made the journey to Ireland "a long, long way to go" indeed. One of the finest of all popular marches, the song remained so closely associated with the war and lovers adrift that, three years later, Val Trainor was not the least hesitant to borrow the title for his and Harry Von Tilzer's equally lively "It's a Long, Long Way to the U.S.A. (and the Girl I Left Behind)."

Harry and brother Albert Von Tilzer, whose surname was actually the pedestrian Gumm, were responsible for as many non-war hits as any other composers of their generation. Albert's "Take Me Out to the Ball Game," "Put Your Arms Around Me, Honey," "Oh, by Jingo! Oh, by Gee! (You're the Only Girl for Me)," and "(I'll Be with You in) Apple Blossom Time" and Harry's "On a Sunday Afternoon," "Wait Till the Sun Shines, Nellie," "A Bird in a Gilded Cage," "I Want a Girl Just Like the Girl That Married Dear Old Dad," "When My Baby Smiles at Me," and "Just Around the Corner" are only a few of their compositions that enjoyed incredible staying power over the years up to the 1960s. Among the most prolific of the war-song composers, Albert wrote 10, Harry 22.

Acclaimed as "It's a Long, Long Way to Tipperary" was on both sides of the Atlantic, in 1915 the American publisher Leo Feist brought out an updated version of the 25-year-old "Are You the O'Reilly ('Blime Me, O'Reilly—You Are Lookin' Well')" and promoted it as "The Tune That Took the Place of 'Tipperary' in the Trenches!" and as "One of the 'Good Old-Timers' Brought 'Up-to-Date!'" Despite the publisher's motto—"You can't go wrong with a Feist song"—the company

misjudged the impact this song would have, as did a news story in the *New York Tribune* of May 7, 1915.

Under the headline, "[Tommy] Atkins Plucks New War Song from an American Chestnut Tree,"* the unnamed reporter boasted that "Are You the O'Reilly" had become the one song that all the British soldiers were singing "now that 'Tipperary' is no longer in vogue." Actually the song never approached the renown of the Tipperary tune despite its jauntiness and P. Emmett's revision of the chorus and addition of several references to World War I in the three verses.

Written in 1890 by vaudevillian Pat Rooney under the title "Is That Mr. Reilly?", the song originated on the burlesque stage. The comedy team of (Ned) Harrigan & (Tony) Hart, almost as familiar at the time as (David) Montgomery & (Fred) Stone, made it famous, singing this version of the chorus:

> Is that Mr. Riley
> They speak of so highly?
> Is that Mr. Riley
> That keeps the hotel?
> Well, if that's Mr. Riley
> They speak of so highly.
> Why, faith, Mr. Reilly,
> You're looking quite well.

British soldiers did accept it briefly as a battle hymn, and Mr. Riley became the man at whom they preferred to direct their innermost thoughts. "Hail Britannia" seemed a bit too formal to sing, and the King would most likely be saved anyway. So the men in the trenches decided to address their comments to the fictitious Irish-American hotel keeper, who far more closely approximated the typical enlisted man's own social status:

> Are you the O'Reilly
> Tha' [who] keeps this hotel?
> Are you the O'Reilly
> They speak of so well?
> Are you the O'Reilly

*The word "chestnut" (as well as "evergreen") was commonly used to designate an old popular song that had recently experienced a revival of popularity.

They speak of so highly?
Gor blime me, O'Reilly,
You are lookin' well.

Another of the great songs designed to cheer up families as well as the boys in the trenches was George Asaf and Felix Powell's "Pack Up Your Troubles in Your Old Kit Bag and Smile, Smile, Smile," which also failed to mention the war while emphasizing the psychological worth of curving one's lips into a smile even in the most life-threatening of situations. Like complaining, another ritual practiced by soldiers through the ages, worrying about the future is fruitless, according to lyricist Asaf.

"What's the use of worrying," he asks; "it never was worthwhile." You're on the battlefield, like it or not, he implies, and uncharted as the future unquestionably is, it's the wise soldier who spends his time concentrating on the pleasures of the present instead of on whatever dangers the future may have in store for him. This *que sera, sera* song, introduced by British singing star Adele Rowland in the London production of *Her Soldier Boy* (1915), was one of only four written during the war to insert a few slang words to refer to smoking as a means of relaxing under tension, most likely tobacco's sole benefit. "While you've a lucifer [match] to light your fag [cigarette]," things never seem to be as bad as they probably are, comments Private Perks, the song's cheerful, daredevil hero.

The next year witnessed the smashing debut of "Colonel Bogey," a sprightly instrumental march by Kenneth J. Alford, the pseudonym of Major F.J. Ricketts, bandmaster of the British 2nd Battalion, Argyll and Sutherland Highlanders. As stirring as any battle anthem written during the Great War, this acclaimed march was revived 41 years later to serve as the themesong for the war film *The Bridge on the River Kwai*. As before, the song proved to be eminently capable of fulfilling its dashing, optimistic role, this time also providing a musical link between World Wars I and II.

One of the better World War II films, for characterization as well as for the suspenseful ending, the movie is set in the hermetic world of a Japanese-operated prisoner of war camp in 1943. The core plot—the building of a railroad bridge to speed the overland delivery of matériel from Bangkok, Siam, to Rangoon, Burma—adroitly brings into play the conflicting philosophies of the camp commander (Sessue Hayakawa) and the martinet colonel-leader (Alec Guinness) of a squad of captured British troops. The deadline given the commander to complete the back-breaking project on time forces him to heap physical and psychological indignities on the captives to compel them into submissiveness.

The colonel is offended by the conversion of his troops into slave laborers, and he stubbornly insists that the principles that govern civilized societies be observed. The commander disagrees; war imposes it own code of conduct that supersedes even the articles of the Geneva Convention pertaining to the treatment of prisoners. The colonel's stance engenders a mixture of bewilderment and grudging admiration among his men. They applaud his feistiness, but question his pledge to retaliate by building the finest bridge in the entire Japanese infrastructure system. And on time.

What they fail to recognize is that their jingoistic colonel is in fact a reincarnated Bogey, strict but fair, a stickler for military decorum, and to the nobility born. His cooperation with his captors is nothing more treasonable than a tangible expression of British superiority, an arrogant implication that his countrymen are simply incapable of doing shoddy work, even under coercion.

Buttressing his determination not only to prevail but also to excel in adversity is the toe-tapping march song, which escorts officers and troops into the prison camp and to the worksites, enlivening them every step of the way. The puff-chested colonel may have been defeated in battle, but he remains relentlessly proud in spirit. He is unquestionably a true lineal descendant of the vintage World War I Bogey, condemned for a time to tolerate the jungle crassness of a people he despises as his inferiors.

Most of 1916 was taken up by the most protracted battle in any war to date. On February 21, the German Fifth Army, under the command of the Kaiser's son, Crown Prince Friedrich Wilhelm, opened its offensive on the fortress town of Verdun, 160 miles east of Paris. Fought in an area smaller than Manhattan Island, Verdun lasted ten months and witnessed the most intensive artillery bombardment ever known. Left in its wake were at least 800,000 French and German casualties, more than half of them deaths, an unparalleled atrocity that shocked the world and verified critics' earlier assessment of the war as unwarranted and merciless.

The progress of the war was on the verge of change by the spring of 1917, but it came too late for an anonymous mother who placed a modest little plaque, still visible despite ravages wrought by time and the weather, on a wall of Vaux, one of the besieged concrete forts on the Verdun battlefield. With a simplicity and tenderness that even the writers of "I Didn't Raise My Boy to Be a Soldier" well might envy, the mother expressed the sorrow of everlasting grief with a remarkable austerity of words:

> To my son,
> Since your eyes were closed, mine have
> Never ceased to weep.

Comrades in Song

For the most part, America's songwriting surrogates took their cue from the British. Up to 1917 they evaded paeans of praise for the soldiers of democracy in favor of pretty and unquestionably sincere sorties into sentimentality designed to tear up the eyes rather than boil the blood. A smattering of prewar songs suddenly re-emerged to find even larger audiences because of their lyrical testimonials to the heartbreak of lovers' separations. The lyrics of Charles K. Harris's "Gee, But I'm So Awful Lonesome" and "No One Else Can Take Your Place," both from 1913, were reinterpreted as apt summaries of the involuntary loneliness thrust upon soldier-sweetheart couples in Europe. Each song spoke more of love than war, but by 1915 they had assumed a poignancy among America's proxy lovers that few other romantic ballads written in peacetime could hope to equal.

"Goodbye, Good Luck, God Bless You," a collaboration by J. Keirn Brennan and Ernest R. Ball, the noted composer of such Emerald Island–tinted songs as "Mother Machree" and "When Irish Eyes Are Smiling," melodiously summarized the anguish of those forced to surrender a young man to combat duty. The two songwriters' "Our Hearts Go Out to You, Canada (Hats Off to You)" was one of the handful of American songs to applaud that north-of-the-border nation's contributions to the Allied crusade in Europe.

George R. Gillespie's "Just an Unknown Soldier" became a most respectable 1915 dirge honoring but one of the many nameless, faceless warriors who had perished while fighting for liberty. Edgar Leslie, Bernie Grossman and Archie Gottler's "The Letter That Never Reached Home" lamented the death of a soldier before he was able to mail it; "Forever Is a Long, Long Time," wrote Darl MacBoyle to the music of Albert Von Tilzer, indicating that the time lapse between goodbye and hello might very well be far longer than anticipated by the optimists in London and Paris.

Oddly, in 1915-16, with patriotic songs at their zenith in the United States, the most famous of them all—"The Star-Spangled Banner"—was subjected to formidable attack. Similar sporadic attempts to dethrone the song as the leading contender for selection as America's national anthem had surfaced in earlier years, but none, before or since, caused a greater stir among defenders and opponents of the song. According to partisans of a substitute national anthem, Francis Scott Key's words were obsolete. Nor were the detractors partial to the melody, which was deemed difficult to sing. In addition, they pointed out that the music was written in three-quarter time, a presumed handicap that could be overcome only by doubling the tempo—actually a minor matter—for the purpose of marching to it. Criticism of the piece had intensified to such a high degree after the Spanish-American War that the formation of an association of America's foremost lyricists and composers was proposed. They were to be charged with composing a new, "more appropriate" contestant for the title of national anthem.

Progress slowed, however, when even the anti-"Banner" forces agreed that the new song should be written not after sober deliberation by a committee, but by virtue of individual inspiration, which, as one spokesman contended, "cannot be had for hire." It was also felt that songwriters, generally believed to function in an obscure world that revolved on an axis of highblown artistic temperament, would never be able to reach any kind of agreement on anything among themselves.

An organization was finally assembled, however, in 1912. Honoring the salutary unanimous vote of its 10,000 members, the National Song Society entered into a provocative "systematic campaign" to introduce the public to worthy replacements for "The Star-Spangled Banner." Greeted with "encouraging results," the society chose "A New National Anthem," which began: "My native land, my country dear, / Where men are equal, free...." Originally published in 1909, the song was revised and republished in 1912 by members of the society. A few new verses were added, but the melody was left untouched.

Proponents of the song remained vociferous on its behalf for the next three years, but to little avail. The campaign for change was a dismal failure, and in 1915 the society undertook to canvass "modern" patriotic songs for a more favorable candidate. This time the winner was "My Own United States," by Stanislaus Stangé and Julian Edwards. Despite the fanfare accompanying the society's adoption of the song as a "suitable national anthem," it never achieved its backers' exalted goal. It was rarely played during World War I. "The Star-Spangled Banner," looked upon for decades by most Americans with reverence, had licked the opposition handily. By executive order, President Wilson officially adopted it as the national anthem in 1916; his order was confirmed by an act of Congress in 1931.

B. America at War, 1917–1918

4. Beating the Victory Drum

[We shall fight] to vindicate the principles of peace and justice . . . and to set up amongst the really free and self-governed peoples of the world such a concert of purpose and of action as will henceforth insure the observance of those principles.

Woodrow Wilson, before a special session of Congress, April 2, 1917

President Wilson sincerely hoped to avoid direct U.S. entanglement in the European war, and he managed to do so for two years and eight months. But German activities in the North Atlantic conspired with diplomatic maneuvering in Mexico to frustrate U.S. neutrality. Unable to compete on the surface with the powerful British Navy to break its blockade of ships entering her own and surrounding waters, Germany countered with the submarine, using it to attack ships plying the Atlantic Ocean with cargoes of munitions for the Allied forces. Targets were selected indiscriminately and, nearly as often as not, the torpedoes found their mark.

On May 7, 1915, a torpedo launched without warning by the German submarine *U-20* hit the unarmed British Cunard passenger liner *Lusitania* off the Irish coast, which Germany had classified as a "war zone." The ship sank in 20 minutes, killing 127 Americans, including the preeminent theatrical producer Charles Froh-

man, and 1,071 persons of other nationalities. The ship was not transporting Canadian troops, as the Germans alleged, but it did contain about 4,200 cases of rifle cartridges for use by British troops.

The Germans, however, had not bothered to find out what the ship might have been carrying. The subsequent uproar in the United States, much of it spread by numerous "Remember the Lusitania" songs, caused Germany to retreat from its shoot-first policy, and its leaders promised not to sink liners without warning or without saving human lives unless the ships attempted to escape or offered resistance.

On February 1, 1917, with the war dragging on and no end in view, the German government reneged and openly vowed to renew its unrestricted submarine warfare. Henceforth, its fleet would shoot on sight all vessels of all countries that it found in waters adjacent to the British Isles and the coasts of France and Italy. An alarmed Wilson broke off diplomatic relations with Germany two days later, an abrupt move the president hoped would deter Germany from carrying out its latest threat.

In mid–March, German submarines torpedoed three American merchant ships, proving that Kaiser Wilhelm II was not bluffing. Nor would he permit his conduct of the war to be weakened by the recent congressional approval, despite fierce filibustering against it by Wisconsin Senator Robert M. Lafollette and other non-interventionists, of Wilson's recommendation that all American merchantmen be equipped with guns and gun crews for defensive purposes.

Of equal consequence in precipitating the United States into war was the earlier release, on February 24, 1917, of a communiqué, decoded by British Naval Intelligence, containing a bold proposal by Alfred Zimmermann, the German foreign minister in Berlin, to the German minister in Mexico City. Alarmed that America very well might enter the war at an early date, Zimmermann called on Mexico to ally herself with Germany once the United States became a belligerent. Mexico's reward was to be the recovery of her "lost provinces" of Texas, New Mexico, and Arizona in the subsequent dismemberment of the United States after the German victory. The appeal to the Mexican government was, of course, quite logical, based as it was on taking advantage of the animosity created by the recent incursions of American soldiers into Mexico.*

Publication of the Zimmermann communiqué fanned anti–German sentiment, particularly in the Southwest, and added to Wilson's growing distrust of Germany. The president was devoted to making the world "safe for democracy" and upholding the rights and liberties of small nations. Stating at a special session of Congress that his only choices were either humiliat-

ing retreat from these ideals or fighting to safeguard them, Wilson advocated the latter approach. Four days later, on April 6, 1917, Congress formally declared that a state of war existed between the United States and the Imperial German government.

The vote was 373 to 50 in the House, 82 to 6 in the Senate. Among the nay voters was Rep. Jeannette Rankin (R–Montana), the first elected U.S. congresswoman in history. She would later cast the only dissenting vote against Franklin D. Roosevelt's declaration of war against Japan on December 8, 1941.

The exhausted Allies, stunned in March 1917 by the overthrow of the Russian Czarist government, welcomed Wilson's war declaration, realizing that only with American troops at their side could they escape defeat. Their nervousness was exacerbated on December 15, 1917, when Vladimir Lenin's Bolsheviks, or Communists, withdrew Russia from the war. Tragically, the Russian pullout enabled the Germans to redeploy huge forces from the eastern to the western front, where they embarked on a series of ultra-bloody offensives beginning in the spring of 1918. The American Expeditionary Force was a major participant in the massive battlefield mayhem that ensued.

Knockout Punches

Despite the vast number of war songs already making the rounds of boot camps and Main Street, U.S.A., and regardless of the similarity of lyrics, anyone who thought American writers had delivered the best or most of their material by the end of 1916 was to be stunned by the flood of songs that cascaded out of American publishing houses after April 1917. War song after war song appeared with the

*Texas gained independence from Mexico in 1836. Nine years later it was admitted as the 28th state in the Union. As a result of America's victory in the Mexican War of 1846–1848, Mexico ceded the present states of California, Nevada, and Utah, parts of Colorado and Wyoming, and almost all of New Mexico and Arizona to the United States.

regularity, and inevitably the monotony, of a metronome's beat.

But until the autumn of 1917, the lyrics of the new songs were of a far different breed. Out went the predictions of a long war. Out went appeals for stoic acceptance of the sacrifices yet to be endured. Lamentations to the desecration of youth and family were significantly reduced, as well as melancholy reminders of prewar years and the accompanying pessimism that their carefree pleasures could be recaptured.

Filling their places came singing diatribes against German soldiers and their leaders, either ridiculing or shaking a collective fist at them. These songs' spirited rhythms contrasted starkly with such a funereal enemy anthem as *Wacht am Rhein.* "We're Going to Take the Sword Away from William," "We're Going to Hang the Kaiser (Under the Linden Tree)," and "We're Going to Take the Germ Out of Germany" boasted three cheeky new Kaiser-bashing tunes, reverberating with the clang of outrage. "We're with You, Tommy Atkins!" roared Darl MacBoyle to a melody by Albert Von Tilzer, in effect canceling any impression by foreigners that Uncle Sam might speak loudly but carry only a tiny twig. Equally insistent on strengthening the British resolve to whip the Germans, "Cheer Up, Tommy Atkins" vowed that "Though they're shooting at your noodle, / With the aid of Yankee Doodle, / You can capture the son of a Hun."

"Boche," a French slang word meaning rascal or blockhead, was already fast becoming a synonym for the German warrior. Of even greater force and soldierly glee was identifying him as a "Hun," which American songwriters overwhelmingly preferred. The word was inserted into the verse or chorus of at least 30 of their biggest-selling tunes before the war ended, as well as into the title of such a song as "Hunting the Hun." Because the Kaiser was the chief Hun, it followed that he would be the perfect target for tunes portraying him as a demented visionary, as in

"All Together ('We're Out to Beat the Hun')":

> One night in sleep the Kaiser thought
> The whole world he could rule;
> And when he woke he started in
> To plan, the poor old fool.

"You Keep Sending 'Em Over and We'll Keep Knocking 'Em Down" thundered the title of Sidney D. Mitchell and Harry Ruby's mid–1917 song, its inflammatory lyric bolstered by the sheet music cover showing a Rambo-like American soldier clutching the barrel of his rifle, ready and able to swat German soldiers daring to invade his dugout. "Where do we go from here, boys, / Where do we go from here?" rang the opening lines of Howard Johnson and Percy Wenrich's popular march, nicknamed the "American Tipperary." Anywhere at all, from "Harlem to a Jersey City pier" was the rowdy answer, just as long as cocksure warriors itching for battle get to see some action pretty soon.

A stronger urge to march onto the battlefield was expressed by W.R. Williams, one of the more gifted of the musical foot soldiers, in "We Don't Know Where We're Going," which was followed by the assertive second half of the title, "But We're on Our Way." The second song to be labeled the "American Tipperary," it presented little difficulty of interpretation among listeners, who correctly assumed that the soldiers' ultimate goal was Berlin. Once there, "'Neath the Stars and Stripes they'll pave the way / To a world democracy"; according to another march, "They're on Their Way to Germany."

Even on leave in such glitzy capitals as Paris, American doughboys were described as capable of cavalierly dismissing the war by joining cabaret performers to sing about the charms of the ladies in such baggy-pants songs as Sam Ehrlich and Con Conrad's "Oh! Frenchy." And the wounded in hospitals were invited to share in the prevailing songwriting humor. "I don't want to get well, / I don't want to get well," was the message of another hit made popular by Eddie Cantor. The reason: "I'm in love with a beautiful nurse [and] having a wonderful time!" A second singing soldier interpolated into the second verse and chorus of the song expects to become so enamoured of his nurse that he goes as far as hoping he'll get shot on the firing line just to get the chance to meet her.

Acting under the persuasive influence of the rapid, decisive American victory in the Spanish-American War, the writers of the new combative songs fully expected a repeat performance. The nation's cause was noble, and hundreds of songs portrayed its sons as fighters for democracy, for liberty, for freedom, and for justice in Europe, while preserving those same virtues in America. Although the Allies had done their best, there was still much to be done. But fear not, the words intoned over and over again, relying more on hyperbole than realistic assessment of conditions to make their main point: Germany will rapidly wind up on the losing side. And the troops destined to transform what once had been viewed as a long haul to victory into a quick fix were chest-thumping, second-to-none superhumans hell-bent for glory, swaggering rather than marching into battle.

The Yanks were coming!

America Goes Over There

Even before the first contingent of Yankee doughboys set foot aboard a troop ship, George Michael Cohan, the master showman and monarch of Broadway, came up with the main dish in America's banquet of war songs. Already noted as the lyricist-composer of a string of hits, including "Yankee Doodle Boy," he had developed into a flag-waving specialist as a means of underscoring his unreserved patriotism.

Cohan wasted no time getting to work on his muscular new march. He hunkered down in the study of his Manhattan apart-ment on Saturday, April 7, 1917, one day after Wilson signed the war declaration. Early Sunday morning, Cohan called his wife and children together to sing the song, written with a stub of a pencil on a scrap of paper in less than two hours.

First came the verse: "Johnny, get your gun, get your gun, get your gun, / Take it on the run, on the run, on the run...." Then Cohan launched into the no-fluff, all-substance first chorus: "Over there, over there, / Send the word, send the word over there, / That the Yanks are coming, the Yanks are coming...." With this single effort, Cohan put a lock on American war songs that continues in effect to the present.

Cohan admitted that the verse owed a debt to the 1886 song "Johnny Get Your Gun," and that he had based the melody of the chorus on a simple bugle call. Admirably straightforward and uncomplicated, both words and melody depended largely on staccato repetitiveness to drum the positive message into the minds of listeners, who found little difficulty memorizing the lyric after a single hearing. As if the song were insufficient to demonstrate Cohan's loyal support of the new American mission, he turned over all his "Over There" royalties to a variety of war charities.

For unknown reasons, the song was not copyrighted as published for six weeks after its completion, rather a startling fact considering its obvious assets. On June 1, 1917, publisher William Jerome, himself a writer of war songs, reregistered it with the Library of Congress. Shortly afterward, "Over There" entered into its warlong service of escorting the boys to the pier and on the march to meet the enemy in France.

Among American battle songs, only "Dixie Land" (also known as "[I Wish I Was in] Dixie" and "Dixie's Land") can be mentioned in the same breath as Cohan's masterpiece. That earlier anthem has long been believed to have been written about 1860 by Daniel Decatur Emmett, an Ohio-born white composer, while he was living on Catherine Street on Manhattan's Lower East Side. A musician of some repute, Emmett had organized the first minstrel company, Bryant's Minstrels, about 1842. Recent scholarship, however, has attributed the song to Ben and Lew Snowden, or other members of their black musical family, many of whom are buried in the same cemetery as Emmett in Mount Vernon, Ohio.

The song was originally performed in one of the Emmett troupe's shows in New York City. A few months later, it was played at the inauguration of Jefferson Davis as president of the Confederate States of America, which in the Civil War practically adopted the song as its national anthem. Reprises of "Dixie" were so common long after the war ended that it ranked high among the most popular songs throughout the final quarter of the nineteenth century.

Together with "You're a Grand Old Flag," which Cohan had written in 1906 for his play *George Washington, Jr.,* "Over There" earned the nation's preeminent song-and-dance man a Congressional Medal of Honor in 1936 for meritorious service in World War I. The occasion marked the first time that Congress had authorized a medal for a writer of songs. The medal, incidentally, was not the regular Congressional Medal of Honor, which is awarded only for personal valor, but a special Congressional Medal, given for specified services to the nation.

Twenty-five years later, the song appeared twice in *Yankee Doodle Dandy,* Warner Bros.' 1942 film biography of Cohan, with the immensely versatile James Cagney as the songwriter. In the film it is sung first by Frances Langford, in a cameo role as Nora Bayes, and reprised in the uptempo final scene by hundreds of confident soldiers marching briskly along a Washington, D.C., street, most likely Pennsylvania Avenue. It became almost as popular with soldiers at the outset of the new war as it had been with their fathers in the old one.

Regardless of the yardstick used to measure the soaring impact and popularity of "Over There" in 1917-18, it is obvious that no one needed to write a successor fight song. Solid as a vein of iron ore, Cohan's feisty lyric said everything that had to be said, and far better than any other march tune ever would — in either of the two world wars. The words are still unparalleled in cheering the Johnnies onward to do battle against the foes of liberty.

They must hurry to Europe, Cohan demands, for the Allies are in desperate need of their help. Goodbyes between sweethearts and families must be brief. Instead of worrying over their safe return, the soldiers' girlfriends and parents should be proud that the overseas-bound boys are undertaking such a dangerous but vital job. By all means, pray for them, but do not pine for their return till victory is achieved. The enemy is warned to beware the presence of the Yanks in the trenches. They will show the Hun what courage is, that the spirit of Yankee Doodle lives on, that the Kaiser will get even more trouble than he asked for, that they are capable of blasting their way into Berlin if need be.

It was abundantly evident from the lyric that Cohan was willing to take on the whole German army by himself, even though at age 38 he most likely would have been denied enlistment and was too old for the draft. Most of the hundreds of other war songs published between April and September 1917 were content to urge Americans into displaying unity of purpose against a common enemy by volunteering for overseas duty. Cohan viewed his function quite differently. He accepted as a given that legions of American males would unhesitatingly rally to the cause. What his song was meant to achieve — and did so brilliantly — was to instill a feeling of invincibility in the recruits' minds. War had come to America from Europe, and now that the United States was in it, there was to be no doubt whatever that it would win.

A single listening to the entire song — the two verses and two choruses — should easily convince anyone that "Over There" is far the most durable of all twentieth-century battle songs. It has no legitimate competitors, only tepid imitators. Unable to break away from its lengthy, intimidating shadow, later World War I writers unhesitatingly appropriated the phrase "over there" — Cohan was the first songwriter to use it as a synonym for the French battlefields — as a part of their own titles and lyrics.

Cohan's march was also the first to settle the ongoing argument between interventionists and isolationists. Unfortunately, the United States was now at war, and it was incumbent on all Americans to cooperate however they could toward winning it. If they couldn't slog through the French mud with Johnny, they surely could give him moral and monetary support.

On October 31, 1917, Leo Feist, Inc., paid Cohan $25,000 for the publishing rights to "Over There," and recopyrighted the song on January 15, 1918. In a series of *Saturday Evening Post* advertisements announcing the coup, Feist termed the amount the "highest price ever paid for a song." The sheet music cover of subsequent editions published by Feist carried the song's most famous illustration. Executed by Norman Rockwell, whose artwork on numerous *Saturday Evening Post* covers would in time bring him fame and fortune, it showed four soldiers, one playing a banjo, relaxing in a tent while singing what the publisher termed "Your Song — My Song — Our Boys' Song!"

Unfortunately, the years immediately preceding Cohan's death were anything but pleasant for the songwriter-playwright-performer. In 1940 he appeared for the last time on a Broadway stage in *The Return of the Vagabond*, which closed after seven performances and prompted his vow that "I'll never come to New York again. They don't want me any more." Tired and ill, he went into reluctant retirement.

On a summer night in 1942, when American troops were again on the march over there, Cohan dressed himself against the protest of his nurse and went for an automobile ride up and down his still-beloved Broadway. The trip gave him his last glimpses of the city's bright lights. In October he became critically ill, and on the evening of November 5, 1942, after touching the hand of his close friend, lyricist Gene Buck, he died. "Over There" was played in funeral march tempo at Cohan's funeral in New York City's St. Patrick's Cathedral two days later.

Another of his successful World War I songs, "Stand Up and Fight Like H---," copyrighted September 30, 1918, never remotely attained the stature or popularity of "Over There," but, again, the lyric is a model of the brevity and bellicosity that distinguished all of Cohan's war songs. "There never was a Prussian or any other man / Who'd ever stand a chance to whip one good American," he declares, adding:

> "Stand up and fight,
> Fight for the Right,
> Don't give the foe a chance;
> Just grab a gun
> And shoot the Hun,
> And drive him out of France.
> Show Kaiser Bill you're out to kill,
> Fill him with shot and shell,
> And see that he gets what's coming to
> him,
> Stand up and fight like h---!"

What Made It All Worthwhile

Several other songwriters followed Cohan's example of reinforcing patriotism by tackling two of the most prominent questions — one old, the other new — that were still troubling the American consciousness after April 6, 1917. Replying to lingering doubts that it was necessary for the nation to enter the war was Jean C. Havez and Louis Silvers's "Root for Uncle Sam," a resounding call to dissenters to "Give up your peaceful notions now, / The time has come to fight! / We might be wrong in some things, boys, / But this time we are right!":

Come on, you Yankee boys and girls,
It's time to show your nerve,
We're out to give the enemy
The licking they deserve.
Although at peace they've sunk our
    ships,
As friends could never do,
They've turned their guns upon our
    flag,
I won't stand that, will you?

"Loyalty Is the Word Today (Loyalty to the U.S.A.)," declared lyricist Dee Dooling Cahill, urging her countrymen to "stand by our flag and our country today":

'Tis no time for doubt, 'tis no time to
    pause;
With love and with faith we'll be true
    to our cause;
Defending our land, protecting our
    trust,
For freedom we'll fight, and die if we
    must.

Similarly pleading for unanimous support of America's entry into the war were Irving Berlin, Edgar Leslie, and George W. Meyer, whose collaboration on "Let's All Be Americans Now," one of the better hymns to homefront solidarity, appealed directly to each individual American's conscience, or sense of duty:

Lincoln, Grant, and Washington,
They were peaceful men, each one;
Still they took the sword and gun
When real trouble came.
And I feel somehow
They are wond'ring now
If we'll do the same.

To poet and playwright Percy Mackaye and composer Reginald DeKoven, who was widely respected for his wedding song "Oh, Promise Me," from the 1890 operetta *Robin Hood*, America's entry into the war was necessary in order to complete the "Battle-Call of Alliance" among nations destined to combine their fire and manpower to free the subjugated:

Arise! Renew with nobler dreams,
The faith we name our own;

The bugle calls to vaster schemes
Which God hath dreamed alone.
To save a planet's liberties
He joineth now our hands
With brothers fighting overseas
Among the ruined lands.

One unambiguous answer to the question "What are we fighting for?" was furnished by the writers of "When There's Peace on Earth Again." Echoing the hope of the anguished that the current war would be the last war, the lyric responded in the simplest of terms that "We're fighting now for wars to cease / So all the world again may live in peace." Like clouds, the battlefields "will fade away," songwriters Roger Lewis, Bob Crawford, and Joseph Santly averred, and "turn to meadowlands where children can play." As for the ultimate objective of the United States,

When battles have been fought and
    won,
No conquest will we seek;
We'll have a "Brotherhood of Man,"
With justice for the meek.
No more will hearts be bowed in pain,
For happiness will rule the world again.

Equally idealistic in defining Uncle Sam's motives was "That's What We're Fighting For," written by Clifton S. Anthony, himself an army sergeant. To him, America's dual purposes for fighting included the familiar one of ending the Kaiser's tyranny, to which he added the growing hope that this war—supposedly mankind's final war—would result in liberty and freedom forever in all nations of the world:

To sheathe the sword that's drawn in
    shame,
To hold aloft our country's name,
To end the dream that Might is Right,
To flash the ray of freedom's light,
For he that bled ten million hearts
Must never have his say.
So with Old Glory unfurled,
We'll show him he can't rule the world;
That's what we're fighting for.

Then, in one of the more reflective passages in the music of war, Anthony looked with confidence to the future, when the eagle would be replaced by the dove:

> The years have gone and men have
>   passed
> That liberty might reign;
> For those who died lift up your hearts,
> For you who live will have the gain.
> The time has come to end this war
> And war forever more.
> So tell to him who dares to ask
> What are we fighting for?

Although the United States was not above seeking revenge for the havoc German U-boats had wreaked on passenger ships in the Atlantic, its sole objective in waging the war was the restoration of peace and liberty abroad, according to Eleanor Everest Freer:

> For the freedom of all nations
> We are on our way to France,
> And to fight against oppression
> God has given us this chance.
> Who can e'er forget the anguish
> Of the women in the waves,
> As the Lusitania's masthead
> Sank to please the Prussian knaves.

"We're Bound to Win"

Cohan's ultraconfidence in the Yanks' war worthiness helped greatly to advance the conviction among Americans that victory would soon be theirs. Even more powerful in the morale-building department, however, were constant melodious reminders that the nation had won every war it had ever fought, a historical fact that after the Vietnam War was no longer valid. America's success in the Revolutionary War, War of 1812, Mexican War, and Spanish-American War was cited over and over again.

The Civil War was regarded as a victory, an understandable designation by songwriters. Practically all of them were either born or pursuing careers above the

Mason-Dixon Line and apparently, as their lyrics implied, they were satisfied with the Union victory. But most never failed in their World War I songs to equate General Robert E. Lee and the Confederate Army with bravery, even if tested under fire in a lost cause.

Typical of the frequent allusions to past military glories was the super-chauvinistic "Enlist! for the Red, White and Blue," which relayed the following appeal to service-nervous young men yet to volunteer to carry on the tradition:

> From Washington to Sixty-One
> Our forefathers fought so true;
> In Ninety-Eight they knew their slate,
> So you see it's up to you.
> So while you may, join in the fray
> Before the battle's through,
> Just don't be late, it's simply great
> To enlist for the Red, White and Blue!

The valor displayed by earlier Americans was used frequently throughout the war to inspire the France-bound troops. "We're Bound to Win with Boys Like You," James Kendis, James Brockman, and Nat Vincent confidently declared in early 1918. "We've read on hist'ry's pages / Of the deeds our sons have done, / So it's up to ev'ryone now / To go and get the Hun," says the mother in the song as she watches her son march away:

> "It was boys like you at Valley Forge
>   with Washington,
> And boys like you were Minute Men at
>   Lexington;
> You built up this wonderful nation and
>   then,
> When Lincoln called for volunteers,
>   you answered again.
> It was boys like you who fought with
>   Grant and Sherman,
> And with Lee 'way down in Dixie, too;
> And this land will always be
> A land of liberty,
> For we're bound to win with boys like
>   you!"

"Boys, don't forget the U.S.A.!" the reminiscing Civil War veteran cries out to a group of young men marching to a recruiting office in "Call of a Nation."

> "In the days of Sixty-One our country
>   called us,
> And with buoyant hearts we hastened
>   to obey;
> Down this little street we marched
>   together,
> The most of us have long since passed
>   away.
> But thank God I am spared to see you
>   leaving,
> To wave the banner Lincoln loved to
>   see.
> When the Yankee emblem flies
> Then the Yankee heart replies:
> 'For America, for love and liberty.'"

"Flag of Victory" Songs

By midsummer 1917, with the United States newly enrolled in the combat in Europe, American battle-song production had surpassed that of the British and French, just as her political and military leaders had taken on an independence of action in the conduct of the war. America was scrupulously referred to as an "associated power," not one of the Allies. Songwriters, too, divorced themselves from British influences to concentrate on U.S. troops and the sweethearts and families they had left behind them.

By late 1917, American war songs were more numerous than the combined output of the British, Canadian, French, Belgian, and Italian writers, whose recopyrighted war songs du jour dwindled to a not-so-precious few. And the lyrics of the Yankee tunes were unmatched in their contempt for Kaiser Wilhelm II. It was he who had borne the brunt of Allied distemper since the war began, not Franz Joseph, Emperor of Austria and King of Hungary, who started it. The Americans carried on the tradition with a vengeance.

To be sure, patriotic tunes celebrating the virtues of democracy as symbolized by the Stars and Stripes were still being

written after April 1917. But by then the flag was presenting a new face to the world. Far from playing its accustomed peacetime role as a colorful national emblem flying aloft over military cemeteries and public buildings, it was now being trumpeted as the one banner in the world qualified to lead both American and Allied forces to victory. It was, as several lyrics proudly stated or implied, the only flag bearing "colors that never run."

In previous years, even including 1914 through 1916, songwriters had regarded the flag quite differently. In their hands it had been molded into a cherished symbol to be adored, indeed worshipped, by native and naturalized Americans alike wherever and whenever it was unfurled. Nature had created it, and it was God Himself who had participated in the design process. As a gift from heaven, the flag was imbued with divinity and idealized as the "starry emblem of God's chosen land," as songwriters J. Will Callahan and Ernest R. Ball maintained in "The Story of Old Glory, the Flag We Love." As the chorus of that 1916 song noted,

> The angels up in heaven took a fleecy
>   cloud of white
> And fashioned it into a banner fair,
> Then striped it with the crimson of the
>   dawn's eternal light,
> With just a bit of sky to hold the stars
>   a-gleaming there;
> Then with their wings they fanned it
>   till its spangled folds unfurled
> In radiant splendor o'er the throne
>   above,
> Then God Almighty blessed it as He
>   gave it to the world;
> That's the story of Old Glory, the flag
>   we love.

With America's entry into the war, however, the flag was elevated from its traditional position as the emblem of a peaceful nation to the symbol of a defiant democracy on a holy mission, waving over a variety of lands and the seas, proclaiming the imminent return of liberty to the oppressed. Charles H. Newman's words for

"The Most Beautiful Flag in the World," copyrighted October 1, 1917, serenaded Old Glory both in its old context as an unsullied source of national pride and in its new context as the insurer of success on the battlefield. The first verse was traditional in the purest sense of the word:

> The brightest stars from heaven
> Are in your field of blue,
> Your stripes are from the rainbow,
> Taken out of heaven, too.
> They made you with the greatest care,
> And when you were unfurled,
> God gave as His gift to America
> The most beautiful flag in the world.

Then, in the transitional second verse, Newman added an international flavor in order to underscore the Red, White and Blue's unquestioned superiority as the world's chief defender of freedom:

> "I swear to always honor you
> At home and far away,
> To fight for your protection
> Even as I am today.
> A hundred million people
> Will proudly do the same;
> And that is why, Old Glory,
> You bear an honored name."

Another song, Thomas H. MacDonald's "We'll Fight for Each Star in the Flag," also from 1917, reconstituted Old Glory into the preeminent battle standard. Flush with predictable outrage, the lyric eschewed any attempt to prettify the flag, preferring instead to flavor the author's allegiance to it with a "Don't Tread on Me" bluntness. The "color of white stands for all that is right," MacDonald wrote, "Protecting the weak 'gainst the strong, / And the red is a signal of danger to all / Who would dare offer insult or wrong." No longer regarded merely as richly decorative colors set in perfect harmony on a field of cloth, the Red, White, and Blue suddenly evolved into a messenger delivering a clear warning directly to the enemy. As the lyric declared:

> Now the Stars and Stripes with its
>   colors so bright

We will follow where e'er it may guide,
For its color of blue means a purpose
    that's true
In a cause for which thousands have
    died.
Where e'er it may be on the land or the
    sea
It must be respected by all,
For no yellow is found in that flag that
    we love,
Ev'ry bluff we'll be ready to call.

"It's war again, so rally 'round the flag, boys," Theodore A. Metz demanded in his own 1917 song, reminding one and all of its power to inspire:

> Fight for the flag, boys, Red, White
>   and Blue,
> Do as your dads did in Sixty-Two;
> And when the bullets fly
> You will hear the battle cry:
> "Fight for the flag, boys, Red, White
>   and Blue,
> Come on! Fight for the Red, White
>   and Blue!"

Henry Ford's Crusade

In the words of songwriter-entertainer Irving Caesar, the American war songs of 1917-18 were written to "spread hope and comfort, no more, no less. They gave people the first outright and encouraged them to seek the second on their own. If the tunes also gave Americans something happy to sing along with or something to laugh at, so much the better."

Born in 1895, Caesar was proud of the fact that he had been born on July 4, qualifying him as the true "Yankee Doodle Boy" among songwriters; Cohan's birthdate was July 3. A lifelong pacifist, Caesar was writing songs during all of America's twentieth-century conflicts up to and including Vietnam, but none of the 2,000 credited to him can be called a fighting war song. "I was afraid some people might think I was trying to glorify war as a challenge to the human spirit," he once said. "Actually, extremely few of my associates who did write of war glorified it. I think they should be applauded for that, since it was an easy trap to fall into once American boys began fighting for their lives. The writers honored bravery, but they refused to praise the circumstances that gave rise to it. And they were very sincere in their patriotism."

In 1914, Ford Motor Company hired the 19-year-old Caesar as an assembly line worker in its Queens factory. Later that year, he was advanced to clerk-typist in Ford's Eastern headquarters in the sister borough of Manhattan. Caesar's proficiency in shorthand, a rare specialty for a man, brought him to the attention of Henry Ford himself, who promoted the aspiring songwriter to be his personal stenographer. In 1915 the carmaker invited the young man to join his ill-fated venture to end World War I. In addition to his stenographic duties, Caesar served as a freelance correspondent, supplying the press with daily releases on the progress of his employer's peacemaking efforts.

Feeling that the United States had no stake in the outcome of the war, Ford had allied himself with peace activists like the Hungarian-American pacifist Rosika Schwimmer. All firmly believed that the war could be ended by what they termed "continuous meditation" between a U.S. "commission" and Scandinavian and other European political leaders.

Hoping to reach that goal, Ford chartered the Scandinavian-American liner *Oskar II* in the late summer of 1915 to carry the delegation to Europe. He offered use of the so-called "Peace Ship" to President Wilson, whose equivocation on accepting the proposal pestered Ford so much that he abruptly took charge of the expedition himself. He then invited more than 100 corporate and political luminaries to join him. Almost all declined.

When the *Oskar II* sailed from New York on December 4, 1915, 120 persons were aboard, including Ford and Caesar. About half of the passengers were journalists sent by a variety of newspapers, many of them already deriding the

expedition as a ship of fools. Just before departing, Ford made more headlines by recommending that the men in the trenches strike to force an immediate peaceful settlement.

Less than three weeks after the ship docked in Norway, a disillusioned or nervous Ford booked passage on another ship for the return trip to the United States. He left the peace commissioners, who had spent most of their shipboard time arguing policy and procedures, to devise some way of stopping the war as best they could on their own. A little later Rosika Schwimmer dropped out of the delegation, and Caesar also disembarked to make a brief personal tour of Norway and Sweden.

Unlike Ford, who turned his company into a leading supplier of armaments once the United States entered the war, Caesar never actively supported the war effort. Indeed, his experience on the Peace Ship only increased his contempt for war in particular and military officers and politicians in general. In late 1916, he temporarily submerged his displeasure at the dismal prospects for world peace by projecting a hopeful note into the lyric of "When the Armies Disband." The song marked Caesar's first collaboration with his newly found Brooklyn friend, and budding genius, George Gershwin. Although the song was never published, their on-and-off writing partnership continued until the early 1920s. From it, in 1918, came one of the biggest song hits of each man's career, "Swanee," which Al Jolson's singing, tap dancing, and cupped-hand whistling turned into the most successful tune to emanate from the long-running 1917-18 Broadway musical *Sinbad*. As might be expected, Caesar's all-time favorite war song was not "Over There," much as he admired its spirit, but "I Didn't Raise My Boy to Be a Soldier."

The gregarious lyricist knew all the songwriters of both world wars and often acted on their behalf during difficult negotiations between the Song Writers' Protective Association and music publishers on royalty-payment issues. But he remained aloof from war-song hysteria. The closest he came to catching it was collaborating, under his birthname of Isador Caesar, with Al Bryan on the lyric and music for "The White House Is the Light House of the World" in 1918. The thrust of the lyric, as with the one written to Gershwin's melody, was definitely antiwar in that both Caesar and Bryan invoked Wilson's cherished hope that the new peace would bring permanent healing in its wings. Twenty-five years later, Caesar wrote the words to two ditties exhorting children to obey the directions of air-raid wardens; the songs were really extensions of his earlier series of children's *Songs of Health, Safety*, and *Friendship*. In a third mild World War II song, written with his usual collaborator,

Gerald Marks, and Al Koppell, Caesar encouraged a distraught little boy to "Be a Good Soldier (While Your Daddy's Away)."

At his best when writing happy tunes, the Lower East Side–born Caesar, who in 1994 married for the first time at age 99, wrote the lyrics to such breezy Broadway hits as "I Want to Be Happy," "Tea for Two," and "Sometimes I'm Happy." His witty lyric for "Crazy Rhythm," with music by Joseph Meyer and Roger Wolfe Kahn, testified to his mistrust of jazz, then rolling along 1920s Broadway and threatening to displace the romantic ballads and novelty songs that claimed Caesar's undying affection. Written in 1928, the song appeared in Broadway's *Here's Howe*.

5. The Song Deluge

Of the 35,600 American patriotic and war songs *copyrighted* by literally thousands of writers between mid–1914 and mid–1919, about 20 percent, or 7,300 can be verified as having been *published*, a slim minority that nonetheless surpasses the 15 percent, or 19,000, of the 127,000 copyrighted World War II songs. Most of the World War I songs were published by the authors themselves or by small independent firms doing business beyond the borders of such major metropolitan areas as New York City, Chicago, and Boston. Since songs published months after their copyright registration were rarely noted in the Library of Congress' annual *Catalogue of Copyright Entries*, the precise number of published works is impossible to ascertain. Compounding the problem was the appearance of printed copies of scores of war songs that had never been copyrighted, a procedure practiced by the smallest of the mom-and-pop publishing shops scattered especially throughout the Midwest.

Surprising as it may be to learn that Americans turned out so many war songs, the count should not amaze. The songwriting community was extremely active in the teens. The *CCE*s list the titles of 111,973 songs of all descriptions between August 1914 and August 1919. In 1915, the first full year of the war, 21,170 songs were copyrighted in America. The total dropped slightly to 20,049 in 1916, then rose to 21,079 in 1917. In the Armistice year of 1918, copyrighted songs numbered 24,858. In the final five months of 1914, 8,288 songs had been copyrighted; another 16,529 were copyrighted from January to August of 1919.

What is amazing is the ratio of war songs to total songs copyrighted in the final two years of the war. In 1915, only about 5 percent of the registered songs can be classified as patriotic or war; in 1916, about 25 percent. Perhaps as many as 10 percent of the 1915-16 copyrighted songs were doubtless inspired by American troops' forays into Mexico. In 1917, about 40 percent of registered songs referred exclusively to World War I. In 1918, the ratio was ratcheted up to about 70 percent. Thus, of the 87,156 songs copyrighted between January 1915 and December 1918, about 36 percent — 31,900 — dealt with the war, a strikingly high percentage. Judged by their titles, it is evident that even the earliest war-based songs increasingly centered on America's deepening concern over the carnage in France rather than on the dangers lurking south of the border.

Adding in the 404 patriotic/war songs copyrighted during the last five months of 1914 and the 3,300 during the first seven months of 1919 raises to 35,600 the grand total of songs touching on some aspect of World War I, including the hundreds of post–Armistice marches and ballads greeting the warriors on their return trip back home, celebrating their victory, and warmly recording the reuniting of families.

This unparalleled number of songs devoted to a single subject documents the magnitude of the horror that consumed Americans before, and especially during, the country's military participation in the war. More men than ever before were being sent to fight, and not only on the ground, where the lethal effectiveness of recently developed weaponry was verifiable by counting the dead. Battles were also being waged in the air and beneath the water. Peaceful countries were being overrun, their villages charred to ashes, their civilian populations brutalized.

The only war-associated tragedy from which Americans were shielded was the specter of invading armies and the subsequent despoliation of their cities and countryside. Even the surge of patriotism that drove thousands of young men into volunteering for active service in the spring of 1917 was mitigated that autumn by the widening fear that their only reward would be death or disfigurement.

Equally instrumental as war fears in generating the huge array of World War I songs was the predominant show business role played by musical performers in the halcyon days of vaudeville. Whether appearing at New York City's Palace Theatre, that awesome ultimate goal of all two-a-day acts since its opening in 1913,* or touring tiny towns' variety houses, all musical stars constantly sought new material to introduce to audiences. Songwriters answered the call by greatly escalating their creation of war songs both to satisfy the performers' needs and to advance their own careers in the expanding market awaiting the arrival of the newest battle-related tunes. With the war the most

discussed subject of the time, the writers and pluggers made themselves readily available to audition songs dealing with marching soldiers and letter-writing sweethearts in the hope that singers and dancers would add them to their repertoires.

Other contributors to building the need for new songs were sheet music, piano roll, and phonograph manufacturers, all of which were actively engaged in popularizing the latest tunes. Instrumentalists as well as stage and vaudeville stars recorded songs: Al Jolson, Eddie Cantor, George Jessel, and Irene Castle, Nora Bayes (born Doris Goldberg), Elsie Janis, Fanny Brice, Eva Tanguay, Sophie Tucker, Belle Baker (billed as the "Bernhardt of Song"), and scores of others. By means of their recordings, a song popular in New York City would be equally well known on the West Coast in a matter of days.

Repetitive hearings, however, usually led to a decrease in sales, regardless of the initial popularity of individual songs. So the public kept demanding new ones, exerting still more pressure on performers to provide them. The days when a few choice songs were enough to accompany a singer on a cross-country tour were over. During World War I, most ticket-buyers in the largest to the smallest communities quickly learned all hit songs by heart and, save for the trusty few that served as an artist's signature song (like Adele Rowland's "Smiles"), customers rarely became excited for long about paying more money to hear them again.

Never before had so many songs in such a short time span inundated Americans with vivid descriptions of the miseries common to entire populations at war, particularly the Belgians and French. The conflict was lengthening into a killing marathon between factions either too stubborn or too foolish to resolve their

*After 19 glorious years of vaudeville, the Palace succumbed to the inevitable by adding films to its live variety entertainment in 1932, and beginning in 1935 it devoted itself entirely to movies. Another citadel of vaudeville, the Apollo, opened its doors the same year as the Palace — 1913 — on West 125th Street, the major boulevard of Harlem. Both landmarks are still in operation, the Palace as a legitimate theater, the Apollo as a venue for occasional live acts and pop artists' concerts.

differences at a peace table. At least a half-dozen American-written songs even dramatized the death of young men on the battlefield, a sober subject almost completely ignored by songwriters in previous wars, and in World War II as well. As late as August 1919, nine months after the war ended, songs were still being published to remind Americans of the heavy toll in lives and property the war had exacted on a significant portion of Western Europe.

The Pulpers

Throughout the period, the music of a vast number of war songs was credited to persons whom music professionals categorized as "pulp composers." Sometimes associated with publishing houses, but usually not, these commercial melodists accepted lyrics written mostly by female neophytes who had been invited through ads in music trade periodicals to submit their poems, to which the pulpers would promptly add the music for a stipulated fee. Sometimes, in lieu of a fee for the pulpers' services, the agreement between the two parties would state that any royalties earned on their speculative efforts, if and when published, would be shared equally by the collaborators.

More often than not, however, according to songwriter Irving Caesar, who was acquainted with several of the pulpers, the music-makers would pocket the fee and send the completed songs back to the lyricists, who were expected to market them on their own to publishers indicating interest in adding to their reservoirs of war songs. More gambler than poet, the average correspondent was reminiscent of the mail-order bride of the Old West, sending off a lyric instead of a photograph, dreaming of a happy, fruitful union with a prospective publisher.

How many of these assembly-line compositions actually wound up in print cannot be determined with exactness, since only a relative few were copyrighted or recopyrighted as published, according to

the Library of Congress' *Catalog of Copyrighted Entries* and card index of musical compositions. Typically, sheet music copies of the songs for which the lyricists were able to find publishers ended up moldering on the shelves of local printing companies, which customarily billed all expenses to the lyricist. He or she was also expected to take charge of distributing the copies to community music stores, a generally dismal occupation for persons without professional songwriting credentials. Rarely were the songs treated to mass-market exposure; the typical small-town publisher was simply unable to gain access to the nationwide distribution channels available to the major music firms operating out of New York City, Chicago, and Boston.

The major pulp composers displayed wanton proficiency—some would call it profligacy—in setting undistinguished war poems to music. In 1918, for example, when the by-mail partnership activity reached an incredible level, Leo Friedman, associated with North American Music Publishing Co. in Chicago, was credited with writing the music for 698 songs, 65 percent of them qualifying as war songs. The composer of such respectable non-war song hits as "Let Me Call You Sweetheart" and "Meet Me Tonight in Dreamland," Friedman was the only pulper to shepherd practically all of his war-song collaborations through the publishing process. The result of Friedman's entrepreneurship was the appearance of his name on more than 1,000 of the 7,300 World War I songs verified as published between August 1914 and August 1919. Regardless of the frequent title redundancies and unquestionable artistic deficiencies of his lyricists, Friedman's creativity stuns the mind. His published output is unrivaled by any other composer in the history of American war music. Nor was he averse to supplying the melodies for songs bearing identical titles. His name was appended as composer of four songs entitled "Dear Old U.S.A."; two of them were registered in 1918, the other two the following year. He also composed five songs entitled "Victory," and four others that inserted that word in longer titles between late 1918 and early 1919.

R(aymond) A. Browne was listed as the composer of 543 songs in 1918, 60 percent of them war-based. His totals for the preceding three years were 275 (50 percent), 1917; 77 (10 percent), 1916; and 92 (3 percent), 1915. The name of J.E. Andino appeared as composer of 580 songs in 1915, 811 in 1916, and 565 in 1917, about 60 percent of the total directly relating to the war. Apparently exhausted by 1918, Andino's production plummeted that year to a mere 103 songs, 65 percent carrying war themes.

Of all these men, none came even close to compiling the song inventory credited to E.S.S. Huntington, the Babe Ruth of the pulping profession, whose collaborative efforts in 1918 totaled 2,995 tunes, or an average of eight a day. Slightly more than 75 percent of them qualify by title as war songs. Only nine songs had carried the Huntington name in 1915, none of them concerning the war. The next year, however, his productivity soared to 944, including 180 war songs. In 1917, 520 of Huntington's 1,485 copyrighted songs related to the war.

From the doggerel titles of the songs on which composer Huntington collaborated, it is clear that he was willing to accommodate his lyricists' subject matter regardless of how many times it had already been duplicated. Some, like "Sure, We'll Win," one of the hundreds of his compositions predicting Germany's defeat, were models of the simple declarative statement. Others exuded contempt, particularly for the much-maligned Kaiser, who was mentioned by name or title or identified by innuendo in the titles of 46 Huntington songs in 1918. "There's a Sick Man in Europe" proclaimed one of his least incendiary songs, followed by the prophetic "Kaiser's Doom," which sought to add to the emperor's misery by letting him dangle in midair while trying to decipher whether his and his nation's fate

would be surrender or annihilation.

Huntington in the single year of 1918 provided the melodies for such unpublished songs as "When Our Boys Come Home," "When Our Boys Come Back Home," "When Our Boys Come Marching Home," "When Our Boys Come Marching Home Again," "When Mother's Boy Comes Marching Home," "When Our Soldier Boys Return," "When Our Soldier Boys Get Back to the U.S.A.," "When I Get Home," and "When I Return to My Home Sweet Home." Countless of his other songs welcomed the troops back to America between January and August 1919; Huntington apparently found the victory bandwagon irresistible and accelerated his contributions accordingly, disregarding the similarity of the titles and lyrics submitted to him.

Actually, very few sheet music copies of his and Browne's and Andino's published songs are in existence today. Were more of their songs to be certified as published, which is extremely doubtful, the number of American patriotic and war songs marketed between August 1914 and the end of July 1919 would swell to more than 12,000. Only Friedman and Browne were members of the American Society of Composers, Authors and Publishers, which was founded in 1914.

Contributing to the verification problem has been the disappearance over the years of nearly 100 percent of the World War I music publishing companies. Not only did all the tiny publishers shuffle off their mortal coils, but so did most of the largest of the New York City firms through merger, bankruptcy, or the partners' deaths or arguments. Disappearing in the wake of their demise were most of the records pertaining to the songs the firms had published.

Most songs copyrighted between 1914 and 1919, of course, had nothing to with the war. The annual copyright figures clearly show that the America of the period was resoundingly music-conscious and interested in a variety of rhythms and topics. Fortunately, a substantial number of the nation's foremost songwriters —

George M. Cohan, Irving Berlin, Victor Herbert, Sigmund Romberg, George W. Meyer, Harry and Albert Von Tilzer, Charles K. Harris, Jerome Kern, Walter Donaldson, James V. Monaco, and James F. Hanley among them—were on hand to cater to the insatiable demand for songs, even though the majority of their war tunes do not represent their finest work, or only a tiny part of it.

Nonetheless, 1918 witnessed the publication of almost 200 war songs by only four of New York City's biggest music publishers. Of the 87 songs issued by Leo Feist, Inc., 73 were concerned with the war; Jerome H. Remick's 139 included 40 war songs. Waterson, Berlin & Snyder Co. published 39 war songs among the 112 it released that year. For Shapiro, Bernstein & Co., the figures were 42 war songs out of the company's total of 131.

Although not particularly active in the songwriting craft before 1914, American women were responsible for at least one-half of all the country's copyrighted World War I songs. Sometimes one woman wrote both words and music; more often she collaborated with a partner. Lyrics rather than melodies were their preference, and about nine of every ten works written by women were musicalized by the pulpers. Since it was common at the time for many songwriters of both sexes to use only the initials of their first and middle names when registering a song, it is impossible to determine precisely how many songs were written or co-written by women. But female productivity most likely accounted for about 60 percent of the war's 35,600 copyrighted patriotic and war songs.

Most of the women's earliest efforts were written as patriotic anthems praising the American flag and the republic for which it stood, or as pleas to end the war before the United States was swept into its vortex. After 1917, they began specializing in miss-you songs and others centering on the pain of grieving for the missing or dead, rather than urging the troops onward, although a few staunchly defended the American crusade as a most noble one,

and quite likely the only means of lifting the embargo on world peace. Immediately after the war, women surpassed their male counterparts by a ratio of 1½ to 1 in the number of songs hailing the victory and the valiant troops most responsible for securing it.

A minimum of their songs became even vaguely popular, chiefly because almost none were accepted by the first-rank publishing houses. Not even the three new ones written by Carrie Jacobs-Bond, a most successful woman composer with "I Love You Truly," "A Perfect Day," and "Just a-Wearyin' for You" already to her credit, proved to be commercially successful. She did score a slight success with "His Buttons Are Marked 'U.S.'," which she wrote in 1902 and recopyrighted in 1918. It was republished by her own firm, Carrie Jacobs-Bond & Son, which maintained offices in Chicago at 746 So. Michigan Avenue. In the song, an admiring little girl salutes her father, dressed in an army uniform, which she describes as a "dandy, fine new brown suit with buttons marked 'U.S.'" To the child, the letters spell "us," which she interprets as meaning that her soldier father still belongs to her and her mother, despite his temporary liaison with Uncle Sam.

A Hostile Environment

The average American's opinion of Germany underwent a wrenching sea change in the spring of 1917 that routed the country from the cautious toleration that had characterized the previous two years. Wilson's own Committee on Public Information, ostensibly a fact-gathering organization, became an agency for circulating virulent anti–German propaganda. The CPI rivaled journalists, academicians, and the embryonic advertising industry in promoting not only the war effort but, above all, fierce loyalty to what was loosely termed "Americanism"—meaning, one must assume, unshakable confidence in the wisdom of the government's switch from neutrality to federation with the embattled Allies.

As rage against the enemy climbed, even the German language was removed from some school curricula, and German operas and symphonies were cut from many American repertories. The war prevented some German musicians from visiting America and even prompted the deportation of Karl Muck, the celebrated conductor of the Boston Symphony Orchestra, who was suspected of harboring pro-enemy sentiment.

Also coming under attack were the "friendless and starving" war refugees who had fled various European countries for America. They had sworn allegiance to the United States upon their arrival, but now some were repaying the welcome they received by abusing and reviling Uncle Sam. He had gathered these thankless, "empty-handed" newcomers close to his bosom and given them food and clothing, according to one song, but many of them were refusing to honor their oath to aid him in time of peril.

"If you don't like Uncle Sammy, / Then go back to your home o'er the sea, / To the land from where you came, / Whatever be its name, / But don't be ungrateful to me," argued Thomas Hoier and Jimmie Morgan in their mid-war diatribe. Personalizing the disconsolate tall man with the high hat and the whiskers on his chin, the songwriters let him issue his own complaint to the ungrateful:

> "If you don't like the stars in Old
>   Glory,
> If you don't like the Red, White and
>   Blue,
> Then don't act like the cur in the story,
> Don't bite the hand that's feeding you."

As reflected in most of the patriotic anthems early in the war, American public opinion from the beginning of the war tended to support the Allies. Americans had ties of race, language, culture, and political ideals with England and bonds of strong friendship with France, none of which had a substantial counterpart in

their relations with Germany. Only in communities where the German or Irish heritage was strong was there likely to be a large pro–German (or anti–British) following. Irish-Americans, for example, were particularly incensed at England's ruthless suppression of the "Easter Rebellion" in Ireland in April of 1916, and their anger at times erupted into vocal and written protests against what they felt were increasingly intense American overtures to assist the British war effort.

Both sides in the war made their propaganda appeals to American opinion. German "atrocities" were magnified, even invented, by the British and French. Such exaggerated stories were often accepted as sober truth, while German propaganda was most often spotted as such and discounted accordingly. It was in this new atmosphere of often gratuitous contempt that many American citizens with Teutonic-sounding names sought to avoid the guilt by association aroused by their German heritage. One Maude Krieger, for example, felt the need to Gallicize her surname into the milder Cregier. It was Maude's daughter, Gertrude, who in later years gave birth to Shirley Temple.

Depression Revisited

With battlefield stalemate running counter to assurances that the Americans would bring a swift end to the war, songwriters in the fall of 1917 began reflecting the public's disenchantment by adhering more faithfully to the sobering, dog-eared messages popularized by their 1914–1916 predecessors. Confidence in victory, pride in heroes, and love of home land—the sole positive themes of warfare—were not dismissed outright. But the chastened writers downplayed them to coordinate their lyrics with the overall dimming of optimism.

Many in the new song collection stoked domestic passions by conjuring up mental and emotional responses to the fond farewells being exchanged by parents and children and between sweethearts in even more sentimental terms than those written in the previous two years. No longer were the British and French the only troops being sent to the trenches. Americans were also fighting there, and it was they who were attracting major songwriter attention and sympathy. The battle song became a scarce commodity for sale to the public. Mary Earl's pretty "My Sweetheart Is Somewhere in France" and "I'm Proud to Be the Sweetheart of a Soldier," for example, ably represented the abrupt change in content and tone, concentrating not on the war but on the individual soldier's predicament. Mary Earl, incidentally, was one of the four pseudonyms used by Robert A. King, whose non-war compositions included "Beautiful Ohio" and "I Ain't Nobody's Darling."

Equally redolent with love for and admiration of the warriors were Raymond B. Egan and Richard A. Whiting's mellifluous "Throw Me a Kiss (From Over the Sea)" ("press it, caress it, address it to me, dear"); Snyder and Doctor's "I'm Hitting the Trail to Normandy (So Kiss Me Goodbye)"; and M. Russell Brown's "When You Kiss Your Soldier Boy Goodbye." Carrying the alternate title of "Our Boys Are Off to France," Brown's song reprised the familiar chin-up lecture that the distressed lover has a duty to give her soldier a smile to take along, despite the breaking of her heart. Consoling wives and sweethearts was Al Bryan, Edgar Leslie, and Harry Ruby's "The Girl He Left Behind Him (Has the Hardest Fight of All)." She may not have to face the foe over there, the song concedes, "but in her heart she has a sorrow to bear" while waiting "for a word from her soldier lad."

Lew Brown, who in the 1920s would become a charter member of the fabulously successful (Buddy) DeSylva, Brown, and (Ray) Henderson songwriting trio, offered some consolation in his lyric to Albert Von Tilzer's mellow "Au Revoir, But Not Goodbye (Soldier Boy)." In their followup "I May Be Gone for a Long, Long Time," however, Brown overlay his lyric with a veneer of distressing realism that even the

most hopeful were incapable of ignoring completely. Brown also collaborated with composer Will Clayton for the only slightly more upbeat "(Watch, Hope, and Wait) Little Girl ('I'm Coming Back to You')."

Almost harrowing in musicalizing the words a young soldier might speak not at home, but on the trampled soil of the battlefield itself, was George L. Boyden's "If I'm Not at the Roll Call (Kiss Mother for Me)." About to go "over the top," the doughboy reveals his wish to a comrade, doubting that "after the fighting is done" he will be alive to respond when the sergeant calls out the names of his troops to learn which of them have survived the attack: "Won't you be kind to my mother, / Just for her soldier son?" he asks. "Tell her I know how she loves me, / And prays for me constantly. / May angels attend her, / Brave comrade, befriend her / And kiss her goodbye for me."

Another suitably searing love song, but of a different stripe, was Al Bryan and Fred Fisher's "Lorraine, My Beautiful Alsace-Lorraine," which recalled pleasant memories of the "quaint old-fashioned people" who inhabited ancient little villages in Alsace-Lorraine, then under German control. (After the war, the country was retroceded to France.) There was also the somber "The Tale the Church Bell Told," Sam M. Lewis, Joe Young and Bert Grant's soliloquy on the war's destructiveness as viewed from a churchyard tower. The distant hammering booms of cannon and shattering cries of young and old have displaced the chirping of birds, which once had blessed the landscape with an aura of serenity. "Someone will answer for this vi'lence," the songwriters vow.

"Let the Chimes of Normandy Be Our Wedding Bells" was only one of the sentimental ballads scripted by Paul B. Armstrong to the music of F. Henri Klickmann. Its forlorn lyric complemented the respectably tender melody, but having plodded along on a predictable course, the words provided only momentary illumination on how one set of separated lovers was reunited symbolically rather than face to face before the song fizzled to the ground. The same writers' "There's a Little Blue Star in the Window (and It Means All the World to Me)," "Old Glory Goes Marching On," and "Will the Angels Guard My Daddy Over There?" suffered a similar fate.

To Mother and Home

Although many American war-song lyrics centered on lovers' farewells, an even larger number dwelled on mothers, with a blend of gentility and pathos worthy of Dickens. It was she whom the songwriters considered to suffer the greatest emotional pain and grief when the young man in the family was pressed into service. Of the scores of published songs concentrating on mother-son partings and mutual loneliness, about 35 qualified as transient hits, like Raymond B. Egan and Richard A. Whiting's prescient "The Bravest Heart of All."

The characters in that song were the familiar mother and baby son who are waving farewell to the father, off on his way to France. His leaving adds to the mother's worries—well founded, as history would prove—that someday the little boy will also board a transport ship to fight for his country. "My little laddie dear," the mother sings, "There's a day I fear, / When you will be so brave and tall":

> "Someday you'll be a man, sir, and
>   then you'll answer
> To dear Old Glory's call;
> Like your dad you'll sail away
> With a heart so brave and gay.
> But when you depart,
> Then your mother's heart
> Will be the bravest heart of all."

The finest of the mother songs rang with praises of the women's steadfastness in accepting the potential sacrifice of their sons as their major contribution to the war effort. Some writers specialized in these songs, like Andrew B. Sterling and

Arthur Lange, who collaborated on three: "America, Here's My Boy," "A Mother's Prayer for Her Boy Out There," and, with an assist from Alfred Solman, "Just a Letter for a Boy Over There from a Grey-Haired Mother Over Here." Imbued with appeals to God and faith in the power of prayer, the typical mother song was more religious than secular in tone and tempo, often approaching the exalted status of a hymn to peace. "Soldier boy, you've gone away, / In my heart I hope and pray / That you will return some day," sings the mother in Walter Hirsch and Frank Magine's "Bring Back My Soldier Boy to Me." Lonesome and careworn, she prays to God each night that He will "watch him, protect him, while he's across the sea."

Some of the songs, major as well as minor, were most likely biographical. This was especially discernible in the scores of earnest but leaden lyrics written by women, like Brenta F. Wallace and Mercy P. Graham's for "Boy of Mine," which adequately combined motherly pride and concern for one son serving overseas:

> "Boy of mine, boy of mine,
> Let your courage prove so true
> That the whole [world] shall be heaven
>   on earth.
> Oh, boy of mine, I'll pray for you."

"There's a Battlefield in Ev'ry Mother's Heart" stressed the conflicting emotions suffered by mothers in search of assurances that their sons would soon be returned to them, yet constantly agonizing that they already may have become battlefield casualties. "There's a battle raging down in each mother's heart," the Howard E. Rogers lyric states. "There's a struggle tearing it apart, / Mem'ries so tender of her boy 'out there' / She won't surrender, but fights her despair."

Particularly exquisite was the sentiment written into "I Can't Stay Here While You're Over There," which expressed another mother's impossible dream of joining her boy in France and consoling him:

"I wish that I could share
All of your troubles and care;
I know you need me there
Just to comfort you now.
You'll always be my baby to me,
In dreams I seem to see
You back on my knee.
You know you are my pride and joy
And my place is by your side.
I can't stay here while you're over there."

Taking the insistent songwriter advice to "Write to Your Dear Sweet Mother (If It's Only a Line)," the boys at the front wrote most of their musical letters not to their sweethearts, but to their mothers. It was they who were the soldiers' first love, and separation had only intensified the devotion they shared. Thus, declarations of undying love of mother pervaded the young men's epistles, along with comforting declarations of their good health and spirits, as voiced in "Oh, Moon of the Summer Night (Tell My Mother Her Boy's All Right)," and "Cheer Up, Mother, It's All Right Now and Everything Is All O.K."

Indeed, as in Jack Caddigan's lyric to "Mother, I'm Dreaming of You," the sentiment and phrasing so closely resembled that of the typical love song from soldier to wife or girlfriend that its message seems more appropriate to a Cub Scout or a very young and lonely lad at summer camp:

"Mother, I'm dreaming of you, dear,
Here in the campfire's glow,
And in all my dreams
I'm seeing, it seems,
That home I used to know.
I feel your arms twine about me,
I feel you kissing me, too,
And I know I've been blessed,
For at night when I rest,
Mother, I'm dreaming of you."

Responding to the numerous mid-war victory songs designed to prop up the spirits of servicemen as well as civilians, many of the doughboy-to-mother songs sought to repay the favor by consoling the home front. Either uninformed or dismissive of credible evidence emanating from the battlefield, the soldiers in the songs rarely omitted their unswerving belief that the day would surely soon arrive when they would come "Back to Mother and Home Sweet Home."

The Mary Earl lyric of "Cheer Up, Mother," for example, contains a soldier's plea to his mother to replace the "teardrop in your eye" with a smile:

"We'll come back with colors flying
After the war clouds roll by,
Homeward bound then
We'll come sailing, mother.
We will win out, never fear;
Dad came home from fields of glory,
Maybe I'll repeat his story,
So cheer up, mother dear."

Bringing that dream to fruition, however, would require massive assistance from at-home Americans of both sexes and all ages. Again, the songwriters strengthened the victory message by advocating various means by which mothers could contribute even further to the war effort. "We'll Do Our Share (While You're Over There)" became the clarion call of mothers who felt that knitting socks and writing letters were inadequate to the task of safeguarding their sons till Uncle Sam, his arm around the shoulder of a returning soldier, stepped up to mothers everywhere and said, "Mother, Here's Your Boy." That title of an excellent Sidney D. Mitchell–Archie Gottler–Theodore Morse postwar collaboration would, in time, say it all. If home was where the heart is, the young soldier would find peace and security in his mother's welcoming embrace. Certainly, the expectation of their eventual reunion was worth any additional sacrifice mothers could endure to speed the boys on their offensive "to cross the Rhine." The Gus Kahn words to "For Your Boy and My Boy (Buy Bonds! Buy Bonds!)" best served the purpose of enlisting mothers and all other civilians as co-equal shareholders in victory:

Hear the bugle call,
The call to those who stay at home;

You are soldiers all,
Though you may never cross the foam.
Keep Old Glory waving
Proudly up above,
Praying, working, saving
For the ones you love.

Nor were the mothers of France forgotten. In "Girls of France" the professional writing team of Al Bryan, Edgar Leslie, and Harry Ruby praised all mothers, especially the younger ones, "for leading your sons like Joan of Arc," an attribution that mothers of whatever age or country were definitely not entitled to. They undoubtedly did inspire, which itself was a significant act of bravery considering the dread and loneliness they were facing. But they led no troops, nor did they fight in the trenches.

Since, in the words of one mother song — "That's a Mother's Liberty Loan" — the giving up of her son to the military "to fight for you and me" represented her investment in the future, it followed quite naturally that America itself would come to be identified as a loving female parent whose cry for help should not be ignored in a time of crisis. Such an appeal was sounded in mid–1917 by Grant Clarke and Jean Schwartz, whose "America Needs You Like a Mother (Would You Turn Your Mother Down?)" was used as an Army recruiting song:

> America has been a mother
> To the children of the world;
> She has taken to her bosom
> Ev'ry homeless boy and girl.
> Now we find she's in trouble,
> Danger's lurking all around.
> America needs you like a mother,
> Would you turn your mother down?

Furthermore, the lyric maintained, the munificence for which America was renowned should be repaid by the beneficiaries:

> We know that there are diff'rent kinds
>   of children,
> There are some who love to roam;
> Then again there's some who love their

mother,
They would rather stay at home.
Still, with all our many faults and failings,
She remains our only friend.
Just like many loyal children,
We should help her to the end.

Tear-Evoking Reminiscences

Rarely absent from these kinds of homefront-involvement songs were sentimental references to the mothers' selflessness, gentility, and model parenting. They were undoubtedly worthy of their siblings' devotion, even if the songwriters' often blatant efforts to wring the last teardrop from the eyes of listeners — and sometimes performers, too — eventually converted the ladies' virtues into clichés. All the mothers, for example, were "old and gray," leading one to surmise that no American woman under the age of 40 had given birth to a son. The mother in one lyric was not only old with hairs of gray, but bent with age as well. Another was feeble, in effect converting her from an object to be admired for her fortitude into one to be pitied for her infirmities. The mothers' eyes were perennially "tear-dimmed" while reading their soldier boys' letters, a condition that very well might have existed, but soon descended into triteness through absurd repetition. Their sons were always their "pride and joy," a common phrase that conveniently rhymed with "boy." And their eyes, when lifted from their sons' letters, were inevitably transfixed on the "vacant chairs" the young men had occupied before they left the home for the battlefield.

It is a curious fact that of the thousands of published World War I songs, only one — and a minor one at that — referred in its title to Christmas, the most festive and sentimental of all holidays. The gathering together of the family around the Yule tree, their happiness diminished by the absence of soldier sons, would not be expressed in song until 1943, when Kim Gannon, Walter Kent, and Buck

Ram produced the memorable "I'll Be Home for Christmas (If Only in My Dreams)," one of World War II's most popular ballads.

Far from detracting from the popularity potential of the mother songs, the ever-present sentimentality the lines exuded was greeted warmly by the typical music fan. Even non-war songs were permeated with endless tearful proclamations of parental love, the premonition that the girl (or boy) of one's dreams would vanish into the arms of another, the longing to return to childhood, and the decision to desert the cold, impersonal city to return to the warmth of the farm down in Dixie.

Without in any way demeaning the quality of many of the popular non-war ballads of the 1914–1919 period, it is a fact that the vast audiences, hip deep in the mist of nostalgia, simply adored graceful melodies with maudlin lyrics. The more lugubrious, the better; the more saccharine, the sweeter. Thus, the sorrowful themes of the majority of the war songs were designed to fit snugly into the prevailing taste in popular music, guaranteeing song-writing success.

Since the typical mother-oriented song was actually a love note, the need of the writers to depend on bromidic recollections of pleasures eroded by time and circumstance was inescapable. The public had been conditioned to tearful contemplation, and the war only buttressed the foundation on which Americans' attachment to the past rested. Ernest R. Ball's "Turn Back the Universe and Give Me Yesterday" (1916) was unmatched in expressing ardor to trade in the present for the long ago. But, then, except for the occasional rag or comic novelty tune performed by vaudevillians, many songs relied on forlorn reminders of lost youth or dreams unfulfilled for popularity.

The singer in Howard Johnson and Theodore Morse's "M-O-T-H-E-R (a Word That Means the World to Me)," from 1915, for example, acknowledges without a hint of embarrassment that "M is for the million things she gave me"; another showers praise on his mother's native land in the lyric to "Ireland Must Be Heaven (for My Mother Came from There)," a 1916 paean also written by Johnson in collaboration with Joseph McCarthy and Fred Fisher. Like the melancholy protagonist in "Mammy's Dixie Soldier Boy" (1918), these young men wanted nothing more than to return to their roots, whether in Swanee or elsewhere, and to the arms of their loving mother, ever on the watch for her wandering son's reappearance.

Grant Clarke and James V. Monaco's 1915 "hometown" song success, "I Want to Be There," recorded the wistful wish of a traveler to return to his childhood home. "Among the shady nooks," he will "see how mother looks" and romp again in familiar places with "my old dog Rover, / Who gets the mail and wags his tail all over." Nat Vincent and Ted Shapiro's 1918 non-war "It's a Long Way Back to School Days" perfectly exemplified the desire to push the war aside and bask again in the innocent delights of childhood. The final line written by these two deans of déjà vu, "We'd all love to be there once again," was an apt summary of the public's disenchantment with the present.

These and numerous other expressions of the typical American's desperation for the reuniting of families exerted a powerful influence on the war-song writers. Especially after the Armistice, they flooded music stores with tunes celebrating the happiness of the homeward-bound soldiers. The boys had survived the war and, as they soon would learn, so had the cherished home fires, courtesy of their mothers, who had kept them burning throughout. Although interrupted, family life had been preserved. It was the perpetual hope of restoring this togetherness that had provided the major stimulus for the doughboys' display of battlefield courage and helped to assuage their loneliness.

Because mothers so indelibly represented the past and childhood, few listeners of J. Keirn Brennan and Ernest R. Ball's "You're the Best Little Mother That God Ever Made" (1916) would blanch at the Victorian-flavored excessiveness of such lines as "God made you, dear mother, / And then broke the mold." Similarly, female sweethearts were depicted as angelic, and with good reason, according to most ballads of the time. They were, after all, destined someday to become mothers themselves; therefore, they were continuously described as demure, beautiful princesses, which was exactly as Ray White and Jim Schiller portrayed "My Dream Girl" in 1918. As the lyric notes: "God put the sunshine in your smile, / Into your hair the moon's bright beams, / Into your lips the reddest of roses, / Then made your teeth of pearl. / The blue of the skies / He put in your eyes...."

Edna Stanton Whaley and F.H. Bishop had provided another dream girl in 1917 in "Evening Brings Rest and You," which publisher M. Witmark & Sons advertised as a "song full of sunshine and love." The remembrance of the daily parting smile between a civilian husband and his wife was a source of comfort that helped to shorten his workday "till the light fades away, / And evening brings rest and you."

The song's kinship with "Smiles" is apparent; had Whaley and Bishop incorporated a military setting into the lyric, it well might have served as a first-rate war song. Their girl was exactly the type that soldiers fantasied about during their nightly reveries in the trenches. Thoughts of her induced contentment: she was well worth fighting for. After Armistice Day it was she, along with a proud mother, whom the soldiers in the welcome-home war songs expected to find at dockside.

Like Father, Like Son

Compared with mothers and sweethearts, fathers were almost completely ignored by the war-song writers unless they were serving overseas with the armed forces. Then it was to God that their children turned to petition for their safety in a series of usually sorrowful, often melodi-ous, prayers. The daddy songs ran a distant second in popularity to those revolving around mothers, largely because of the lyrics rather than the melody, which at times was most respectable. The mother songs could usually overcome the sugary-sad appeals to God to watch over the boys over there; mothers were expected to talk that way. Fathers, on the other hand, were to be honored for controlling their emotions in times of distress, disdainful of serving as candidates for pity.

Thus, songs with teary-eyed daughters, and sometimes sons, as the centerpiece abounded. Lacking virtually any significant differences among them, all begged for the sight of the soldier-parent emerging from the horizon like the morning sun, his fighting days behind him and ready to resume the role of magistrate and benefactor of the little universe that was his family. "Bring Back My Daddy to Me" was the doleful cry of one little girl whose father had gone off to war. "I don't want a dress or a dolly," she adds in the musicalized prayer by William Tracey, Howard Johnson, and George W. Meyer, just the embrace of the adult man in her life. The song sold well, striking as it did a highly responsive chord because of the dramatic increase in the number of youngsters made fatherless by the war. The girl pictured on the sheet music cover was Madge Evans, then a child actress who in the 1930s became one of the movies' most glamorous leading ladies, starring in such films as *Dinner at Eight* (1933), *David Copperfield* (1935), and *Pennies from Heaven* (1936).

Another heart-rending song, by Sam M. Lewis, Joe Young, and Jean Schwartz, presented a baby girl who "toddles up to the telephone, / And whispers in a baby tone: 'Hello Central, give me No Man's Land, / My daddy's there.'" What she wants to know, she tells the operator, is why her mother starts to weep when, during prayers, the child says "Now I lay me down to sleep." Equally sad—albeit highly effective—in dramatizing the heartsickness of the innocent was "Just a Baby's Prayer at Twilight," Lewis, Young, and M.K.

Jerome's recitation of the words spoken by another little girl fearful for the safety of her daddy.

For Geoffrey O'Hara's "Over Yonder Where the Lilies Grow," the Norman Rockwell cover showing a youngster pinning a flower on a soldier intensified the pathos of the child-without-father syndrome. "My Daddy's Star," with the Ivan Reid lyric joined to a lovely melody by Peter DeRose, featured on the cover a girl child gazing affectionately up at a French sky seeded with stars, one of them displaying her deceased father's likeness in the heavens.

Only rarely were little boys written into these songs of supplication. And when they were, as in "Wake Me Early, Mother Dear," "Take a Letter to My Daddy 'Over There,'" and "Somewhere in France Is Daddy," their personality and physical features were scarcely distinguishable from those for which their little sisters had been traditionally admired. The boys were presented as petite role models of decorum and charm, their voices gentle, their hair clustered in curls and cheeks indented with dimples, their heavenly incantations more pleading than demanding.

In "Wake Me Early, Mother Dear," by Alex Sullivan and Arthur Lamont, a three-year-old lad bids his mother goodbye after singing, "Last night I dreamt dear daddy called me / Far across the sea, / And I must go, / 'Cause he can't come home to me." Just as his nightly dreams revive images of his father, so do they transport the toddler overseas to his dead parent's side. Another little child directed her prayer to the highest earthly authority in Lew Porter's "Hello! Gen'ral Pershing (How's My Daddy Tonight)?"

For the most part, the primary duty of stay-at-home fathers in the songs was to prod their sons into proving their masculinity by emulating the elder man's own battlefield heroics. War does demand such selfless devotion to duty, but that kind of fatherly counseling was hardly comforting to other parents worried about the well-being of their soldier sons. In such a song as "Daddy's Land," for example, a dying soldier outlines his family's military history to his captain, proud to the end that he had added to its glory:

"My dad left his birthplace when only
    a boy
To fight for the land of the free;
He fought with Grant," said the lad
    with a sigh,
"With Sherman he marched to the sea.
Now I've done the same for his country
    and name,
And it's all that he'd wish me to do;
Please tell them at home how I died
    here alone
And prayed for the Red, White and
    Blue."

Songwriter J. Francis Kiely's mortally wounded soldier's fondest hope is that he has matched his father's valor in an earlier war and that his own brave service in the new one will help to restore peace to his homeland:

"I've fought for the land of my daddy,
For daddy fought for mine;
When Lincoln called for volunteers,
Why, he was there in line.
I've just one wish," he whispered,
"Before the last command;
May God help my United States
Bring peace to daddy's land."

In J. Will Callahan and Paul C. Pratt's "Your Daddy Will Be Proud of You," a model warrior of a father writes to his son, hoping that he will follow the example he has set for him. The young man's survival is of secondary interest, even if devoutly wished; he is over there to do a job, and the father, perhaps vicariously reliving his own past, demands that he do his very best at it:

"I followed Teddy up the San Juan
    Hill,
Now you know what you're to do.
Just write me that you're well,
Then wade in and give 'em hell,
[Just put the map of France
On the seat of William's pants],
And your daddy will be proud of you."

Battlefield Sweethearts

In third place, behind mothers and girlfriends, in reaping songwriters' sympathy and admiration were members of the American Red Cross — Irving Berlin's "Angels of Mercy" in World War II. One of the first such tributes to win multitudes of admirers, Will Mahoney's "The Girl Who Wears a Red Cross on Her Sleeve," concentrated on the pride of one "gray-haired mother in a far-off town" with only female offspring to her credit. "I would be glad / If I had a lad / To fight for his country like a man," the mother confides. But, she quickly adds, "And though I had no boy, / It just filled me with joy / To give my darling girl when war began."

That other mothers should display identical pride in the role their daughters can play in the war is implied throughout the song, provided that a little cross of red adorns the youngsters' uniforms. Serving soldiers at the front, each "works with the heart of an angel / 'Mid the sound of the cannon's roar." She is caring "with love so sweet and tender / For the sons of the mothers who grieve, / And many are the hearts that are grateful tonight / To the girl who wears a red cross on her sleeve." As Mahoney and other songwriters pointed out, often quite graphically, the roles played by Red Cross nurses were far more valuable than merely wrapping bandages and sewing bits of clothing.

"Let's Help the Red Cross Now" advocated support of the organization by indicating how selflessly its nurses were performing their duties in the midst of danger. "When shot and shell are flying, / They help the sick and dying, / Cooling each fevered brow," revealed songwriter Ted S. Barron:

> On ev'ry field of battle
> They are always to be found;
> To do their duty bravely without fear,
> They carry off the wounded
> While the shells are bursting 'round.
> It is their prayers our dying soldiers
>   hear.

Addressing the imperative of civilians' lending a helping hand to the uniformed ladies was Lew Orth's "Don't Forget the Red Cross Nurse," which described its nurses as mothers to the soldiers in their care, dainty and demure to be sure, but nonetheless "always in the thickest of the fray":

> On the field of battle 'mid cannon's
>   roar and rattle,
> She will think of your life first.
> She may be somebody's wife,
> Still she's willing to give up her life;
> To the wounded she brings joys,
> Our hats off to her, boys!
> So don't forget the Red Cross nurse.

The injured soldier in Byron Gay's "My Angel of the Flaming Cross" bestows a heavenly glow on the typical battlefield nurse, possessed of the highly vaunted "golden hair and eyes of blue," who saved his life:

> "There's an angel over there,
> An angel from I know not where;
> Smiling sweetly through her tears,
> She drove my fears away.
> Little girl who nursed me through,
> I owe my life to you;
> Oh, come back,
> Love that I found and lost,
> My angel of the flaming cross."

Like the lyrical "That Red Cross Girl of Mine," essentially a love poem from a soldier to his healer and savior, Gay's soliloquy was only one in the series of songs in which a doughboy shyly admits that he has fallen in love with a heroic Red Cross nurse. How powerful that love could be was the motivating force behind one recovering soldier's love "for some noble girlie all in white" in Harry Bewley and Theodore Morse's "My Red Cross Girlie (the Wound Is Somewhere in My Heart)." In this instance, the "wound" has been inflicted not by shot or shell, but by Cupid:

> "My Red Cross girlie, for you I'm call-
>   ing,
> Though you're many miles away.

My Red Cross girlie, for you I'm fall-
ing,
Longing for you night and day.
I need you, sweetheart, for I am
wounded
By a cunning fellow's dart;
But don't swoon, dear,
For the wound, dear,
Is only somewhere in my heart."

Adding to the divinity of the battlefield nurse was "There's an Angel Missing
in Heaven," which concludes with the
parenthetical reason for her absence:
"(She'll Be Found Somewhere Over
There)." Commenting that "There's a Cross
/ And it stands for atonement, / Bringing
hope to both you and to me," the singing
soldier continues:

"There's a Cross
At the end of my string of pearls—
My Rosary, my Rosary.
There's a Cross,
A Red Cross that means mercy,
Devotion and tenderest care.
There's an angel who's missing from
heaven,
She'll be found somewhere over there."

Despite the infusion of poetry into the
lines, the second verse of the song nonetheless ranks among the most realistic
descriptions of war's desolation in the
popular music of the time. It also added
more than a modicum of stature to the
bravery of the young women who shared
the battlefield horrors and hopes of the
men they had volunteered to serve:

Picture the maimed and the dying,
Picture the crushing of youth;
Picture the blackness of fear, the doubt
Of Virtue and Right and of Truth.
Then picture this angel of mercy,
Like Bethlehem's Star in the night;
She brings us the message that God is
still living,
And that Might will be conquered by
Right.

Lyricist H. MacDonald Barr's equally
poetic lines in "Angel of No Man's Land"
also saluted the ever-dependable Red Cross

nurse and "all her noble band" as the sole
purveyors of comfort and love on the
whole of the Western Front:

O, a soldier may walk with a martial
tread
In the midst of a crimson stream;
He may leap from the trench and
plunge ahead
Where the battle may deadly seem.
Though foes are near, he knows no
fear,
He's fighting to win or die;
Nor, if he fall, does he vainly call,
For the angel is passing by.

In "The Rose of No Man's Land," the
"one real rose the soldier knows" is the
Red Cross nurse, the "work of the Master's
hand":

Out of heavenly splendor,
Down to the trail of woe,
God in His mercy has sent her,
Cheering the world below.

Although George M. Cohan's "Their
Hearts Are Over Here" never mentions the
Red Cross, he dedicated the song to the
organization and donated the entire proceeds from sales to furthering its war-relief
efforts.

Among the tributes bestowed on
International Red Cross workers was
Arthur J. Lamb and F. Henry Clique's
(Klickmann's) "The Bravest Heart of All,"
a tribute to Edith Cavell, an English nurse
and matron of a Red Cross hospital in
Brussels. Arrested in 1915 by German
authorities, she pled guilty to harboring
Allied prisoners, some of whom she had
helped to escape to the Netherlands. She
was shot by a firing squad that October.
The dramatic illustrated cover of the sheet
music, published only a few weeks after
her death, shows her standing in front of
her executioners resolutely determined to
accept the inevitable in the same stoic
manner as a male prisoner of war.

Receiving less but equally sincere
kudos was the Salvation Army, its female
members known familiarly as "Salvation
Sal" (or "Rose") and "Army Lassie." The

best known of the praise songs was "My Doughnut Girl," which in 1919 cast a kindly backward glance at the lassies who had "helped us through / As you toiled in the trenches / For the Red, White and Blue!" Lyricist Elmore Leffingwell continued in the second verse:

When the shrapnel flew fast
And our fellows were gassed,
You sang and baked and prayed;
As we bent back the line
Of the Hun toward the Rhine,
Cheered on by the doughnuts you
made!

6. A Few Smiles

The briefly popular balladeer Jack Frost successfully tempered his emotive and transitory "When a Boy Says Goodbye to His Mother (and She Gives Him to Uncle Sam)" and "A-M-E-R-I-C-A (means 'I Love You, My Yankee Land')" with one of the better comic gang or "rube" songs. The first, but assuredly not the last, of its kind in the songwriters' kit bag of novelty tunes, the song saluted the ease with which the farm boy-turned-soldier is able to transfer his indomitable fighting spirit from the cornfield to the battlefield. "Giddy Giddap! Go On! Go On! (We're on Our Way to War)," hollers Frost's protagonist, the very model of the brave rural warrior, to his barracks buddies.

The best gang song, Lloyd Garrett's "Private Arkansaw Bill (Yip-I-Yip and a Too-Ra-Le-Ay!)," revolved around a hillbilly song, the only one fiddler Bill could play, and its morale-building effects on himself and his bunkhouse compatriots. The "haunting strain" crept into every "weary brain," encouraging the recruits to relieve their tension by singing their fears away. William Herschell and Barclay Walker's soldier-friendly "Goodbye, Ma! Goodbye, Pa! Goodbye, Mule, with Yer Old Hee-Haw!" was still another tribute to the derring-do of yokels, ready to slam the enemy at the first opportunity, their nerve and verve ever in tow.

To further counteract the sad songs more conducive to depression than exhilaration, publisher Leo Feist made available for the "piano, player-piano, and talking machine," a number of tunes guaranteed to provoke smiles rather than tears. To save paper, Feist printed them in the new "patriotic war size"—about two-thirds that of the standard sheet music cover. To promote impulse buying, the company advertised all the songs in the popular weekly journal *The Saturday Evening Post* and exhibited them prominently in such merchandising emporia as Woolworth, Kresge, Kress, McCrory, Kraft, and Metropolitan stores. "War isn't all battle, mud, and devastation—there are rays of sunshine, smiles, and good fellowship, too," wrote the Feist copywriter, most likely exempt from the draft, on the reverse side of Grant Clarke, Howard E. Rogers and George W. Meyer's humorous "(If He Can Fight Like He Can Love) Goodnight, Germany." "If you could visit the trench, the dugout, and the billet Over There, you'd hear the boys singing—singing from reveille to taps," the copywriter added.

The Feist song that shed the most sunshine as a "sure cure for gloom and grouch" was "Good Morning, Mr. Zip-Zip-Zip!", Robert Lloyd's brightly entertaining salutation to the rawest of recruits just emerging from the obligatory trip to the boot camp barber. Shorn of his locks like an undernourished Samson, the youngster is pleased to discover that, rather than setting him apart, his closely clipped hair has earned him the respect of the "veterans" surrounding him. Mr. Zip-Zip-Zip's hair is cut just as short as theirs, the song notes, and the youngster is qualified for admittance into their fellowship.

That Feist ranked as the most productive publisher of war songs, both serious and humorous, was due in large measure to the philosophy that guided the firm's executives during the countrywide singathon of 1917-18. "A nation that sings can never be beaten—each song is a milestone on the road to victory," read the copy of advertisements that ran throughout much of 1918 in *The Saturday Evening Post*.

The purpose of the ads was to generate sales of the company's 80-page, 4 by 5½-inch pocket-size music book *Songs the Soldiers and Sailors Sing*, which saddle-stitched together 127 Feist war songs and retailed for 15 cents a copy. Feist gave itself a hearty part on the back with the assertion that "music is essential" in times of adversity, and it promoted the songs as indispensable to the war effort. "The producer of songs is an 'ammunition' maker,'" the ad copy continued. "The nation calls upon him for 'ammunition' to fend off fatigue and worry."

Another winning comic novelty song from Feist was "There'll Be a Hot Time for the Old Men (While the Young Men Are Away)." Containing at least a kernel of truth in the title, the song was a worthy precursor of the better-known World War II lament of the loveless lady who, after surveying the civilian market eligible for dates, concludes that "They're Either Too Young or Too Old." Half spoken and half sung by Bette Davis in *Thank Your Lucky Stars*, this Frank Loesser–Arthur Schwartz song was nominated for the 1943 Academy Award.

Popularized by singer Emma Carus, the 1917 Grant Clarke and George W. Meyer tune declared that "All the old men read the papers and laughed / When all the young men were caught in the draft." Men of fifty were feeling "mighty nifty" because

they were spared from military service. "Young men are sailing ev'ry day," the lyric notes, presenting old-timers with the provocative challenge: "Who will love the girlies while they're away?" The answer was fairly obvious:

> While the young men stayed here
> They had ev'ry maid here,
> Things have changed somehow.
> And the real old fellow
> Never was so mellow
> As he is right now.
> It's not very hard to figure them,
> All the old men think they're young
>   again.

Songs with the potential for evoking more resentment than merriment, however, were rare throughout the war. Jeff Branen and Arthur Lange's treatise on civilian duplicity—"Brother Bill Went to War, While I Stayed Home and Made Love to His Best Girl"—was the only other one to combine irony and humor while addressing one of the average doughboy's most pervasive fears. It failed to attract many buyers, which very well might explain why no more songs of the type were published.

An appeal to keep addicted troops supplied with smoking tobacco, in particular the "Genuine Bull Durham" brand used in rolling their own cigarettes, was issued by Vincent Bryan, the author of the words of "In My Merry Oldsmobile," and Harry Von Tilzer in late 1917. By that time, as Bryan points out in "The Makin's of the U.S.A. (A Plea in Song for Tobacco for the Boys Over There)," American-grown tobacco had become a scarce commodity, roiling nerves and eroding morale. It was not that the European Allies were unwilling to share their tobacco; it was a matter of preference for the accustomed.

The Yanks generally found all foreign tobacco unfit for consumption. The English, French, and Italian varieties were far too strong to satisfy their taste, and the smokes captured "from the Huns are like limburger cheese." The solution, according to the song: each American must "get a sack of good tobacco / And send it to your Yankee soldier right away." That, Bryan declared, was the surest way to prove that the domestic front was solidly behind them.

Written long before health concerns began dampening the demand for cigarettes, the Bryan–Von Tilzer song accomplished its goal. Tobacco became a priority American export, prompting a thank-you letter, dated August 11, 1917, from the commanding colonel of the U. S. Marine Corps Headquarters 5th Regiment, Expeditionary Force. Addressing it to the editor of the *New York Sun*, the colonel, presumably while contentedly puffing away, wrote: "In behalf of the men of the 5th Regiment of Marines I wish to extend to you our heartiest thanks for the generous quantity of cigarettes which you so kindly sent to us here in France where they are so much needed; for, although there is French tobacco to be had, it is not at all to our liking." He concluded that "in our few leisure moments, when we relax and think of home, to be able to smoke an American cigarette" was a genuine boon to the troops. Somewhere, squatting in his dugout and lighting up, Private Perks was most likely nodding his head in agreement.*

The frequent unavailability of various hard-to-get commodities, from rubber and gasoline to beef and flour, was regarded by most civilians as more of an annoyance than a crisis. Tolerating deprivation without complaint became a sort of badge of solidarity with the troops. Not very much time elapsed before the songwriting community turned the rationing of favored goods into a source of amusement.

According to the do-without-with-cheer message preached in "Keep Cool! The Country's Saving Fuel (and I Had to Come Home in the Dark)," the willingness to walk rather than drive to and from work, regardless of inconvenience or weather, was a sure sign of one's patrio-

tism. Another example was the nonchalant acceptance of shortages of electricity and heat, cigarettes and sugar, comfort and sleep by a well-adjusted married couple. As Mary tells John in another highly amusing novelty song, "I'll Do Without Meat and I'll Do Without Wheat but I Can't Do Without Love," homefront sacrifice may indeed promote character-building, but it does have its limits:

> "I'll keep ev'ry rule
> And try to keep cool
> While prices are soaring above;
> I'll do without meat
> And I'll do without wheat,
> But I can't do without love."

The lyricist, Arthur J. Lamb, was the author of the words of the far better-known "Asleep in the Deep" and "A Bird in a Gilded Cage." Composer Frederick V. Bowers, a popular minstrel and vaudeville singer, entertained the armed forces in three wars, the Spanish-American War and World Wars I and II.

Unquestionably, the most popular song cementing the bold new fellowship of Americans and Allies was "Hail! Hail! the Gang's All Here." Not written as a war song, it was nevertheless greeted as one by troops wishing to suck on the pacifier of cheerfulness. Even more contemptuous of fate than "Pack Up Your Troubles," the barrack-room ballad helped them to celebrate their own transformation from callow youth into thumb-in-your-eye soldiers. Problems may come and problems may go, the D.A. Esrom-Theodore Morse song concedes, adding the carefree tag line, "What the deuce [hell] do we care." In addition to its war service, the tune has survived over the years since 1917 to become the chief themesong of defiant merriment whenever crowds of males get together, regardless of the purpose. It served an identical role in the Great War, and still ranks high among the best-remembered

---

*Actually, musical praises of smoking tobacco were common at the time. One of the best known of them, the novelty "Nic' Nicotine," written in 1912 by John W. White, defined it as a "jolly good fellow" who is "never unruly, this friend of yours truly; / He'll stick to you rain, hail, or shine."

chants sung on land, on the sea, and above all by comrades grouped around a piano in a foreign bistro.

D.A. Esrom was the pen name of Theodora Morse, composer Theodore's wife, who in the 1920s wrote the words to "Wonderful One," "Three O'Clock in the Morning" (using the pseudonym Dorothy Terriss), and "Siboney." Theodore's biggest hit ballads were "M-O-T-H-E-R" and "Dear Old Girl."

In a rare display of acknowledging a classical songwriting source, "Hail! Hail! the Gang's All Here" also carried the name of a third writer, Arthur Sullivan, the composing half of the world-famous Gilbert and Sullivan team. The song's melody was derived from two themes, "Come, Friends, Who Plough the Sea," a tenor solo, and "With Catlike Tread," a choral air, that Sullivan had written for Act Two of *The Pirates of Penzance* in 1879.

Countdown to Mediocrity

Nineteen seventeen was a banner year for popular song hits, among them "The Bells of St. Mary's," "Darktown Strutters' Ball," "Johnson Rag" and "Tiger Rag," "Oh Johnny, Oh Johnny, Oh!", "Rose Room," "For Me and My Gal," and Sigmund Romberg's sweetheart, sweetheart, sweetheart song, "Will You Remember?" Jerome Kern's "Till the Clouds Roll By," was not a war song, but its comforting recommendation to seek shelter from the pitter-patter of raindrops was surely applicable to persons anxious to escape the interminable news reports on the lack of progress toward victory in France. But of all that year's remembrance songs to mesmerize great numbers of persons both in and out of the services, none approached the vaulting popularity of "Smiles," ultimately the most satisfying of all World War I ballads. Appropriately, the cover of the original 1917 sheet music was decorated with the smiling face of a raven-haired beauty.

Interpolated the next year into Pass-

ing Show of 1918, it was sung by the Broadway singing star Nell Carrington. Containing the happy admission that "Dearie, now I know / Just what makes me love you so, / Just what holds me and enfolds me / In its magic glow," the J. Will Callahan–Lee S. Roberts song was so identifiable with lovers' determination to resume relationships that it served coincidentally as a commentary on love affairs sundered by the war.

No other lyric of the time made a clearer distinction between the remembered smile endowed by happiness and the far more elusive one that stubbornly glows with hope through tears of sadness. There are smiles that make us happy, the lyric states, and there are smiles that make us blue. Some are capable of stealing away the tear drops; others have a tender meaning visible only to the eyes of lovers. And, the singer is pleased to note, "The smiles that fill my life with sunshine / Are the smiles that you give to me."

Not until late 1942, when Irving Berlin's "White Christmas" became a bestseller, would another non-war song distill nostalgic reminders of the pleasurable past so winningly.

Carrying the most stirring melody of all the sweetheart songs, George A. Norton's "'Round Her Neck She Wears a Yeller Ribbon (for Her Lover Who Is Fur, Fur Away)" has become more identified in recent decades with the American frontier, its original turf, than with the battle-grounds of 1917 France. Thanks for the transfer of locale go largely to director John Ford, who used it numerous times as a farewell march in his Western films of the 1940s and 50s. This song and the lively old traditional march "Garry Owen" were two of his favorites. He even picked up the title almost verbatim for his 1949 adventure classic *She Wore a Yellow Ribbon*, starring John Wayne and Joanne Dru. Sporting three sets of new lyrics by M. Ottner and Leroy Parker, the song was reprised throughout the picture.

Except for the revised lyric, the 1917 Norton adaptation was an unoriginal addition to the war-song parade. As pointed out by musicologist Theodore Raph, the first version was published about 1838 under the title "All Around My Hat" and became a modest hit in England as well as in America. The original words are attributed to J. Ansell, the melody to John Valentine. By the end of the nineteenth century, both words and music had been modified numerous times by U.S. cavalry soldiers, who used it as a marching song. The ribbon in the title is believed to refer to the familiar yellow piping worn by the horse soldiers on their blue uniforms, often given to their sweethearts as a love token. Norton, incidentally, also authored the words of composer Ernie Burnett's "Melancholy," renamed "Melancholy Baby" in 1911, and W.C. Handy's superlative "Memphis Blues."

Like the Norton tune, a few Great War songs were as catchy as the opening production number in a Broadway musical. Similarly, the finest ballads were so professionally crafted that, removed from their military setting, they could have been interpolated into a Broadway score. But as the months passed, the marketplace for songs quickly resembled an insatiable maw, ever eager for more songs to digest. The hundreds that were published simply overwhelmed the public; the result was that even many respectable songs were neglected by potential buyers unable to keep up with publishers' offerings.

Yet the constant demand for songs that uplifted the spirit or dispensed compassion led hordes of inexperienced songwriters to follow Cohan's lead, rushing to publishing offices with copy-cat versions of earlier hits, hoping to cash in on the public's vigorous interest in marches and ballads with a decidedly American accent. Unfazed by a common lack of Cohan's melodic and versifying gifts, the writers poured out a remarkable glut of bravado lyrics, anodyne platitudes, and redundant victory vows. Some boasted adequate shelf lives, but most perished instantly.

By late 1917, the assembly line was replacing originality. The hack was competing with the craftsman, the superior war songs colliding with the mundane. The lyric and melodic deficiencies of the latter were patently obvious, inhibiting their sheet music and record sales. So poor were most of them that the frequent appearance of new battle songs and lovers' laments gradually cast suspicion on the worth of the highest-caliber creations that occasionally went to market.

Chief among the reasons for what amounted basically to creative inertia was the surfeit of minor publishers, essentially vanity houses organized to provide amateurs with the means to see their names on song covers. The companies asked little in the way of quality, and that was exactly what their stables of writers brought to them. Few of the latter apparently recognized the need of seriously overhauling their works before final submission. That the obscure writers were often the firm's owners or partners, or related to them, only increased the chances that their contributions would misfire. Little wonder that the tiny firms, unable to take advantage of the big publishers' vast distribution networks, were more or less forced to pass sheet music copies on to family and friends to entice an audience for them.

A few of these inexperienced publishers were even headquartered in New York City, the country's music capital, operating out of offices from the downtown financial district all the way up to Harlem, about 140 blocks to the north. The majority, however, were found in other cities of varying sizes throughout much of the northern half of the United States. Calling Chicago home were Will Rossiter and Co. ("*the* Chicago publisher"), Frank K. Root & Co., and Ted Browne Music Co., each quite respectable in its song selections.

The third highest concentration of music publishers, all of them decidedly below par when compared with the New York and Chicago firms, was in Boston and surrounding communities. Boston was dubbed the "Birthplace of Ballads," although it lacked the credentials for such an honor, by Louis J. Fay, himself a song-writing publisher with offices in the Massachusetts capital.

Other active but marginal companies were based in Hartford and New Haven, Conn.; Philadelphia, Pittsburgh, Williamsport, and Scranton, Pa.; Washington, D.C.; Cleveland, Columbus, Dayton, and Norwalk, Ohio; Indianapolis, Ind.; and St. Louis and Kansas City, Mo. Even such unlikely places as Elizabeth, N.J., Providence, R.I., Rochester, N.Y., and Exeter, N.H., were home to several tiny song-publishing firms. The highly regarded Sherman, Clay & Co. maintained one office in San Francisco and another in New York City.

By 1914 most of the New York City music publishers had vacated West 28th Street between Fifth and Sixth avenues, formerly the main thoroughfare of Tin Pan Alley. One major exception was Jerome H. Remick & Co., a rare hold-out from the exodus to uptown, which continued to occupy a brownstone building on the street as well as maintain a branch facility in Detroit. It was Remick that George Gershwin, then 17, joined in 1915 as a song plugger, working ten hours a day for the magisterial salary of $15 a week. Two years later, he was graduated to rehearsal pianist for Jerome Kern and Victor Herbert's Broadway musical *Miss 1917*.

The intensely busy Leo Feist organization operated out of its own building at 231-235 West 40th Street. Waterman, Berlin & Snyder Co. settled in a suite in the Strand Theatre Building on the corner of Broadway and West 47th Street, where it remained until 1919, when its chief client, partner Berlin himself, established his own independent company. Giant Shapiro and Bernstein was housed around the corner at 224 West 47th Street; the Chas. K. Harris firm, operated by the famous songwriter himself, was situated in the Columbia Theatre Building on the opposite corner of Seventh Avenue and West 47th Street, near the offices of Harry Von Tilzer, a former partner in Shapiro and

Bernstein and the man most responsible for launching the career of Berlin, whom he hired as a song plugger for his own publishing firm, which he had opened in 1902.

Broadway Music Corp., headed by another Von Tilzer named Will, was one of six music publishers bearing a West 45th Street address, including the hyperactive Joe Morris Music Co., at number 145. Occupying their own nearby buildings were publishing powerhouses M. Witmark & Sons, with branch offices in Chicago, Philadelphia, Boston, San Francisco, and London; Chappell & Co.; T.B. Harms; and G. Schirmer, Inc. About 40 blocks to the southeast was the venerable Carl Fischer organization, where it remains to this day. The prices of these companies' music sheets ranged from 10 cents up to 50 cents, depending on the track record of the individual writers.

Off the Assembly Line

Throughout the course of World War I — and of World War II, for that matter — the melodies of the war-based marches and love songs were clearly superior to the lyrics. In only a few instances — "Over There," "Goodbye Broadway, Hello France," and "Till We Meet Again," for example — did the words rise to the professionalism of the music. Such obviously talented wordsmiths as Andrew B. Sterling, J. Will Callahan, Raymond B. Egan, Lew Brown, Al Bryan, Ballard MacDonald, and Gus Kahn were able to arouse patriotism or pity without falling prey to pomposity or over-sentimentality. But theirs was a skill that few of the other wartime lyricists were equipped to challenge.

Unfortunately, it was the below-par lyricists' heavy reliance on boilerplate that classified the bulk of their probings into the major catastrophe of their time as ephemeral rather than profound. True, the wordsmiths were not totally to blame for their lack of ingenuity. They were circumscribed at the outset of each composition by the paucity of subject matter available to them. So it was perhaps to be expected that their lyrics soon began giving the distinct impression that the writers spent their time riffling through a file of stock phrases rather than creating from scratch. Not only were the song titles overripe with redundancy; so were the verses and choruses.

More than a few established song-writers and most of the novices unhesitatingly dubbed American soldiers as "Sammies" from "Sammy Land." Indeed, so many lyrics inserted "over there" and "long way" into their titles that the phrases quickly trailed off into tedium, as did the constant references to the American flag as "Old Glory" or the "Red, White and Blue." Many of the song titles were long, often windy, consisting of up to 19 words, some of them enclosed inside parentheses, a nod to the custom of Victorian novels and vaudeville to condense the territory covered by a book or song on the title page.

"It's a Long Way from Here to 'Over There'" and "It's a Long, Long Way to Berlin but We'll Get There" were only two examples of cliché dependency. "It's a Long Way to Dear Old Broadway" became a success, but not for its title familiarity as much as for its being popularized by singer Elsie Janis and the lyric's casual relationship to Cohan's "Give My Regards to Broadway," written for *Little Johnny Jones* in 1904. Janis, at the top of the doughboys' list of favorite female traveling entertainers, was the Marlene Dietrich of World War I. The uncontested "Sweetheart of the A.E.F.," she served numerous tours of duty at the front, singing, dancing, chatting with the boys in uniform, doing handsprings and imitations of celebrities. Sometimes she performed alone; other times she was with members of her "gang" of kindred performers. Sometimes she dressed in fatigues, but she always wore her trademark black velvet tam. Her vivaciousness earned her another title, that of "playgirl of the Western Front," from the churlish critic Alexander Woollcott,

later to be immortalized on stage and screen as "The Man Who Came to Dinner."

Two other lyric fragments from the past that became commonplace were "Yankee Doodle" and "Home Sweet Home," each used to excess in hopes of spurring widespread acceptance of the newest tune to recycle them. "Yankee Doodle's Going to Berlin" and "When I Come Back to You (We'll Have a Yankee-Doodle Wedding)" at the beginning of American participation in the war, and "Dreaming of Home Sweet Home" and "All Aboard for Home Sweet Home" at the end, were but four of the numerous tunes to prey upon shopworn titles.

The melody of "Yankee Doodle" has been traced to the reign of Charles I in seventeenth-century England, when it was sung to ridicule the "Roundheads," the Puritan supporters of Parliament who opposed the King in the English Civil War. The melody has also been identified with the "Danza Esparta" of old Biscay and as a vintage song of France, the Netherlands, and many other countries.

The verses relating to the American colonists are believed to have been written between 1755 and the early 1770s by Dr. Richard Schuckberg (or a "Dr. Schack," according to some authorities), a British army surgeon, most likely in derision of the motley band of Colonial soldiers then fighting the Canadian French. The song reached its popularity zenith, of course, as a favorite anthem of the colonists during the Revolutionary War. "Home Sweet Home," among the best-known songs of all time, was written as far back as 1823 by John Howard Payne (words) and Sir Henry Bishop (music) for the British opera *Clari*, or *The Maid of Milan*.

The World War I lyricists' overuse of "foam" as a substitute for ocean can be loosely attributed to poetic license. On closer inspection, however, it is apparent that the word was inserted so often because it rhymed conveniently with roam and home, as in "where e'er they roam" and "thinking of home sweet home." Another common synonym, "sea," could be rhymed with such a huge assortment of words — verbs, nouns, pronouns, adjectives, and adverbs — that its consistent usage was inevitable from the moment the first American troops boarded a transport ship to carry them across the Atlantic Ocean.

The same rhyming possibilities encouraged lyricists' overindulgence in the word "fray" as a substitute for battle or war; "grit" for determination; "foe" for enemy; and in such expressions as "shot and shell" for bombardment, "true blue" for faithfulness, "doing your bit" for participating in the war, and "do or die" for fighting unto death. Other regulars were the use of "bugle" to announce the "call to arms" and rampant predictions that once the war was over, Americans again would live in "clover." Likewise, the assurance that the "Kaiser will be wiser" after the Yanks taught him the right way to fight a war quickly lost its initial cleverness by being subjected to consistant usage.

Far too many songs issued identical threats to "get the Kaiser's goat," meaning to frustrate the imperial German leader into reversing his victory expectations, or to grab him by his familiar gray goatee. So, too, did they insert numerous slangy assertions that the Yanks would "can" or "kan," meaning get rid of, the Kaiser. Eventually their excessive dependence on virtually the same phrasing to make the same point nullified whatever propaganda value the boast might have had. And the constant calling for "Hats Off" and "Three Cheers" to salute the flag and marching troops, as well as on "winding up the watch on the Rhine" as a victory vow, was simply too abundant to permit these phrases to retain any effectiveness.

Inappropriate end-rhyming was distressingly common among lyricists who showed little compunction over forcing singers to strain the limits of pronunciation or syllabification with such pairings as rocky/khaki, home/poem, porter/water, wise/advice, and Verdun/burden. The frequent coupling of "again" with such words as "lane" and "pain" was allowable, since many persons of the time pronounced all three as rhymes. Sometimes, to preserve authentic end-rhymes, the lyricists engaged in absurd word inversion. It usually succeeded artistically, but too often resulted in such awkward phrasing as: "Our children love Old Glory / And learn that name to spell" from "A-M-E-R-I-C-A (Means 'I Love You, My Yankee Land')", or the following from "Any Old Place the Gang Goes (I'll Be There)": "A lad named Ford fell overboard and a cry for help he gave; / Mike's company dove in the sea, their comrade's life to save." A third example was provided by the song "It's a Long, Long Way to the U.S.A. (and the Girl I Left Behind)":

> To his pal he's softly saying,
> "Tell the little girl for me,
> Night and day how I was praying
> Her dear face once more to see."

Similarly trite was the overuse of diminutives emphasizing the youth of most of the troops and the girls back home. Unlike the World War II writers, who almost always referred to the combat forces as men, the World War I lyricists looked upon them as "boys" or "laddies." Sweethearts were designated as "girlie" or "dearie," their childlike qualities accented by the constant modifying adjective "little."

This condescending tone was applied even to married ladies, leading several songwriters into demeaning their presence or, except for Red Cross nurses, their presumed feeble participation in the war effort. "What an Army of Men We'd Have (If They Ever Drafted the Girls)," written by Al Piantadosi and Jack Glogau as late as 1918, added insult to injury by portraying young females as merely morale-building love objects without the slimmest potential for fulfilling difficult military assignments.

Andrew B. Sterling–Alfred Solman's "We'll Keep Things Going Till the Boys Come Home (Won't We, Girls?)" further satirized women as incapable of handling even the simplest of typically masculine chores, such as working as trolley conductors, tending bar, and pounding out weapons on factory assembly lines. Agreeing with the writers that "ev'ry girl must do her little bit," and that a "girl will take the place of ev'ry man," the young females in the song coyly express somewhat uncertain willingness to "cast aside the paint and powder puff" to show the world "we've got some noodle":

> Mother's taking father's job,
> He was a steeplejack,
> She wears a pair of overalls
> That buttons up the back;
> And she'll have a ripping time some
> day
> When she climbs up a stack!

Try as they might to lend their freshly scrubbed helping hands and manicured nails to the battalions of homefront workers, older women were likewise held by songwriters to be incapable of escaping from inborn incompetency:

> Aunt Priscilla, just to show
> She couldn't hold aloof,
> Now runs an elevator,
> Isn't that sufficient proof?
> And the other night she got mixed up
> And ran it through the roof!

That the war-song melodies for the most part far exceeded the lyrics in quality is clearly evident from listening to a scattering of, say, 50 of even the best-known World War I songs. Rare indeed were such evocative lines as Ballard MacDonald and Edward Madden's quatrain describing the aftermath of the shelling of a Belgian village that lay in the pathway of invading troops. "Forsaken, alone, amid tumbled-down stone / In the dust of what once was a home, / Two little tots lay as the close of the day / Cast its shadow o'er heaven's blue dome," the lyricists wrote.

"So Long, Mother," "I Wish I Had Someone to Say Goodbye To," "Cheer Up, Father, Cheer Up, Mother," and "On the Road to Home Sweet Home" were other examples of lyric-cribbing centered on love and farewell. The slightly better-than-usual "Caroline (I'm Coming Back to You)" had the distinction of bearing the name of a new composer, James McHugh, on the title sheet. In later years McHugh, often in collaboration with lyricist Dorothy Fields, became a major stage and Hollywood songwriter, winning six Academy Award nominations along the way. Among the many Fields-McHugh standards are "I Can't Give You Anything But Love," "Don't Blame Me," and "I'm in the Mood for Love."

"The Girl Behind the Man" was a repetitive urgent request for the moral support of girlfriends back home. Also superfluous were the ritualistic "I'll Love You More for Losing You a While" and "Don't Try to Steal the Sweetheart of a Soldier," which, like an excerpt from a behavioral manual, instructed lady loves that they were bound to honor their commitment to be faithful for the duration. The latter song, with a lyric by Al Bryan and music by the inestimable vaudeville duo of (Gus) Van and (Joe) Schenck, issued the strongest warning to flirtatious men. "He marched off and left his girl behind him, / On the battlefield of France you'll find him," wrote Bryan. He then asks: "Are you on the square with his sweetheart fair / While he's over there? / 'All is fair in love and war,' they say, / But would you steal his girl away?" Then Bryan shook the finger of condemnation at deceiving 4-Fs, then called "slackers," eager to take advantage of a boyfriend's absence:

> Though he's over there and she's over
> here,
> Still she's always in his heart;
> They may not meet again to love each
> other,
> Still he prays that he'll come back
> some day.
> While he fights for you and me
> To protect our liberty,
> Don't try to steal his girl away.

Mounting the Pulpit

Inevitably, some writers segued into the manufacture of routine hymns, which at the time were expected to merge patriotism with intensely spiritual acceptance of the sacrifices the word often implies. Vincent Shaw's solemn "God Bring You Safely to Our Arms Again," enriched by the Kate Gibson lyric, thanked American soldiers for their courage while reminding them that the thoughts and prayers of their loved ones accompanied them along the battlefield. A rare quality song to emanate from the religious armory, which was also a source of the surfeit of heart-rending daddy and mother and service flag songs, it almost succeeded in living up to its publisher's rather overblown description as "The Song-Message with a Melody That Haunts."

Another satisfactory hymn summoned up a symbol of the past to instill a positive reaction to the present crisis. The lyric of "Liberty Bell (It's Time to Ring Again)," by Joe Goodwin and Halsey K. Mohr, skillfully joined two major conflicts together, pointing out that the purpose of the current war was to defeat the tyrants who wanted to stifle American freedom, that precious legacy bequeathed by the Revolutionary War. (Carrying a sturdy message applicable to future dangers, the song enjoyed a brief revival in America after France fell to the Nazis in the late spring of 1940.) With "I Think We've Got Another Washington and Wilson Is His Name," music publishers and writers James Kendis and James Brockman also merged the American Revolution and World War I, elevating their leaders to front rank among the nation's heroes.

Also deleterious to originality was the habit of many songwriters to serve as listener or observer of events in the lives of the men, women, and children who peopled their war songs. A mother's prayer for her soldier son is often overheard and then retold in storyteller fashion in the lyric. Or the songwriter pretends to read a soldier's letter and proceeds to divulge the contents.

Or he stands over a worried child cuddled in a mother's lap and then records their conversation. This literary device did project a sense of realism, in that the lyricist is supposedly dealing with actual words spoken by real people in true-to-life situations. But it also tended to dilute the quality of the song by casting the lyricist as a reporter rather than creative artist.

A popular cheerleading exercise that never lost its propaganda effectiveness was beginning hundreds of war-song titles with the unifying words "Let" or "Let's"—("Let's All Do Something [Uncle Sammy Wants Us Now"]; "Our" ("Our Boys Across the Sea"); and "We," "We're," "We've" or "We'll" ("We'll Carry the Star-Spangled Banner Through the Trenches"). Still another participatory title-starter was "When We," to indicate the promising future: ("When We March Through Germany"). Literally hundreds of titles inserted "When" somewhere, usually at the beginning. These personalized introductory words did characterize the war as a crusade demanding the full cooperation of every American, not only those in uniform, if victory was to be achieved. The all-inclusiveness of the words and phrases promoted collective prosecution of the war, permitting the writers to exult in their optimistic outlook through thick and thin, while enticing the public at large into sharing it.

Structurally, too many of the war's comic songs relied for effect on catch phrases or punchlines, an already outmoded gimmick used by vaudevillians ever on the prowl for expanding audience approval by adding extra or alternative guffaw-inducing lines into the songs they sang. That songwriters should have taken such a stale artifice to heart is not surprising in light of the fact that many of them wrote for or appeared in vaudeville themselves. Typically consisting of one or a series of two-, three-, or four-line commentaries, the catch phrases were intended to humorously summarize the message the song was written to convey. In "So Dress Up Your Dollars in Khaki (and Help Win

Democracy's Fight)," for example, song-writer Lister R. Alwood issued a plea to civilians to "Let a War Savings Stamp send your money to camp, / And answer the President's call." At the tail end of the lyric appears the alternative catch phrase "Ev'ry Thrift Stamp's a sign that the 'Watch on the Rhine' / Will be wound up fore'er by fall" and "So let's all put the 'pay' into patriot today, / And turn William's Hunny to gall."

Exuding confidence that "We'll Have Peace on Earth and Even in Berlin," James A. Flanagan predicted that it will arrive "When our boys begin to shout, / 'Kaiser Wilhelm, this way out!'" Or, as he reemphasized in the tag lines, "When the German folks get wise / They'll take Wilson's good advice / And they'll drive Kaiser Wilhelm from Berlin."

Although opportunities to illustrate sheet music covers were plentiful during the war years, only Edward H. Pfeiffer, Albert Barbelle, and Norman Rockwell were able to raise the level of their work to art. The best of their covers compare favorably with the four dozen military posters executed by James Montgomery Flagg, the official artist for New York state during the war. Pfeiffer, who sometimes signed his works "Fifer" and "EHP," illustrated more than 1,500 covers from about 1892 to his death in 1932. About 125 dealt with World War I, among them "The Girl Who Wears a Red Cross on Her Sleeve," "It's a Long, Long Way to the U.S.A. (and the Girl I Left Behind)," "Mothers of France," "'Round Her Neck She Wears a Yeller Ribbon (for Her Lover Who Is Fur, Fur Away)," "Take Me Back to New York Town," "We're Going to Take the Germ Out of Germany," "The Man Behind the Hammer and the Plow," and "When I Send You a Picture of Berlin (You'll Know It's Over, Over There, 'I'm Coming Home')."

Born in 1868 in New York City of German immigrant parents, Pfeiffer also designed costume jewelry and illustrated newspaper and magazine articles. His fame, however, rests on his sheet music

works. They vividly attest to an ever-active imagination, but one that was prevented from sacrificing realism for the fanciful by paying scrupulous attention to detail. Pfeiffer's consistent integrity placed his works far above those of his derivative competitors.

It was the lesser artists, not Pfeiffer, Barbelle, or Rockwell, that were stampeded into conformity by the gigantic number of published songs requiring illustrations, mechanically turning out lookalike jut-jawed Yanks, rifles in their hands, lips pursed, poised to advance menacingly against the enemy. Most of the figures were army men; sailors were rarely pictured, and never in battle. The sole U.S. marine known to show up on the cover of a pre–1919 popular song—the march song "Victory"—is shown gripping his trusty rifle with his left hand and the Corps flag with his right, validating the impression that by 1918 all sectors of the music field were playing host to merchants of triviality.

The almost totally inflexible popular song format also acted as a brake on diversity. Practically every war song, whether march or ballad, consisted of two verses and the chorus. Adherence to such strict uniformity forced some writers into excessive dependency on previously published lyrics for ideas, or into variations on their own earlier phrasing, in order to fill out the allocated lines, which at times numbered more than 50. With the subject matter severely restricted to begin with, these freewheeling borrowings led to more than a few title similarities, and, as already noted, an alarmingly high percentage of style and substance duplications.

Another disturbing tendency was the lyricists' custom of throwing in such frequently unnecessary words as "just" to cover eighth notes when no other solution came to mind. Likewise, "old" was inserted far too often for the same reason. Use of that word was appropriate in such a phrase as "Old Glory," a traditional colloquialism for the American flag, but in time it became the chief modifier of a host of nouns, ranging from "old home town" and "old mother" to "old U.S.A." and "old flag" and "old Kaiser" and "old Berlin."

Most of the World War I song titles were, in fact, more than a little stolid. Save for seeking to justify the death of a soldier through such an imaginative phrase as "He Paid His Last Installment on the Price of Victory" in 1918, cleverness was typically not among the songwriters' assets. Their preference for dealing in straightforward accusations and plain Jane romantic pleadings was very much in evidence.

By the time of World War II, however, even the most minor lyricists had acquired the knack of delivering time-worn messages with a vernacular freshness that often won the admiration of singers and listeners. "Cheer Up, Blue Hawaii," written only weeks after the Pearl Harbor aggression, blended comforting nostalgia with hope by referring in the title to the well-known Leo Robin and Ralph Rainger ballad redolent with Waikiki's halcyon days of the 1930s. The warning to persons in the know not to divulge military secrets was succinctly expressed in "Loose Lips Sink Ships," while the best advice to shirkers was condensed in the equally finger-jabbing demand to "Quitcherbeliaken and Help to Win the War."

"The Flag Is Still There, Mr. Key" was an original reminder that no enemy had ever been able to lower the Star-Spangled Banner; "There's a Permanent Wave in Old Glory" made the same point, while paying tribute to the many women who had volunteered for the various services. "Hitler's Getting Littler Ev'ry Day" reduced the Great Dictator to pigmy size. "Back the Attack (Lend 'Em Your Jack)" amusingly encouraged the purchase of War Bonds; "You're Sweet as Sugar and Twice as Hard to Get" used a rationing theme to indicate one doughboy's inability to win the lady of his dreams.

"S-s-s-so Sorry, Mr. Moto," aimed directly at the Japanese, ironically apologized for America's recent piling up of victories in the Pacific by basing its title on a phrase uttered every so often by Peter Lorre in the role of a mild-mannered Oriental detective in the *Mr. Moto* series of low-budget 1930s films. Depending on a business-correspondence formality for unique effect was "The Answer to Yours of December Seventh," cast as a "response" to the Pearl Harbor fiasco that was "delivered" to the Japanese shortly after U.S. forces captured Saipan in 1944.

Also beyond the artistic range of the Great War lyricists were victory and peace predictions that were not clothed in such bland phrases as "when the war clouds have passed" (or "rolled by"). The later war's "When a Speck in the Sky Is a Bluebird," for instance, was an inspired reference to the pending replacement of bombers on the attack with birds on the wing. And few war titles softened the tragedy of missing American planes and their heroic crews over enemy territory better than "There's a Landing Field in Heaven."

First Steps on the Road to Glory

Remnants of the anger aroused by "I Didn't Raise My Boy to Be a Soldier" were suppressed with finality in 1917 by such minor-league songs as "I'm Proud to Be a Soldier of the Allies" and "If I Had a Son for Each Star in Old Glory, Uncle Sam, I'd Give Them All to You." The latter, used to assist the government's 1917 recruitment campaigns, was subtitled "A Mother's Song of Patriotism."

The "Star" in the title referred to the service flag, another overused songwriting subject, with a blue star sewn on a field of red and white as a tribute to each member of a family serving in the military. The flags were usually attached to the façade of the family's house or window of its flat or apartment. When a son or father was wounded, his star was resewn in silver; at his death it was resewn in gold thread. Although dreaded, the term "Gold Star Mother" was nonetheless a source of pride as well as sorrow with some parents whose soldiers had made the supreme sacrifice.

Blissfully unapprehensive of the consequences of going off to war, the mother in "If I Had a Son for Each Star in Old Glory, Uncle Sam, I'd Give Them All to You" expresses satisfaction in watching her son don a uniform and steel himself in traditional manly fashion for the harsh duty ahead. In a move to placate any ill feeling the song might generate among rattled draft-age youngsters, the publisher advertised it as a "corking one-step" as well as a "stirring march."

More pride was expressed by experienced songwriter Bernie Grossman, along with Thomas H. Hoier and Al W. Brown, who hit a bullseye with "There's a Service Flag Flying at Our House." If by chance the family's soldiers are killed, the lyric points out, the heavens each night will be brightened by a cluster of new stars put there to honor their memory.

Unfortunately, the lyric was submerged in an excess of patriotism that tended to equate a family's love of country with the number of male relatives serving in the armed forces. Dispirited mothers were now applauded for willingly giving up their darling boys and watching with admiration as they marched away. Although their hearts may ache, even break, mothers by the millions were "glad they can say / There's a service flag flying at our house," according to the lyric.

The pacific Irving Caesar, who praised writers for not glorifying war, judged this song as bordering on the offensive. The lyric surely exulted in the opportunities that battlefield service provides to the soldier eager to become a hero. In doing so, however, it knocked motherhood off the pedestal that the mammy songwriters of the time had taken great care to construct. This particular mother, far from being depicted as the giver and cautious guardian of life, has taken on the role of an intense zealot on a par with many musical depictions of fathers who placed duty to country above life itself. Though painful, the departure of her son raises in the mother the hope that he may "return with fame and glory," apparently even if

he is maimed making the effort. (Gradually, even grieving sweethearts began urging their boyfiends on to heroism in war songs. One young lady, for instance, assured her departing love that "After the battle is over, then you can come back to me," but only if he has "covered [himself] with glory.")

Shortly afterward, lyricist Grossman atoned for his misdirected enthusiasm by joining Alex Marr for "Say a Prayer for the Boys 'Out There'," a capably turned ballad but far less familiar today than Herb Magidson and James McHugh's World War II Academy Award nominee with almost the same title, "Say a Pray'r for the Boys Over There," introduced by Deanna Durbin in *Hers to Hold* in 1943.

One mildly successful example of cheerleading in 6/8 time, this one bearing a cover illustration of the Statue of Liberty on the march with a soldier at its right and a sailor at the left, asserted that, insofar as the outcome of the war was concerned, "America, It's Up to You." This highly jingoistic tune, along with the lyrical "You're My Beautiful American Rose" and "When You Write, Send a Letter of Cheer," was written by Charles A. Ford, who set up his own music publishing shop on the other side of the Hudson River in Newark, New Jersey. With a flair for self-promotion, he concocted a tag line that combined salesmanship with patriotism. "As you travel along — Hum a Ford song — They're hummers," read the logo on his wartime covers. Only marginally less self-serving was the slogan used by Leo T. Corcoran, a war-music publisher domiciled at 224 Tremont Street, Boston's version of Tin Pan Alley, who praised his selections as "Songs a Little Better Than Seem Necessary."

Since the war was no longer just a European affair, many American music publishers vied with one another and the songwriters to display their patriotism in print. They became adept at inserting pungent little aphorisms on their music covers to remind stay-at-homes that they were duty-bound to contribute whatever they could toward bringing the war to a successful end. "Wheat Wins War — Share It with the Allies for Victory!" served as the slogan on a number of Jerome H. Remick & Co. covers, along with proclamations that "Soap Is Made from Fat / So Don't Waste Soap, / For Germany Has Got to Be Cleaned Up!" and "If You Can't Jab a Bayonet, Grab a Bond!" To prevent meat shortages among the troops, another Remick inducement urged homefront abstinence: "Every Vegetable on the Table Means a Hun on the Run!"

As vital to the war effort as farmers and industrial workers were, only one published song noted their achievements. In his "Proclamation by the President to the People," delivered April 16, 1917, President Wilson had urged the nation to "supply abundant food for ourselves and for our armies and our seamen, not only, but also for a large part of the nations with whom we have now made common cause, in whose support and by whose sides we shall be fighting." Citing the singular importance of foodstuffs, clothing, coal, and steel, Wilson continued:

> We must supply ships by the hundreds out of our shipyards to carry to the other side of the sea, submarines or no submarines, what will every day be needed there, and abundant materials out of our fields and our mines and our factories with which not only to clothe and equip our own forces on land and sea, but also to clothe and support our people, for whom the gallant fellows under arms can no longer work.... The supreme test of the nation has come. We must all speak, act, and serve together!

In effect, the president had provided the impetus for another Remick music-cover tag: "Win the war with BREAD and LEAD!"*

Harry Von Tilzer's "The Man Behind the Hammer and the Plow," subtitled "A Song Every American Should Learn," musicalized Wilson's wartime plea that his fellow countrymen "realize to the full how great the task is and how many things, how many kinds and elements of capacity and service and self-sacrifice it involves." In particular, Von Tilzer credited farmers and factory workers with making "this country what it is today"; i.e., a virtual storehouse of food and weapons needed to stoke the Allied war machine over the long haul. They were depicted as the "gift of God's creation, / The builders of a nation," all honest sons of toil and the backbone of the nation's genius at producing goods.

Together, Von Tilzer rhapsodized, the working man and the serviceman had the power to win for Uncle Sam in this hour of his greatest need. Thus, the song buttressed Wilson's further contention that men "assigned to the fundamental, sustaining work of the fields and factories and mines ... will be as much part of the great patriotic forces of the nation as the men under fire."

Innumerable small-bore songs, like "We'll Do Our Share (While You're Over There)," also sought to adrenalize participation on the home front. "What Are You Going to Do to Help the Boys?" a tuneful and popular 1917 ditty demanded to know. The aforementioned "So Dress Up Your Dollars in Khaki (And Help Win Democracy's Fight)" adopted the purchase of Liberty Bonds as its crusade:

> You're America's friend
> When you're willing to send
> All your savings to serve at the front.
> But the spender sits tight
> And lets his comrades fight,
> He could play the game right but he
>   won't.
> It's all my little bills and it's all your
>   bills, too,

In 1917, Congress passed the first daylight saving time bill to maximize food production during the war. The law was repealed in 1919, over Wilson's veto, because farmers were complaining that the new time system was disorienting their cows and chickens. In World War II, from 1942 to 1945, the United States went on permanent daylight saving time, doubling it to two extra hours in the summer.

That will lick this "Big Bill" over there,
    boys;
So let's dress up our dollars in khaki,
    let's do!
And lick the old Kaiser for fair, boys!

"What are you going to do when our boys come home?" asked Ivan Reid in his and Peter DeRose's song with the same title, protesting civilian inaction in the war effort; "what are you going to say to make them glad?" Then, in an attempt to counter any postwar guilt complex, Reid provides the answer with another question: "Will you tell them that you've tried to do your share / While they were fighting for your freedom over there?" These and other songs served the same purpose as Irving Berlin's "Any Bonds Today?" (1941), the best remembered of all the "Buy Bonds" songs, and the "Buy War Bonds and Stamps for Victory" logo, printed under the likeness of a Minute Man, on World War II music covers and an assortment of patriotic posters.

Jazzing It Up

Serving as antidotes to, and stiff competition with, the melancholy wartime ballads were the hundreds of songs played in ragtime. This comparatively new rhythm, rich in syncopation and spontaneity, was used as a synonym for jazz (or "jas," as some early practitioners spelled and pronounced it), a term which as far as can be determined was coined about 1910. Thanks to a number of incredibly talented black composers and pianists, more often than not one and the same, ragtime began its assault on the popularity of conventional dance music, especially with the younger set, in the late nineteenth century.

It gradually won more and more white converts, and even a degree of respectability, following publication of Scott Joplin's "Maple Leaf Rag" (1899) and "The Entertainer" (1902). Jelly Roll (Ferdinand Le Menthe) Morton's "King Porter Stomp" was a huge 1906 hit, as were Euday Bow-

man's "12th Street Rag" in 1909 and "Junk Man Rag," a minor classic by Luckey (Charles Luckeyeth) Roberts, in 1913. Maurice Abrahams, Grant Clarke and Lewis F. Muir's "Ragtime Cowboy Joe," composed in 1912, still ranks high among the better-known rags of the period.

Eubie Blake was a major exponent of World War I ragtime, along with James P. Johnson, Willie ("The Lion") Smith, and scores of lesser-knowns bearing enviable musical credentials. Among the greatest of all jazz pianists, Smith volunteered for war service, rose to the rank of artillery sergeant while in France, and earned his fearsome nickname by conspicuous bravery under fire. Blake wrote several war songs with fellow black musician and conductor James Reese Europe.

Ragtime, like jazz, is essentially indefinable, depending as it does more on intuition than formal academic training. Louis Armstrong's famous declaration, "If you got to ask what it is, you ain't got it," remains the strongest testimonial to its elusiveness. The typical rag was distinguished by a rapid, energetic beat that accompanied the major theme, in effect adding the propellant that enlivened the old "Negro" blues and spirituals, from which jazz evolved, and moved them into the American mainstream. The very first jazz bands acknowledged their debt to ragtime by loading their repertories with 16-bar and, later, 32-bar rags and two-steps embroidered with improvised variations.

So many rags on practically every subject imaginable became popular during World War I that even the most fashionable white tunesmiths began writing them. Sigmund Romberg, the Hungarian-born composer well indoctrinated in Central Europe's fondness for waltzes, wrote many rags for Broadway. His "Ragtime Pipe of Pan" and "Polo Rag" appeared in *A World of Pleasure*, a 1915 Lou Holtz stage success, and "Rag-Lag of Baghdad" in *Sinbad*, the wartime hit starring Al Jolson. Romberg's "Ragtime Arabian Nights" was a highlight of *Whirl of the World*, with comedian Willie Howard, while his "Galli-

Curci Rag," named after the opera soprano, added sparkle to *Passing Show of 1917.*

Irving Berlin, whom Eubie Blake in later life termed the "greatest of all American songwriters" (George Gershwin ranked second with him), leaned heavily on ragtime as a writing exercise both before and during the war, a tribute to the songwriter's unrivaled ability to conform his immense talent to the latest trend in the musical marketplace. Between 1909, when Berlin's "Yiddisha Rag" was inserted into that year's Ziegfeld Follies, and 1919, he wrote about 30 rags of varying popularity. His biggest hits included "Yiddle on Your Fiddle; Play Some Ragtime," "Sweet Marie, Make a Rag-a-Time Dance Wid Me," "Wild Cherry Rag," and the superlative "That International Rag."

Nominated by Blake as the "finest rag ever written" was Berlin's "Alexander's Ragtime Band." In 1910, with the completion of their new—and ultimately disastrous—Folies Bergère, Broadway's and America's first cabaret theater (later renamed the Fulton), impresarios Henry B. Harris and Jesse Lasky asked Berlin to write a song for Ethel Levey, who was scheduled to star in the three-part opening bill. Everyone agreed that Berlin's initial contribution, "I Beg Your Pardon, Dear Old Broadway," was a poor choice, so Lasky requested a replacement.

Berlin said he had one handy and serenaded him with "Alexander's Ragtime Band," which Lasky accepted on the spot. He gave it, however, not to Miss Levey but to Otis Harlan, who whistled the song only once on the opening night of the theater. A prominent vaudevillian, Harlan in later life appeared in numerous silent and sound films, ending his career by appearing as Cap'n Andy in the 1929 film version of *Show Boat.*

The song was finally sung in late 1910 by Emma Carus, who introduced it on a Chicago vaudeville stage. Then, at the insistence of George M. Cohan, who was blessed with sensitive ears that recognized a hit at first hearing, the song was inserted

into *Friars' Frolic of 1911* and sung by Berlin himself. A few months later, "Alexander's Ragtime Band" was interpolated into Broadway's *The Merry Whirl*, and off it went on the road to stardom.

In 1918, when Al Bryan, Cliff Hess, and Edgar Leslie's "When Alexander Takes His Ragtime Band to France" was published, the writers took for granted that the American public needed no footnote to explain which Alexander the song referred to. They were correct. Everyone knew that America's Alexander the Great simply had to be the leader of a band that played songs in ragtime.

One of the strangest and most artistically profound side effects of World War I was shifting the headquarters of jazz from New Orleans to the northern United States. Since 1897, about 38 square blocks of the city, bounded by Canal and Basin streets, had been officially reserved for the legalized practice of prostitution. Named for Sidney Story, who conceived the idea of curbing the rapid spread of vice throughout New Orleans by confining it to one section, Storyville became home to numerous sporting houses and nightclubs, like Lulu White's Mahogany Hall, on Basin Street, where the greatest jazz musicians flourished.

Storyville also became a magnet for servicemen, even unmusical ones, which did little to burnish the image of God-fearing youth observing the tenets of American morality while fighting for democracy. The blow fell on October 2, 1917. At the insistence of the U.S. Navy, the New Orleans City Council approved an ordinance to close down Storyville. As their audiences dwindled, most of the musicians exited the city and migrated to Chicago, which served as the new jazz capital until 1928, when they drifted east to New York City. Manhattan reigned supreme in jazz circles for the next seven years, until the renaissance of the "Swing Era" beginning in 1935. Mahogany Hall was demolished in 1950.

The fact that ragtime was a distant relative of the insulting "coon" songs and cakewalks failed to stunt its growth between 1914 and 1918. Popularized mostly by white minstrel singers and dancers wearing exaggerated blackface makeup and bizarre costumes, those two types of songs had been around since about 1830. The plantation dialect lyrics, containing line after line of crude racial humor and sketches satirizing — or, more accurately, distorting — black life flourished in minstrel shows. The fact that the humor was written by whites with little insight into black culture or experience was of no consequence to audiences.

More than likely, ragtime's frequent pandering to racial stereotypes attracted rather than repelled many white ragtime adherents in the strictly segregated America of the war years. Many of the songs, to say nothing of the sheet music covers, depicted blacks, frequently referred to as "Ethiopians," as shiftless and lazy, their unwelcome presence inviting derision.

In 1917, Jimmy Marten and Mitch LeBlanc merged the blues with ragtime to produce "Nigger War Bride Blues," as disrespectful and mean-spirited as any song written during the war, which took as its sole purpose the ridiculing of husbandless black wives immersed in even deeper hardship than most of their white counterparts.

But blacks as well as whites wrote such songs. The black writer Maceo Pinkard's "Those Draftin' Blues" (1918) was only mildly less dialectally offensive than usual, although he did compensate for it with "Don't Cry, Little Girl, Don't Cry," a straightforward, if not particularly original, treatment of grief applicable to separated lovers of any race.

On the whole, however, black Americans were not victimized excessively by the war songs, at least when compared with the number of insults written into the non-war ballads and novelties of the time. Use of such words as "colored" and "pickaninny," and such phrases as "Sambo Sammies," was infrequent, as were such demeaning song titles as "When Rastus Johnson Cakewalks Through Berlin" and

"When the Boys from Dixie Eat the Melon on the Rhine."

Not even the most demeaning of the black-oriented songs of the period approached the sarcasm commonly expressed by writers in the previous decade, like "The Booker T's Are on Parade Today," written in 1908 by E.P. Moran and J. Fred Helf, who slightly earlier had collaborated on "Every Race Has a Flag but the Coon." Featured in Lew Dockstader's minstrel shows, their song used one Eph Green, a member of the all-black Booker T Society, as its spokesman. The uneducated Eph informs one and all that Booker T. Washington, who was due to visit the town at any moment, is the "only Washington that's bona-fide; / The rest are imitations." Indeed, it was Booker T, not George the president, who chopped down the cherry tree, crossed the Delaware, never told a lie, and was renowned as "first in war and peace." Booker Taliaferro Washington, the black writer, educator and organizer of the Tuskegee Institute, outlived the song by seven years, dying during the war in 1915.

Some songs, however, did pay tribute to black soldiers, even if condescendingly. Harry Carroll's "They'll Be Mighty Proud in Dixie of Their Old Black Joe" was one. Val Trainor–Harry DeCosta's "When the Lord Makes a Record of a Hero's Deeds, He Draws No Color Line" was another, although this 1918 song, for some unknown reason, restricted praise of the deeds of blacks to those who had fought in the Civil War (first chorus) and the Spanish-American War (second chorus). Oddly enough, there was no third chorus mentioning World War I.

After attempting sincerity to convey the love of one black mother, whose husband was in the war, for her baby son, Mitchell and Gottler's "Mammy's Chocolate Soldier" boomeranged into derision when the mother referred to the boy's "little cheeks of chocolate brown" and "kinkey head." With "You'll Find Old Dixieland in France," Grant Clarke and George W. Meyer, however, collaborated on a genuinely serious tribute to Southern black soldiers serving in World War I. Appropriately, it was popularized mostly by the gifted black performer Bert Williams, who introduced it in the Ziegfeld Follies of 1918.

Curiously, since Italy was fighting on the side of the Allies, it was the Italo-American soldier who bore most of the brunt of nationality ridicule after the United States entered the war. With "Hey, Wop, Go Over the Top!" songwriter Lew Brown displayed a remarkable lack of concern over using a crude appellation for Italians that even in 1918 was not exactly a term of endearment, while undermining the assertion in "America, I Love You" that its people for decades had prided themselves in welcoming all nationalities and races to "settle on their shore."

Similarly subjected to derision, this time strictly because of his dialect, was a former barber, also nicknamed Tony, who was better known as the "Italian ace." Indeed, his unquestioned bravery had earned him dubious celebrity as the "fighting wop." According to the lyric of "When Tony Goes Over the Top," this battle-loving warrior is happy to "grab-a da gun and chase-a da Hun / And make 'em all run like son-of-a-gun!" What's more, the lyric adds, "With a rope of spagett / And a big-a stilette, / He'll make-a the Germans sweat."

"Over the Top"—a familiar phrase denoting the dispatch of troops from trench onto the terrain of No Man's Land—was used as the full or partial title of three dozen tunes. Most, like "Over the Top and at 'Em, Boys!" served as pungent battle cries; two others carrying the identical title of "Over the Top with Jesus" were actually short petitions to the Son of God, beseeching Him to bless the attacking soldiers and assure their safe return.

Irish-Americans, too, surfaced in numerous war songs as the stereotypical boisterous male actively seeking opponents for fisticuffs. It was generally assumed that, either by nature or after imbibing a wee bit too much at the local saloon, they were inclined to fight at the drop of a hat—or a helmet. In short, their scrappi-ness made Irish males perfect warriors, and they ranked as many songwriters' favorite personification of the belligerency that the ideal soldier should display.

Defanging the Dogs of War

To adapt ragtime as a new format for their post–1917 World War I songs, a number of writers reconstituted the rag rhythm into pseudo-march tempo and, even though rags were traditionally word-less, added killer-instinct lyrics merging the new wartime take-no-prisoners men-tality with unassailable optimism. The beat reminded more than a few performers of the shuffle, and they strutted rather than marched to the melodies. And they sang the words with gusto, more appropriate to a vaudeville or burlesque house than to the legitimate stage or dance hall. None of these drawbacks, however, deterred a crack legion of lyricists and composers from en-listing in the ragtime war regiment. Par-ticular favorites were Jack Frost and Harold Neander's "When the Kaiser Does the Goose-Step to a Good Old American Rag," Coleman Goetz and Jack Stern's "We're Going to Celebrate the End of War in Ragtime (Be Sure That Woodrow Wil-son Leads the Band)," and Irving Berlin's "Ragtime Soldier Man."

A similarly rhythmic tribute to the in-vincibility of ragtimers on the battlefield was the aforementioned "When Alexander Takes His Ragtime Band to France," popularized by stage star Belle Baker. Its unveiled threat that Alexander's music would put all the Germans in a trance, allowing the instrumentalists to "capture every Hun, / And take them one by one," proved to be another melodic tonic for chasing war blues away.

Faring better in the popularity polls, stature, and longevity was "Bugle Call Rag," by W.C. ("St. Louis Blues") Handy. Originally a railroad blues song entitled "Ole Miss," the slightly recalibrated word-less song was renamed in 1916 and took on a new life among persons who assumed the title referred to an army bugler's early morning wake-up call. More than likely, the reference was to the trumpet or cornet played in jazz bands, since instrumentalists customarily used "bugle" or "horn" as a nickname for both.

A second "Bugle Call Rag" appeared in 1916, the melody to this one composed by J. Hubert Blake, soon to be known simply as "Eubie." It was definitely a war, or at least an army song as well as an off-hand tribute to the unlucky soldier assigned to shatter the early morning dreams of doughboys. The latter are also congratulated for promptly answering the bugler's unwelcome demand that they rise and, if at all possible, shine.

In mid-1917 along came the one war rag that swept the country, no doubt enhanced by the addition of a better-than-average fighting lyric. "The Ragtime Volunteers Are Off to War," as spirited a song as the war produced, was the work of lyricist Ballard MacDonald and James F. Hanley, an excellent composer who in the early 1920s would provide Fanny Brice with two of her biggest stage hits: "Rose of Washington Square" (Florenz Ziegfeld's [1920] Midnight Frolic) and "Second Hand Rose" (Ziegfeld Follies of 1921).

According to "Ragtime Volunteers," the aging musicians may not have fought since the Spanish-American War of almost 20 years earlier, but their long association with old Colonel Jones's "Jas-bo band" had trained their feet to adapt to a syncopated beat at a moment's notice. Knapsacks on their shoulders, the ragtime "darkies" merrily stomp past the doors of their tearful kin and neighbors—left, right, left, right, the drummer full of pep to keep them in step—determined and unstoppable in war as in peace:

> Ain't that some demonstration?
> Oh! what syncopation!
> Old Colonel Jones look like a pouter
>   pigeon
> As they go swinging by his door;
> Each high brown turtle dove says:
> "Farewell, my lady love,
> The ragtime volunteers are off to war!"

The sheet music cover of Hanley's earlier "A Little Bit of Sunshine (from Home)," written with MacDonald and Joe Goodwin, added novelty to the sermon on the importance of sending letters to servicemen by including the smiling face of one W.J. Reilly, posing as a sailor aboard the U.S.S. *Michigan* who apparently had received a billet-deux just before the picture was taken. A singer of inconsiderable reputation, Reilly was a busy model, appearing on the cover of numerous other war songs, typically in a sailor's uniform.

Hanley repeated the well-worn letter-writing theme in "Never Forget to Write Home" and "Three Wonderful Letters From Home." Along with his ho-hum "We'll Be There on the Land, on the Sea, in the Air" and "Everybody's Knittin' Now," none of the songs foreshadowed his branching out from traditional musical formats into something as intricate as ragtime, but he did so with professional aplomb.

7. On the "Great White Way"

Vital as the Broadway theater was to promoting songs into hit status, comparatively few persons wrote war songs for stage musicals. Even fewer were the patriotic songs they did write that ingratiated themselves with the sheet music- and record-buying public. The World War I stage was overwhelmingly devoted to entertaining people desperate for diversion, not to probing disasters or the motives of the socially wayward, as in later decades. Musicals ruled Broadway to a greater extent than even during World War II. Producers from late 1914 to late 1918 were content to provide lighthearted three-hour escape hatches from the realities of the killing and devastation going on in Europe. They were convinced that their chief assignment was to make certain the war-weary were not confined to living lives that were all Lent and no Easter.

Relatively few war dramas, like *Three Faces East* and *Watch Your Neighbors*, contributed to the growing anti–German feeling by warning that German-Americans were entirely capable by spying for the land of their birth. Most of the plays— *Lilac Time*, *Out There*, *The Big Chance*, *Moloch*, *Marie-Odile*, *The Prince of Pilzen*, *Stolen Orders*, *Seven Days Leave*, *Where Poppies Bloom*, *The Long Dash*,

Under Orders, *Inside the Lines*— eluded the stigma of arousing direct nationality hatred by impartially analyzing battlefield and lovers' misery; no playwright was eager to support or counsel against America's active involvement in the war. For example, producers Arch and Edgar Selwyn raised inoffensiveness to diplomacy in their program notes in the playbill for Roi Cooper Megrue's *Under Fire* (1916) with the following caveat: "This play deals with certain phrases of the Great War and it attempts to be neutral, although its characters, being English, Belgian, French, and German, are naturally partisan. The management earnestly requests, therefore, that no member of the audience will indulge in any unpleasant demonstrations which might be offensive either to others in the audience or to those on the stage." That such a plea was made only shortly after the sinking of the *Lusitania* was, in the opinion of some listeners, incredible.

The best of the World War I plays was actually a comedy, *The Better 'Ole*, which featured Charles Coburn as Old Bill and a few songs by Hermann E. Dareweski and Percival Knight. Later to become one of Hollywood's most gifted character actors, Coburn would win the 1943 Academy Award for Best Supporting Actor for his role in *The More the Merrier*, a comedy that revolved around the housing shortage in Washington, D.C., during World War II.

In Sam Shipman and Aaron Hoffman's *Friendly Enemies*, a German-American renounces any loyalty to Germany; *Allegiance*, written by Prince and Princess Troubetzkoy (Amelie Rives), centered on the conversion of German-Americans living in the United States into intense pro–American partisans. Neither play provoked any demonstrations by the suspicious. Woodrow Wilson made Broadway as well as political history in the late spring of 1917 by becoming the first sitting American president to be impersonated in a musical comedy. The play was *Follies of 1917* (not a Ziegfeld production), and the impersonator was Walter Catlett. He appeared in a tableau named "Columbia Stands by the President," with Allyn King, who was draped in a Statue of Liberty costume and given the symbolic name of "Miss Columbia." Her left arm was wound about "Wilson's" shoulders, indicating quite clearly that both she and the country she represented solidly supported America's entrance into the war.

Getting Together, a pro–British musical play, included British Army soldiers in its huge cast, but the few ditties composed by Lieutenant Gitz Rice, then a member of the First Canadian Contingent serving in France, managed to negotiate the play through the audiences' conflicting emotions by adding light touches to the proceedings. Among the lightest and best of them was Rice's rollicking hit "You've Got to Go In or Go Under," the most successful vaudeville- or music hall–based song to be performed on a Broadway stage during the entire war. More than likely the title was inspired by the British prime minister, Lloyd George, who apparently coined the

phrase and repeated it frequently to inspire his own countrymen and friendly foreigners to give their all in the crusade against Germany.

It was sung by Rice himself in the J. Hartley Manners–Major Ian Hay–Percival Knight play. Warning that "pro–Germans are a danger, / They are lurking at your door," the song was among the strongest uptempo appeals to American males not in uniform to do their bit to win the war. Either assist the Americans and Allies or suffer the consequences of a German victory, Rice threatened. "We know you're not in khaki or in blue, / But you're as big a man and you've a job to do," he sang. Civilians can indeed add muscle to defeating the enemy: "If you can't cross the pond, / Buy a Liberty bond, / And we'll drive them back to Germany."

There were occasionally other war songs performed along New York's "Great White Way," so named for the hundreds of white light bulbs that illuminated theater marquees on Broadway and midtown side streets. Some were distinguished, like the aforementioned "Poor Butterfly." Another one, "Goodbye Broadway, Hello France," written by C. Francis Reisner, Benny Davis, and Billy Baskett for Passing Show of 1917, deservedly blossomed into a first-tier success shortly after its publication on June 20, 1917, earning a reputation as one of the best marches of the war years. "It won't take us long" to help the French win the war, the lyric promised. On the original cover were hand-drawn illustrations of General John J. "Blackjack" Pershing, commander of the American Expeditionary Force, and Marshal Ferdinand Foch, supreme commander of Allied forces on the Western Front, each standing tall above America and France, respectively, shaking hands across the ocean.*

*The patriotic spirit that the writers of "Goodbye Broadway, Hello France" and other World War I songs hoped to stir was properly endorsed by Allen Jenkins in the 20th Century-Fox period musical Tin Pan Alley in mid-1940. Playing a combative Irish janitor named Casey, Jenkins overhears Jack Oakie singing the song. Asked by Oakie how he liked it, Jenkins replies: "After listenin' to it, I'd spit in the eye of the first gink who even looks like he'd get tough with America." His comment was equally appropriate to the America of 1940, then threatened by the specter of involvement in still another devastating war.

But on the whole, when Broadway went to war, it was the performers, not the tunes, that enticed the public into enlisting or buying Liberty Bonds. They carried war songs along with them on their tours of military camps and hospitals both stateside and overseas, but also included in their repertoires were many years-old novelty and tear-jerking songs celebrating mammies, Dixie, and Honolulu. On their travels, many of America's biggest vaudeville, stage, and movie stars boosted morale by entertaining the troops, establishing an honorable show business tradition that would be revived on an even larger scale in World War II.

Ballard MacDonald, Edward Madden and James F. Hanley's misty-eyed "War Babies" was a long-running favorite performed by Al Jolson, already a master of pathos, on the stage of the Winter Garden Theatre. His nightly retelling of this tale of alleged German bestiality toward the Belgians, to be amplified later in "Belgium, Dry Your Tears," and Ben Black's appeal to soldiers to "Bring Back a Belgian Baby to Me," raised audience compassion to the highest pitch it would reach until "My Mammy" came along in 1921. But the little orphans will "share in the joys of our own girls and boys," Jolson assured listeners, adding that "war babies, we'll take care of you."

The great Irish tenor John McCormack earned the nickname of the "Singing Prophet of Victory" by popularizing "Dear Old Pal of Mine," a most respectable "My Buddy" kind of song written by Harold Robè and Gitz Rice, and "Our God, Our Country, and Our Flag." With Eddie Cantor, it was Sidney D. Mitchell and Archie Gottler's energetic "Would You Rather Be a Colonel with an Eagle on Your Shoulder (or a Private with a Chicken on Your Knee)?" which the bubbling Broadway performer had sung and danced into prominence in the Ziegfeld Follies of 1918. Headline vaudevillians Van and Schenck scored with Jack Glogau and Al Piantadosi's "On the Shores of Italy."

Meanwhile, thanks to the federal government's rather hasty construction of wooden structures known as "Liberty Theaters," military camps throughout the nation were visited by lesser-known performers who toured them in slimmed-down versions of many of Broadway's hit plays.

From the Professional Ranks

Most of the men and women who in time would rank as the finest composers and lyricists in Broadway history did not begin their careers during World War I or were only a few minor songs into them. George Gershwin was still a neophyte, albeit an exceptionally promising one, at war's end. His lyric-writing brother, Ira, would not begin collaborating with him until the early 1920s. Richard Rodgers and Lorenz Hart were similarly absent from the musical scene, not to emerge as a triumphant Broadway partnership until 1924, as were Vincent Youmans and Oscar Hammerstein II.

Cole Porter was a mere stripling of 23 when he wrote his first complete stage score, for *See America First*, which opened March 26, 1916, with dancer Clifton Webb in the leading role. Panned by the critics, it closed after only 15 performances, despite the popularity of one song, "I've a Shooting Box in Scotland." Later that year, Porter contributed one minor ballad each to two Jerome Kern shows, *Miss Information* and *Very Good Eddie*.

While in France in 1918, he joined the Foreign Regiment of the 32nd Field Artillery Regiment, which soon transferred him to the Bureau of the Military Attaché of the United States. Porter thus served in the French army as an American citizen under the direct control of the French Foreign Legion. Contrary to the fiction created by Hollywood writers for *Night and Day*, the composer's 1946 filmed "biography," he served his time in Paris, not on the battlefield in the company of fellow legionnaires.

In postwar 1919, Porter supplied a full

stage score to that year's Hitchy Coo revue. Three years later, for Hitchy Coo of 1922, he finally wrote his first war song, a nondescript little postwar number in which the singer, perhaps Porter's alter ego, looks nostalgically back on the time "When I Had a Uniform On."

Jerome Kern, the most prolific, popular, and influential American composer during the war, almost completely ignored it in his music, along with his various collaborators, who included "Jeeves" novelist P(elham) G(renville) Wodehouse. Except for Kern's "We'll Take Care of You All," which referred to extending help to the "little refugees" made homeless by the war in *The Girl from Utah* (1915), the composer dabbled only skimpily in commentaries on the conflict in Europe.

Even in 1917-18, while Americans were fighting abroad, only two of Kern's Broadway shows featured a war-related song. None appeared in *Oh Boy!*, *Miss Springtime*, *Have a Heart*, *Love o' Mike*, *Leave It to Jane*, *Miss 1917*, *Go to It*, *The Riviera Girl*, *Rock-a-Bye Baby*, *Toot Toot*, or *Head Over Heels*. The sole exceptions were *The Canary*, which introduced Kern's "Oh, Promise Me You'll Write to Him Today," and *Oh, Lady! Lady!!*, which debuted his and Wodehouse's "Wheatless Day," an amusing allusion to food rationing. Kern also wrote a rare non-production tune, "If Mr. Ragtime Ever Gets into That War," a bouncy warning to the enemy that ragtimers were singularly capable of functioning at full throttle no matter where they found themselves.

Kern's escapist *Very Good Eddie* (1915) was so popular that two companies played it simultaneously in New York — and on the same block of West 39th Street. It was not difficult to decipher the public's fondness for Kern's music, an ultra-melodious mixture of graceful two-steps and waltzes. The finest wartime example of his facility for composing bestselling scores was *Leave It to Jane*, the 1917 collegiate musical based on George Ade's enormously successful 1904-05 comedy *The College Widow*. *Leave It to Jane* was later pro-

duced as a silent picture and then as a talkie.

Elsewhere, 1917 was a troublesome year. But inside the theaters, *Leave It to Jane* and Broadway's many other divertissements were all that were needed to exorcise wartime fears by means of frothy plots that could have been staged in the pre-1914 years. *Leave It to Jane*'s two hits, the title tune and "Cleopatterer," were revived in 1946 in *Till the Clouds Roll By*, Metro-Goldwyn-Mayer's eye- and ear-filling tribute to Kern. The other *Leave It to Jane* songs, as their titles indicate, were meant to be nothing more than hummable little excursions into love triangles bearing Wodehouse and Guy Bolton lyrics shorn of any relationship to events taking place in the outside world: "A Peach of a Life," "Poor Prune," "Sir Galahad," "There It Is Again When Your Favorite Girl's Not There," Why?", "I'm Going to Find a Girl," "It's a Great Big Land," "Just You Watch My Step," "An Old-Fashioned Wife," "The Siren's Song," "What I'm Longing to Say," "The Sun Shines Brighter," and "The Crickets Are Calling." World War I might just as well have been a fiction created by an ambitious novelist.

Firmly established by 1914 as the nation's entertainment showplace, Times Square was the leading contender for the title of featherweight champion of the American theater. Quite naturally, legions of writers of musical shows settled there, specializing in recreating stock characters who sang their way out of stock situations. One such master of the inconsequential was the resourceful librettist and lyricist Harry B. Smith, who wrote more than 100 musicals. He was able to satisfy the public's fancy for entertainment for entertainment's sake by never permitting an original plot to interfere with his amazing productivity. In short, he gave theatergoers exactly what they wanted, despite the hearty criticism leveled at his works by critics. Even some of his associates were quick to point out his playwriting deficiencies. When the musical *Watch Your Step* opened in late 1914, the program bore the credit-line inscription, "Book (if any) by Harry B. Smith." Unsurprisingly, none of Smith's librettos dealt with the war, and he penned the lyric to but one mild war song—"War Garden." It appeared in *Look Who's Here*, which arrived on the Broadway scene when the war was practically over.

Competing with such other serial musicals as Hitchy Coo, Passing Show, and Ned Wayburn's Town Topics, and outdistancing them all in spectacle and audience reception, the annual Ziegfeld Follies meshed the most lavishly costumed and choreographed production numbers with skits that satirized current events and the notables embroiled in them. All except the war, that is, which all four revue series almost totally dismissed.

Florenz Ziegfeld's World War I productions were staged at the New Amsterdam,* the most opulent theatrical edifice in Times Square, which he opened in 1903 with a production of *A Midsummer Night's Dream*. Beginning in 1915, the 700-seat rooftop theater and supper club known as Aerial Gardens played host to a series of musicals called the Midnight Frolics. One of his favorite composers, the tireless Dave Stamper, wrote the bulk of the scores for 24 of the master producer's extravaganzas, including the Follies of 1914 through 1918 and a number of the Frolics and Nine O'Clock Revues. Of the 50 Stamper songs, only three referred to the war: the breezy "If the Girlies Could Be Soldiers" and "My Little Submarine" (both from Ziegfeld Follies of 1915), and the sedate "When He Comes Back to Me" (Florenz Ziegfeld's [1916] Midnight Frolic).

Another Ziegfeld reliable, Louis A. Hirsch, composer of "Hello, Frisco [Hello]" (from Ziegfeld Follies of 1915) and "The Love Nest" (from *Mary*, 1920), contributed 17 songs to the Follies of 1915, 1916, and 1918. None of them, or any other song in his extensive portfolio, even remotely touched on the war.

Like Ziegfeld, producer Ned Wayburn

occasionally squeezed a war tune into his own Town Topics, if for no other reason than to vary their musical menus. Harold Orlob, whose non-war "Waiting" was the hit of *Listen Lester* in 1918, contributed the most successful Town Topics war song, "In Time of Peace, Prepare for War." His "Johnny Get Your Gun" was interpolated into the 1918 stage show of the same name, and the psychologically rewarding "Here Come the Yanks with the Tanks" into Hitchy Coo of 1918.

A tiny list of American musical shows, like *Johnny Get Your Gun*, revolved totally around men in the armed forces, typically the army. Comedies rather than dramas, they all called on songwriters to add sparkle to the librettos, though neither the plots nor the songs received very high marks in any category. Among them was *What Next?* (1918), with music by Harry Tierney, best remembered today for his lilting score for the 1919 musical comedy *Irene*. Alternating between the swinging and the sedate, the *What Next?* songs ranged from "Get a Girl to Lead the Army" and "If You'll Be a Soldier, I'll Be a Red Cross Nurse" on the one side to "Garden of Liberty" on the other.

Two other Tierney contributions to the canon of war songs were as contradictory in message as those of any other composer. "It's Time for Every Boy to Be a Soldier," he maintained early in 1917. He softened his interventionist stance later that year, however, with the solemn "Universal Peace Song: God Save Us All," set to an Al Bryan lyric that echoed the despair of many American activists whose expectations of a speedy victory were receding in a seemingly endless series of battles:

> The tramp of armies marching
> Now shakes the earth again,
> Two years they have been fighting all
>   in vain.
> Ten million men have fallen,
> Ten thousand more each day,
> For ev'ry one a mother kneels to pray.

---

*The New Amsterdam, which still exists, was converted into a movie house in 1937.

In the second verse, Bryan reverted to the pacifism that distinguished his lyric to "I Didn't Raise My Boy to Be a Soldier." Referring to the war, he wrote:

What matters now who caused it,
What matters who's to blame,
The burden of each prayer should be
    the same.
It's time to stop the slaughter
And lay their swords away;
Let's hope and pray that God will
    speed the day
When love will come to rule the world
    for aye.

Composer Tierney was also the source of an inoffensive little piece of fluff named "My Little Service Flag Has Seven Stars" (1918). The central character was not a family member, but a Ziegfeld girl whose seven admirers had each joined a different branch of the military.

Doing Our Bit, a 1918 Broadway show starring Ed Wynn, continued the pleading for homefront Americans to open their hearts and wallets and volunteer in every way they could toward victory. Sigmund Romberg's contributions included the songs "Doing My Bit," and "For the Sake of Humanity." Another vaguely successful military production, completed in 1918 but staged the next year, was *Toot Sweet*, originally entitled *The Overseas Revue* and written and produced by composer James F. Hanley. The melodies were by Richard A. Whiting, later the father of songbird Margaret Whiting and a major composer under contract with Paramount Pictures, Fox Film, and Warner Bros. in the 1930s. "Louise," "My Ideal," "Beyond the Blue Horizon," "One Hour with You," "On the Good Ship Lollipop," "Hooray for Hollywood," and "Too Marvelous for Words" are only a few of the movie-song hits in Whiting's impressive catalog.

Whiting had composed various war songs before *Toot Sweet*, and a few of them enjoyed sufficient popularity to indicate that here was a new composer to be reckoned with. For *Toot Sweet*, Whiting wrote ten songs, all but one directly relat-

ing to the war: the title tune, "America's Answer," "The Charge of the Song Brigade," "Eyes of the Army," "Just 'Round the Corner from Easy Street," "Rose of Verdun," and "Blighty Bound" ("Blighty" was commonly used as a nickname for home sweet home by British soldiers in France). "Salvation Sal" was one of the half-dozen wartime tributes to the Salvation Army; "Give Him Back His Job," addressed to employers, was the first stage song to hint at the postwar unemployment problem that many a returning serviceman would face.

Absent from *Toot Sweet*, but written by Whiting about the same time, was the most beautiful of all popular American war ballads. Although it retreaded the already familiar theme of the departing male lover, it did so exquisitely. With more than 18 million copies sold since its August 30, 1918, publication date, the blue-chip song is also one of the biggest-ever sheet music sellers. With its slow, dignified waltz tempo adding poignancy to the moving Raymond B. Egan lyric, "Till We Meet Again" so far outstripped all other World War I love songs in restrained sentimentality that it has become an acknowledged classic.

The words ("Smile the while you kiss me sad adieu") never refer directly to the war. Rather, the loneliness to be inflicted on both lovers is the tragedy, regardless of the cause. Only the cover, with the moon illuminating an army officer embracing his beloved, identified it as a war song. In the history of war ballads only Frank Loesser's "Spring Will Be a Little Late This Year" comes close to rivaling "Till We Meet Again" in gracefulness of melody and words. Written in 1944 for *Christmas Holiday*, the Loesser song was sung by Deanna Durbin.

On the Operetta Front

Unquestionably the ranking operetta composer during the war, as he had been as far back as the 1890s, was Victor

Herbert, Ireland's gift to America and Broadway's most versatile songwriter. The grandson of Samuel Lover, author of the novel *Handy Andy*, Herbert was also an accomplished instrumentalist (he was a master of the cello) and conductor. He achieved the highest stature of any composer ever to write for the Broadway stage, and his series of fanciful and buoyant musicals—among them *Babes in Toyland*, *Sweethearts*, *The Red Mill*, *Naughty Marietta*, and *Eileen*—rank foremost in the history of American operetta.

Faithful to the strict limitations imposed on the operetta by tradition and librettists, Herbert was forced to eschew subjects dealing with contemporary history. The contrived world of operetta consisted of the never-never lands of yore, back when qualities resembling knighthood and maidenhood were in full flower, rogues were easily dispensed with, and happy peasants sang and danced with remarkable coordination in the squares and inns of picture-book Central European villages. Typically, the leading figures were disarming, class-conscious royalty who sought to conquer nothing more evasive than the heart of the demurest of ladies. It was love and love alone that drove these musicals. Any problem that threatened to disturb harmony anywhere in the kingdom was dissolved by the time the lovers sang their final curtain-lowering duet.

Even Herbert's modern-dress operetta, *Her Regiment*, which opened November 12, 1917, conveniently brushed the war aside. Set in a French army encampment in Normandy in 1914, it concentrated exclusively on the exaggerated ardor and ritualistic maneuvering of the male lead to win the lady of his dreams. Except for the composer's "Soldier Men" and "'Twixt Love and Duty," far more romantic than martial, the piece was a huge disappointment and closed after only 40 performances.

A staunch Irish patriot throughout his life, Herbert was naturally well aware of the struggles going on in his native Ireland as well as on the Continent, even if he in-

jected them into his musicals only once. *Hearts of Erin* (1917), later renamed *Eileen*, delved into Irish-English relations up to the present, giving the composer a suitable forum for airing his dream that Ireland one day would take its rightful place among the free nations of the world. Between 1914 and 1917, Herbert was president of the Friendly Sons of St. Patrick, organized in 1784 by Irish veterans of the American Revolution. He retired from the position in May of 1917, when the Friendly Sons pledged loyalty to the United States, which only recently had joined Great Britain in the war, without expressing any reservations concerning Ireland's freedom.

Herbert's penchant for defending the Irish as victims of English injustice had led him in 1916 to voice the hope that Germany would defeat England and that America would take no part in the war. In reality Herbert, who for a time was mistakenly judged in some circles to be pro-German, was solidly pro–American, even if anti–English. About one year before America did enter the war, he turned his superb talent toward musicalizing the greatness of his adopted country. He undertook the writing of the background musical score for the silent picture *The Fall of a Nation*, by Thomas Dixon, Jr., a Baptist preacher whose novel *The Clansman* had provided the source of director D.W. Griffith's *Birth of a Nation* in 1915. The book had been turned into a Broadway play in 1905, becoming one of that season's biggest box office disasters.

The Fall of a Nation, heavily influenced by the contemporary songs and sermons urging preparedness, opened in New York City on June 6, 1916. It preached that because America was so unprepared to wage war, it was ripe for conquest by a foreign power, presumably Germany, although that country was apparently never mentioned. The tragic consequences of such a fate struck Herbert as appalling, and he underlined the film's message with customary musical skill and vigor. In the process he wrote what critics at the time termed the finest orchestral accompaniment ever written for a motion picture. Unfortunately, both the film and most of the score have been lost.

Praised in particular was Herbert's series of miscellaneous motifs used to emphasize those portions of the film pointing up the difficulty a democracy faces in preserving liberty. This and the warning that America must be ever vigilant in order to repel foes at home and abroad constituted the picture's major theses. With the help of women warriors, the yoke of the conqueror is finally thrown off, democracy is restored, and a greater America rises, now totally prepared to assert itself in any crisis.

For *The Century Girl*, which opened November 6, 1916, Herbert wrote "When Uncle Sam Is Ruler of the Sea," among the most virile of his marches and an extraordinarily effective piece of pro–United States propaganda. The next year, in his maiden participation in the Ziegfeld Follies, he composed the music for a special flag-waving finale to Act I. Included was his "Can't You Hear Your Country Calling," which glorified America and assured victory over the Central Powers. Lastly, in 1918, Herbert's ultra-patriotic *The Call to Freedom*, an eloquent cantata for solo, chorus, and orchestra, again upheld the ideals of American liberty.*

Although it is true that Herbert's lyrical "When You're Away," written in late 1914 for *The Only Girl*, which opened November 2, 1914, in New York City, was acceptable as a wartime farewell song, it saw only limited service. As with most of his songs, a voice comparable with that of an opera star was required to sing it, so renditions were rare and usually restricted to orchestras staffed with the most highly trained instrumentalists.

Equally adaptable to wartime was the composer's "Tramp, Tramp, Tramp," an excellent marching tune sung by the leading male character, Captain Richard Warrington, and his band of Louisiana mercenary soldiers in *Naughty Marietta* (1910). The forceful Rida Johnson Young lyric contained all the ingredients that any later war song would need to qualify as a first-class battle cry, from the singers' pledge to fight for what they believe to be right to their readiness to "do or die" for their cause. Indeed, those very sentiments were pressed into service so often in the war songs of 1917-18 that the phrases grew hackneyed. Rarely, however, did the melodies challenge Herbert's mastery of the composing art.

Dead at the relatively early age of 65 on May 26, 1924, Herbert was aptly eulogized two days later by fellow composer and music critic Deems Taylor in the *New York World*: "Losing Victor Herbert, the music world loses someone it will never quite replace. He was the last of the troubadours. His musical ancestor was Mozart and the family of which he was so brilliant a younger son numbered Offenbach, Delibes, Bizet, the Strausses, and Arthur Sullivan among its elders. What he had was what they all had, the gift of song [that] bubbled and sparkled and charmed."

Rudolf Friml, who along with Sigmund Romberg rivalled but never surpassed Herbert in composing operettas, wrote dozens of lilting melodies between 1914 and 1918 for such shows as *High Jinks, Katinka, Sometime, The Peasant Girl, Kitty Darlin', You're in Love*, and *Glorianna*. No war song appeared in any of them, a significant loss to American patriotic music, since it soon became evident that this musical master, who studied under the classical composer Anton Dvorak, was capable of writing marches on a par with anyone else's when called on to do so. In the 1920s, such stirring theatrical pieces as "Song of the Mounties" (*Rose-Marie*), "Song of the Vagabonds"

Unknowingly, perhaps, Herbert was an early songwriting upholder of women's rights. In The Only Girl, *after three new husbands have sung of their disenchantment with marriage, their insulted wives present their side of the story, declaring that the men are the cause of most of the problems. The song was entitled "Equal Rights" (also known as "Why Should We Stay Home and Sew?").*

(*The Vagabond King*), "The Regimental March" (*The White Eagle*), and "The March of the Musketeers" (*The Three Musketeers*) verified his exceptional talent for concocting best-selling martial airs.

Romberg, on the other hand, composed a number of mildly popular war songs, all of them emanating from Broadway shows, although his most famous wartime musical, *Maytime* (1917), was bereft of them. "When the Colored Regiment Goes Off to War," a patronizing march, went into *Ruggles of Red Gap* in 1915, and the above-average "Ring Out, Liberty Bell" into Passing Show of 1917. For Al Jolson, he wrote the lighthearted laments "Never Trust a Soldier" (*Dancing Around*, 1914) and "Don't Be a Sailor" (*Robinson Crusoe, Jr.*, 1916).

Romberg also supplied the score for two war-centered Broadway musical comedies. The first was the American version of *Her Soldier Boy* (1916), with "A Married Man Makes the Best Soldier" (sung by John Charles Thomas), "Mother," and "Ragtime Fight." The second show, *Over the Top*, also in 1916, marked the Broadway debut of the composer's briefly popular title tune and the teenage brother and sister team of Fred and Adele Astaire.

Like Friml, Romberg had expertise at writing marches, although the best were reserved for the Broadway of later years. The still-familiar "Drinking Song" and "Students' Marching Song" were highlights of *The Student Prince* (1924), "The Riff Song" of *The Desert Song* (1926), "Your Land and My Land" of *My Maryland* (1927), and "Stout Hearted Men" of *The New Moon* (1928).

Murdering the Bugler

It was left to the indispensable Irving Berlin, like Cohan a sincere superpatriot, to create the best known of all the World War I comic tunes. He also sang it, both in his 1918 Army show *Yip, Yip, Yaphank* and in his 1942 stage hit, *This Is the Army*. Despite the brevity of his appearance in the

1943 film version of the latter show—he was on screen for only about four minutes—Berlin and the revived song managed to steal the movie from such other luminaries as Joan Leslie, George Murphy, and Ronald Reagan.

The appeal of "Oh! How I Hate to Get Up in the Morning" is a testament to Berlin's knack for condensing whatever message he wanted to convey into the fewest pertinent words, sprinkling wit over them, and wrapping everything into an immensely singable package. If any military regulation weighs more heavily on the psyche of young recruits, only recently deprived of their habit of lounging in bed long after the first glimmer of dawn's early light, it was, and still is, being startled from their dreams by the piercing command emitted by a bugler at reveille. Like the automatons they have become, the freshmen soldiers reluctantly answer the challenge by rising and fumbling about for scattered pieces of their uniform. Their sole wish, universal in its application, is to slough off the morning ritual and roll over again in the sack. Still dearer to the typical soldier's heart was Berlin's vow to bring an end to the daily torture by muffling the bugle call for good:

> "Someday I'm going to murder the
>   bugler,
> Someday they're going to find him
>   dead;
> I'll amputate his reveille, and step
>   upon it heavily,
> And spend the rest of my life in bed."

Berlin's narrator even swears to "get that other pup: / The guy that wakes the bugler up," but his dream is an idle wish.

Others have performed the song over the years—Jack Haley, for example, in the 1938 20th Century–Fox film *Alexander's Ragtime Band*. But it is doubtful that any one of them was better suited by temperament or appearance than army enlistee Berlin, who was promoted to sergeant in 1918. His slight stature, closer to that of the unsoldierly Charlie Chaplin in *Shoulder Arms* than the rugged William ("Wild Bill")

Donovan of "Fighting 69th" fame, dispelled rather than created fear. He was the perfect embodiment of the little man with big ideas, resentful of the military and courting failure in it. Berlin's blank, unaggressive stare and matter-of-fact singing voice only added pathos to the figure of a woeful dogface issuing a threat that he has neither the instinct nor the nerve to carry out.

The show opened in July 1918 at Camp Upton's Liberty Theatre in the Long Island community of Yaphank. All profits were earmarked for the erection of a "community home" where friends and relatives of the officers and men in training could be made comfortable when visiting the camp, which was basically a staging area for New York City–area soldiers on their way to France. The show was transferred, along with 350 Camp Upton trainees (called "Yip, Yip, Yaphankers") in the cast, on August 19, 1918, for a short run at New York City's Century Theatre, before it was transferred to the Lexington Theatre on September 2.

Nine of the 12 other *Yip, Yip, Yaphank* songs were related to military life or the war itself, including the sentimental "Dream On, Little Soldier Boy" and the mother song "I Can Always Find a Little Sunshine in the YMCA"; the humorous "Kitchen Police; Poor Little Me"; and the lively triad of "The Ragtime Razor Brigade," "Send a Lot of Jazz Bands Over There," and "We're on Our Way to France." (That Berlin seemed to regard the show before rehearsals began as something of a lark can be inferred from his description of *Yip, Yip, Yaphank* as a "military musical mess" on the registration form when he copyrighted "Ding Dong.")

One bright non-war exception was "Mandy," which Berlin interpolated the next year into the Ziegfeld Follies of 1919, with Eddie Cantor reintroducing it. This edition of the Follies, incidentally, featured a character named Woodrow Wilson, marking the second time that the president was impersonated in a Broadway musical. As fate would have it, the finest song

written for *Yip, Yip, Yaphank*, and one of the greatest American anthems of all time, never appeared in it. Berlin considered the song too sentimental and at the last minute dropped "God Bless America" from the score.

Unlike "America the Beautiful," the Berlin song's only serious rival for nomination as the country's unofficial national anthem, both the words and the melody of "God Bless America" were written by the same person. The words to the first song, which helped to stimulate patriotic fervor during the Spanish-American War, were written in 1895 by Katharine Lee Bates, a professor of English at Wellesley College. The melody, however, was based on "Materna," which Samuel Augustus Ward had composed in 1888 as a setting for an anonymous author's poem "O Mother Dear, Jerusalem."

Ironically, it was on a patch of land near Camp Upton in Yaphank that the pro–Nazi German-American Bund set up the most elaborate of its own camps in the late 1930s. Called Siegfried, it was used to train American children and youths, who wore German uniforms, marched to German songs, and waved German swastikas. Their hours there were devoted to mastering stiff-necked Prussian discipline, memorizing German genealogy and ideology, and reciting the greatness of the Führer in much the same way as their counterparts in the Hitler Jugend were being taught throughout Germany.

More than two decades later Berlin conceived and produced *This Is the Army*, his successor service show with a new cast and new songs for a new war. This time all the proceeds were donated to the Army Emergency Relief Fund. The show played the Broadway Theatre throughout the latter half of 1942, and featured 300 doughboys and a 50-piece orchestra led by Corporal Milton Rosenstock. Sergeant Alan Anderson, son of playwright Maxwell Anderson, served as stage manager. Instrumental in assembling the production crew was Staff Sergeant Ezra Stone, then a producer, director, and actor with Army

Special Services. He was far better known at the time, however, as "Henry Aldrich" in the popular weekly radio program *The Aldrich Family*, based on characters created by Clifford Goldsmith for his 1938 hit Broadway play *What a Life*. The weekly half-hour radio program ran from 1939 to 1953.

Far more Berlin song hits came from the World War II show than from *Yip, Yip, Yaphank*: "I Left My Heart at the Stage Door Canteen," "With My Head in the Clouds," "I'm Getting Tired So I Can Sleep," and the songwriter's optimistic reverie to the end of all warfare, "This Time (Is the Last Time)." The biggest hit of all was "This Is the Army, Mr. Jones," the classic warning to one recruit, a sort of Mr. Everyman, that the pleasures he enjoyed as a civilian had been put on ice for the duration, from a private telephone to breakfast in bed. Along with the minor "My Sergeant and I Are Buddies," a reminder that the best way to advance one's own interests is to cozy up to persons in authority, both songs served as cogent reminders that Berlin's expertise at pounding out humorous lyrics had remained intact between the wars.

In only one way did the 1942 show depart from its predecessor. *This Is the Army* included two new Berlin songs honoring members of sister services, the Army Air Corps ("American Eagles") and the Navy ("How About a Cheer for the Navy?").*

None of Berlin's other published World War I songs equalled the popularity of "Oh! How I Hate to Get Up in the Morning," although he wrote as many of them as any other songwriter. "The Voice of Belgium" was a creditable recitation of the horrors inflicted on that small nation by the German army; obversely, "They Were All Out of Step but Jim" was a comic exposé of an awkward young re-

cruit's inability to cope with synchronized drilling, and the result that he marches to his own drummer. "For Your Country and My Country," "Let's All Be Americans Now," "True Born Soldier Man," and "Over the Sea, Boys" expressed pride in country and confidence in victory. "Daddy, Come Home" and "Kiss Your Sailor Boy Goodbye" dwelled on the sorrowful partings of soldiers from children, parents, and lovers.

Among his stage songs, "Homeward Bound" was written for superstar dancers Vernon and Irene Castle in the heavily ragtime-based *Watch Your Step*, which premiered in New York City on December 8, 1914. Invited by producer Charles B. Dillingham to appear in the musical was a comedian and juggler named W.C. Fields. On the road in Australia at the time, Fields was delayed by the presence of German submarines in the Pacific. He finally found a captain of a freighter bound for San Francisco who was willing to take him aboard. Fields finally got to New York City, but the day after the show opened, his act was cut out of it.

Besides performing the tango and turkey trot in the musical, the Castles introduced their famous "Castle Walk" to the tune of Berlin's "Syncopated Walk." *Stop! Look! and Listen!* the following year introduced "The Sailor Song" and "When I Get Back to the U.S.A." Helping to brighten the Ziegfeld Follies of 1918 were "I'm Gonna Pin My Medal on the Girl I Left Behind" and "The Blue Devils of France."

Berlin's "Smile and Show Your Dimple," still another in the platitudinous series of goodbye songs, centered on a departing soldier's final request in a brave farewell. It became only mildly popular, repeating as it did the customary entreaty to a "little girlie" not to grieve. Better she "sprinkle just a twinkle, / Light your face up, / Just brace up and smile," Berlin advised, adding

---

On June 25, 1942, Robert P. Patterson, Under Secretary of War and president of Army Emergency Relief, wrote to Berlin: "I want to express my deep appreciation for the splendid contribution you have made to Army Emergency Relief. As writer and producer of 'This Is the Army,' you have given most generously of your time, talents and money. We want you to know that the Army is very grateful...."

that "it will soon be over, / Then he'll come marching back to you."

The song, however, had theatrical history written into it. In 1933, Berlin rewrote the lyric and slightly revised the melody of both verse and chorus before inserting the song into his score for Broadway's *As Thousands Cheer*. Renamed "Easter Parade," the song developed into one of the songwriter's and Broadway's all-time biggest hits.

No Strangers to Song Hits

The fact that most of the high-profile lyricists and composers were unable to enhance their fame and fortune by writing World War I songs that have stood the test of time in no way diminishes the professionalism they brought to creating them. A few songs from such brand-name composers as Cohan, Berlin, Whiting, Hanley, and Walter Donaldson have retained an air of familiarity about them, but they are the occasional exceptions to the rule. As recently as the early months of 1993, for example, a Delta Air Lines radio and television commercial began playing "Over There" as the background theme for the company's inducement to choose that carrier as the fastest and most comfortable way to get "from here to over there," as the tag line phrased it. The lyric was not sung; the tune was sufficient to identify it. Another World War I hit, "Colonel Bogey," served as the themesong for Getty Oil Company's commercials from the mid- to late 1980s.

The overwhelming majority of the war ballads, even those that avoided dating themselves by omitting specific mention of the conflict, have not enjoyed very many reprises since their pre–Armistice heyday. It was a fate shared by all the songs written by the novices, whose works unanimously went out of hearing range permanently with the termination of the war. Nonetheless, an impressive number of the professional writers had been, or were about to be, highly proficient contributors

to American popular music. Some of them, like the Von Tilzers, had begun their enviable careers before 1914; others, like Gus Kahn and Arthur Freed, reached their professional writing pinnacles during the peaceful interregnum between 1919 and 1939.

The major writers not only were prolific during the war, but also accounted for most of the song successes. Lyricist Al Bryan collaborated on 30 of them; ranking second was Irving Berlin, who wrote the words and music to 23 songs and collaborated with Edgar Leslie and George W. Meyer on another one.

Three quarters of a century later, even the biggest World War I song hits ring the bell of recognition almost exclusively among the elder generations. Younger persons may have heard a number of them, but their tendency to dismiss them as artifacts of a past too distant to serve as commentaries on their own times is widespread. The intrinsic sentimentality of the ballads is surely so foreign to contemporary musical tastes that the songs are equated with grainy television reruns of the Mack Sennett comedies of the same period, and rejected as antique curiosities. Or they are associated with the ornately dressed, usually plump beauties seen in the silent dramatic films of the period, which now seem so totally divorced from reality as to define irrelevancy.

Long the victims of neglect, and at times derision, the songs do mirror the styles and mores of their birthyears. Yet many of the writers and their tunes are integral to the study of popular American music in the first four decades of the twentieth century. Their own names as well as those of their songs occupy honored places in its development.

Composer Gus Edwards, whose name appeared on 12 World War I songs, was a much-respected Tin Pan Alleyite for such earlier songs as "School Days," "Sunbonnet Sue," "By the Light of the Silvery Moon," "In My Merry Oldsmobile," and "If I Were a Millionaire." A charter member of the American Society of Composers,

Authors and Publishers, he was responsible for discovering a distinguished array of talented youngsters—Elsie Janis, Eddie Cantor, Walter Winchell, and George Jessel, each of whom collaborated on at least one World War I song, and in postwar years Ray Bolger, Eleanor Powell, and the singing Lane Sisters, including Priscilla. The redoubtable Edwards's generous passing out of first big breaks to aspiring entertainers earned him the title of "Star Maker," also the name of his "life story," filmed by Paramount in 1939 with Bing Crosby.

Fred Fisher, who composed the comic "Oui, Oui, Marie"* and six other war songs, may well be anonymous in the 1990s, but he was respected in his day for such antique perennials as "Come, Josephine, in My Flying Machine," "Peg o' My Heart," "Dardanella," and that famous themesong of what was then the nation's second largest city, "Chicago." Among Percy Wenrich's all-time standards are "Put on Your Old Gray Bonnet," "Moonlight Bay," and "When You Wore a Tulip and I Wore a Big Red Rose."

Abe Olman's four World War I tunes achieved only moderate success compared with "O Johnny, O Johnny, O!" and "Down Among the Sheltering Palms." Pete Wendling's peacetime song hits included "Oh! What a Pal Was Mary," "There's Danger in Your Eyes, Cherie," "Red Lips, Kiss My Blues Away," and "On the Street of Regret." Ragtimer Eubie Blake's reputation rests far more on "I'm Just Wild About Harry" and "Memories of You" than on any of his war songs.

The four novelty war songs of Con Conrad, the pseudonym of Conrad K. Dober, failed to attract very much attention, but in later years his "Memory Lane," "Barney Google," "Margie," "Ma, He's Making Eyes at Me," and "The Continental" assuredly did. Among Harry Carroll's non-war melodies were those for "By the Beautiful Sea," the Chopin-based "I'm

Always Chasing Rainbows," and "The Trail of the Lonesome Pine," all of which towered over his nine songs with war themes.

Composer Jean Schwartz's "Chinatown, My Chinatown" was almost surpassed in sales by his "Rock-a-Bye Your Baby with a Dixie Melody," thanks to Al Jolson's fondness for it. Egbert van Alstyne became renowned not for his 14 war songs, but for "In the Shade of the Old Apple Tree," "Pretty Baby," "Drifting and Dreaming," and "Your Eyes Have Told Me So." Charles K. Harris's "After the Ball," written in 1892, totally overshadowed the 11 war songs that bore his name. Despite the initial success of Al Piantadosi's "I Didn't Raise My Boy to Be a Soldier" and 12 other war-related songs, none ever came close to rivaling the composer's "The Curse of a Breaking Heart" in popularity, or for that matter in mawkishness.

Maceo Pinkard's name is associated more with "Gimme a Little Kiss, Will 'Ya, Huh?" and the effervescent "Sweet Georgia Brown" than with his five novelty or sentimental war songs. Composer M.K. Jerome's "My Wild Irish Rose," "Bright Eyes," and "My Little Buckaroo" stimulated far more sales than any of his World War I tunes. A generation later he received Academy Award nominations for "Sweet Dreams, Sweetheart," sung by Joan Leslie and Kitty Carlisle in *Hollywood Canteen* (1944) and for "Some Sunday Morning," from *San Antonio* (1945). "It's Victory Day" won him a United States Treasury Department Silver Medal shortly after the end of World War II.

It was not until after the Armistice that the active Harry Ruby, collaborator on 11 fighting and homefront songs, and lyricist Bert Kalmar formed one of the most successful of Broadway partnerships. "So Long—Oo-Long," "My Sunny Tennessee," "Who's Sorry Now?", "Thinking of You," "Hooray for Captain Spaulding" (Groucho Marx's theme song), and "Never-

*The song was one of actress Betty Grable's favorite "oldies," and she sang "Oui, Oui, Marie" in the 1948 20th Century–Fox musical When My Baby Smiles at Me.

theless" are among the team's chief song successes. For the title of the duo's 1950 biography, MGM selected their "Three Little Words," written ten years earlier. Red Skelton essayed the part of Ruby, Fred Astaire that of Kalmar. The songmen's two war-song collaborations were "Girls of America, We All Depend on You" and "I've Got a Red Cross Rosie Going Across with Me," both published in 1917.

Joseph A. Burke composed seven war songs, but his failure to hit paydirt did not prevent his becoming Warner Bros.' first successful composer under contract in the early talking-picture era. For *Gold Diggers of Broadway* (1929), he wrote two immense hits: "Painting the Clouds with Sunshine" and "Tip Toe Through the Tulips (with Me)." A third movie-based success was his "For You." Composer-lyricist Arthur Lange, whose "America, Here's My Boy" served as a popular recruiting song in 1917, headed the music department of MGM beginning in 1929. In 1937, while working for 20th Century–Fox, he was musical director for *On the Avenue*, which featured six new tunes by fellow wartime songwriter Irving Berlin.

Two other minor wartime writers, Sam H. Stept and Bud Green, later to collaborate on movie songs, hit their stride well after the Armistice. Composer Stept's "This Is Worth Fighting For" and "Don't Sit Under the Apple Tree (with Anyone Else but Me)" rank among the best of the World War II songs. Among Green's collaborative highlights are "Alabamy Bound," "I'll Always Be in Love with You," "That's My Weakness Now," "Once in a While," and "Sentimental Journey."

The Word Merchants

Similarly few lyricists were able to pen many war songs that rose above the commonplace, practiced as a number of the writers were. Andrew B. Sterling authored the words to seventeen such songs, but not even "Merrily We'll Roll Along" attained the stature of "Hello, Ma

Baby," the first well-known song to mention the telephone, which he had written in 1899 with Joseph E. Howard, another relatively minor war-song composer, with five to his credit. "Meet Me in St. Louis, Louis," "In the Evening by the Moonlight," and "When My Baby Smiles at Me" are other notable non-war Sterling songs.

Hollywood honored Howard in 1947 with the pseudo-biographical *I Wonder Who's Kissing Her Now*, also the title of his and Harold Orlob's best-known ballad, starring Mark Stevens as the songwriter. One of Howard's contemporaries, Ernest R. Ball, was portrayed by crooner Dick Haymes in the 1944 film *Irish Eyes Are Smiling*.

Howard Johnson, the author of 22 war-song lyrics, was also responsible for the words of that incomparably tearful tribute to motherhood: "M-O-T-H-E-R." Eight war songs, including "You Keep Sending 'Em Over and We'll Keep Knocking 'Em Down," helped to advance lyricist Sidney D. Mitchell's career, but the movies gave him a greater impetus. Writing mostly for 20th Century–Fox in the 1930s, Mitchell versified Shirley Temple songs ("At the Codfish Ball," "Toy Trumpet"), several others for Sonja Henie ("One in a Million," "Who's Afraid of Love?"), and the lovely "Twilight on the Trail," an Oscar nominee from *The Trail of the Lonesome Pine*.

Lyricist Edgar Leslie and composers E. Ray Goetz and George W. Meyer's "For Me and My Gal" far outshone any of their World War I songs. Leslie, an early collaborator with Harry Warren, also wrote the words to "Among My Souvenirs," "Moon Over Miami," and "The Moon Was Yellow," a rare hit tango. Meyer wrote the melodies of 13 war songs, at least half of which gained a fair degree of popularity. In 1942, he collaborated with Stanley Adams and Abel Baer on "There Are Such Things," one of the best of the World War II songs. Its encouraging words that people will again see a peaceful sky if only they retain their trust in what the future will bring were sung into prominence by the then 25-year-old Frank Sinatra.

Two other 1920s Warren partners were Sam M. Lewis and Joe Young, whose names were coupled on twelve war songs and separately on four more with varying success. Far better remembered is their later teamwork on "My Mammy," "I'm Sitting on Top of the World," "Dinah," and "I Kiss Your Hand, Madame." Young was not present when Lewis wrote the words to another standard, "Street of Dreams." The reverse was true when Young authored "In a Shanty in Old Shanty Town" and "I'm Gonna Sit Right Down and Write Myself a Letter."

Warren's most consistent collaborator, Al Dubin, was represented in the war with four songs, including the mildly popular "The Dream of a Soldier Boy." It was as Warner Bros.' chief contract lyricist in the early to mid–1930s, however, that he gained renown after writing the words to "Forty-Second Street," "Shuffle Off to Buffalo," "Shadow Waltz," "I Only Have Eyes for You," and dozens of other screen hits that secured his reputation as a major Hollywood lyricist.

In 1943 Dubin was reunited with his sometimes World War I collaborator, composer James V. Monaco, to write songs for *Stage Door Canteen*. Included was the Oscar nominee "We Mustn't Say Goodbye," crooned by pop singer Lanny Ross. Outranking L. Wolfe Gilbert's Great War song lyrics were his words for "Waiting for the Robert E. Lee," one of Al Jolson's all-time favorites; the Latin-tinged "Mama Inez"; and "The Peanut Vendor."

Foremost among the accomplished versifiers to practice during the war — even if not all that successfully — was Gus Kahn, who in the early 1920s collaborated with composer Isham Jones on three mammoth hits, "Swingin' Down the Lane," "I'll See You in My Dreams" (incidentally the title of Kahn's 1952 filmed biography), and "It Had to Be You." Kahn also lyricized "Toot, Toot, Tootsie! (Goodbye)," "Memories," "Ain't We Got Fun," "Side by Side," "Flying Down to Rio," "The

Carioca," and "One Night of Love," among many other songs.

The most quickly identifiable name of a World War I lyricist belongs to Arthur Freed, who — like fellow war writer Earl Carroll, later a producer and director of such stage revues as Earl Carroll Vanities and Earl Carroll Sketch Book — compiled a list of enviable credits in the postwar entertainment field. Freed began his theatrical career in vaudeville with Louis ("April Showers") Silvers. His two war songs, "Belgium, Dry Your Tears" and "Over in Hero-Land," failed to give the slightest indication of the fame that was to be his after motion pictures found their singing voice in late 1927 with *The Jazz Singer*. In 1929 he teamed with composer Nacio Herb Brown to write songs for MGM musicals and several dramas and adventure films. From their partnership came "Broadway Melody," "You Were Meant for Me," "Singin' in the Rain," "Pagan Love Song," "Temptation," "All I Do Is Dream of You," "You Are My Lucky Star," and "Good Morning."

Beginning in the late 1930s, Freed gradually turned from versifying to producing musical films. For the next 19 years, it was he who added even more glitz and glamour to MGM's enviable parade of song-and-dance extravaganzas with *Meet Me in St. Louis* (1944), *The Harvey Girls* (1946), *Good News* (1947), *Easter Parade* (1948), *On the Town* (1949), the third filmed version of *Show Boat* (1951), *A Royal Wedding* (1951) *An American in Paris* (1951), the matchless *Singin' in the Rain* (1952), *The Band Wagon* (1953), and *Gigi* (1958).

Although the Russian-born Herman Paley was responsible for a few war songs, he, too, like Freed and Earl Carroll, branched out into other areas of the entertainment field after the war. It was as a publishing and radio executive that he made his reputation. Paley had organized various World War I shows that toured Europe; in World War II he directed musicals for presentation at the Stage Door Canteen.

Obviously, the "Big Two" of World War I musical comedy—Kern and Berlin—achieved such renown in later years that they fully deserve the universal acclaim awarded to them for their theatrical and film songs. Kern's *Show Boat* alone would place him in a special niche among Broadway's foremost composers. His songs for such other post–Armistice stage hits as *Sally*, *Sunny*, *The Cat and the Fiddle*, *Music in the Air*, and *Roberta* (which introduced "Smoke Gets in Your Eyes") strengthened his already solid reputation and, beginning in 1935, led to his Academy Award–winning West Coast career as a composer of Hollywood musicals.

Berlin's stage shows, from the *Music Box Revues* of the early 1920s to *Face the Music* and *As Thousands Cheer* in the 1930s, *Annie Get Your Gun* in 1946, and *Call Me Madam* in 1950, gave ample evidence of the flourishing of his musical genius well beyond the end of the Great War. Also boasting musical roots in the war years, insignificant as they were, was Cole Porter. He eventually also won superstardom with such tunes as "Night and Day" (1932), "I Get a Kick Out of You" (1934), "Begin the Beguine" and "Just One of Those Things" (both 1935), and "Easy to Love" and "I've Got You Under My Skin" (both 1936), in addition to numerous other hit songs written for a score of distinguished stage and screen musicals between *Paris* (1928) and *Silk Stockings* (1954).

The Working Girl
from Armentières

Probably the most universally familiar song late in the war was "Mad'moiselle from Armentières," better known at the time by its alternate fractured–French title of "Hinky-Dinky Parlez-vous." A basically ribald song more appropriate to servicemen on leave than those on the march, it is believed to have been written in 1918. It was based partly on "Skiboo," a nineteenth-century favorite with British soldiers serving with Field Marshal Horatio Herbert Kitchener in the Sudan, and partly on the even older folk song "Mademoiselle de Bar-Le-Duc." Kitchener, incidentally, was one of the few British leaders who believed at the outset that World War I would last a number of years rather than months. At the time, he was serving the government as secretary of state for war.

The author of the Armentières song, who missed out on a fortune in royalties, is unknown, as is the mademoiselle. Unfounded rumors circulated during the war identified her as "Marie Lecocq," a barmaid in an unnamed small French café in Armentières, a northwest French town near the Belgian border. True or false, Mlle. Lecocq was ideally cast as the adjunct sweetheart of millions of homesick soldiers who never tired of serenading her imaginary charms, companionship, kisses, and availability—at least in their dreams.

Geoffrey O'Hara's whimsical "K-K-K-Katy," advertised alliteratively in 1918 by publisher Leo Feist as the "Sensational Stammering Song Success Sung by the Soldiers and Sailors," quickly became associated with the waning months of the war through the personage of one Jimmy, a "soldier brave and bold" but "just a gawk" when it came to women. The tongue-tied lover, nervous in the presence of his g-g-g-girlfriend, seemed to typify in some minds the difficulty encountered by the shy soldier while saying goodbye. If the girl was not the source of his insecurity, the fear of going into battle would do, and so the novelty love song faced little trouble adapting to the wartime environment.

The perennially popular "Caissons Go Rolling Along" had been written in 1908 in honor of the field artillery by Edmund L. Gruber, a member of the West Point graduating class of 1904 who was later promoted through the ranks to brigadier general. Thanks to John Philip Sousa, who made a brilliant band arrangement of it in 1918 under the title "The United States Field Artillery March," Gruber's song won the widest possible acceptance with troops marching over hill, over dale, and along the dusty trail.

Probably the most famous alumnus of the World War I field artillery was President Harry S Truman, who sailed for France aboard the *George Washington* on March 30, 1918. A captain in the 129th Field Artillery of the 35th Division, he took part in battles in and around the Vosges Mountains, St. Mihiel, Meuse-Argonne, and Somme-Bourevilles. Returned to the United States aboard the German passenger ship *Zeppelin* on April 19, 1919, he was discharged from the service on May 6.

The Caissons song's only serious rival during the war was the equally pulsating navy anthem, "Anchors Aweigh," also a carryover from the past. The composer, Charles A. Zimmerman, was the Naval Academy's musical director and bandmaster when he wrote the famous song. It had become a tradition with him to write songs for the academy's graduating classes, and the Class of 1907 requested a march that would inspire as well as serve as a football marching song. The result was the "March of the Class of 1907," now known as "Anchors Aweigh."

The first time it was heard in public was at the Army-Navy football game in 1906, which was played at Franklin Field in Philadelphia. As Zimmerman undoubtedly hoped, Navy won the game, 10-0, finishing the season with an 8-2-2 record. Alfred H. Miles, a member of the 1907 graduating class, authored the first—or "football"—chorus to the classic salute to America's seafaring service. George D. Lottman later made several revisions to the first as well as the second chorus. The date when "Anchors Aweigh" was officially adopted as the academy's "fight song" is unknown.

The prewar years were also called on for two other immensely popular military tunes. The first, the traditional "You're in the Army Now," was derived, like Cohan's "Over There," from a bugle call, or was a clever imitation of one. Its lyric, more realistic of the enlisted man's life than that of any other army march, warns recruits that "You'll never get rich / A-diggin' a ditch." It is not known who wrote the song, when they wrote it, or who it was—if not the original lyricist—who added the serviceman's earthy touch to the song by substituting "You son-of-a-bitch" for "A-diggin' a ditch."

The Civil War year of 1863 was tapped for "When Johnny Comes Marching Home," which was revived in splendid fashion, so much so that it served as the best and most popular "welcome home" march of the Great War. The writer's name has yet to be verified; the most likely candidate is Patrick S. Gilmore, then the official bandmaster of the Union Army. Henry Clay Work's equally famous "Marching Through Georgia," also a Civil War song, provided the melody for the popular 1917 anthem "Marching Song of Freedom." "Dixie" was similarly revived, providing the melody for Edmund Vance Cook's "U.S.A. Forever," published July 31, 1918, and for D.B. Coats's "Freedom Land," published November 9, 1918.

Pushing Toward the Rhine

Several signals that the war was coming to an end were appearing even before the run of *Yip, Yip, Yaphank*. On April 21, 1918, the Allies scored a major psychological as well as military victory with the death of Manfred von Richthofen, the war's dashing "ace of aces" better known as the "Red Baron." Credited with shooting down 80 Allied planes, Richthofen was aloft in his maroon Fokker triplane near Sailly-le-Sec, Somme, France, when members of the Australian 24th Machine Gun Company and the Australian Field Artillery's 53rd Battery opened fire. The plane staggered and then glided a couple of hundred yards before crashing just north of the Bray-Corbie road, a mile and one-half inside contested territory held precariously by the Australians.

Richthofen's body was taken to Poulainville, five miles from the crash site, and laid in a hangar belonging to the Australian Flying Corps. The question of exactly who killed him has never been completely resolved. He was buried with full military honors by the British and Australians on the afternoon of April 22 in a cemetery in Bertangles, near a Royal Air Force base. The prestigious British aviation weekly *The Aeroplane* praised the dead warrior as a "brave man, a clean fighter, and an aristocrat." On July 14, 1918, command of the Richthofen Wing of the German Air Service was passed on to Lieutenant Hermann Goering.* Seven years after the Armistice, on November 20, 1925, Richthofen's remains were reburied in Invaliden Cemetery in Berlin. The military parade accompanying him to the gravesite was the largest and most glittering spectacle Germany had seen since the war.

Songwriters, of course, were keeping close tabs on developments in Europe, the most significant of them the faltering of the once highly touted "Hindenburg Machine," which had developed severe engine trouble. "The Road to Berlin's Getting Shorter," comedian Eddie Cantor acutely observed in his lyric to the mid–1918 song. So short, in fact, that the seemingly bloated effusiveness of Andrew B. Sterling and Arthur Lange's "(When Yankee Doodle Marches Through Berlin) There'll Be a Hot Time in the U.S.A." was greeted as gospel by all but a few war-watchers. Like the songwriters, they, too, were unable to visualize any detours on the path to the German capital. The Yanks will soon be hauling down the "Kaiser's black flag," Sterling reported, while informing him in no uncertain terms that "he can kiss himself goodbye":

> Here they come, here they come,
> And the drums are beating,
> There'll be no retreating,

> They'll be there,
> They'll be there,
> For there's vict'ry in the air!
> And they'll win, yes, they'll win,
> Then they'll flash the news to old
> Broadway;
> And when Yankee Doodle marches
> through Berlin,
> There'll be a hot time in the U.S.A.**

With perception about to become reality, and with the Allies and Americans clearly taking the offensive, other tune-smiths fired off a new fusilade of songs bearing fierce-sounding titles that caromed from derisive to boastful. "Bing! Bang! Bing 'Em on the Rhine!", urged singer Blanche Ring to standing ovations. This song, along with "I'd Like to See the Kaiser with a Lily in His Hand," "We're All Going Calling on the Kaiser," "Keep Your Head Down, 'Fritzie Boy'," "We Stopped Them at the Marne," and the ironic response to the peacemakers' pleas, "Let's Bury the Hatchet (in the Kaiser's Head)," were only six of the insults lobbed at Wilhelm II in the first sustained outpouring of contempt for the enemy since the halcyon days of mid–1917.

Once again, according to the lyrics, the Yanks were prepared to emulate the charge of bulls along the streets of Pamplona and put into action, as it were, George M. Cohan's toxic warning that "We'll never stop until we cop / The Kaiser in Berlin."

"Germany, You'll Soon Be No Man's Land," blustered another 1918 song with typical chip-on-the-shoulder jauntiness, followed in short order by the equally threatening "Just Like Washington Crossed the Delaware (General Pershing Will Cross the Rhine)" and "When Pershing's Men Go Marching into Picardy," all of them accurately gauging the orgasmic heights to

---

The leading U.S. air ace in World War I was Eddie (Edward Vernon) Rickenbacker, who was credited with destroying 26 enemy planes. He later became an executive with several airlines, including Eastern Airlines, which he built into a major passenger and cargo carrier.

**The most renowned of the "hot time" songs, "There'll Be a Hot Time in the Old Town Tonight," was written in 1886 by Theodore Metz, then conductor of the pit orchestra for (James) McIntyre and (T.K.) Heath's Minstrels. Unrelated to war, it nonetheless was a favorite marching song with American soldiers in the Spanish-American War 12 years later. Metz also composed the equally sassy "Ta-ra-ra Boom-de-Ree."*

which victory expectations in the United States had risen. The over-optimists were further cheered by "We'll Nail the Stars and Stripes to the Kaiser's Door" and "We'll Make the Germans All Sing 'Yankee Doodle Doo.'"

Even stubborn realists found something to sing about with the less sanguine but still assertive "We'll Lick the Kaiser If It Takes Us Twenty Years." The highly effective "We'll Knock the Heligo — Into Heligo — Out of Heligoland!" was little more than an awkward singing pun, referring to the German island fortress on the Kiel Canal, with "Heligo" acting as a polite substitute for the no-no word "hell."

Sam M. Lewis, Joe Young, and Bert Grant's hair-raising "The Worst Is Yet to Come" gleefully reduced the Imperial German leader to a cornered bully:

> Oh! Willie, Willie, wild fellow,
> Growing up so high,
> You'd better order your coffin now
> Because you're gonna die!

They further mocked the Kaiser for his tendency to overreach: "You tried to put the whole world on the bum; / Now, you crazy Kaiser, you've gotta give up!"

Similarly downplaying fear of Germany was "We Don't Want the Bacon (What We Want Is a Piece of the Rhine)," which substituted "Rhine" for "Rind" while prophesying that "Wilhelm the Gross" would soon be crowned "with a bottle of Budweiser," presumably wielded by a Yank. Another of many songs to pledge that the Yanks would emerge victorious from the conflict was "The U.S.A. Will Lay the Kaiser Away," with its boastful forecast that "Our guns will roar and our great airplanes will soar, / We'll march to Berlin in the spring; / We'll win our way and you'll soon see the day / When everlasting peace on earth we'll bring."

It was evident that by using their songs as both shield and weapon, the writers were doing their bit more brazenly than ever before. Enemy forces were hanging on the ropes, ripe for a knockout, as was the Kaiser himself, who was fiercely reindicted for a plethora of criminal activities. The United States, now on the move, could not possibly lose the war, the lyrics stressed. The most powerful protagonist in the war, America was determined to end it by autumn.

Menacing the German army more directly than most of the songs was J. Edwin and Lincoln McConnell's "Goodbye, Germany" — which could easily have been detonated against the Nazis a generation later:

> We have watched you make your dirty
> fight,
> Watched as you trampled ev'ry Right,
> Trampled helpless people 'neath your
> heel,
> Now the hand of power you shall
> surely feel.
> My country is a land
> Where the hearts of men beat true,
> And when you murder the people
> Of this grand old nation,
> You'll get what's coming to you.

The prime example of the renewal of optimism among the troops was "Merrily We'll Roll Along," Andrew B. Sterling and Abner Silver's tip-of-the-cap salutation to American sailors in recognition of the successes they were experiencing. The march toward victory, having moved for months at what seemed a glacial pace, had now gained momentum. The battles, at least shorter now if not less fierce, usually ended in the surrender or retreat of enemy forces.

As the devil-may-care lyric pointed out, the Americans were swaggering again up to enemy lines, triumph entrenched in their minds, no longer frustrated by incessant stalemate. It was not with trepidation they faced battle, but merriment. Anxiety over the next encounter had been replaced by eagerness for it to begin, at least according to the songwriters. Like battalions of tanks, the Yanks were rolling onward, masters of the ground and sea, sweeping the Germans from their path. "And when ev'rything's all over / We'll roll the Kaiser over, / Then we'll all come rolling home," Sterling boasted.

Meanwhile, legendary optimist George M. Cohan uncharacteristically sought to tamp down the public's possibly premature renewal of confidence. The July 19, 1918, copyrighted title of his new song addressed to soldiers was the mood-leveling "When You Come Back (If You Do Come Back, There's a Whole World Waiting for You)." After a few weeks' reflection, he canceled any lingering doubts he might have had on the prospects for victory, and on August 9 recopyrighted the piece as "When You Come Back (and You Will Come Back, There's a Whole World Waiting for You)."

A similar title alteration was made to "(Watch, Hope and Wait) Little Girl (Until I Come Back to You)." Just before the October 3, 1918, publication of the six-month-old Lew Brown–Will Clayton song, the title was switched to the more affirmative "(Watch, Hope, and Wait) Little Girl ('I'm Coming Back to You')."

With the Armistice, the lyric-writing team of Lewis and Young promptly joined forces with Walter Donaldson for the first and greatest of all comedy songs looking beyond the present into the future. Few war songs of any kind surpassed its immense popularity, the result of its being syndicated across the country, thanks chiefly to Nora Bayes's recording of it only weeks after war's end.

Donaldson, later the composer of "My Mammy," "Carolina in the Morning," "My Buddy," "Yes Sir, That's My Baby," "Love Me or Leave Me," "What Can I Say After I Say I'm Sorry?", "At Sundown," "My Blue Heaven," "Little White Lies," and dozens of other vastly popular songs, was a prolific writer throughout the war. "The Army's Full of Irish," "I've Got a Ten-Day Pass for a Honeymoon for the Girl I Left Behind," and "We're Coming Back to You When the Fighting Days Are Through" received only minimal attention. Donaldson's "Don't Cry, Frenchy, Don't Cry,"

however, attracted an enthusiastic international public that wanted to believe its tantalizing promise that "peaceful stars" will soon begin to "heal the scars of Flanders."

A far greater audience became enamored of his "How 'Ya Gonna Keep 'Em Down on the Farm (After They've Seen Paree)?" Provoking laughter rather than sighs of hopefulness, this postwar song centered on the forthcoming return of a country lad to the sticks, unfolding his father's and mother's humorous lament that their young Reuben will no longer display any interest whatsoever in working with a rake or a plow. Having spent so much time in Paris, the corrupted youngster most likely will carry on in the United States the way he did over there, "jazzin' aroun'" Broadway and "paintin' the town." Chances are also pretty good that he'll dally over his barnyard chores while dreaming of the charms of those delightful, roving-eye French girls, Reuben's frustrated father groans. But even he admits in an insightful aside: "Who the deuce can parley vous a cow?"*

Mission Fulfilled

By late summer of 1918, newspapers were reporting that even more of the fearsome German offensives were being halted decisively. Bulgaria surrendered in September, Turkey in October. That same month, Germany and Austria-Hungary issued peace feelers through the neutral Swiss and Swedish governments. German armies were still intact, however, and held an unbroken line on foreign soil.

But morale among civilians and the armed forces had nearly collapsed, dramatized by a mutiny in the German High Fleet at Kiel on November 4, which convinced government leaders that further prosecution of the war would be fruitless. Songwriter Leon DeCosta's mid–1917 pre-

*This song contains the most familiar of the alternative catch phrases found in World War I songs. Often substituting for "They'll never want to see a rake or a plow, / And who the deuce can parley-vous a cow?" was the couplet: "Imagine Reuben when he meets his pa, / He'll kiss his cheek and holler 'oo-la-la!'"

diction had at last come true: "Let them [the Germans] know that the bird of America / Is a dove and an eagle in one, / We'll tramp, tramp, tramp, / Till the work of the Yanks is done."

The Kaiser abdicated in the face of an armed revolution on November 9, ending the long rule of the Hohenzollern dynasty, which had also served as a point of ridicule for many songwriters. His abrupt departure marked the beginning of Germany's turbulent experiment with democracy. He was immediately succeeded by a provisional German People's Government headed by the Socialist deputy Friedrich Ebert. To prevent a destructive invasion of their country, the Germans accepted Marshal Foch's terms for an armistice. In a railway car near Compiègne, France, which served Foch as headquarters, they signed the document at 5 A.M., November 11, to become effective six hours later—11 A.M. in Paris, 12 noon in Berlin.*

Songwriters Ed Morton, James E. Dempsey, and Joseph A. Burke's "Greatest Day the World Will Ever Know" had finally arrived, as had fulfillment of Charles K. Harris's early February 1918 vision of "our laddie boys" on their way back home "With their bright smiling faces, / No scars and no traces of dark, weary nights spent alone":

> What a wonderful, wonderful dream it
>   would be
> If the mothers could live just to see
> Their boys safe at home sleeping,
> No heartaches or weeping,
> What a wonderful, wonderful dream.

Under the Armistice and the threat of occupation of the industrial Ruhr, Germany agreed to pay the European Allies the tremendous sum of $33 billion in reparations. The new states of Poland, Czechoslovakia, and Yugoslavia, initially named the "Kingdom of Serbs, Croats and Slovenes," emerged from the breakup of the Austro-Hungarian Empire and the detaching of Polish territory from Germany and Russia. Austria was separated from Hungary and forbidden to unite with its former German ally. The Baltic states of Estonia, Latvia, and Lithuania were freed from Russian control and granted independence. The January 1917 dream of Wilson—and of the mother in "I Didn't Raise My Boy to Be a Soldier"—for a "League of Peace" to check aggression collectively seemed well on the way toward actuality when the League of Nations Covenant was incorporated as a part of the Treaty of Versailles.

Fearing legislative defeat of his unpopular proposal for American membership in the league, and consequently U.S. rejection of the entire treaty, Wilson resolved to appeal directly to the public over the heads of the Senate. He entered into a vigorous cross-country campaign, rousing much popular enthusiasm, but ended it in tragedy. Under the strain of the effort—36 formal addresses in addition to numerous rear-platform speeches at whistle stops—the president suffered a paralytic stroke that for months made him an almost helpless invalid. He had not fully recovered at the time of his death in 1924.

His solicitous wife, Edith Bolling Wilson, became his surrogate and steward to such a degree that critics dubbed America's First Lady the "Acting First Man." She secluded the president from friends and shielded him from sound advice while the ill man in the White House clung to his insistence that the proposal be approved exactly as he had written it or not at all.

Despite its standing as a subject of major controversy, league membership failed to impel very many America songwriters to assume the thankless task of propagandizing its pros and cons. Some remembered too vividly the antagonism incurred by their participation in the 1915-16 isolationist-interventionist fracas. War had

---

In one of the more ironic historical somersaults, it was in Compiègne on June 21, 1940, that a revengeful Hitler dictated armistice terms to a defeated France in the same railway car. He then had it and the nearby monument to the 1918 French victory transported to Berlin.

come to America after all, and the song-writers had absolutely nothing to do with influencing the course of history.

There is no record of any published song written by professionals that could be interpreted as pro- or anti–League of Nations. Only six minor pieces, including "At the League of Nations' Ball," made passing reference to the organization. Even Irving Caesar, who heartily subscribed to the league's principles, refrained from mentioning it in his postwar songs. In effect, songwriters were determined to sidestep this controversial issue altogether. Ironically, the melody of "When Johnny Comes Marching Home," already in revival as a welcoming anthem to returning doughboys, was given a new lyric and widely circulated as an anonymously written parody of Wilson's plan for the league:

A League of Nations has no place,
    hurrah, hurrah,
'Til we become a coward race, hurrah,
    hurrah;
And never shall we yield again
To weasel words of weasel men,
And we're all so glad to breathe the air
    again.

Opposition to the League of Nations Covenant, spearheaded by Sentors William E. Borah of Idaho and Henry Cabot Lodge of Massachusetts, proved superior to support for it. On November 19, 1919, the Senate rejected the Treaty of Versailles three times and promptly adjourned *sine die*. Sincere isolationists particularly feared the League as a "super state" that would destroy American independence and drag the country into quarrels in which it had no concern, two charges that would be leveled to a less intense degree during the founding of the United Nations in 1945.

Nevertheless, attempts at reaching a compromise continued in the Senate. On March 19, 1920, members again voted down the treaty, 49 to 35, in effect keeping the United States still technically at war with Germany and insuring that the league's peacekeeping potential as overseer of international disputes would fail to

materialize. On May 21, Congress by joint resolution declared that the war with Germany and Austria-Hungary was ended. Wilson vetoed the measure, which did not allow for American participation in the League of Nations, as an "action which would place an ineffaceable stain upon the gallantry and honor of the United States." On July 21, 1921, however, the joint resolution was renewed, passed, and signed by the new president, Warren G. Harding. Treaties of peace with Germany, Austria, and newly independent Hungary were negotiated by his administration and finally approved by the Senate on October 18, 1921, almost three years after the Armistice.

Meanwhile, a brand new death threat had descended over much of the world in 1918 in the form of a devastating disease incorrectly diagnosed as the "Spanish Flu." It is still not known what caused the outbreak or exactly where it originated, except that it most probably was incubated somewhere in Asia. What was known was that no vaccine was available to combat it, and that the killing force of the disease was frequently enhanced by pneumonia. So lethal was the new influenza strain that it literally could kill a person overnight.

The disease was pandemic, and by the end of the winter of 1918-19, an estimated two billion people around the world had fallen victim to it. The influenza claimed as many lives in a single year—between 20 and 40 million—as had died in the four-year "Black Death," the bubonic plague that ravaged Europe from 1347 to 1351. In October 1918, the month before the Armistice, about 196,000 Americans died of it, some 80,000 more than the nation had lost in the whole of World War I.

Several minor songwriters somehow managed to treat the killer flu with humor. Few subjects, regardless of how tragic, have ever been entirely free from tuneful levity. Emulating the light touches inserted by other writers into their novelty war songs were Narcissus L. Bush, whose "Spanish Flu Blues" possibly amused a few listeners, and Helen Pettigrew, whose "Oh,

You Flu!" attempted to defuse fear of the disease by dousing its ravages in ragtime.*

Goodbye to France

Irving Berlin's name again appeared on the war scene on November 12, 1918, this time as author of a new song relishing in the preparations leading to the departure of the first American troops from the Continent back to the United States. A melodious reverse reply to "Goodbye Broadway, Hello France," Berlin's "Goodbye, France" bore a front cover that also harkened back to the earlier march. As might be preferred by a young man bred, if not born, on New York City's Lower East Side, an American and a French infantryman have replaced Pershing and Foch to shake hands while the Statue of Liberty sheds her light on both.

From Egan and Whiting came "Hand in Hand Again," the twosome's lovely sequel to "Till We Meet Again," which reunited the formerly distressed lovers. Their tender parting now superseded by a joyful homecoming embrace, they summarized their own and other couples' happiness in the chorus:

> Ev'ry heart is lighter,
> Ev'ry smile is brighter,
> Sad "Adieu" is changing to "Hello"
>   again.
> Sorrow walked before us
> But a prayer watched o'er us;
> We strayed far but here we are,
> Hand in hand again.

Considering the surfeit of war-mother songs already in print, it was not surprising that the ladies of the household should be rewarded just before the end of the conflict with several more well-meaning, if undistinguished, pats on the back. The first, the trite and teary "The Bravest Battle of the War Was Fought in a Mother's Heart," unfortunately presented mothers

as more to be pitied than honored. Another song, containing the message "Mothers of America (You Have Done Your Share)," was given frequent airings by Eva Tanguay, whose studied insouciance while performing had earned her the frivolous title of the "I Don't Care Girl." Motherhood, however, was one subject she did care about, and deeply. She sang the song so often that it became identified solely with her, and such lines as "You have given to the strife / Your heart, your soul, your life" cogently summarized her philosophy.

A facsimile of the singer's handwritten description of the tune as "our greatest war song written to date," appeared on the sheet music cover. Her tribute, however, was not only self-serving, but preposterous as well. Published in September 1918, the year that Congress designated Mother's Day, it was one of the country's last war songs, but in no way did it challenge "Over There," "Goodbye Broadway, Hello France," or about 40 others in quality or originality. Nevertheless, her song did perform the valuable function of focusing again on the immense debt of gratitude the nation undeniably owed female parents.

About eighteen months earlier, in 1917, Al Selden's lyric to Sam H. Stept's "(When We Reach That Old Port) Somewhere in France" had taken specific note of America's obligation to France for her support in the Revolutionary War. He'll be back, the departing youth told his sweetheart, "When it's all over there / And with France our debt is squared, / When with Germany we're through." An identical, simultaneous message had been relayed by Mary Earl in "Lafayette (We Hear You Calling)," as well as by numerous other writers with a sense of history. On November 11, 1918, the debt was stricken from the books. America had paid it in full.

To do so, the millions of Johnnies

World War II events were similarly open to indelicate humor to make a point. On October 2, 1945, Al Neveloff copyrighted the genuinely unfunny "The Japs Were Surprised When They Were Atomized."

who got their guns had to struggle side by side with the Allies through villages blasted into fire-blackened hells in Chateau-Thierry, Soissons, Saint-Mihiel, the Argonne, and La Marne. Now they had come back to march triumphantly in parades along the main streets of their home towns, the Stars and Stripes flying high above their heads, cheers reverberating in their ears.

The soldiers of the Great War had finally reached the end of the long, long trail.

8. Homeward Bound

"We'll be over,
We're coming over,
And we won't come back
Till it's over, over there!"

As George M. Cohan had predicted some 18 months earlier, it *was* over, over there and the boys at last were coming back. With the conflict at an end, Americans celebrated Thanksgiving Day 1918 about two weeks before its official arrival, which since Lincoln's time had been the last Thursday of November. "Ring Out! Sweet Bells of Peace," William H. Gardner and Caro Roma's exhilarating sigh of relief at Germany's capitulation, became one of the first songs to raise patriotism to its highest peacetime pitch in decades.

The reason for all the cheering, melodically summarized by Peter Call and Artie Bowers, was that "The American Boys Whipped Germany." Besides relief that the deadly struggle had ended, many postwar songs expressed the pride that all Americans undeniably felt for their boys in khaki, blue, and olive green. "When the boys were under fire, each one / Firmly backed up the Red, White and Blue!", wrote Eva C. Hardy in her praiseworthy victory song; "'Twas then the Yanks victorious marched into Germany. / America, we're proud of you!" And now, in Sam Habelow's words, "They're Coming Back,"

back from hell, those same Yanks who had left as boys and were returning as men, those heroes, those victors in the greatest war the world had yet witnessed:

> Our boys in blue and khaki
> Showed that they were plucky
> When they took their stand in that
>   foreign land;
> We'll welcome them, each one,
> Yes, ev'ry mother's son.

The mere expectation of the hugs and kisses to be exchanged by returning servicemen and their loved ones was sufficient to instantly cancel the wartime jitters endemic to battlefield and home front alike. Disrupted lives were now on the mend; plans could be laid without concern that the war-free future would disallow them.

Scarcely had the Armistice taken effect on November 11 when other songwriters joined the homecoming parade, switching overnight from musical denigrations of the enemy and sad lovers' farewells to fast-tempo encomiums honoring America's freedom-loving tradition and the heroes who had so successfully upheld it. But a funny thing happened on the way to the victory parties. The publication of so many postwar war songs—about 1,450—reemphasized the lasting emotional impact that the war was to have on the population. The same trauma that had precipitated the writing of thousands of war ballads and attack songs from April 1917 to early November 1918 was also responsible for the hundreds of patriotic songs that inundated the country up to midsummer of 1919. Unlike the months immediately following the end of World War II (September–December 1945), when only comparatively few songs referred to the Allied victory or the defeated Axis, the eight-month period between November 1918 and August 1919 produced a staggering number of copyrighted World War I–based songs. When they finally petered out, they had accounted for roughly 22 percent, or 3,300, of the 16,529 songs copyrighted during the first seven months of 1919.

Apparently determined to keep the war-song franchise alive, the minor writers especially resuscitated the fight-on themes of old with moth-to-flame consistency. Hundreds of songs carrying such outdated and trite titles as "Everything Will Be Silent in the Kaiser's Den When the Yankees Swat Berlin," "Remember the Lusitania," and "Answer the Call to the Colors," which advertised the need for additional recruits, went on stream for months after peace was declared. "The Prayer to Whip the Kaiser Is Our Dollar Bills," advised a latecoming Liberty Bond song published April 8, 1919, or almost five months to the day following Wilhelm II's abdication.

"On Boys, On to Berlin!" published June 3, 1919, was still urging American and Allied troops onward almost seven months after they had achieved victory. The most flagrant disregard of historical fact, "We Are Going to Help the Allies Win the War," was copyrighted June 19, fully seven months into the postwar period. Also popping up Zelig-like were dozens of unoriginal songs that cashed in on the commercial success of one of the

war's truly great marches by bidding good-bye to France and hello to Broadway.

Undoubtedly, the late publication dates of the many song anomalies indicated the usual time lag between the writing of a song and its appearance in print, especially by small firms unaccustomed to observing strict deadlines and suffering from clogged pipelines. Then, too, it is entirely possible that the amateur writers, fearful that peace inevitably would dampen enthusiasm for their efforts, were determined to get their songs into sheet music format regardless of the outdated themes. None of the late-arriving 1919 battle songs, however, induced a public too busy at the job of celebrating to pause very long and reflect on the brutality and heroism that had made the victory possible.

As might be expected, the most productive of the 1919 songwriting participants were the pulpers. It was they who wrote the bulk of the cheerful "welcome home," "well done, boys," and flag-waving exercises honoring America's triumphant troops. The new peace reactivated the inexhaustible creative juices of the "Big Four," and they proceeded to pour out a spectacular assortment of "victory is ours" tunes throughout the first half of the year. Back in harness was a regenerated J.E. Andino, whose compositions had dropped from 565 in 1917 to 103 in 1918. For the first seven months of 1919 his output climbed to 210, with about 50 percent of the songs referring to the war. Leo Friedman wrote the melodies of 1,116 more songs, about 40 percent of which vividly recalled World War I, including the tardy "We're Going to Win the War," copyrighted February 21, 1919, and "We Are After Kaiser Bill," copyrighted April 19, 1919. The superman composer's 487 published war songs in 1919 represented more than one-third of the 1,435 such songs known to have been published that year. Of R(obert) A. Browne's 288 January–August songs, 55 percent referred to the late war. The unstoppable E.S.S. Huntington added 2,178 more to his copyrighted song catalogue, about 40 percent treating the war as if it were still in progress.

The January–August period also agitated three new pulpers into action. They were not nearly so prolific as the preceding four heavyweights, although they were most likely encouraged by their example to join the mass-production line. Roy Hartzell, the pseudonym of composer Glenn Ashley, attached his name to 177 postwar songs, about half of which resurrected war-in-action themes. Although neither Frank W. Ford nor Artie Bowers, both associated with Authors & Composers Service Co., had written more than a smattering of songs before 1919, each blossomed into a full-fledged postwar pulper. Of Ford's 175 songs copyrighted in 1919, 40 percent qualified as war songs; of Bowers's 350, about 50 percent did, including songs like "When the Yanks Get Into Berlin," published May 20, 1919, fully six months after the Yanks actually got there. Despite relentless servings of this eight-month smorgasbord of war songs, only one, "How 'Ya Gonna Keep 'Em Down on the Farm (After They've Seen Paree)?", was an unqualified hit and subsequently attained the stature of a standard.

Overwhelmingly, the marches that had escorted the troops into battle were superior to those that welcomed them home, even including those written by the acknowledged talents. One exception, Byron Verge's stirring "My Uncle Sam," outdistanced all postwar competitors in the realm of pride in country. The United States has always been a staunch supporter of liberty, Verge wrote. In addition, as World War I proved, its historical resolve "to help the weak and strong, / Defend the good and right the wrong" remained as steadfast a principle as ever.

Salute to the Marines

The third major U.S. military service anthem was a largely unheralded, elderly veteran of the late war, which it preceded by decades. Its exact date of composition

and authors are unknown. "The Marines' Hymn" was familiar to relatively few persons who were not members or fans of the Corps, being only slightly more widely recognizable in 1918 than Victor Herbert's robust "All Hail to You, Marines!" But the song won mountains of praise in 1919, after the Corps finally copyrighted it on August 18. With a genealogy as complex as that of any other pre–1900 song, "The Marines' Hymn" poses no problem regarding the source of the melody. It is the authorship of the words that is difficult to trace.

The march tune was adapted about 1880 from the song "Couplets des Deux Hommes d'Armes" (or "The Gendarmes' Duet"), written by the classical composer Jacques Offenbach for his opéra bouffe *Genviève de Brabant*. The original work, in two acts, opened in Paris on November 19, 1859. A three-act version was presented the day after Christmas in 1867, and it was for this expanded work that Offenbach added "The Gendarmes' Duet." The work was staged in New York City on October 22, 1868, the same year that the duet first appeared on sheet music.

The original four stanzas of the hymn dutifully glorify a few pre–World War I Marine engagements that had won the respect of the nation and earned the Corps distinction as America's premier fighting force. Three persons have been credited, at various times, with writing one or more of the stanzas, but verification is elusive. L.Z. Phillips was named the lyricist on the 1919 copyrighted edition. Marine Colonel Henry C. Davis has been mentioned as the probable writer of the third and fourth stanzas about 1911. According to other sources, it was USMC General Charles Doyen who wrote the words of the fourth stanza.

The entire four-part lyric, but not the music, was printed in the June 16, 1917, issue of the New York City periodical *The National Police Gazette*. The earliest known printing of all the stanzas *and* the music was an uncopyrighted sheet music edition dated August 1, 1918, which carried the notation "Printed but not published by the U.S.M.C. Publicity Bureau, 117-19 E. 24th St., New York, N.Y."

The source of the first stanza has been traced to 1805, when the Corps flag bore the inscription "To the shores of Tripoli," a reference to President Thomas Jefferson's dispatching the Marines that year to tame the Barbary pirates scattered along the coast of northwest Africa. The second familiar phrase, "From the halls of Montezuma" (actually the Castle of Chapultepec), has suggested to some that the original writer was a Marine who had served in the Mexican War of 1846–1848, when the Corps took part in the capture and occupation of Mexico City. It was probably he who reversed the chronological order of the two historical incidents so that the opening line read, "From the halls of Montezuma / To the shores of Tripoli."

As music scholar James J. Fuld pointed out in 1985, it is assumed that this first stanza was a poem, since it was most likely written years before Offenbach composed "The Gendarmes' Duet." In 1929, the commandant of the Marine Corps authorized the three stanzas of the hymn that appear in Part III of the present volume as the official version of the song. In 1942, the commandant approved the alteration of the fourth line of the first stanza that now reads "In the air, on land and sea," indicating the expanded role of the Corps over the years.

The song went through a number of revisions and new arrangements in subsequent years, among the finest of them Maxwell Eckstein's version, published in 1943. With its tail-end declaration that the streets of heaven itself are guarded by United States Marines, the hymn went a long way in depicting them as God's chosen warriors, fearless and unyielding. At first hearing the passage may seem an overcooked piece of public relations puffery, but nonetheless it is an effective tribute to the Corps' distinguished service at Belleau Wood and elsewhere in World War I and throughout the Pacific in World War II.

Peace and Contentment

Harry H. Zickel's "Allied Victory March" was only one of the scores of published postwar songs that bore the word victory somewhere in their titles. It had appeared frequently throughout the war, but only as a goal awaiting achievement. Now, with the songwriters' vision fulfilled, "victory" signalled the bright beginning of a new era free from casualty lists and military funerals.

Peace was another most-favored word, along with democracy, both also used to excess, but understandably so. America had proved to be the chief adhesive that bound together the Western democracies; unquestionably, her troops were chiefly responsible for the victory and the restoration of peace. Besides the march, the waltz was also called on to proclaim the sweetness of victory ("Liberty Waltz") and to serenade the victors then on their voyage home ("You'll Be Welcome as Flowers in the Maytime").

Not strictly a war-remembrance song, Sam M. Lewis, Joe Young and Walter Donaldson's "You're a Million Miles from Nowhere When You're One Little Mile from Home" fit the bill by emotionally condensing the quiet despair that settles over the homesick of any and all nationalities under adverse circumstances. Another non-war song that nonetheless gave voice to the regenerated hope for permanent peace on the scarred European soil was "The World Is Waiting for the Sunrise," introduced in January 1919 in the London stage production *Perrot Players*.

The lovely melody was composed by Ernest Seitz, the cautiously optimistic words by vaudeville and stage actor Eugene Lockhart. He would later appear in numerous talking pictures, equally at home playing genial or cowardly characters. Among his better-known roles were those of Regis in *Algiers* (1938), for which he was nominated for an Academy Award for Best Supporting Actor, Stephen A. Douglas in *Abe Lincoln in Illinois* (1939), the alcoholic Dr. Prescott in *The Sea Wolf*

(1941), and the starkeeper in the 1956 film version of *Carousel*. Lockhart's wife, Kathleen, was a film actress, as was his daughter, June.

A little tardy in entering the musical scene were two exceptional ballads prompting memories of lovers' wartime separations. The first, "I Know What It Means to Be Lonesome," could easily have been written two years earlier. It was a collaboration by war-song writers James Kendis and James Brockman, in company with Nat Vincent, whose "I'm Forever Blowing Bubbles" was an even bigger 1919 hit for the three collaborators.

The second wartime reminder was "Tell Me (Why Nights Are Lonesome)." The lyric by J. Will Callahan, who had written the words to "Smiles," was appropriate to lovers of either sex, in war or peace, faced with the painful necessity of saying goodbye and watching the setting of the sun behind the figure of their departing companions. The lovely Max D. Kortlander melody was a perfect counterpoint to the sentimental message, and the song enjoyed tremendous temporary success.

Most of the other love songs, now shorn of their former incantations to rely on patience and hope to heal the wounds of loneliness, enjoyed only fleeting approval. A time of joy was at hand, and ballads were really not required to sustain it. Relieved of the need to shield their fears for the safety of battlefront-bound doughboys, people happily permitted uptempo celebratory tunes to replace the tender love songs of only yesterday.

For the most part, the new romantic tunes were lively. Addison Burkhardt and Fred Fisher's "When Yankee Doodle Sails upon the Good Ship 'Home Sweet Home'," for instance, merrily catalogued the pleasures awaiting the soon-to-be-discharged servicemen. A minority were lyrical, like Will R. McDowell's "My Heart Will Love It E'er," a pretty addition to the nation's stockpile of love ballads. In this instance, however, the recipient of the writer's adoration was not a woman, but the American flag.

The limelight of publicity shone most brightly on General Pershing, who, as exemplified by songs like Eugene West's hero-oriented "P-E-R-S-H-I-N-G," received the lion's share of tuneful praises, making him the leading man of song until Charles A. Lindbergh flew across the Atlantic on his own in 1927. President Wilson, who like Pershing had been celebrated in numerous wartime songs, became another subject of idolatry after the Armistice, as well as the symbol of the nation's hope that his peace-making expedition to France would succeed even beyond his expectations.

But even the lowliest doughboy merited adulation for a difficult job well done. J. Ernest Reels, D. Rosenwein and H. Rosenthal's "When the Boys Come Marching Home," among the best of the homeward-bound songs, lumped members of all the services, regardless of rank or age, together as "our boys in uniform," each equally deserving of the nation's applause. Earl Fuller's "When the Old Boat Heads for Home" with its cargo of triumphant defenders of freedom skillfully re-emphasized a familiar message:

> We've never lost in a fight,
> We never fight till we're right;
> Our boys don't know defeat and they
>   never will,
> We've proved that to old Kaiser Bill.

Some 200 other songs published between November 1918 and June 1919 expressed similar pride in America's newest heroes.

For the first time in years, the smiling rather than wan faces of soldiers' children began appearing on daddy-song sheet music covers. In one of the best of them, "Clap Your Hands, My Baby (for Your Daddy's Coming Home)," a mother encourages her baby son to share her happiness:

> "Let your mamma see you smile,
> No more we'll be alone.
> Oh! how happy you will be
> When your daddy bounces you on his
>   knee;
> So clap your hands, my baby,
> For your daddy's coming home."

Held in the child's hand for this Frankie Williams–Edward G. Nelson song was a picture of his fighting father in an Army uniform. Also from composer Nelson, with an assist from lyricist Bud Green, came "Welcome Home" ("We've kept our home-fires a-burning while yearning for you"), a simple and straightforward greeting repeated by Will D. Cobb and Gus Edwards in their lively march "Welcome Home, Laddie Boy, Welcome Home."

Ragtime continued to influence songwriters, with DeWitt H. Morse and William H. Farrell's "When I Get Back (From Over There)" promising that the conclusion to the war will be celebrated most fittingly with a "great big ragtime jubilee." To Harry Carroll, Southerners were destined to be rewarded with the best and presumably most boisterous of all homecoming parties "At the Dixie Military Ball."

The Light Touch

Also included in the peacetime collection were songs that encouraged people to relax in the comforting arms of comedy, all of them comparatively mediocre in the remembered luster of such a predecessor as "How 'Ya Gonna Keep 'Em Down on the Farm (After They've Seen Paree)?" Among the catchiest was "Oh! What a Time for the Girlies (When the Boys Come Marching Home)," written by Lewis, Young, and Ruby, which spelled out some of the delights fostered by lovers' reunions. "He's Had No Lovin' for a Long, Long Time," contributed by William Tracey and Maceo Pinkard, urged every young lady to give her boyfriend "all the kisses that you've saved for him."

Sam Ehrlich and Con Conrad picked up from where they left off in "Oh! Frenchy" by reversing the sex of the singer in their new novelty tune "Frenchy, Come to Yankee Land." This time "Frenchy" is a French army soldier, not a female cabaret singer, whose absence is regretted by one Rosie Green, who "went across the sea" for unknown reasons and fell in love with him. Even though she caught soldier Jean playing up to "K-K-K-K-Katy" and walked out on him, Rosie sends a cablegram from home declaring that she has forgiven his philandering, still loves him, and misses his kisses. "Pack up your la-la's in your old kit bag," she implores, book passage on a westward-bound ship, and come join her in the good old U.S. of A.

No classic, the song helped to bridge the transition from wartime tragedy to peacetime gaiety. Even love lost had become a subject that could be treated lightly without fear of resentment. The inimitable Scotsman Harry Lauder, an entertainer of international stature, best projected the happiness of the postwar world with his own composition "Don't Let Us Sing Anymore About War, Just Let Us Sing of Love."

In the somewhat degrading but lilting "Five Women to Every Man," Louis Herscher, Sam Downing, and Joseph A. Burke zeroed in on the love-starved veteran. With single women estimated to outnumber single men by a five-to-one ratio in postwar America, the writers advised lame-ducks to "go and get your share of live women." Conceding that "it costs a lot to cultivate a Mormon's taste," they quickly added that playing the field is well worth the frustration and expense, since the writers "hate to see good women go to waste."

George Jessel and Harry Ruby, already show business stalwarts, set their perky 1919 song "And He'd Say 'Oo-La-La! Wee-Wee!'" in liberated Paris, where some doughboys presumably were using those two phrases as passwords to romance. Mesmerized by the "naughty little glance" sent his way by a "sweet young girl one day in France," soldier Willie Earl muses, "This little girl is meant for me, / No more I'll cross the sea, / I'll stay in Gay Paree." The fact that he could speak only the few French words he'd learned in the trenches failed to put a damper on his ardor:

Ev'ry day you would hear him say to
    his babee,
"Your talk I do not know but I
Will manage to get by
With my oo-la-la! and wee-wee."

Also falling back on a bogus French accent
was Eugene West and Joe Gold's "Ze
Yankee Boys Have Made a Wild French
Baby Out of Me," billed as a Parisian girl's
version of "How 'Ya Gonna Keep 'Em
Down on the Farm?"

Lew Porter, Alex Sullivan, and Max
Friedman shunned humor for their "Give
a Job to the Gob and the Doughboy" (for
each had "helped to make the whole world
free"), an appropriate decision considering
that their song hit a sensitive nerve among
the many postwar civilians and ex-servicemen scouting around for work:

Are you ready with job that's steady
Now that they are coming back once
    more?
Don't forget them and be proud to let
    them
Have the jobs they held before.
They were glad to fight for us both
    night and day,
Show them that you're willing to repay.

Irving Berlin, however, shortly afterward became the sole songwriter to treat
the job search with comic relief and a dash
of sweet revenge. He did his own job so
well that the words offended no one; most
people probably chuckled at Berlin's wry
humor while nodding their heads in satisfaction. It will never be known whether
the young man in "I've Got My Captain
Working for Me Now," introduced by Eddie Cantor in the Ziegfeld Follies of 1919,
was the same fellow who had schemed to
murder the bugler. Nonetheless, Berlin's
lyric was equally pungent in betraying the
resentful ex-doughboy's contempt for
authority as personified by his one-time
commanding officer, who also had traded
in his uniform for civilian garb.

Back home and working again in the
family business is former Private First
Class Johnny Jones. Learning that his

captain needed a job, he bowed to the latter's track record as a white-collar func-
tionary and "made him a clerk in my
father's factory," where Johnny keeps him
"wrapped in work up to his brow." He
smugly reports that he makes the captain
"open the office ev'ry morning at eight, / I
come around about four hours late." One
can picture the delighted grin on Johnny's
face as he adds: "Ev'rything comes to those
who wait: / I've got my captain working
for me now."

That vaudevillian Johnny Burke could
score a success, even if short-lived, with
the satirical "I Was a Soldier" was a testament to the healing power of humor,
which by late 1919 had acclimated postwar
audiences to appreciation of lighthearted
tunes dealing directly with combat. George
A. Norton's 1917 version of "'Round Her
Neck She Wears a Yeller Ribbon" had
sketchily presented the doughboy lover as
a coward, but never explained the exact
reasons for his fleeing from his battlefront
brethren.

On the other hand, Burke's song,
written for Passing Show of 1920, pain-
stakingly detailed the woes encountered by
another young man out to save his own
skin, the least welcome of all former
soldiers at a time of protracted hero worship. He had looked forward to the trip to
France and basked in the cheers of the
crowds, only to discover that the big shells
fired by German guns, countless "cooties"
in the trenches, hand-to-hand combat,
homesickness, and fright combined to
compel him to retreat quickly to the rear
"when the fighting it grew thick."

Berlin's and Burke's drollery, however,
did not serve as preamble to an outpouring of additional musical jibes at military
service. Americans were confronted with
far more important matters, like burying
the last of their dead and caring for the
wounded. Not until 1946, the year after
World War II ended, would "I've Got My
Captain Working for Me Now" enjoy a
brief revival. It was given to Bing Crosby
and Billy DeWolfe to reprise in brilliant
fashion in Berlin's film musical Blue Skies.

Contrasting starkly with the vaudeville ditties, marches, and love songs were the small number that recalled the dead, who for the most part were neglected by songwriters, immersed as they were in the euphoria of victory. Harry Hamilton and Ed Thomas's "The Boys Who Won't Come Home," a lovely threnody, recounted one gray-haired mother's bereavement over the loss of her army son. Murmuring sadly, she dutifully reminds listeners that though many servicemen will not be aboard the incoming troop ships, neither they nor their valor should be forgotten. Their lives cut short, they now lay in Flanders Fields and other Continental cemeteries, far away from the precious country they once called home.

Touching on the same subject were Al Jolson and Harold Atteridge, whose "Don't Forget the Boys Who Fought for You and Me" served as an invocation to remember and respect the sacrifices made not only by the servicemen, but also by their loved ones. Duncan J. Muir's reverential "They Sleep in Fields of Battle" similarly pleaded with celebrants to remember the deceased heroes.

"Where Is the Boy Who Went Over the Sea?" asked Marie Rich in her post–Armistice song, one of the dozens that, if actually written by mothers who had lost sons in France — and there is no reason to think they were not — focused on the heartbreak of women whose loss was not to be assuaged by listening to the peal of victory bells. Sharing her loneliness were Martha J. Callahan ("Don't Forget the Mother Who Is Waiting Home in Vain") and Nellie Dean ("Beneath the Battlefields of France a Boy Lies Sleeping"), two more musical mementoes attesting to the sorrow visited upon thousands of parents whose dreams of a reunited family were not to be realized.

The war's most famous poem, "In Flanders Fields, the poppies grow / Between the crosses, row on row...," was written by John McCrae, a Canadian poet and physician who served in the war up to his death in 1918. It was set to music more than 20 times in postwar America, eight of them published in 1918, the most renowned version by John Philip Sousa. Fifteen more elegies to the Flanders Fields war dead, who only "short days ago" had "lived, felt dawn, saw sunset glow, / Loved and were loved," but now lay silent in that graveyard's hallowed ground, were published in 1919 by such composers Charles Gilbert Spross, Arthur William Foote, F. Henri Klickmann, Mark Andrews, Homer N. Bartlett, George W. Parrish, and Emerson L. Stone.

The Decade That Roared

Post-Armistice American society was beset by so many contradictions that it is difficult to conceive of a decade less likely to roar with prosperity and hedonism than the 1920s. Peace closed defense factories, idling thousands of workers and slamming the door in the faces of many more thousands of veterans seeking entry into the labor market. The country had definitely not been transformed into the paradise that some wartime songwriters had intimated it would be.

Hardly had people begun reassuming life free from draft calls and basic training regimen when they were hit by ravaging inflation, which was brought under control only by an equally severe, but brief, recession. Wall Street, long a focal point of interest for capitalists, became a target for terrorists on Thursday, September 16, 1920, when a bomb exploded outside J.P. Morgan & Company at No. 23. Thirty persons were killed instantly or died shortly afterward, and more than 300 were injured.

Foreign anarchists, possibly German or Italian, or more than likely Russian, were suspected of planting the bomb in a horse-drawn wagon parked near the fabled "House of Morgan." No group, however, took responsibility for the crime. No one was convicted of it, nor was the precise nature of the bomb ever established. The pockmarks it inflicted on the building are still visible.

The next day, September 17, the Sons of the American Revolution sponsored a celebration of the 133rd anniversary of the adoption of the Constitution. It was held at the Sub-Treasury Building, opposite the Morgan bank's headquarters. Although not scheduled to be sung during the festivities, the strains of "The Star-Spangled Banner" echoed through the canyons of the financial district.

The crowd began singing it impromptu after one of the speakers declared that the person or persons guilty of the act of violence "should be killed like a snake." This was neither the first nor the last time the famous anthem would be called upon to promote solidarity against the foes of the United States, whether operating overseas or locally. It was patently obvious that the campaigns of the National Song Society and other groups of detractors to demote the "Banner" from its towering ranking among the nation's patriotic songs would never succeed. However difficult it might be to sing and however passé its words might be, no other song better expressed love for the "land of the free and the home of the brave," despite songwriters' numerous attempts from 1914 to 1918 to replace it with a new national anthem.

Meanwhile, the "pings" of crystal raised in victory toasts were muffled by Prohibition, which beginning in January 1919 turned off saloon spigots and closed down manufacturers, distributors, and retailers of booze. Temperance—a kindlier word than abstinence—became the largely ignored law of the land, which had been set into motion partly by some vociferous, vengeful agitators who falsely believed that German-Americans controlled the liquor industry. Following passage of the Eighteenth Amendment, the Volstead Act survived Wilson's veto and outlined how enforcement of the new law would be achieved. New badges of courage that became almost as common as the medals displayed with pride on soldiers' uniforms began springing up the country over. These were the white ribbons worn by Temperance Movement supporters who had taken the pledge never to imbibe alcoholic beverages.

Unfortunately from their viewpoint, the law was ridiculed in songs like the contagious "Prohibition Blues," written in 1919 by singer-songwriter Nora Bayes, who had introduced "Over There" in the late spring of 1917, and the popular author Ring Lardner. And so consistently was the Volstead Act disregarded that J. Russel Robinson and Billy Curtis could contend with justification in mid–1920 that "Prohibition, You Have Lost Your Sting." Surely, when it came to legislating morality, no laboratory was ever more ill-suited to the task than 1920s America.

Even the World War I Marine general, Smedley D. Butler, given a leave of absence to accept the post of Philadelphia's director of safety, was unable to staunch the thirst for outlawed spirits in the City of Brotherly Love. One year after his appointment, the number of arrests for Prohibition violations had more than quadrupled, but the rate of convictions was still below 4 percent. Most law enforcers treated lawbreakers with a leniency bordering on consent. H.L. Mencken's definition of Prohibition as a conspiracy by small-town residents jealous of the good life believed to be enjoyed only by bibulous city dwellers was not very far from the truth.

But Philadelphia was not the only big city to default on its anti-drinking crusade. New York police authorities estimated in 1926 that the city had 20,000 speakeasies operating openly and going full blast. Sporting such raffish names as the Hotsy Totsy Club and Kit Kat, many were operated by female celebrities, like singer Helen Morgan and the wisecracking Texas Guinan.

Parched throats could be soothed in neighboring countries, too, where demon rum and other disreputable substances were readily available, or by contracting for the services of bootleggers. Activated by ever-rising consumption levels, these purveyors of America's own home-grown hooch, nicknamed "bathtub gin," contributed mightily to satisfying home as well as speakeasy demand. The exchange of dollars for jiggers shunted gigantic profits into the coffers of organized crime, which made a killing by acting as middleman between distiller and customer.

Songwriters, as usual, took careful notes on these developments, reveling in their potential for humorous treatment. In Edward Laska and Albert Von Tilzer's "Alcoholic Blues," a discharged soldier laments the evils not of drinking, but of being cut off from legitimate sources of booze. The Prohibition movement itself was the target of the amusing laments "America Never Took Water and America Never Will," by wartime writers J. Keirn Brennan, Gus Edwards, and Paul Cunningham, and Harry Ruby's "What'll We Do on a Saturday Night — When the Town's Gone Dry?"

Irving Berlin's witty "(I'll See You in) Cuba" reminded patrons that bars were still flourishing in that little nation south of the border. An early song success by Harry Warren, the future "Father of the Hollywood Musical," tempted binge-minded people northward to Canada in the anti–Prohibition favorite "Hello, Montreal," wherein the parched protagonist cheerily bids goodbye to Broadway to make whoop-whoop-whoopee night and day in the Province of Quebec.

The public nemesis known as taxes had risen to Himalayan heights to pay the huge expenses of waging the war. Even a one-cent "war tax" on letters, lifting the cost of a first-class postage stamp from 2 cents to 3 cents, had been levied in 1917. Like the Prohibition writers, Jack Yellen and Milton Ager gave tax collecting a humorous slant that amused the public, at least for a short period. Unlike the upbeat message that Irving Berlin would deliver in "I Paid My Income Tax Today" in 1942 — that since the government was spending most of its tax receipts on defeating the Axis, it was therefore entitled to all the money it could get — "Don't Put a Tax on

the Beautiful Girls" took a far different tack. Warning in the verse that his congressman will lose his vote if he doesn't heed his complaint, the singer of the Yellen-Ager song protests that he is simply unable to live without love, which requires money to cultivate. "You can tax my business and all that I own, / But have a little pity, / Leave my pleasures alone," he pleads, tongue firmly in cheek, rather than knife at the throat.

The anti-tax rhetoric circulated by the song may not have been the chief agent of reform, but Congress did drastically reduce taxes, although not until 1927. Persons with annual incomes of $1 million that year paid less than $200,000 in federal taxes. A married man with a $7,500 income paid about $60, or 1.5 percent, after the $3,500 exemption for the happy couple. The overwhelming majority of the people paid no federal taxes at all.

The decade was also notable for a grandiose scheme to outlaw war, undoubtedly spurred onward by reminders of the Great War. Under the Kellogg-Briand Pact, designed to usurp the role of the impotent League of Nations, war was renounced and made illegal in the hope that no nation would wish to be branded a criminal by the rest of the world. Named for its chief authors and sponsors, American Secretary of State Frank B. Kellogg, who was awarded the Nobel Peace Prize, and French Foreign Minister Aristide Briand, the pact was signed with appropriate fanfare in Paris on August 27, 1928, and eventually ratified by 63 nations. Ironically, its signers included Germany, Italy, Japan, and the Soviet Union. The U.S. Senate approved the pact with but one dissenting vote, and President Hoover signed it on July 24, 1929.

Only the latest exercise in exaggerated expectations, Kellogg-Briand perfectly reflected the temper of the time in the new Golconda — the one that delighted in carefree, energetic dances like the Charleston, Black Bottom, and Varsity Drag,* and

*All three songs were introduced in Broadway musicals: "Charleston" (by Cecil Mack and Jimmy [James P.]

entertained visions of eternal prosperity guaranteed by an ever-bullish stock market fueled mostly by speculation. Of all the popular songs written in the 1920s, the one that best summarized the national mood was unquestionably "I'm Sitting on Top of the World," which was where many people sat out the latter half of the decade. Business was roaring and profits were soaring. It *was* a good time, at least on the surface.

Emulating the superstardom of many 1920s figures in the entertainment world—Jolson, Cantor, Rudolph Valentino, Janet Gaynor and Charles Farrell, Rudy Vallee, Paul Whiteman, and scores of other household names—were sports figures whose feats have since become legendary. Jack Dempsey's name was synonymous with boxing excellence, Bill Tilden's with tennis, Bobby Jones's with golf. Red Grange, three-time All-American halfback for the University of Illinois, was Mr. College Football. Baseball, of course, belonged to one George Herman Ruth, the "Babe," the "Bambino," the wild man of the American pampas, the extrovert with the spindly shanks and bulging waistline—and very likely the greatest player ever to wear a baseball uniform.

Overseeing the merrymaking and hoopla was the phlegmatic Calvin Coolidge, formerly vice president under matinee idol Warren G. Harding, whom he succeeded in 1923. Swearing to do as little as humanly possible to "interfere" in the marketplace, Coolidge was ideally suited by temperament and philosophy to preside over the laissez-faire America of that swaggering decade. He never tired of asserting that the "chief business of the American people is business," and that the "man who builds a factory builds a temple; the man who works there worships there."

But there was trouble in paradise. In 1931 the Paris peace pact was grounded in much the same manner as Henry Ford's

Peace Ship when Japan launched its campaign for the conquest of Manchuria, renamed Manchukuo. Prosperity was wiped out by the mother of all depressions, and the tribal dances so loved by sheiks and flappers were superseded by the melancholy strains of "Brother, Can You Spare a Dime?"

Battlefield Reruns: Films on World War I

Echoes of the late war's rumble of canons dissolved in the All-American pursuit of wealth and happiness, as did artistic works referring to it, save the novel. In the movies, still unable to speak or reproduce the sounds of artillery throughout most of the 1920s, such stars as Chaplin, Valentino, Mary Pickford, Douglas Fairbanks, Sr., Harold Lloyd, Stan Laurel and Oliver Hardy, Lillian Gish, Gloria Swanson, and John Barrymore amassed fortunes for themselves and their studios by concentrating on comedies, romances, overcooked melodramas, and swashbuckling escapades into exotic backlot lands that enthralled viewers unfamiliar with fairy tales or bereft of imagination.

Serious films with a war theme turned into an endangered species, practically on the edge of extinction. Even Buster Keaton's fact-based rendering of an adventurous, albeit misfit, Civil War hero in the silent classic *The General* (1927) placed that war and the runaway locomotive engine in a humorous context.

The few World War feature films produced in America between 1914 and 1918 had fallen into two categories: slapstick comedies like *Shoulder Arms* and melodramatic propaganda pieces like *Patria*, a silent film serial with Irene Castle; *No Man's Land*; and *The Claws of the Hun*. Billie Burke essayed the role originated in 1917 on the stage by Fay Bainter in *Arms*

[continued] *Johnson) appeared in* Runnin' Wild, *1923;* "Black Bottom" *and* "Varsity Drag" *(both by Buddy DeSylva, Lew Brown, and Ray Henderson) appeared in* George White Scandals, *1926, and* Good News, *1927, respectively.*

and the Girl. War Brides coupled Richard Barthelmess with Alla Nazimova, the legendary Russian-born actress who had starred in the short 1916 play upon which the movie was based.*

Among the most successful of the films was D.W. Griffith's *Hearts of the World*, the "inspiration" for Lee Johnson's briefly popular 1918 song with the same name. Dorothy and Lillian Gish starred in the Griffith work, which also introduced bit player Noel Coward to films. Only 19 at the time, he appeared in a walk-on part pushing a wheelbarrow. In late 1918, French director Abel Gance released his monumental *J'accuse/I Accuse*, a three-hour masterpiece excoriating war as futile from every standpoint imaginable. *Pershing's Crusade* briefly featured child actress Lillian Roth, better remembered for her early sound movie musicals and especially for her sensational autobiography, *I'll Cry Tomorrow*, in 1955.

In the 1920s, Wallace Beery and Raymond Hatton continued the comedy tradition, teaming up for such lightweight war-based diversions as *Behind the Front* and *We're in the Navy Now*. Griffith's *Isn't Life Wonderful* (1924) was a rare silent film dealing with the assorted miseries inflicted on Germany in the wake of the late war. The fabled director's recipe for preventing their repetition was strict international adherence to the brotherhood of man doctrine, marking the first artistic plea for people to overcome their petty ideological differences on behalf of world peace since the anti-interventionist songs of 1914–1916.

The same reluctance to deal seriously with war themes characterized the legitimate stage, which also preferred wearing a smile to flexing the muscles of memory. The high renaissance of musical comedy arrived on Broadway in 1919, bringing with it a Who's Who of glittering performers, songwriters, librettists, dance directors,

and costume and set designers who influenced the sumptuous style and frivolous tone of this most impressive American art form for decades to come. Carryover composers from the war years easily assumed command of the stage—Cohan, Berlin, Donaldson, Friml, Kern, Romberg, Porter, Harry Tierney, Harry Ruby, and James F. Hanley—along with such gifted newcomers as Vincent Youmans, the Gershwin brothers, DeSylva, Brown, and Henderson, Rodgers and Hart, and at decade's end, James McHugh, Arthur Schwartz, and Harold Arlen. From their musicals emanated about half of the biggest song hits between 1919 and 1929, an astronomical percentage, ranging from "A Pretty Girl Is Like a Melody" and "I'm Just Wild About Harry" at the beginning to "What Is This Thing Called Love?" and "With a Song in My Heart" at the end.

The titles of their musical shows— *Sunny*; *No, No, Nanette*; *Helen of Troy* (New York); *Kid Boots*; *Oh, Kay!*; *The Girl Friend*; *Good News*; *Whoopee!*; *Rio Rita*—served as enticing invitations to fluffy little sorties into artificial worlds submerged in cheerfulness, where nothing more sinister than a lovers' spat was permitted to usurp the enthusiasm for trivia shared by cast and audience. Youmans's *Hit the Deck* (1927), one of the rare musicals of the time with a military background, spun around the love affairs of sailors on leave, as Leonard Bernstein's *On the Town* would in World War II. Except for Cupid's arrows, not another shot was fired in either play. Even the unusually sober subplots of *Show Boat*, also 1927, which featured a marriage on the rocks and touched on miscegenation and the abysmal working conditions of American blacks, were downplayed into insignificance by the lyrical Kern songs. Welcomed with enviable enthusiasm, the music stole the show from the dramatic overtones written

As fate would have it, Nazimova's final screen role was in another war drama, Since You Went Away, *in 1944. Although her appearance as an immigrant defense plant worker is brief, she made the most of it with her inspired recitation of the last four and one-half lines of Emma Lazarus's sonnet "The New Colossus," which in 1903 was inscribed on a bronze plaque and placed inside the base of the Statue of Liberty.*

into the Edna Ferber novel, Oscar Hammerstein II's libretto, and "Ol' Man River."

It was not that certain political events of the 1920s would exert no influence on the history to be acted out in later decades; their significance was simply unnoticed or ignored. Benito Mussolini, the father of modern fascism, marched on Rome and forced Italy's King Victor Emmanuel III to appoint him to the post of premier in 1922.

The next year, Adolf Hitler launched his infamous Beer Hall Putsch to depose the Bavarian government in Munich and, accordingly, the Weimar Republic itself in Berlin. His failure landed him in a cell in Landsberg fortress, where he dictated the highly revealing *Mein Kampf (My Struggle)* to amanuensis Rudolf Hess. In the Soviet Union, Joseph Stalin in 1928 began his reign as a more powerful, vengeful, and bloodthirsty dictator than any czar who had ruled before him.

Some songwriters and music publishers, perhaps more prescient than politicians, detected in these distressing events the possibility of another widespread conflict and issued citizen alerts. "We Want Peace," subtitled "The March of Peace," served as Fritzie and Charles Haubiel's 1925 admonition against war by graphically reviving some of the horrors of the last one. Dorothy Alexander's 1927 "Sleep, Soldier Boy (Sailor)," dedicated to "those who had served on land and sea," reminded listeners of the imperative of preserving peace. The battle is over and peace is all around us, she wrote, pleading that the world permit the dead to sleep on among the blessed.

In 1929 the valor of the ordinary seaman in the U.S. Navy was properly honored in Harold L. Cool, Arthur J. Daly, and Tommy Christian's "Gunner Jim." A long song consisting of four verses and 19 four-line choruses, it unfolded the adventures of a gunner on the cruiser *Pride* in World War I. Normally a carefree sailor, Jim dies in battle, proving that he is a fierce fighter for democracy as well as a convivial shipmate. Reminding the public of the essential worth of the rigorous

training and discipline endured by army cadets was the 1928 debut of the foot-pounding "West Point March," with the lyric by Alfred H. Parham and music by Captain Philip Egner.

Movie Songs

Because World War I had been so widely discarded by the artistic community and the public in the years immediately following the Armistice, it came as no great surprise that Metro-Goldwyn-Mayer's *The Big Parade*, with popular stars John Gilbert and Renée Adorée, became one of the most successful films of 1925. It stood out in its uniqueness. To adults it was a poignant memento of a tragedy thrust upon a world unprepared to cope with its violence. To pre-teenagers it was a history lesson, or at least a novelty, far removed from the typical fare they had been weaned on since making their childhood voyages to the neighborhood movie house.

Besides being a tremendously effective saga of one young socialite's terrifying experiences on a French battlefield, the picture was also responsible for popularizing a war song, the first from a 1920s film. The work of Al Dubin and James McHugh, "My Dream of the Big Parade" was the latest in a succession of songs stretching back to the mid-teens used to publicize a film. Irving Berlin had created such tunes, along with Ernest R. Ball, Richard A. Whiting, Ray Henderson, and George Gershwin.

Unless the songs became popular on their own, they were rarely heard inside the theaters that played the films. The instrumental background scores accompanying the action on the screen were commissioned by the studios, and it was this music, played by pit orchestras or solo pianists, that held viewers' often rapt attention, not the promotional pieces. The Dubin-McHugh song, however, had become a success independently, and so it was interpolated at will by the instrumentalists into the theme music written for the film.

Earlier, in 1924, McHugh, with Al Dubin, Irving Mills, and Irwin Dash, had published another war song, "Hinky Dinky Parlay Voo?" Actually the slightest revision of "Mad'moiselle from Armentières," the new adaptation comprised twenty new five-line verses and attracted a respectable public, largely because of its comic, but nostalgic, comparisons of 1920s culture with that of the war years. Uninhibited flappers had replaced the demure ladies of yesterday, skimpy bathing suits their decorous beachwear—but saddest of all, beer was no longer cheap or all that easy to find, the authors lamented.

Additional war pictures and songs were slow to travel the trail to the box office. The 1926 film version of the Broadway play *What Price Glory*, another powerful indictment of war despite its dependency on rowdiness for widespread appeal, introduced Erno Rapée and Lew Pollack's lovely "Charmaine," a perennial hit and the first popular song to be recorded on Fox Film's early sound process known as Movietone. Except for the musical soundtrack, the picture was silent and starred Victor McLaglen and Edmund Lowe in the roles originated on the stage by Louis Wolheim and William Boyd—the stage actor, not the future cowboy hero of the *Hopalong Cassidy* film series.

Wings, in 1927, with a very young Gary Cooper in the secondary role of a World War I pilot, provided eye-filling aerial photography along with a better-than-average story, and it won the first Academy Award for Best Picture. Cooper reprised the role of an American soldier in two other World War I films that featured popular songs. For *Lilac Time* (1928), adapted from the World War I play, L. Wolfe Gilbert and Nathaniel Shilkret wrote "Jeannine, I Dream of Lilac Time"; Lou

Davis and J. Fred Coots's "A Precious Little Thing Called Love" brightened the sound track of the first film rendition of *The Shopworn Angel*, also 1928.

With "Together," DeSylva, Brown, and Henderson managed to write not only a resounding hit for the Broadway show *Manhattan Mary* (1928), but also a song that would become richly associated with World War II, one of only four such revivals of romantic ballads from the 1920s. Inserted in 1944 into David O. Selznick's *Since You Went Away*, the pleasant waltz repeated its success for two very sound reasons. First, the conventional melody reminded older viewers of the happier pre-World War II and Depression eras of only 16 years earlier. Equally welcome was the sentimental lyric, particularly the concluding lines of the first chorus. It is there that the singer attests to eternal devotion by promising that the lovers will always be together, if only in memory, which underscored the lonely existence of one wife (Claudette Colbert) as she awaits the fate of her missing soldier husband. With many women viewers sharing an identical quiet desperation, the song seemed to be addressed to them. Indicating the strength of the mid-war revival of "Together" was its appearance no fewer than 12 times in 1944 on *Your Hit Parade*, radio's weekly compendium of the best-selling and most bandleader- and disk jockey–requested popular songs.*

Also making the rounds in 1928 was Sidney Holden and Otto Motzan's "Pick a Rose in Picardy," a very pretty remembrance song that harkened back to the site of "Roses of Picardy," its sorrowful lyric assuring that one lady's love for her dead soldier survived, strong as ever, 12 years after the battle that claimed his life. In Rosamond and J.W. Johnson and Bob Cole's "The Old Flag Never Touched the Ground," a 1901 war-reminder song

---

*Other revived songs included "I'll Get By" (Roy Turk and Fred E. Ahlert, 1928), reprised by Irene Dunne in A Guy Named Joe in 1943 and Dinah Shore in Follow the Boys in 1944; "Miss You" (Charlie, Harry, and Henry Tobias, 1929); and "(I Love You, I Love You, I Love You) Sweetheart of All My Dreams," by Art and Kay Fitch and Bert Lowe (1926), the themesong of Thirty Seconds Over Tokyo in 1944.

successfully revived in 1928, the American flag was presented as the "emblem of sweet liberty" that had "been in many a fix / Since seventeen seventy-six" but still flew above the land it so proudly symbolized. May it ever so wave over a land at peace, the writers prayed.

As the ebullient Twenties began to give way to the dismal Thirties, writers and producers dipped deeper into the recent past for material, some of it centering on World War I. Buster Keaton scored a minor success in 1930 with *Dough Boys*, also known as *The Big Shot*, which related the tale of a young bumbler who joins the army hoping that his spiffy uniform will win him the girl of his dreams. Laurel and Hardy's *Pack Up Your Troubles* (1932) treated combat with slapstick humor, and in that regard was another unusual departure from standard 1930s movie-making.

Far more notable were films that took as their purpose not to entertain for profit, but to propagandize against warfare, using psychological implants from the last big war as the prime example of a world gone awry. The career and martyrdom of Nurse Edith Cavell during the war, for instance, were relived in the 1928 film *Dawn* by Sybil Thorndike, three years later to be created Dame Commander of the British Empire. R(obert) C(edric) Sherriff's play *Journey's End* (1929), a depressingly realistic analysis of the obscene waste associated with war was welcomed on both sides of the Atlantic. An infantry captain in World War I, Sherriff a few years later wrote the screenplay for such successful films as *Four Feathers, Goodbye, Mr. Chips*, and *Odd Man Out*.

The 1930 film version of *Journey's End* also garnered critical praise, as did director G.W. Pabst's German classic *Westfront 1918 / Comrades of 1918*. The year's greatest acclaim, however, was reserved for the superlative *All Quiet on the Western Front*, America's first truly significant all-talking picture and still widely considered the finest antiwar film ever produced. Presenting a view of World War I from the perspective of a sensitive young German soldier named Paul Baumer, played by Lew Ayres, the story line traces his disintegration from gung-ho volunteer recruit to cynical, battle-weary veteran, still giving his all but expecting little of value from it.

Change the soldier's surname to Smith or Jones, and Paul's story of the loss of bravado and idealism would have applied to many young American men between late 1917 and mid–1918. They, too, had lusted at the outset of their military service for a taste of battle, eventually hating every minute on the firing line, their innocence destroyed and self-esteem rendered valueless by the inconclusiveness of their deadly struggles and uninterrupted death of comrades.

Containing the greatest series of battle scenes on film, all performed under an El Greco sky, the picture is handicapped by Ayres' sometimes stilted acting style, more suitable to silent than sound films, and a poor soundtrack. But the expert cinematography by Arthur Edeson, editing by Edgar Adams, screenplay by George Abbott, and adaptation by Maxwell Anderson compensated for those flaws. So, too, did the competent acting by Louis Wolheim and Slim (George) Summerville, the latter a one-time Keystone Kop in the Mack Sennett days of one-reel comedies, and, above all, Lewis Milestone's direction, which by itself would have welded *All Quiet on the Western Front* into an honored place on the list of Hollywood's greatest achievements.

The memorable final scene of Ayres's hand reaching for a butterfly on the battlefield, only to recoil from it after he is shot to death by a French soldier on the day the Armistice is declared, remains the most poignant and powerful metaphor of the senselessness of war. The winner of the 1930 Best Picture Academy Award, the film was banned from Nazi Germany by Minister of Public Enlightenment and Propaganda Joseph Goebbels in 1933.

Only 22 when he made the film, Ayers later conceded that acting in it had powerfully influenced his decision to seek conscientious objector status when he was called to military duty in 1941. He cited in particular the brutal realism of *All Quiet on the Western Front*, as well as the film's expertly symbolizing the tragedy of young men used as cannon fodder in wars started and continued by their elders. Also influenced by playing the title role in nine *Dr. Kildare* films from 1938 to 1942, however, Ayers distinguished himself in World War II, serving almost four years as a noncombatant medic and chaplain's aide.

Hollywood's 1932 translation of Ernest Hemingway's novel *Farewell to Arms*, which recounted the star-crossed love affair between a World War I soldier (Gary Cooper) and a nurse (Helen Hayes), was a much-honored film that gave Cooper his finest role up to 1941, when his portrayal of *Sergeant York* earned the actor his first Academy Award.* The original *Farewell to Arms* was far more succinct and grittier than Selznick's dazzling 1957 remake (with Rock Hudson and Jennifer Jones as the lovers), and it was the inspiration behind the popular title song, written by Allie Wrubel and Abner Silver in 1932 as a promotional piece.

Fox's *Cavalcade* was based on the 1931 Noel Coward stage extravaganza that had whipped up patriotism in Britain to a fever pitch not seen since 1918. The lavish production required 22 sets, hundreds of costumes, and a cast of 250. The Fox translation was equally spectacular, and in 1933 it became the third of Hollywood's World War I pictures since 1928 to win the Academy Award. An episodic rendering of the triumphs and tragedies affecting the British upper-class Marryot family, the screenplay covered the period from December 1899, the year of Coward's birth, to New Year's Eve, 1932. (Coward's play had stopped at December 31, 1931.) Sheltered from turmoil by two generations of Victorian prosperity, the family suddenly experiences the ravages of war. The father,

played by Clive Brook, is sent with his regiment to relieve Mafeking in the midst of the Boer War of 1899–1901. (In 1939 the South African–born Ian Hunter, playing Shirley Temple's father, would be sent on the same expedition in *The Little Princess*, one of the last of the American films dealing with the age of Victorian conquests.)

Disruptive as the Boer War is to the Marryots, it proves to be insignificant compared with World War I. Again, family members are involved in battlefield bloodshed, which is depicted brilliantly in a four-minute "marching on to victory" montage sequence designed by William Cameron Menzies, a giant in Hollywood's cadre of art directors. After noting the widespread pessimism generated by the futility of postwar disarmament talks, the film ends without offering anything in the way of consolation. Most likely, it implies, the rest of the twentieth century will not be any better than the first third, an enlightened conclusion considering that Hitler assumed the chancellorship of Germany only a few months before the picture was released.

The Doleful Decade

One of the more unforgettable decades of the twentieth century, if for reasons vastly different from those that turned the untormented Twenties into a mantra for nostalgia, the 1930s introduced the largest number of war films and songs since the teens. The majority of them were very good and many became highly popular. The revival of interest in war themes was understandable. Battles were fought, or nearly broke out, in a host of lands in Europe, Asia, and Africa between 1936 and 1939.

Few popular songs or films, however, referred directly to current events. The marches and loneliness ballads were written

A virtual one-man army, the pacifist-leaning Alvin Cullum York was credited with singlehandedly killing 20 German soldiers and capturing 132 while taking a hill during a battle in the Argonne Forest on October 8, 1918, five weeks before the Armistice.

mostly to summon up reminders of the late Great War. The hope was that recollections of it might somehow dissuade persons the world over from falling victim to another interlude of pain and slaughter. Such warnings were pertinent, even if most democratic leaders were in the dark over how to fend off the insatiable demands of a passel of amoral strongmen in positions of absolute power.

In 1936, Mussolini annexed Ethiopia (Abyssinia). Hitler publicly repudiated the entire Treaty of Versailles and, in bold defiance of it, occupied and then remilitarized the Rhineland, which comprised all territory west of the Rhine River that had been separated from Germany to serve as a buffer between that nation and France. That same year, Generalissimo Francisco Franco led an insurrection against the leftist republican government in Spain. By the time it ended in 1939, the civil war had claimed some 500,000 lives. Mussolini sent weapons and men to Franco, as did Hitler. Dispatched to Spain by Air Marshal Hermann Goering was the Condor Legion, which became famous, or infamous, with the bombing of Guernica, the incident that inspired Picasso's pictorial masterpiece with the same name. Premier Stalin, meanwhile, subverted the Loyalist cause and absconded with it before the government fell.

In 1937, Japan began its full-scale offensive against China in hopes of gaining control of at least five of that country's northern provinces. In March 1938, Hitler announced to nearly a half-million cheering supporters from the balcony of the Imperial Hotel in Vienna the completion of the unlawful *Anschluss* (Austria's union with Germany). Next on the Führer's timetable of conquest was the Sudeten area, which fringed the western end of Czechoslovakia and faced German territory to the north, west, and south. It was there that most of the republic's large German population lived, and on September 30, 1938, Mussolini, British Prime Minister Neville Chamberlain, and French Premier Edouard Deladier meekly ceded the Sudetenland to Hitler.

Despite his vow not to devour more territory, the predatory dictator in effect absorbed the rest of the country in March 1939, turning the Czech and Moravia regions into German protectorates. Not to be outdone by his neighbor to the north in the land-grabbing sweepstakes, Mussolini in April 1939 added the formerly independent state of Albania to the realms he ruled in the name of Victor Emmanuel III.

That November, the Soviet Union charged into Finland, which Stalin finally conquered in 1940 after a massive, sustained assault that left thousands of his soldiers frozen to death in statue-like clusters in temperatures 30 to 40 degrees below zero. His pyrrhic victory cost him mightily: about 200,000 troops killed and 1,600 tanks and 975 aircraft destroyed compared with fairly minor Finnish losses. As his reason for the invasion, Stalin charged that Finnish artillery had deliberately killed a Russian soldier in preparation for a full-scale attack on the Soviet Union. At the time, the U.S.S.R. had a population 45 times larger than Finland's and an equally overwhelming superiority in arms and troops. Later in 1940, Stalin reclaimed Estonia, Latvia, and Lithuania, freed in the wake of the 1918 Armistice, as protectorates and annexed Bessarabia and part of Bucovina from Rumania.

Curiously, no American songs referred to any of these pocket wars up to the closing months of 1939. Not even the gallant resistance by the Finns, which earned worldwide admiration, elicited a single American musical piece in its honor, save for a few minor attempts at adding English words to Jean Sibelius's tone poem *Finlandia* (1900). Most popular songs of the time came from film and stage musicals, and neither amusement forum displayed very much interest in responding to the bellicose activities that were again darkening the sky over Europe in the opening scenes of what Churchill later would term the "gathering storm."

Nor did the New York World's Fair, which set down its trademark trylon and perisphere in Flushing Meadows, Queens, early in the summer of 1939. War was absent from its "World of Tomorrow" exhibits, such as General Motors Corporation's "Futurama." What all the manufacturers preferred to highlight was the expected upsurge in work, travel, and household efficiencies to be derived from using their products in the United States of distant 1960.

Back to the Past

A few films skillfully recreated a World War I ambience as the backdrop for many of Hollywood's top stars. In *Mata Hari* (1931), Greta Garbo essayed the part of the glamorous Dutch dancer (Margaretha Geertruida Zelle) and paramour of men in high places whom the French executed as a German spy in 1917. Director Ernst Lubitsch's *Broken Lullaby*, also known as *The Man I Killed* (1932), was a sufficiently fierce denunciation of war that starred Phillips Holmes, who himself would be killed in an air crash while serving in World War II.

Viva Villa! with Wallace Beery as Pancho the Bandit, recalled the Pershing expedition into Mexico. It was released in 1934, one year before the politically active Mexican director Fernando de Fuentes's *Vamonos con Pancho Villa/Let's Go with Pancho Villa. Under Two Flags* and *The Road to Glory*, the latter boasting a screenplay collaboration by William Faulkner, in 1936 reintroduced the horrors of war on land. *The Lost Squadron* (1932) centered on airborne warfare, as did *Ace of Aces* (1933), with Richard Dix as a sculptor who enlists as a pilot in World War I. The exemplary *Dawn Patrol* was filmed twice, first in 1930 with Richard Barthelmess and Douglas Fairbanks, Jr., as the stars and again in 1938 with Errol Flynn and David Niven. Each version derived character and plot authenticity from the story by John Monk Saunders, a one-time second lieutenant in the U.S. Army Air Corps. Director Frank Borzage's touching *Little Man, What Now?* (1934) traced the increasing

victimization of a young German couple, charmingly played by Douglass Montgomery and Margaret Sullavan, trying to fathom the abrupt transformation of their war-free country into a virtual prison by the newly installed Nazi government.

The General Died at Dawn (1936), with a screenplay by Clifford Odets, touched on the Communist-Nationalist enmity in China; *The Last Train to Madrid* (1937), directed by James Hogan, and *Blockade* (1938), with a script by John Howard Lawson, explored an identical murderous grab for power in the context of the Spanish Civil War. *Suzy* (1936) cast Cary Grant in the role of André Charville, a fictional fighter pilot ace, presumably the French equivalent of Germany's "Red Baron."

They Gave Him a Gun (1937), with Spencer Tracy and Franchot Tone, indicted World War I and the Depression as the causes of one young veteran's gravitating into a life of crime because of his expert training in the use of handguns and inability to find a job. *Lancer Spy*, released the same year, probed the byzantine world of the First Great War's espionage operatives. Frank Borzage's *Three Comrades* (1938) centered on a trio of disillusioned German veterans of World War I, played by Robert Taylor, Franchot Tone, and Robert Young. It made a respectable attempt to analyze the causes of Germany's postwar instability, choosing the lack of economic opportunity as the chief culprit. But the love story revolving around Taylor's unfortunate love affair with Margaret Sullavan—the screen's greatest female sufferer, and one of its finest actresses—tended to shift the film's focus from social commentary to romance. The dialogue throughout, however, is remarkably literate, doubtless helped along the way by co-screenwriter F. Scott Fitzgerald. The novel on which the film was based was by Erich Maria Remarque, also the author of *All Quiet on the Western Front* and himself a survivor of the World War I trenches.

In much the same way as had the more notable of the 1915–1917 stage dramas,

Anatole Litvak's *Confessions of a Nazi Spy* (1939) brought the subject of impending doom up to date by disclosing Nazi Fifth Column activities in New York City's heavily German-American Yorkville section on the Upper East Side. Anna Neagle played the title role in *Nurse Edith Cavell*; James Stewart replaced Gary Cooper for the 1940 remake of *The Shopworn Angel*. Meanwhile, on the comedy front, the Marx Brothers in 1933 starred in their all-time best film, *Duck Soup*, a brilliant, catch-all lampoon on diplomats, fascism, and war.

More common were films that indirectly espoused the growing American interventionist movement by upholding the power and majesty of the British Empire, exemplified to perfection by the demeanor and dulcet tones of such actors as Ronald Colman, Errol Flynn, and David Niven. England, after all, was regarded as a reliable ally, a bastion of parliamentary government, and a friend, soon to be in need, that unselfishly had undertaken the white man's burden of occupying about one-fifth of the world's land area in the name of the King.

Frankly Anglophile and propagandist, such adventure films as *The Lives of a Bengal Lancer* (1935), *The Charge of the Light Brigade* (1936), *Wee Willie Winkie (1937)*, and the 1939 trio of *Gunga Din, Four Feathers,* and *The Light That Failed* portrayed the British as benevolent disciplinarians and the world's insurance policy that any rebellion attempts by colonists would be crushed forthwith. Surely, these pictures implied, the Brits could be counted on to stand up with identical firmness to any would-be conqueror striding like a colossus on European soil.

Indeed, at the close of *The Sea Hawk* (1940), actress Flora Robson, in the role of Queen Elizabeth I, delivers the strongest film meditation up to that time on British determination to thwart any invasion of her tight little island. She is referring to the formidable skill of the sixteenth-century English privateers at plundering Spanish ships, but her speech has an unmistakable Churchillian ring to it. The English, she warns, are confronted by the "grave duty" of preparing "our nation for a war that none of us wants" and have tried "by all means in our power to avert." But, she adds, "When the ruthless ambition of a man threatens to engulf the world, it becomes the solemn obligation of all free men to affirm that the earth belongs not to any one man but to all men, and that freedom is the deed and title to the soil on which we exist." The invasion of the Spanish Armada that had threatened the England of Queen Elizabeth I failed; so will the "Operation Sea-Lion" invasion planned by Hitler, the actress implies.

Several other films, a number of which were based on Broadway plays by Robert E. Sherwood, later to become one of President Roosevelt's chief speechwriters, confronted the fascist threat in exclusively symbolic terms. In *The Petrified Forest* (1935), for example, the unwelcome intrusion of hostile forces into the lives of typical small-town Americans added political relevance to the gangster motif that dominated the screenplay. Antiwar sentiment also turned Sherwood's *Idiot's Delight* (1938) into a successful movie, not because of its often clouded preparedness message, but because of the marquee power of Clark Gable and Norma Shearer. In *Abe Lincoln in Illinois* (1939), Sherwood used the tumult surrounding the Civil War president's first inauguration to imply the need of identical strong (i.e., Rooseveltian) national leadership to contend with the mounting problems confronting contemporary Americans.

With director Frank Capra, Hollywood's chief exponent of the nobility of the "common man," at the helm, audiences in both 1937 and 1939 were witnesses to two remarkable films that touched on the dismal conditions then enveloping Europe. The first picture dealt with the likely onset of a new Armageddon, the second with the necessity of fighting against all odds to defend the principles for which America had stood for almost 150 years.

Lost Horizon, starring Ronald Colman as Robert Conway, a celebrated antimilitarist soldier and diplomat, is set for the most part in the sheltered Himalayan paradise that novelist James Hilton dubbed "Shangri-La." Nestled in the "Valley of the Blue Moon" (actually Tibet), the community is isolated from an increasingly troubled world. It is a place of permanent peace and security, free from crime, envy, illness, and the eternal struggle to survive. Its highly cultivated people obey but one rule, "Be kind," which their astute leader hopes can serve as a lesson to an outside world rushing headlong into chaos.

Realizing that his life is approaching its end, the High Lama (Sam Jaffe) conspires to kidnap Conway. A kindred spirit, he was selected by the old man to succeed him upon his death. It will be only through the dedicated peacemaking efforts of an enlightened man like Conway that the world can be saved from its own bestiality. He will continue the High Lama's work, using Shangri-La as the model upon which all civilization should be based. So influential on Conway is the philosophical example set by the High Lama that the former risks life and limb to return to Shangri-La,* which he had reluctantly left to ameliorate the restlessness of his younger brother, played by John Howard — who, incidentally, became an authentic hero in World War II, winning the Navy Cross and Croix de Guerre for valor.

The second Capra film, *Mr. Smith Goes to Washington*, ranks with *Let Freedom Ring!* (also from 1939) as the most patriotic motion picture made in America in the 1930s. James Stewart, perfectly cast in the title role of a small-town idealist and emblem of the "little people," is appointed U.S. senator to fill out the term of the recently deceased incumbent. His mentor, the governor of the state, is actually putty in the hands of a cadre of political hacks and a self-serving newspaper publisher who are accustomed to molding people in their image to further their selfish interests. Instead of acting out his per-

ceived role as the innocent lamb in a cage of hungry lions, Mr. Smith subverts their cause by assuming Lincoln-like statesmanship when required. Forced to pit his crusade to establish a camp for poor boys against the corruptness of his back-home sponsors, he whips them all, including the state's senior senator and the powerful publisher, portrayed masterfully by Claude Rains and Edward Arnold, respectively.

It would be crediting Capra with an excess of perspicacity to infer from his film that the Mr. Smiths of the world, like America itself, will always win over the evil-doers (e.g., the Axis Powers) that hope to destroy it. But the imminence of a new world war was circulating across the land when the picture was released, and Capra convincingly stumped for the preservation of American traditions of liberty and freedom for all. When Mr. Smith visits the Washington Monument, Lincoln Memorial, and other historical landmarks, the audience shares in his pride; like the young senator, they hear snatches of "Columbia, Gem of the Ocean" and other patriotic anthems in the background, which further motivates them into reflecting on the nation's glorious history.

Ever the realist, however, Capra does not send the publisher or any of his cohorts to prison for their chicanery. Such people have always been with us, the director implies, and always will be, hence the need to be ever on the defense against their accumulation of power. In fact, Arnold did reappear two years later in Capra's *Meet John Doe*, again playing the evil manipulator of public opinion.

In one *Mr. Smith* scene, dictators from two unnamed foreign countries are shown watching the give-and-take that characterizes the U.S. Senate in action. Surely, Capra intimates, this is a healthy political process unknown in their own countries, where opposition parties were outlawed. "Liberty is too precious a thing to be buried in books," an impassioned

---

*Shangri-La subsequently became the name of the presidential retreat in the Maryland mountains. Since the mid-1950s it has been known as Camp David.

Mr. Smith observes on the Senate floor, pleading with his fellows to acknowledge their debt to America with action rather than empty rhetoric. And the final point of the film—that even the most politically naïve of young men can emerge unscathed, with their ideals intact, from a hostile environment—represented Capra's most eloquent defense of fighting for one's ideals regardless of the odds.

On December 15, 1941, actor Stewart was a leading player in Norman Corwin's hour-long patriotic drama *We Hold These Truths*, which was aired by the Columbia Broadcasting System, National Broadcasting Co., and Mutual Broadcasting System. Essentially an appeal for American unity in the new war, the program also starred Lionel Barrymore, Walter Huston, Edward G. Robinson, and Orson Welles. The background music was composed by Bernard Herrmann, who a few months earlier had provided the musical score for Welles's *Citizen Kane*. The radio program was said to have been heard by 60 million persons, the largest audience to date to tune in to a dramatic performance on radio.

Other important war films, each begun in 1939 but released in 1940, were frankly propagandistic warnings to Americans that events in Europe might well force them once more to shuck off the chrysalis of non-involvement. For example, MGM took on the war in its own dramatic terms with director Borzage's *The Mortal Storm*, based on the novel by Phyllis Bottome. Both graphically portrayed the rise of the Nazi movement and its cruel effects on simple German villagers, including the two lovers played by James Stewart and Margaret Sullavan. Touching only obliquely on Nazi anti-Semitism, despite the inclusion of a concentration camp scene, the picture skirted the issue by referring to Viktor Roth, a Jewish professor of medicine played by Frank Morgan, as a "non-Aryan." Perhaps wary of being charged with advocating an American rescue of Germany's Jews, studio executives obviously decided that discretion in such a sensitive matter was preferable to specific-

ity. *Escape*, another anti-Nazi exposé, roughly covered the same territory, and almost as well.

Robert E. Sherwood's *Waterloo Bridge* was a *Camille*-like romance with Robert Taylor and Vivien Leigh. Most of the Broadway play and the film version was set in World War I England; only briefly (at the beginning and end) does it concern itself with World War II. Even after 22 years have elapsed, the tragedy thrust upon the two lovers by the earlier war continues to haunt army officer Taylor. Implicit in his emotional torture is the likelihood that younger men and women will be confronted by similar tragedies as a result of the new war against Hitler. Alfred Hitchcock's *Foreign Correspondent*, like his *Lady Vanishes* in 1938, failed to identify the country responsible for spreading chaos across its own frontiers, but few viewers could escape the British director's implication of Germany as the center of international intrigue and treachery.

Warner Bros.' *Roaring Twenties* reenacted battlefield terrors of World War I while performing a critical autopsy on Prohibition. Adhering to the studio's long-standing advocacy of social reform, especially where gangsterism and poverty were concerned, the picture devotes most of its running time to life in the economically depressed America of 1919 as exemplified by three ex-soldier buddies (James Cagney, Humphrey Bogart, and Frank McHugh), who turn to bootlegging to survive. Their postwar careers wreak havoc on themselves and on innocent civilians caught in the crossfire of their rivalry to control the ever-increasing market for their illegal wares. The same studio's *Fighting 69th* refreshed memories of the exploits of that fabled World War I infantry unit, subtly indicating that the United States, if need be, would be capable of fielding new fighting forces of equal distinction. Actor George Brent played "Wild Bill" Donovan, Jeffrey Lynn was poet Joyce Kilmer, and Pat O'Brien was ideally cast as Father Francis P. Duffy.

Charles Chaplin, absent from the

screen since *Modern Times* (1936), reap-peared in 1940 to play the dual role of a timid Jewish barber, who was also an amnesiac veteran of World War I, and Adenoid Hynkel, the all-powerful, egotis-tical ruler of Tomainia, in the guardedly interventionist *Great Dictator*. The fact that the peerless comedian bore a striking resemblance to Hitler, and the ghetto barber to Hynkel, made abundantly clear that Tomainia, the land of the "double cross," was Chaplin's artistic substitute for the Führer's Germany.

Nor was there any doubt that Jack Oakie, in the finest performance of his career as the beer-bellied Benzino Napa-loni, the braggadocian dictator of Bac-teria, was Mussolini. Playing the bemed-alled Hermann Goering was Billy Gilbert as "Field Marshal Herring." Joseph Goeb-bels, renamed "Herr Garbitsch," was rep-resented by the velvet-voiced Henry Daniell, who three years later would dou-ble as Joachim von Ribbentrop in the book-based *Mission to Moscow*.

The first film in which Chaplin's speaking voice was heard (he had sung a few verses of a slightly risqué tune in *Modern Times*), *The Great Dictator* neatly balanced pathos with ridicule in a brilliant probing of Jewish life in Nazi-occupied Germany, while portraying Hynkel as an arrogant bumbler. By mid–1940, however, the real dictator was ruler of all the lands from Berlin to Paris, as well as Denmark and Norway, and his anti–Semitism had been displayed to the world with absolute clarity even before *Kristallnacht* in 1938. Chaplin was funny; Hitler definitely was not.

Unsurprisingly, the picture offended Hitler, reviled by Chaplin as the "beloved phooey" in one scene and as a "medieval maniac" in another. President Roosevelt, assistant secretary of the navy in World War I, however, was delighted by it. One of the 10 films nominated by the Academy of Motion Picture Arts and Sciences as the Best of Picture of 1940, *The Great Dic-tator* lost out to *Rebecca*.

The Chaplin "biography" was also en-hanced by Meredith Willson's excellent background score. Particularly effective was the composer's musical accompani-ment to Chaplin's interpretative ballet symbolizing the Great Dictator's unbridled ambition for world conquest. The globe is his balloon, and accordingly Hynkel bal-ances one on his right index finger, spins it wantonly, and bounces it off his head, back, and even his derrière. Then, after he fondles it too tightly in a childlike display of covetousness, the balloon explodes in Hynkel's face, reducing him to tears.

The War-Song Revival

But for the most part, Hollywood's examinations of military matters took their cues from the 1930 movie version of *Hit the Deck*. The peacetime navy was a par-ticular favorite with the studios. Ships lay at anchor, usually in New York City or San Francisco waters free from torpedoes and mines, and stayed there for the dura-tion of the picture. Their decks served as impressive props for spectacular musical numbers written by such exceptional tal-ents as Al Dubin and Harry Warren (*Ship-mates Forever*, 1935), Irving Berlin (*Follow the Fleet*, 1936), and Cole Porter (*Born to Dance*, 1936).

The inevitability, even the possibility, that the happy-go-lucky, girl-crazy sailors might be called on to activate the guns standing guard over the battlewagon dance-floors was shrugged aside. The occasional injection of scenes showing ships riding ocean waves with authority, however, was designed to assure audiences that America's first line of defense was entirely capable of protecting the nation if and wherever necessary. Typically gleaned from news-reels and the navy's own documentary films, these up-anchor showcases almost always featured at least the opening strains of "Anchors Aweigh" in the background.

West Point cadets dazzled by parading in choreographed unison in army films, in-dicating that the academy was still capable of training first-rate marchers who could double as battlefield commanders when required. But, as *Flirtation Walk* (1934) and *Rosalie* (1937) demonstrated, it was the songs and romance between Dick Powell and Ruby Keeler and Nelson Eddy and Eleanor Powell that stimulated box office receipts. Rarely did the West Pointers or their hardened supervisors engage in anything more physical than a football game. Only in such an innovative film as *Test Pilot*, a 1938 non-musical, did Hollywood hint at the necessity of research projects to improve the capabilities of American military equipment, in this instance aircraft. And all the testing was done by two civilians, played by Gable and Spencer Tracy.

A number of the better military songs of the 1930s became even bigger hits during the World War II years. Dick Powell introduced Al Dubin and Harry Warren's "Don't Give Up the Ship," also known as "Shipmates Forever," which matched the title of the 1935 film in which it was first heard. More popular and professional than Lew Brown, W.A. Timm and Jaromir Vejvoda's earlier "Here Comes the Navy," the melody of which was based on "The Beer Barrel Polka," the Powell tune was reprised over and over again years later by the singer himself during World War II war bond drives and trips to naval installations.

In 1937, the handsome Warner Bros. troubadour sang "The Song of the Marines," another Dubin-Warren hit written for *The Singing Marine*. The U.S. Marine Corps honored the song by adopting it as its "unofficial" anthem. An exceptional send-off march urging a Sally and a Sue not to be blue when the boys leave them for duty, it was kept very much alive during the war, again through the courtesy of Powell's ebullient vocalizing.

Dubin and Warren had also collaborated on one of the finest of American "torch" songs relating to veterans and the Depression. The year was 1933. For the concluding production number in *Gold Diggers of 1933*, they wrote "Remember My Forgotten Man" in an attempt to arouse the Depression-ravaged public to the hardships being suffered by World War I veterans. Many of them had joined the disastrous "Bonus March" rally in Washington, D.C., in the late summer of 1932. The marchers' immediate goal was to sway the government to release the money promised to veterans in 1925, seven years after the war. The money had been pledged by President Calvin Coolidge partly to compensate for the refusal of the federal government to grant six months' pay to World War I doughboys at the time they were being mustered out of the service. But the bonus amounts, ranging from $500 to $1,000, had been issued as federally guaranteed bonds redeemable in 1945, or 27 years after the Armistice.

The song, like the Bonus March, appealed for immediate payment, in effect pleading that the government acknowledge the plight of thousands of unemployed ex-servicemen. Certainly, no song surpassed E.Y. Harburg and Jay Gorney's "Brother, Can You Spare a Dime?", written at the depth of the Depression in 1932 for the Broadway revue *Americana*, in dramatizing the misery of veterans reduced to begging to survive. But "Remember My Forgotten Man" came closer than any other of the period.

The World Will Always Welcome Lovers

As surely as "Together" insinuated itself into public favor during the 1940s, so did "As Time Goes By," written in 1931 by Herman Hupfeld. A sailor in World War I, Hupfeld became a fairly successful singer and composer-lyricist who wrote several songs in both wars and entertained the troops in military camps and hospitals in World War II. Originally a torch song sung by Frances Williams in *Everybody's Welcome*, the inherently optimistic "As Time Goes By" has become as closely linked to *Casablanca* as "Over the Rainbow" has to *The Wizard of Oz*. In each instance, the song and the movie are inseparable.

An exemplary war picture although it contains no battle scenes, *Casablanca* was helped along the popularity road by its name recognition as one of the six strategic points where Allied troops landed during the "Operation Torch" invasion of North Africa, and as the site of the midwar meeting of Roosevelt, Churchill, and their chief aides. Outfitted with a custom-fitted cast that could have been assembled in Hollywood's version of heaven, the picture was solely responsible for reviving the 12-year-old song. It did the job so well that "As Time Goes By" joined *Your Hit Parade* on March 20, 1943, for the first of its 21 appearances on the program. Portions of it are played three times in the film by Dooley Wilson—or, rather, dubbed by an unbilled soloist, since Wilson was unable to play the piano.*

Premiered November 26, 1942, at New York City's Hollywood Theatre (later the Mark Hellinger), *Casablanca* was based on the unproduced play *Everybody Goes to Rick's* by Murray Burnett, a New York City school teacher, and Joan Alison, a socialite and theater-loving friend. Voted Best Picture of 1943, the film acutely reflected American indecisiveness in 1939–1941 and then its post–Pearl Harbor outrage.

The picture concentrates on the lovelorn tale of Rick Blaine (Humphrey Bogart), an expatriate American and owner of the Café Americain in what in late 1941 was still unoccupied French Morocco. He is the epitome of the disillusioned, self-indicted alcoholic, an idealist who has turned his back on a "crazy world" that even after fighting one massive war in recent years still refuses to conform to the ideals of individual liberty and justice for all. A one-time gun-running supporter of the defeated Spanish Republican Army in the 1936–1939 civil war, he has since isolated himself from involvement in Europe's perennial troubles, convinced that further disillusionment will be his only reward.

Maintaining a quiet contempt for the fascist forces leagued against his congenital sense of fair play, Rick is determined to sidestep overt action altogether. The war, after all, has made his business prosper. His saloon and casino are jammed night after night with well-heeled refugees from conquered countries eager to drink and gamble away the hours while awaiting the chance to bargain with a demimonde of unsavory characters for a seat aboard the all-important night flight to Lisbon and freedom. Their fate is of no consequence to Rick, and his typical curt manner toward everybody, regardless of ideology, deflects importunities to transform him into a friend or partisan in any cause other than his own survival.

Yet this intensely private man has a conscience. His strong moral sense finally overcomes his cynical neutrality, and he commits himself to assist in the escape of a heroic anti–Nazi underground leader. He turns himself inside out to become a resistance fighter without orders or uniform, knowing that his change of heart will exact a heavy price. He sells his café and resolves to live the life of a condemned war criminal, ever on the run from the evil he has challenged.

To compare the philosophical outlooks of *Casablanca* and, say, the popular late 1930s play (and Frank Capra film) *You Can't Take It with You* is to discern the great degree to which Americans had been forced to mature in the intervening five years, much the same as they had between 1914 and 1917. George S. Kaufman and Moss Hart's amiable characters showed absolutely no interest in involving themselves in the complicated world outside the family. All they wanted was to be left alone to pursue their offbeat enterprises.

The 58-key piano used in Casablanca *was sold for $154,000 on December 17, 1988, to Eric Vance, a U.S. representative of C. Itoh & Co., a Japanese trading company. Vance said he had bid on behalf of a Japanese collector, whose name he did not disclose. The sale took place at Sotheby's, an auction house in New York City. Among the disappointed bidders was Donald Trump.*

Their home was their cloister, its doors serving as barriers against intruders who might shock them into reality. Such contented isolationism was no longer possible by 1941.

Harold Rome, who in postwar years was to add the Broadway musicals *Call Me Mister*, an entertaining 1946 saga of lame ducks adjusting to civilian life, and *Fanny* to his Broadway credits, was no stranger to songs of patriotism or ridicule before World War II burst upon the world stage. His "Franklin D. Roosevelt Jones" had been the hit of the pro-labor stage show *Sing Out the News*, produced in 1938 by the International Ladies Garment Workers Union. Sung in the show by Hazel Scott and a black chorus during a Harlem christening scene, it was a favorite with British troops during the Dunkirk evacuation of 1940. Two years later it was revived by 20-year-old Judy Garland in *Babes on Broadway* as a tribute to the wartime president.

Rome's irreverent "Four Little Angels of Peace" (1937) was the first song to poke serious fun at contemporary political leaders, whether they be aggressors or appeasers. His angels consisted of Hitler, Mussolini, Stalin, and Neville Chamberlain. The later *Lunchtime Follies* placed several more of his war songs in a popular revue setting that was frequently staged in defense plants throughout much of 1943.

In Peace and War

Kate Smith, radio's "Songbird of the South," most likely had no idea of the latent wartime significance of Edward Pola and the Austrian-born Franz Steininger's year-old "Marching Along Together" when she first sang it in 1933 using Mort Dixon's English lyric. Like the words to "We're All Together Now," written by Hollywood's workaholic Robin and Rainger for the full-length animated cartoon *Gulliver's Travels* six years later, those to "Marching Along Together" were easily adaptable to the wartime climate. Dixon's original Great Depression invitation to Americans to

bond themselves together one to the other by sharing smiles and tears until the clouds roll by was equally valid throughout the war years.

E.Y. Harburg and Harold Arlen's "God's Country," written in 1937 for Broadway's *Hooray for What?*, reappeared to advantage two years later in MGM's *Babes in Arms*, with Mickey Rooney and Judy Garland sharing it to fortify the pride Americans should take in being citizens of the greatest land of earth. An identical theme was expressed the same year by Maxwell Anderson and Kurt Weill, an excellent composer and recent émigré from Nazi Germany, in "How Can You Tell an American?" from their stage musical *Knickerbocker Holiday*, and by Benjamin Edwards Neal for his mildly popular "I Am an American!" Clearly apparent from these and other such songs was that the World War I writers were not unique in promoting patriotism at a time of increasing peril.

Like a number of World War I ballads, songs with sentimental lyrics sutured to gracious, danceable rhythms in the late 1930s proved irresistible to millions of future soldiers and sweethearts. One such song was "I'll Be Seeing You," which in early 1945 provided the musical backdrop for the picture of the same name starring Ginger Rogers, Joseph Cotten, and Shirley Temple. The Irving Kahal–Sammy Fain song had been written in 1938 for the Broadway show *Right This Way*. The next year it was interpolated into the *Royal Palm Revue*.

Neither outing attracted the attention the song deserved, and it remained in relative seclusion for almost seven years, when the war, the film, and the popular chanteuse Hildegard revived it, bringing out the tender significance of its deeply nostalgic lines of remembered love. The song tied with "You'll Never Know" as the most popular World War II song; both appeared 24 times on *Your Hit Parade*. "I'll Be Seeing You" ranked first for ten weeks, "You'll Never Know" for nine weeks.

Another sterling example of a charming foxtrot with later wartime significance was Ruth Lowe's "I'll Never Smile Again (Until I Smile at You)," copyrighted August 24, 1939, on the eve of the outbreak of World War II. Popularized mainly by Tommy Dorsey's Orchestra, the tune grew into one of the greatest of all American farewell ballads. It was the first "war" song to make the *Your Hit Parade* program, landing in ninth place on July 20, 1940, exactly five years to the day after the show was first broadcast. It reappeared fifteen more times on the program, seven of them as the nation's number one popular song.

On the night and early morning of November 8-9, 1938, Hitler's government allowed gangs of Nazis to rampage across the country, killing and arresting Jews, burning their synagogues, and smashing the display windows of their shops.* The anti-Semitic orgy became known as *Kristallnacht*, so named for the broken glass that littered the streets on the morning of the 9th. Two days later, the twentieth anniversary of the end of World War I, Americans celebrated Armistice Day. In New York City, Kate Smith strode to the CBS microphone and, in sturdy tones vibrant with emotion, sang the biggest hit of her career. A few weeks earlier, she had asked Irving Berlin to write a patriotic song for her. Instead of creating a new one, he reached into his discard file and retrieved a 1918 song that had lain dormant during the intervening two decades. It proved to be the perfect choice, representing the finest embodiment of love for America to emerge from the little soft-spoken Jewish immigrant from czarist Russia. As his legacy to the generations to come, Berlin donated all of the song's substantial royalties to the Campfire Girls and Boy and Girl Scouts of America.

Less than a year away, the Second World War was soon to temporarily unite the country of his birth and the one he consistently enriched with his talent as allies in one of the most perilous challenges either nation had faced. Smith sang the simple, heartfelt words, written only a few months before the conclusion of World War I, as well as anybody else ever would. After invoking God to stand beside the United States and guide it through the night with a light from above, the singer asked for His blessing. More than any other pre-war song, "God Bless America" contained a plea to which peace-loving peoples everywhere could readily subscribe.

Heading Skyward

With the U.S. Navy, Army Field Artillery, and Marine Corps boasting their own official songs, the only other major military service lacking one in early 1939 was the Army Air Corps. A few writers had made futile attempts to fill the gap. Ian Hackerman, John W. Bratton and Leo Edwards's "Wings Over America" failed to make the grade in 1935, as did Evelyn O. and Alexander P. DeSeversky's most respectable "Over the Land and Over the Sea (Song of the American Air Force)" in 1937. But the Air Corps was not to be denied an anthem, and it got it in a unique way.

In 1939, it conducted a nationwide contest in *Liberty* magazine in hopes of finding the ideal song. One of the competitors was Air Corps Captain Robert M. Crawford, a graduate of Princeton University and the Juilliard School of Music, as well as an author, conductor, teacher, and composer of numerous instrumental works. Responding to the magazine's invitation, he submitted the lively "Army Air Corps" in praise of America's flying service. He won the first prize of $1,000, and the Corps happily accepted it as its

*November 9 has played an unusual number of important roles in German history. That was the date in 1918 that Kaiser Wilhelm II abdicated. On November 9, 1923, Hitler was arrested after his Munich "beer hall putsch" was crushed in Bavaria. On November 9, 1989, the East Germans breached the Berlin Wall for the first time, signaling the end of the Cold War for Germany and, eventually, the rest of the world.

official anthem—just in time, one might say, to participate in a new conflict in which the men of the sky would again excel at their myriad assignments.

As macho a promotional song as has ever been written, "Army Air Corps" put the world on alert that the country's bold pilots were not the least bit shy about zooming into the skies, forever willing and able to dogfight every enemy plane out of them. From the opening words, "Off we go into the wild blue yonder," to the final "Nothing'll stop the Army Air Corps!" the song is unmatched in advocating the power of positive thinking among men who "live in fame, / Or go down in flame."

As a sop to listeners' sensibilities, the phrase "off on one helluva roar" was softened to "off on one terrible roar" for radio and early television audiences. After 1948, when the government divided flying responsibilities among the Air Force, the Army, the Navy, and the Marines, Crawford's song underwent a few word and phrase changes and was retitled "The U.S. Air Force."*

Several later Crawford songs further testified to his pride in the Corps. One of them, "Born to the Sky," became the official song of the Air Transport Command, in which Crawford served as major in World War II. Another, this one displaying refreshing candor, was entitled "Kill the Bastards!", the most explicit fighting song of the Second World War.

The decade of the 1930s had not quite expired when RKO circulated *The Story of Vernon and Irene Castle* among the nation's movie houses. No 1939 film better anticipated the impending switch in screenplay content, and Hollywood films would never be quite the same again. Within a matter of months, cameras would be trained on dramatic and comic characters preparing for, and then fighting in, the new war. Choruses would continue to sing

and dance, but the first priority of lyricists was to promise victory on the battlefield, not economic recovery at home, which had arrived as a result of the national defense buildup. Even B pictures, the co-features on double bills, often propped up their customary lightweight scenarios with a serious wartime reference or two.

Dwelling on the career of World War I's favorite ballroom-dancing twosome, *The Story of Vernon and Irene Castle* starred Fred Astaire and Ginger Rogers. Vernon, an Englishman, enlisted in the Royal Flying Corps in 1915 and ended his life in the service of the United States by training student pilots at the Fort Worth, Texas, Army Air Force base. In 1918 his plane crashed, killing him instantly. The death of the entertainer gave the film a rare unhappy ending, especially for a musical, that audiences were as yet unready to accept. It was the only Astaire-Rogers picture to lose money and concluded their screen partnership for ten years, when they appeared together one more time in *The Barkleys of Broadway*.

The only new song in the picture, the very pretty "Only When You're in My Arms," might have served as a theme for wartime lovers, but failed to do so. The composer was Con Conrad, a veteran of the World War I songwriters' brigade, who only five years earlier had furnished Fred and Ginger with the Academy Award–winning "The Continental" for their second feature film together, *The Gay Divorcee*. But that was long ago. The song had been written in an age that now bore only the slightest relevance to current events, even among adults who had lived through it.

America's between-the-wars isolationism and innocence, already imperceptibly receding, were about to be shocked entirely out of existence by an aggression in Eastern Europe that in a short time would enflame much of the civilized world.

The Army Air Corps was given its exclusive Broadway salute in 1944 with Winged Victory, *translated the next year into a film that featured many Hollywood stars who had enlisted in the service. In earlier years, such Hollywood films as* I Wanted Wings *and* A Yank in the RAF *(both from 1941) had promoted Air Force enlistment while advocating close cooperation between American and British air forces.*

9. Documenting
the Dangers

*I shall give a propagandist reason for starting the war, whether it is plausible
or not. . . . The victor will not be asked, later on, whether he told the truth or
not. In starting and waging a war, it is not Right that matters, but Victory. Have
no pity.*

Adolf Hitler, August 1939

Gleiwitz in 1939 was a 663-year-old obscure, gritty industrial German town in Prussian Silesia, just over the border from Poland. At summer's end, it fulfilled its destiny of playing a pivotal role in world history similar to that of Sarajevo in 1914.

Early in the morning of September 1, about 100 Germans wearing Polish uniforms broke into the radio station in Gleiwitz, shouted into the live microphone that Poland had captured the town and that it was time for all Poles to make war on Germany. Before fleeing the town, the "invaders"—actually SS men recruited by Reichsfueher Heinrich Himmler—killed a German concentration camp prisoner, also dressed in a Polish uniform, who had been sent to Gleiwitz expressly to be murdered. They left him behind as evidence that troops of both countries had indeed been involved in a battle.

This seemingly minor incident had been planned by Major General Erich von Manstein, chief of staff of the German Army Group South, in the hope of insti-

gating full-scale war by means of a sham skirmish involving "Polish terrorists." According to von Manstein's reasoning, Hitler would be given a justifiable excuse for sending soldiers into Poland to punish the criminals and the officials who ordered the attack. Another significant participant in the plan was Admiral Wilhelm Franz Canaris, a wily and brilliant conspirator who was then chief of Abwehr, the Nazis' major intelligence-gathering system that, in time, expanded its operations to cover espionage, counterespionage, and sabotage.

Hitler's original plan was to send 16 separate small Abwehr-led combat teams into Poland on the morning of Sunday, August 27. Moving surreptitiously farther and farther into the country only a few hours in advance of German troops, the teams were to destroy airstrips, blow up bridges, and cut telephone and telegraph wires. Hitler postponed the plan on August 25, however, for reasons still unclear. All the teams were halted in their tracks.

All except one, that is, which could

131

not be reached. This "lost" team attacked and defeated a superior Polish force, and in the process fired the first shots in World War II, about one week before the staged Gleiwitz affair. Curiously, the attack was dismissed by the Poles, who failed to respond to it militarily or diplomatically.

While the Gleiwitz operation was under way, one and one-half million German troops were massed at the Polish border, awaiting the call to action, which came at 4:45 A.M., September 1. Plotted with incredible attention to detail, the Nazi invasion ranks as one of the most meticulously planned military campaigns in the history of warfare. Shortly after the fake Polish soldiers hurried away from Gleiwitz, German panzer divisions and squadrons of Stuka dive bombers burst into Poland at 20 different points. At 10 A.M. the same day, Hitler announced that German military units had "returned the fire" initiated by the bogus Polish soldiers.

The Führer knew he had a free hand in attacking Poland. Only days before, he had concluded with the Soviet Union a trade pact and then a non-aggression pact which guaranteed that Joseph Stalin would not interfere with Hitler's war. The German dictator also gambled that the West would not mount a major offensive during the Polish campaign, and he was correct. Poland, the fifth greatest military power in the world, surrendered just 27 days after the invasion, indicating quite clearly that not even a country with an army 1.7 million strong was able to withstand the fury of the *blitzkrieg* (lightning war), which destroyed 75 percent of all of Poland's airplanes in the first 24 hours of battle.

Faithful to the terms of its recently executed mutual-assistance pact with Poland, Great Britain declared war on Germany on September 3. Also pledged to protect Poland, France followed five hours later. Without issuing a formal declaration of war, Hitler had deliberately shoved the world into a furious conflagration that would last six years. The result was an estimated 100,000,000 casualties worldwide, including at least 60 million deaths.

The United States lost about 405,000 lives compared with the 116,500 of World War I. The wounded totaled about 672,000. World War II cost the United States more than $250 billion, increasing the national debt five-fold. More than 10 million American men and women, including about 700,000 blacks, served in the armed forces.

The Poles did mount a heroic defense of Warsaw, but they were no match for the Luftwaffe, which reduced the capital city to rubble and many of its inhabitants to starvation by September 25. Calling on Frédéric Chopin, its radio station throughout the brief defense periodically broadcast the opening notes of the composer's *Polonaise* (in A-flat, Opus 53) to inform the world that Warsaw had not been surrendered.

Observing Hitler's command, the Nazi invaders displayed neither pity nor mercy during the invasion or during the long occupation of Poland that ensued. Nor did the Soviets, who, despite a non-aggression treaty with Poland, attacked the country from the east on September 17, the day after signing a peace treaty with Japan, which had been skirmishing with the Soviet army along the Mongolian border.

The Awakening 2

The shock of Hitler's bludgeoning his way into Poland was not sufficient to send America's tunesmiths swiftly into action. Like their forebears in the first two years of World War I, they remained unsettled on the sidelines, as did the United States itself. This state of affairs was only one in a chain of striking similarities that portrayed World War II as little more than a delayed continuation of the earlier conflict, with Adolf Hitler instead of the exiled Kaiser Wilhelm II, who was to die in Switzerland in 1941, in the starring role.

Many people still looked upon World War I as an unalloyed disaster; World War II was regarded at the outset in much the same way. Only 21 years had elapsed between the end of the First Great War and the beginning of the second. The millions of Americans over the age of 40 had little difficulty recalling the bloodletting meted out by World War I, and most were understandably upset over the likelihood that a reprise was in the making, this time to be performed on an even larger world stage.

In their opinion, World War I had solved nothing; rather, the European Allies' stringent peace terms had laid the cornerstone for the new war now under way. Even the three major combatants were the same. Once more it was England, once dismissed by a contemptuous Napoleon as a "nation of shopkeepers," and France versus Germany.

It was a different story in England, however, where the military services, as in 1914, were beefing up their ranks, and factories their armament production, in response to the new aggression that had rendered the government's appeasement policy worthless. Sensing the suffering to be borne by their countrymen, British songwriters were quick to give voice to the overarching sadness felt by the troops and the loved ones they were leaving behind. They had performed an identical service 25 years earlier. The names of their songs were different, but the themes closely approximated those of the war songs of 1914–1916.

From Eric Maschwitz and Manning Sherwin came not only the first World War II ballad, but also one of the most poignant of the thousands of such songs to be inspired by that conflict. Inserted into the 1940 London revue *New Faces*, "A Nightingale Sang in Berkeley Square" was a lyrical metaphor for dreams gone astray, unfolding as it did the story of a couple who had met for the first time in Mayfair and, despite the fact that the whole world seemed to be in a topsy-turvy state, fallen in love. The romantic background refrain provided by the nightingale will not be heard again for a long, long time, the lyric implies, having been diminished by Hermann Goering's Luftwaffe to a fondly re-

membered echo from the sunnier days of prewar England.

About the same time, along came a second well-remembered war song, this one by Ross Parker and Hughie Charles, that merged four standard wartime emotions. Sung throughout the war, particularly at its most depressing moments, "There'll Always Be an England!" underscored all loyal Britons' respect for their impressive heritage, symbolized by the sheet music cover photograph of Anne Hathaway's cottage in Stratford-on-Avon.

The picture prompted reminders of the glory years of the English Renaissance, when Shakespeare ruled the world of poetry and drama and England ruled the seas after erasing the threat posed by the Spanish Armada. Wedded to the resolve to fight the enemy on land, on the sea, and in the air were three more: never to submit to the conquering hordes, absolute confidence in final victory, and determination to preserve centuries-old ideals and traditions that not even Napoleon I or Wilhelm II had been able to destroy.

Realistically, however, the country's survival in 1939 depended not on languishing in the prestige of the past. It was the disturbing present that mattered. According to the song, England would remain free only if her people recognized the extent of the new German threat and were willing to make the sacrifices needed to counter any assault the enemy might launch against them. In an optional aside to the lyric's call for British soldiers and civilians to prepare for the worst, writers Parker and Charles cast an interventionist eye across the Atlantic. Somehow, and soon, they urged, America must be awakened to the clear and present danger stalking Europe, and they suggested that it was in the United States' own vital interest to help England save the world from the scourge of Nazism.

Written that same year by Parker and Charles, the ballad "We'll Meet Again," elevated to prominence by singer Vera Lynn,*

*Miss Lynn's jaunty recording of "We'll Meet Again" was reprised to great ironic effect at the conclusion of

developed into a bigger hit in America than in Britain by virtue of the later recording by the Ink Spots, a popular American black quartet. The lyric's plea for estranged couples to keep smiling till blue skies drive the dark clouds from view may have raised some spirits, even though the authors frankly admitted they didn't know when or how the current crisis would be reversed in the lovers' favor.

Edward Pola and Tommy Connor's "Till the Lights of London Shine Again" was a sentimental, short-lived followup to the nightingale song, dwelling on the darkened streets of the English capital, their neon signs turned off, their residential lights shrouded by layers of drawn curtains from German bombers from dusk to dawn. Meanwhile, Michael Carr's "Somewhere in France with You," became the first love song to assure members of the overseas British Expeditionary Force that their absent sweethearts were marching alongside them, at least in spirit.

Among soldiers of the sky, the jolly "I've Got Sixpence (As We [I] Go Rolling Home)" became a popular themesong first with the Royal Air Force and later with the U.S. Army Air Force. Brimming with the same spirit of fellowship that two decades earlier had turned "Hail! Hail! the Gang's All Here" and "Merrily We'll Roll Along" into megahits, it was written by Desmond Cox, Elton Box, and Desmond Hall. The song splendidly highlighted the closely knit camaraderie of British pilots and crew impelled into harm's way to intercept superior Luftwaffe aircraft over London and to drop their own bombs over Germany. Americans, too, warmed to its carefree lyric, especially the references to the pleasures of playing the role of off-duty spendthrift, which for enlisted

men in particular was impossible unless they were independently wealthy.

If the wives back home received any money at all from their military men, they should consider themselves lucky, the song pointed out. The singing husbands simply refuse to be burdened with domestic woes; the hazards of their present occupation were more than enough to contend with. The single lads, in the meantime, revel in the absence of demanding wives who most likely would only take their pay and then go about deceiving them. Two years later, however, Eric Maschwitz and Michael Carr's vastly popular "He Wears a Pair of Silver Wings" restored public pride in the aerial service by shedding a more favorable and serious light on one of its bravest members.

America Marches in the Song Parade

What Americans did excel at before the country dispatched its own troops to halt the fascist aggression was jump-starting sympathy for the victims of the new conflict through a few popular songs, usually solemn, sometimes distinguished. Again, as at the outset of World War I, only a tiny number voiced support for U.S. involvement in the new European conflict, typically limiting it to supplying the Allies with desperately needed armaments. Reckless indeed would be the songwriter who sought to undermine America's neutrality by even suggesting that the country might be forced into a battlefield reunion with Britain and France.**

That possibility was clearly evident, however, tempting much of the population into retreating behind the friendly walls of escapism rather than confronting the heartache and expense that a second trip "over

---

[continued]   director Stanley Kubrick's Dr. Strangelove, or How I Learned to Stop Worrying and Love the Bomb. Heightening the black comedy aspects of the classic 1964 film, the song is heard in the last scene when, thanks to the unreformed Nazi scientist, Dr. Strangelove, the earth experiences mushrooming nuclear annihilation.

**In 1940, about three percent of the 41,847 copyrighted songs were patriotic or war-related; in 1941, about 10 percent of the 50,454 songs; in 1942, about 75 percent of the 53,636 songs; in 1943, about 60 percent of the 48,398 songs; in 1944, about 50 percent of the 51,525 songs; and in 1945, about 40 percent of the 63,817 songs.

there" would entail. Only rarely did American songwriters uphold either the interventionist or the isolationist cause, and then only mildly. Most copyrighted songs that did take a stand one way or the other almost never received the apostolic blessing of the major publishers, and died unrecognized by everyone except their writers. Those that did find their way into print were about evenly matched philosophically. "This Ain't Our War" and "Let's Stay Over Here" supported the isolationist cause; "Let's Stand Behind Great Britain" and "Thumbs Up to the British" argued that keeping Britain supplied with arms was absolutely necessary to prevent her defeat. Virtually ignored in song from 1939 through 1941, the upstart Hitler was subjected to only one fiery admonition from American shores. "There'll Be No Goosestep Over Here," songwriters L. McDonald and M.G. Thomas informed the Nazi leader.

The meager number of "America First" songs were balanced by the correspondingly scant appeals for America to "wake up and prepare" or, as some tunes phrased it, to "be alert." Extremely few— "Allies Marching On," for example— vibrated with admiration of the faltering British and French, or, like "We've Just Begun," heartily endorsed the revitalization of America's defense industries and armed forces. John Philip Sousa's old preparedness theme was on the way to making a comeback, surely but slowly.

More prevalent were the prayers to God for peace, or for divine guidance in case of war, that were recited in the innumerable hymns. Alternating between interventionism and isolationism, the lyrics clearly defined the quicksilver reflexes of an American public vacillating between using the Atlantic Ocean to transport goods to a longtime ally or as a wide moat to shut the nation off from participation in the problems of the rest of the world.

The vast majority of the new songs reprised the 1914–1916 patriotic petitions to venerate a country enriched by a constitution embodying the highest political and social ideals. Between the end of 1939 and the end of 1941, hundreds of lively American-written marches pledged renewed allegiance to the flag and proclaimed the virtues of democracy. Songs fostering love of country greatly overshadowed the comparatively few requiems to the death of freedom in other lands. With their frequent references to the torch held high by the Statue of Liberty, the patriotic-song lyricists frankly sought to commit the public, regardless of political persuasion, to keeping its flame forever burning.

The year 1940 witnessed the debut of Don Raye and Al Jacobs's "This Is My Country (to Have and to Hold)," an admirable inspirational hybrid that coupled toughness with sensitivity. Particularly effective when sung by a male chorus, its usual format, the song qualified as a restrained member of the "Keep America Free" movement. Far better in melody and message than any of its World War I predecessors, "This Is My Country" superbly awakened Americans to the price they might have to pay for exempting themselves from a foreign crisis that in time well might threaten their own nation and themselves.

Every war needs valid reasons for people to support it, and Eddie DeLange and Sam H. Stept's memorable "This Is Worth Fighting For" enumerated enough of them to tempt even the most stubborn isolationist to desert the cause in favor of espousing world democracy. Now troubled with worry and woe, America is a unique nation unashamed of its idealism and proud of its achievements in preserving the liberty of its citizens, the songwriters pointed out. She has served admirably for decades as the democratic model envied by people the world over. Nothing must be allowed to extinguish the light she continues to shed over European nations again at war. And nothing shall, the writers implied.

In only one major area did the World War II songwriters vary their subject matter from that of their World War I counterparts. Rather than ridicule minorities, a few went so far as to suggest that one hoped-for result of overthrowing the manipulators of international chaos would be the integration of all Americans into one society, blind to nationality and color. "Ballad for Americans," a narrative solo for baritone written in 1940 by John Latouche and Earl Robinson in praise of ethnic and racial harmony, was one such work. Far more dramatic than 1915's "America, I Love You," it reasserted the older song's pride in the nation's commitment to extend the hand of welcome to all peoples. Relaying a message that some listeners for unsustainable reasons found offensively leftist rather than patriotic, "Ballad for Americans" won only short-lived popularity, despite its appearance in the 1940 Broadway revue *Sing for Your Supper* and the superb recording made that same year by Paul Robeson. The cantata would have to wait almost a decade before its revival on the CBS network's *Pursuit of Happiness* radio program in 1949 temporarily lifted it from obscurity.

Several rungs farther up on the artistic ladder was Robinson's second salute to America's role as host country for the oppressed of all nationalities, creeds, and colors. According to the Lewis Allan text for "The House I Live In (That's America to Me)," America deserved special humanitarian recognition for creating a melting pot within its borders, which the lyricist identified as the greatest of all the nation's innumerable virtues. Like "Ballad for Americans," however, this dramatic monologue, certainly among the finest pieces of American patriotic music, did not find widespread acceptance at first. Although it was movingly sung by the Delta Rhythm Boys, a black quartet, at the conclusion of *Follow the Boys* in 1944, it was not until the next year, when Frank Sinatra sang it in *The House I Live In*, that a substantial portion of the public was exposed to the work. Mervyn LeRoy, who coproduced and directed the short documentary film

on the evils of intolerance, won a special Academy Award that year for his pioneering effort.

In the summer of 1941, Metro-Goldwyn-Mayer released *Lady Be Good*, a frothy musical typical in its cheerful, uncomplicated approach to solving marriage and career problems. The film sported several new and old songs, dancing by Eleanor Powell, and a disinterred plot centering on the struggles of a husband-and-wife team (Robert Young and Ann Southern) to make it big in the songwriting business. The studio permitted the war to creep briefly into the screenplay, giving rise to the high point of the picture, which was underscored by the new Jerome Kern song MGM had bought to add nostalgia to the scene.

According to legend, unverifiable but quite possibly true, Oscar Hammerstein II telephoned Kern one day to read a poem he had written shortly after the Nazis marched unopposed into Paris. Like all Broadway composers before Hammerstein teamed up with Richard Rodgers for *Oklahoma!* in 1943, Kern was unaccustomed to setting music to words. The composer recognized the rare quality of the lyric, however, and musicalized it as a modified cabaret song. It was handed to Miss Southern, who introduced "The Last Time I Saw Paris" in *Lady Be Good* while her face was superimposed on a montage of film clips showing the French capital in its between-the-nightmares glory years. The lyric, one of Hammerstein's finest, unfolds the love affair, temporarily ended but never to be forgotten, between the writer and the city he lived in as a young man. At its core are the author's ruminations on the sorrow and pity of the June 1940 surrender of the beautiful City of Light to the Nazi invaders. The simple, dignified melody was one of the most familiar of 1941 and earned Kern his second Academy Award for Best Song.*

Like many of the earliest World War I

Kern won his first Oscar for "The Way You Look Tonight," from Swing Time *(1936). In later years he was nominated four more times for "Dearly Beloved" (*You Were Never Lovelier, 1942*); "Long Ago (and Far Away)"*

and World War II songs, "The Last Time I Saw Paris" was short on interventionism but long on sympathy for victimized Europeans that at times bordered on despair. Falling back on George Washington's admonition that tyranny, like hell, is not easily conquered, the passionate song lyric presented Hitler's Germany as a worldwide menace, but it refrained from suggesting any measures to combat it. Still to come from songwriters were powerful warnings aimed either at Americans to take action against the Nazis or at the Nazis themselves to be wary of arousing the wrath of the mighty but slumbering United States, a gross error that had doomed the Kaiser a quarter-century earlier.

You're (Back) in the Army Now

Among the most significant and best-remembered actions undertaken during the second Roosevelt Administration was congressional passage, on September 14, 1940, of the first peacetime Selective Service Training Act in the nation's history. Six weeks later, on October 29, only days before the presidential election between F.D.R. and Wendell L. Willkie, the government sponsored a national lottery. Newspaper photographs and newsreels recorded its initiation, showing the blindfolded secretary of war, Henry L. Stimson, reaching into a fishbowl and plucking a chit of paper with 158 written on it. That was the serial number designating the first 6,000 registrants between the ages of 21 and 35 to be drafted into the army. An identical lottery had been filmed by Movietone newsreel cameramen in April 1917, with the blindfolded vice president, Thomas Riley Marshall, drawing the first serial number.

Unlike 1917, many young men, and their families as well, looked upon the draft as something of a lark. After all, a little exercise and discipline very well might be of benefit, and the pay of $21 a month was in addition to free meals, lodging, and the other perquisites of military life. The training program was widely regarded as no more serious than a tour of duty in the Civilian Conservation Corps (CCC), which was also supervised by the army. Men of varying backgrounds, from unsophisticated farm hand to big-city slicker, would be herded together in hastily constructed government collectives, perform bothersome tasks under duress, spend off hours in strange towns, and, viewed hopefully, learn something of lasting value.

Quickly latching on to the induction blues were a number of minor songwriters who celebrated the average conscript's new lifestyle with humor rather than the heartrending pathos reminiscent of the draft calls of 1917. America, after all, was not at war, only playing at it. Mack Kay's cheery "Goodbye Dear, I'll Be Back in a Year" was written to placate distressed sweethearts, Maury Coleman Harris's lyrical "Dear Mom" to console troubled mothers. "He's 1-A in the Army (and He's A-1 in My Heart)" was a catchy mock tribute by Redd Evans from one girlfriend to her departing conscript lover; "I Feel a Draft Coming On," by Clarence Kulseth and J. Fred Coots, was an amusing antidote for youngsters stricken with fishbowl fever.

The funniest of the draftee-oriented songs, "Is It Love (or Is It Conscription)?", popularized by band-vocalist Doris Day, not so innocently wondered whether the dislike of trudging off to boot camp was not the real reason for the current marriage epidemic. Could the urge to take a wife be traced to Cupid or to Congress, songwriters Lou Singer and Walter Bishop asked after watching more and more altar-shy males scurrying around for suitable mates who would secure their exemption from the draft.

[continued]   (Cover Girl, 1944); "More and More" (Can't Help Singing, 1945); and "All Through the Day" (Centennial Summer, 1946).

Poking harmless fun at the low starting salary earned by the apprentice warriors was "$21 a Day — Once a Month," written by Ray Klages and Felix Bernard for *Top Sergeant Mulligan*. An inconsequential 1941 remake of the inconsequential World War I–based silent film, directed by James Hogan in 1928, the new version nevertheless bristled with authoritarianism by starring Nat Pendleton, a one-time professional wrestler, in the title role. The song also sounded a serious note by suggesting that serving Uncle Sam was well worth any sacrifices it might entail.

Balancing these comic tunes was Henry Tobias and Henry Russell's "If Mother Could See Me Now (Marching with My Army Pal)," which sought to inject soldierly pride into recruits. In the most melodious of the new love songs, Stanley Cowan and Bobby Worth's "'Til Reveille," the lonely draftee is content to spend the hours between taps and the wake-up call in the ageless pursuit of dreaming of his sweetheart. The period's best new marching song was Willie Lee Duckworth's "Sound Off," with its 20 tough drill-instructor verses based on *The Cadence System of Teaching Close Order Drill*, an instructional manual written by retired army colonel Bernard Lentz. Most of the song's popularity stemmed from the recording made by the deep-throated singing bandleader Vaughn Monroe.

Handled with a flair for comedy, the apprentice doughboys' inevitable boot camp misadventures were unquestionably such stuff as farce is made of. Ever receptive to themes on which to base formula films, Hollywood instantly recognized the commercial windfall to accrue from dropping non-military types into a highly disciplined culture that abridged personal freedom and penalized offenders. World War I Broadway had savored the profit to be made from servicemen shows. Now it was the movies' turn to rake in the customers.

Within a few months, out of the studios poured a brand new creation — draftee-oriented, Chaplinesque slapstick comedies and musicals that predated the cartoons of Bill Mauldin, who later would chronicle the more embittering aspects of the war through the characters of Willie and Joe and the eternal klutz, Private Berger. The new movies attracted stupendous crowds and introduced the first of the World War II march songs performed on screen by ensembles of singers and dancers.

On Land and Sea and in the Air

Except for 1941's *Caught in the Draft*, with a young Bob Hope jumping consistently from the top of a piano to the floor to dodge servitude by developing flat feet, the major entries in the new round of film comedies were carried by Bud Abbott and Lou Costello. In that single year, this pair of experienced performers from burlesque and the legitimate stage "served" in three branches of the military — the army, the navy, and the Air Corps. And they and other males in the casts actually engaged in a few battlefield maneuvers, inserting a realistic touch here and there to counterbalance the shenanigans that pervaded all their films.

Joining the comedians in two of their military musicals were the Andrews Sisters, already renowned for their precise singing synchronization and bouncy deliveries. Put all these performers together, add a couple of lively songs and one or two ballads, and life in the armed forces took on a tuneful, if often frenzied, hilarity not seen since the custard pie–throwing days of World War I's silent screen. The format would continue well into later decades, courtesy of such Dean Martin and Jerry Lewis 1950s Paramount films as *At War with the Army*, *Jumping Jacks*, and *Sailor, Beware*. Columbia Pictures' *Stripes*, with Bill Murray and John Candy cast as typical uniformed misfits, was a derivative comedy hit of the 1981 season. In 1994 it was *In the Army Now*, starring Pauly Shore, that put the wackiness back into war films.

In *Buck Privates*, the first of the

Abbott and Costello military vehicles, the new songs included a peppy salute to army draftees, "You're a Lucky Fellow, Mr. Smith." A convincing plea that the recruits should regard their training to defend America as a privilege rather than an inconvenience, the song was sung by Patti, Maxene, LaVerne, and an energetic chorus on Universal Pictures' highly respectable reconstruction of Grand Central Station. The picture also debuted the pretty "I Wish You Were Here," the first of America's World War II sentimental "letter-writing" songs from draftee to back-home sweetheart, which is sung by Jane Frazee.

The hit of the picture, and an Academy Award Best Song nominee to boot, was "Boogie Woogie Bugle Boy (of Company B)," which surpassed even the mid-picture reprise of the 21-year-old "(I'll Be with You in) Apple Blossom Time" in popularity. No one was eager to murder this hip bugler, most likely because he laced his solos with a boogie beat that hypnotized the jitterbug generation. Even the titles of boogie woogie tunes attracted indoctrinated youngsters, who flocked to live or canned renditions of finger-snapping tunes bearing such unromantic titles as "Beat Me Daddy, Eight to the Bar," "Scrub Me, Mama, with a Boogie Beat," and "Bounce Me, Brother, with a Solid Four."

Much of the credit for reviving boogie woogie deservedly belonged to Earl ("Fatha") Hines, whose recording of "Boogie Woogie on St. Louis Blues" became an instant 1939 classic. But it was the popularity of the bugle boy song that propelled the genre into a major musical experience, and it quickly became the "ragtime" of World War II. Just as firmly rooted in jazz antiquity, boogie woogie was the medium used to play the blues on piano, livening them up with swinging improvised riffs.

For Bud and Lou's *In the Navy*, the new and talented partnership of Don Raye and Gene DePaul added clout to military songs with the fighting lyric to "We're in the Navy," which warned saber-rattling nations everywhere that if they want a slugfest with Uncle Sam, they'll get one—and they won't win it. The picture's other two navy songs, "Off to See the World" and the comic "A Sailor's Life for Me," were far closer in content and execution to the songs of the carefree 1930s musicals—Irving Berlin's "We Saw the Sea," from *Follow the Fleet*, for example—than to the typical war tunes to come.

The Andrews Sisters were replaced in the singing department for *Keep 'Em Flying* by Dick Powell, then at the ebb of his musical comedy days, and Martha Raye. Non-relative Don Raye and DePaul contributed the songs for this weak-sister U.S. Army Air Corps feature, which included their respectable march "Let's Keep 'Em Flying" and a ballad dedicated to the conventional homesick recruit, "The Boy with the Wistful Eyes."

Columbia Pictures, never ranked high on the list of musical-producing Hollywood studios, was nonetheless the first to release a draftee-based extravaganza, insuring its box office prominence by co-starring Fred Astaire and Rita Hayworth. In *You'll Never Get Rich* (1941), Fred is called away from his Broadway dance-direction chores into the army, where between musical routines he naturally pursues the glamorous Rita. The songs were all by Cole Porter, making him the first major American composer (and lyricist; he was both) to write a complete score for a major World War II "military" film.*

The songs ranged from the jovial "I'm Shootin' the Works for Uncle Sam," sung by a huge crowd comprising band musicians, chorus girls, redcaps, and onlookers,

---

Rita Hayworth ranked second to Betty Grable as the war's favorite pinup girl, particularly in the still photograph showing her clad in the black negligee she wore in the 1942 film You Were Never Lovelier. *The most popular pinup in World War I was the beautiful British actress Gladys Cooper, who later in life was nominated for three Academy Awards for Best Supporting Actress (*Now, Voyager, 1942; The Song of Bernadette, 1943; *and* My Fair Lady, 1964).

marching through another Grand Central Station replica to cheer the neophyte soldier off, to "Since I Kissed My Baby Goodbye." The first American-written farewell song of the new war and one of the year's Academy Award nominees, it is played and sung by a quartet of black soldiers and danced by Astaire while he is confined to the guardhouse for slugging his sergeant and an officer — Rita's brother, no less.

At age 52, Irving Berlin in 1940 still had a bright future to escort an accomplished past. He joined the World War II song parade earlier than any other major songwriter and for two years led all his fellow professionals in the number of commercial successes, just as he had in 1918. In "It's a Lovely Day Tomorrow," his winsome ballad from *Louisiana Purchase*, a 1940 Broadway musical, Berlin focused his attention on the fear drifting from Europe over America. His poignant lyric urged people to retain their optimism as best they can by feasting their tear-dimmed eyes on the prospect of the happier days bound to come.

That same year, Mickey Rooney and Judy Garland, the fresh-face stars of the musicals *Babes in Arms* and *Strike Up the Band*, became the best-known members of the first Hollywood contingent to hop aboard MGM's "Metro Bond Train." Like the Al Jolsons and Mary Pickfords of the Great War, they crisscrossed the country, greeting gigantic crowds of fans at railroad stations, and entertaining them there or on movie house stages in selected cities. The purpose of the immensely popular promotion was to pump up sales of U.S. Defense bonds and stamps. Mickey and Judy were a roaring success wherever they went, as were other film and theatrical personalities who appeared in cameo roles in later war bond rallies the country over, all of them responsible for adding millions of much-needed dollars to Uncle Sam's coffers throughout the war.

What the initial run of the Metro Bond Train lacked was a jaunty, tuneful song to add zest to the bond drives and

impetus to impulse buying. Revivals of the old "Liberty Bond" songs simple would not do. So Irving Berlin furnished the perfect candidate in 1941, and "Any Bonds Today?" was selected as the official theme-song of the National Defense Savings Program. Bearing a cover picture of a smiling Uncle Sam doffing his hat in thanks to purchasers of government bonds and stamps, the song was the only notable one devoted to enticing the public into voluntarily financing the defense buildup and, later, the war. In a typical patriotic gesture, the songwriter assigned the copyright to Henry Morgenthau, Jr., the secretary of the treasury.

Also from the resourceful Berlin's pen in 1941 came the stirring "Arms for the Love of America," written in honor of the U.S. Army Ordnance and dedicated to its chief officer, Major General C.M. Wesson. The only well-known songwriter in World War II to honor the American Red Cross, Berlin dedicated his lovely "Angels of Mercy" to that organization. Rather than rest on his laurels with these four hits behind him, he remained in harness, the most significant of his World War II songs yet to be written.

Berlin was the only songwriter to write more than one mammoth hit during both wars, but he was not the only holdover from World War I to publish songs between 1939 and 1945. A number of other older writers — James V. Monaco, Al Bryan, Al Dubin, Al Piantadosi, Abner Silver, Edgar Leslie, M.K. Jerome, Lew Brown, Jerome Kern, and Sam H. Stept among them — were active professionally in World War II. Besides Berlin, only George W. Meyer, Monaco, and Kern were able to match or surpasse the success they had achieved in the previous war.

Another sturdy promotional song, but not by Berlin, was the fund-raising "'V' Song," which quickly became identified with America's "Bundles for Britain" program. Through it, volunteers collected and shipped such donated essentials as clothing, blankets, and canned goods to English families desperately in need of them. The song represented a welcome change of pace for writer Saxie Dowell, whose nonsensical "Three Little Fishies" was played so often throughout 1939 and 1940 as to constitute a national menace.

Another Era Ends

With the prayerful "My Own America," popularized by singer Tony Martin, lyricist-composer Allie Wrubel in 1941 became the first Hollywood contract songwriter to write a successful war song. Unlike Berlin, Kern, Porter, Gershwin, Rodgers, and a handful of other heavyweights who had established their reputations on Broadway before freelancing for film musicals, Wrubel was a Hollywood discovery who earned his livelihood by writing on freelance assignment for the studios. His score for Warner Bros.' *Flirtation Walk* was his most successful West Coast endeavor of the 1930s.

Wrubel's appeal to God to watch over America's destiny was more solemn than all but a very few of the scattering of other war songs published in 1941. The inspiration behind "My Sister and I," a very pretty song by Hy Zaret, Joan Whitney, and Alex Kramer, was the best-selling book of the same name. In it, author Dirk van der Heide related memories of a happier Holland shared by two Dutch children before, as the lyric notes, the warm and lovely world they knew suddenly disappeared under the terror imposed by the Nazi occupation. In its own poignant way, "My Sister and I" was the Dutch equivalent of World War I's "Lorraine, My Beautiful Alsace-Lorraine."

"The Things I Love," by classical violinist Harold Barlow and Lewis Harris, was another lovely addition to the growing literature of songs that doubled as romantic ballads and sober meditations on the perils confronting the United States. The evocative lyric persuasively recalled simple pleasures of the prewar past — the glow of sunset in the peaceful summer sky, the sound of a sweet voice whispering "I love

you" — while obliquely lamenting their possible loss in a world once more at war. The music was based on Tchaikovsky's "Melody" (Opus 42, No. 3), another example of the frequent borrowings from classical composers for popular songs in the early 1940s. Meredith Willson's moving tribute to the Red Army, "And Still the Volga Flows," was adapted from Rachmaninoff's *Second Piano Concerto*.

Dedicated primarily to the English, but also to other peoples already subjugated by the Nazis, was the four-star early 1941 hit "The White Cliffs of Dover," by Nat Burton and Walter Kent. Merging tender reminders of the past with optimism, the lyric praises the pluck of the Britishers, whom Burton recalled with fondness for displaying cheery thumbs-up salutations to one another even amid the air raids that were turning London to shambles.

Presented as a mother's prayer to her child, most likely one of the many youngsters being evacuated to safer havens in the English countryside and abroad, the words offered comfort to parents and dislocated children alike even more compellingly than MGM's *Journey for Margaret*, which starred Robert Young and Margaret O'Brien. More than five decades later, the song's promise that bluebirds will once again fly over a country at peace remains a stunning textbook example of how to deliver a simple message of hope universal and eternal in its application to victims of warfare anywhere at any time.

Of comparable stature in the 1941 popularity polls, and even more familiar to succeeding generations, was the melancholy Frank Loesser–Jule Styne hit from the co-feature film *Sweater Girl*. Introduced by starlet Betty Jane Rhodes, "I Don't Want to Walk Without You" so well documented the emotional suffering caused by soldier-sweetheart separations that it retained its immense initial appeal throughout the war.

According to the majority of these early songs, the war was already disrupting American lives, leaving young and old freighted down with worry and aghast at the crushing power of the reinvigorated German war machine. They found some relief when Churchill succeeded Chamberlain as prime minister on May 10, 1940. But not even that cigar-chomping, tenacious bulldog of a leader could prevent the fall of France one month later.

Beating the Victory Drum 2

The tens of thousands of songs copyrighted by Americans between October 1939 and October 1945 dutifully appealed to patriotism and touched on the anxiety and sadness—and at times the humor—inherent in the strife of warfare. The total was almost four times higher than the number of such songs cobbled together by the World War I writers. To accommodate this creative upsurge, almost three times as many music-publishing firms were in operation between 1939 and 1945 as between 1914 and 1918. Some of their songs found their way onto the Broadway stage, as others had in the Great War; many more of them traveled the well-worn path to Hollywood. Most were independent, or non-production tunes, depending exclusively on bandleaders and disk jockeys for public hearings. No song publisher, however, came close to dominating the war-song market as had Leo Feist, Inc., the great assembly line publisher of World War I.

Numerous calls to arms were again issued, prodding young men into volunteering rather than awaiting the draft notice. Mother and sweetheart goodbye and miss-you songs proliferated, along with the familiar "Yanks are coming" and "marching on to victory" songs and "we'll be back" assurances. Battles were memorialized—some, like Bataan and Corregidor, to be cast in an elegiac mode; others, like Guadalcanal and Iwo Jima, properly celebrated as the notable historical achievements they were.

The highly emotional responses these events aroused found semi-artistic outlets

in the birth of a few successors to the earlier war's pulpers. Their combined songs, however, numbered in the hundreds, not thousands, as was true of E.S.S. Huntington and his fellow melody manufacturers. But the names of Lew Tobin, Bob Carleton, Eddie Keenan, J. Charles McNeil, Ray Hibbeler, Aaron A. Clark, Burrell Van Buren, and Leo and Hector Richard appeared frequently on the sheet music covers of minor World War II tunes. As before, most of the lyrics of their songs were written by women; also as before, the lyrics throbbed with lethal warnings identical with those written in 1917-18. Refusing to stray onto any side issues, the new lyricists also concentrated on heckling the enemy, dooming them all to a trifecta of despair, disintegration, and defeat.

Vanity publishers in particular helped greatly to fuel the furious outpouring of pre- and post–Pearl Harbor war songs. Such small but active firms as Yankee Music Publishing Corp. in Manhattan and Victory Songs on Staten Island, N.Y., specialized almost exclusively in them, as did Echoes of Victory Music Publishing Co. in Detroit; D & L Victory Music Publishers in Kansas City, Mo.; Patriotic Music Publishing Co. in Chicago; and Nordyke Publishing Co. in Hollywood.

As had happened to Sir Arthur Sullivan in the World War I years, another and far greater classical composer was called on to provide the antecedent for the most familiar—and shortest— musical phase of either war. Consisting of a mere four notes, Beethoven's so-called "Fate" motif—the first two bars of his *Fifth Symphony*—was the equivalent of three dots and a dash. In Morse Code the symbols stand for the letter V, which is also recognizable as the Roman numeral for five. To the Allies "V" was shorthand for "Victory" and served as Churchill's optimistic trademark, which he popularized by raising the first two fingers of his right hand when appearing before audiences and photographers. Later in the war, Josephine Fester Royle turned the *Fifth Symphony* into a chorale by adding cheerleading words to the first movement. Her adaptation was entitled "Voices of Victory."

Spirited and uplifting as many of the major and minor World War II songs were, none was able to cushion the crushing realization that the First World War had vacated its role as the "war to end all wars." Once again young men — soon to include Americans — were engaging in battlefield homicide on foreign lands, both they and their forlorn sweethearts daring to trust in the same desperate hope voiced by one departing soldier of the World War I generation. His plaintive message was still timeless, his determination to salve the worries of his lady love with the balm of optimism as applicable to lovers in 1941 as they had been in 1917. Revived by Vera Lynn and other singers while Europe waited for the second coming of the Yanks, the old song again lifted hearts with its compassionate appeal for patience and faith in the future:

> "Smile the while you kiss me sad adieu,
> When the clouds roll by I'll come to
>   you;
> Then the skies will seem more blue,
> Down in lover's lane, my dearie.
> Wedding bells will ring so merrily,
> Ev'ry tear will be a memory;
> So wait and pray
> Each night for me,
> Till we meet again."

Part II
Published Patriotic and War Songs of World War I

The following list of American World War I patriotic and war songs is the most comprehensive compilation of its kind. It includes the titles of such songs published in the United States from August 1914 to August 1919, or eight months after the Armistice brought that war to its conclusion. Songwriters, especially the amateurs, continued to pour out patriotic tunes after November 11, 1918, to welcome American troops back home, rejoice with them in their victory, and glory in the return of peace to the world.

As mentioned in the text on World War I, Americans copyrighted almost 36,000 war-based songs during that conflict. Only 20 percent or so, including all the songs published by the major New York City publishing houses, can be verified as having been published; all of those appear on the list. The overwhelming majority of the songs were merely registered with the Copyright Office of the Library of Congress in Washington, D.C., as unpublished; these titles are not included.

Also excluded are the hundreds of World War I songs written and originally published in Great Britain, Canada, France, Belgium, Italy, and other combatant nations. The only exceptions are such songs as "Keep the Home-Fires Burning ("Till the Boys Come Home)," "Roses of Picardy," and about a dozen others that were recopyrighted in the United States during the war years and that attracted vast audiences in America as well as overseas.

Some of the patriotic and war songs registered as unpublished between 1914 and 1919 — perhaps hundreds of them — were later made available on sheet music, published privately by the writers themselves or by small, local printing presses or minor publishing firms with extremely limited distribution networks. Sales were few in such cases and the songs quickly went out of print. Unless these songs were recopyrighted as published, or included in the Library of Congress' extensive sheet music archives or card index of musical compositions, there was no publication record to enable their inclusion in the World War I song list.

The major source for compiling the list was *The Catalog of Copyright Entries* for the years 1914–1919. The lyrics of the less familiar songs were sought in the Library of Congress, the Lincoln Center Library for the Performing Arts, the New York Public Library, and the war-music collections of sheet music dealers and were read whenever available to confirm their qualification for inclusion in either the patriotic or war category. However, since sheet music copies of at least 75 percent of even the major published songs are impossible to find, it was necessary to classify most of the songs as patriotic or war-based strictly according to their titles as listed in the *CCE* volumes.

The titles of unavailable songs containing such words or phrases as "Kaiser," "Sammy," and "Fighting Yankees" were easy to identify as war songs. Those without such clear guideposts were excluded from the list. Songs referring to the tragedies suffered by parents (e. g., "When a Blue Service Star Turns to Gold") and the loneliness of sweethearts ("I'll Be Waiting Over Here 'Til It's Over, Over There") were automatically accepted as war songs. The many additional published love and loneliness songs bearing titles that fail to make specific reference to World War I were disqualified, since they may well have referred to civilian lovers temporarily separated under circumstances unassociated with the war.

An asterisk (*) before a title means that the complete lyric of the song appears in Part III of this book.

A

A.D. 1968 Hun Retrospection. L: Franklin Clark Sawhill; M: Kathryn I. White, 1918

Abie, My Soldier. L: Alfred Olenick; M: Leo Bennett, 1917

Add a Star to Your Service Flag for Each Fighter You Take Back. L: D.B. Portnoy; M: Leo Friedman, 1919

Aeroplane Song. L&M: Karl Merkau, 1917

*(After the Battle Is Over) Then You Can Come Back to Me. L: L. Wolfe Gilbert; M: Anatol Friedland, 1918

After the Battle Wild. L&M: Dave Bailey, 1919

After the Boys Return. L&M: Andrew A. Dorsey, 1918

After the Kaiser. L: O.P. McFerren; M: Ruth Repine, 1918

After the Kaiser. L: A.A. LeBlanc; M: Roy Hartzell, 1919

After the Peace Was Won. L: I. Snyder; M: Artie Bowers, 1919

After the Storm the Sun Will Shine. L: L.D. Strong; M: Artie Bowers, 1919

After the Victory (March). M: Paul Gardie, 1917

After the War. L&M: Why Oakland, 1917

After the War. L: C.S. Blackschleger; M: Mary E. Cox, 1918

After the War (March). L: J.A.L. Waddell; M: Rocco Venuto, 1918

After the War. L&M: D.J. Strong, 1919

After the War. L&M: Mrs. Emmett Eling, 1919

After the War. L: Mary S. Wiggins; M: Leo Friedman, 1919

After the War Is Done. L: N. Humphrey; M: Leo Friedman, 1918

After the War Is Over. L&M: Charles A. Trader and Eddie Elliott, 1916

*After the War Is Over. L&M: James W. Casey, 1917

After the War Is Over. L&M: L.E. Hempy, 1917

After the War Is Over. L: Frederick H. Green; M: Arthur A. Penn, 1917

After the War Is Over. L&M: Lew Porter, 1917

After the War Is Over (Waltz). L&M: Lucile D. Weigrand, 1917

After the War Is Over. L: M. Dick; M: Artie Bowers, 1919

After the War Is Over. L: Ada Conrad; M: Leo Friedman, 1919

After the War Is Over, I'm Coming Back to You. L&M: Charles T. Keating, 1918

After the War Is Over (What Will That Meeting Be Like?). L: John Kirby; M: Bernie Grossman and John Kirby, 1918

After the War Is Over, Where Will the Kaiser Go? L&M: F.C. Stoutenburg, 1918

*After the War Is Over (Will There Be Any "Home Sweet Home"). L: E. J. Pourmon and Joseph Woodruff; M: Harry Andrieu, 1917

After the War Many a Chair Will Be Vacant. L: H.D. Shaiffer; M: Clarence Kohlmann, 1918

After the War, Sweetheart. L: P. Klingelhoefer; M: Leo Friedman, 1918

After This War Is Over. L: J. Burnham; M: Edward Wunderlich, 1915

After This War Is Over. L: Mary O'Gorman Hess; M: Harry Stirling, 1915

Ah Didn't Raise Mah Boy to Be a Slacker. L&M: Al Hart, 1917

Ah'm Goin' Over de Top. L: Ruth Gardner; M: Leo Friedman, 1918

Ain't You Proud of Your Old Uncle Sam? L&M: F. Arl and H.S. Inger, 1918

The Airman. L&M: A.L. Fuqua, 1919

Alexander's Band Is Back Home Again. L: S.E. Topping; M: George Graff, Jr., 1919

Alexander's Band Is Back in Dixieland. L: Jack Yellen; M: Albert Gumble, from stage production Sinbad, 1918

All Aboard for America, the Land of the Stars and Stripes. L&M: A.J. Vitelli, 1919

*All Aboard for Home Sweet Home. L&M: Addison Burkhardt, Al Piantadosi, and Jack Glogau, 1918

All Aboard for the U.S.A. L: M.T. Jackson; M: Leo Friedman, 1919

All Aboard to Can the Kaiser. L: C.E. Little; M: "Dixie Land," 1917

All Dressed in Khaki. L: K.F. Gargan; M: Leo Friedman, 1919

*All for America! L&M: Josie Bleuler, 1917

All for Liberty. L: Cleland Butcher; M: Carrie Brooks Patche, 1918

All for My Flag and You. L: B.O. Carpenter; M: Leo Friedman, 1919

All for Norah Daly. L&M: Eliza Doyle Smith, 1918

All for the Boys Who've Gone Away. L&M: H.S. Cohen, 1918

All for the Red, White and Blue. L: S.E. Carter; M: Arthur Stanley. 1919

All for Uncle Sammy. L: Vyrta Evans; M: Roy Hartzell, 1919

All Hail, America! L&M: C.W. Laufer, 1918

All Hail, Flag of the Free! L&M: W.W. Moore, 1917

All Hail, My Land, to Thee. L&M: Thomas A.Y. Hodgson, 1918

All Hail! Rejoice! (Easter Anthem). M: Alfred Judson, 1919

All Hail the Flag. L: George M. Beckett; M: H.C. Gilmour, 1917

All Hail to Marshal Joffre. M: F.C. Wight, 1917

All Hail to Our Flag. L&M: Virginia Tryon Kent, 1917

All Hail to Our Flag So Grand. L: J.E. Codley; M: Robert H. Brennen, 1918

All Hail to Our United States. L&M: William S. Cudlipp, 1915

All Hail to the Flag. L: J.H. Hosterman; M: Stephen Miles Turner, 1917

All Hail to Thee, America. L&M: Peter P. Bilhorn, 1917

All Hail to Thee, America. L&M: Mrs. J.P. Shanks, 1918

All Hail to Thee, America. L: Eugenie Savoie; M: Leo Friedman, 1919

All Hail to Thee, Columbia (March). L&M: M.J.E. Hartman, 1918

All Hail to You, Marines! L: Richard J. Beamish; M: Victor Herbert, 1918

All Hail, U.S.A. (March). L&M: Theodore Schroeder, 1917

All of No Man's Land Is Ours. L: James Reese Europe and Noble Sissle; M: Eubie Blake, 1919

All on Account of the War. L: Edward Madden and Ballard MacDonald; M: James F. Hanley, 1916

All the Real Americans Are Doing Their Bit. L: H.E. Chase; M: Leo Friedman, 1919

All the World Loves the U.S.A. L: F.D. Brewer and V. Smigell; M: Beatrice R. Brewer, 1919

*All Together ("We're Out to Beat the Hun"). L: E. Paul Hamilton; M: M.L. Lake, 1918

All We Can Say Is God Bless You (America Is Proud of You). L: Edmond J. O'Connell and Harry C. Pyle, Jr.; M: Louis Thomas, 1917

Allegiance. L&M: Julia Smith, 1918

Allied Liberty World Song. L&M: J.M. Hardy, 1919

Allied March to Freedom. M: F. Paolo Tosti, 1915

Allied Soldier's Anthem. L: A. McC. McHenry; M: P.B. Story, 1918

Allied Victory. M: A. Amato, 1917

Allied Victory (March). M: Harry H. Zickel, 1918

Allieds Victorious (March). M: Albert Rossi, 1918

Allies. L: Hester Hexmit; M: J.B. Herbert, 1917

Allies (March). M: Chester Pizzino, 1918

The Allies and Uncle Sam. L&M: L. Dupree, 1918

The Allies' Anthem. L&M: F. Seaborne, 1918

Allies Flower Garden Ball. L&M: Willie Weston, 1918

Allies March. M: Joseph Biondi, 1918

Allies March to Berlin. L: C. Lester; M: Artie Bowers, 1919

Allies Triumphal March. M: Frederick M. Bryan, 1919

Allies United for Liberty (March). M: Paolo Signore, 1918

The Allies' Welcome to the States. L: Margaret Busby; M: Leo Friedman, 1919

Aloha, Soldier Boy. L: Sidney Carter; M: Walter Smith, 1918

Along Comes the Yankee Soldier. L: A.P. Thomas; M: Robert H. Brennen, 1917

Alsace Beside the Meuse. L: M.E. King; M: Rollin C. Ward, 1918

Alsace Lorraine (on to Paris or Berlin). L: L. Wolfe Gilbert; M: Lewis F. Muir, 1914

Always Stick to Your Uncle Sam. L: T. Sims, Jr.; M: Fred Campion, 1918

America. L: Samuel Francis Smith; M: A.B., Davenport, 1915

America. L: Samuel Francis Smith; M: Fritz Gaul, 1916

America. L: Samuel Francis Smith; M: C.F. Smith, 1916

America (March). L: Samuel Francis Smith; M: Alessandro Liberati, 1916

America. L: William Cullen Bryant; M: Carl Busch, 1916

*A-M-E-R-I-C-A. L&M: May Greene and Billy Lang, 1917

A-M-E-R-I-C-A (A Patriotic Song). L&M: Burton J. McPhee, 1917

America. M: Charles William Reiser, 1917

America. L&M: Henry Lena, 1917

America. L: Samuel Francis Smith; M: Daniel Webster, 1917

America. L: Samuel Francis Smith; M: Albrecht Pagenstecher, 1917

America. L: Samuel Francis Smith; M: C. Forman Smith, 1917

America. L&M: Elsie G. Nardin, 1918

America. L: Lily Peter; M: Leo Friedman, 1918

America. L: Samuel Francis Smith; M: D.A. Brown, 1918

America (National Anthem). L: L. Wagner; M: F. Fettinger, 1918

America. L: Louis Wagner; M: Hermann M. Hahn, 1919

America. L: J.C. Lawffer; M: Leo Friedman, 1919

America, All Hail. L: C.D. Hilton; M: D.B. Towner, 1918

America All the Time. L: H.J. Kingsley; M: Carrie North Thrall, 1916

America Always, First and Last, If You're Loyal to Uncle Sam. L&M: Lew Sully, 1917

America, America (March). L&M: Clarence E. Billings, 1915

America! America! (War Song). L: Rollin J. Wells; M: Anna W. Poole, 1917

America, America. L: Mrs. J. Sturdivant; M: Leo Friedman, 1918

America, America (Marching Hymn). L&M: Ada H. Kepley, 1918

America, America, Hurrah! L&M: G.R. Pritchett, 1919

America, America March. M: Clarence E. Billings, 1917

America, America! The Best Land on Earth. L&M: Harvey Erwin Bruce, 1918

America, America, the Land of Freedom's Right. L: Ida Merritt; M: Leo Friedman, 1919

America, America, Your Flag Has Come to Stay (March). L&M: R.W. Lavery, 1918

America and France. L: D. Stewart; M: Leo Friedman, 1919

America, Awake. L: Lila J. Davis; M: G.E. Johnson, 1918

America, Awake Ere Liberty Is Gone. L&M: Thomas A.Y. Hodgson, 1918

America Awakes. L: A.W. Woodruff; M: Caroline B. Lavoux, 1918

America! Beloved by All. L: F.H. Ackermann; M: Daniel Protheroe, 1917

America, Beloved Land (A Patriotic Anthem). L&M: J.I. Taylor, 1917

America, Blest Land of Freedom. L: Ivor C. Parry; M: T.G. Thorburn, 1918

America Born Anew. L&M: R.A. Hilton, 1918

America Calls. L&M: Annie M. Bassett, 1917

America Calls. L&M: L.I. Thompson, 1918

America Can Count on Me (Song of Allegiance). L&M: W.C. Wakefield, 1916

America, Dear America. L&M: W.V. Hyde, 1917

America Forever (March). M: Yves Arnandez, 1917

America Forever (March). L: H.A. Freeman; M: E.T. Paull, 1917

America, God's Chosen Land (A Patriotic Song). L&M: M.B. Hafer, 1918

America Goes Forth to War (March). L: Louis W. Reynolds; M: R.S. Flagler, 1918

America Exultant (March). M: Al Hayes, 1917

America First. L&M: James Brockman, 1915

America First (March). M: F. H. Losey, 1915

America First. M: John Philip Sousa, 1916

America First. L: A.E. Mottram; M: J.A. Swenson, 1916

America First. L&M: Anderson Green, 1916

America First. L: M.A. Karr; M: L.S. Moses, 1917

America First (March). L: John Menown; M: Howard Kocian, 1917

America First (A Patriotic Song). L: H.E. Winegar; M: P.B. Story, 1918

America First and Last (March). M: Adam Preston [Henry J. Sawyer], 1917

America First Is Our Battle Cry! 'Tis the Land We Love. L: J. Will Callahan; M: Eddie Gray, 1916

America, First, Last and All the Time (March). M: Edgar Krones, 1918

America First, the Land of Our Choice. L: A.H. Ben-Oliel; M: Richard W. Oliver, 1916

American Flag. L: Joseph Rodman Drake; M: R.H. Prutting, 1915

America Flag Song. L: Henry Van Dyke; M: Lawrence Camilieri, 1919

America Flag Waltz. M: J.J. Tingstad, 1917

America for All. L: G.B. Croft; M: Leo Friedman, 1919

America for Americans. L: Jessie Cannon Hurd; M: Florence Baker, 1916

America for Humanity (March). M: Charles F. Stayner, 1916

America for Me. L: E. Russell; M: Carl Heil, 1915

America for Me. L: Henry Van Dyke; M: Ella L. Smith, 1918

America for Me. L: H.L. Cheyney; M: Leo Friedman, 1919

America, For Thee. L: Mrs. A. Elgutter; M: Leo Friedman, 1918

America Forever (March). L&M: Jack Mahoney, 1914

America Forevermore. L&M: Catherine H. Skinner, 1918

America, Glorious Land of Freedom. L&M: S.S. Meyers, 1918

America Goes Forth to War. L: Louis W. Reynolds; M: R. S. Flagler, 1917

America, Here's My Bond. L: G. Davis; M: Leo Friedman, 1918

America, Here's My Boy. L: Andrew B. Sterling; M: Arthur Lange, 1917

America, Here's My Uniform, Give Me Back My Job. L&M: Hope Seiberlick, 1919

America, Here's to You. L: M.B. Mount; M: Roy Hartzell, 1919

America, He's for You. L&M: Andrew B. Sterling, 1918

America, Home Sweet Home. L&M: Carrie M. Brooks, 1917

*America, I Love You. L: Edgar Leslie; M: Archie Gottler, 1915

America, I Love You and I Hear You Calling Me. L: Susie Nelson Fergerson; M: Courtney Allemong, 1917

America, I Love You and I'm Here to Prove the Same to You. L: H.E. Menne; M: M. Alice Menne, 1918

America, I'm with You. L: O.D. Castro; M: Robert Van Sickle, 1918

America in No Man's Land. L: Mrs. A.W. Hill; M: Leo Friedman, 1919

America in War. L&M: J.B. McPhail, 1918

America, Ireland Loves You. L&M: E.H. Kelly, 1917

America Is Calling. L: C.M. Ray; M: "A.B.M.," 1918

America Is Calling Me. L&M: Roscoe S. Jones, 1917

America Is Calling You. L&M: May Mills Fuller, 1917

America Is Calling You. L: J.J. Cunningham; M: Roy Hartzell, 1919

America Is Proud of You, Boys. L: E. Moran; M: Antonio Galvan, 1918

America Is Ready. L: J.B. Cassidy; M: N. DeRubertis, 1917

America Is Victorious. L: John Chirgwin; M: Leo Friedman, 1919

America, It's Up to You. L&M: Charles A. Ford, 1917

America, It's Up to You. L: Horace Haws; M: Alevia R. Chins, 1917

America, Land of My Adoption. L&M: Margaret Burns, 1917

America, Lead the Way (A Patriotic Song). L&M: A.A. Dart, 1917

America Leads the World. L: C. Weber; M: W.H. Brown, 1919

America Loyalty March. M: Ernest Hand, 1917

America, Make the World Safe for Democracy. L: Rudolph DeVivo; M: Sol P. Levy, 1918

America March of Peace. M: Platon Brounoff, 1916

*A-M-E-R-I-C-A (Means "I Love You, My Yankee Land"). L&M: Jack Frost, 1917

America Must Win. L: C.A. Mulliner; M: J.C. Halls, 1918

America, My America. L&M: George Thornton Edwards, 1914

America, My America. L: Ray B. Powers; M: Edith Powers, 1917

America, My America. L&M: Mary C. Brunning, 1919

America, My Bride. L&M: Laura Buchanan, 1917

America, My Country (March). M: J. Owen Long, 1916

America, My Country. L&M: George Thornton Edwards, 1916

America, My Country (New National Anthem). L: Jens K. Grondahl; M: E.F. Maetzold, 1917

America, My Country. L: Lena S. Hesselberg; M: Edouard Hesselberg, 1917

America, My Country. L: O.J. Johns; M: Marvin Radnor, 1918

America, My Country Dear. L&M: W.W. Barker, 1918

America, My Country Great and Free. L&M: George Warren Hayford, 1917

America (My Country, 'Tis of Thee). L: Samuel Francis Smith; M: Mary Ely Phelps, 1916

America (My Country, 'Tis of Thee). L: Samuel Francis Smith; M: A.A. Springmeyer, 1917

America (My Country, 'Tis of Thee). L: Samuel Francis Smith; M: A.D. Liefeld, 1917

America (My Country, 'Tis of Thee). L: Samuel Francis Smith; M: A.L. Faust, 1917

America (My Country, 'Tis of Thee). L: Samuel Francis Smith; M: S.S. Townsend, 1917

America, My Country, 'Tis of Thee (New Tune). L: Samuel Francis Smith; M: F.E. Cook, 1918

America, My Home. L&M: A.R. Wilcox, 1918

America, My Home. L&M: H.R. Detweiler, 1919

America, My Home So Fair. L&M: A.H.
Aarons, 1918

America, My Homeland. L&M: Laura
Walker Colgrove, 1917

America, My Homeland (Song of the States).
L&M: H.C. Eldridge, 1917

America! My Homeland. L: Henry Treleaven;
M: Richard Blaine, 1918

America, My Homeland. L: Ruth E. DeBoer;
M: Leo Friedman, 1919

America, My Land. L: May Hewes Dodge;
M: John Wilson Dodge, 1918

America, My Native Land. L: J. Lyddane;
M: S.B. Jackson, 1918

America, My Sweet Land. L&M: Jacob S.
Rosenberg, 1918

America Needs You. L: Clara Kennedy; M:
P.B. Story, 1917

*America Needs You Like a Mother (Would
You Turn Your Mother Down?). L: Grant
Clarke; M: Jean Schwartz, 1917

America, Now's the Time. L: Carrie A.
Clione; M: George Graff, Jr., 1919

America, O Land of Love. L&M: Robert A.
Rogers, 1919

America, Oh! America (National Anthem).
L: Carter S. Cole; M: Alexander Mac-
Fayden, 1916

America, Oh Noble Name. L: W.W. Thum;
M: Patrick O'Sullivan, 1917

America, On America (the Land of Love and
Song). L&M: S.J. Mooney, 1918

America, Our Blessed Land. L: Fred Freder-
ickson; M: Leo Friedman, 1918

America, Our Country (Battle Hymn). L&M:
Louis Oesterle, 1919

America, Our Fatherland. L&M: A. Lynn
Colman, 1914

America Our Land Shall Be (A Patriotic
Song). L: George Stewart; M: E.S. Lorenz,
1918

America, Our Mother Land. L&M: Grace
Wilbur Conant, 1919

America, Our Pride. L&M: Louis Oesterle,
1917

America, Our Wondrous Home. L&M: F.
Crane and G. Klein, 1919

America Over All (March). M: C.H. Jonas,
1915

America, Peace Makes Thy Fame. L: Samuel
Francis Smith; M: Henry Carey, 1915

America, Prepare. L: Nathan Caleb House;
M: Elizabeth deS. Day, 1916

America, Prepare. L: Elizabeth Herbert
Childs; M: Ribé Danmark, 1916

America Prepared (March). M: Henry C.
Theis, 1916

America Saved the Day. L&M: Harry L.
Brown, 1918

America Saved the Day. L&M: W.R.
McCracken, 1919

America, So Fair and Free. L&M: E.H.
Purcell, 1915

America, Star of the West. L&M: Theresa
L.T. Hoppe, 1914

America Still Stands for Liberty. L&M: J.E.
Kirkham, 1918

America the Beautiful (March). M: Will C.
Macfarlane, 1918

America, the Land We Love. L&M: F.B.
Sheehan, 1916

America, the Name We Love. L: Blanche
White; M: Leo Friedman, 1919

America, the Paradise for Me. L: Isabella
Bisel; M: Andrew J. Schorr, 1918

America, the Sweet Land of Liberty. L:
John Pankey; M: Leo Friedman, 1918

America, the World Is Proud of You. L&M:
Anita Stewart, 1918

America, the World Loves You. L&M: G.A.
Delaney, 1919

America, They Are Both for You. L: Samuel
Joseph Perrault; M: Armand John Piron,
1917

America, Thou Land of Hope. L&M: H.
Wickman, 1919

America, Thou Victorious One. L&M: C.
Hulse-Petrilla, 1919

America, To Thee (A Patriotic Hymn).
L&M: Grace F. Bullock, 1917

America Today (March). M: A.W. Swallen,
1916

*America Today. L: Herbert Moore; M:
W.R. Williams, 1917

America Triumphant. L: John Hayes
Holmes; M: Clifford Demarest, 1915

America United. L&M: D.A. Sullivan, 1917

America, United We Stand. L: Alice Parker
Hall; M: Carl Muehling, 1918

America Victorious. L&M: Helen A. Jackson, 1918

America Victorious (March). M: Bertha G.
Storer, 1918

America Victorious. L&M: Sophia L. Mc-
Millan, 1919

America Victorious, America Forever. L&M:
C.B.Y. Tompkins, 1918

America, We Are Ready (A Patriotic Song).
L&M: W.F. Herman, 1917

America, We Come. L&M: C. Durham, 1917

America, We Come Home to Thee. L&M: Peter Furtyo, 1919

America, We Love Her. L: Mabel Eggum; M: Leo Friedman, 1918

America, We Love You. L: Eugene Wade; M: Leo Friedman, 1918

America, We Love You First. L&M: A.P. Ross, 1918

America, We Love You Truly. L: B. Motsch; M: Eugene Platzmann, 1918

America, We Need You. L: O. Harter; M: A.L. Gardey, 1918

America, We Need You Most of All. L: Arthur A. Foley; M: E.W. Madigan, 1917

America, We Owe It to You. L&M: J.D. Damascus, 1919

America, We Protect You Day and Night. L: Rolland Urban; M: Leo Friedman, 1918

America, We Will Pray for Thee. L&M: Otto Palm, Jr., 1918

America, We'll Die for You. L: Mabel B. Evans; M: Leo Friedman, 1919

America, We'll Never Say Die. L&M: F.S. Balliett, 1918

America, We'll Stand by You. L&M: Daisy Crookham, 1918

America, We're Coming Back. L: A.V. Stark; M: Leo Friedman, 1919

*America, We're Proud of You. L&M: Eva C. Hardy, 1919

America, We're Proud to Fight for You. L&M: William DeLuca, 1918

America Will Fight for Freedom and for Right. L: Peter DeLinde; M: Mary Hotchkiss-Love and E. Horneman, 1918

America Will Lead to Victory. L: E.E. Furman; M: Mrs. J.H. Valentine, 1917

A-M-E-R-I-C-A Will Surely Stop Old Kaiser Bill (Then All Hoo-Ra!). L: C. Rowmand; M: A.S. Palmer, 1918

America Woke Up at Last. L&M: Harry Heine, 1917

America, You Are a Nation All Adore. L&M: B.L. Glickman, 1919

America, You're My Darling. L&M: E.J. Hennessy, 1918

America'll Win the War. L&M: Mary Scott Bywater, 1918

American Anthem. L&M: Reba Ray, 1919

American Army Hymn. L: Allen E. Cross; M: Mark Andrews, 1919

American Army Song. L: L.A.R. Clark; M: T.Y. Cannon, 1917

American Battle Cry (A Liberty Slogan for 1917) L&M: F.J. O'Neill, 1917

American Battle Hymn. L: C. Sullivan; M: Leo Friedman, 1919

*American Beauty. L: Al Bryan and Edgar Leslie; M: M.K. Jerome, 1918

American Beauty, Do Your Duty to the Land of the Fleur de Lis. L: Harold L. Cool; M: Arthur J. Daly, 1917

American Bells (March). M: Ammon E. Cramer, 1918

American Born (March). M: Eugene R. Kenney, 1914

*The American Boy for Me. L&M: Bessie Westphal, 1916

American Boys. L&M: Frances Kubik, 1919

American Boys in France (March). L&M: Jessie Wilde Jocelyn, 1918

The American Boys Whipped Germany. L: Peter Call; M: Artie Bowers, 1919

American Bugle Call. L&M: Julius Schmidt, 1917

The American Colors (March). M: Frank A. Panella, 1916

American Consecration Hymn. L: Percy Mackaye; M: Francis MacMillen, 1918

American Crusaders. L&M: Frances Belohlavek, 1918

American Crusaders (March). M: Will Wood, 1918

American Eagle. L: O.M. Lund; M: H.G. Gerrish and C.E. Berggren, 1918

American Eagle. L: W.H. Gordon; M: Mildred Crawford, 1918

American Eagle and Airplane One-Step. L&M: O.D. Hopkins, 1918

American Flag. L: Joseph Rodman Drake; M: Frederick W. Wodell, 1914

American Flag. L: Joseph Rodman Drake; M: Heinrich Jacobsen, 1915

American Flag. L: D.E. Parks; M: C.E. Coleman, 1916

American Flag. L&M: Malcolm Baggett, 1918

American Flag. L: Joseph Rodman Drake; M: J.H. Swanger, 1918

American Flag. L&M: T.F. Gattle, 1919

American Flag. L: Josephine Hayes; M: Leo Friedman, 1919

American Flag Song. L: Henry Van Dyke; M: Lawrence Camilieri, 1919

American Flag Waltz. M: J.J. Tingstad, 1917

American Hearts (March). M: Charles K. Harris, 1916

American Honor (March). M: H.J. Crosby, 1919

American Hymn (Speed Our Republic). L&M: Matthias Keller, 1917

American Hymn. L&M: Mrs. G.R. Brown, 1918

American Hymn (Inspire, O God, Our President). L: Huhe Malcolm McCormick; M: Giacomo Quintano, 1918

American Ideals (March). M: Wisden J. Potts, 1917

American Independence (March). M: Charles C. Sweeney, 1915

An American Irishman's Wish. L&M: Bob Simmons, 1917

American Jubilee (Patriotic March). M: Edward B. Claypoole, 1916

American Loyalty (March). L&M: Bessie Walker-Knott, 1918

American Loyalty March. M: Ernest Hand, 1916

American Lullaby. L: Ada Maynaden; M: Leo Friedman, 1918

American Marines (March). M: Yves Arnandez, 1917

American National Anthem. L: "A.M.D.G."; M: W.J. Grunebaun, 1916

American National Hymn. M: Alfred F. Denghausen, 1916

American National Hymn. L: Samuel Francis Smith; M: G.L. Weitz, 1917

American National Waltz. M: J.M. Schaeffer, 1916

American Patriot (March). M: J. Frank Frysinger, 1916

The American Patriotic Spirit (March). M: O.J. Tharp, 1918

American Red Cross March. M: Louis Panella, 1919

American Red Cross Nurse. L&M: Vincent A. Valentini, 1918

American Sailor. L&M: A.S. Josselyn, 1918

American Soldier. L&M: M.A. Jackson, 1919

American Soldier. L: F.O. Ruess; M: Arthur Stanley, 1919

American Soldier (March). L&M: Byron Verge, 1919

American Soldier in France. L: E. Clinton; M: "Shepherd Boy," 1917

American Soldiers' War Song. L&M: Robert Uhlmann, 1918

American Stars in the Blue. L&M: John Rommel, 1916

American Triumphal March. M: Burnes E. Head, 1917

American Victory March. M: Charles A. Ware, 1915

Americana's Boys. L: F. Huber; M: E.H.F. Weis, 1917

Americanization March (March of Peace and Prosperity). M: A.H. Huesgen, 1917

Americans Abroad (A Patriotic Song). L: Emery Anderson; M: Martin Greenwald, 1917

Americans All. L&M: L. C.M.C. Cheves, 1918

Americans First. L&M: Kate Ayres Robert, 1917

Americans, Get in This Fight! L: J. Cohen; M: Roy Hartzell, 1918

Americans in France. L&M: Jacob S. Rosenberg, 1919

Americans on the Marne. L: Florence Good Stauffer; M: Leo Friedman, 1919

Americans One and All. L: Edith Crosby Wilcox; M: Leo Friedman, 1918

America's America. L: Samuel Francis Smith; M: William J. Faulkner, 1917

America's Answer. L: Samuel Francis Smith; M: William J. Faulkner, 1917

America's Answer. L: Raymond B. Egan; M: Richard A. Whiting, from stage production *Toot Sweet*, 1919

America's Answer. M: Dora R. Croft, 1919

America's Army. L: M. Messick; M: Leo Friedman, 1919

America's Awakening. L&M: Fred J. Eddy, 1916

America's Battle Cry. L: N. Frances; M: P.B. Story, 1918

America's Call. L&M: Ella Agnes McDonough, 1917

America's Call. L: A. Ceylia; M: Leo Friedman, 1918

America's Call to Arms. L&M: Katherine Daly, 1917

America's Crusaders (March). L&M: Charles Fonteyn Manney, 1918

America's Dashing Yankee Boys. L&M: P.T. Hickman, 1919

America's Daughter (A Red, White and Blue Girl). L&M: C.L. Cobb, 1918

America's Day. L&M: Martin Joseph Mahony, 1917

America's Destiny (March). M: G.E. Holmes, 1916

America's Final Stand. L: O.A. Haas; M: Leo Friedman, 1918

America's Final Word. L: C.J.W. Mulvey; M: A.M. Lupe, 1918

America's Flag Song (The Flag That Enlightens the World). L&M: William J. Faulkner, 1916

America's Greatest Victory. L: E. Boruff; M:
Leo Friedman, 1919

America's in Line. L&M: Joseph J. Miller,
1917

America's Leader, Woodrow Wilson. L:
L.A. Keenan; M: Rubey Cowan, 1916

America's Love Song (to Her Boys). L&M:
Maude M. Price, 1918

America's Marching Song. L: M.A. Maxon;
M: C.M. Maxon, 1917

America's Marseillaise (A Patriotic Song).
M: James Chadwick, 1918

America's Message (A Universal Anthem). L:
Harvey Worthington Loomis; M: A.E.
Johnstone, 1917

America's Prayer (A Hymn). L&M: Mark I.
Knapp, 1917

America's Prayer. L: Josephine Maurine; M:
Leo Friedman, 1919

America's Proud of You (March). L&M:
A.J. Hiller, 1917

America's Rally Song. L: Minnie Coleman
Martin; M: Kate Gilmore Black, 1917

America's Red, White and Blue. L: A.B.
Williams; M: T.L. Wittrock, 1917

America's Slogan. L&M: Clara L. Baker, 1917

America's Slogan (Fall In, Fall In, and Give
Them All We've Got). L: W.H. Bright; M:
C.K. Denlinger, 1918

America's Sons Stand Together (March). L:
Jack Gartland; M: J.S. Cascio, 1916

America's the Word for You and Me. L&M:
J.J. Tanner, Jr., 1918

America's Vow. L: Mrs. J. Kavanaugh; M:
Artie Bowers, 1919

America's Winning the Day. L: M. Norton;
M: Leo Friedman, 1919

Among the Other Flags. L: E.B. Zanen; M:
Robert H. Brennen, 1918

Anchor and Star March. M: John Philip
Sousa, 1918

*Anchors Aweigh. L: Capt. Alfred H.
Miles/ George D. Lottman; M: Charles A.
Zimmerman, 1907

*And He'd Say "Oo-La-La! Wee-Wee!"
L&M: George Jessel and Harry Ruby, 1919

*And Then She'd Knit, Knit, Knit. L: Eddie
Moran; M: Harry Von Tilzer, 1917

*Angel of No Man's Land. L: H. MacDon-
ald Barr; M: Grant Colfax Tullar, 1918

Angels, Guard the House Where Hangs a
Golden Star. L: F.E. Loner; M: Ernest
Toy, 1918

Angels of the Cross of Red (Waltz). M: John
D. McDonald, 1918

Another Gallant Soldier. L&M: Maud Bell,
1919

*Answer Mr. Wilson's Call. L&M: Billy
Gould, 1917

Answer the Call to the Colors. L&M: Marie
Dudley, 1919

Answer to Just a Baby's Prayer at Twilight
(for Her Daddy's Over There). L: Sam M.
Lewis and Joe Young; M: M.K. Jerome,
1918

Answer to the Call. L: W.D. Hearon; M:
Artie Bowers, 1919

Answer Uncle Sammy's Call. L: Clifford
Martin Eddy, Jr.; M: Kay S. Dover, 1917

Answer Your Country's Call! L: Helen Farr
Tolman; M: Finch Elbert Lewis, 1917

Answering Liberty's Call (March). M: C.
Corvers, 1917

Anthem of Liberty. L&M: R. Hekeler, 1918

Anthem of the Free. L: Matthew P. Brady;
M: Walter Keller, 1916

*Any Old Place the Gang Goes (I'll Be
There). L&M: William J. McKenna, 1918

Anything! Everything! For Our Brave Boys!
L: Alfred Olenick; M: Walter C. Simon,
1918

Appeal to Loyalty. L: L.L. Calvert; M: Leo
Friedman, 1919

Arc of Peace. L&M: F.J. Lowe, 1915

Are You Going to Shoot Some Other Girlie's
Daddy? L: George Graff, Jr.; M: Alfred
Solman, 1915

Are You Helping the Boys Over There?
L&M: Emma M. Sheets, 1919

*Are You Lending a Hand to Yankeeland?
L: J. Will Callahan; M: Blanche M. Tice,
1918

Are You Prepared for the Summer? L: Bert
Kalmar and Edgar Leslie; M: Jean
Schwartz, 1916

Are You Ready to Fight for Uncle Sam? L:
H.W. Newport; M: Luther A. Clark, 1918

Are You Ready to Go to War? L&M: J.H.
Schaffer, 1916

Are You Ready to Stand Behind the Gun?
(March). L: Edith Waite Colson; M: N.R.
Smith, 1917

*Are You the O'Reilly? ("Blime Me,
O'Reilly—You Are Lookin' Well"). L&M:
Pat Rooney (original version), 1890; P.
Emmett (new version), 1915

Aren't You Glad You're Living in the
U.S.A.? L: Glavenie M. Levett; M:
William Busé, 1915

Arise, America. L&M: George Warren Hayford, 1917

Arise, Arise, America. L: Unknown; M: Bernardo Jensen, 1917

Arise! Arise! To Arms! L: Lena Kellogg; M: Grover Tilden, 1919

Arise, Come Forth, Crusaders. L&M: Frederick Adam Babcock, 1918

Armed for the Battle, Americans Are We. L: P.S. Pirtle; M: Leo Friedman, 1919

Army and Navy March, L&M: Ernest Marsh, 1919

Army Mule. L&M: D.J. LaRocca, Larry Shields, and Henry Ragas, 1918

Army of Democracy. L&M: F.A.A. Robertson, 1918

The Army's Full of Irish. L: Bert Hanlon; M: Walter Donaldson, 1917

'Arrah, Me Kaiser, I'm a-Comin'. L&M: Grace F. Sullivan, 1917

*As Her Soldier Boy Marched By. L&M: Lena Leonard Fisher, 1917

As I Yearn for the Dawn of Peace. L: M. Macon; M: Leo Friedman, 1919

As She Changed That Star of Blue to One of Gold. L: T.H. Waldron; M: Leo Friedman, 1919

As We Carry the Stars and Stripes Through Old Berlin. L&M: J.T. Loveland, 1918.

As We Go Marching Through Germany. L&M: Edith DeLorne, 1918

Asleep in France. L&M: Stephen Shannon, 1919

At Rest Beneath the Red, White and Blue. L: J.A. Scheutz; M: Leo Friedman, 1919

At That Alabama Regimental Ball. L&M: Dave Harris, 1917

At the Call of the Bugle (A Patriotic Song). L&M: J.B. McPhail, 1918

At the Dawn of Peace. L&M: L.L. Thollehaug, 1918

At the Dixie Military Ball. L: Ballard MacDonald; M: Harry Carroll, 1918

At the "Funny Page" Ball. L&M: Lloyd Garrett, 1918

At the League of Nations' Ball. L&M: Fred Whitehouse, Murry Mencher, and Jack Bennett, 1919

At the Soldiers' Camp (March). M: Carl Wilhelm Kern, 1919

At the Yankee Military Ball. M: Harry Jentes, 1918

At Them, Uncle Sam! L: S. and L. Tucker; M: Will Pease, 1917

A'top of the World, Our Flag. L&M: John D. McDonald, 1918

Atta Boy, Sammy, Go Get That William Goat! L&M: A.S. Rhodes, 1918

Au Revoir. L: Will D. Cobb; M: Gus Edwards, 1918

Au Revoir, but Not Goodbye (Soldier Boy). L: Lew Brown; M: Albert Von Tilzer, 1917

Au Revoir France, Hello Broadway. L: M.V. Goar; M: Leo Friedman, 1919

Au Revoir, Soldier Boy. L: Louis E. Holcomb; M: Ernest B. Clifton, 1918

Aw, Sammy! L: H. Sanborn; M: Geoffrey O'Hara, 1918

Awake, America! L&M: J.F. Gaithness, 1917

Awake, America! L&M: Cornelia E. Palmer, 1917

Awake, America! L: E.S. Peets; M: Wilson G. Smith, 1918

Awaken Now, Ye Patriot Nation! L: A.W. Neeli; M: Leo Friedman, 1918

The Awakening of the Lion (March). M: "Brepsant," 1918

Away from Home in a Foreign Land. L&M: Andrew J. Schorr, 1917

Away with the Kaiser. L&M: Emma M. Rummel, 1919

B

Babes of France (March). L&M: Luella Osborne, 1917

Baby Jim. L&M: John B. Archer, from stage production *Red Letter*, 1918

Baby's Prayer for Papa. L: Madge Keller; M: Leo Friedman, 1919

Baby's Prayer Will Soon Be Answered. L&M: Gus Van, Joe Schenck, and Billy Baskette, 1919

Back from France. L&M: Al Segal, 1918

Back from Over There. L: J. Treis; M: John P. Selas, 1918

Back from the Trenches. L: Gifford Wood; M: Frank Pace, 1917

Back Home Again. L: Bill Dee; M: R.W. Dutton, 1919

*Back Home I'll Come. L&M: Edmund M. Capen, 1917

Back Home I'll Go to Mother. L: M.A. Beales; M: Leo Friedman, 1918

Back Home in the U.S.A. L&M: Mildred Toombs, 1919

Back in Dear Old U.S.A. L: Mrs. W.H. States; M: Roy Hartzell, 1919

Back in the U.S.A. L: B.F. Inman; M: Eugene E. Noel, 1917

Back the Man Behind the Gun. L&M: Herman Wasserman, 1918

Back to Mother and Home. L: Edna Hubert; M: Leo Friedman, 1919

Back to Mother and Home Sweet Home. L&M: "Biese and Klickmann," 1918

Back to the Old Folks and the U.S.A. L: C.E.L.L. Rupp; M: George Graff, Jr., 1919

Back to the U.S.A. L&M: Robert G. Kneedler, 1918

Back Up Our Boys Over There. L&M: E.G. Allen, 1918

Backed by the Red, White and Blue. L&M: A.A. Mills, 1917

Banner of Democracy (March). M: Al Hayes, 1917

Banner of Liberty. L: W. O'Connor; M: Artie Bowers, 1919

Banner of Mercy. L&M: E.M. Sheridan, 1917

Banner of the Free. L&M: M.E. Hogan, 1919

The Banner's Wave (March). M: Frederick A. Williams, 1918

Batter Up. L: Harry Tighe; M: Harry Von Tilzer, 1918

Battle Call. L&M: W.W. McKee, 1918

*Battle-Call of Alliance. L: Percy Mackaye; M: Reginald DeKoven, 1917

Battle Cry. L: Mrs. C.F. Golay; M: Leo Friedman, 1918

Battle Cry. L: R.A. Dean; M: Leo Friedman, 1919

Battle Cry. L: J. Wilde; M: Leo Friedman, 1919

Battle Cry for Liberty and Arms. M: O.S. Grinnell, 1918

The Battle Cry Is Ringing. L: Etta Babler; M: Leo Friedman, 1919

Battle Cry of America. L: L.W. Baldridge; M: Leo Friedman, 1919

Battle Cry of Peace. M: J. Tim Brymn, 1915

Battle Cry of Peace. L: Henry T. Bunce; M: William Donaldson, 1916

Battle Cry of the Republic in 1918. L: E.B. Ashcraft; M: Roy Hartzell, 1919

Battle Cry of the U.S.A. (A Patriotic Song). L: Bob Spender; M: Lou Thompson, 1917

Battle Cry of the U.S.A. L: J.J. Walsh; M: Leo Friedman, 1919

Battle Cry (On to Victory). L&M: Bertha Reade Fike, 1918

Battle Field. L: Selma Payne; M: Leo Friedman, 1918

Battle Flags of Liberty and Freedom. L&M: A.F. Shaw, 1918

Battle for Democracy. M: Frank Fuhrer, 1918

Battle Hymn. L&M: F. Burnell, 1918

Battle Hymn of Democracy. L&M: H.B. Seely, 1917

Battle Hymn of Democracy. L&M: E.M. Cox, 1919

Battle Hymn of Freedom. L: J.M. Young; M: Constance G. Young, 1918

Battle Hymn of Freedom. L&M: J.E. Douglass, 1918

Battle Hymn of Liberty. L&M: J.J. Ridgway, 1918

Battle Hymn of the Liberty Army of the U.S.A. L: G. Enggaard; M: John Hartmann, 1918

Battle in the Air. M: Harold Spencer [Henry S. Sawyer, Jr.], 1917

Battle in the Sky. M: J. Luxton, 1915

Battle Line of Liberty (March). L&M: Louis S. Florence, 1918

Battle March. L&M: Annie A. Ferree, 1917

Battle March of Liberty. L&M: Theodore Henckels, 1918

Battle of Argonne (March). M: V. Huber, 1919

Battle of Liberty. M: Charles Brunover, 1918

Battle of the Marne. L&M: J. Luxton, 1916

Battle of Ypres. M: Gaston Borch, 1918

Battle on the Marne. M: Gaston Borch, 1918

Battle Prayer. L: William Borden Gilbert; M: C.B. Lufburrow, 1918

Battle Song of America, 1917. L: L.B. Couch; M: "Maryland, My Maryland," 1917

Battle Song of Peace. L: Charlotte Porter; M: Helen A. Clarke, 1916

Battlefield. L: L. Millhouse; M: Mabel Millhouse, 1918

Battlefields of France. L&M: P.J. O'Neill, 1918

Bayonet Song. L: Horatio G. Winslow; M: Robert P. Boyd, 1918

Be a Grand Soldier Man for Uncle Sam. L: L.N. Dexter; M: Leo Friedman, 1918

Be a True American. L: J. Will Callahan; M: Frank H. Grey, 1917

Be a War Daddy. L&M: Al Piantadosi, 1917

Be Brave and True (A Patriotic War Song). L: H.E. Spinner; M: Frank W. Hall, 1919

Be Brave, My Boy, Be Brave. L&M: W.A. Freese, 1918

Be Prepared. L&M: Belle Schrag, 1916

Be Prepared, Our Nation's Emblem (New National Song). L&M: W.M. Wood, 1916

Be Proud, Mother Dear, I'm a Volunteer. L: J.J. Wingrave; M: William J. Herbst, 1918

Be Sure to Get the Kaiser, Too. L: Joe Fried and Arthur C. Wilson; M: Arthur C. Wilson, 1918

Beast of Berlin (We're Going to Get Him).
L&M: John Clayton Calhoun, 1918

Beautiful America (National Song). L&M:
M.E. Streeter, 1917

Beautiful Liberty Flag. L&M: J.I. Horton,
1917

Because We Did Our Bit. L: T.K. Diehl; M:
Leo Friedman, 1919

Because You Love Your Flag, Your Girl and
Liberty. L&M: Jack Salden, 1917

*Because You're Here. L: Harold Robe; M:
Gitz Rice, 1919

Before the Boys Leave Home. L: Frank L.
Stanton; M: Flavil Hall, 1917

Beginning of the End (Sammie's Marching
Song). L&M: G. Newton Negus, 1918

Behold Us, Kaiser Wilhelm, We Arise to
Wipe the Sting. L&M: Harold J.W. Williams, 1919

Belgium and Lorraine. L: E.F. DuPree; M:
Leo Friedman, 1919

Belgium, Brave Be. L&M: W.I. Chambers,
1918

*Belgium, Dry Your Tears. L: Arthur Freed;
M: Al Piantadosi, 1918

Belgium Forever. L: Yvonne Townsend; M:
Natalie Townsend, 1914

Bell of Freedom. M: Karl Lenox, 1915

Belle Story's Liberty Waltz Song. L: Darl
MacBoyle; M: J.M. Rumshisky, from
stage production *Everything*, 1918

Bells and Guns of Freedom. L: G.B. Whitney; M: I.E. Jones, 1918

Beloved America, Great Land of Liberty
(Thou Art My Home). L&M: Bertha M.B.
Taylor, 1918

Beloved Land (A Patriotic Hymn). L: Elizabeth Calvert; M: R.S. Yeomans, 1915

Beneath the Battlefields of France a Boy Lies
Sleeping. L&M: Nellie Dean, 1918

Bereaved Mother. L: Lovina Warren; M:
Leo Friedman, 1919

Berlin Bound. L&M: James Kendis, James
Brockman, and Nat Vincent, 1918

Berlin Bound. L&M: R.L. Peak, 1919

Berlin or Bust. L: Will Addison; M: Charlie
Thompson, 1917

Berlin or Bust (March). L: Llewella Pierce
Churchill; M: E.R.R. Ort, 1918

*Betty's Basting Belly Bands for Belgians. L:
Charles Roy Cox; M: Dick Lerch, 1915

Beware, Kaiser Bill, Beware! L&M: W.L.
Walton, 1918

Beyond the River Rhine. L: M.S. Sweeney;
M: Felix West, 1917

Big Chief Kill-a-Hun. L: Al Bryan and Edgar
Leslie; M: Maurice Abrahams, 1918

*The Biggest Thing in a Soldier's Life (Is the
Letter That Comes from Home). L:
Robert F. Roden; M: Edward G. Nelson,
1918

*Billy Boy. L: Lester A. Walton; M: Luckey
Roberts, 1917

Billy Boy, the Late Kaiser. L&M: E.G.
Clark, 1919

*Bing! Bang! Bing 'Em on the Rhine! L&M:
Jack Mahoney and Allan J. Flynn, 1918

Birth of a Nation. L: Thomas S. Allen; M:
Joseph M. Daly, 1915

Birthplace of Sweet Liberty. L: Bertie A.
Ballal; M: J.F. Zimmermann, 1919

The Black Boys Are Coming, Mr. Kaiser. L:
C.H. Parker, Jr.; M: Samuel H. Speck,
1918

Black Jack (March). M: Fred K. Huffer, 1918

The Blessing of Peace. M: E.S. Hosmer, 1919

Blest Home of Peace. L&M: James V. Reid,
1916

*Blighty (The Soldier's "Home Sweet
Home"). L: R.E. Weston; M: Bert Lee,
1916

Blighty Bound. L: Raymond B. Egan; M:
Richard A. Whiting, from stage production *Toot Sweet*, 1919

The Blue and the Gold. L: J.R. Hawkins;
M: Leo Friedman, 1919

The Blue and the Gray. L: L.P. Burke; M:
Joseph T. Murphy, 1918

Blue Devils of France. L&M: Irving Berlin,
from stage production Ziegfeld Follies of
1918, 1918

The Blue Star Turned to Silver, Then to
Gold. L: M.H. Abell; M: James G. Ellis,
1918

A Blue Star Turns to Gold. L&M: F.A.
Murphy, 1918

Blue Star, You Have Turned to Gold. L:
M.G. Vaughn; M: Leo Friedman, 1919

Blue Stars Turned to Gold. L: M.G. Darby;
M: K.D. Stewart, 1919

Blue—White—Red (March). M: St. Servan-
Marie, 1917

The Boast of Germany. L: Langley Lowe;
M: Leo Friedman, 1919

Bobby, the Bomber. L: Charles R. McCarron; M: Carey Morgan, 1918

The Boche Called the Kilties the Ladies from
Hell. L&M: Rose Pringle, 1918

Bonds of Liberty. L: Mrs. C.K. Banfield; M:
Leo Friedman, 1918

Bonnie Land of Freedom. L&M: E.D. Moyer, 1917

Boom-a-Laddie-Boom! (A Juvenile Patriotic March Song). L&M: John S. Ruhlman, 1917

Boom! Bang! Bing! Our Boys Are Now on Their Way to Berlin. L&M: A.M. Thatcher, 1918

Boots, Boots, Boots. L: Blanche Merrill; M: Jean Schwartz, 1918

Bound for Berlin. L&M: Billy Burns, 1917

Bound to Win. L&M: H.R. Doorly, 1918

Bow Down to Uncle Sam. L&M: Lester J. Wilson, 1917

Boy From No Man's Land. L&M: George J. Schratz, 1919

The Boy I Sent Over There. L: E.E. Rodemacher; M: P.M. Brown, 1918

Boy in Blue. L: J. Smith; M: Leo Friedman, 1918

Boy in Khaki. L: C.M. Scott; M: Leo Friedman, 1918

Boy of Mine (March). L: William Creager; M: James A.N. Caruso, 1917

*Boy of Mine. L: Brenta F. Wallace; M: Mercy P. Graham, 1918

The Boy Over There. L: Myrtle Classen; M: Leo Friedman, 1918

The Boy Scout's Letter to His Soldier Brother. L: J.M. Clayton; M: Paul C. Pratt, 1918

The Boy That Is Somewhere in France. L&M: George W. Robinson, 1918

The Boy That Went. L: K.P. Crowninshield; M: George Lowell Tracy, 1917

The Boys and Flag. L&M: R.F. Edwards, 1918

The Boys Are Back. L: W.A. Vollmeke; M: Leo Friedman, 1919

The Boys Are Coming Home. L&M: Edwin L. Taylor, 1919

The Boys Are Coming Home Again. L: Fannie Fahm; M: Artie Bowers, 1919

The Boys Are Marching On. L: Mrs. M.H. Davis; M: Artie Bowers, 1919

The Boys Are Now Returning. L&M: E.C. Nelson, 1919

Boys from the U.S.A. L&M: Anna Lemke, 1918

Boys from the U.S.A. L: L.W. Mendum; M: Leo Friedman, 1919

Boys from Yankee Land. L&M: H.R. Franks, 1917

Boys, Get Ready! (March). L&M: Reginald DeKoven, 1918

Boys, Go Defend! (March). L&M: R.W. Patrick, 1917

Boys in Blue. L&M: C.P. Cox, 1918

Boys in Blue and Khaki. L&M: Mabel Ensley, 1918

Boys in Blue, in Khaki, Too. L: L.Y. Lenhart; M: I. Clark Hall, 1917

Boys in Brown. L&M: H.D. Bradford, 1917

Boys in Brown (They'll Get the Kaiser's Goat). L&M: D.F. Hallahan, 1918

Boys in France. L: C.E. Smith; M: Leo Friedman, 1919

Boys in Khaki (March). L&M: W.L. Lawson, 1917

Boys in Khaki. L&M: L.E. Laughner, 1918

Boys in Khaki. L: R. Erickson; M: Leo Friedman, 1918

Boys in Khaki. L&M: M.E. Rich, 1918

Boys in Khaki. L: C.H. Quinlan; M: E.S.S. Huntington, 1918

The Boys in Khaki Are Coming Back Bye and Bye. L: E.J. Briggs; M: Leo Friedman, 1919

Boys in Khaki Brown. L: C.A. Brooks; M: Leo Friedman, 1918

Boys in Khaki (There Is No Blue Nor Gray). L: John A. Rutherford; M: Joseph L. Bickerstaff, 1918

Boys in Navy Blue. M: John Philip Sousa, 1917

Boys in Navy Blue. L: T.W. Sageman; M: A.A. Thielke, 1918

Boys of Company I (March). M: Mrs. W.D. Eyre, 1917

Boys of Liberty. L: B.J. Scully; M: Eugene Platzmann, 1918

Boys of '17. L&M: Nellie Miles, 1917

Boys of Stars and Glory. L: E.A. Jaras; M: Frank W. Ford, 1918

Boys of the Blue and Gray (29th Division March Song). L&M: J.D. Felsenheld, 1918

Boys of the Grand Old U.S.A. L: R. Creswell; M: Leo Friedman, 1918

Boys of the Red, White and Blue. L: E. McCune; M: Lew Jacobs, 1918

Boys of the U.S. Camp in France. L&M: R.H. Watson, 1919

Boys of the U.S.A. L: Mrs. D. Crossley; M: Robert H. Brennen, 1917

Boys of the U.S.A. L: J.E. Palmer; M: E.P. Atlins, 1918

Boys of the U.S.A. L: M. Hollinshead-Hubbell; M: J.S. Howe, 1918

Boys of the U.S.A. L: J.R. Berry; M: Leo Friedman, 1918

Boys of the U.S.A. L: Frona O. Hall; M: L.O. Streeter, 1918

Boys of the U.S.A. L: M.G. Brown; M: Carl Seyb [Floda Fisher], 1918

Boys of the U.S.A. L: L.S. Martin; M: Leo Friedman, 1918

Boys of the U.S.A. L&M: Mrs. A.B. Stewart, 1918

Boys of the U.S.A. L: C. Fahlsing; M: Artie Bowers, 1919

Boys of the U.S.A. L: E. Kelley; M: Wille Wagner, 1919

Boys of the U.S.A. L: Julia E. Charlton; M: Leo Friedman, 1919

Boys of the U.S.N. (Waltz). L&M: Laura G. Pringle and E.P. Belcher, 1918

Boys of Uncle Sam. L&M: T.C. Trent, 1917

Boys of Uncle Sam. L: F.H. Ackermann; M: Daniel Protheroe, 1917

Boys of Uncle Sam (March). M: James P. Johnson and William H. Farrell, 1917

Boys of Uncle Sam (Our New Battle Song). L&M: James Cameron, 1917

Boys of Uncle Sam. L: C.C. Smith; M: Leo Friedman, 1918

Boys of Uncle Sam. L&M: Helen Mildred Knight, 1918

Boys of Uncle Sam. L&M: William Hewitt, 1918

Boys of Uncle Sam. L&M: Emma Benedict, 1918

Boys of Uncle Sam. L: A.W. Olson; M: Roy Hartzell, 1919

The Boys of Uncle Sam Will Be There. L&M: D. Clifford, 1917

The Boys Over There. L: Jennie Langley; M: Leo Friedman, 1918

The Boys Over There. L: P. Johnson; M: Roy Hartzell, 1919

The Boys They Call the Yanks. L&M: Elizabeth McLean, 1918

Boys, We Are Proud of You. L&M: Niel O'Brien, 1919

Boys, We're Going Through. L&M: James Jones, 1918

The Boys Who Always Proved True. L&M: Ida Brownlow, 1919

*The Boys Who Fight for You. L&M: Ralph Hyatt, 1918

The Boys Who Fought in the Trenches. L: T.L. Jordan; M: M.B. Cowart, 1917

*The Boys Who Won't Come Home. L: Harry Hamilton; M: Ed Thomas, 1919

Brave American Boys (March). M: Gustave Schumann, 1916

The Brave and the Free (Patriotic March Song). L&M: W. Brown Leonard, 1918

Brave Are the Boys That's Gone. L: P.L. Perkins; M: Leo Friedman, 1918

Brave Boys. L: Mrs. A. Callender; M: Leo Friedman, 1918

Brave Boys Are They. L: S.H. Birdsall; M: Leo Friedman, 1919

Brave Boys of the U.S.A. L: F.J. Boyer; M: Leo Friedman, 1918

Brave Boys of Yankee Land. L: Mary J. Fitzgerald; M: Leo Friedman, 1919

Brave Boys Somewhere in France. L: Mrs. C. Whitford; M: Leo Friedman, 1918

Brave Gallant Defenders. L: C.R. Osgood; M: Z.M. Parvin, 1918

Brave-Hearted Mother. L: Eleanor Gorman; M: Leo Friedman, 1919

Brave Soldier Boy Waltz. M: Adam Preston [Henry J. Sawyer], 1918

Brave Soldier Boys. L&M: F.B. Hartmaier, 1917

Brave Yankee Middies of the U.S.A. L&M: Effie Louise Koogle, 1918

Brave Yankee Sammy. L: Mrs. P.J. MacKermon; M: Leo Friedman, 1918

The Bravest Battle of the War Was Fought in a Mother's Heart. L: Thomas P. Hoier and Paul Beggs; M: Al W. Brown, 1918

The Bravest Heart of All (A Tribute to Edith Cavell). L: Arthur J. Lamb; M: F. Henri Clique [Klickmann], 1915

*The Bravest Heart of All. L: Raymond B. Egan; M: Richard A. Whiting, 1917

Break the News to Mother. L&M: Charles K. Harris, 1897, revised 1917

*Bring Back a Belgian Baby to Me. L&M: Ben Black, 1918

Bring Back, Bring Back, Bring Back the Kaiser to Me. L: Adele Rowland and Ed Moran; M: Harry Von Tilzer, 1917

*Bring Back My Daddy to Me. L: William Tracey and Howard Johnson; M: George W. Meyer, 1917

Bring Back My Daddy to Play Santa Claus. L&M: D. Davidson, 1918

*Bring Back My Soldier Boy to Me. L: Walter Hirsch; M: Frank Magine, 1918

Bring Back My Soldier Man to Me. L&M: Joseph Pafumy, 1915

Bring Back That Dear Boy to Me. L: Mrs. J.G. Rollins; M: Leo Friedman, 1919

Bring Back the Flag. L&M: "Vivian-Fagin-Roberts," 1917

Bring Him Back, Boy of Mine. L&M: Ella B. Davis, 1918

Bring Home the Victory. L: Howard J.
Green; M: Harry H. Roese, 1917

*Bring Me a Letter from My Old Home
Town. L: A.G. Delamater; M: Will R.
Anderson, 1918

Bring Our Heroes Home. L&M: Frank
Kiefel, Sr., 1919

Bring Peace, We Pray. L&M: Flora Cathcart,
1914

Bring Us Back the Dear U.S.A. We Left
Behind. L: V.D.P.A. Stebor; M: Leo
Friedman, 1919

Britons, Rally 'Round the Union Jack!
L&M: C.S. MacDonald, 1918

Broad Stripes and Bright Stars. L&M:
Charles F. Stayner, 1917

Broadway Tipperary. L&M: George M.
Cohan, from stage production *Hello,
Broadway*, 1915

Brother Bill Went to War, While I Stayed
Home and Made Love to His Best Girl. L:
Jeff Branen; M: Arthur Lange, 1915

Brought Back Victory Again. L&M: Jacob
Gabriel, 1918

The Brown Skin Boys Are Coming. L&M:
G.A. Lewis, 1918

Buddie Boy, How's Ev'ry Little Thing with
You? L&M: Geoffrey O'Hara and Theodore Morse, 1919

Buddy's Coming Home. L: T.B. Limbocker;
M: Leo Friedman, 1919

Bugle Call (A Patriotic Hymn). L: D.O. Col-
lings; M: Robert Sauer, 1917

Bugle Call. L: William Mahard Davidson;
M: G.M. Rohrer, 1918

Bugle Call. L&M: Sadie D. Burgess, 1918

Bugle Call March. M: Adam Preston, 1918

Bugle Call Rag. L&M: J. Hubert ("Eubie")
Blake and Carey Morgan, 1916

Bugle Call Rag (Old Miss). M: W.C. Handy,
1916

Bugle Call to Peace. L: Herbert McNenny;
M: Dawley Troth, 1916

The Bugle Calls to Clasp the Hands Across
the Sea. L&M: Florence Reed Howard, 1917

Bugle Song. L&M: Constance Cutmore, 1917

Building Ships for Uncle Sam. L&M: William
Lillie, 1918

Bullets and Bayonets (March). M: John
Philip Sousa, 1919

Bury the Hun. L&M: Archie Coates, 1918

But the Allies Took Will Out of William,
and Then They Kicked B Out of Bill. L:
C.A. Wicklund; M: Leo Friedman, 1919

Buy a Bond. L: E.H. Douglas; M: Leo
Friedman, 1918

Buy a Bond. L&M: Julia Britt, 1918

Buy a Bond. L: Richard Fechheimer; M:
W.B. Kernell, from stage production
Goodbye, Bill, 1918

Buy a Bond. L&M: G.W. Sharpe, 1918

Buy a Bond. L&M: Mrs. A. Long, 1919

Buy a Bond, Boys, Buy a Bond, Girls!
L&M: I.M. Cassel, 1918

Buy a Bond, Buy a Bond for Liberty. L&M:
Erle Threlkeld, 1918

Buy a Bond for Liberty. L&M: J.L. Fitzhenry, 1918

Buy a Liberty Bond. L: J.J. McMillan; M:
Sidney V. Dudley, 1918

Buy a Liberty Bond. L: John H. Jones; M:
Hattie May Jones, 1918

Buy a Liberty Bond. L: M.C. Ward; M: Leo
Friedman, 1918

Buy a Liberty Bond. L&M: Lynn F. Cowan,
1918

Buy a Liberty Bond. L: B.B. Rees; M: Leo
Friedman, 1918

Buy a Liberty Bond. L&M: Morris Leibson,
1918

Buy a Liberty Bond. L: J. Ensign; M: Vincent J. Nery, 1918

Buy a Liberty Bond for the Baby. L: Ed
Moran; M: Harry Von Tilzer, 1917

Buy a Liberty Bond [War Saving Stamp]
(Free Alsace-Lorraine). L&M: Laura
Sedgwick Collins, 1918

Buy a Liberty Bond Now. L&M: Statia
O'Donnell, 1918

Buy a Liberty Bond Today. L&M: Carrie
Krieger Holbrook, 1918

Buy Our Bonds. L&M: J.H. Densmore, 1918

By-O Baby Bunting (A Lullaby for Putting
the Huns to Sleep). L&M: Helen Howard
Lemmel, 1918

By the Boys of the Red, White and Blue.
L&M: C.E. Mathias, 1918

By the River Rhine. L: Mary M. Mellinger;
M: Carl Bendel, 1915

Bye and Bye You'll See the Sun a-Shining. L:
Ed Moran and Vincent Bryan; M: Harry
Von Tilzer, 1918

Bye, Bye, Baby Dear, Pappa's Baby-Soldier
Baby. L&M: Roy L. Burtch, 1918

C

*The Caissons Go Rolling Along. L: Robert
M. Danford, William Bryden, and Edmund
L. Gruber; M: Edmund L. Gruber, 1908

The Call. L&M: Paul V. Clark, 1917

The Call (March). M: Egbert Van Alstyne, 1918

A Call Across the Ocean Deep. L: J.P. Wright; M: R.W. Gebhardt, 1918

The Call for Peace. L&M: Pauline M. Hill, 1916

The Call for Volunteers. L&M: Emily Cox, 1917

Call of a Nation. L&M: Fred E. Ahlert; M: Pete Wendling, 1916

Call of a Nation. L: H. Helling; M: Leonarde Yellman, 1916

*Call of a Nation (March). L&M: Edward J. Boyle, 1918

Call of America. L: F.J. Dalrymple; M: Leo Friedman, 1918

Call of Columbia (March). L: Cullom Standing; M: I. Torrill, 1918

Call of Freedom. L&M: F. Holland Dewey, 1917

Call of Liberty. L: I.G. Hall; M: Leo Friedman, 1918

Call of the Allies (March). L: Jack Coleman; M: J.L. O'Connor, 1918

Call of the Allies. L: J.H. Calhoun; M: Leo Friedman, 1919

Call of the Brave. L: Jack Adams; M: Leo Friedman, 1918

Call of the Flag. L: L.D. Westfield; M: H. Aide, 1917

Call of the Flag. L&M: M.E. Sheehan, 1917

Call of the Nation. L&M: Elizabeth Shirley, 1918

Call of the Sammies (A Patriotic Song). L&M: T.O. Glazier, 1918

Call of the Stars and Stripes (March). L: Frederic T. Cardoze; M: H.D. Thomas, 1918

Call of the U.S.A. L&M: J.J. Donahue, 1918

Call of Uncle Sam. L: John Adam Kuta; M: Lawrence Thomas Kuta, 1917

Call of Uncle Sam. L&M: Horace P. Gates, 1917

Call of Uncle Sam. L&M: J.H. Cobel, 1919

The Call—the Yankees Are Coming (March). L&M: Ole Vikoren, 1918

A Call to All. L&M: Leon Berg, 1918

Call to Arms. L&M: U.E.N.E. Hayden, 1917

Call to Arms. L&M: F.M. Chacon, 1917

Call to Arms. L: J.H. Lewis; M: J.H. Lewis and Georges Clerbois, 1917

Call to Arms (March). L&M: M.R. Bonnell, 1917

Call to Arms (Our Country Calls). L: Edward T. Glynn; M: E. Brown, 1917

Call to Arms (March). M: Bert R. Anthony, 1918

Call to Arms. L&M: Clara B. Groves, 1918

Call to Battle. L: E.E. Rexford; M: Samuel W. Beazley, 1915

Call to Battle. M: J. Lawrence Erb, 1915

Call to Battle. L: M.J. Harris; M: Mrs. M.J. Harris, 1918

Call to Freedom. L&M: Victor Herbert, 1918

Call to Liberty. L&M: J.J. Bunting, 1918

Call to Peace (March). L: M.A. Rehling and A.G. Corless; M: E. Edwin Crerie, 1914

Call to Peace. L&M: Eva B. Deming, 1916

Call to Service. L: M.E. Sweeney; M: Leo Friedman, 1919

Call to the Boys in Blue. L: Mrs. C.T. Mitchell; M: Al Pleau, 1918

Call to the Colors. L: Harold Atteridge; M: Sigmund Romberg, from stage production *Dancing Around*, 1914

Call to the Colors. L&M: Mae Robison, 1918

Call to the Flag (March). M: John Jancsek, 1917

Call to the Flag. L: Loretta Bishop; M: Leo Friedman, 1918

Call Us Buddies from U.S.A. L&M: James H. Underdue, 1918

Called to Service. L: Grace Gordon; M: Adam Geibel, 1917

Called to the Colors. L: L.M. Belyea; M: Roy Hartzell, 1919

*Camouflage. L&M: L. Wolfe Gilbert and Anatol Friedland, 1917

Camouflage (March). L&M: H.B. Blan, 1918

Camp Custer (March). M: Robert Meier, 1917

Camp Custer March. M: Edward A. Schroeder, 1917

Camp Dix. L: Unknown; M: W.L. Gardner, 1918

Camp Sheridan (March). M: H.H. Dunkeson, 1918

Can America Depend on You? L&M: F.E. Oliver, 1917

Can the Kaiser. L&M: Thomas Williams, 1917

Can the Kaiser. L&M: J.B. Herbert, 1917

Can the Kaiser. L: E.P. Smith; M: Edwin Soley, 1917

Can the Kaiser. L&M: A. Wadkins and T. Fennell, 1917

Can the Kaiser Teach the Irish to Talk Dutch? (March). L: E.L. Shadomy; M: Theodore H. Northrup, 1916

Can You Say That You've Done Your Share? L: Henry Fink and Lew Porter; M: Abner Silver, 1918

Canada, Our Canada. L: Henry Chadwick; M: H. Dellafield, 1916

Can't You Hear Your Country Calling. L: Gene Buck; M: Victor Herbert, from stage production Ziegfeld Follies of 1917, 1917

Can't You Hear Your Uncle Sammy Calling (He's Calling You and Me). L: Cal DeVoll; M: Ed Ritchie and Cal DeVoll, 1917

The Cantonment (March). M: E.H. Frey, 1917

Caroline (I'm Coming Back to You). L: Jack Caddigan; M: James McHugh, 1916

Carry On! L: Sherman E. Grau; M: Beverly Bunt, 1918

Carry On (A Patriotic Song). L&M: E.T. Ellsworth, 1918

Carry On! (March). M: Matilee Loeb-Evans, 1918

Carry On! (March) M: Monroe A. Althouse, 1918

Carry On, America. L&M: M.E. Williams, 1918

Carry On, America, and Help Them Hold the Lines. L: Medora B. Pulver; M: N. Hoffman, 1918

Carry On, Boys. L&M: R.G. Morton, 1918

Carry On, Boys. L: J.B. Figaro; M: Frank W. Ford, 1918

Carry On! Carry On! Old Glory (March). L: Richard D. Ware; M: David Stevens, 1917

Carry the Flag to Victory. L: Lizzie DeArmond; M: B.D. Ackley, 1917

The Cause of Liberty. L: M.L. Corkum; M: Leo Friedman, 1919

The Cavalry Soldier (March). M: J.O. Brockenshire, 1917

Charge, Boys, the World Is All Before You (March). L: Ellen Barbour Glines; M: F. Porrata-Doria, 1918

Charge of the Song Brigade. L: Raymond B. Egan; M: Richard A. Whiting, from stage production *Toot Sweet*, 1919

The Charm of Old Glory. L&M: W.I. Chambers, 1918

Chateau-Thierry (March). M: Eddie Mahoney, 1919

Cheer, Boys, Cheer. L&M: William Clews, 1918

Cheer, Oh Cheer, Oh Cheer Old Glory. L&M: William Wood, 1918

Cheer the Boys. L: William T. Robertson; M: Leo Friedman, 1918

Cheer Up, America (A Patriotic Song). L&M: C.E. Braun, 1918

*Cheer Up, Father, Cheer Up, Mother. L: Al Bryan; M: Herman Paley, 1918

Cheer Up, France, We're on Our Way (March). L: Frank Smith; M: Arthur Lupton, 1918

*Cheer Up, Mother. L&M: Mary Earl, 1917

Cheer Up, Mother. L: M.L. Tillapaugh; M: Leo Friedman, 1918

Cheer Up, Mother. L&M: C.E. Alderman, 1918

Cheer Up, Mother. L: M.D. Ferguson; M: A.L. Gardey, 1918

*Cheer Up, Mother, It's All Right Now and Everything Is All O.K. L&M: Tod Weinhold, 1918

*Cheer Up, Tommy Atkins. L: Will J. Hart; M: Edward G. Nelson, 1918

Cheer Up, Uncle Sam. L&M: Simon Sarche, 1917

Cheerfully Serving the King. L: Cora C. Russell; M: George C. Stebbins, 1918

Cheers for the Boys in the Army. L: Casper Nathan; M: J.F. Ruskin, 1918

Cheers for the Red, White and Blue. L&M: W.H. Potstock, 1917

*Cheers to Our Khaki Lads. L&M: H. Marie Cass, 1919

A Cheery Smile Is as Good as a Mile on the Road to Victory. L&M: Anita Stewart, 1918

Cheese It! We Should Worry! In Good Old U.S.A. (A Patriotic Bigger Navy Song). L&M: Frederick Hall, 1915

Children of Liberty (A Patriotic Song). L&M: H.B. Seely, 1917

A Children's War Hymn. L: Eva Moyniham; M: F.A.J. Hervey, 1918

Chimes of Normandy. L: Al Bryan; M: Jack Wells, 1917

The Choice of All the Flags. L: F.J. Kinney; M: Leo Friedman, 1919

Chosen Boys of Uncle Sam. L: H. Rowley; M: Leo Friedman, 1918

Christ Leads to Victory. L: Franc Bentley Henderson; M: J.W. Henderson, 1917

A Christian Soldier's Dying Words. L: Willie McKean; M: Frank W. Ford, 1919

Christmas Stockings to Somewhere in France. L: S.J. Dracas; M: Leo Friedman, 1919

Church Bells Tolled in the City. L: Alga Hennig; M: Leo Friedman, 1919

Civilization Peace March. M: Victor Schertzinger, from silent film *Civilization,* 1916

*Clap Your Hands, My Baby (for Your Daddy's Coming Home). L: Frankie Williams; M: Edward G. Nelson, 1918

Clarion Call. L: Joseph W. Hallam; M: Lily Wadhams Moline, 1918

Colonel Bogey. M: Kenneth J. Alford, 1916

Colored Soldier Boys of Uncle Sam (We're Coming). L&M: W.H. Nickerson, 1918

Colors (A Patriotic March Song). L&M: I.W. Partin, 1916

*The Colors That Will Not Run. L: Dora Hendricks; M: Charles H. Gabriel, 1918

Columbia (A Patriotic Service). L: C.S. Brown; M: Charles H. Gabriel, 1917

Columbia, Arise. L: E.E. Hewitt; M: Charles H. Gabriel, 1917

Columbia, Freedom Is Your Name. L&M: S.L. Simpson, 1918

Columbia Victorious. L: Maurice Freeman; M: Ralph Garren, 1917

Columbia's Banner. L: Francis Scott Key; M: J.R. Sillince, 1918

Columbia's Banner on the Sea. L&M: William Arms Fisher, 1917

Columbia's Call. L: George L. Cobb; M: Bob Wyman, 1917

Columbia's Call. L&M: A.K. Lympero, 1917

Columbia's Calling You, Laddies. L&M: Virginia Roberts, 1917

Come Across. L: Grace C. Foote; M: John Hermann Loud (verse), Myra E. Ficke (chorus), 1915

Come Across, Yankee Boy, Come Across. L: Al Bryan; M: Fred Fisher, 1918

Come Along, Boys, We're with You, Mr. Wilson. L&M: Minnie Lee Jeffords, 1917

Come Back, General Pershing, We'll Make You President. L&M: "Dr. Smiles" [Nathan L. Teeple], 1919

Come Back, My Hero, Won't You? L&M: M.E. Forsyth, 1919

Come Back, My Love (A New War Song). L&M: M.M. Watson, 1918

Come Back, There'll Be a Welcome for You. L&M: John L. Jones, 1917

Come Back to Normandy. L&M: Walter Smith, 1917

Come Battle, My Boy, for the Right. L&M: M.L. Dick, 1919

Come, Be a Red Cross Nurse for Me. L&M: Leila E. Burgess, 1918

Come, Boys, and Fight for Your Country. L&M: Louis Oesterle, 1919

Come, Boys, Be Ready to Fight for Our Country. L&M: D. Primavera, 1917

Come, Boys, Come Let Us Rally Around the Flag. L: F.M. D'Auby; M: Robert H. Brennen, 1917

Come, Boys, Let's Join the Army! L: J.A. Cooper; M: Leo Friedman, 1918

Come, Boys, the Bugles Are Calling. L&M: Bessie May Dudley, 1917

Come Buy a Liberty Bond. L&M: Kate Green Hoof, 1918

Come Buy a Thrift Stamp. L: Julia Britt; M: Leo Friedman, 1919

Come Home, My Hero, My Soldier. L: T. August; M: E. Gary, 1918

Come O'er the Sea and Help Us Make Democracy the Best. L: John Philips; M: Frank W. Ford, 1918

*Come On, America! L: Edmund Vance Cooke; M: Kenneth M. Murchison, 1918

Come On, Boys! L&M: Arthur Dixon, 1917

Come On, Boys, and Fight for the Red, White and Blue! L: Anna R, Kostakos; M: Clem F. Goyke, 1917

Come On, Boys, Over the Top! L&M: Bonia Dean, 1918

Come On, Come On, Our Nation Needs You Now (To Arms, To Arms, Ancestors Taught You How). L: R.R. Parrish; M: Henry Clay Work, 1917

Come On, Come On, They're Calling You and Me. L: J.F. Jones; M: Theodore Tinnette, 1918

Come On, Let's Hooverize. L: M.S. Graybill; M: B.S. Hannah, 1918

Come On '19, We're Going to Win This War. L&M: Guy A. Surber, 1918

(Come On Over Here) It's a Wonderful Place. L: William Jerome; M: Seymour Furth, 1916

Come On, Rally 'Round Our Flag, Boys. L: Terry C. Elmendorf; M: Charles N. Schneider, 1917

Come Over and Help Us. L: Laura O. Plank; M: Miriam Hannaford, 1918

Come Over the Top. L: F.D. Randle; M: Felix West, 1918

Come Over the Top with Me (The Nation's Call). L: A.M. White; M: J.F. Keilty, 1918

Come Under the Folds of the Red, White and Blue. L: S. Packard; M: R. Blamquist, 1918

Come Where the Poppies Grow. L: Arthur J. Lamb; M: Irving Cortland Sanders, 1918

Coming Back to Our Own U.S.A. L&M: R.H. Bocock, 1918

Coming Home. L&M: Mrs. A.E. Leslie, 1919

Coming Home. L&M: Sarah D. Pfersick, 1919

Coming Home. L: A.F. Van Dyke; M: Leo Friedman, 1919

Coming Home, for the Battle Is Over. L: C.H. Lucas; M: Edouard Hesselberg, 1919

Coming Home to Mother. L: Harry Rasmussen; M: Leo Friedman, 1919

Coming Through the Rhine. L: Ben Ryan and Arthur Fields; M: Walter Donovan, 1918

Commander-in-Chief (Marshal Ferdinand Foch). M: F.H. Losey, 1918

A Common Volunteer. L: F.M. Lehman; M: F.M. Lehman and Claudia Lehman Mays, 1917

Comprenez-Vous, Papa. L: Al Bryan; M: Ray Lawrence, 1918

Comrades in Arms. L&M: Julian Jordan, 1918

Comrades in Arms, Let's Rally, Boys! (March). L&M: G.S. Barlow, 1917

Conquer the Kaiser (March). L: R. Hurd; M: Ernest Steiberitz, 1917

The Conquering Hero. L: Mrs. M.L. Munch; M: Artie Bowers, 1919

Conscientious Objector's Lament. L&M: Davy Burnaby and Gitz Rice, 1918

Conscription (March). M: Thomas S. Allen, 1916

Content. L: Grenville Parr; M: Norman G. Notley, 1916

Contest of the Nation. L: Elizabeth F. Guptill; M: Archibald Humboldt, 1918

The Country Backs You, Mr. Wilson. L: Charles Hope Waggener; M: R.J. Mazza, 1917

The Country Calls (March). L&M: A.F. Ischinger, 1918

Cover with Flowers Each Hero's Deep Bed. L: W.N. Hull; M: H.C. Verner, 1914

Cradle of Liberty (March). M: Alfred E. Joy, 1915

Cradle Song of the War. L: "N.S.D."; M: Margaret Ruthven Lang, 1916

The Creed of America. L: L.C. Sears; M: Leo Friedman, 1918

Cries of War. L: R.R. Estell; M: Leo Friedman, 1919

The Cross Beside the Flag (A Patriotic Service). L: Jesse Brown Pounds; M: J.H. Fillmore, 1918

The Cross That Saved the World Before Will Save the World Today. L: Arthur Lamb; M: Alfred Solman, 1918

Crossing the Rhine. L: A.H. Harvey; M: Frederick Melville, 1918

Crusader and Tommy. L: Clifford Grey; M: Herman Finck, 1918

Cry of Democracy. L&M: Charles S. Overholtz, 1919

Cry of Liberty. L: W.N. Garvin; M: Vashti Rogers-Griffin, 1917

Cupid in War Time. L: J.E. Smith; M: Leo Friedman, 1919

Cursed Be the War. L: R.D. Lafontaine; M: Artie Bowers, 1919

D

Daddy, Come Home. L&M: Irving Berlin, 1918

Daddy Darling, Here's Your Angel Child. L: Grant Clarke; M: George W. Meyer, 1918

Daddy, I Want to Go. L: Joseph F. Dunn; M: Edward Stembler, 1915

Daddy Is a U.S. Aeorplane Man. L: C.M. Diefembach; M: Jack Berger, 1918

Daddy, Please Don't Let Them Shoot You. L&M: J.O. Donovan, 1915

Daddy's Come Home to Mother and Me. L: L. Angrove; M: George Graff, Jr., 1919

Daddy's Gone to Fight the Hun, Hurray, Hurray, Hurray! L&M: L.J. Pollak, 1918

*Daddy's Land. L&M: J. Francis Kiely, 1918

*A Daddy's Prayer. L&M: Harold B. Freeman, 1918

Daddy's Return. L&M: H.J. Rouse, 1919

Danger Ever Braving, Facing Ev'ry Foe. L: E. Houlton; M: Leo Friedman, 1919

A Dash of the Red, White and Blue. L&M: Gene Quirk, 1918

Davy of the Navy, You're a Wonderful, Wonderful Boy. L&M: Harold Dixon, 1918

Dawn of a Lasting Peace. L&M: B.J. Shanley, 1918

Dawn of the Peaceful Age. L: G.R. Sinning; M: Otto Merz, 1916

Day of Liberty. L&M: Mrs. Edward M. Bush, 1919

The Day That the War Is Over. L: R.L. Ekstrand; M: Leo Friedman, 1918

De World Sho Is a-Fightin' Mad (A Negro War Song). L&M: John H. Jones, 1917

Dear America. L: Lucy D. Faulkner; M: Hazel M. Bleecker, 1918

Dear Heart Across the Ocean. L: Anne L. McKinley; M: Leo Friedman, 1918

Dear Land of Freedom. L&M: A.C. Weeks, 1917

Dear Land of Freedom. L&M: F. Hermans, 1918

Dear Little Mary, Soldiers' Nurse. L&M: F.G. McPherson, 1918

Dear Little Red Cross Nurse. L&M: A.P. Trubey, 1918

Dear Old America. L&M: Ammon E. Cramer, 1917

Dear Old America. L: A. Cooper; M: Leo Friedman, 1918

Dear Old America, You Played the Winning Hand (Waltz). L&M: J.J. Frederick, 1918

Dear Old Dad's Farewell to Me. L&M: A.B. Carter, 1918

Dear Old Fighting Boys (March). L: C.M.S. McLellan; M: Herman Finck, from stage production *Around the Map*, 1915

Dear Old Flag. L&M: Frank Emerald, 1917

Dear Old Flag. L: Grant Colfax Tullar; M: I.H. Meredith, 1917

Dear Old Flag. L&M: Eliza Ramsey, 1918

Dear Old Flag. L&M: Orando Cowles, 1918

Dear Old France (March). M: Charles R. Stickney, 1918

Dear Old France—Uncle Sam He Hears You Calling. L&M: J.J. Mahoney, 1917

Dear Old Glory. L: M.W. Cummings; M: William T. Evans, 1918

Dear Old Glory. M: Bernard Hamblen, 1918

Dear Old Glory (A Patriotic Song). L&M: J.D. McCarthy, 1918

Dear Old Glory. L&M: E.C. Harrington, 1919

Dear Old Glory. L: P.J. Tobler; M: Artie Bowers, 1919

Dear Old Glory Land. L&M: Marcellus [J.J. McCabe], 1917

Dear Old Ma. L&M: Jack Frost and Henry S. Sawyer, 1915

Dear Old Pal of Mine. L: Harold Robè; M: Gitz Rice, 1916

Dear Old Red, White and Blue. L&M: J.A. MacMeekin, 1916

Dear Old Uncle Sam. L&M: E.J. Dowis, 1915

Dear Old U.S.A. L: R. Hallock; M: Leo Friedman, 1918

Dear Old U.S.A. L: A. Thornton; M: Leo Friedman, 1918

Dear Old U.S.A. L&M: Mrs. E.E. McCollum, 1919

Dear Old U.S.A. L: Callie Greer; M: Leo Friedman, 1919

Dear Old U.S.A. L: Mrs. R.H. Isley; M: Leo Friedman, 1919

Dear U.S.A. (March). L: M.E. Jones; M. Henry F. Smith, 1919

Dearest Land of All. L: Edward Lockton; M: Nellie Simpson, 1918

Death and Mother on the Battlefield. L&M: Mabel Bolma, 1919

De-De-Moc-Cra-Cy. L: Jonnie Johnson Shaw; M: C.A. Williams, 1918

Defend America (March). L: Rufus Stickney; M: Arthur Hadley, 1917

Defend Our Land (A Patriotic Song). L&M: Albert S. Crockett, 1917

Defend the Flag. L&M: William J.O'Gorman, 1917

Defend the Red, White and Blue. L: L. Michael; M: Everett J. Evans, 1918

Defenders. L&M: Arthur Farwell, 1918

Defenders of Freedom and Right. L: Paul Karlowitz; M: Leo Friedman, 1919

Dem German Dutch. L: "Harbington"; M: J.B. Herbert, 1917

Demobilization. L: C. Grahme; M: Charles H. Enyap, 1919

Democracy. L&M: Paul McMichael, 1918

Democracy. L: Paul T. Allen; M: P.F. Brady, 1918

Democracy. L: William Mill Butler; M: Carrie Jacobs-Bond, 1918

Democracy. L: J. Fuhrman; M: Leo Friedman, 1918

Democracy (March). M: Harry H. Zickel, 1918

Democracy. L: Mrs. Z. Jones; M: Leo Friedman, 1918

Democracy. L: Paul T. Allen; M: P.F. Brady, 1918

Democracy. L: E.L. Klein; M: Earle Scott, 1918

Democracy. L: William Cary Duncan; M: Anselm Goetzl, from stage production *Royal Vagabond*, 1919

Democracy. L&M: N.V. Turner, 1919

Democracy. L: F.K. Tomer; M: Artie Bowers, 1919

Democracy. L: Joseph Dutton; M: Harold Jarvis, 1919

Democracy. L&M: W.E. Gordon, 1919

Democracy. L: J.D. Wilson; M: Leo Friedman, 1919

Democracy and Liberty. L: Robert James Brennen; M: Leo Friedman, 1919

Democracy and Liberty Are What We're Fighting For. L&M: Dave Brown, 1918

Democracy Calls. L&M: John Morison, 1917

Democracy Forever (March). M: G.S. Cash, 1917

Democracy Forever (March). M: Neil Morét, 1918

Democracy Forevermore. L: L.D. Manuel; M: Leo Friedman, 1919

Democracy, Humanity Forever! (March). L&M: A.S. Gay, 1918

Democracy in the U.S.A. L&M: Joseph Simms, 1919

Democracy March. M: Egbert Van Alstyne, 1919

Democracy Shall Live Forever! L&M: E.W. Ericson, 1918

Democracy, Sweeping On. L: Walter Crips; M: George V. Rankin; French lyric by Louis Delamarre, 1918

Democracy's Call (Swat the Bugaboo) (March). L&M: M.E. Gray and M. Lhevinne, 1917

Democracy's Love Song. L&M: D.B. Alfred [D.A. Blackman], 1918

The Devil's Farewell to Kaiser Bill. L&M: B.R. Hall, 1918

Did You Send Your Knight to Battle? L: Gordon Johnstone; M: Shepard Kram, 1918

Dirge for a Fallen Soldier. L: George Henry Boker; M: Bryceson Treharne, 1917

Division Eighty-Nine. L: May M. Bowman; M: Ernest R. Kroeger, 1919

*Dixie Volunteers. L: Edgar Leslie; M: Harry Ruby, from stage production Ziegfeld Follies of 1917, 1917

Do, Do Your Best for Uncle Sam. L&M: G.E. Stephens, 1917

Do Not Shun Your Uncle Sam. L: E.E. Hollingsworth; M: Leo Friedman, 1918

Do We Remember Dewey at Manilla, Do We, Do We (Yer Bet Your Life We Do). L&M: Harry DeCosta, 1918

Do Your Bit. L&M: Flora L. Belford, 1917

Do Your Bit. L&M: Archie MacDonald, 1917

Do Your Bit. L&M: E.K. Baldwin, 1917

Do Your Bit. L&M: M. Adam Preston [Henry J. Sawyer], 1918

Do Your Bit (and We'll Beat Those Doggone Submarines). L&M: S.H. Love, 1918

Do Your Duty and Fight for Uncle Sam. L: A.E. Leitkam; M: Leo Friedman, 1918

Do Your Duty, Boy. L&M: I.L. Parker, 1918

Do Your Little "Bitty-Bit" (Right Now). L&M: Frances Belohlavek, C.C. Perkins, and Edmund Braham, 1917

Does It Pay to Raise Your Boy to Be a Soldier? L: Fred S. Daniel; M: William Bettmann, 1916

Doing My Bit. L: Harold Atteridge; M: Sigmund Romberg, from stage production Doing Our Bit, 1917

Doing Their Bit. L: M.E. Kerr; M: Roy Hartzell, 1918

Dolly McHugh (March Ballad). L: Marie Wardell; M: Muriel Pollock, 1914

Don't Be a Sailor. L: Harold Atteridge; M: Sigmund Romberg, from stage production Robinson Crusoe, Jr., 1916

Don't Be a Slacker. L: E. Bond; M: Leo Friedman, 1918

Don't Be a Slacker, Send Some Tobaccer to the Boys in France. L&M: Leslie Duckers, 1918

Don't Be a Slacker, Uncle Sam Wants a Backer. L&M: J.J. Monaghan, 1918

Don't Be Afraid, Uncle Sammy. L&M: A.C. Littlefield, 1917

*Don't Be Anybody's Soldier Boy but Mine. L: Joe Lyons; M: Frank Magine, 1918

Don't Be the Last to Go. L&M: L.V. Williamson, 1917

Don't Become a Slacker. L: James Ollie Burns; M: Leo Friedman, 1918

*Don't Bite the Hand That's Feeding You. L: Thomas P. Hoier; M: Jimmie Morgan, 1915

*Don't Cry, Frenchy, Don't Cry. L: Sam M. Lewis and Joe Young; M: Walter Donaldson, 1919

Don't Cry, Little Girl, Don't Cry. L&M: Maceo Pinkard, 1918

Don't Do Your Best, Do Your Damn Best. L&M: C.H. Wheatley, 1918

Don't Forget the Boys in Blue Are Going Over, Too. L&M: Harold Mack [Harold J. McKinley], 1918

Don't Forget the Boys Who Fought for You and Me. L: Al Jolson and Harold Atteridge; M: Fred E. Ahlert, 1919

Don't Forget the Girl Who's Waiting in the Good Old U.S.A. L: M.C. Peninger; M: Nellie Green, 1918

Don't Forget the Girl You Left Behind. L: Howard King; M: Raymond White, 1917

Don't Forget the Girlies When You're on the Other Side. L&M: Gretchen Schumm Smith, 1918

Don't Forget the Girls in the U.S.A. L&M: Elsie Maye Beamgard, 1917

Don't Forget the Mother Who Is Waiting Home in Vain. L&M: Martha J. Callahan, 1919

*Don't Forget the Red Cross Nurse. L&M: Lew Orth, 1917

Don't Forget the Red Cross Nurses. L: Harry S. Lee; M: Dorothy Rosine, 1918

Don't Forget the Salvation Army. L: Jimmie Lucas; M: Billy Frisch, 1919

Don't Forget to Write, My Dear. L&M: Elgin Mason, 1918

Don't Forget Us, Yankeeland (March). L&M: F.H. Robertson, 1918

Don't Forget Your Dear Old Mother. L: H.H. Schultz; M: Courtney and J. Edwin Allemong, 1916

Don't Forget Your Loved Ones at Home. L&M: R.T. Green, 1918

Don't Forget Your Soldier Boy. L: C. Purcell; M: Leo Friedman, 1919

Don't Go Back on Your Uncle Sam. L&M: W.H. Hyde, 1918

Don't Grieve, Mother Dear. L: Mrs. S.D. Brunk; M: Leo Friedman, 1919

Don't Harm the Flag That Protects You. L: M.V. Lawrence; M: Leo Friedman, 1918

Don't Let a Slacker Win Your Heart. L&M: Nick Hall and Harry Harris, 1918

Don't Let a Stain Touch the Folds of Old Glory. L: H.L. Purdy; M: Artie Bowers, 1919

Don't Let Him Linger When His Leave Is Over (A.W.O.L. Song). L&M: George M. Cohan, 1918

*Don't Let Us Sing Anymore About War, Just Let Us Sing of Love. L&M: Harry Lauder, 1918

Don't Lose Your Heart to the Lily of France. L: E. LeDoux; M: E. LeDoux and Archie Dionne, 1917

Don't Marry a Slacker's Girls. L: G. Dattilo; M: Minnie May Bauer, 1917

Don't Play with Uncle Sammy. L: H.L. Blumberg, 1918

Don't Put a Tax on the Beautiful Girls. L: Jack Yellen; M: Milton Ager, 1919

Don't Quit Till Every Hun Is Hit. L: L.S. Smith; M: Martin Greenwald, 1918

Don't Say Goodbye, We're Coming Back. L: G.W. Gage; M: L.D. Hall, 1918

Don't Sigh, Mother, Don't Cry Over Me. L&M: H.S. Booth and Edward J. Henley, 1918

Don't Steal My Yankee Doodle Dandy. L: Bud Green; M: Edward G. Nelson, 1918

Don't Take My Darling Boy Away. L: Will Dillon; M: Albert Von Tilzer, 1915

Don't the Kaiser Care? L: Mrs. J. Meyers; M: Leo Friedman, 1919

Don't Tread on Me. L&M: Anna M. Spring, 1916

Don't Trifle with a Soldier's Heart Unless You're Going to Love Him True. L: Arthur J. Lamb; M: Frederick V. Bowers, 1918

Don't Try to Steal the Sweetheart of a Soldier. L&M: Mary Earl, 1917

*Don't Try to Steal the Sweetheart of a Soldier. L: Al Bryan; M: [Gus] Van and [Joe] Schenck, 1917

Don't Turn My Star to Gold. L: Mrs. S.V. Heaton; M: Leo Friedman, 1919

Don't Turn Your Back on Uncle Sam. L&M: Ted Billings, 1918

Don't Weaken and Stick Till the Boys Come Home. L&M: Helen Trix, 1918

Don't Worry for the Yankees; Hold the Line. L&M: W.J. Seabrook, 1919

Don't Worry When the War Will End. L&M: A.V. Fiske, 1918

Don't You Hear Uncle Sammie Calling? (A Patriotic Song). L&M: A.P. Dawson, 1918

Doughboy Jack and Doughnut Jill. L: Marcus C. Connelly; M: Gitz Rice, 1919

Doughboy March. M: E.W. Berry, 1919

Doughboy Wishes. L: D.A. Ulwelling; M: Artie Bowers, 1919

Doughnut Girl. L: H. Earnest; M: Leo Friedman, 1919

Down Deep in a Submarine. L&M: Harry D. Kerr, 1915

*Down in the U-17. L: Roger Lewis; M: Ernie Erdman, 1915

Down the Trail of the Old Dirt Road. L: Richard Howard; M: Nat Vincent, 1918

Down the Wrong and Raise the Right. L: M.R. McKee; M: P.B. Story, 1918

Down with the Enemy, Up with Our Flag. L&M: A.K. Harsch, 1917

Down with the Kaiser. L&M: Lees and Carroll [David Masterton Lees], 1917

Down with the Kaiser. L&M: O.I. Janke, 1918

Down with the Kaiser, On to Berlin. L: Rufus Kemp, Jr.; M: Roy Hartzell, 1918

Down with the Kaiser (What the Allied People Say). L: F.A. Baker; M: C. deVaux Royer, 1918

Downfall of the Kaiser. L: W.J. Brennan; M: Leo Friedman, 1918

Dream of a Soldier Boy. L: Al Dubin; M: James V. Monaco, 1917

Dream On, Little Soldier Boy. L&M: Irving Berlin, from stage production *Yip, Yip, Yaphank*, 1918

Dreaming of Home Sweet Home L: Ballard MacDonald; M: James F. Hanley, 1917

Dreaming of the Dawn of Peace. L&M: Julian Jordan, 1916

Dreaming Sweet Dreams of Mother. L: Jack Caddigan; M: James H. Brennan, 1918

Dress Up Your Dollars in Khaki Today. L&M: J.W. Callicotte, 1918

Drive the Devils Back! L&M: T. Sigurdson, 1918

Drop the Battle Flag and Drum. L: G.R. Sinning; M: Will Held, 1917

Dry Your Tears. M: Charles K. Harris, 1917

Dumpty Deedle de Dum Dee. L&M: Walter Donaldson, 1915

Duty Calls Me O'er the Sea. L: C. Monroe; M: Arnulf Cintura, 1918

The Duty of All. L: Tracie Lowry; M: Leo Friedman, 1918

The Dying Sammie. L&M: Harry White, 1918

The Dying Soldier. L: Sarah Wykes; M: Claude Wellington, 1915

Dying Soldier Boy. L: Katherine Kaiser; M: Leo Friedman, 1919

A Dying Soldier's Message. L: Mrs. J. Cox; M: Paul Shannon, 1915

E

Each Boy Is a Hero to Someone Tonight. L: E.B. Myers; M: Robert Van Sickle, 1918

*Each Stitch Is a Thought of You, Dear. L: Al Sweet; M: Billy Baskette, 1918

Eagle of Justice. L: William Stapper; M: Frank W. Ford, 1919

The Eagle Screams (March). M: Arthur O. Carlstedt, 1918

Eagles of the West. L&M: L. Arbor, 1917

Echoes from the Front. L: Morde Smith; M: Charles T. Edwards, 1917

Echoes of Liberty, Our Country's Dream. L&M: A.W. Van Dorston, 1917

The 89th Division (March). M: Forest Cook Castle, 1918

Emblem of Freedom (March). M: G.R. Preston, 1918

Emblem of Liberty. L: Harriet A. Sherman; M: C. Frederick Toenniges, 1918

Emblem of the Just (A Patriotic Song). L: W.A. Reller; M: John Biondi, 1918

Emblems of Uncle Sam. L: Mary Ruth Myer; M: Everett J. Evans, 1918

England, My England. L: W.E. Henley; M: Healey Willan, 1914

England, My England. L: W.E. Henley; M: Alfred Hiles Bergen, 1918

*Enlist! for the Red, White and Blue. L&M: W.T. Holmes, 1917

European Armageddon. L: A. Uptegrove; M: Carl Heil, 1915

Europe's Big War. L: R.H. Malcolm; M: Edward Wunderlich, 1915

Every Bond We Sell. L&M: M.F. Paschkes, 1918

Every Boy's a Hero in This War Today. L: Myles McCarthy; M: Chauncey Haines, 1918

Every Girl Is Knitting (for Some Mother's Son in France). L&M: "Hawley & Bellaire," 1917

Every Girl That Has a Heart Loves a Soldier. L: C.F. Whaley; M: Katharine Hoffman, 1918

Every Girlie Loves a Soldier. L&M: Charles Bayha, 1917

Every Man That's American Will Fight for the U.S.A. L&M: James Wright, 1917

*Every Mother's Son. L&M: Calla Gowdy Gregg, 1917

*Every Mother's Son Must Be a Soldier (A Patriotic Song on Preparedness). L: W.H. Pease; M: Leola E. Pease, 1916

Every Night He Goes Over the Top. L: Howard Johnson and Alex Gerber; M: George W. Meyer, 1918

Every Place That Wilson Goes, Mrs. Wilson Goes Along. L&M: Charles R. McCarron, Carey Morgan, and Henry Lewis, 1919

Every Star in Our Flag Tells a Story. L&M: F.B. Teeling, 1918

Everybody Does the March Step Now. L: Harry S. Lee; M: J.B. Wells, 1917

Everybody Hit for Victory. L: Harry S. Lee; M: William Barnes [John Barnes Wells], 1918

Everybody Hooverize. L: Maude Burnette; M: Leo Friedman, 1919

Everybody Loves a Sammy. L&M: Russell C. Goldberg, 1918

Everybody Loves a Soldier. L&M: K.C. Murphy, 1917

Everybody Loves a Soldier Boy. L: J.E. Wall; M: Harris O'Farrell, 1918

Everybody Ready for War. L&M: Joseph Parrino, 1917

*Everybody Welcome—Everything Free (That Is the Slogan of the K of C). L: Alex Sullivan; M: Thomas Egan, 1918

Everybody's Knittin' Now. L: Joe Goodwin; M: James F. Hanley, 1917

Everyone Can Lick the Kaiser If He Wants To. L&M: Harold A. Frey, 1918

Everyone Over the Top! L&M: L.J. Burt, 1918

Everyone Will Say, Oh, Long Live the U.S.A.! L&M: Billy Gibson, 1918

Everyone's a Good American. L: E.S.S. Huntington; M: Edward Hutchinson, from stage production *Mutt and Jeff in College*, 1915

Everything Will Be Silent in the Kaiser's Den When the Yankees Swat Berlin. L&M: A.W. Hamm, 1918

Everywhere Over There. L: J.Y. Carter; M: Frank W. Ford, 1918

Ev'ry Sammy Needs His Smokin' Over There. L: Richard W. Pascoe; M: Monte Carlo and Alma Sanders, 1917

Ev'rybody's Fighting in the U.S.A. L: D.F. Reed; M: Leo Friedman, 1919

Exit the Kaiser (March). L: Edwin K. Hurlbut; M: F. Marsena Paine, 1918

Eyes of the Army. L: Raymond B. Egan; M: Richard A. Whiting, from stage production *Toot Sweet*, 1919

Eyes of Uncle Sam. L&M: F.M. Kaylor, 1917

*E-Yip-Yow! Yankee Boys, Welcome Home Again! L: Bob F. Sear; M: Al W. Brown, 1918

F

Fair Flag of Liberty (U.S.A. National Song). L&M: Jack Randall, 1917

Fair Land of Freedom (Victory Ode). L: F. Denison; M: A.A. Stanley, 1919

Fairest Flag Beneath the Sky. L: F.W. Herzberger; M: Liborious Semmann, 1917

Faithful Dying Soldier. L: H.J. Willis; M: Leo Friedman, 1919

Fall in, Boys! L&M: Barclay Walker, 1917

Fall in, Boys! (A Recruiting Song). L: A. Revere and H.L. Wynne; M: M. Paul Jones, 1918

Fall in for Your Motherland. L: Woodrow Wilson [from speech]; M: Frank Black and John L. Golden, from stage production *Army Play-By-Play*, 1916

Fall in Line (March). M: Arling Shaeffer, 1917

Fall in Line Behind Old Glory. L&M: C.B. Bartle and J.P. Keough, 1917

Fall In, U.S.A.! L: Azubah J. Latham; M: William J. Kraft, 1917

Fall of a Nation. L: D.O. Cornell; M: Leo Friedman, 1919

Fall of the Kaiser. L: T.P. Lipton; M: Leo Friedman, 1919

Fallen Heroes. L: A.W. Mackay; M: Edouard Hesselberg, 1919

Far Across the Ocean Blue (Goodbye, Little Girl, I'm Going Far Away). L: W.E. Roush; M: Charles L. Johnson, 1918

Far Away Across the Atlantic (March). L: John Newton; M: Walter Webb, 1918

Far Away in France. L&M: Gitz C. Rice, 1918

Fare Thee Well, Soldier Boy. L&M: James Wright, 1918

Farewell, America. L: M.H. Carter; M: Leo Friedman, 1918

Farewell, America. L: E. Johnson; M: Leo Friedman, 1918

Farewell, Kaiser. L: R. Sheeler Campbell and W.F. Lintt; M: W.F. Lintt, 1918

Farewell, Little Mother, So Long, Dear Old Dad. L: Bertha Hanilla; M: Leo Friedman, 1918

Farewell Mother, Sweetheart, Wife. L: F.E.W. Torrey; M: H.L. West, 1918

Farewell, My Soldier. L: M.L. Murphy; M: William Owens, 1918

Farewell, My Soldier Boy. L: Lena Guilbert Ford; M: Mary Davies, 1915

Farewell, Soldier Boy. L: William D. Totten; M: J.E. Butler, 1917

Farewell, Soldier Boy. L&M: Della Hamilton, 1918

Farewell, the Trumpet Calls Me. L: F.A. Miller; M: Leo Friedman, 1918

Farewell Till We Return Some Day. L: H. Brouseau; M: Eddie Jackson, 1918

Farewell to Fighting Sammy. L&M: Frank Templeton, 1918

The Farther We Are from Our Home Town, the Nearer We Are to Berlin. L: Frank Lalah; M: Robert H. Brennen, 1918

(The Fatherland, the Motherland) The Land of My Best Girl. L: Ballard MacDonald; M: Harry Carroll, 1914

15th Infantry. L&M: Andrea Razafkeriefo, 1919

59th Over Here Association March. M: Ernest Ester, 1919

Fight, Boys, Fight! L&M: Sue Robinson Swayne, 1918

Fight, Boys, Fight, We're All Back of You! L&M: R.W. Billings, 1918

Fight, Fight, Fight! L: Mrs. W. Ray; M: Leo Friedman, 1919

Fight for Dear Old Glory. L: S.R. Slater; M: J.A. Folkes, 1918

Fight for Freedom. L&M: J.T. Haile, 1919

Fight for Liberty. L: G. Eixmann; M: Leo Friedman, 1918

Fight for Mother Land. L&M: S.A. Massell, 1915

Fight for Our Uncle Sam. L&M: Gertrude Watson, 1917

Fight for the American Flag. L&M: Heinrich Bauer, 1915

Fight for the Dear Old Flag. L&M: Ida Jennings, 1918

Fight for the Flag. L&M: Eva Louise Bradley, 1918

Fight for the Flag. L&M: Ruth Oellig Dorrah, 1918

*Fight for the Flag, Boys, Red, White and Blue. L&M: Theodore Metz, 1917

Fight for the Flag We Love. L: Clarence Zollinger; M: Billy Smythe, 1917

Fight for the Red, White and Blue. L: William H. Barry; M: Ernest Menna, 1917

Fight for the Red, White and Blue. L&M: J.J. Neenan, 1918

Fight for the U.S.A. (March). L: Jack Gregg; M: Lou Jennus, 1917

Fight for the U.S.A. L&M: Tipton Mayne, 1917

Fight for the U.S.A. L&M: Jack Neville, 1917

Fight for the U.S.A. L&M: G.M. Sommers, 1918

Fight for Uncle Sam. L: E. Ayo; M: Harry Werton, 1917

The Fight Is On (March). L: J.R. Shannon; M: Carl D. Vandersloot, 1918

Fight On, America! L&M: Jean Taggart, 1918

Fight On, American! L&M: Mrs. Ray Myers, 1918

Fight On (Vict'ry Will Surely Come)! L: Ed Drake; M: Charles Rosen, 1918

Fight the Good Fight. L: J.S.B. Monsell; M: R.M. Stults, 1914

Fight the Hard Fight. L: J.S.B. Monsell; M: LeRoy M. Rile, 1917

Fight with Tommy in the Trenches (on the Firing Line). L: Herbert Thompson; M: Willis Richfield, 1914

Fight Your Battle with a Pray'r. L: Ida B. Brown; M: Leo Friedman, 1919

Fighters of the U.S.A. L&M: Lucy T. Fowler, 1918

Fighting Boys from the U.S.A. L&M: O.N. Miller, 1918

The Fighting Fifteenth. L: J.C. Crisler; M: Amber G. Lasley, 1918

The Fighting First (March). L&M: M.K. Fowler, 1917

Fighting for France and You. L: Grace Grinsted Arundel; M: C.H. Arundel, Sr., 1918

Fighting for Freedom. L&M: Hermia E. Blasius, 1918

Fighting for Freedom. L: A.G. Catlin; M: D.J. Michaud, 1918

Fighting for Freedom. L&M: Willis L. Smith, 1919

Fighting for Freedom and You. L: Grace G. Arundel; M: C.H. Arundel, Sr., 1918

Fighting for Our Flag on the Fields of France. L: Cecelia M. Cook; M: Alfred Damm, 1917

Fighting for the Stars and Stripes. L: W. Brownlee; M: Leo Friedman, 1918

Fighting for the U.S.A. L: Leo Wood; M: Courtney Allemong, 1917

Fighting for the U.S.A. L&M: D.G. Van Arsdell, 1917

Fighting for the U.S.A. L: C. Masters; M: Leo Friedman, 1918

Fighting for You. L&M: F.H. Robertson, 1917

Fighting in France. L&M: Honor Bright, 1918

The Fighting Irish 69th Are Coming Home Today (A Come-All-Ye to the 69th New York Regiment). L&M: W. Croxton, 1918

Fighting Mechanics (March). L&M: B.B. Miller, 1918

Fighting Men. L: M.A. DeWolfe Howe; M: George W. Chadwick, 1917

Fighting Navy (of the Good Old U.S.A.). L: Sam Keane; M: Stanley Henry, 1917

Fighting Sammies of the U.S.A. (the Land of the Free). L&M: F.G. McPherson, 1917

Fighting 69th. L: Jerome J. McCuen; M: Everett J. Evans, 1918

Fighting Sixty-Ninth. L&M: Anna L. Hamilton, 1918

Fighting Soldier Man. L: C.R. Meyer; M: Grace Moser, 1918

Fighting the Hun (March). L&M: E.L. Aikin, 1918

Fighting Tommies (Great Britain's Pride) (March). M: John Boulton, 1918

Fighting 28th. L: R. Moody; M: Walter Wiesbauer, 1919

Fighting U.S. Marine. L: C.H. Hogue; M: B. Heisel Harrison, 1918

Fighting with the Allies. L: C.W. Allen; M: Leo Friedman, 1918

Fiji Sammies. L&M: Phil Lyon, 1917

Fill the Flag. L&M: Edith Ella Davis, 1918

Fill Up the Ranks, Boys! (or, Make It Four Million Strong). L: J.V. Bogert; M: Leo Friedman, 1919

Firmly Stand for the Right. L: Anna B. Russell; M: George C. Stebbins, 1918

First Regiment March. M: Maude Drake, 1918

Five Women to Every Man. L&M: Louis Herscher, Sam Downing, and Joseph A. Burke, 1919

The Flag. L: Edith Sanford Tillotson; M: C. Harold Lowden, 1917

Flag Ever Glorious. L&M: W.D. Chenery, 1916

The Flag Goes By. L: Henry Holcomb Bennett; M: Carrie Bullard, 1918

Flag I Love. L: James Rowe; M: C.C. Stafford, 1918

Flag I Love. L: Ireta Alexander; M: Leo Friedman, 1919

The Flag of a Country That's Free. L&M: Richard Lawley, Jr., 1918

Flag of a Thousand Years. L&M: Nat S. Hart, 1917

Flag of All Flags. L: Anonymous; M: Susan E. Watson, 1917

Flag of Freedom. L: M.J. Simpkins; M: Edith W. Currie, 1917

Flag of Freedom. L: Oliver Wendell Holmes; M: C. Whitney Coombs, 1917

Flag of Freedom. L: E.E. Hewitt; M: B.D. Ackley, 1917

Flag of Freedom (the Stars and Stripes). L&M: John Wilton, 1917

Flag of Glory. L: Roy Stevenson; M: Arthur Claasen, 1917

Flag of Humanity (March). M: Al Hayes, 1917

Flag of Liberty. L&M: C. Price and C. Botefuhr, 1918

Flag of Liberty. L: K. Cruikshank; M: Robert H. Brennen, 1918

Flag of Liberty. L: E. LaPlace; M: "Anonymous French Melody," 1918

Flag of Liberty, Union and Peace. L: Elberta Kate Shipley; M: Laura Sedgwick Collins, 1915

Flag of Mine. L: Albert F. Madison; M: D.C. Schnabel, 1917

Flag of My Country. L&M: William J. Going, 1916

Flag of My Country (A Patriotic Song). L: M.J. Gilbride; M: Thomas Rennie, 1917

Flag of My Country. L: M.J. Gilbride; M: Charles Corbeau, 1918

Flag of My Country, the Girl of My Heart. L: Etta W. Miller; M: Reginald Bellin, 1919

Flag of My Heart. L: William F. Kirk; M: G. Ferrari, 1917

Flag of My Heart and Home. L&M: Ben Aaronson, 1917

Flag of My Land. L: T.A. Daly; M: Charles A. Chase, 1917

Flag of Our Country. L: Edgar Brazelton; M: Orrin B. Crane, 1917

Flag of Our Liberty. L: H.F. Alber; M: Leo Friedman, 1918

Flag of Our Nation. L: James Ollie Burns; M: Leo Friedman, 1918

Flag of Our Nation. L&M: R.F. Bryan, 1919

Flag of Peace (March). M: E.G. Ruth, 1915

Flag of the Free. L: W.C. Brookshire; M: Leo Friedman, 1918

Flag of the Free (New National Anthem). L: C.S. McLaury; M: A.W. Sutherland, 1918

Flag of the Red, White and Blue. L: R.T. Moore; M: Leo Friedman, 1918

Flag of the True. L: C.S. McLaury; M: A.W. Sutherland, 1918

Flag of the True. L: E.E. Hewitt; M: B.D. Ackley, 1918

Flag of the Union. L&M: C.S. Mackenzie, 1917

Flag of the U.S.A. (March). L: Belle Schlosser Collins; M: Will Kurtz, 1917

Flag of the U.S.A. L&M: L.C. Gibson, 1917

Flag of the U.S.A. L: B.E. Bilzing; M: Leo Friedman, 1918

Flag of the U.S.A. L&M: W.S. Knodle, 1918

Flag of the U.S.A. L&M: J.J. Donahue, 1918

The Flag of Uncle Sammy and the Jack of Johnny Bull. L&M: G.E. Miller, 1917

Flag of Us All. L: Minnie L. Upton; M: Edward Moore, 1918

Flag of Victory (March). M: C.C. Crammond, 1916

Flag of Victory (March). M: Peter Tesio, 1918

The Flag Our Fathers Flew (March). L&M: W.R. Smith, 1916

The Flag—Our Flag. L&M: Cary C. Countryman, 1917

Flag Song. L: Wilbur D. Nesbit; M: Harry S. Cyphers, 1916

Flag Song. L&M: Grace U. Bergen, 1917

The Flag That Betsy Made. L: G.H. Sharp; M: A. Pearsall, 1918

The Flag That Counts in This Cruel War Is the Dear Old Stars and Stripes. L: Mrs. G. Dunn; M: Leo Friedman, 1919

The Flag That Flies for Liberty. L: S. Iannone; M: Merritt E. Gregory, 1917

The Flag That Frees the World. L&M: Herbert L. Smith, 1917

The Flag That Has Never Retreated. L: Annie June Johnson; M: Frederick L. Hogan and Lowry U. Demings, 1918

The Flag That Knows No Fear. L&M: A.J. Granger, 1917

The Flag That Makes Us One. L: Frederick Henry Skyes; M: Louis Adolphe Coerne, 1917

The Flag That Never Knew Defeat. L: Ella Mackay; M: Leo Friedman, 1919

The Flag That Protects (Is the Red, White and Blue). L: Augusta Eiterman; M: A.D. Magbee, 1918

The Flag That Rules Them All. L&M: Marguerite Campbell, 1919

The Flag That Sets Us Free. L&M: Hattie E. Green, 1917

The Flag That Waves on High. L: G. Schott; M: Robert H. Brennen, 1918

The Flag That We Love. L&M: J.P. Delaney, 1917

The Flag That Will Never Know Defeat. L&M: Thomas Hamilton, 1918

The Flag—The Flag. L: Susie Workman; M: Leo Friedman, 1919

The Flag, the Rose, and You. L: Edward W. Schaub; M: Alfred Damm, 1918

The Flag They Love So Well. L: Henry J. Zelley; M: W. Philip [Phillip Wuest], 1918

The Flag We Adore. L: F.M. Hanley; M: George F. Hamer, 1917

The Flag We Love. L&M: J.H. Kurzenknabe, 1918

The Flag with a Single Star. L: Gattie Nottage; M: Leo Friedman, 1919

Flag Without a Stain. L&M: C.A. White, 1914/1918

Flag Without a Stain. L: P.S. Wright; M: Vida Hinkle Baird, 1916

Flags of France. L: Grace Ellery Channing; M: James H. Rogers, 1918

Flags of Freedom (March). M: John Philip Sousa, 1918

Flags of Liberty. L&M: A.H. Schaeffer, 1918

Flanders Dead. L: Della Brown; M: Leo Friedman, 1919

Flanders Fields. M: Alfred Hiles Bergen, 1918

Flanders Requiem (America's Answer). L: R.W. Willard; M: Frank LaForge, 1919

The Flatfoot (March). L: C. Lawson; M: Arnold Krueger, 1918

The Fleur-de-Lis Shall Bloom Again. L&M: A. Bowes, 1918

Fleur-de-Lis Waltz. M: John Martel, 1918

Fling the Banner to the Breeze. L: P. Kane; M: George Lowell Tracy, 1918

Flower of Salvation That Bloomed on No Man's Land. L&M: Leo Wood, 1919

Flowers of Peace. M: J.M. Baldwin, 1919

Flying Colors (March). M: Will Wood, 1917

Flying Fighters for Freedom. L&M: Marion L. Wood, 1918

Flying Squadrons (March). M: Carl Lawrence, 1918

Flying the Red, White and Blue. L&M: A. McPherrin Frazier, 1917

The Foe That Would Strike Old Glory Would Strike Your Mother, Too. L&M: W.C. Stewart, 1918

Follow Me to Germany and Victory. L: Will J. Hart; M: Edward G. Nelson, 1918

Follow Old Glory (March). L&M: Marie O. Sprinkle, 1918

Follow the Dear Old Flag. L&M: Bert Rourke, 1918

Follow the Flag (March). M: Albert Franz, 1915

Follow the Flag (A Patriotic Song). L&M: Nina M. Paddack, 1916

Follow the Flag. L: Walter Winchell; M: Roy Mack, 1917

Follow the Flag (March). M: Edgar LaRue, 1918

Follow the Flag. L: Elizabeth Zerrahn; M: C.Z. Bradley, 1918

Follow the Flag. L&M: Juanita Tramana, 1918

Follow the Flag (A Patriotic Song). L&M: J.B. McPhail, 1918

Follow the Flag. L: E. O'Donnell; M: Roy Hartzell, 1919

Follow the Flag of the Free. L&M: Amanda Kennedy, 1918

Follow the Flag of the U.S.A. L&M: J.J. Moritz, 1917

Follow the Flag Wherever It Leads. L&M: F.B. Young, 1918

Follow the Flag You Love. L: William Jerome and Coleman Goetz; M: Archie Gottler, 1916

*For a Girl Like You. L: Sgt. Dave M. Allan, Jr.; M: Sgt. C. Truman Collins, 1918

For a Worldwide Democracy. L: W. Clark; M: W. Clark and John C. Hustad, 1918

For All and Forever (March). M: Harry J. Lincoln, 1919

For All the States—One Flag, the Stars and Stripes—Our Pride. L: E.C. Geneux; M: Clifton Keith, 1917

For America. L: Ethel Mann Curtis; M: Agnes Mynter, 1917

For America (Our Khaki Boys' March Song). L&M: C.E. King, 1918

For America. L: Miss B. Thompson; M: Leo Friedman, 1918

For America and Liberty (March). L: L.L. Davis; M: Earl V. Moore, 1918

For America Needs Us All Now. L&M: Fred Parsons, 1918

For an Eagle's Wings! L: Sarah Stokes Hackett; M: Harvey Worthington Loomis, 1917

For Brave Men and They [Are] from the Mighty U.S.A. L: W.D. Jiam; M: Leo Friedman, 1918

For Country and You. L&M: Iva Catalana, 1919

For Dear Old Glory. L&M: Erick O. Peterson, 1918

For Dear Old Glory. L: Henry Fisher; M: Jack Burdette, 1919

For Dear Old Uncle Sam. L&M: Charles F. Stayner, 1915

For Democracy. L: Emma Johansen; M: Rose J. O'Brien, 1918

For Democracy (March). L&M: Victor E. Moser, 1918

For Democracy. L&M: C. Faine, 1919

For Democracy. L: Charles Ferrara; M: Leo Friedman, 1919

For Democracy and You (March). L: Minnie A. Storer; M: Robert M. Storer, 1918

For Dixie and Uncle Sam. L: J. Keirn Brennan; M: Ernest R. Ball, 1916

For Every Tear You've Shed, I'll Bring a Million Smiles. L: Ben Bard; M: Ray Lawrence, 1919

For Ev'ry Golden Star on Earth There's a Golden Star in the Sky. L: G. Gutensky; M: Leo Friedman, 1919

For Flag and Country. L: Erma Clarke; M: H.A. Dinsmore, 1917

For France. L&M: A.W. Moss, 1918

For France and Uncle Sam. L&M: Tony Fasone, 1918

For Freedom and for Peace. L: Edwin Spicer [E.M. Crossman]; M: Arthur A. Penn, 1917

For Freedom and Humanity. L: Peter J. McAvoy; M: Henry Haas, 1917

For Freedom for All and Forever Floating the Flag of the U.S.A. L&M: R.N. Doore, 1918

For Freedom's Cause (March). L: E.E. Good; M: Marvin Radnor, 1918

*For God, America and You. L&M: Louis J. Fay and Bennie McLaughlin, 1917

For God and Our Country (March). M: A.J. Schindler, 1918

For God, for Home, for Country. L: J.A. Coutts; M: R.L. Knowles, 1915

For He Fights for Home and Old Glory. L&M: James Chadwick, 1917

For He's an American. L&M: Helen R. Smith, 1918

For Home and Country and the Right (March). L: J.W. O'Brien; M: P.B. Story, 1917

For Home and Liberty (A Patriotic Song). L&M: Henry Wylee [G.H. Hutchinson], 1917

For Home and Liberty (March). L&M: Julian Jordan, 1917

For Home and the Nation. L&M: S.D. Thurmond, 1918

For Home Sweet Home and Uncle Sam. L: Stanley Murphy; M: Alfred Solman, 1916

For I See the Flag of Uncle Sammy. L: J.L. Davis; M: Arthur Stanley, 1919

For Justice We Must Fight. L: A.F. Delmargo; M: Irving Gingrich, 1918

For Liberty. L: Charles W. Gordon; M: Katherine Gordon French, 1917

For Liberty. L: Ethel J. Gardner; M: J.E. Miller, 1918

For Liberty. L: M.E. Allen; M: Leo Friedman, 1919

For Liberty. L: Minnie A. Cork; M: Leo Friedman, 1919

For Liberty (March). M: S.E. Morris, 1919

For Liberty and Freedom. L: Mrs. E.F. Skinner; M: Leo Friedman, 1918

For Liberty and the Old Red, White and Blue. L: Clayton Bahm; M: Leo Friedman, 1919

For Love and Liberty. L&M: J.E. Boyd, 1918

For Love and Old Glory. L: E. Hadley; M: Frank W. Ford, 1918

For Marching Men. L: Theresa V. Beard; M: H. Clough-Leighter, 1919

For Mother and the U.S.A. L: F.J. Zaffke; M: Leo Friedman, 1918

For Mother, Home and Country (March). L&M: James Austin Bostwick, 1917

For My Country and My Flag. L&M: Harry Farmer, 1917

For My Land, My Flag, and You. L: Daniel Olsen, Jr.; M: J.A. Heaton, 1917

For Old Glory and Liberty. L&M: J.W. Yoder, 1917

For Old Glory and All Humanity. L: T.B. Nikral; M: Leo Friedman, 1919

For Old Glory and Ohio (March). L&M: M.W. Townsend, 1918

For Old Glory, Uncle Sam, We Are Preparing [Performing]. L&M: Walter Irving, 1917

For Our Boys Are Coming Home. L: N. Hamilton; M: George Graff, Jr., 1919

For Our Country and Our Flag (March). L&M: Eugene R. Kenney, 1917

For Our Dear Old Glory. L: Mary Compagnon; M: Everett J. Evans, 1918

For Our Great Democracy. L: Alice Edwards Blair; M: R.A. Browne, 1918

For Our Soldier Boys. L&M: Rose A. Ulrich, 1917

For Peace and Liberty (A Patriotic Song). L&M: D.E. Morgan, 1917

For Right and Liberty. L&M: Joseph Elton, 1918

For Right We Fight. L: J.N. Nugent; M: Leo Friedman, 1919

For Sammy and France. L: P.L. Schwartz; M: Leo Friedman, 1919

For Surely I Will Come Back to You. L&M: Robert Lloyd, 1918

For the Allies and the U.S.A. L&M: Jessie Wells, 1919

For the Boys Over There. L: Gus Kahn; M: Egbert Van Alstyne, 1918

For the Boys Who Cross[ed] Over the Waves. L&M: W.S. Wymer, 1918

For the Dear Old U.S.A. L: Irene McGinley; M: Leo Friedman, 1918

For the Eagle, God, and Liberty. L: E.H. Tessman; M: Leo Friedman, 1918

For the Flag and America. L&M: Charles Dennée, 1917

For the Flag and Uncle Sam. L&M: O.B. Brown, 1917

*For the Freedom of All Nations. L&M: Eleanor Everest Freer, 1917

For the Freedom of the World (The Song of Nations). L: Edmund Vance Cooke; M: J.S. Zamecnik, 1917

For the Good Old U.S.A. L: S. Bodine; M: Leo Friedman, 1919

For the Grand Old Flag and You. L: M. Haynes; M: Robert Van Sickle, 1918

For the Home and the U.S.A. L: Mayme Bradburne; M: Leo Friedman, 1919

For the Honor of the Day, Hip-Hip Hooray!

L: R.H. Burnside; M: Raymond Hubbell, 1916

For the Honor of the U.S.A. L&M: W.J. Lysaght, 1917

For the Honor of Uncle Sam. L&M: James A. Dillon, 1917

For the Land and Flag You Love (March). L&M: F.A. Nick, 1917

For the Men at the Front. L: John Oxenham; M: N.C. Morgan, 1918

For the Old Red, White and Blue. L: George Lyman; M: Leo Friedman, 1918

For the Old Red, White and Blue. L: I.C. Bott; M: Leo Friedman, 1918

For the Old Red, White and Blue. L: K.M. O'Kelly; M: R.A. Browne, 1918

For the Red, White and Blue. L: Mrs. W. Baxter; M: George Graff, Jr., 1919

For the Red, White and Blue. L: M. Offinger; M: Leo Friedman, 1919

For the Red, White and Blue, Dears, and You. L&M: M.J. Whitely, 1917

For the Sake of Dear Old Glory. L: E. Mushake; M: Leo Friedman, 1919

For the Sake of Humanity. L: Harold Atteridge; M: Sigmund Romberg, from stage production *Doing Our Bit*, 1918

For the Sake of Old Glory. L&M: J. Hodgson Hartley, 1918

For the Soldier That Fights for You. L: M.P. Gauss; M: Fred A. Reynolds, 1918

For the Sons of U.S.A. L&M: Nell Marshall, 1918

For the Stars and Stripes. L: V.H. Hartman; M: Harry Weston, 1918

For the Stars and Stripes and You. L&M: F.V. Tapley, 1919

For the Stars and Stripes We'll Live and Die. L: A. Garrasi; M: A.W. Speed, 1914

For the World and the U.S.A. (March). L&M: Gertrude E. Buck, 1918

For Thee, America. L&M: C.T. Schubarth, 1917

For Thee, O Dear, Dear Country. L: J.M. Neals; M: Homer N. Bartlett, 1918

For They Are True Americans. L: Silas Lodge; M: Albert Franz, 1918

For Uncle Sam. L: Bob Lawton; M: Max O'Neill, 1918

For Uncle Sam and You. L: W.L. Wright; M: Leo Friedman, 1918

For Uncle Sam and You. L: J.B. Satterlee; M: R.V. Haywood, 1918

For Uncle Sam Is a Grand Old Man. (A Patriotic Song). L&M: Clara T. Rice, 1918

For Uncle Sam Is Doing Right. L: V. Gelatha; M: Leo Friedman, 1918

For U.S.A. L&M: Alma Bates, 1918

For Victory. L: Frederick M. Davis; M: A.F. Heckle, 1918

For We Are the Boys of U.S.A. (War Marching Song) L&M: J.D. Jelita, 1918

For We'll Welcome Them All. L: L.W. Deuty; M: Leo Friedman, 1919

For World Democracy (March). M: V.A. Knauss, 1918

For You, America. L: Fannie Fahm; M: Artie Bowers, 1919

For You and Dear Old Uncle Sammy. L&M: L.E. Cole, 1918

For You and Uncle Sam. L&M: LaFrance Meneritti, 1918

For You, Little Girl, and Old Glory. L&M: Zeni Mac, 1918

*For Your Boy and My Boy (Buy Bonds! Buy Bonds!) (March). L: Gus Kahn; M: Egbert Van Alstyne, 1918

For Your Country and My Country. L&M: Irving Berlin, 1917

Forest Hill Liberty March. M: P.H.V. Trier, 1917

Forever Is a Long, Long Time. L: Darl MacBoyle; M: Albert Von Tilzer, 1917

Forget Me Not, My American Rose. L&M: Ray Sherwood, 1918

Forth to the Fray! (March). L&M: George Dudley Martin, 1918

Forward, America! (A Patriotic Hymn). L: James H. Dillard; M: Yves Arnandez, 1918

Forward, American Soldiers! L: Leonore McCurdy; M: Sara C. David, 1917

Forward, Boys! (March). M: A.M. LoScalzo, 1918

Forward, Ever Forward (March). L&M: George T. Johnson, 1918

Forward, Forward, America's Son! L: P.L. Haims; M: Leo Friedman, 1918

Forward March! L: T. Walton; M: Leo Friedman, 1919

Forward March All! L: N. Williams; M: Leo Friedman, 1919

Forward March! Columbia's Calling. L&M: Sister M.J. Quinn, 1918

Forward March! Mississippi Volunteers. L: Robert Levenson; M: George L. Cobb, 1917

Forward to Honor March. M: Paul Gardie, 1917

Forward to Victory. L: William T. Pettengill; M: Duke M. Farson, Jr., 1918

Four Years More in the White House. L: Thomas P. Hoier; M: Jimmie Morgan, 1916

Four Years of Fighting. L: Stephen Miller; M: Leo Friedman, 1919

France. L&M: Rosamond Booth Sheppard, 1918

France, America Loves You. L&M: C. Butterfield, 1918

France Is Calling. L: H.D. Shaiffer; M: Clarence Kohlmann, 1917

France-Land Lullaby. L&M: Lena Leonard Fisher, 1918

France, to You. L&M: Gerda Wisner Hoffmann, 1918

France Was a Friend Indeed. L: C.A. Paul; M: Leo Friedman, 1919

France, We Have Not Forgotten You. L: Grant Clarke and Howard Johnson; M: Milton Ager, 1918

France, We'll Rebuild Your Towns for You. L&M: Jack Coogan, 1918

Franco-American (March). M: Mary L. Leonard, 1917

Freedom. L: W. Handreck; M: Samuel H. Speck, 1918

Freedom. L&M: Mrs. M.A. Williamson, 1918

Freedom. L&M: L.R. Freeman, 1918

Freedom (A Patriotic Song). L: R.A. Wilson; M: J.C. Merthe, 1918

Freedom and Glory (March). L: Wallace Rice; M: Edward C. Moore, 1918

Freedom and Honor (March). M: B.F. Corbett, 1917

Freedom and Liberty. L: W.P.J. Murray; M: Robert H. Brennen, 1918

Freedom and Peace (An Order of Service for Use in Time of War). L&M: Grace Wilbur Conant, 1917

Freedom Bells. L&M: Arthur F. Fuller, 1918

Freedom Call. L&M: J. Brightwell, 1918

Freedom for All. L: Anna M. Reilly; M: J.W. Becktold, 1918

Freedom for All. L&M: Frank M. Cornell, 1919

Freedom for All. L: A.L. Trailor; M: Leo Friedman, 1919

Freedom for All Forever. L&M: B.C. Hilliam, 1918

Freedom for All Forever. L&M: Bertha H. Dible, 1918

Freedom for All Forever. L: Edward F. Cogley; M: William E. Bock, 1918

Freedom for All Forever (The Motto of the U.S.A.). L&M: Mary A. Jones, 1918

Freedom Forever (March). M: George Bowen, 1915

Freedom Forever. L: Frederic Smith; M: L.C. Wedgefurth, 1918

Freedom in Red, White and Blue (March). L: F. Quinn; M: Fred A. Reynolds, 1918

Freedom Land. L: D.B. Coats; M: based on "Dixie," 1918

Freedom of the Sea. L: J. Joseph Goodwin; M: "Marcellus," 1917

Freedom of the Sea. L: Marjorie Hills; M: Porter Steele, 1917

Freedom of the Seas. L&M: William Arms Fisher, 1917

Freedom of the Seas. L&M: E.C. Bruen, 1917

Freedom of the Seas. L: Henry M. Wharton; M: George A. Norton, 1917

Freedom of the Seas March. M: Walter Esberger, 1918

Freedom of the World. L: Harold Adam Houtz and Jasper Turano; M: William Laurence Gibson, 1918

Freedom of the World. M: E.C. McCaw, 1918

Freedom's Altar. L: Allen E. Cross; M: Walter Ruel Cowles, 1918

Freedom's Battle Hymn. L&M: William J. Tobin, 1918

Freedom's Battle Song. L: Katharine Lee Bates; M: Lawrence Camilieri, 1917

Freedom's Call. L&M: M.H. Weyrauch, 1917

Freedom's Call. L: F.P. Copper; M: Gerald Tyler, 1918

Freedom's Call. L&M: F.H. Cesander, 1918

Freedom's Call. L: H. Edler; M: Leo Friedman, 1919

Freedom's Day. L: Frederick L. Myrtle; M: Edward H. Lemare, 1919

Freedom's Flag. L&M: J.H. Powers, 1917

Freedom's Flag. L: O.T. Dozier; M: Elbert B. Fowler, 1917

Freedom's Flag. L: S.E. Mekin; M: Alfred Wooler, 1918

Freedom's Hope. L: E.L. Rowles; M: Leo Friedman, 1918

Freedom's Land. L&M: R.H. Locke, 1917

Freedom's Land, I Answer to Your Calling. L&M: J.W. Lambert, 1918

Freedom's Song. L&M: John S. Hoppes, 1918

Freedom's Victory. L&M: D. Colvin, 1918

Freedom's War. L: William O. Stoddard, Jr.; M: G.A. Tuttle, 1917

Freeman's Hymn (A Wartime Supplication). L&M: Andre Benoist, 1918

The French Trot. L: Jack Frost; M: F. Henri Klickmann, 1918

*Frenchy, Come to Yankee Land. L: Sam Ehrlich; M: Con Conrad, 1919

Frenchy-Koo. L: Billy Baskette; M: Maceo Pinkard, 1919

Frieden (Our Boys Are Coming Back). L&M: D. Meyerowitz, 1918

Friends of France (March). L: Mary Gardenia; M: J.H. Densmore, 1917

From a Soldier's Sweetheart. L: Bertha Rowland; M: Leo Friedman, 1919

From Berlin to Donegal (March). L&M: C.H. Wheatley, 1918

From Blue to Gold. L: W.H. Worts, Jr.; M: Leo Friedman, 1919

From God the Victory. L: "From the Bible"; M: Charles H. Gabriel, 1917

From No Man's Land to Yankee Land. L: E.H. Schulte; M: Harry J. Lincoln, 1919

From the Aisne to the Rhine. L: A.J. Casey; M: Leo Friedman, 1919

From the Battlefields of France. L: J.J. Noonan; M: Eugene E. Noel, 1918

From the Girls of the U.S.A. L: M. DiMora; M: Leo Friedman, 1919

From the Hudson to the Rhine. L: J.A. Brex, Sr.; M: Leo Friedman, 1919

From the Shores of No Man's Land. L: Leopold Liebl; M: Leo Friedman, 1919

From the West (March). M: H.J. Woods, 1918

From Valley Forge to France. L&M: Mary Earl, 1918

From Yaphank to You. L&M: H.D. Hoberman, 1917

The Further It's from Tipperary. L&M: Bide Dudley, John Godfrey, and James Byrnes, from stage production *Odds and Ends of 1917*, 1917

The Further We Get from the Hudson, the Nearer We Get to the Rhine. L: Louis E. Thayer; M: Victor M. Paulson, 1918

G

The Gang's All Here. L&M: The Rev. J.B. Bair, 1918

Garden of Liberty. L: Al Bryan; M: Harry Tierney, from stage production *What Next?*, 1918

Gathering Clouds. L&M: Edmund Parlow, 1915

Gee, but It's Good to Be Back, Back to the U.S.A. L&M: Jesse Winne, 1918

Gee, but It's Good to Get Home. L: O.G. Griswold; M: Jane Jewett Draper, 1916

Gee, but It's Great to Get Back Home. L: P.J. Dixon; M: Floyd E.Whitmore, 1919

Gee, Don't It Feel Good to Be Back Home Again? L: Louis Oswald; M: Joseph Psota, 1919

Gee, I Wish I Had a Soldier Boy. L&M: Dixie Gray, 1918

Gee, I Wish I Was a Man of War. L: M. Tokarich; M: Leo Friedman, 1918

*(Gee! What a Wonderful Time We'll Have) When the Boys Come Home. L&M: Mary Earl, 1917

General Joffre Grande Marche Militaire. M: Jules Bolle, 1916

General John J. Pershing—the Fighting Man. L: E.J. Goodwin; M: Leo Friedman, 1918

*General Pershing (March). L: J.R. Shannon; M: Carl D. Vandersloot, 1918

General Pershing (March). M: Cora E. Edgerly, 1918

General Pershing and His Men. L: M.M. Duffee; M: Luther A. Clark, 1917

General Pershing and His Soldiers Overseas. L&M: Joseph Casey, 1919

General Pershing of the U.S.A. L&M: W.H. Bennett, 1918

*General Pershing's March to Berlin. L&M: Daniel LaGrove, 1918

The German Blues, It's Neutral. L: Bob Lurtey; M: L.E. Zoeller, 1916

The German Empire. L: J.F. Beckwith; M: Carl Heil, 1915

The German War. L: Mrs. J.M. Palmer; M: Carl Heil, 1915

The Germans Must Pay for It All. L: J.P. Carnevar; M: Leo Friedman, 1919

Germany and the U.S.A. L: C.H. Roberson; M: Harry J. Bowers, 1918

Germany Is Dished. L: Will A. Heelan; M: Seymour Furth, 1915

Germany, Oh Germany. L: H. Anderson; M: Leo Friedman, 1919

Germany, Oh Germany, Why Don't You Set Old Ireland Free? L&M: Jess Dorman, 1916

Germany, You'll Soon Be No Man's Land. L: James E. Dempsey and Tom Kennedy; M: Joseph A. Burke and Sam Downing, 1918

Germ-on-Knee (Germany). L&M: Abe Haytreot, 1918

Get a Bond, Boys, and Be Happy. L: J.W. Spencer; M: P.B. Story, 1917

Get a Girl to Lead the Army. L: Al Bryan; M: Harry Tierney, from stage production *What Next?*, 1918

Get Behind Old Uncle Sam. L&M: Edward Oliver, 1918

Get Behind the Man Behind the Gun. L: M.F. Collins; M: Cyril Sargent, 1917

Get Busy Over Here or Over There. L&M: Edward Laska, 1918

Get Him, "Me und Gott." L&M: Gertrude Upson, 1918

Get in Line. L: W.W. Reid; M: B.D. Ackley, 1917

Get in Line, Now's the Time (A Recruiting Song). L&M: Charlotte Druh, 1917

Get Out of Belgium, Bill. L&M: E.R. Houston, 1918

Get Out on the Firing Line. L&M: M.V. Thornberry, 1919

Get the Kaiser. L&M: A.F. Day, 1918

Get There, Sammies, and Get There Quick! (March). L: W.L. Colby; M: Thomas Lester, 1917

Giddy Giddap! Go On! Go On! (We're on Our Way to War). L&M: Jack Frost, 1917

The Gink They Call the Kaiser. L: W.T. Sleeman; M: Leo Friedman, 1918

The Girl at Home. L&M: F. Marion Ralston, 1917

The Girl Behind the Man. L&M: Mary Earl, 1917

The Girl Behind Will Stand Behind the Boy Behind the Gun. L&M: Jack Mahoney, 1918

Girl—Goodbye, I'll Be All Right, All Right. L: Cornelia Otis Skinner; M: Roy Atwell, 1918

*The Girl He Left Behind Him (Has the Hardest Fight of All). L: Al Bryan and Edgar Leslie; M: Harry Ruby, 1918

The Girl He Left Behind Him Over There. L: B.E. Sotters; M: Leo Friedman, 1919

The Girl I Left at Home. L: L.M. Snare; M: A.A. Sandefur, 1918

The Girl I Left Back There. L&M: Alfred Jordan, 1919

The Girl I Left Behind in America. L&M: Bertha W. Gardner, 1918

The Girl I Left Behind Me Is Before Me All the Time. L&M: Jack Mahoney, 1917

A Girl in Dixie in the Days of 1860 (Loved a Yankee Soldier Boy). L&M: Bob Yosco, 1915

Girl of the U.S.A. L: Evelyn Staples; M: Leo Friedman, 1919

The Girl Over Here Sighs for Her Boy Over There. L: P.F. Fort; M: Leo Friedman, 1919

The Girl That He Loves Best (March). M: Edward M. Corliss, 1918

The Girl That I Love Over There. L&M: A.W. Packard, 1918

*The Girl Who Wears a Red Cross on Her Sleeve. L&M: Will Mahoney, 1915

Girls of America, We All Depend on You. L: Edgar Leslie and Bert Kalmar; M: Harry Ruby, 1917

*Girls of France. L: Al Bryan and Edgar Leslie; M: Harry Ruby, 1917

The Girls We Leave Behind. L: Arthur F. Holt; M: William T. Pierson, 1917

Girls, Write a Word to the Boys. L&M: E.F. Knapp, 1918

Give a Cheer for the Boys Over There. L: Roy M. Evans; M: Leo Friedman, 1918

*Give a Job to the Gob and the Doughboy. L: Lew Porter and Alex Sullivan; M: Max Friedman, 1919

Give a Little Credit to the Navy. L: Buddy DeSylva and Gus Kahn; M: Albert Gumble, 1918

Give Him Back His Job. L: Raymond B. Egan; M: Richard A. Whiting, from stage production *Toot Sweet*, 1919

Give Honor to the Soldier Boy. L: Dora Ludwig; M: Leo Friedman, 1918

Give Me a Girlie to Love Me and I'll Fight Like the Devil for You. L: E.J. Kelly; M: J. Haunschild, 1918

*Give Me a Kiss, Mirandy ('Cause I'm Going Over There). L: Forrest S. Rutherford; M: Althea J. Rutherford, 1917

Give Me Back My Husband, You've Had Him Long Enuff. L&M: J.J. Davilla, 1917

Give Me Back My Uniform with the Corporal Stripes. L: Louis Effron; M: George Graff, Jr., 1919

Give Me the Stars in Old Glory. L: Dora R. Croft; M: Leo Friedman, 1918

Give the Sammie Credit. L&M: Albert Schmid, 1919

Give Them Victory. L: T.A. Gardner; M: Leo Friedman, 1918

Give Three Cheers and a Hurrah! L: O.N. Ritzman; M: Leo Friedman, 1919

*Give Three Cheers for "Unc' Sam's" Soldiers. L&M: Maurice G. Attree, 1918

Give to Us Peace. L: Henry F. Chorley; M: C. Harold Lowden, 1915

Give Us a Song, Cried Our Soldiers (March). L&M: Duncan J. Muir, 1917

Give Us Back Our Jobs. L&M: C.C. Muth, 1919

Give Us Peace Again. L&M: H. A. Rosenbaum, 1915

Give Us the Days of Eternal Peace. L: Joe Learner; M: Cy J. Briefer, 1917

Gloriosa Patria. L: Helene H. Boll; M: Horatio Parker, 1915

Glorious Banner. L: "From the Bible"; M: Charles H. Gabriel, 1917

Glorious Emblem of the Free. L: Lizzie DeArmond; M: D.B. Towner, 1918

Glorious Flag. L&M: S.C. Salzer, 1917

Glorious Red, White and Blue. L&M: L.H. Eaton, 1917

Glorious Stars and Stripes. L&M: H.A. Blackburn, 1914

Glorious Stars and Stripes. L&M: J.M. Smith, Jr., 1918

Glory — Glory — Fight We Must! L: Mrs. C. O'Conner; M: Leo Friedman, 1918

The Glory of Peace (March). M: E.T. Paull, 1914

Glory of the U.S.A. (March). L&M: R.K. Jones, 1917

Go and Teach the Kaiser How to Sing the Marseillaise (Then Come Marching Home to Me). L&M: Forrest E. Wilson, 1918

Go Fight, My Boy, My Boy a Soldier. L: M.S. Huston; M: Roy Hartzell, 1919

Go Get the Kaiser. L: B.L. Lunau; M: Ambrose V. Keenan, 1917

*Go, Lad, and May God Bless You. L: Haven Gillespie; M: Henry I. Marshall, 1917

Go On, My Boy, Your Country Needs You. L&M: E.D. Horgan, 1917

Go On or Go Under. L: A.A. Miller; M: J.E. Ecker, 1918

Go On, Uncle Sam (March). L&M: F.B. Crittenden, 1917

Go Over the Top. L&M: John Wilson, 1918

Go Right Along, Mr. Wilson (and We'll All Stand by You). L&M: A. Seymour Brown, 1915

Go, Soldier Boy. L&M: Maud Jewell, 1918

Go to It, America, You Are the Melting Pot of the World. L&M: Jennie Wolff, 1918

God Be with My Wandering Boy Tonight. L: Eddie Dorr and Bob Schafer; M: Lew Porter and Jim Quigley, 1918

God Be with Our Boys Tonight. L: Fred G. Bowles; M: Wilfrid Sanderson, 1918

God Bless America. L: George William Douglas; M: Reginald DeKoven, 1917

God Bless Him! My Boy! L: Fay R. Hunt; M: Wilbur Watson, 1917

God Bless Our Allies. L: A. Aird, Sr.; M: Leo Friedman, 1918

God Bless Our American Boys. L&M: Mary A. Micholson, 1919

God Bless Our Boys. L: Henry J. Zelley; M: Philip Wuest, 1918

God Bless Our Boys, Our Dear Boys. L&M: Violet Hall, 1917

God Bless Our Land. L&M: Annie Gorans, 1918

God Bless Our Soldier Boys. L: Orley S. Johnston; M: Russell C. Poyster, 1918

God Bless Our Soldiers All. L: Margaret Tate; M: Leo Friedman, 1919

God Bless the Boys of Uncle Sam. L: Albert Finn; M: Mae Miller, 1917

God Bless the Dear Old Stars and Stripes. L&M: G.E. Jackson and F.E. Mendenhall, 1917

God Bless the Red Cross. L&M: L.C.M.C. Cheves, 1918

God Bless the Soldier Boy. L&M: W.E. Edmiaston, 1918

God Bless the Yankee Boys. L&M: H.W. Ellerton, 1917

God Bless You, Boy in Blue. L&M: Floyd Delker, 1918

God Bless You, Boys of Yankee Land (March). L&M: T.E. O'Brien, 1918

God Bless You, Sammy. L&M: C.A. Barry, 1918

God Bless You, Sammy. L: H. Stephenson; M: Roy Hartzell, 1919

God Bless You, Sammy Boy. L&M: Gertrude Marrack, 1918

God Bless You, U.S.A. L&M: O.H. Oakley, 1917

God Bless You, Woodrow Wilson. L&M: Charles C. Wright, 1914

God Bring Back Our Boys Safe Home Again. L&M: H.C. Weasner, 1918

God Bring You Safely to Our Arms Again. L: Kate Gibson; M: Vincent Shaw, 1917

God Guide Our President (National Prayer). L: J.M. Lydon; M: Theodore H. Northrup, 1915

God Has Blessed You and Me When He Gave Us Liberty. L&M: H.V. Coyle, 1917

God Is Our Refuge (Anthem for Peace After Victory). M: Mark Andrews, 1919

God Keep and Guide Our Men. L: Wilbur Chapman; M: May Agnes Stephens, 1918

God of Our Country. L: James Rowe; M: Anthony J. Showalter, 1918

God Save America. L&M: Laura Walker Colgrove, 1917

God Save America. L: Charles F. Lee; M: Louise S. Stevenson, 1918

God Save America. L: W. Franke Harling and Frank Conroy; M: W. Franke Harling, 1919

God Save Our President. L&M: Viola C. Snider McManis, 1917

God Save the President. L: W. Franke Harling and Frank Conroy; M: W. Franke Harling, 1918

*God Spare Our Boys Over There. L&M: William Jerome and J.F. Mahoney, 1918

God Speed the Day We Get the Kaiser's Goat. L&M: A.D. Kahler, 1918

God Speed Them Home Again. L&M: A.H. Walls, 1919

God, the All-Terrible! Give to Us Peace. L: Author unknown; M: E.J. Bonhomme, 1918

God Will Give You Peace. L: Margaret Churchill; M: A. Haertel, 1919

God's Country (American Anthem). L&M: Robert Sturmberg, 1916

God's Country, the U.S.A. L&M: F.S. Porter, 1918

God's Liberty Flag. L: Hortense D'Arblay; M: Edna Marione; English lyric by Harold Emery-Jones, 1918

God's Message of Victory (The Red Cross So True). L&M: Margaret Conway, 1918

God's with You, My America. L: H.D. Wixson; M: Roy Hartzell, 1918

Going Back H-O-M-E. (March). M: Kenneth S. Clark, 1917

Gone to Get the Kaiser. L: F.M. Timmons; M: Frank W. Ford, 1918

Going On and Over. L: P.R. Minahan; M: Florence Bettrey, 1917

Going to Can the Kaiser. L&M: Edna Coburn, 1918

Going to France. L&M: Mary D. Ramseur, 1918

Going to Lick the Kaiser. L: L.A. Perdue; M: Edith Houston Halberg, 1918

Going to See the Kaiser in Berlin. L: W. McDaniel; M: Frances Ann Wade, 1918

Going to Victory. L&M: Lawrence Love, 1917

Golden Bells of Peace. L: H.L. Frisbie; M: Peter P. Bilhorn, 1917

Golden Service Star. L: W.R. Thompson; M: Robert H. Wilson, 1918

Golden Star. L: Mrs. N.C. Gauntt; M: Leo Friedman, 1919

Good Luck and God Be with You, Laddie

Boy. L: Will D. Cobb; M: Gus Edwards, 1917

Good Luck, God Bless Our U.S. Soldier Boys. L: Louise Hollenbeck; M: J.F. Langan, 1918

Good Luck to the Boys of the Allies. L&M: Morris Manley, 1915

*Good Luck to the U.S.A. L: Arthur J. Lamb; M: Frederick V. Bowers, 1917

Good Luck to Yankee Soldiers. L: John Phoenix; M: Leo Friedman, 1918

*Good Morning, Mr. Zip-Zip-Zip! L&M: Robert Lloyd, 1918

Good Night, Kaiser. L&M: A.J. Tuxworth, 1917

Good Old Navy. L: R. Payne; M: Leo Friedman, 1918

Good Old U.S.A. L: Jack Drislane; M: Theodore Morse, 1916

Good Old U.S.A. L: W.R. Shearer; M: Leo Friedman, 1918

Good Old U.S.A. L&M: L. "Willis"; M: Leo Friedman, 1919

Good Old U.S.A. L: Maite Herr; M: Leo Friedman, 1919

Good Old U.S.A. and You. L&M: V.H. Mattson, 1918

Good Ole' U.S.A. L: S. Fink; M: Leo Friedman, 1919

Good Soldiers. L: Arthur Page; M: N.S. Waldo, 1914

Goodbye, Alexander (Goodbye, Honey-Boy). L&M: Henry S. Creamer and Turner Layton, 1918

Goodbye All, Take Care of My Yankee Friend. L&M: E. Fortunata, 1918

Goodbye, America (March). L: W.J. McKeever; M: James A. Brennan, 1917

Goodbye, America (March). M: James M. O'Keefe, from stage production *Leave It to the Sailors*, 1918

Goodbye and Good Luck, Boys (March). L&M: "Hassall and DeLuca," 1917

*(Goodbye and Luck Be with You) Laddie Boy. L: Will D. Cobb; M: Gus Edwards, 1917

Goodbye, Barney Boy. L: J. Keirn Brennan; M: Theodore Morse, 1918

Goodbye, Bill. L: Richard Fechheimer; M: W.B. Kernell, from stage production *Goodbye, Bill*, 1918

Goodbye, Bill Kaiser, Goodbye. L: F. Frazier; M: Ida K. Mervine, 1918

Goodbye, Billy Hohenzollern, Goodbye. L: R.R. Davidson; M: E.A. Lord, 1918

Goodbye Blighty, Hello France. L&M: Elmer Joyner, 1919

Goodbye Boys, Come Back Soon and Bring Back Home the Bacon. L: Herman Koenig; M: Barrington L. Brannan, 1917

Goodbye Boys, So Long. L: H.C. Dorsey; M: B.J. Wrightsman, 1918

*Goodbye Broadway, Hello France. L: C. Francis Reisner and Benny Davis; M: Billy Baskette, from stage production Passing Show of 1917, 1917

Goodbye, Daddy Dear. L&M: Ben Black, 1918

Goodbye, Dear Boys, Goodbye. L: Mae Curtis; M: Leo Friedman, 1918

Goodbye, Dear Old America. L&M: J.A. Provenzano, 1918

Goodbye, Dear Old France, Goodbye. L&M: Mrs. H.R. Scott, 1919

*Goodbye, Dear Old Girl, Goodbye. L&M: E.J. Pourmon, 1917

Goodbye, Dear Old U.S.A. L: E.L. Madocks; M: Leo Friedman, 1918

Goodbye, Dear Old Yankee Land, Hello France. L: Ruth Long; M: Leo Friedman, 1918

Goodbye, Dear Ones, Goodbye. L&M: Maud J. Howe, 1918

Goodbye Dear Sweetheart, Goodbye Dear Mother, Too. L&M: Ella Myers Gasber, 1918

Goodbye, for I Must Go. L&M: G.E. Chilton, 1918

*Goodbye, France. L&M: Irving Berlin, 1918

Goodbye, France. L&M: L.R. Ice; M: Leo Friedman, 1919

Goodbye, France. L: Mrs. H. Gilbertson; M: Leo Friedman, 1919

Goodbye France, Goodbye. L: Mrs. F. Uher; M: Artie Bowers, 1919

Goodbye France, Hello America. L: M. Kenny; M: Artie Bowers, 1919

Goodbye France, Hello Broadway! L&M: W.F. Wells, 1918

Goodbye France, Hello Broadway. L&M: Mabel Fuller, 1919

Goodbye France, Hello Broadway. L: A.E. Aker; M: Leo Friedman, 1919

Goodbye France, Hello Broadway. L: E.L. Webb; M: Artie Bowers, 1919

Goodbye, France! Hello, Miss Liberty. L&M: Homer A. Rodeheaver, 1918

*Goodbye, Germany. L: J. Edwin and Lincoln McConnell; M: J. Edwin McConnell, 1918

Goodbye, Germany. L: H. Newingham; M: Leo Friedman, 1918

Goodbye Girlie, I Must Leave You. L&M: M.G. Fitzgerald, 1918

Goodbye, Good Luck, God Bless You. L: J. Keirn Brennan; M: Ernest R. Ball, 1916

Goodbye, Good Luck, My Soldier Boy. L: Kathleen Yarck; M: Lillian Kuhlman, 1917

Goodbye, Honey Boy, Goodbye (A Patriotic Poem and March). L&M: Isabel Wister, 1917

Goodbye, Kaiser Bill. L&M: J.L. Waldorf, 1918

Goodbye, Kaiser Bill. L: M. Jones; M: Leo Friedman, 1919

Goodbye L'il Liza Jane, Hello Alsace-Lorraine. L: H. McNutt; M: Karl Johnson, 1918

Goodbye, Little Berlin. L: M.E. Herring; M: Leo Friedman, 1918

Goodbye, Little French Girls, Goodbye. L: B. Lowmiller; M: Leo Friedman, 1919

Goodbye, Little Girl, for a While. L: Herbert H. Power; M: Walter H. Curtis, 1918

Goodbye, Little Girl, Goodbye. L: Will D. Cobb; M: Gus Edwards, 1917

Goodbye, Ma! (Soldier's Song). L: Jennie Mitchell; M: George Lowell Tracy, 1918

Goodbye, Ma! Goodbye, Pa! Goodbye, Mule, with Yer Old Hee-Haw! L: William Herschell; M: Barclay Walker, 1917

Goodbye, Mary, It Won't Be Long Till I Come Back. L: B.B. Kent; M: Frank W. Ford, 1918

Goodbye, Miss Liberty. L&M: Rosalie O'Neal, 1919

Goodbye, Mollie Darling (March). L&M: George Spink, 1917

Goodbye, Mollie May (March). L&M: Michael J. Fitzpatrick, 1917

Goodbye Mother, Don't Forget the Boys That Won't Come Home. L: Edward L. Pyers; M: Artie Bowers, 1919

Goodbye, Mother, Don't You Worry Over Me. L&M: Robert T. Fleming, 1919

Goodbye Mother, I'll Return Some Day. L: W.H. Powell; M: Leo Friedman, 1918

Goodbye Mother, Old and Gray. L: Dillies Forton; M: Leo Friedman, 1918

Goodbye Mother, So Long Dad, Hello Uncle Sam. L: W.E. Browning; M: Christian A. Grimm, 1917

Goodbye, My Boy, and God Bless You. L: Ina Duley Ogdon; M: Charles H. Gabriel, 1918

Goodbye, My Brave Soldier Husband. L: Irene Loder; M: Leo Friedman, 1918

Goodbye, My Chocolate Soldier Boy. L: R. Graham; M: James White, 1918

Goodbye, My Dear Old Mother. L: Fred W. Zilz; M: Leo Friedman, 1918

*Goodbye, My Hero. L&M: Ernest R. Hech, 1918

Goodbye, My Laddie! L: Leona Upton; M: Robert Ashford, 1918

Goodbye, My Little Lady. L: Joe Goodwin; M: James F. Hanley, 1917

Goodbye, My Only Sweetheart. L: J.O. Dyer; M: Isabella Dyer, 1918

Goodbye, My Pretty Baby. L: Walter Hirsch; M: Howard Steiner, 1917

*Goodbye, My Soldier Boy. L&M: Calla Gowdy Gregg, 1917

Goodbye, My Soldier Boy. L&M: Hettie King Hankins, 1918

*Goodbye, My Soldier Boy (March). L&M: June Bauer, 1918

Goodbye, My Soldier Boy (God Bless You). L: B.B. Fleishman; M: F.S. Iula, 1918

Goodbye, My Soldier Boy, Goodbye. L: Adam Speace Moore; M: Robert Marlowe Jandus, 1918

Goodbye, My Sweetheart, I Am Going. L: Jay Tyler; M: E.S.S. Huntington, 1918

Goodbye, My Sweetheart, I Go to Fight for Country and My Flag. L&M: James L. Halloran, 1917

Goodbye, My Yankee Soldier Boy. L&M: W.J. Satchell, 1917

Goodbye, New Hampshire and the U.S.A. L: Alice Riley; M: Leo Friedman, 1918

Goodbye, Old Glory's Calling Me. L: J.J. Coughlin; M: Luther A. Clark, 1917

Goodbye, Old Khaki Kid. L: Lee M. Walker; M: Arthur Lamont, 1918

Goodbye, Sal (March). L&M: Ella Rebecca Miller, 1917

*Goodbye, Sally (Good Luck to You). L&M: Sam Habelow, 1919

*Goodbye, Sammie! (Gee, I'm Glad to See You Go!). L: Samuel L. Gassel; M: Albert Tusso, 1918

Goodbye, Sammy Dear. L&M: C.W. Hatch, 1918

Goodbye, Shot and Shell. L: Lou Spero; M: Gerald Peck, 1919

Goodbye, Slim. L&M: Walter Donaldson, 1918

Goodbye, So Long, Little Sweetheart. L&M: Andrew Mack, 1917

Goodbye, [My] Soldier Boy. L: J.Ernest Reels and D. Rosenwein; M: J. Ernest Reels, 1917

Goodbye, Soldier Boy. L&M: Lulu M. Crockett, 1918

Goodbye, Sweet Annabelle. L: Edward W. Schaub; M: Alfred Damm, 1918

Goodbye, Sweetheart, Be Good to Uncle Sam. L&M: Lillian Ramona Morin, 1918

Goodbye, Sweetheart, Goodbye. L: Anthony Mancuso; M: Leo Friedman, 1918

Goodbye, Sweetheart, Goodbye (March). L&M: Bennie Branch, 1918

Goodbye Sweetheart, I'm on My Way to War. L: J.H. Mark; M: Leo Friedman, 1918

"Goodbye," That Means You. L: Andrew B. Sterling; M: Arthur Lange, 1917

Goodbye to Germany. L: J.A. Wright; M: Frank W. Ford, 1919

Goodbye to No Man's Land. L: Walter J. Monahan and L.E. Segal; M: L.E. Segal, 1919

Goodbye to the Dream of the Huns. L: H.J. Emmons, 1919

Goodbye to You, to Sue, and Uncle Sammy, Too. L: V. Allison; M: Leo Friedman, 1918

Goodbye, Uncle Sam, Goodbye. L: T.J. Geyer; M: Leo Friedman, 1918

Goodbye, Uncle Sam, We Are on Our Way to Fight for the U.S.A. L: I.M. Flower; M: Leo Friedman, 1919

Goodbye, United States. L&M: T. Bruce, 1918

Goodbye, U.S.A. L&M: Guy A. Surber, 1918

Goodbye, Virginia. L: Grant Clarke; M: Jean Schwartz, 1915

Goodbye, We Are Off to France. L&M: Sylvia Ramsey, 1918

Goodbye, William, Goodbye. L&M: A.A. Dart; M: Edward Auten, Jr., 1918

The Goose Step. M: Eugene Platzmann, 1915

Grab a Hoe, Hoe, Hoe. L: Junie McCree; M: Edward Stembler, 1917

The Grand Old Army Wilson Sends to France. L: P. Reynolds; M: C.R. Wenzel, 1917

The Grand Old Flag Over There. L: G.W. McCauslen; M: Louis Panella, 1918

Grand Old U.S.A. L&M: A. Stevens, 1917

Grandma's Little Soldier Girl. L&M: Natalie Whitted Price, 1919

Grant Us Peace. L: M.L. Hunter; M: David E. Grove, 1916

Gratitude from Our Allies. L: John Chirg-

win; M: Leo Friedman, 1919

A Grave in France. L: Nora Moore; M: Rudolph Ganz, 1918

A Gray-Haired Mother's Praying to Bring Her Boy Back Home. L&M: J.I. Soukup and H. Price, 1917

Great God of Liberty (A Patriotic Anthem). L&M: M.O. Burford, 1918

Great Peace. L: Psalm 119; M: J.B. Herbert, 1917

The Great World War. L: U.G. Foster; M: Leo Friedman, 1919

The Greatest Battle Song of Them All. L: Al Friend and Sam Downing; M: Harry Ruby, 1916

*The Greatest Day the World Will Ever Know. L: Ed Morton and James E. Dempsey; M: Joseph A. Burke, 1918

Greatest Little Mother in the World. L&M: Willie Weston, James Kendis, James Brockman, and Nat Vincent, 1918

Greatest Nation on Earth. L&M: Charles Abbate, 1917

The Greatest Thing That Came from France. L: Harry Pease; M: Edward G. Nelson, 1919

Grogan of the Fighting Sixty-Ninth. L: P.J. Carey; M: Harry Murphy, 1918

Guard House Blues. L&M: Ben Garrison, 1919

Gunner's March. M: Carlo Graziani-Walter, 1918

H

Hadn't Bill Forgotten to Reckon with Uncle Sam? L: C. Ratcliff; M: J.A. Halls, 1919

Hail, America. L&M: A.G. Spencer, 1917

Hail America, Our Cry! L: Charles Keeler; M: Hugo Riesenfeld, 1918

Hail, American Soldier (March). L&M: Alice G. Arthur, 1918

Hail, Columbia. M: Maurice F. Smith, 1917

Hail, Flag of Freedom! L: W. McClare; M: Alfred Pennington, 1918

Hail! Freedom's Land. L&M: Justin McCarthy, 1917

Hail, Hail, America! L&M: Marion S. Harris, 1917

Hail, Hail, Land of Freedom! L&M: George Chittenden Turner, 1915

*Hail! Hail! the Gang's All Here. L: D.A. Esrom; M: Theodore Morse and Arthur Sullivan, 1917

Hail, Land of Liberty! (National Hymn). L&M: Alfred F. Denghausen, 1917

Hail, League of Nations! L: N.D. Sweeny; M: Leo Friedman, 1919

Hail, Loved America (A National Hymn). L&M: Waldo Reed, 1918

Hail, Starry Banner. L&M: Emma Lois Reardon, 1917

Hail, the Conquering Hero Comes. L: C.C. Whelen; M: J.W. Rey, 1919

Hail the Dawn of Peace. L&M: Nell Marshall, 1918

Hail to America! L&M: G. Herb Palin, 1917

Hail to America! (March). L&M: Fred K. Huffer, 1917

Hail to Old Glory (March). M: Fred Jewell, 1918

Hail to Old Glory Forever. L&M: Lucia Wells, 1917

Hail to Our Flag (A Patriotic Anthem). L: Frederick H. Mortens; M: A. Maloof, 1916

Hail to Our Flag. L: E.D. Platt; M: Roy Hartzell, 1919

Hail to the Boys from France! L&M: Mary Howes Sparkman, 1919

Hail to the Flag. L&M: J.G. Bush, 1917

Hail to the President! (March). M: Frederick Coit Wight, 1916

Hail to the Red Cross Nurses. L&M: Leonore Hoppes Armor, 1918

Hail to the Spirit of Freedom (March). L&M: W.C. Handy, 1915

Hail to the Stars and Stripes. L&M: Joseph Miller, 1919

Hail to Uncle Sam (March). M: Ernest Weber, 1916

Hail, U.S.A.! L&M: Justin McCarthy, 1915

Halt the Hun! L: M.C. Egan; M: Leo Friedman, 1919

*Hand in Hand Again. L: Raymond B. Egan; M: Richard A. Whiting, 1919

The Hand That Rocks the Cradle (Is the Hand That Rules the World). L: Jeff Branen; M: Evans Lloyd, from stage production A Courtship in Song, 1917

Hands Around the World. L: Alfred S. Eiseman; M: A. Baldwin Sloane, 1917

Hands Off Our U.S.A. L&M: Rosie Hendricks, 1917

Hands Off the U.S.A. L: G. Garrett; M: Ralph Keefer, 1916

Happy Sammies. M: Leo DeVal, 1917

Happy Soldiers. L&M: Grace Hill, 1919

Hark, Hear the Bugle Calling! L: Mrs. J. Anderson; M: Rea Wallace and Mrs. J. Anderson, 1917

Hark, the Bugle Calls "Away"! L&M: I.C. Tirrell, 1918

Hark, 'Tis a Call. L: E.E. Hewitt; M: Charles H. Gabriel, 1917

Hark to the Call of Freedom! L&M: G. deVeuve, 1917

Hark, to the Country's Call. L&M: J.H. Calisch, 1917

Hark to the President's Call, Boys! L: Harry Wolfe; M: Rosalind Linnette, 1918

Hark! Uncle Sam Is Calling. L&M: Mrs. William Wegener, 1919

Hats Off, Salute Old Glory! L: J.L. Ripper; M: John E. Brown, 1918

Hats Off! The Flag! L: Henry Holcomb Bennett; M: Charles E. Burnham, 1919

Hats Off! The Flag Goes By (A Patriotic Song). L: Henry Holcomb Bennett; M: R.B. Lynch, 1917

Hats Off to All America and to the Old Red, White and Blue. L: Peter W. Kehlenbach; M: Elizabeth S. Howe, 1919

Hats Off to Dear Old Glory, and Hurrah for Uncle Sam! L&M: Charles M. McIntyre, 1915

Hats Off to President Wilson. L&M: H.J. Williams, 1919

Hats Off to the Boys from Yankee Land. L: G.A. Childers; M: Leo Friedman, 1919

Hats Off to the Boys in Khaki. L: S.H. Weaver; M: Leo Friedman, 1918

Hats Off to the Flag. L&M: James G. Dailey, 1917

Hats Off to the Red, White and Blue (March). L: Chester R. Hovey; M: Ralph F. Beegan, 1918

Hats Off to the U.S.A. L: H.E. Jaynes; M: Henry Kailimai, 1918

Hats Off to Uncle Sam (March). M: Emily D. Wilson, 1918

Hats Off to Uncle Sam. L&M: C.M. Rautenberg, 1918

Have Courage, My Boys, We're Coming Right from the U.S.A. L&M: P.J. O'Reilly and R.M. Rogers, 1918

Have You Bought a Liberty Bond? L: Bernard Brodie; M: J. Carlton Podolyn, 1918

Have You Seen the Lad Called a Slacker? L&M: D.T. Atkinson, 1917

He Does His Sentry Duty Like a Man. L&M: Joe Guinan, 1918

He Fell in France. L&M: Bates Torrey, 1918

He Fought That All the World Be Free. L: John Robertson; M: Ian Donnachaidh, 1919

He Gave His Life in Flanders. L: D.E. Feldhausen; M: Leo Friedman, 1919

He Gave Us Wilson. L&M: Charles R. Campbell, 1918

He Paid His Last Installment on the Price of Victory. L&M: R.F. O'Shaughnessy, 1918

He Said We Couldn't Do It but We Did. L&M: Nell Marshall, 1918

He Sleeps Beneath the Soil of France. L&M: Tell Taylor, 1917

He Sleeps in Sunny France. L: C.G. Robinson; M: Kathryn I. White, 1919

He Was a Soldier from the U.S.A. (Fighting for His Native Land). L: J. Fred Lawton; M: Howard Kocian, 1914

He Was My Buddy. L&M: Cliff Hess and Arthur Fields, 1919

He Was Only a Private. L&M: William Main, 1918

Hear the Call. L&M: C.B. Iliffe, 1918

Hear the Call (A Liberty Bond Song). L&M: E.T. Welsh, 1918

Hear the Peace Bells Ring Ding Dong. L&M: Arthur N. Green, 1918

Hear Uncle Sammy Calling to the People Ev'rywhere. L: W.H. Shirley; M: Kathryn I. White, 1918

Hear Your Country's Call (A Patriotic Song). L: Anonymous and J. Fletcher; M: J. Fletcher, 1917

Hear Your Uncle Sammy Calling. L: Mrs. W.J. Hart; M: E.S.S. Huntington, 1918

Heart of America (March). M: Arthur Pryor, 1917

Heart of America. L: Sophia Beck; M: Leo Friedman, 1919

Heart of the World. L&M: George B. McConnell, 1915

Hearts of America (March). M: A.C. Gardner, 1916

Hearts of the World. L&M: Lee Johnson, from silent film *Hearts of the World*, 1918

Hearts of the World, We Are Sending Our Sweethearts to You. L: George Graff, Jr.; M: Bert Grant, 1918

Heatless, Meatless, Wheatless Days. L: J. Thinnes; M: Roy Hartzell, 1919

The Heavens Are a Mother's Service Flag. L: Nathan A. Conney; M: J. Edward Woolley and Paul L. Specht, 1917

The Heav'n Sent Stars and Stripes. L: Fred Earp; M: Leo Friedman, 1919

Heep Plenty Hun Scalps! L: Franklin Clark Sawhill; M: Kathryn I. White, 1918

He'll Come Back from Somewhere (A Patri-

otic Song). L: H.H. Blake; M: W.G. Yule, 1918

Hello, America, Hello. L&M: George Fairman, 1917

Hello, America, I'm Home Again. L: Nelle Earle; M: Leo Friedman, 1919

Hello Boys, Hello Boys. L: J.A. Brex, Jr.; M: Leo Friedman, 1919

Hello Broadway, Goodbye France. L&M: Bettie Skinner, 1919

Hello Broadway, Goodbye France. M: R.A. Walter, 1919

Hello Central, Give Me France. L: James M. Reilly; M: Harry DeCosta, 1917

Hello Central, Give Me France. L: J.L. Poston; M: Leo Friedman, 1919

*Hello, Central! Give Me No Man's Land. L: Sam M. Lewis and Joe Young; M: Jean Schwartz, 1918

Hello Central, Is My Daddy There? L&M: Mollie [Julia M. Moore], 1918

Hello! Gen'ral Pershing (How's My Daddy To-Night?) L&M: Lew Porter, 1918

Hello! Miss Liberty. L&M: Dave Brown, 1919

Hello, Mother, I'm Back Home. L&M: Bobby Heath, 1919

Hello, My Darling Mother. L&M: Barney Goldstein, 1918

Hello Red, White and Blue, America and All (Hello Allies, Too). L: John J. Puderer; M: C.H. Iddings, 1917

Hello Sammy, Here's My Son. L: V.R. Coon; M: Leo Friedman, 1918

Hello There, Uncle Sammy! And How Do You Do? L: G.A. Miller; M: William A. Schilling, 1918

Help Bring Our Stars and Stripes Across the Rhine (March). L&M: R.H. Unterdorfel, 1918

Help Carry the Red, White and Blue. L: Mrs. F.M. Waggener; M: Leo Friedman, 1918

Help Civilize the Huns. L: A.D. Kingsley; M: Leo Friedman, 1918

Help Hoover Win the War. L&M: Ada Mae Collins, 1918

Help Our Boys in Khaki Win the Fight. L: S.A. Drew; M: S.A. Drew and Louis Boos, 1918

Help Put the Kaiser Out. L: A.L. Hodgers; M: Leo Friedman, 1918

Help Sammy Fight It Out (The Great Drive Song). L: Carrie McCune; M: Wilhelm Schroder, 1918

Help Save Our Boys and Old Glory. L&M: J.W. O'Brien, 1918

Help to Bring the Boys Back Home. L&M: Ellis Levy, 1918

Help to Make a Happy World. L: Elsie Duncan Yale; M: Adam Geibel, 1917

Help Uncle Sam Down the Kaiser. L: M.M. Holtz; M: Leo Friedman, 1918

Help Uncle Sam Win. L: W.R. Goslin; M: Clarence Kohlmann, 1917

Help Your Own Country. L: Mary Jardim; K: Leo Friedman, 1918

Helping the Soldiers to Win. L: L.D. Strong; M: Leo Friedman, 1918

Helping to Hel-met the Kaiser (March). L: C.W. Towne; M: G. Nocet, 1918

Henry Ford's March. M: Per Selander, 1916

Hep, Hep, All Keep Step! L&M: F.A. Grant, 1918

Her Boy Up in the Blue. L&M: Belle McNeir, 1918

Her Charming Soldier Boy. L: E. Cross; M: Artie Bowers, 1919

Her Country's Call. L&M: Frances Atwell, 1917

Her Lad Who Never Returned. L&M: L.E. Brown, 1919

Her Only Boy. L&M: Carrie Baker, 1919

Her Only Son. L: J.M. Achen; M: Leo Friedman, 1918

Her Soldier Boy. L: S.F. Blair; M: Artie Bowers, 1919

Her Soldier Boy. L: J.W. Utterback; M: Leo Friedman, 1919

Her Soldier Over There. L: L.B. Hoffer; M: Leo Friedman, 1918

Her Soldier Sweetheart's Farewell. L&M: G.L. Riggs, 1918

Her Sweetheart Went Across the Sea. L&M: James B. Love, 1919

Her Yankee Boy. L: A. Thornton; M: Leo Friedman, 1919

Her Yankee Soldier Boy. L&M: J.F. Langan, 1917

Herald of Peace (March). M: E.T. Paull, 1914

Here Are My Sons, Dear U.S.A. L&M: Abraham J. Goldberg, 1918

Here Come Our Boys (March). M: Louis Gerber, 1918

Here Come the Khaki Boys. L&M: H.L. Cramm, 1918

Here Come the Yanks with the Tanks. L. Ned Wayburn; M: Harold Orlob, from stage production Hitchy Coo of 1918, 1918

Here Comes America. L&M: Ed Rose and Jack Glogau, 1918

Here Comes Our Uncle Sam Now. L: Mrs. H.C. Keitz, 1918

Here Comes Uncle Sam. L: C.W. North; M: W.H. Graham, 1917

Here I Am, Uncle Sam. L&M: E.L. Powell, 1917

Here I Am, Uncle Sammy, Take Me. L: Dean T. Wilton; M: James McHugh, 1917

Here They Come (Left, Right — Left, Right). L&M: Sadie E. Simpson, 1918

Here We Are, All Americans. L&M: Sadie Willson Brown, 1917

Here We Are, Lafayette. L&M: C.A. Pfeiffer, 1918

Here We Come (March). L&M: Mary E. Turner, 1918

Here We Come, America. L&M: Charles Manney, 1917

Here We Come, Ye Sons of France. L: Dow Vroman; M: Henry Tussing, 1917

Here's My Hand, Uncle Sam, for I Hear Them Calling Me. L: G.H. Brooks; M: Leo Friedman, 1918

Here's to Our Aeroplane Heroes So Brave. L&M: F.W. Stodgell, 1919

Here's to Our Boys. L: Mary Bertha Rice; M: C.I. Thoma, 1918

Here's to Our Boys. L: G.E. Boyd; M: Leo Friedman, 1919

Here's to Our Country's Freedom. L&M: Harold Partington, 1916

Here's to Our Flag. L&M: Helen Savage McKay, 1917

Here's to Our Sailors. L: I.M. Heskett; M: Leo Friedman, 1919

Here's to Our Sailors in Blue. L: Eva A. Ball; M: Amber G. Lasley, 1918

Here's to Our Soldier Boys. L&M: H. and Babe Mayhall, 1918

Here's to the Boys in Khaki. L&M: Charles H. Forsythe, 1918

Here's to the Boys of the U.S.A. L: Frederick H. Green; M: Harry Verona, 1918

Here's to the Flag. L&M: Frank Sherwood, 1917

Here's to the Flag. L: K.M. Fargo; M: E.D. Palmer, 1917

Here's to the Flying Corps. L&M: Ann and Elizabeth Oles, 1918

Here's to the Land of the Stars and Stripes. L: Willis N. Bugbee; M: Edna Randolph Worrell, 1917

Here's to the Land of Uncle Sam. L: George F. Jordan; M: R.S. Browne, 1917

Here's to the Soldier. L: Ida L. Simpson; M: Leo Bennett, 1917

Here's to the Sons of the Flag. L: George Morrow Mayo; M: Alla Pearl Little, 1918

Here's to You, America. L: Fred W. Zilz; M: Leo Friedman, 1919

Here's to You, Fighting Men. L&M: Mabel Baker, 1918

Heroes Are a Mother's Service Flag. L: Nathan A. Conney; M: J. Edward Woolley, 1918

Heroes in Khaki. L: Mrs. S. Tuttle; M: Al Farnham, 1919

Heroes of Liberty. L: Norma Bernards; M: Edward I. Pfeiffer, 1919

Heroes of '17. L&M: Grace C. Persike, 1917

Heroes of the Flag. L&M: Gordon V. Thompson, 1919

Heroes of Today. L&M: Ethel Low Clays, 1918

Heroic Mother. L&M: Katharine Dewson Gostin, 1918

Hero's Return (March). M: H.J. Crosby, 1918

Hero's Return. L&M: Geraldine Krause, 1919

He's a Soldier for the Red, White and Blue. L&M: F.F. Dawdy, 1918

He's a Soldier of the U.S.A. L: Dan J. Wall; M: James White, 1914

He's a Traitor to the Union Boys in Blue. L&M: Billie Jones, 1917

He's All Shot to Pieces by the French Girls' Eyes. L&M: John Stark, 1917

He's Coming Home. L: Rida Johnson Young; M: Sigmund Romberg, from stage production *Her Soldier Boy*, 1916

He's Coming Home. L: Bob Schafer; M: Frank Papa, 1919

He's Doing His Bit (for the Girls). L: Bert Hanlon; M: Harry Von Tilzer, 1917

He's Everybody's President Now. L&M: John T. Mills, 1914

He's Gone to Fight for America. L: B. Peck and E. Ott; M: E.S.S. Huntington, 1918

*(He's Got Those Big Blue Eyes Like You) Daddy Mine. L&M: Lew Wilson and Al Dubin, 1918

He's Had No Lovin' for a Long, Long Time. L: William Tracey; M: Maceo Pinkard, 1919

He's in Uncle Sam's Marines. L&M: F. Seaborne, 1918

He's Just a Common Private Soldier. L&M: Walter Fryburg and Cyrille Lamar, 1918

He's Mother's Sailor Boy. L: B. Cohen; M: Carl R. Zerse, 1918

He's My Boy. L&M: Lou Klein, 1918

He's Now Upon the Sea. L: Mrs. Lucius Hardage; M: Flavil Hall, 1917

He's Sadder Now but Wiser Is the Kaiser. L: I.L. Baer; M: Edgar Rollman, 1918

He's the American Boy. L&M: Louis F. Grabs, 1917

*He's Well Worth Waiting For. L: Garfield Kilgour; M: Harry Von Tilzer, 1918

He's Your Boy and My Boy, Daddy. L: E. Thornton; M: Robert Van Sickle, 1917

Hey, Wop, Go Over the Top! L&M: Lew Brown, 1918

Highlanders, Fix Bayonets! L: William J. Pitts; M: Geoffrey O'Hara, 1915

Hip, Hip, Hooray! L: Mrs. W.E. Wood; M: Leo Friedman, 1918

Hip-Hip Horray for Our Red Cross Nurses. L&M: I.M. Cassel, 1918

Hip, Hip Hooray for the Grand Old U.S.A. L&M: H.R. Fletcher, 1917

Hip, Hip, Hooray for the U.S.A.! L&M: H.C. Hardley, 1918

Hip! Hip! Hooray, We Are Marching Away (March). L&M: Barney Toy, 1917

Hip! Hip! Hurrah! We Are Coming Home Some Day. L: A.R. Salsgiver; M: Leo Friedman, 1919

His Buttons Are Marked "U.S." L: Mary Norton Bradford; M: Carrie Jacobs-Bond, 1902/1918

His Daddy Was a Soldier. L: L. Jackson; M: Artie Bowers, 1919

His Land of the Red, White and Blue. L: Lillian Knox; M: Genevieve Scott, 1914

His Last Message from France. L: Mary Huber; M: Hermann M. Hahn, 1918

Hit the Trail for Europe! (Marching Song of the Sammy). L&M: Jack Neilan, 1918

Hock the Kaiser. L&M: James H. Hall, 1917

Hock the Kaiser. L&M: C.J. Novak, 1918

Hoe Your "Little Bit" in Your Own Backyard. L: Dee Dooling Cahill; M: J.E. Andino, 1917

Hold 'Em Back Till We Get There, That's All! L&M: Jack Frost, 1918

Hold Fast, Tommies, Here Comes Uncle Sam! L: Mrs. W.C. Cochran; M: Leo Friedman, 1918

Hold the Foe at Bay. L: C. Guibor; M: Leo Friedman, 1918

Hold the Line. L: G.G. Currie; M: Robert H. Brennen, 1918

Hold the Line (or, Bearing the Banner of the Free). L: A. Spalding; M: G. Maxwell, 1918

Hold the Line, For We Are Coming. L: E.J. Tyner; M: Leo Friedman, 1919

Hold the Line, Lads, We Are Coming! L: Dixie Gray; M: Leo Friedman, 1918

Hold the Line, We're Coming, Boys, We're Coming Millions Strong. L: M.N. Keith; M: Leo Friedman, 1918

Holy Father, Cheer Our Way. L: R.H. Robinson; M: Irving Gingrich, 1919

Home Again. L: Rida Johnson Young; M: Sigmund Romberg, from stage production *Her Soldier Boy,* 1916

Home Again. L: William Cary Duncan; M: Alexander Johnstone, from stage production *Flood of Sunshine,* 1919

Home Again. L: J.G. Sherman; M: Leo Friedman, 1919

Home Again. L&M: L. Zumwalt, 1919

Home Again (America for Me). L: Henry Van Dyke; M: E. Philleo, 1919

Home Again, Boys, Home Again, Back Across the Sea. L&M: Harry L. Brown, 1919

Home Again to Drive All the Tears Away. L: Bartley Costello; M: James W. Casey, 1919

Home Again to Home Sweet Home. L&M: C.B. Weston, 1918

Home! Boys, Home (March). L: H.W. Noyes; M: A.B. Swan, 1918

Home from Berlin. L: Mrs. O. Abbey; M: H. Richard, 1919

Home from the Front. L&M: H.R. Kienzle, 1918

Home from the Plains of France. L&M: Forest Lohr and John Weibel, 1919

Home Guards March. M: Charles Southwell, 1918

Home of Liberty. L&M: Frank A. Daniels, 1916

Home of the Red, White and Blue (March). L&M: J.T. Young, 1918

*The Home Road. L&M: John Alden Carpenter, 1917

H-O-M-E Spells Where I Long to Be. L: J. Fred Lawton; M: Will E. Dulmage and Eddie McGrath, 1918

Home Sweet Home Will Be Sweeter. L: B.S. Buhrmester; M: George Graff, Jr., 1919

The Homecoming (March). M: Foster A. Beck, 1918

Homecoming Week in France. L&M: Seneca G. Lewis, 1918

*Homeland (I Can Hear You Calling Me). L: James E. Dempsey; M: Joseph A. Burke, 1918

Homeward Bound. L&M: Irving Berlin, from stage production *Watch Your Step,* 1915

Homeward Bound. L: Howard Johnson and Coleman Goetz; M: George W. Meyer, 1917

Homeward Bound (March). M: P.F. Brady, 1918

Homeward Bound. L: V.A. Marsh; M: Herman A. Hummel, 1919

Homeward Bound. L: Susanna Dicker; M: Leo Friedman, 1919

Homeward Bound. L&M: Isabell L. Hempstead, 1919

Homeward Bound Blues. L&M: J. Clifford Powers and Eugene Platzmann, 1918

Honor the Army That Died for You. L: Mrs. J. Fitzgerald; M: Leo Friedman, 1919

Honor the Red, White and Blue. L: B.D. Coulter; M: Robert H. Brennen, 1917

Honor to Our Nation (March). M: Alfred E. Joy, 1917

Honor to Our Soldier Boys. L&M: Mrs. F.E. Bowman, 1918

Honor to Our Soldier Boys. L&M: Arnettie Washington, 1919

Honor's Call (A Patriotic Song). L&M: John W. Metcalf, 1917

Hooray for Uncle Sam! L&M: Della Williams Paine, 1917

Hooray, Hooray for Dixieland and Yankee Doodle, Too! L&M: Minnie B. Allyn, 1919

Hooray, We're Coming Home! L: R.W. Lockard; M: E. Riley, 1918

Hoover Hooverized. L&M: Mrs. Melrose Scales, 1918

Hooverization of Our Nation. L&M: E.K. Failor, 1918

Hooverizing. L: Lily Younkin; M: Leo Friedman, 1918

A Hope for Peace (Waltz). M: Jesse Darnell, 1917

Hope of the World (Patriotic Song). L&M: A. Fieldhouse, 1919

Hopeful Sammies. L&M: Herlen de la Barre Sohm, 1918

Hosanna. L&M: Arthur Farwell, 1918

The Hour I Was Told of His Death. L&M: Ida E. Scafe, 1919

Hour of Peace. L: M.J. Schmidt; M: Leo Friedman, 1919

How America Can Win. L: Beatrice Barnes; M: Leo Friedman, 1918

How Are the Styles Since the Boys Came Home? L: Verna Schields; M: Leo Friedman, 1919

How Did the Yanks Get Across? L&M: Charles R. McCarron and Carey Morgan, 1918

How Glad I Am I'm a Yankee Man. L&M: N.W. Foust, 1918

How I Love a Soldier Boy. L&M: Fay Watters, 1918

How Many Blocks to France? L: L. Treadway; M: Leo Friedman, 1919

How Sleep the Brave? M: Walter Wild, 1918

How We Love You, Dear Old Glory, You're the Greatest Flag on Earth. L&M: Glenn C. Leap, 1917

*How 'Ya Gonna Keep 'Em Down on the Farm (After They've Seen Paree)? L: Sam M. Lewis and Joe Young; M: Walter Donaldson, 1919

Humanity March. M: J.L. Fitzhenry, 1918

The Hun Drive. L&M: R.L. Webb, 1918

The Hun Is on the Wave. L: M.B. Marshall; M: Albert Hodgson, 1918

Hun on the Run. L: Ora E. Sempre; M: Christian A. Praetorius, 1918

Hun on the Run. L: M. Abernathy; M: Artie Bowers, 1919

A Hundred Million Strong (A War Song for the Nation). L: Andrew F. Underhill; M: Robert E.S. Olmsted, 1917

*Hunting the Hun. L: Howard E. Rogers; M: Archie Gottler, 1918

Hurrah, All Wars Are Over! (International League of Nations Song). L&M: Felix Heink, 1918

Hurrah for America! (March). M: Tobia Acciani, 1918

Hurrah for America! L: A. Lindner; M: Leo Friedman, 1918

Hurrah for America! L&M: G.W. Clark, 1919

Hurrah for America! (Let's Say It Again). L: M.E. Root; M: Arthur Stanley, 1919

Hurrah for My Native Land! L&M: W.O. Hood, 1914

Hurrah for Old Glory (A Patriotic Song). L&M: F.C. Lampham, 1917

Hurrah for Old Glory! L: W.M. Ruggles; M: Leo Friedman, 1919

Hurrah for Our Boys! L: H.C. Brooks; M: Laura Sedgwick Collins, 1918

Hurrah for Our Sammies! L: S.J.N. Brock; M: Leo Friedman, 1918

Hurrah for Our Soldier Boys! L: Fanna Simmerman; M: Leo Friedman, 1918

Hurrah for President Wilson! L&M: Virginia E. Young, 1915

Hurrah for the Allied Fleet! L&M: Pearl Beale and O.B. Woodruff, 1918

Hurrah for the Army and Navy! L&M: M.M. Osborne, 1917

Hurrah for the Army and Navy! L: Maud Thompson; M: John Tasker Howard, Jr., 1918

Hurrah for the Boys. L&M: Freeman B. Van Horn and Elsie Shepard Van Horn, 1918

Hurrah for the Boys from Yankee Land! L&M: E.P. Wideman, 1919

Hurrah for the Boys in Khaki. L&M: F.M. McFarland, 1918

Hurrah for the Boys in Khaki. L&M: Anna V. Smock, 1918

Hurrah for the Boys That Have Gone Over There! L&M: N.F. Schill, 1919

Hurrah for the Flag! L: C.S. Nutter; M: Genevieve Scott, 1914

Hurrah for the Flag of America! L&M: J.A. Hansen, 1918

Hurrah for the Liberty Boys, Hurrah! (March). L&M: E.T. Paull, 1918

Hurrah for the Marines! L: A.T. Ouellette; M: Leo Friedman, 1919

Hurrah for the Red, White and Blue. L&M: O.E. Howard, 1918

Hurrah for the U.S.A.! L: Mrs. S. Hangsrud; M: Leo Friedman, 1919

Hurrah for Uncle Sam! L&M: Howard Sargent, 1917

Hurrah for Uncle Sam! L: L.M. Cooper; M: Leo Friedman, 1918

Hurrah for Uncle Sammy! L: Mrs. E.O. Davis; M: Roy Hartzell, 1919

Hurrah for U.S.A. (March). L&M: John Castricone, 1918

Hurrah for Wilson and the American Race! L: L. Martino; M: Leo Friedman, 1918

Hurrah for Wilson's Braves! L&M: A. May Brannan, 1918

Hurrah! Hurrah! America! L: Wessie Buchanan; M: Frank W. Ford, 1919

Hurrah, Hurrah America, Hurrah for Uncle Sam! L&M: Julius Carl, Jr., 1918

Hurrah, Hurrah for America! L&M: Minnie B. Allyn, 1918

Hurrah! Hurray! for Uncle Sam. L&M: Mary F. Smyth Davis, 1917

Hurrah, Hurrah, We'll Set the Belgians Free! L&M: Miles Fay, 1917

Hurrah, I'm Bound for France Today! L&M: C.B. Shivers, 1918

Hurrah, U.S.A.! L&M: G.H. Wilson, 1918

Hurrah, We're Going to Berlin! L: J.H. Mills; M: Leo Friedman, 1918

Hurrah, We're Off for France! L: T. Lynch; M: Leo Friedman, 1918

Hurrah When Sammy Comes Marching Home. L: M.C. Prell; M: F. Allen, 1918

Hurray, America! L&M: G.W. Hassler, 1917

Hurray for Peace with Victory. L: G.H.W. Cloud; M: Walter Lewis, 1918

Hymn for America. L: A. Codington; M: Joseph Maerz, 1917

Hymn for America. L: William Adams Slade; M: Lawrence Camilieri, 1918

Hymn in Time of War. L: Arthur C. Cove: M: G.A. West, 1918

Hymn of Patriotism. L: Emile Voûte; M: C. Lillian Griffin, 1917

Hymn of Peace. L&M: H.J. Sattler, 1915

Hymn of Peace and Good Will. L: Edwin Markham; M: William Arms Fisher, 1918

Hymn to America. L: W.C. Langdon; M: B.C. Peters, 1916

Hymn to Democracy. L: J.M. Dorey; M: E.A. Mueller, 1918

Hymn to Freedom's Cause. L: Roland Covert; M: Oscar Miller, 1918

Hymn to Old Glory, the Star-Spangled Flag of the Free. L: W.E. Minshall; M: W. Drobegg, 1915

Hymn to the Hun. L&M: J.S. Pamplin, 1918

Hymn to the United States of America. L&M: W.C. Holmes, 1918

I

I Ain't Got Weary Yet. L: Howard Johnson; M: Percy Wenrich, 1918

I Ain't Had No Lovin' Since You Went Away. L&M: Harry Ruby, 1919

I Am a Real American. L&M: H. Abbott Danforth, 1917

I Am an American. L&M: W.B. Garrabrants, 1918

I Am Coming Home to You. L: J.V. Jewett; M: Leo Friedman, 1919

I Am Fighting for America and You. L&M: Barney O'Mara, 1917

I Am Fighting for Country, for You and Little Nell. L&M: Billie Jones, 1917

I Am for America First, Last, and All the Time. L&M: L.J. Martin, 1917

I Am Glad My Boy Is Brave Enough to Fight. L: E.J. Lancaster; M: Roy Hartzell, 1918

I Am Lonely for You (Trench Song). L&M: H.T. Stanton, 1918

I Am Longing for the Dear Old U.S.A. L: F.J. Corhominis; M: Leo Friedman, 1918

I Am Marching Away to Be a Soldier. L: Myrtle Lynch; M: Leo Friedman, 1918

I Am on My Way to Glory. L&M: E.A. Lewis, 1917

I Am 100% American, Are You? L: Bernice Bateman; M: L. St. Clair, 1918

I Am Proud to Be the Mother of a Soldier Boy. L&M: R.N. Moffat, 1916

I Am Proud to Be the Sister of a Soldier. L: E.S. Perkins; M: George Graff, Jr., 1919

I Am Sending Criss-Cross Kisses to Someone's Soldier Boy. L: George B. Alexander, M: May Green and Billy Lang, 1918

I Am Uncle Sam's Yankee Doodle Boy. L&M: F.A. Hinderman, 1918

I Am Waiting for You, Soldier Boy. L: Mrs. W. Roberts; M: Leo Friedman, 1918

I Belong to Uncle Sam. L&M: L.F. Day, 1917

I Belong to Uncle Sammy and I Come From the U.S.A. L&M: Alan Green, 1918

I Can Always Find a Little Sunshine in the YMCA. L&M: Irving Berlin, from stage production *Yip, Yip, Yaphank*, 1918

I Cannot Bear to Say Goodbye. L&M: Anita Owen, 1918

*I Can't Stay Here While You're Over There. L: Lew Brown and Al Harriman; M: Jack Egan, 1918

I Did Give My Boy to Uncle Sammy. L: W. Speck; M: Robert H. Brennen, 1918

I Didn't Raise My Boy to Be a Coward. L: F.G. McCauley; M: C.C. Case, 1917

I Didn't Raise My Boy to Be a Slacker. L&M: Theodore Baker, 1917

I Didn't Raise My Boy to Be a Slacker. L: Happy Mack; M: Eugene Platzmann, 1917

I Didn't Raise My Boy to Be a Slacker. L&M: J.H. Boyd, 1917

I Didn't Raise My Boy to Be a Slacker. L: Helen Wall; M: Leo Friedman, 1918

*I Didn't Raise My Boy to Be a Soldier. L: Al Bryan; M: Al Piantadosi, 1915

I Didn't Raise My Dog to Be a Sausage. L: Charles R. McCarron; M: Herman Paley, 1915

I Didn't Raise My Ford to Be a Jitney. L&M: Jack Frost, 1916

*I Don't Know Where I'm Going but I'm on My Way. L&M: George Fairman, 1917

*I Don't Want to Get Well. L: Harry Pease and Howard Johnson; M: Harold Jentes, 1918

I Dreamed of Peace. L&M: Virginia Thornberry, 1919

I Dreamt I Saw You Crossing No Man's Land. L&M: H.B. Collier, 1918

I Dreamt My Daddy Came Home. L: Joe Darcey; M: Lew Porter, 1918

I Dreamt That the Whole World Was Free. L&M: Joe Cronson, 1918

I Gave My Love to a Sailor Boy. L: Kathryne Reich; M: Artie Bowers, 1919

I Guess That I'll Do My Bit. L&M: T.B. Sullivan, 1918

I Hate to Lose You. L: Grant Clarke; M: Archie Gottler, 1918

I Have Bought a Liberty Bond. L&M: John S. Dunham, 1918

I Have Come Back for a Last Goodbye. L&M: Lloyd Garrett, 1918

I Have Nothing Else to Do but Fight for You. L&M: E.S. Gudelj, 1917

I Haven't Got Time for Anyone Else 'Till John Gets Home. L&M: James V. Monaco, 1917

I Hear Columbia Calling, Goodbye Motherland. L&M: Leland Johnson, 1918

I Hear My Country Calling. L&M: George L. Boyden, 1917

I Hear the Bugles Calling, Millie. L: T.U. Coe; M: Leo Friedman, 1919

I Hear Thy Country Calling (A Mother's Farewell to Her Son). L&M: D.F. Hallahan, 1918

I Hear Uncle Sammy Calling Me. L: L.A. Sparks; M: Leo Friedman, 1918

I Heard a Soldier Sing. L: Herbert Trench; M: Jessie L. Pease, 1915

I Know What It Means to Be Lonesome. L&M: James Kendis, James Brockman, and Nat Vincent, 1918

I Learned to Love Old Glory When I Knelt at Mother's Knee. L: William Taylor; M: Leo Friedman, 1919

I Love a Soldier in a Uniform. L: Robert Garland; M: Jean Bonner, 1915

I Love Each Star in Old Glory. L: Barney Newlin; M: W.H. Nelson, 1917

I Love My Country. L&M: W.H. Howells, 1918

I Love My Uncle Sammy. L&M: John H. Trayne, 1917

I Love My U.S.A. L&M: Joe Cronson, 1916

I Love Soldier Boys, Don't You? L&M: A.H. Wynkoop and Joseph Meagher, 1917

I Love the Flag That Waves for Me. L: N. Armstrong; M: Leo Friedman, 1918

I Love the Name of America. L: P. Barnhill; M: George Graff, Jr., 1919

I Love the Stars and Stripes. L&M: Herbert J. Millington, 1916

I Love the U.S.A. L&M: Will Hardy, 1914

I Love You, Columbia! L: Arthur A. Chief; M: E.F. Niel, 1918

I Love You, Dear Old U.S.A. L&M: Olaf M. Hansen, 1917

I Love You, Soldier Boy, and Your Uniform. L: Suella Fryer; M: Leo Friedman, 1918

I Love You, Uncle Sammy, True. L&M: Mrs. R.E. Slesnick, 1918

I May Be Gone for a Long, Long Time. L: Lew Brown; M: Albert Von Tilzer, from stage production Hitchy-Coo of 1917, 1917

I May Not Have Reared My Boy to Be a Soldier. L&M: Bernarr Macfadden, 1917

I May Stay Away a Little Longer. L: Lew Brown; M: Albert Von Tilzer, 1918

*I Miss Daddy's Goodnight Kiss. L&M: James Kendis, James Brockman, 1918

I Need Someone Just Like You. L: Myrtle Efting; M: Al Weston, 1917

I Never Knew How Much I Loved My Soldier Boy Until He Marched Away. L&M: Leon P. Rundell, 1917

I Never [Didn't] Raise My Boy to Be a Soldier, But. L: H.G. Mayes; M: Richard Ferber, 1918

I Raised My Boy a Soldier to Be. L&M: Marietta Nourse Blythe, 1917

I Raised My Boy to Be a Soldier. L: Emma M. Sheets; M: Leo Friedman, 1917

I Raised My Boy to Fight for His Country. L&M: N. Kearney, 1916

I Raised You for a Soldier, Lad. L: I.B. Liesmann; M: Leo Friedman, 1918

I Saw Lafayette Shake Hands with Washington. L&M: R.H. Farrell, 1918

I See Our Flag There. L&M: R.R. Parrish, 1917

I Stand for America. L&M: Luella Logsdon, 1917

I Take My Hat Off, Boys, to the U.S.A. L&M: Hattie Trice, 1919

I Thank You, Mr. Hoover (That's the Best Day in the Year). L&M: Clarence Gaskill, 1918

I Think I'll Wait Until They All Come Home. L: Marcus C. Connelly; M: Gitz Rice, 1919

I Think We've Got Another Washington and Wilson Is His Name. L&M: James Kendis and James Brockman, 1915

I Think We've Got Another Washington and Wilson Is His Name. L&M: George Fairman, 1917

I Tried to Raise My Boy to Be a Hero. L&M: Frank Huston, 1916

I Want a Soldier Boy to Correspond with Me. L&M: F.L. and R.T. Morehead, from stage production *Somewhere in America*, 1918

I Want a Submarine. L: P.A. Draper; M: Paul Argyle, 1918

I Want a Yankee Sailor Boy. L&M: J.T. Brodzinski, 1917

I Want My Daddy. L&M: Morris Manley, 1916

I Want to Be a Hero Same as Dad. L: T.J. Reynolds and M.W. Reimer; M: M.W. Reimer, 1918

I Want to Be a Sammie. L&M: Margaret Strub, 1918

I Want to Be a Soldier. L&M: A. Brangman, 1917

I Want to Be a Soldier. L: E.B. Chandler; M: Frank W. Ford, 1918

I Want to Be a Soldier Boy. L&M: Levi Bryant, 1917

I Want to Be a Soldier Boy. L&M: D.W. Guise, 1918

I Want to Be a Soldier Like My Dad. L: Arthur Fields; M: Theodore Morse, 1918

I Want to Be a Soldier Like Papa. L: Bertha Oakley; M: Frank W. Ford, 1918

I Want to Be an Oy, Oy, Oyviator (A Yiddisha Plea). L&M: Harry DeCosta, 1918

I Want to Be Loved by a Soldier. L: Henry Fink; M: Abner Silver, 1918

I Want to Come Back to You. L&M: Leo Wood, 1917

I Want to Go Back to Blighty. L: Lee M. Walker; M: William B. Davidson, 1918

I Want to Go Back to My Own Dear Land. L&M: John Chapman, 1918

I Want to Go Back to the Army. L&M: Earle W. Johnston, 1919

I Want to Go Back to the U.S.A. L: A.E. Hazall; M: Leo Friedman, 1919

I Want to Go Back to the War. L: Henry Blossom and Percival Knight; M: Raymond Hubbell, from stage production *Among the Girls*, 1919

I Want to Go Home. L&M: Gitz Rice, 1917

I Want to Live Where Old Glory Waves. L: Mae Kirkpatrick; M: Myrtle Oak, 1917

I Want Uncle Sam to Build a Navy That Can Lick All Creation. L: W.H. Pease; M: W.H. Pease and O.E. Hermann, Jr., 1916

I Will Fight for the Red, White and Blue. L: Emma C. Browning; M: E.B. Hutchison, 1918

I Will Wait Until You Come Back. M: M. Angelo Pennella, 1917

I Wish I Could Be a Soldier Boy. L&M: S.H. Dorsey, 1918

I Wish I Had Someone to Say Goodbye To. L: Joe Goodwin; M: Halsey K. Mohr, 1918

I Wish the War Was Over. L: William Simon; M: Harry Stirling, 1915

I Wish You All the Luck in the World. L&M: Abe Olman, 1917

I Wonder If She Is Waiting in Her Old New England Town. L: Arthur J. Lamb and Dave Reed; M: Frederick V. Bowers, 1917

I Wonder What He's Doing Tonight. L: Joe Goodwin; M: James F. Hanley, 1917

I Wonder What They're Doing Tonight (at Home Sweet Home). L: Bernie Grossman; M: Al Piantadosi, 1916

I Wonder What's Ze Matter Wiz My Oo-La-La (Come What May, I Can't Say Oo-Ze-Oo-La-La-La-La). L: Jack Frost; M: F. Henri Klickmann, 1919

I Wonder Where My Boy Is Now. L&M: Angelo Pennella, 1918

I Won't Be in Line When the Boys Come Marching Home. L: Anthony Marino; M: Barrington L. Brannan, 1919

I Work for Uncle Sam. L&M: A. A. Dart and Edward Auten, Jr., 1918

I Would Not Have Your Comrades Call You Slacker. L: R.M. Stevens; M: Leo Friedman, 1918

*I Wouldn't Steal the Sweetheart of a Soldier Boy. L: Al Bryan; M: Herman Paley, 1916

I'd Be Proud to Be the Mother of a Soldier. L&M: Charles Bayha, 1915

I'd Feel at Home If They'd Let Me Join the Army. L: Jack Mahoney; M: Albert Gumble, 1917

I'd Gladly Be a Wounded Soldier (If You'll Be My Red Cross Nurse). L&M: Remo Taverna, 1918

I'd Like to Be the First to Carry the Flag Through Berlin. L&M: Ida McPeak, 1918

I'd Like to See the Kaiser with a Lily in His Hand. L: Howard Johnson and Henry Leslie; M: Billy Frisch, from stage production *Doing Our Bit*, 1918

I'd Love to Punch the Kaiser. L: Mrs. J.N. Stotelmeyer; M: Roy Hartzell, 1919

*(If He Can Fight Like He Can Love) Goodnight, Germany! L: Grant Clarke and Howard E. Rogers; M: George W. Meyer, 1917

If I Am Not at the Roll Call (Kiss Mother

Goodbye for Me). L&M: George L. Boyden, 1917

If I Die Somewhere in France. L&M: Lily Sincere Ahrens, 1918

If I Had a Son for Each Star in Old Glory. L: James E. Dempsey; M: Joseph A. Burke, 1917

If I Had a Son for Each Star in Old Glory, Uncle Sam, I'd Give Them All to You. L: Richard Glass; M: Harry Tierney, 1917

If I Had Ten Lives to Give Away, I Would Give Them for the U.S.A. L&M: E.L. Lerch, 1918

If I Only Had the Kaiser Now. L&M: G.G. Wright, 1918

If I Should Get a Cross for Bravery. L&M: Joseph Callju, 1918

If I Were a Grown-up Soldier and You a Mercy Maid. L&M: H.C. Eldridge, 1918

If Mr. Ragtime Ever Gets Into That War. L: Schuyler Greene; M: Jerome Kern and Otto Motzan, 1916

If One of the Shells Bears Your Name. L: M.M. Nelson; M: Leo Friedman, 1919

If Sammy Simpson Shot the Shutes [Chutes], Why Shouldn't He Shoot the Shots? L: Ed Moran; M: Harry Von Tilzer, 1917

If the Blue Star Should Turn to Gold. L: Florence Armstrong; M: Leo Friedman, 1919

If the Girlies Could Be Soldiers. L: Gene Buck; M: Dave Stamper, from stage production *Ziegfeld Follies of 1915*, 1915

If the Kaiser Had His Way. L: Chauncey Long; M: C.E. Keller, 1918

If the Kaiser Were Wiser (He'd Keep Far Away). L: Pete Kramer and Jack Singer; M: Morris Perlman, 1917

If They Want to Fight, All Right, But Neutral Is My Middle Name. L&M: Jack Frost and James White, 1915

If They'd Only Fight the War with Wooden Soldiers. L: Bert Fitzgibbon; M: Theodore Morse, 1915

If This Should Be Our Last Goodbye. L: Bernie Grossman; M: Alfred Solman, 1917

If Uncle Sam Needs a Helping Hand. L: R.M. Stevens; M: Leo Friedman, 1918

If War Is What Sherman Said It Was. L: Andrew B. Sterling; M: Albert Gumble, 1915

If We Had a Million More Like Teddy [Roosevelt]. L&M: Charles Bayha, 1917

If We Knock the Germ Out of Germany. L: R.C. Leighton; M: Roy Hartzell, 1919

If We Never Come Back. L&M: J.J. Dinkins, 1918

If We Only Had Another Washington. L: Harry Bertini; M: Jack Gold, 1915

If You Do Your Bit, They'll Never Put America Down. L: P.A. Brophy; M: Robert C. Buckley, 1917

If You Don't Like Our President Wilson, You Knife the Land That Feeds Us All. L&M: Charles Flagler and W.R. Williams, 1917

If You Don't Want to Fight for Uncle Sammy, Then You Don't Need to Fight for Me. L: W.O. Witscher; M: A.R. Smith, 1917

If You Fight for Your Country Like You Fought at Home. L&M: Harry DeCosta, 1917

If You Just Must Go to War, Bring the Kaiser Back. L&M: Garland Tucker and Harry Baisden, 1918

If You Like Your Uncle Sammy, Buy a Bond. L: J.A. Hurst; M: Leo Friedman, 1918

If You'll Be a Soldier, I'll Be a Red Cross Nurse. L: Al Bryan; M: Harry Tierney, from stage production *What Next?*, 1918

If You're a True American, You're All Right. L: H. Weston Gill and H.P. Lombard; M: H.P. Lombard, 1917

If You're Going to Join the Army, Play the Game. L&M: Ella L. Smith, 1918

If You're Going to Live with Uncle Sammy, Why Don't You Work for Him? L: Mrs. O.A. Miles; M: Leo Friedman, 1918

I'll Be a Sammy's Sweetheart. L: F.M. Blackwell; M: Leo Friedman, 1918

I'll Be Back, So Keep the Lovelight Shining. L: William Lazarus; M: Harley E. Cash, 1919

I'll Be Over Your Way in the Mornin', Bill. L&M: Harry Ruby, 1918

I'll Be Praying Just for Victory and You. L&M: Charmian Reid, 1918

I'll Be Somewhere in France. L: George V. Hobart; M: Raymond Hubbell, from stage production Ziegfeld Follies of 1917, 1917

I'll Be There, Laddie Boy, I'll Be There. L: Jack Frost; M: E. Clinton Keithley, 1918

I'll Be Waiting for You, Soldier Boy. L&M: C.N. Guttenberger, 1918

I'll Be Waiting, My Soldier Boy, for You. L&M: J.Hodgson Hartley, 1918

I'll Be Waiting Over Here, Dear. L: Grace F. Poe; M: Leo Friedman, 1919

I'll Be Waiting, Sweetheart, in the U.S.A. L&M: Jewell Ellison, 1918

I'll Bet Bill's Sorry Now. L: Irene Severson; M: Leo Friedman, 1919

I'll Come Back and Be Your Soldier Boy. L: Sandy Chapman and Bert Meyers; M: Joe Solman, 1918

I'll Come Back to You, Dear Mother, or Fill a Hero's Grave. L: W.A. Lee; M: Frank J. Ford, 1918

*I'll Come Back to You When It's All Over. L: Lew Brown; M: Kerry Mills, 1918

I'll Come Sailing Home to You (a Long Way from Broadway). L: Stanley Murphy; M: Harry Carroll, 1917

I'll Die Like a True American. L&M: T.C. McCauley, 1917

I'll Do the Fighting—You Back Me with Powder and Something to Chew. L: J. Smith; M: Harry Franklin, 1918

I'll Do the Same as My Daddy. L&M: James L. Dempsey, 1918

*I'll Do Without Meat, I'll Do Without Wheat, But I Can't Do Without Love. L: Arthur J. Lamb; M: Frederick V. Bowers, 1918

I'll Fight for My Country and You. L&M: Miriam Florence, 1917

I'll Fight for the U.S.A. L&M: Dot E. Bennett, 1918

I'll Fight for the U.S.A. L&M: Julia E. Brownlie, 1918

I'll Fight for Uncle Sam and You. L&M: Bertha Reade Fike, 1918

I'll Gladly Be a Wounded Soldier If You Will Be My Red Cross Nurse. L&M: Remo Taverna, 1918

I'll Gladly Give My Boy to Be a Soldier. L: Bert Hudson; M: Everett J. Evans, 1916

I'll Go Back to the Red, White and Blue. L&M: Lorena E. Divet, 1916

I'll Have a Date for Ev'ry Night When I Get Home from France. L: Margaret B. Ogden and Julia G. Holmes; M: Julia G. Holmes, 1919

I'll Help to Put the Finish to the Submarine. L: W.E. Riedel; M: Leo Friedman, 1918

I'll Keep a Bright Light Burning. L: Vileta Nelson; M: Leo Friedman, 1919

I'll Love You More for Losing You a While. L: Raymond B. Egan; M: Richard A. Whiting, 1917

I'll Make You Proud of Me, Mother. L&M: Will Wood, 1918

I'll Never Go to War Again. L: William Aronheim; M: Gus Aronheim, 1917

I'll Pray for You and You Must Pray for Me. L&M: Edward St. Quentin, 1918

I'll Rush Old Glory Into Germany. L: Beverly Creech; M: Leo Friedman, 1918

I'll See You Later, Yankee Land. L&M: Charles K. Harris, 1917

I'll Soon Be Coming Back to You. L: E.M. Solloway; M: J.E. Andino, 1917

I'll Take a Gun and Fight for You. L&M: Calvin A. Barnett, 1917

I'll Take My Little Rifle and Go Bang, Bang, Bang! L: Hugh F. Palmer; M: Harry E. Ransom, 1918

I'll Take Old Glory with Me, Dear (and in My Heart You'll Be). L: B.M. Graybill; M: August Halter, 1918

I'll Wait for You. L: Gus Kahn; M: Egbert Van Alstyne, 1919

I'll Wait Till the War Is Won. L&M: W.J. Fader, 1918

I'll Wed the Girl I Left Behind. L&M: Will Dillon, 1917

I'm a Lanky Yankee Doodle Man. L: J.E. Lyman; M: R.A. Browne, 1918

I'm a Nephew to Uncle Sam. L: W.E. Sagmaster; M: Leo Friedman, 1918

I'm a Regular Daughter of Uncle Sam. L&M: Edgar Allen, 1917

I'm a Soldier. L: Emma Breiting; M: Loa Scheeler and J.M. Schergen, 1918

I'm a U.S. Soldier. L&M: Sue Stevens, 1918

I'm a Yankee Doodle Soldier Boy. L&M: W.E. Earle, 1918

I'm an American, That's All. L: Harry D. Kerr; M: Johann C. Schmid, 1915

I'm Back from the Battle, Mother. L: Cyrus H. Young: M: Grace Young, 1919

I'm Coming Back to America and You. L: S.B. Rifkin; M: Leo Friedman, 1918

I'm Coming Back to You. L&M: Luke S. Murdock, 1918

I'm Coming Back to You. L: Harry E. Rose; M: Anson C. Jacobs, 1918

I'm Coming Back to You. L: Bertie A. Ballat; M: J.F. Zimmermann, 1919

I'm Coming Back to You, Old Tipperary. L: C.B. and Mabel Lawlor; M: Alice Lawlor, 1915

I'm Coming Back to You, Poor Butterfly. L: Andrew Donnelly; M: Raymond Hubbell, 1917

I'm Coming Home. L: A. Wilkinson; M: Fred A. Reynolds, 1919

I'm Coming Home, Dear Mother. L: Mrs. A.E. Jones; M: Artie Bowers, 1919

I'm Coming, Uncle Sammie, Watch for Me, Miss Liberty. L: H. Cliff Hill; M: George Behr, 1917

I'm Crazy About My Daddy in a Uniform. L: Charles R. McCarron; M: Carey Morgan, 1918

I'm Fighting for You (March). L&M: W.A. Perry, 1917

I'm Fighting for You and Liberty. L&M: N. Yellenti, 1918

I'm for Neutrality. L&M: Charles Robert Parker, 1915

I'm Giving You to Uncle Sam. L: Thomas H. Ince; M: Victor Schertzinger, 1918

I'm Glad I Live in the U.S.A. L: M.L. Babcock; M: Franz Von Hoffman, 1915

I'm Glad I Went Over to France. L: Kenneth Graham Duffield and Alice Monroe Foster; M: Fay Foster, 1919

I'm Glad My Sweetheart's in France. L: Bertha Lee; M: Leo Friedman, 1919

I'm Glad My Sweetheart's Not a Soldier. L&M: Hank Hancock and Tom McNamara, 1915

I'm Glad to Be Back in the U.S.A. L&M: Carl E. Summers, 1919

I'm Glad to Be the Mother of a Soldier Boy. L: Rene Bronner; M: Frederick V. Bowers, 1918

I'm Glad We're Neutral. L: F.A. Randall; M: Ray Waters, 1915

I'm Goin' to Break That Mason-Dixon Line (Until I Get to That Gal of Mine). L: Al Bryan; M: Jean Schwartz, 1919

I'm Goin' to Fight My Way Right Back to Carolina. L&M: Billy Baskette and Jessie Spiess, 1918

I'm Going Away to Fight for My Good Old U.S.A. L: Harry H. Rubinstein and E.B. Gregory; M: Henry V. D'Iorio, 1917

I'm Going Back to the U.S.A. L: Louise Anthony; M: Leo Friedman, 1919

I'm Going 'Cross to France. L&M: G.A. Knight, 1918

I'm Going Home Without You, Comrade. L: A.E. Denning; M: Leo Friedman, 1919

I'm Going to Be a Soldier. L: F.H. Luce; M: Leo Friedman, 1919

I'm Going to Be a Soldier and Fight for the U.S.A. L&M: Charles Haller and Ernest S. Stafford, 1917

I'm Going to Be a Soldier for Dear Old Uncle Sam (March). L&M: N. Dantzic, 1918

I'm Going to Follow the Boys (March). M: James V. Monaco, 1917

I'm Going to Join the Army and Help Fight Germany. L: Dwight Hostetler; M: Leo Friedman, 1918

I'm Going to Lend My Man to Uncle Sam. L&M: J.A. Richard, 1917

I'm Going to Raise My Boy to Be a Soldier and a Credit to the U.S.A. L: J. Will Callahan; M: Leo Friedman, 1916

I'm Gonna Pin My Medal on the Girl I Left Behind. L&M: Irving Berlin, from stage production Ziegfeld Follies of 1918, 1918

I'm Hitting the Trail to Normandy (So Kiss Me Goodbye). L&M: Charles A. Snyder and Oscar Doctor, 1917

I'm in France and You're in Tennessee (but You Just Keep on Haunting Me). L: Harold Berry; M: Leo Friedman, 1919

I'm in Love with a Daughter of Dixie (America's Tipperary). L&M: Nell Madigan, 1918

I'm in Love with Uncle Sammy (March). L&M: O.M. Ford, 1917

I'm in the Army. L&M: Victor Ormond, 1917

I'm in the Army Now. L&M: Charles Bayha, 1917

I'm Just a Lonesome Boy, and I'm Looking for a Lonesome Girl. L: May Greene; M: Billy Lang, 1918

I'm Just a Sammy, a Blue-Blooded Yank. L&M: Nora T. Ricketts, 1918

I'm Knitting a Rosary. L: Robert Levenson; M: Vincent Plunkett, 1918

I'm Lonely Tonight for Broadway. L: H.R. Moynes; M: Leo Friedman, 1919

I'm Lonely Tonight for Dixie Land. L: H.S. Lang; M: Leo Friedman, 1919

I'm Mother's Sailor Boy in Blue. L: S. Covey; M: Artie Bowers, 1919

I'm Neutral. L: Herman Gautvoort; M: Leon DeCosta, 1916

I'm Not Going to Buy Any Summer Clothes But a Uniform of Blue. L: Harry Pease; M: Gilbert Dodge, 1917

I'm Off for a Place Somewhere in France, But I'm Coming Back from Berlin (March). L: Alexander C. Fortner; M: Kitt G. Sapp, 1917

I'm Off to the War. L: J.W. Montgomery; M: E.M. McDonough, 1918

I'm on My Way Back Home Again. L: Mrs. F. McGregor; M: Gene Rawty, 1919

I'm on My Way to France. L: E.E. Bort; M: Leo Friedman, 1918

I'm Over Here and You're Over There. L: Harold Atteridge; M: Jean Schwartz, 1918

I'm Over, Not Under, in France. L: W.H. Durbin; M: Leo Friedman, 1918

I'm Proud My Boy's a Soldier. L&M: A. Geddes, 1917

I'm Proud to Be a Soldier of the Allies. L: Vern Irvine; M: Bern Done, 1918

I'm Proud to Be a [the] Son of Uncle Sam. L: S.E. Levine; M: George Weiss, 1917

I'm Proud to Be of Service to My Country. L&M: The Great Howard [Howard Miller], 1918

I'm Proud to Be the Sweetheart of a Soldier. L&M: Mary Earl, 1917

I'm Proud to Be the Sweetheart of a Soldier. L: J. Flanagan; M: Thomas Rennie, Jr., 1918

I'm Proud to Serve the Land That Gave Me Birth. L: C. Davis; M: Sam Brobst, 1918

I'm Raising My Boy to Be a Soldier to Fight for the U.S.A. L: Leo Ryan; M: Mrs. Leo Ryan, 1917

I'm Satisfied with Uncle Sam. L&M: Marvin Lee and Terry Sherman, 1916

I'm Sure I Wasn't Raised to Be a Soldier (But I'll Fight for Dear Old Red, White and Blue). L&M: Charles R. Campbell, 1916

I'm the Man That Got the German Kaiser's Goat. L&M: "The Christophers," 1917

I'm Uncle Sammy's Soldier. L&M: W. Tankersley, 1917

I'm Waiting for My Country to Call Me. L: C.L. Jewell; M: Leo Friedman, 1918

I'm Writing to My Soldier Boy Over There. L&M: Grace Goff, 1918

I'm Writing to You, Sammy. L: Lew Brown; M: Al Harriman, 1917

In a Place Called No Man's Land Across the Sea. L: H.P. Martin; M: Leo Friedman, 1918

In All Our Rejoicing as the Boys Come Home, Let Us Pray for the Ones Who Stay Over. L&M: George MacFarlane and Harry DeCosta, 1919

In Chateau-Thierry, Where My Darling Sleeps. L&M: Jennie M. Flynn, 1919

In Dear Old U.S.A. L: Elbert Sward; M: T.W. Harrison, 1916

In Dear Old Yankee Land. L&M: J.H. Voss, 1916

In Faraway France. L&M: Joe Seiler, 1918

In Flanders Fields. L: Lt. Col. John McCrae; M: Alfred Hiles Bergen, 1918

In Flanders Fields. L: Lt. Col. John McCrae; M: Benjamin F. Cliffe, 1918

In Flanders Fields. L: Lt. Col. John McCrae; M: Jennette Loudon, 1918

In Flanders Fields. L: Lt. Col. John McCrae; M: Allan Robinson, 1918

In Flanders Field. L: Lt. Col. John McCrae; M: O.M. Oleson, 1918

*In Flanders Fields. L: Lt. Col. John McCrae; M: Frank E. Tours, 1918

In Flanders Fields. L: R. Contant; M: Leo Friedman, 1918

In Flanders Fields. L: Lt. Col. John McCrae; M: Charles Gilbert Spross, 1919

In Flanders Fields. L: Lt. Col. John McCrae; M: Arthur William Foote, 1919

In Flanders Fields. L: Lt. Col. John McCrae; M: Mary Wyman Williams, 1919

In Flanders Fields. L: Lt. Col. John McCrae; M: F. Henri Klickmann, 1919

In Flanders Fields. L: Lt. Col. John McCrae; M: Mark Andrews, 1919

In Flanders Fields. L: Lt. Col. John McCrae; M: Homer N. Bartlett, 1919

In Flanders Fields. L: Lt. Col. John McCrae; M: Emerson L. Stone, 1919

In Flanders Fields. L: Lt. Col. John McCrae; M: Frederick Rocke, 1919

In Flanders Fields. L: Lt. Col. John McCrea; M: Henry E. Sachs, 1919

In Flanders Fields. L: Lt. Col. John McCrea; M: Edith L. Neumann, 1919

In Flanders Fields. L: Lt. Col. John McCrae; M: Edouard J. Bonhomme, 1919

In Flanders Fields. L: Lt. Col. John McCrae; M: George W. Parrish, 1919

In Flanders Fields. L: Lt. Col. John McCrae; M Arthur H. Turner, 1919

In Flanders Fields. L: Lt. Col. John McCrae; M: Lola Blanks, 1919

In Flanders Fields. L&M: R.L. Finch, 1919

In Flanders Fields (An Answer). L: Henry Polk Lowenstein; M: Nell Marshall, 1918

In Flanders Fields (The Answer). L: C.B. Galbreath; M: A.C.W. Burton, 1918

In Flanders Fields the Poppies Grow. L: Lt. Col. John McCrae; M: John Philip Sousa, 1918

In France with Pershing. L&M: A.H. McOwen, 1917

In Her Little Blue Bonnet with the Red Ribbon on It, She's Salvation Sal. L: Bide Dudley; M: Frederic Watson, from stage production Come Along, 1919

In Honor of Our Country (A Reverie). M: K. Pearce, 1915

In Liberty's Name (March). L&M: Edward O. Schaaf, 1918

In My Dream of the U.S.A. L&M: Dean T. Wilton, 1918

In My Dreams This World Had Peace Again. L&M: D. O'Brien and Frank Wallen, 1916

In No Man's Land. L: H.M. Martin; M: Leo Friedman, 1919

In No Man's Land Are the Sammies. L: Al C. Corcoran; M: Roy Hartzell, 1919

In No Man's Land Tonight. L&M: John Collins, 1919

In Peace and War. L: C. Bentley; M: Carl Heil, 1915

In Peace for Ever and Ever. L&M: Joseph Digiorgio, 1916

In the Dawning of the Morning When the Boys Come Marching Home. L&M: Joseph Atkins, 1918

In the Dear Old U.S.A. L&M: C.P. Smith, 1917

In the Good Old U.S.A. L: Jasper Laird; M: Leo Friedman, 1918

In the Heart of No Man's Land. L&M: J.T. Haddow and James T. Hadden, 1918

In the Heart of No Man's Land. L: Betty Gray; M: Leo Friedman, 1919

In the Land of Liberty. L: I.M. Price; M: Leo Friedman, 1919

In the Land of Liberty, Now That's Where I Want to Be. L&M: C. Mortland, 1917

In the Land of the Free and the Brave. L: Ed E. Davis; M: William Dick, 1917

In the Land of U.S.A. L&M: Louis Lehner, 1917

In the Land Where Poppies Bloom. L: Billy Baskette; M: Gus Van and Joe Schenck, 1918

In the Muddy Trenches. L&M: M.C. Paxton, 1919

In the Ranks of the U.S.A. L&M: C.R. Carson, 1917

In the Service of the King. L: Elsie Duncan Yale; M: Adam Geibel, 1917

In the Trenches. L&M: E.P. O'Leary, 1918

In the Trenches. L&M: J. DeLancey, 1918

In the Trenches. L&M: W.R. Prince, 1918

In the Trenches, Mother Darling. L: O.L. McSharry; M: Roy Hartzell, 1919

In the Uniform of Uncle Sam. L&M: H.T. Schultze, 1918

In the U.S. Radio. L&M: J.B. Rowden, 1918

In the War of Hearts and Eyes. L&M: Emma Carus, Ernest Breuer, and J. Brandon Walsh, 1915

In This Last Great War. L: Harry Meyers; M: George D. West, 1914

In Time of Peace, Prepare for War. L: Eddie Cavanaugh; M: Bob Allan, 1915

In Time of Peace, Prepare for War. L: Robert B. Smith; M: Harold Orlob, from stage production Town Topics, 1916

In Yankee Doodle Land. L&M: Art Williams, 1918

Infantry. L&M: Cedric W. Lemont, 1917

Invincible America (March). M: H.T. Woods, 1919

Invincible America (March). M: H.J. Crosby, 1916

Invincible U.S.A. (March). M: Francis A. Myers, 1919

Ireland Is Your Home Sweet Home. L: Charles Horwitz; M: Al H. Wilson, 1917

The Irish Kaiser. L&M: Edwin Forrest Kamerly, 1917

An Irishman Was Made to Love and Fight (March). M: Joseph H. Santly, 1919

*Iron Men. L&M: J. Harley Coyle, 1919

Is My Papa Now in France? (or, A Child's Prayer for Daddy). L: G.B. Pratt; M: Norman C. Remich, 1918

Is It a Long Way to Tipperary, the Kaiser Will Be There. L: W.H. Pease; M: O.E. Herrmann, Jr., 1915

Is Your Blood Red, White and Blue? L: William R. Cushman; M: A.F. Frankenstein, 1917

I'se Got a Flag What's Red, White and Blue. L&M: A.C. Reed, 1919

Ismailia (March). M: Nat Stockdale, 1915

It Came in Freedom's Name. L: R.H. Pallister; M: Leo Friedman, 1918

It Didn't Take the Yankees Long. L: G. Detberner; M: Leo Friedman, 1918

It Don't Seem the Same Since the Boys Marched Away. L&M: Yvon O. Brosseau, 1917

It Gets a Little Shorter Every Day. L: George Kershaw and Garfield Kilgour; M: Harry Von Tilzer, 1918

It Is the Royal Standard of the U.S.A. (A Soldier's Love Song). L&M: H.M. Andersen, 1916

It Is Up to Uncle Sam. L&M: "The Boys and Sisk & James," 1918

*It Isn't Any Fun to Be a Soldier (A Nation's Plea for Peace). L&M: Charles E. Wood, 1915

It Must Be the Spirit of '76. L: William Jerome; M: Arthur N. Green, 1917

It Must Have Been Some Wonderful Boy

(Who Taught Her How to Love). L&M: William Tracey and Jack Stern, 1918

It Shall Be Done (The Dixie Division Song). L&M: Alexander Beach Pooley, 1918

It Takes a Man Like Wilson to Wear the White House Shoes. L&M: Earl H. Coffey, 1918

It Takes the Red Cross to Help Uncle Sam Win the War. L: J. Carter; M: Frank W. Ford, 1918

It Takes Your Uncle Sammy to Finish Up the Scrap. L: A.F. Shaw; M: Howard E. Hitchcock, 1917

It Won't Be Long Before We're Home. L: Paul Cunningham; M: Joseph E. Howard, 1918

It Won't Be Long Till I Come Back. L: Edward Plottle; M: Floyd E. Whitmore, 1918

*It Won't Be Long (Till the Boys Come Marching Home). L&M: Frankie Williams, 1918

It's a Grand Old Flag to Fight For (March). L: J.H.G. Fraser; M: D.E. MacPherson, 1917

It's a Hard Job to Lick the Kaiser. L: R. Sheeler Campbell; M: William F. Lintt, 1918

It's a Long, Long Time (Since I've Been Home). L&M: Josephine E. Vail, 1916

It's a Long, Long Way Back to the Good Old U.S.A. L: S.A. Rosendahl; M: W.C. Sumner, 1917

It's a Long, Long Way from the U.S.A. L&M: Langton Marks, 1918

It's a Long, Long Way to My Old Home Town. L&M: Andrew Mack, 1917

It's a Long, Long Way to Old Broadway. L: Southard P. Whiting; M: J.H. Riggs, 1918

It's a Long, Long Way to Somewhere in France. L: F.M. D'Auby; M: Leo Friedman, 1918

It's a Long, Long Way to the Battlefields of France. L&M: Thomas McCloskey, 1918

It's a Long, Long Way to the U.S.A. (and My Own Little Home Sweet Home) L&M: Zeph Fitzgerald, 1917

*It's a Long, Long Way to the U.S.A. (and the Girl I Left Behind). L: Val Trainor; M: Harry Von Tilzer, 1917

*It's a Long, Long Way to Tipperary. L: Jack Judge; M: Harry Williams, 1912

It's a Long Way Across the Ocean. L: J. Woodworth; M: Leo Friedman, 1918

It's a Long Way from Berlin to Broadway. L&M: Harold B. Freeman, 1917

*It's a Long Way from Here to "Over There." L&M: Lew Peyton, 1918

It's a Long Way to Berlin (The Song of the Soldier and Sailor). L&M: Francis J. Lowe, 1915

It's a Long Way to Berlin But We'll Get There (March). L: Arthur Fields; M: Leon Flatow, 1918

*It's a Long Way to Dear Old Broadway. L&M: Ernest Breuer and George Fairman, 1918

It's a Long Way to Europe but Teddy [Roosevelt] Knows the Way. L&M: H.V. Irvine, 1917

It's a Long Way to France. L: Francis Preston; M: Leo Friedman, 1918

It's a Long Way to [the] Front in Flanders. L: J.B. Lykins; M: Leo Friedman, 1919

It's a Long Way to Germany. L&M: J.W. Woller, 1917

It's All for the Flag and You. L&M: Robert D. Quinn, 1917

It's All Over Now. L&M: Frankie Williams and "The Kreys," 1918

It's All Over, Over There. L: G. Gilard; M: C. Dennis, 1918

It's America First. L&M: G.G. Wright, 1916

It's Been a Long Time Since I Said Goodbye (But I Soon Will Say Hello). L&M: H.J. Richter, 1918

It's de Kaiser Bill fo' Me. L&M: J.E. Thomas, 1918

It's Goodbye Germany and Kaiser Bill Forever. L&M: Walter Smith, 1918

It's Goodbye to His Submarines and All His Zeppelins. L&M: Emile Hoyaux, Sr., 1918

It's Great to Be a Soldier. L&M: J.L. Sullivan, 1917

[Oh!] It's Great to Be a Soldier of the U.S.A. L&M: Beth Mack, 1917

It's Great to Be a Son of Uncle Sam. L&M: E.R. Horst, 1919

It's My Flag, Too. L: Lizzie DeArmond; M: Charles H. Gabriel, 1918

It's Not the Uniform That Makes the Man. L: Henry Blosson; M: A. Baldwin Sloane, from stage production *A Trip to Washington*, 1917

It's Over, Over There. L&M: Mary Wyman Williams; M: Leo Friedman, 1919

It's Over — Over There. L: I.W. Lennox; M: Leo Friedman, 1919

It's the Flag. L&M: Lottie W. Simmons, 1918

It's the Flag That God Has Blessed. L: Eleanor Dudley; M: Artie Bowers, 1919

It's the Good Old U.S.A. L: F.A. Shattuck; M: George Graff, Jr., 1919

It's the One That Is Left Behind. L&M: Elwood S. Harris, 1917

It's the Spirit of Yankeeland. L&M: James Wright, 1917

It's the Star-Spangled Banner. L&M: Arthur F. Faneuf, 1917

*It's Time for Every Boy to Be a Soldier. L: Al Bryan; M: Harry Tierney, 1917

It's Up to the Yankees. L&M: C.M. Levett, 1918

It's Up to Uncle Sam. L&M: "The Boys and Sisk and James," 1918

It's Your Flag and Mine. L: F.C. Smith; M: C.W. Hatch, 1917

I've Adopted a Belgian Baby. L&M: Louis Weslyn, Ben Kutler, and Marian Pollock, 1918

I've Done My Bit for Uncle Sam (Will You Do Your Bit for Me?). L: Joe Davis; M: George F. Briegel, 1919

I've Got a Red Cross Rosie Going Across with Me. L: Edgar Leslie and Bert Kalmar; M: Harry Ruby, 1917

I've Got a Ten-Day Pass for a Honeymoon for the Girl I Left Behind. L&M: Ballard MacDonald, James F. Hanley, and Walter Donaldson, 1917

*I've Got My Captain Working for Me Now. L&M: Irving Berlin, from stage production Ziegfeld Follies of 1919, 1919

I've Got the Army Blues. L&M: L. Wolfe Gilbert and Carey Morgan, 1916

I've Taken My Stand for Uncle Sam. L: B. Lumbert; M: Leo Friedman, 1918

J

Jane (March). M: Halsey K. Mohr, 1916

Jerry, Mon Cheri. L: Stanley Murphy; M: Harry Tierney, 1918

Jerry, You Warra a Warrior in the War. L: Dannie O'Neill; M: Billy Baskette, 1919

Jim, Jim, Don't Come Back Till You Win. L: Ben Ryan and Bert Hanlon; M: Harry Von Tilzer, 1918

Jim, Jim, I Always Knew That You'd Win. L: Ben Ryan and Bert Hanlon; M: Harry Von Tilzer, 1918

*Joan of Arc, They Are Calling You. L: Al Bryan and Willie Weston; M: Jack Wells, 1917

Joan of Arc, They're Calling You. L&M:

Frank Sturgis, from stage production This Way Out, 1915

Johnny Get Your Gun. L: Bartley Costello; M: Harold Orlob, from stage production Johnny Get Your Gun, 1918

Johnny, Get Your Gun, Put the Kaiser on the Run, Just as Your Dad Would Do! L: J.G. Knight; M: E.J. Lee, 1917

Johnny Jones, He Didn't Know His Left Foot from His Right. L&M: Cary Johnson, 1918

Johnny on the Spot. L&M: George Thornton Edwards, 1917

Johnny's in Town. L&M: Jack Yellen, George W. Meyer, and Abe Olman, from stage production Ziegfeld Follies of 1919, 1919

Join the Army for Peace Instead of War. L&M: G.J. Kock and Louis Herscher, 1915

The Joy of Peace. L&M: Lucy Lee Voorhees, 1919

Junior Sammies. L&M: Olive M. Stilwell, 1919

*Just a Baby's Prayer at Twilight. L: Sam M. Lewis and Joe Young; M: M.K. Jerome, 1917

Just a Baby's Letter (Found in No Man's Land). L: Bernie Grossman; M: Ray Lawrence, 1918

Just a Faithful Wife's Prayer for Her Husband Somewhere Over There. L: V.A. Fenner; M: John S. Caldwell, 1918

Just a Letter for a Boy Over There from a Grey-Haired Mother Over Here. L&M: Andrew B. Sterling, Arthur Lange, and Alfred Solman, 1918

Just a Little After Taps. L: Richard Fechheimer; M: W.B. Kernell, from stage production Goodbye, Bill, 1918

Just a Little Flag with One Bright Star of Gold. L&M: J.B. Holmes, 1919

Just a Little Star of Gold. L: Mabel J. Nagel; M: Leo Friedman, 1919

Just a Little War Baby. L&M: Mary E. Turner, 1918

Just a Lock of Baby's Hair (That's Your Daddy's Treasure Over There). L: J.S. Brothers, Jr.; M: H.C. Elsesser, 1918

Just a Mother Who's Watching and Waiting for Her Boy Who Will Never Return. L&M: James Wright, 1919

Just a Mother's Dream (When Shadows Fall). L: Bernie Grossman; M: Frank Magine, 1918

Just a Plain Soldier Man, That's All. L&M: S.J. Meinert, 1916

Just an Unknown Soldier. L&M: George R. Gillespie, 1915

Just as Great as My Hate Is for War, Just as Great Is My Love for You. L&M: Dick Howard, 1915

*Just as the Sun Went Down. L&M: Lyn Udall, 1918

Just Back from France. L: Tony Ferrazzano; M: R. DeLuca, 1918

Just Before the Battle. L&M: Mrs. M. Mc-Colgan, 1918

Just Buy a Liberty Bond. L&M: J.C. Denker, 1919

Just for the Sake of You, Mother. L&M: Lew Schaeffer, 1917

Just for You and the U.S.A. L: H.W. Smith; M: Leo Friedman, 1918

Just for You, Dear. L: Gus Sullivan and George B. Pitman; M: George B. Pitman, 1917

Just Give Me a Week in Paris. L: Alex Sullivan; M: Lynn F. Cowan, 1918

Just Keep the Roses a-Blooming Till I Come Back Again. L: Robert Levenson; M: George L. Cobb, 1918

Just Leave It to Your Uncle Sam. L: W. Richardson; M: Julius Kranz, 1918

*Just Like Washington Crossed the Delaware (General Pershing Will Cross the Rhine). L: Howard Johnson; M: George W. Meyer, 1918

Just Over There (March). L&M: R.L. Apgar, 1918

Just Put Us on Your List, Dear Uncle Sam. L&M: Caroline Louise Sumner, 1917

Just 'Round the Corner from Easy Street. L: Raymond B. Egan; M: Richard A. Whiting, from stage production *Toot Sweet*, 1919

Just Send the Word to the Kaiser That We're Coming Over There. L: Garry James; M: Harry Weston, 1918

Just Tell Old Glory. L: George Halligan; M: Ark Arkenson, 1918

Just the Glorious U.S.A. L&M: Mrs. A.G. Benfield, 1917

Just Think of What a Soldier Has to Go Through in This War. L: E.G. Hitchcock; M: H.E. Hayden, 1915

Just Volunteer Today. L&M: Fannie Fahm, 1918

Just Welcome Them. L: C.J. Roberts; M: Leo Friedman, 1919

Just Yankee Soldier Boys. L: Mrs. P.E. Turner; M: H.T. Comerford, 1919

K

Kaiser. L: Vincent Healy; M: Leo Friedman, 1918

The Kaiser and His Goat. L: John W. Russell; M: Hugo Herzer, 1918

Kaiser Bill. L&M: Gale M. Barton, 1917

Kaiser Bill. L: L.Y. Lenhart; M: Inez C. Hall, 1917

Kaiser Bill (March). L: L. Osborn; M: Rose Wood, 1917

Kaiser Bill. L: Raymond B. Egan; M: Egbert Van Alstyne, 1918

Kaiser Bill. L: S.E. Darby, Jr.; M: A. Baldwin Sloane, from stage production *Look Who's Here*, 1918

Kaiser Bill. L&M: D. Harrington, 1918

Kaiser Bill. L&M: J. I. Taylor, 1918

Kaiser Bill and the Yankee Jake. L: J.L. Sherman; M: Artie Bowers, 1919

Kaiser Bill, Goodnight. L&M: John W. Betscher, 1918

Kaiser Bill, Goodnight. L&M: "The Selbys," 1918

Kaiser Bill Has Met His Waterloo. L: Hilda Eisner; M: Leo Friedman, 1919

Kaiser Bill Will Not Be There. L&M: H.E. Humphreys, 1918

Kaiser Bill, You've Got a Lot to Answer For. L: William Hallen; M: Al Beatty, 1917

Kaiser Bill's Doom. L&M: S.B. Soard, Sr., 1918

Kaiser Bill's End. L: M.A. Cross; M: Leo Friedman, 1919

Kaiser Bill's Finish. L: Myrtle Merritt; M: Leo Friedman, 1919

Kaiser Blues. L: J.C. Jones; M: Frank W. Ford, 1918

Kaiser Bound for Hell. L: J.P. Stoll; M: Leo Friedman, 1919

The Kaiser Condemned. L&M: R.F. Edwards, 1918

Kaiser-Eat-Us. L&M: Jesse G.M. Glick and Robert Starkey, 1918

The Kaiser Has Committed Suicide. L: R.A. Dillavon; M: Leo Friedman, 1919

The Kaiser in the Soup. L&M: L. Thomas, 1919

The Kaiser Man. L&M: R.G. Lee, 1916

The Kaiser Rides in His Armored Car. L&M: M.V. Bixby, 1918

The Kaiser Wants to Rule the World. L: R.A. Conrad; M: Leo Friedman, 1919

Kaiser Wilhelm. L: F.A. Salter; M: Leo Friedman, 1918

The Kaiser Will Be Wiser When the Yankees

Take Berlin. L: L. Leslie and George H. Kelley; M: L. Leslie, 1918

The Kaiser Will Be Wiser When Uncle Sam Is Through. L&M: C.T. McClelland, 1917

The Kaiser Will Be Wiser When We Reach Berlin. L: Charles Capehart; M: R.A. Inch, 1918

Kaiser William, What Will You Do on That Day? L: F.D. Welch; M: Leo Friedman, 1918

The Kaiser's Aspirating. L: J.J. Cross; M: Leo Friedman, 1918

The Kaiser's Band Is Going to Play a Yankee Melody. L&M: Morris Silnutzer, 1918

Kaiser's Blues. L: R.G. Moffett; M: Samuel H. Speck, 1918

The Kaiser's Crazy. L: W. McDaniel; M: Frances Ann Wade, 1918

The Kaiser's Dead March. L&M: E.L. Kyle and E.F. Swindell, 1918

Kaiser's Doom. L: T. Jones; M: T. Jones and F. Henri Klickmann, 1918

The Kaiser's Dream. L&M: R. Bevington Lynn, 1918

The Kaiser's Dream. L: M.F. Childs; M: Leo Friedman, 1918

The Kaiser's Dream. L: S.B. Owens; M: Leo Friedman, 1918

The Kaiser's Dream. L&M: C.E. Hull, 1919

The Kaiser's Dream. L: Margaret S. Williams; M: Leo Friedman, 1919

The Kaiser's Finish. L: John H. Jones; M: Leo Friedman, 1919

The Kaiser's Funeral March. L&M: Daniel LaGrove, 1918

The Kaiser's Goat. L&M: A.H. Harvey, 1918

The Kaiser's Goat's Gone Up in Smoke. L: Katharine Wright; M: Leo Friedman, 1919

The Kaiser's Goodbye to His Submarines and All His Zeppelins. L&M: Emile Hoyaux, Sr., 1918

The Kaiser's Got the Blues (He's Got the Weary Blues). L&M: Domer C. Browne, 1918

The Kaiser's Got the Blues Since Uncle Sam Stepped In. M: F.D. Waldron, 1918

The Kaiser's Message. L: N.M. Gordon; M: Leo Friedman, 1918

The Kaiser's Military Ball. L: C.S. Guilford; M: Charles L. Johnson, 1918

The Kaiser's Mistake. L: Harry DeLaney; M: Leo Friedman, 1918

The Kaiser's Mistake. L: B.S. Stovall; M: Leo Friedman, 1918

The Kaiser's Nightmare. L: Thomas Harris; M: Leo Friedman, 1918

The Kaiser's Over There. L&M: Edith Gill, 1918

The Kaiser's Pants Afire. L: W.J. Irving; M: W.L. Schaub, 1918

The Kaiser's Retreat. L&M: C.M. Stark, 1919

Kamerad. L: John Gordon; M: Leo Friedman, 1919

Kamerad, Kamerad. L&M: William G. Makray, 1919

Keep a Steady Heart Till the Boys Return. L: Richard W. Pascoe; M: Monte Carlo and Alma Sanders, 1918

Keep Cool! The Country's Saving Fuel (and I Had to Come Home in the Dark). L&M: Charles R. McCarron, 1918

Keep Heart for the U.S.A. L&M: Lula Jones, 1919

Keep Me on the Firing Line. L&M: E.A. Lewis, 1917

Keep Old Glory Floating. L: E. Blackford; M: Robert H. Brennen, 1918

Keep Old Glory in the Air. L: J.G. Weyer; M: Leo Friedman, 1919

Keep Our Colors Waving. L: E.E. Hewitt; M: B.D. Ackley, 1918

Keep the Boys Happy While They're Away. L&M: William G. Henry, 1918

Keep the Flag on High. L: H.P. Tallmadge; M: Oliver Washburn Gushee, 1917

Keep the Glory in Old Glory. L: E.B. Gamble; M: Artie Bowers, 1919

Keep the Glow in Old Glory. L: A.H. Ben-Oliel; M: Charles H. Gabriel, 1918

Keep the Guns Still Booming. L: N.L. Houser; M: Leo Friedman, 1919

Keep the Home-Fires Bright. L&M: R.L. Fletcher, 1918

Keep the Home Fires Burning. L&M: Sarah A. Blackman, 1917

*Keep the Home-Fires Burning ('Till the Boys Come Home). L: Lena Guilbert Ford; M: Ivor Novello, 1915

Keep the Home Push Up for Pershing. L: Sidney D. Mitchell; M: Archie Gottler, 1918

Keep the Homes Together, Mother, That's All We're Fighting For. L: W.C. Keene; M: Bessie L. Keene, 1918

Keep the Kaiser Running. L: E.E. Waldrep; M: Leo Friedman, 1919

Keep the Love Spark Burning in Your Heart. L: Arthur J. Lamb; M: Alfred Solman, 1918

Keep the Lovelight Burning. L: Roger Lewis and Bobby Crawford; M: Billy Baskette, 1918

Keep the Lovelight Burning in the Window (Till the Boys Come Marching Home). L: Jack Caddigan; M: James McHugh, 1917

Keep the Old Flag Flying. L: C. Davis; M: Otto Merz, 1918

Keep the Same Old Love in Your Heart for Me (and Don't Forget Your Soldier Boy). L&M: Frankie Williams, 1918

*Keep the Trench Fires Going (for the Boys Out There). L: Ed Moran; M: Harry Von Tilzer, 1918

Keep Up Your Courage Till I Come to You. L&M: B.F. Dennis, 1918

Keep Your Eye on Uncle Sam. L&M: M.M. Speik, 1918

Keep Your Head Down, Allemand. L: Joe Franken; M: C.F. Dobbs, 1918

Keep Your Head Down, "Fritzie Boy." L&M: Gitz Rice, from stage production Getting Together, 1918

Keeping the Shine in Old Glory. L: Dora Hendricks; M: Charles H. Gabriel, 1918

Khaki and Navy Blue. L&M: G.E. Crump, 1917

The Khaki and the Blue (The New Battle Cry of Freedom). L&M: W.J. Trainer, 1917

The Khaki and the Blue (March). M: Salvatore Tomaso, 1918

The Khaki and the Blue. L: Mrs. N. Forden; M: Leo Friedman, 1918

The Khaki and the Blue. L&M: Mary Maude Mitchell, 1918

The Khaki and the Blue (Victory Song). L: W.H. Bishop; M: G.F. Genung, 1919

The Khaki and White. L: Ned Zola; M: J.J. DeLos Santos, 1918

Khaki Bill (March). L&M: Harry L. Watson, 1917

Khaki Boy. L&M: C.E. Wilkerson, 1918

Khaki Boy. L&M: Emily G. Blagdon, 1918

Khaki Boy. L&M: Amelia Renowski, 1919

Khaki Boy, Here's Our Hand. L&M: E.W. Cribb, 1919

Khaki Boys. L: Louis Bertrand; M: Florence E. Gale, 1918

Khaki Boys. L&M: M.B. Dobbins, 1918

Khaki Boys of U.S.A. L: Ella M. Smith; M: Howard I. Smith, 1917

Khaki Boys of the U.S.A. L: C.E. Alderman; M: Robert H. Brennen, 1917

Khaki-Clad Heroes. L: A. MacKintosh; M: Leo Friedman, 1918

Khaki-Clad Soldier Lad of the U.S.A. L: M.E. Lyons; M: Leo Friedman, 1918

Khaki Is the Color. L: Winnifred McGowan; M: Louise Clarke, 1918

Khaki Lads and Blue-Clad Jackies, Here at Home We're Backing You. L&M: J.H. Lyons, 1918

The Khaki Lads Are Coming. L: J.J. Leonard; M: Leo Friedman, 1919

The Khaki Lads Return. L: E. Parker; M: Artie Bowers, 1919

Khaki Sammy. L&M: John Alden Carpenter, 1917

The Khaki, the Blue and the Gray. L&M: J.C. Edwards, 1918

Kicking the Kaiser Around. L: Howard Johnson; M: Harry Jentes, 1918

The Kid Has Gone to the Colors. L: William Herschell; M: E.T. Hawson, 1917

Kid the Kaiser. L: Calvin A. Barnett; M: C.M. Runyan, 1918

Killed in Action. L: C.S. Farriss; M: Leo Friedman, 1919

Kiss Mother's Dear Sweet Lips for Me, Old Pal, If You Get Home. L&M: Charles Jordan, 1919

The Kiss She Gave (A Soldier Ballad). L: Wirt B. King; M: H.J. Young, 1918

Kiss the Stars and Stripes for Me. L: L.B. Lowmiller; M: Leo Friedman, 1918

Kiss Your Little Sammy Goodbye. L&M: Don Sillaway, 1917

Kiss Your Sailor Boy Goodbye. L&M: Irving Berlin, 1917

Kiss Your Soldier Boy Goodbye. L&M: Ray Girard, 1917

Kitchen Police; Poor Little Me. L&M: Irving Berlin, from stage production Yip, Yip, Yaphank, 1918

*K-K-K-Katy. L&M: Geoffrey O'Hara, 1918

Knights of the Air. L&M: Earl Carroll, 1919

Knit, Girls, Knit. L: Howard Johnson and Harry Pease; M: Harry Jentes, 1918

Knitting. L&M: Muriel Bruce and Baron Aliott, 1915

Knitting. L: Frank L. Armstrong; M: Anna Priscilla Risher, 1917

Knitting. L: L.V. Brophy; M: Roy Hartzell, 1918

Knitting a Sock. L: A.M. Fielding; M: Leo Friedman, 1918

Knitting for Our Soldiers. L&M: Margaret Ruthven Lang, 1919

Knock the Germ Out of Germany. L&M: W.A. Miller, 1918

Knocking the Kaiser. L&M: J.P. White, 1918

Knocking the K Out of Kaiser (Canada Spelt With a K). L&M: B.C. Hilliam, 1917

L

The Lad in the Khaki. L: W. Frederic Fadner; M: H.L. Sorensen, 1917

The Lad in the Uniform. L: G.N. Reis; M: G.A. Schnabel, from stage production *The Maxixe Girl*, 1915

Laddie Boy. L: Will D. Cobb; M: Gus Edwards, 1918

A Laddie in France Is Dreaming, Little Girlie, of You. L: E. McGrath; M: Will E. Dulmage, 1918

Laddie in Khaki (the Girl Who Waits at Home). L&M: Ivor Novello, 1915

The Laddie We Love So Well. L&M: William Treloar, 1918

The Laddies Who Fought and Won. L&M: Harry Lauder, 1916

Lady, Lady, Take Your Hoe. L&M: Ralph L. Grosvenor, 1918

Lafayette. L: J.G. Ginn; M: Leo Friedman, 1918

Lafayette. L: Wellington Cross; M: Ted Shapiro, 1919

Lafayette, Goodbye. L: Percy Dillon; M: Artie Bowers, 1919

Lafayette, They've Paid Their Debt. L: Clayton Phillips; M: Leo Friedman, 1919

Lafayette, We Are Here. L&M: Clark Hill, 1919

Lafayette, We Are Here. L: H.D.S. Coates; M: M.A. Coxon, 1919

*Lafayette (We Hear You Calling). L&M: Mary Earl, 1917

Lafayette, We're Going Over. L&M: Ray Girard, 1917

Lafayette, We're Here. L: Phil Scott; M: Ward Edwards, 1918

The Land and Flag. L&M: S.S. Merriman, 1918

Land Beyond Compare. L: T. Henckels and Henry Van Dyke; M: T. Henckels, 1917

Land o' Glory (March). L&M: C.M. Schofield, 1917

Land of Liberty. L&M: E.H. Scott, 1917

Land of Liberty (A National Anthem). L&M: C.M. Pyke, 1917

Land of Liberty (A Patriotic Song). L&M: F. Lines, 1917

Land of Liberty. L&M: John Tafte, 1918

Land of Liberty. L&M: F.R. Parker, 1918

Land of Liberty—America. L: B.M. Allern; M: Leo Friedman, 1918

Land of Mine, L: Wilbur D. Nesbit; M: J.G. MacDonald, 1917

The Land of My Best Girl (the Fatherland,

the Motherland). L: Ballard MacDonald; M: Harry Carroll, 1914

Land of Our Hearts. L: John Hall Ingham; M: J. Henry Francis, 1919

Land of the Brave and Free. L: Edward G. Allanson; M: Charles Miller, 1916

Land of the Free. L&M: A.N. Hosking, 1918

Land of the Free. L: G.D. Miryalis; M: Frank W. Ford, 1919

Land of the U.S.A. L: Una Marie Hale; M: Lucy D. Holt, 1918

The Land That Finished Kaiser Bill. L: M.F. Gran; M: Leo Friedman, 1919

Land We Love. L: John R. Wreford; M: H.A. Henry, 1917

Land We Love. L: C.B. Pittington; M: Artie Bowers, 1919

The Lanky Yankee Boy I Sent Away. L: Harry Williams; M: Grace Henkel, 1918

Larry and the 5th Brigade. L: C.J. Kinkaid; M: Everett J. Evans, 1918

The Last Appeal, O Germany. L: L. Warren Johnson; M: Andrew J. Schorr, 1918

The Latest from France. L: Franklin C. Sawhill; M: Kathryn I. White, 1918

Laurels of Victory. L: A.G. Corless; M: E. Edwin Crerie, 1918

Lead, Columbia. L&M: William Dearness, 1917

Lead On, America. L&M: Jean Gebhart, 1918

Lead On, O Flag! L: Helen O'Donnell; M: M.M. Shedd, 1917

Lead On, O Patriotic America. L: W.C. McCorkle; M: Leo Friedman, 1918

League of Nations (March). M: William T. Pierson, 1919

League of Nations. L: Mrs. A.B. Longsdon; M: Artie Bowers, 1919

League of Nations. L&M: E.V. Cabbage, 1919

Leave It to the Navy. L: R.N. Moffat; M: Hale E. Dewey, 1918

Led by the Red, White and Blue. L: E. Jensen; M: H.G. Gerrish, 1918

Lend a Hand (A Liberty Loan Song). L: E.D. Kennedy; M: Victor Albert, 1918

Lend a Hand to Uncle Sam. L&M: Eva Bartlett Watson, 1917

Lend a Hand to Wilson. L: Caroline Nye; M: Neenah Lapey, 1917

Lending Her Boys to France. L: L. Crook; M: Jack Burdette, 1919

Let Freedom Ring. L: E.B. Lausaune; M: George Graff, Jr., 1919

Let Me Kiss the Flag Before I Die. L: Arthur J. Lamb; M: Frederick V. Bowers, 1918

Let Our Stars and Stripes Forever Wave. L&M: A. Holloway, 1917

Let Peace Be with Us Forever. L&M: O.L. Cunningham, 1915

Let Peace Go Marching On. L: L.C. Shea; M: Paulina Dinwiddie, 1915

Let the Chimes of Normandy Be Our Wedding Bells. L: Paul B. Armstrong; M: F. Henri Klickmann, 1918

Let the Flag Fly! L&M: L. Wolfe Gilbert, 1917

Let the Starry Flag Advance. L: T.W.B. Crafer; M: Percy Fullinwider, 1918

Let the Whole World Cheer America. L&M: J.H. Cleveland, 1918

Let Them Fight. L: Evan Sicks; M: Carl Heil, 1915

Let Us All Fight with All Our Might for Good Old Uncle Sam. L: T. McLarnon; M: Leo Friedman, 1918

Let Us All Salute Old Glory for the Boys. L: O.G. Speak; M: Artie Bowers, 1919

Let Us All Shout Wilson and Hurrah! L&M: Amanda Mae Humason, 1918

Let Us All Take a Crack at the Kaiser. L: G.G. Hill; M: Leo Friedman, 1918

Let Us Begin to Prepare. L: John Brack; M: Mr. and Mrs. James McEvans, 1917

Let Us Boys Fight for Our Nation and Stick to the U.S.A. L: Victor Haimovitch; M: F.M. Gensberger, 1917

Let Us Fight with All Our Might! L&M: E.D. Cartledge, 1917

Let Us Gather Around Old Glory. L: J. McCarthy; M: Leo Friedman, 1918

Let Us Have Peace. M: Otto Motzan, 1915

Let Us Make the World Safe for Democracy (March). L&M: A.H. Simms, 1918

Let Us Pray for Peace, Dear Old U.S.A. L&M: C.W. Paul, 1915

Let Us Say a Prayer for Daddy. L&M: Lew Schaeffer, 1917

Let Us Stand by the President. L&M: B. Anna Rosenberg, 1917

Let Your Country's Flag Be Your Guiding Star. L&M: H. Fuller Wright, 1916

Let's All Be a Service Star. L: L. Wagner; M: Angelus Stuart, 1919

*Let's All Be Americans Now. L&M: Irving Berlin, Edgar Leslie, and George W. Meyer, 1917

*Let's All Do Something (Uncle Sammy Wants Us Now). L: Andrew B. Sterling; M: Arthur Lange, 1917

Let's All Go Over to France. L: J.W. Illingworth; M: E.H. Feather, 1917

Let's All Join the Red Cross Band. L: H.W. Rotavele and Henry J. Secord; M: Michael Jackson, 1917

Let's All Respond to the Call. L: L. Smith; M: Leo Friedman, 1918

Let's All Swat the Kaiser. L&M: Lucius M. Carr, 1918

Let's Be Neutral in the U.S.A. L&M: Walt Russell and Hap Whalen, 1917

Let's Be Prepared. L: Bobby Heath; M: Billy James, 1916

Let's Be Prepared for Peace or War. L&M: R.A. Browne, 1916

Let's Be Ready, That's the Spirit of '76. L: Charles Bayha; M: Rubey Cowan, 1916

*Let's Bury the Hatchet (in the Kaiser's Head). L&M: Addison Burkhardt, 1918

Let's Cheer the Boys Along. L: Agnes E. Lenard; M: Leo Friedman, 1918

Let's Fight for the U.S.A. L: Antoinette K. Fellows; M: Christian A. Grimm, 1917

Let's Finish the Job and Buy (for Victory). L: John Menown; M: Gertrude Watsorg, 1919

Let's Get Over Into France (March). L: R.S. Cooper; M: Martin Greenwald, 1917

Let's Give a Little Credit to the Boys. L&M: A. Cafiero, 1918

Let's Go (A Battle Song for a Fighting Throng). L&M: J.C. Eldridge, 1917

Let's Go (A Patriotic Song). L&M: S.M. McMillan, 1918

Let's Go, Boys, Let's Go! L: R.E. Porter; M: Leo Friedman, 1918

Let's Go, Boys, Let's Go! L: Ouverture Alston; M: M. Toussaint, 1919

Let's Go Over the Top, Boys! L: A.A. Tyson; M: Sallie Tyson Maner, 1918

Let's Have Liberty Till the End. L&M: J.L. Gwirtz, 1917

Let's Help the Red Cross Now. L: Raymond B. Egan; M: Richard A. Whiting, 1917

*Let's Help the Red Cross Now. L&M: Ted S. Barron, 1917

Let's Keep the Glow in Old Glory. L: Wilbur D. Nesbit; M: F. Henri Klickmann, 1918

Let's Rally. L: Lindsay S. Perkins; M: Otto Motzan, 1917

Let's Rally, Boys (Our Allies' Delight). L&M: G.S. Barlow, 1918

Let's Smoke the Kaiser Out. L: Julia Anding; M: Leo Friedman, 1918

Let's Turn to the Sunshine Again. L: William Tracey; M: Maceo Pinkard, 1919

Letter from France (or, Bosche Kultur). L: O.A. Nelson; M: E. Anderson, 1918

Letter from No Man's Land. L&M: Harold B. Freeman, 1918

The Letter That Never Reached Home. L: Edgar Leslie and Bernie Grossman; M: Archie Gottler, 1916

A Letter to Mother from Her Soldier Boy. L: E. Baumberger; M: W. Morris, 1918

A Letter to My Sammy. L: G.L. Hendricks; M: Roy Hartzell, 1919

L-I-B-E-R-T-Y. L&M: Ted S. Barron, 1917

Liberty. L&M: Charles H. Gabriel, 1917

Liberty. L: S.E. Reece; M: Clara May Callahan, 1917

Liberty (U.S.A. Emblem Song). L&M: Ella T. Crawford, 1917

Liberty. L: C.E. Keith; M: Leo Friedman, 1918

Liberty. L: Sarah West; M: Leo Friedman, 1918

Liberty. L&M: J.L. Burke, 1918

Liberty. L&M: W.A. Crause, 1918

Liberty. L: I.W. Sims; M: Lloyd Melvin Manners [Warner C. Williams], 1918

Liberty (March). M: William Grindrod, 1918

Liberty. L: Genevieve Bower; M: Ruth Libby, 1918

Liberty. L&M: J.M. Stinson, 1918

Liberty (A Patriotic Song). L&M: William D. O'Brien, 1918

Liberty (A Patriotic Song). L: C.C. Stern; M: T.M. Williams, 1918

Liberty. L: T. Fazioli and Joseph Anzivino; M: Gene Rawty, 1919

Liberty. L: Elizabeth Ivers; M: Leo Friedman, 1919

Liberty. L&M: C.H. Lynch, 1919

Liberty. L: L. Pierce; M: Billy Held, 1919

Liberty. L: R.G. Stringer; M: George Graff, Jr., 1919

Liberty, America Forever! (Our National Song of Peace). L&M: J. Austin Springer, 1915

Liberty and Peace. L&M: George W. Gates, 1918

Liberty and Peace Forever (March). M: Angelo Vascial, 1918

Liberty Awakening (U.S.A. Hymn of Freedom). L&M: P.J. Jersey, 1919

Liberty Battle Hymn. L&M: C.R. Morse, 1918

Liberty Bell. L: J.M. Humphrey; M: Charles H. Gabriel, 1915

Liberty Bell. L: M.A. Feldman; M: Roy Hartzell, 1919

The Liberty Bell Is Ringing. L&M: Dallas Boudeman, 1916

*Liberty Bell (It's Time to Ring Again). L: Joe Goodwin; M: Halsey K. Mohr, 1917

*Liberty Bell, Ring On! (March). L: Haven Gillespie; M: Albert William Brown, 1918

Liberty Bell Song. L&M: J.A. McNulty, 1915

The Liberty Bells Are Ringing (A Patriotic Song). L: M. Probasco; M: Metta J. Shoemaker, 1917

Liberty Bond. L: Ida Welch; M: Leo Friedman, 1918

Liberty Bond Magee. L: John Barclay; M: Charles McNaughton, 1918

Liberty Bonds. L&M: Mrs. I.J. Davis, 1919

Liberty Bonds Song. L&M: James M. Lathrope, 1918

Liberty Calls. L&M: C.B. Reynolds, 1917

Liberty Chimes (A Patriotic Review). L&M: Karl Lenox, 1918

Liberty, Dear Liberty. L: Robert N. Ogden; M: Arthur Olaf Andersen, 1918

Liberty Fight (or, Uncle Sam's on the Job). L&M: N.F. Nixon, 1917

Liberty for All (March). M: Alfred Francis, 1918

Liberty for All (March). M: Floyd E. Whitmore, 1918

Liberty for the World. L: W.A. Bryan; M: Edouard Hesselberg, 1919

Liberty for the World. L: I.A. Reeves; M: Leo Friedman, 1919

Liberty Forever (March). M: Bert Brown, 1917

Liberty Forever. M: Enrico Caruso and Vincenzo Bellezza; English version by Frederick H. Martens, 1918

Liberty Forever (March). M: D.J. Michaud, 1918

Liberty Forever. L: A.E. Sager; M: Leo Friedman, 1919

Liberty Forever (March). M: H.J. Crosby, 1919

Liberty Forever in the U.S.A. L&M: S. J. Chamberlain, 1917

Liberty Glide. L: Collin Davis; M: Joseph E. Howard, from stage production *In and Out*, 1918

Liberty Host. L: C.O. Lind; M: Artie Bowers, 1919

Liberty Hymn. L&M: Susan C. Treynor, 1918

Liberty, I Hear You Calling Me. L: M.F. Deibel; M: Al Farnham, 1919

Liberty Lads (American Triumphal March). M: Lee Orean Smith, 1917

Liberty Loan March. M: John Philip Sousa, 1917

Liberty March. L&M: C.A. West, 1917

Liberty March. M: J. Frank Frysinger, 1918

Liberty March. L: F. Eikenkoeter; M: Stefanie Tuscan, 1918

Liberty Military March. L&M: Antonio Scato, 1917

Liberty, O Liberty. L&M: Isadore H. Weinstock, 1918

Liberty, Oh Liberty. L: Tom Kennedy; M: Frank W. Ford, 1918

Liberty on Guard. L: A.S. Rabador; M: Leo Friedman, 1918

Liberty Shall Never Die. L&M: Otto Brand, 1918

Liberty Shall Not Die. L: Henry I. Myers; M: Isidore Luckstone, 1918

Liberty Song. L: Samuel Francis Smith; M: J.M. Wilson, 1917

Liberty Song. L&M: Bessie Lane Bean, 1918

Liberty Song. L&M: N.J. Young, 1918

Liberty Song's Bugle Call. L: Charles L. Church; M. A.L. Church, 1918

Liberty Spirit (March). M: August J. Lotz, 1916

The Liberty Statue (Is Looking Right at You). L: Arthur Guy Empey; M: Charles R. McCarron and Carey Morgan, 1918

Liberty, Sweet Liberty. L: C. Carter; M: George Thornton Edwards, 1917

Liberty That Shall Not Pass Away. L: M. Lundy; M: Carol Sweely, 1918

Liberty Triumphant. M: G.A. Sahlin, 1915

Liberty Until the End. L&M: Jay L. Gwirtz, 1918

Liberty Victorious. L: S.L. Nichols; M: Jack Berger, 1919

Liberty Waltz. M: J. Bodewalt Lampe, 1918

Liberty Waltz. M: Mrs. W.E. Osborne, 1918

Liberty Waltz. L&M: Paul Driscoll, 1919

Liberty, You're My Sweetheart. L&M: George C. Pennington, 1918

Liberty's Battle Song. L&M: William J. Faulkner, 1917

Liberty's Call. L: Eleanor Scott Sharpless; M: W.L. Nassau, 1916

Liberty's Colors Are Flying. L: A.J. McIntosh; M: Leo Friedman, 1918

Liberty's Tribute. L&M: Della Kopp, 1917

Light of Freedom. L: Robert Owen Foster; M: Willard Patton, 1918

The Light of the World Is Uncle Sam. L&M: Sue Greenleaf, 1917

The Light That Shines Forever (Is the Light at Home Sweet Home). L&M: Jaan Kenbrovin, 1918

Lillies of France. L&M: Alan McDougall, 1918

Lily and the Frog (Let Me Be Your Little Froggie). L: Grant Clarke; M: Abe Olman, 1916

Line Up, America, Line Up Behind Your Walls. L&M: C. Mussman, 1917

Line Up for Uncle Sam. L: Martha S. Gielow; M: Don Richardson, 1916

Lining Up in France (A Patriotic Song). L&M: Hiram A. Grover, 1918

Listen! Hear the Boys in Khaki Sing. L&M: J.B. Nye, 1918

Listen to the Bugle Call. L&M: Virgie D. Simpson, 1917

Listen to the Knocking at the Knitting Club. L: Bert Hanlon; M: Harry Von Tilzer, 1917

Little Baby Bond. L&M: Leon Berg, 1918

Little Belgian Children. L&M: Nell Marshall, 1918

*A Little Bit of Sunshine (from Home). L: Ballard MacDonald and Joe Goodwin; M: James F. Hanley, 1918

Little French Mother, Goodbye. L&M: Jack Caddigan and Chick Story, 1919

The Little Girl Who Represents the Red, White and Blue. L: E.L. Sharpe; M: L.B. Baldwin, 1918

Little Gold Star. L: Will M. Maupin; M: J.A. Parks, 1918

Little Good for Nothing's Good for Something After All. L: Lou Klein; M: Harry Von Tilzer, 1918

The Little Gray Mother's Only Son. L: Mrs. F.C. Smith; M: Leo Friedman, 1919

Little Red Cross Mother, You're the Greatest Mother of All. L: Vernon T. Stevens; M: J. Stanley Brothers, Jr., 1918

Little Red Cross Nurse. L&M: John H. McDonald, 1918

Little Sammies to the Front (March). M: Carl Sontag, 1919

Little Sammy. L: C.F. Golay; M: Leo Friedman, 1918

Little Sammy's Lamentations. L: S.G. Browman; M: Leo Friedman, 1919

Little Soldier March. M: Adolph Linden, 1919

The Little Town—Belgian 1914. L: Katharine Adams; M: Seneca Pierce, 1917

Little Uncle Sam Will Win. L&M: Michael Toolan, 1918

The Lone Soldier. L: A.M. Kline; M: Leo Friedman, 1919

The Lone Star in the Window. L: C.W. Westbay; M: Leo Friedman, 1919

Lonely Boys in France. L: Lillian Hartley; M: Leo Friedman, 1919

The Lonely Grave of Our Soldier Boy. L: J. Campbell; M: Luther A. Clark, 1918

Lonely Soldier Boy. L: Mrs. L. Laplante; M: Leo Friedman, 1919

Long Boy. (See "Goodbye, Ma! Goodbye, Pa! Goodbye, Mule [With Yer Old Hee-Haw!]")

*A Long Fight, A Strong Fight. L: Leona Upton; M: Robert Armstrong, 1917

Long Live Democracy! L&M: A. Fieldhouse, 1919

Long Live Our America! L&M: Dan E. Wheeler, Emma P. Stretch, and George B. Wheeler, 1917

Long Live Our U.S.A. (March). M: H.C. Miller, 1917

Long May She Wave. L&M: Barclay Walker, 1917

Long Wave Old Glory. L&M: B.A. Colby, 1917

A Long Way from Uncle Sammy. L: Dora Driver; M: Leo Friedman, 1918

Longing for Her Soldier Boy. L&M: Fred Wissmann, 1919

Longing for the U.S.A. L: Mrs. R.M. Horne; M: Leo Friedman, 1919

Longing for You and the U.S.A. (Battlefield Days). L: James A. Sussman; M: Irving Bruckman, 1918

Look Out, Berlin! L: Lawia King; M: Leo Friedman, 1919

Look Our for Squalls, Kaiser Bill. L: E.H. Fitzpatrick; M: Harry Frey, 1917

Look Out for Uncle Sam. L: Charles A. Kells; M: E.S.S. Huntington and Charles A. Kells, 1918

Look Out for U.S.A. L&M: Mrs. W.C. Davidson, 1918

Look Out Over There. L&M: Pvt. John J. McCarty, 1918

Look What My Boy Got in France. L: Will Dillon; M: Con Conrad, 1918

Lorraine, My Beautiful Alsace-Lorraine. L: Al Bryan; M: Fred Fisher, 1917

Lost on the Lusitania. L: Edith Williams; M: Barclay Walker, 1917

Lovable Lou, I'm Dying to Come Back to Louisiana and You. L&M: Harry DeCosta, 1919

Love and War (March). M: R.G. Gradi, 1915

Love, Joy and Peace. L: Gene McDole Hay; M: H.C. Jordon, 1917

A Love That Is Red, White and Blue. L&M: Violet Shore, 1918

Love the Flag (March). M: Nellie M. Bour, 1917

Love to My Home in America. L&M: P.C. Jordan, 1918

Loving U.S. Sailor Boy. L: A. Mueller; M: Leo Friedman, 1918

Loyal Americans. L&M: John Hardy, Jr., 1918

Loyal Dominion (March). M: Clarence Lucas, 1915

Loyal Red Cross. L: A. Suhr; M: Leo Friedman, 1918

Loyal to the Flag. M: Theodore Henckels, 1918

Loyal to the U.S.A. L&M: G.L.K. Secord, 1917

Loyalty (A Flag Song). L: Elsie Janet French; M: H.W. Fairbanks, 1917

Loyalty. L&M: J.A. Hansen, 1918

Loyalty (March). L&M: Hortense D. Mercer, 1918

*Loyalty Is the Word Today (Loyalty to the U.S.A.). L: Dee Dooling Cahill; M: J.E. Andino, 1917

Loyalty to Our Flag. L: A. Teague; M: Leo Friedman, 1919

Luck Be with You, Soldier Boy. L&M: D.M. Franz, 1918

Lullaby of War (While Your Daddy's Far Away). L&M: Robert S. Kampman, 1917

Lusitania. L: A.H. Garcia; M: Leo Friedman, 1918

Lusitania. L&M: Charles Moody, 1919

Lusitania Memorial Hymn. L: O. Greig; M: Orrin E. Henry, 1915

M

Machine Gun March. M: Julius Wuerthner, 1918

*Madelon. L: Louis Bousquet; M: Camille Robert; English lyric by Al Bryan, 1918

Mad'moiselle from Armentières. L&M: Unknown, 1918

Mail a Letter to France. L&M: Jane Carter, 1919

Make Cupid Darts, My Dearie, Instead of Shells and Guns. L&M: Eva Macy Waton, 1918

Make the Kaiser Lay His Big Gun Down. L&M: Thomas Gibson, 1919

Make the Old Flag Proud of You. L&M: Edna McFarland, 1919

Make the World Safe for Democracy. L&M: R.L. Smith, 1917

*Makin's of the U.S.A. (A Plea in Song for Tobacco for the Boys Over There). L: Vincent Bryan; M: Harry Von Tilzer, 1918

Mama, Where Is Papa, Tell Me Why He Don't Come Home. L&M: A.H. Wood, 1918

Mama's Captain Curly Head. L: Eddie Moran; M: Harry Von Tilzer, 1918

Mammy's Chocolate Soldier. L: Sidney D. Mitchell; M: Archie Gottler, 1918

*Mammy's Dixie Soldier Boy. L&M: Norman L. Landman, 1918

The Man at the Front (Preparedness). L: Martha Newland; M: Violet W. Rucker, 1916

*The Man Behind the Hammer and the Plow. L&M: Harry Von Tilzer, 1917

The Man in the Battle Plane. L: W.F. Boosey; M: Emma Stephens, 1917

The Man of the Hour (March). L&M: Cordelia Muir, 1917

The Man of the Hour (Wilson Is His Name). L&M: Robert Mortimer, 1916

The Man on the Firing Line. L: Mrs. M.C. Mahoney; M: Leo Friedman, 1919

The Man Who Put the Germ in Germany. L&M: Nora Bayes, Sam Downing, and Abe Glatt, 1918

Many a Heart Is Broken for the Dear One That's Gone. L&M: Kenneth Malcolm Roberts, 1919

Many a Soldier Boy Will Be There. L: Mrs. W.T. Brophy; M: Arthur Stanley, 1919

March Along (or, We'll Wait for the Homecoming Day). L&M: C.H. Eppelsheimer, 1918

March, March, March Away. L&M: Miss M. Lockwood, 1917

March of Liberty. L&M: Herbert L. Smith, 1917

March of Peace. M: Robert L. Knecht, 1915

March of Preparedness. L&M: B.R. Jolly, 1916

March of the Allies. M: Meta Ellsworth, 1915

March of the Allies. M: H.E. Kent, 1918

March of the Allies. M: Viva Harrison, 1918

March On (Allied Triumph Song). L&M: H.C. Barber, 1918

March On (Triumph Song of the Allies). L&M: H.C. Barber, 1919

March on, Americans! (American Marseillaise). L: Grace McKinley; M: Mabel McKinley, 1918

March on, Boys, March On! L: D.R. Enness; M: Frank Samson, 1918

March on, Liberty Boys, March On! (March). L&M: F.J. Wilmington, 1918

March on, March on, March Right on to Old Berlin! L: A.M. Brown; M: Sidney M. Oscher, 1918

March on, March on, With Our Comrades Over There! L: Lew Colwell and Ernie Aldwell; M: Pete Wendling, 1918

March on to Victory. L: Ella M. Bangs; M: Charles H. Gabriel, 1916

March on, Ye Brave Sons of Washington. L&M: F. Hackert, 1918

March Patriotic. M: Newell Cummins, 1917

March to the Front. L&M: S.L. Goldman, 1917

March to Victory. L&M: R.L. Fletcher, 1918

March to Victory. L&M: Elsa Lachenbruch, 1918

March Victorious. M: Mrs. John P. Murphy, 1917

March We on for America (A National Hymn). L&M: Mrs. J.L. Lake, 1917

Marche des Heros. M: David Dick, 1917

Marche L'Humanité. L&M: Georges Milo; English lyric by J.E. Turcot, 1914

Marching on to Victory. L&M: J. Friedlander, 1918

Marching on to Victory for Us. L&M: Mabel R. McKay, 1918

Marching Song. L&M: David Donald, 1917

Marching Song of Democracy. M: Percy Aldridge Grainger, 1916

Marching Song of Freedom. Revised lryic and melody based on Henry C. Work's "Marching Through Georgia," ca. 1863/ 1917

Marching Song of the 122nd Field Artillery. L: Bert L. Taylor; M: S.W. Hubbard, 1917

Marching Song of the 318th Engineers. L: Frank Fox; M: D.R. Godfrey, 1918

Marching Through Berlin. L&M: William Warren, 1918

Marching Through Berlin. L: Eva Tressler; M: Leo Friedman, 1919

Marching Through Germany. L&M: Thomas W. Tresidder, 1918

Marching Through Germany. L: P.C. Rawlings; M: Henry Clay Work, 1918

Marching Through Germany. L: L.E. Price, Jr.; M: George Lowell Tracy, 1918

Marching Through Old Berlin. L: C.B. Van Derbur; M: Leo Friedman, 1918

Marching Through Paris. L: R.C. Miller; M: Leo Friedman, 1919

Marching Through Rhineland. L&M: Hal E. Goodwin, 1918

Marching to Berlin. L&M: M.M. Kreling, 1918

Marching to Germany. L: J.W. Eller; M: Roy Hartzell, 1919

Marching to Victory. L&M: M.S. Linn-Parr, 1917

Marching to Victory. L&M: Irene Fraser Anderson, 1918

Marching to Victory. L&M: Ella M. Bates, 1919

Marine Band March. M: M.C. Bales, 1918

Marine Corps of America (March). M: William Fredrick Barmbold, 1918

The Marines. L&M: A.G. Wobus, 1918

The Marines. L: D.B. Portnoy; M: George Graff, Jr., 1919

*The Marines' Hymn. L&M: Unknown or unverified, 1918

A Married Man Makes the Best Soldier. L: Rida Johnson Young; M: Sigmund Romberg, from stage production *Her Soldier Boy*, 1916

Marshal Ferdinand Foch (March). M: F.H. Losey, 1918

Marshal Joffre (March). M: Ruth Garland, 1917

Mary Lee (Merrily I'll Come to You). L: Harold Robè; M: Gitz Rice, 1918

The Mascot I Took to France. L: A.S. Rabador; M: Leo Friedman, 1918

May God Send You Safely Back to Me. L: C.S. Guilford; M: R.A. Browne, 1918

McCarthy in Picardy. L: William Massa; M: E.S.S. Huntington, 1918

The Meaning of America Today. L: R. Vonhauten; M: Roy Hartzell, 1918

Meet Me Tonight in Berlin. L: D.R. Resseguie; M: Leo Friedman, 1919

Meet Me When I Come Back Home. L&M: Clara H. Rees and Richard A. Whiting, 1915

Memories of France. L: Emma Bowden; M: Ernest Otto, 1919

The Men Behind the Guns. L&M: Mrs. A.B. Stewart, 1918

The Men Behind the Men Over There. L: R.G. Williams; M: Leo Friedman, 1918

Men, Men and More Men! (The Hymn Universal). L&M: C.M. Swingle, 1917

Men of America (March). L: F.B. Taylor; M: W. Bonney, 1918

Men of America, We're Mighty Proud of You. L: Joseph P. Gorman; M: Mary Catherine Taylor, 1918

Men of the Draft Army (March). L: Rutherford B.H. Macrorie; M: Daniel Webster, 1918

Men of the Merchant Marine. L&M: John Livingstone, 1918

*Merrily We'll Roll Along. L: Andrew B. Sterling; M: Abner Silver, 1918

The Message (A Patriotic Song). L: J.W. Van Winkle; M: J.H. Morris, 1918

Message from Home. L&M: N.H. Hopkins, 1918

Message from Home. L&M: Olive Prince, J. Russel Robinson, and Spencer Williams, 1918

Message from Home to Our Boys Out There. L: Jane Overton; M: Gerald Ames, 1918

Message from Over There. L: L.B. Richards; M: Leo Friedman, 1919

The Message of America. L&M: Joe Miller, 1917

Message of Peace. L&M: W.C. Reed, 1919

Message of Victory. L&M: William T. Pettengill, 1918

Message to France. L&M: Henry Harrison Lessew, 1918

Message of the Service Star [Flag]. L&M: W.W. Smith, 1918

Message to My Land Across the Sea (A Patriotic Home Song). L&M: L.E. Allen, 1918

Messiah of Nations (A Patriotic Song). L: James Whitcomb Riley; M: John Philip Sousa, 1918

Mighty America (March). M: A.L. Maresh, 1917

Mighty American Army. L&M: Thomas W. Tresidder, 1918

Mikie Wore the Khaki. L: Mrs. G.L. Smalley; M: George Graff, Jr., 1919

Military Decoration Dance. L: Al Bryan; M: Jean Schwartz, from stage production *Shubert Gaities of 1919*, 1919

Military Fox Trot. L: Rida Johnson Young; M: Augustus Barratt, from stage production *Little Simplicity*, 1918

Military Life for Me. L: Helen S. Woodruff; M: Madelyn Sheppard, 1918

Military Stamp. L: Rida Johnson Young; M: Sigmund Romberg, from stage production *Her Soldier Boy*, 1916

Military Step. L: Will J. Harris; M: Harry I. Robinson, 1917

Military Waltz. L&M: Frederic Knight Logan, 1917

Militia of the U.S.A. (March). L: M. O'Malley; M: Thomas Carver, 1918

*A Ministering Angel. L: Charles Dunlop; M: William Leigh, 1916

Miss Liberty. L: W.J. Burke; M: Robert H. Brennen, 1918

Miss Liberty. L: Mrs. G.L. Harpst; M: Leo Friedman, 1919

Miss Liberty, You're Calling Me. L: H.L. Hankins; M: James B. Young, 1918

Missing Airman. L: Mrs. N.E. Coan; M: Leo Friedman, 1918

Mister Wilson, We Are Grateful to You. L&M: R. Wilkinson, 1919

Mollie's Hero at the Front. L&M: Jannie E. Wright, 1917

Molly, I'm Coming Home Again. L&M: Newton Alexander, 1915

'Mong the Lillies Over There. L&M: Shad J. Tinsley and "Schoor," 1919

The Moon's Message to the Soldier. L&M: W.B. Robinson, 1918

*Most Beautiful Flag in the World. L: Charles H. Newman; M: Jack Glogau, 1917

*Mother. L: Rida Johnson Young; M: Sigmund Romberg, from stage production *Her Soldier Boy*, 1916

Mother Americans. L&M: Edward Walter Buchanan, 1918

Mother and Home Sweet Home. L&M: Pommé Panchot, 1919

Mother and Uncle Sam. L&M: S.T. Rablen, 1915

Mother Dear, I'm Returning to You Again. L&M: Silvio Previtale, 1919

Mother Dear, We'll Come a-Marching Back to You. L: C.C. Brigham; M: Leo Friedman, 1918

Mother (Dreaming of Him Over There). L&M: Sylvia Ramsey, 1919

Mother, Farewell. L: C.A. Demo; M: Leo Friedman, 1919

Mother, Here's Your Boy. L&M: Sidney D. Mitchell, Archie Gottler, and Theodore Morse, 1919

Mother, I'd Fight the World for You. L: I.C. Bingler; M: Leo Friedman, 1919

Mother, I'll Come Back to You a Better Boy. L: Clara Armstrong; M: F. Henri Klickmann, 1919

*Mother, I'm Dreaming of You. L: Jack Caddigan; M: Chick Story, 1918

Mother, I'm Going Over. L&M: James O. Scott, 1918

Mother, I'm Not Sleeping or Dead. L&M: Adelaide Walther, 1919

Mother Is Dreaming of You. L: H.H. Archer; M: Roy Hartzell, 1918

Mother, Is Your Boy Over There? L&M: G.W. Stroud, 1918

Mother Kissed Him and Let Him Go. L&M: T.S. Reimestad, 1918

Mother o' Mine. L&M: Joseph H. Hughes and H. Richardson, 1918

Mother, Why Don't Brother Come Home? L: C.B. Dickson; M: Leo Friedman, 1919

Mother, You're Sunshine to Me. L&M: Norrie Bernard, 1919

Motherland (March). L&M: William J. Fagan, 1914

Mother's Absent Soldier Boy. L: L: Barrigher; M: Roy Hartzell, 1918

A Mother's Answer to the Call. L: E.B. Graham; M: Anthony S. Lohman, 1918

Mother's Baby Boy Is Gone. L: B. Cassity; M: Leo Friedman, 1918

Mother's Boys Are Marching to the Front. L: L.A. Meyer; M: E.S.S. Huntington, 1917

The Mothers Far Away. L: Sylvan Smith; M: Leo Friedman, 1918

A Mother's Farewell. L: C.L. Austin; M: Roy Hartzell, 1918

A Mother's Farewell. L: Mrs. J.L. Muncie; M: E.S.S. Huntington, 1918

A Mother's Farewell. L: Mabel B. Holden; M: Leo Friedman, 1918

A Mother's Farewell to Her Soldier Boy. L: Mrs. Clay Wiseman; M: Leo Friedman, 1918

A Mother's Goodbye to Her Soldier Boy. L&M: L.E. Keiser, 1918

Mothers' Hall of Fame. L: Addison Burkhardt; M: John T. Hall, 1918

Mother's Hero Sons. L: Ethel Mae Imrie; M: J.W. Rey, 1919

Mother's Khaki Boy. L: G.M. Nelson; M: Leo Friedman, 1918

Mothers of America. L&M: M.M. Parker, 1918

Mothers of America. L&M: T.P. White, 1918

*Mothers of America (You Have Done Your Share!). L: Harry Ellis; M: Lew Porter, 1918

Mothers of Democracy March. M: Frank A. Panella, 1919

Mothers of France. L: David J. Friedman; M: Jean Walz, 1917

*Mothers of France. L&M: Leo Wood, 1918

The Mothers of Our Nation Are Crying for Peace, Not War. L&M: Edward J. Henk, 1917

A Mother's Parting Words to Her Boy. L: M.E. Herron; M: Leo Friedman, 1919

A Mother's Prayer. L&M: Christine M. Smith, 1918

A Mother's Prayer. L: J.W. Moody; M: G.L. Smink, 1918

A Mother's Prayer at Eventide for Her Soldier Boy. L&M: Emily D. Wilson, 1918

*A Mother's Prayer for Her Boy Out There. L: Andrew B. Sterling; M: Arthur Lange, 1918

*A Mother's Prayer (for Her Boy "Over There"). L: Harold L. Cool; M; Arthur J. Daly, 1918

A Mother's Prayer for Her Soldier Boy. M: Wolff N. Rostakowsky, 1918

A Mother's Prayer for Her Soldier Boy. L: Mrs. R.T. Whiteley; M: Charles A. Gregory, 1918

A Mother's Prayer Will Bring Her Boys from Over the Sea. L&M: Novella A. Monroe, 1919

A Mother's Reverie. L: E.E. Leonard; M: Leo Friedman, 1918

Mother's Sitting Knitting Little Mittens for the Navy. L: R.P. Weston; M: Herman E. Darewski, 1915

Mother's Soldier Boy. L&M: V.H. Maves, 1918

Mother's Soldier Boy. L: Florence McVay; M: Frank W. Ford, 1919

A Mother's Son in France. L&M: Charles R. Moore, 1918

Mothers, Sweethearts, Wives Rejoice, Coming Are the Soldier Boys! L&M: C.H. Petrillo, 1919

Mother's Waiting for Her Boy. L&M: L.H. Daniels, 1919

Motto of Uncle Sam. L&M: M.B. Baker, 1917

Move a Little Bit of Broadway to Paris and Make the Boys Feel Right at Home. L&M: Sam Landers and Mary Donoghue, 1918

Mr. Kaiser, You'll Be Wiser. L: "Vittazelle"; M: John Stillwell, 1918

Mr. Kaiser, You'll Be Wiser (for You'll Dance to the Tune of Yankee Doodle Doo). L&M: F.E. Mathewson, 1918

Mr. Sousa's Yankee Band. L&M: J. Farrell and G. Greene, 1918

Mr. Wilson Is President Again. L&M: Charles Abbate, 1917

Mr. Wilson, President of Our Nation Grand. L&M: H.J. Bischoff, 1917

Mr. Wilson, United We Stand to Make Old

Glory Wave for Peace All O'er the Land. L&M: Louis Pasciuti, 1917

Mr. Wilson, We're All with You. L&M: Bernie Grossman, Herman Jacobson, and Maurice Abrahams, 1915

Mr. Woodrow Wilson Is Our Man. L: J.O. Connor; M: George Graff, Jr., 1919

Mr. Yankee Doodle, Are We Prepared? L: Joseph J. Barry; M: George H. Taylor and George H. Malmgren, 1916

*My Alsace Lorraine (On to Paris or Berlin). L: L. Wolfe Gilbert; M: Lewis F. Muir, 1914

My America. L&M: James G. Dailey, 1916

My America. L: James Rowe; M: Anthony J. Showalter, 1918

My America. L: L. English; M: Roy Hartzell, 1919

My American Boy in France. L: Evelyn Wylie; M: Leo Friedman, 1919

My American Rose. L&M: Ethel Low Clays, 1918

*My Angel of the Flaming Cross. L&M: Byron Gay, 1918

My Aviator Man. L: G.C. Thacker; M: Leo Friedman, 1919

My Barney Lies Over the Ocean, Just the Way He Lied to Me. L: Sam M. Lewis and Joe Young; M: Bert Grant, 1919

My Beau Who's in the Army. L: Daisy Bell; M: Leo Friedman, 1918

My Beautiful Country. L: Mrs. J.D. Lehalle; M: Robert H. Brennen, 1917

My Belgian Rose. L&M: George Benoit, Robert Levenson, and Ted Garton, 1918

My Beloved Flag. L: H.A. Sarzynick; M: Frank W. Ford, 1919

My Bit-of-a-Girl (All Day Long I Think of You). L: Leslie Stewart; M: Malcolm MacKenzie, 1918

My Boy. L: Frances Tileston Breese; M: Bruno Huhn, 1917

My Boy (A Patriotic Song). L: A.T. Cook; M: P.B. Story, 1917

My Boy and Your Boy. L: Mell Faris; M: Helen Bates Faris, 1918

My Boy, He Just Can't Help from Being a Soldier. L&M: J.E. McGirt, 1917

My Boy Went Yesterday. L: Mrs. J. Fields; M: R.A. Browne, 1918

My Boy Will Be a Soldier When He's Needed. L&M: Dallas Boudeman, 1916

My Boy's a Soldier. L: C.A. Doak; M: Leo Friedman, 1918

My Brother Is a Soldier. L: Lura Baxter; M: Leo Friedman, 1918

My Brother Is a Soldier of the U.S.A. L: M.M. Manford; M: Leo Friedman, 1919

My Brown-Eyed Soldier Boy. L: C.E. Beck; M: Eugene Platzmann, 1918

My Choc'late Soldier Sammy Boy. L&M: Egbert Van Alstyne, 1919

My Country (March). M: W.C. Kihnlein, 1916

My Country. L&M: Frank Von Neer, 1917

My Country. L: M.S. Woolf; M: George Fred Lindner, 1919

My Country (New National Song). L&M: H.J. Koerner, 1919

My Country, America. L: Samuel Francis Smith; M: J. Fletcher, 1917

My Country and My Home. L&M: J.H. Boschen, 1917

My Country and You. L&M: H.H. Petz, 1918

My Country Calls. L: Annie Nelson; M: Robert H. Brennan, 1918

My Country Calls, I Come, I Come! L&M: W.K. Fobes, 1917

My Country Calls to Me, Dear. L: Lottie B. Larson; M: Roy Hartzell, 1918

My Country Forever. L: H.W. Yeager; M: Lee S. Roberts, 1917

My Country—God's Country. L: P.L. Beatty; M: Arthur A. Penn, 1918

My Country, I Hear You Calling Me. L: Bernie Grossman; M: Dave Dreyer, 1916

My Country, I Love You (March). M: B.N.B. Miller, 1918

My Country, I'm for Thee. L&M: Cordelia Ford, 1917

My Country—My Flag. L: H. Arnold; M: Leo Friedman, 1918

My Country, My Mother and Thee. L&M: J.M. Winship, 1918

My Country Needs Me. L: Aziz Kadora; M: Charles Warren, 1917

My Country Needs Me, Mother. L&M: Belle Williams, 1917

My Country Needs My Aid. L: A. Landry; M: Leo Friedman, 1918

My Country, Oh, My Country (A Patriotic Hymn). L: Emma L. Wulff; M: Cora Young Wiles, 1918

My Country Right or Wrong. L: Cecil Mack; M: Chris Smith, from stage production Ziegfeld Follies of 1915, 1915

My Country, the United States. L: W. Heine and W. Uffelmann; M: Leo Friedman, 1919

My Country, 'Tis of Thee. L: Samuel Francis Smith; M: Solon Willey Bingham, 1916

My Country, 'Tis of Thee. L&M: Charles Jacobs and Milton H. Cohn, 1917

My Country, 'Tis of Thee. L: Samuel Francis Smith; M: George Beaverson, 1917

My Country, 'Tis of Thee. L: Samuel Francis Smith; M: C.T. Schubarth, 1917

My Country ('Tis of Thee). L: Samuel Francis Smith; M: M.E. Florio, 1917

My Country, 'Tis of Thee. L&M: Martha M. Csicsics, 1918

My Country, 'Tis of Thee. M: O. M. Oleson, 1918

My Country, 'Tis of Thee. L: Samuel F. Smith; M: E.B. Hagar, 1918

My Country, U.S.A. L: Mary Wert; M: Casper G. Haynes, 1917

My Country's Calling Me. L: Ervin R. Miller; M: Charles F. Roberts, 1918

My Country's Flag. L&M: J.D. Wood, 1917

My Daddy Has Gone After the Kaiser. L: Elizabeth Cornelius; M: Leo Friedman, 1919

My Daddy Will Never Come Home. L: J.A. Hoff; M: Leo Friedman, 1919

My Daddy's Coming Home. L&M: D.W. Cooper, 1918

*My Daddy's Star. L: Ivan Reid; M: Peter DeRose, 1918

My Dear-O (March). L&M: Helen Howarth Lemmel, 1918

My Dear Old Yankee Land. L: F.M. D'Auby; M: Roy Hartzell, 1919

My Dearest Boy. L: Annie Ferrezzano; M: Al Farnham, 1919

My Doughboy (March). M: Hugo Frey, 1917

*My Doughnut Girl. L: Elmore Leffingwell; M: Robert Bertrand Brown, 1919

My Dream of Peace. L&M: Halsey K. Mohr, 1918

My Flag. L&M: George M. Cohan, from stage production Hello, Broadway, 1915

My Flag (A Patriotic Song). L: J.L. Hartenberger; M: Hermann M. Hahn, 1918

My Flag. L: B. Buhle; M: Roy Hartzell, 1919

My Flag and Country. L: G.J. Brothers; M: Anonymous, 1918

My Flag Forever. L&M: James G. Dailey, 1919

My Flag, My Girl and Me. L&M: Elsie F. Mount, 1918

My Fleur-de-Lis in France. L: Jean Millet; M: Douglas Holmes, 1919

My Free United States. L&M: Lillian Langdon and Mildred Manning, 1918

My Girl From the U.S.A. L: Max C. Freedman; M: George B. McConnell, 1918

My Glorious Stars and Stripes (March). L&M: J.N. Burke, 1917

My Golden Star. L: Mrs. L.E. Gilbert; M: Leo Friedman, 1919

My Good Old Uncle Sam. L&M: Reverda L. Cross, 1915

My Great Big Gun That Will Get Old Kaiser Bill. L&M: Ed Voge, 1918

My Heart Belongs to the U.S.A. L: William A. Halloran, Jr.; M: Byron Hamilton, from stage production *You Know Me, Al*, 1918

My Heart Is with the U.S.A. L&M: Farrar Burn, 1915

My Heart Will Love It E'er. L&M: Will R. McDowell, 1919

My Heart's in the Trenches of France. L: L. Lockney; M: L.E. Bachherms, 1918

My Hero Daddy. L: E.L. Gordon; M: Leo Friedman, 1919

My Heroes of the U.S.A. L: K.D. Pearson; M: Roy Hartzell, 1919

My Home, My Country. L&M: G.H. Nolton, 1918

My Jack Is Safely Back. L: V.J. Wakefield; M: Artie Bowers, 1919

My Khaki Boy. L: B.E. Mohr; M: Frank W. Ford, 1918

My Khaki Boy. L&M: Mildred Stratton, 1919

My Land. L&M: Robert Emmet Moore, 1917

My Land (A Patriotic Ode). L: Thomas Davis and Frank W. Gunsaulus; M: Daniel Protheroe, 1918

*My Life Belongs to Uncle Sam (but My Heart Belongs to You). L: Schulyer Greene; M: Otto Motzan, 1914

My Little Lad in Khaki Clad Is Coming Home to Me. L: F. McGuire; M: Luther A. Clark, 1918

My Little Service Flag Has Seven Stars. L: Stanley Murphy; M: Harry Tierney, 1918

My Little Soldier Girl. L: Effie Struthers; M: Leo Friedman, 1918

My Little Submarine. L: Gene Buck; M: Dave Stamper, from stage production Ziegfeld Follies of 1915, 1915

My Little Yankee Girl. L&M: Henry K. Sommer, 1917

My Lonely Fleur-de-Lis. L: Bobby Crawford; M: Frank Magine, 1918

My Love's in the Army—Is Yours? L: J.W. Spencer; M: Leo Friedman, 1918

My Mamma Needs Me Here Till Daddy Comes Home. L: Herman Kahn; M: Roy Ingraham, 1918

My Mem'ry of You, Little Sweetheart, Will Keep Up My Spirits in France. L&M: F.W. Christianson, 1918

My Midwest Yankee Home. L: W.B. Emerson; M: A.M. Laurens, 1918

My Mother Raised Her Boy to Be a Soldier. L&M: Jack Crawford, 1915

My Mother's Lullaby. L&M: Harold B. Freeman, 1917

My Native Land. L: J. Pedro; M: Carl Heil, 1915

My Native Land, My Country. L: L.E. Baumberger; M: W. Morris and E. Baum, 1918

My Old Man Is in the Army Now. L: Roy K. Moulton; M: S.R. Henry and D. Onivas, 1917

My Own America, I Love but Thee. L&M: Edna Randolph Worrell, 1916

My Own United States. L&M: Stanilaus Stangé and Julian Edwards, 1915

My Phi Delta Soldier Boy. L&M: B.J. Mechling, 1918

My Pledge, I Shall Stand by Our Land to Eternity. L: J. Keirn Brennan; M: Ernest R. Ball, 1918

My Rainbow Ribbon Girl. L&M: Gus Edwards, 1919

*My Red Cross Girlie (the Wound Is Somewhere in My Heart). L: Harry Bewley; M: Theodore Morse, 1917

My Rich Uncle Sam (March). L&M: E. Vernick, 1918

My Sailor Laddie. L: M.H. Fancher; M: Leo Friedman, 1919

My Salvation Army Girl. L: Jack Mason; M: Al Piantadosi, from stage production *Who Stole the Hat*, 1918

My Salvation Nell. L: J. Brandon Walsh; M: Jack Norworth, 1919

My Service Flag. L&M: F.C. Breuer, 1918

My Service Flag for You. L: Grace Lord; M: Jesse M. Winne, 1918

My Soldier Boy. L&M: C.W. Fuller, 1917

My Soldier Boy. L: Ruth Allen; M: George D. Ingram, 1917

My Soldier Boy. L&M: Lester Brockton, 1918

My Soldier Boy. L&M: Henry A. Dienst, 1918

My Soldier Boy. L&M: I.V. Hollenbeck, 1918

My Soldier Boy. L: W.L. Van Vecton; M: Roy Hartzell, 1918

My Soldier Boy. L: I. Nord; M: Leo Friedman, 1918

My Soldier Boy. L: A. Suhr; M: Leo Friedman, 1918

My Soldier Boy. L: Mrs. J.W. Cox; M: Leo Friedman, 1918

My Soldier Boy. L: E.C. Miller; M: Leo Friedman, 1918

My Soldier Boy (March). L&M: Henry Haas, 1918

My Soldier Boy. L&M: Ethel W. Mitchell, 1918

My Soldier Boy. L: M. Fritsche; M: Leo Friedman, 1918

My Soldier Boy. L: Charles Tripp; M: Leo Friedman, 1918

My Soldier Boy. L&M: Levessa Gross, 1919

My Soldier Boy Is Coming Home. L&M: Mrs. T.R. Prideaux, 1919

My Soldier Boy, Over the Top! L: Adalina Cady; M: Artie Bowers, 1919

My Soldier Boy Will Not Return. L: Maude Darling; M: Leo Friedman, 1918

My Soldier Boy, You Are Leaving Me. L: Edna A. Ritchie; M: Leo Friedman, 1919

My Soldier Boy's Farewell. L&M: A.W. LeMieux, 1918

My Soldier Boy's in Europe. L: F.D. Smith; M: Leo Friedman, 1918

My Soldier Brother. L&M: C. Stephenson, 1917

My Soldier Has Been Called. L&M: S.E. Collins, 1918

My Soldier Lad (Mon Soldat). L: R. Brisson; M: Louis Payette; English lyric by Clarence Lucas, 1915

My Soldier of 1918. L: B.R. Scott; M: Roy Hartzell, 1919

My Soldier of the Sea. L: Mrs. W.R. Brown; M: Leo Friedman, 1919

My Soldier Sweetheart. L: E. Van Cortebek; M: Charles H. McCurrie, 1918

My Soldier Sweetheart. L&M: G.M. Johnson, 1919

My Son! L&M: Carrie Jacobs-Bond, 1918

My Son, You're Country Is Calling. L&M: Milton C. Bennett, 1917

My Star (Service Flag). L&M: Elsa Maxwell, 1918

My Sweetheart Across the Sea. L: Louise Anthony; M: Leo Friedman, 1919

My Sweetheart Far Over the Sea. L&M: Ada H. Kepley, 1919

My Sweetheart in the Homeland. L: F.N. Shankland; M: Leo Friedman, 1919

My Sweetheart Is a Soldier in France. L&M: Carrie Beebe, 1918

My Sweetheart Is a Soldier of the U.S.A. L&M: R.L. Varnado, 1919

My Sweetheart Is Over the Ocean. L&M: Frederick Leber, 1918

My Sweetheart Is Somewhere in France. L&M: Mary Earl, 1917

My Sweetheart Soldier Boy. L: B.W. Butler; M: Leo Friedman, 1918

My Sweetheart Was a Hero. L&M: Alfred LaMarche, 1916

My Sweetheart's a Sailor. L: R.T. Prowse; M: D.F. Prowse, 1918

My Uncle Sam. L&M: H.J. Smith, 1917

My Uncle Sam. L&M: Byron Verge, 1919

My Uncle Sam's a Soldier. L&M: A.R. Howe, 1916

My Uncle Sammy Gals. L: Jack Frost; M: F. Henri Klickmann, 1918

My Victory Land. L&M: Harry S. Krossin, 1919

My Yankee Boy. L: Bernie Grossman and Billy Frisch; M: Alfred Solman, 1917

My Yankee Lad. L: Georgia Rials; M: Leo Friedman, 1919

My Yankee Land (March). L&M: William DelHarta, 1917

My Yankee Land. L&M: H.S. Krossin, 1918

My Yankee Sweetheart. L: Francis Erhard; M: J. Edward Fefel, 1914

Myself—My Country and You. L&M: H.W. Snyder, 1918

N

The Name of France. L: Henry Van Dyke; M: James H. Rogers, 1919

The Nation Calls Us (A Patriotic Song). L&M: H.M. Omar, 1918

Nation of Nations. L&M: H.G. Schuette, 1918

National Army Man. L&M: Clifton Crawford, 1917

National Army March. M: Edmund Braham, 1918

The National Call. L: I.O. Neal; M: Roy Hartzell, 1918

National Defense (March). M: J. Bodewalt Lampe, 1916

National Honor (March). M: James L. Harlin, 1917

National Hymn. L: Samuel Francis Smith and C.W. Levalley; M: C.W. Levalley, 1917

National Pride (March). M: G.H. Bishop, 1917

National Spirit March. M: S.E. Hummel, 1917

Nation's Awakening (March). L&M: Lucien Denni, 1917

The Nation's Call. L&M: C.R. Meyer, 1918

The Nation's Call. L: M.L. Pennybaker; M: Leo Friedman, 1918

The Nation's Call for Humanity and Right. L&M: N.A.W. Carty, 1918

A Nation's Hymn. L&M: St. John Byer, 1917

The Nation's Prayer. L&M: Jennie Collins, 1918

The Nation's Prayer. L: E. Hahn; M: Leo Friedman, 1918

The Nation's Rosary. L&M: Sarah C. David, 1918

Naval Review and March of Liberty. M: G. Wayne Ewell, 1918

Navy Blues. L: Alex Rogers; M: Luckey Roberts, 1918

The Navy Forever (March). M: J.M. Maurice, 1917

Navy League March. M: E.W. Berry, 1918

Navy One-Step. L&M: Daisy M. Pratt Erd, 1918

Navy Song. L&M: F. Holland Dewey, 1917

The Navy Took Them Over and the Navy Will Bring Them Back. L: Howard Johnson; M: Ira Schuster, 1918

Neal of the Navy. L&M: Charles Bayha, 1915

Neal of the Navy. L&M: Douglas Bronston, 1915

Near a Little Brook in Flanders. L: R.E. Kelly; M: Leo Friedman, 1919

Near My Heart a Star of Gold Is Shining. L: A. Dietrick; M: Margaret Neidig, 1919

'Neath Old Glory (March). M: Ralph Kirkland, 1914

'Neath Stars and Stripes (March). L&M: C.M. Pyke, 1917

'Neath the Banner of Glittering Stars (March). L&M: E.R. Wolfe, 1918

'Neath the Banner of the Free (March). L&M: J. Van Hoorebeke, 1919

'Neath the Dixie-Doodle Flag. L&M: C.M. Schofield, 1917

'Neath the Flag of the U.S.A. L&M: Risca Williams, 1917

'Neath the Folds of the Red, White and Blue. L: Jockey Russell; M: Edward J. Mellinger, 1915

'Neath the Old Red, White and Blue. L&M: George T. Wilson, 1914

'Neath the Old Red, White and Blue. L&M: Ethelyn Glasser, 1918

'Neath the Poppies They're Sleeping. L&M: A.V. Stark, 1919

'Neath the Red, White and Blue. L: R.G. Scott; M: Frank W. Ford, 1918

'Neath the Shadow. L&M: Anna Barron McKay, 1918

'Neath the Standard of the Stars. L: N.C. Heisler; M: M.B. Parrish, 1917

'Neath the Starry Skies of France. L: J. Koehler; M: Leo Friedman, 1919

'Neath the Stars and Stripes (March). M: R.S. Morrison, 1917

'Neath the Stars and Stripes (A Patriotic Anthem). L&M: J.L. Lanin, 1918

Negro Yanks. L&M: Marie Coleman, 1919

Nephews of Uncle Sam. L: George Graff, Jr.; M: Bert Grant, 1917

Neutral (March). M: Harry J. Lincoln, 1915

The Neutral Waltz. M: Frank Lollick, 1916

Neutrality (March). L: Gertrude P. Ganung; M: Theodore H. Northrup, 1915

Neutrality. L&M: John Hahn, Jr., 1916

Neutrality March. M: Mike Bernard, 1915

The Neutrality of the Dear Old U.S.A. L: G.R. Leonard; M: Edward Wunderlich, 1915

Neutrality Rag. L&M: James White and Jack Frost, 1916

Neutrality Waltz. M: Gertrude E. Buck, 1915

*Never Forget to Write Home. L: Ballard MacDonald; M: James F. Hanley, 1917

Never Let America Desert Her Post. L: Elizabeth Ebling; M: Leo Friedman, 1918

Never Let Old Glory Fall. L: J.C. Beaumont; M: I.M. Owens, 1917

Never Swap Horses When You're Crossing a Stream. L: Harold Robè; M: Jesse Winne, 1916

Never Trust a Soldier. L: Harold Atteridge; M: Sigmund Romberg, from stage production *Dancing Around,* 1914

The New America. L: Samuel Francis Smith; M: S.L. Fulford, 1916

New America. L: W.E. Davis; M: W.E. Davis and H. Bossert, 1917

New America. L&M: R.A. Hilton, 1917

The New "America." L: Samuel Francis Smith; M: E. Whitfors, 1918

New America. M: Ernest H. Wilkins, 1919

New Battle Cry of Freedom. M: George F. Root, 1918

The New Code of Honor Our World's Fighting For (America Leads in That War). L&M: Lillian A. Turner, 1917

New Columbia (A Patriotic Song). L: T.J. Mitchell; M: D.T. Shaw, 1917

The New Europe (March). M: J. Mazza, 1918

New Freedom. L: Blanche Cain; M: Leo Friedman, 1919

New Glory Added to Old Glory. L&M: Solon W. Bingham, 1918

New Liberty (March). M: Harry J. Lincoln, 1917

New National Anthem, America. L&M: C. Condie, 1917

New National Hymn. L&M: Henry Graham, 1914

New National Hymn (America, the Land of Liberty). L: Hannah M. Graham; M: Francis C. Huston, 1916

New National Hymn. L&M: B.J. Hoffacker, 1919

New Old Glory. L: Lou Singletary Bedford; M: Horace Neely Lincoln, 1918

The New Patriotism. L: Marion Mills Miller; M: Laura Sedgwick Collins, 1916

New Serenade (to the Service Star). M: W.H. Neidlinger, 1918

Nigger War Bride Blues. L: Jimmy Marten; M: Mitch LeBlanc, 1917

Night on the Field of Battle. L&M: E.O.B. Gilbert, 1917

Night Time in the Trenches. L&M: Blanche Bruner, 1919

No Braver Soldiers Can Ever Be Than Our American Boys. L&M: G.H. Means, 1919

No Flag Like the Red, White and Blue. L&M: Charles K. Harris, 1917

No Foe Shall Invade Our Land (American Children's Pledge). L: Agnes R.L. Pratt; M: Alfred Hallam, 1917

No Man's Land. L: Glen MacDonough; M: Raymond Hubbell, from stage production *Heart o' th' Heather*, 1916

No Man's Land in Memory. L&M: C.T. Burneson, 1919

No Man's Land Was Yankee Land. L&M: James J. McGrath, 1919

*No Matter What Flag He Fought Under (He Was Some Mother's Boy, After All). L: J. Will Callahan; M: F. Henri Klickmann, 1915

*No One Said Goodbye to Me. L: L.B. Arthur; M: B.S. Edwards, 1914

No Place Like the U.S.A. L&M: Clare Kummer, 1914

Noble Troops of Uncle Sam. L: Ollie Brown; M: Leo Friedman, 1918

Nobody Knows How I Miss You, Dear Old Pal. L&M: Eddie Dorr and Lew Porter, 1919

Nobody's Licked the Yankees Yet. L&M: A.F. Way, 1918

Noontide Prayer for Our Boys Over There. L&M: James G. Dailey, 1918

Not a Streak of Yellow in the Stars and Stripes. L: T. Philip Harris; M: Haldor Lillenas, 1917

Nothing's Too Good for Uncle Sammy. L&M: Harvey Burton, 1916

Now All the World's at Peace. L: Fleta Jan Brown; M: Peter DeRose, 1918

Now and Forever, America First (March). L&M: Daniel LaGrove, 1918

Now I Lay Me Down to Sleep. L&M: C.A. Pfeiffer, 1918

Now Listen! The War Is Over, Now Then What Next? L&M: George L. Rothermel, 1919

Now Our Boys Are Coming Home. L: J.G. Dofflemeyer; M: Artie Bowers, 1919

Now That the War Is Over. L&M: G. Howlett, 1919

Now That the War Is Over. L: V. Mancuso; M: George Graff, Jr., 1919

Now That the War Is Over (A Toast). L&M: G. Howlett Davis, 1919

Now That the War Is Over, Send Him Home to Mother. L&M: Nellie G. Moore, 1919

Now That We've Got the Kaiser. L: S.W. Velker; M: Leo Friedman, 1919

Now the Stars and Stripes Are Flying Over There. L: Mrs. M.J. Lott; M: Leo Friedman, 1919

Now the War Is Over. L&M: Peter Wylie, 1919

Now the War Is Over and the Victory's Won. L: Jack Lloyd; M: Leo Friedman, 1919

Now the War Is Over, to My Homeland I'll Return. L&M: Mary E. Howell, 1919

Now There Isn't Any Kaiser Any More. L: Ross Kiner; M: J.J. Frederick, 1918

Now They Call It Yankeeland. L&M: Harold Shaw, 1918

Now Watch Our Sammies! L: J. Randale; M: Leo Friedman, 1918

Now We're Marching. L&M: J.B. Waterhouse, 1917

Now's the Time to Wake Up, America. L: Anna B. Haines; M: Arné Emerson, 1918

O

O, America, America, We Hail Thee! L&M: Marjorie Bell Johnson, 1918

O, Country, My Own Dear Country. L: Charlotte Gaines; M: Samuel Richard Gaines, 1918

O! France. L: H.B. Edwards; M: John Pearson, 1918

O, Glorious Land! L&M: J.M. Long, 1917

O, Glorious Land, America. L&M: Fred Doeppers, 1917

O, God of Armies. L: M. Woolsey Stryker; M: T. Frederic H. Candlyn, 1916

O, God of Nations. L: Samuel Francis Smith; M: George Beaverson, 1917

O, It's Bill, Bill, Murderer Bill. L&M: Perley M. Helms, 1918

O, Lafayette, We're Here (March). L&M: H.W. Geiger, 1918

O, Land of Truth and Liberty. L&M: S.H. Hodges, 1917

O, Land We Love. L: William Charles O'Donnell; M: Mary Vincent Whitney, 1915

O Let the Nations Be Glad (Thanksgiving Anthem). L: Anonymous; M: Ralph Kinder, 1918

O Native Land! L: S.E. Mekin; M: Alfred Wooler, 1918

O, Peerless Flag! L&M: William Arms Fisher, 1917

O Sammie, Get Your Gun Right Away! L&M: G.L. Spining, 1918

O Sergeant, Have a Heart. L: William Herschell; M: Barclay Walker, 1918

O Soldier Mine. L&M: Cora M. Gibson, 1919

O, the Girl I Left Behind Me. L&M: Charles G. Comegys, 1918

O, Uncle Sam, How Glad I Am That I Belong to the U.S.A. L&M: Kathryn Seacord, 1919

O, Valiant Sons! L: "M.K."; M: Vernon Eville, 1918

O Willie, We're After You! L&M: Russ C. Moon, 1917

O! You La La. L: Lew Brown; M: Harry Tush, 1918

The Ocean Must Be Free. L&M: D. Kohn and L. Flint, 1917

Ocean Waves, Bring Back My Boy. L&M: D.E. Williams, 1918

The O.D. Boy (The Olive Drab Boy). L: A.W. Patterson; M: George P. Howard, 1918

Ode to Our Flag. L: S.F. Emanuel; M: Leo Friedman, 1919

Ode to the Flag. L: W.R. Thompson; M: H.P. Jackson, 1917

Ode to the Soldiers. L: Mrs. F. Elsner; M: Leo Friedman, 1918

O'er the Top We'll Go! L: "MM and FP"; M: J.C. Marks, 1918

Off for France. L&M: Jack Richman, 1918

Off to France! L&M: J.B. McPhail, 1918

Off to Join the Army. L: Selena Richardson and H.W. Gericke; M: H.W. Gericke, 1918

Off to the Front (March). M: Charles Huerter, 1918

Off to the Front. L: L.E. Dunkin; M: Leo Friedman, 1918

Off to the Front. L: T. Lilley; M: Robert Thompson, 1918

Off We Go to France. L: Louise Tipton Weaver; M: J.S. Sweet, 1918

Oh, America! L: Uebbing; M: George Graff, Jr., 1919

Oh Boy, It's Over! L: Emil Ludekens; M: Henry Jacobsen, 1919

Oh Boy, We're Back in the U.S.A.! L: N.S. Scales; M: Leo Friedman, 1919

Oh Danny, Love Your Annie (Like You Learned It Over There). L: Ray C. Spencer; M: Sid Reinherz, 1919

Oh, Flag of My Nation! L: J.L. Langford; M: Roy Hartzell, 1919

Oh! Frenchy. L: Sam Ehrlich; M: Con Conrad, 1917

Oh God! Let My Dream Come True! L: Blanche Merrill; M: Al Piantadosi, 1916

Oh, Heroes from the Battlefield. L: Anthony S. Lohman; M: Harry F. Kissell, 1919

Oh, Hock the Kaiser! L&M: R.H. Bonnell, 1917

*Oh! How I Hate to Get Up in the Morning. L&M: Irving Berlin, from stage production *Yip, Yip, Yaphank*, 1918

Oh! How I Want You! L: Arthur J. Lamb; M: Clarence M. Jones, 1916

Oh! How I Wish I Could Sleep Until My Daddy Comes Home. L: Sam M. Lewis and Joe Young; M: Pete Wendling, 1918

Oh, How We Love You, Red, White and Blue! L&M: Imelda and Bernard Doyle, 1918

Oh, I'm Glad I'm a Yankee Lad! L: D. Lochrie; M: Leo Friedman, 1919

Oh, It's Great to Be a Private in the Army! L: Walter J. Coe; M: Paul Kellogg, 1918

Oh! Jack, When Are You Coming Back. L: Andrew B. Sterling; M: Arthur Lange, 1917

Oh, Let It Wave (Our National Flag Song).
L&M: Sigler Pennell, 1917

Oh, Liberty! L&M: H.B. Edwards, 1918

Oh! London, Where Are Your Girls Tonight?
L: R.P. Weston; M: Bert Lee, 1918

*Oh, Moon of the Summer Night (Tell My
Mother Her Boy's All Right). L&M: Allan
J. Flynn, 1918

Oh Mother, Weep Not for Your Sons. L&M:
Mrs. J.A. Wills, 1919

Oh Mr. Kaiser. L&M: A.R. Spessard, 1918

Oh Mr. Kaiser, You Will Soon Be Wiser
When You Meet Old Glory's Sons. L:
Camille Louis; M: John Jerreld, 1918

Oh, Noble France, We Heard Your Call. L:
John Allen Cooke; M: John Thomas
Malool, 1918

Oh! Oh! It's All Over with the Boches!
L&M: Albert Platt, 1918

Oh, Pres'dent Wilson, What Will You Do
Next? L: R.W. Rees; M: Leo Friedman,
1919

Oh, Promise Me You'll Write to Him Today.
L: Harry Clarke; M: Jerome Kern, from
stage production Canary, 1918

Oh, Red Is the English Rose. L&M: Cecil
Forsythe, 1916

Oh, Sammy! L: Marjorie Munn; M: Adelia
Baker Graham, 1918

Oh, Santa Claus, Send Daddy Back to Me.
L: Phil Ponce; M: Sid Metchell, 1917

Oh, Soldier Boy. L&M: Mrs. L.R. Hertlein,
1917

Oh, Soldier Boys So True. L: M.P. Kellar;
M: Se Deviner, 1918

Oh, the Boys Are Coming Home Now! L:
M.S. Duke and I.W. Anthony; M: Leo
Friedman, 1919

Oh, the Dear Old Flag of the U.S.A. L: Van
H. Terry; M: Tony Denufri, 1918

Oh, the Star-Spangled Banner! L: E.J. Murphy; M: Leo Friedman, 1919

Oh, the Yankee Boys Have Got the Stuff! L:
W.R. Geiling; M: Leo Friedman, 1919

Oh, Think of the Boys Over There. L: Margaret A. Wills; M: Ed Wills, 1918

Oh, to Hades with Kaiser Bill! L: B.M.F.
McKellar; M: Leo Friedman, 1919

Oh Uncle Sam, Man of the Hour. L: E.B.
Zanen; M: Leo Friedman, 1918

Oh, Uncle Sammy, We Do Anything You
Say. L&M: G.M. Gonzalez, 1918

Oh, We Won't Be with You Tomorrow (Today We March Away). L&M: George L.
Boyden, 1917

Oh! What a Lovin' the Girls Will Get When

the Boys Come Home. L&M: Howard
Johnson, Harry Pease, and Harry Jentes,
1919

*Oh! What a Time for the Girlies (When the
Boys Come Marching Home). L: Sam M.
Lewis and Joe Young; M: Harry Ruby,
1918

Oh Will-Yum (A Soldier's Song). L&M: Dorr
Wilder, 1918

Oh, Won't the Eagle Scream! L: Bertha S.
Tiffany; M: Bernice A. Wiseman, 1918

Oh! You La! La! L: Lew Brown; M: Harry
Tush, 1918

Oh, You U-Boat. L&M: H. Bright, 1918

The Ohio Troops (March). L: Frank J.
Daley; M: Raymond P. Paul, 1917

Old Bill Bluff. L&M: John Prindle Scott,
1917

The Old Flag Forever (A National Anthem).
L: Unknown; M: William H. Reussenzehn,
1917

The Old Flag Right or Wrong. L&M: Charles
J. Mann [C.T. Meissner], 1918

The Old Flag's Calling You (A Patriotic
Song). L&M: E.A. Cranston, 1917

Old Glory. L: W.E. Hazlett; M. R.J. For-
mica, 1916

Old Glory (Song of Preparedness). L: Edwin
Skedden; M: Edwin Skedden and Katherine
Pike, 1916

Old Glory (Unison Song). L: James Whitcomb Riley; M: Henry B. Roney, 1916

Old Glory. L: Virginia Roberts; M: Cordelia
Wood, 1917

Old Glory. L&M: Emma Louise Ashford,
1917

Old Glory. L&M: E.M. Birch, 1917

Old Glory. L&M: Karl Sutter, 1917

Old Glory. L&M: H.F. Baldwin, 1917

Old Glory (A Patriotic Song). L: Thomas J.
Duggan; M: Homer N. Bartlett, 1917

Old Glory (March). L&M: C.L. Gillam, 1917

Old Glory (National Hymn). L&M: William
Cutty, 1917

Old Glory. L: J. Nisbet; M: Oscar Williams,
1918

Old Glory. L: B.E. Roberts; M: Leo Friedman, 1918

Old Glory. L: J.H. Michaels and J.W. Miller; M: J.W. Miller, 1918

Old Glory. L&M: H.J. Lebo, 1918

Old Glory. L&M: E.P. Anderson, 1918

Old Glory. L: Mrs. T. Grigg; M: Roy Hartzell, 1919

Old Glory. L: Dora Ginette; M: Leo Friedman, 1919

Old Glory (The New Star-Spangled Banner). L: N.F. Nixon; M: "After the original," 1918

Old Glory and Permanent Peace. L&M: Jared Barhite, 1918

Old Glory Entwined with the Flags of the Allies. L&M: N.F. Nixon, 1917

The Old Glory Flag (March). L&M: Edwin Lowe, 1918

Old Glory Goes Marching On. L: Paul B. Armstrong; M: F. Henri Klickmann, 1918

Old Glory Goes Over the Top. L&M: H.A. Ryan, 1919

Old Glory, I'll Fight for You. L: James Daley; M: Marie Armstrong, 1917

Old Glory Is Calling. L: R.J. Caskey; M: Roy Hartzell, 1919

Old Glory Is the Sign. L: J.G. MacDermid; M: James Gardner, 1917

Old Glory Is Waving. L&M: Charles Fonteyne Manney, 1917

Old Glory Leads. L: J.H. Lowden Potts; M: Leo Friedman, 1919

Old Glory Mine (A Hymn to Our Flag). M: Alfred Marschner, 1917

Old Glory on a Foreign Shore. L: C.S. Guilford; M: Edward Kloepfer, 1917

Old Glory, Our Shield. L: H.W. Newton; M: W.J. Jarrell, 1918

Old Glory Over Berlin. L: Gladys Drumm; M: Leo Friedman, 1919

Old Glory, She Waves for You. L: H.W. Yeager; M: H.C. Webb, 1917

Old Glory, the Flag of Our Nation. L: Dora A. Spittle; M: Frank W. Ford, 1918

Old Glory, the Flag That Floats O'er the U.S.A. L&M: F.E. Hathaway, 1917

Old Glory, the Flag We Love. L: W.J. Blake; M: Leo Friedman, 1918

Old Glory, the King of Kings. L: W.L. Brannon; M: Leo Friedman, 1918

Old Glory, the Red, White and Blue. L&M: Sara C. David, 1917

Old Glory Triumphal March. M: C.E. Duble, 1919

Old Glory Unfurled. L&M: Effie Louise Koogle, 1918

Old Glory Will Be Flying When the Kaiser Is Dead. L: Mrs. A.D. Miller; M: Leo Friedman, 1918

Old Glory Will Be There. L&M: G.W. Armstrong, 1917

Old Glory, Your Flag and Mine. L: Gus Sullivan and George B. Pitman; M: George B. Pitman, 1917

Old Glory's Call. L&M: G.R. Clinton, 1918

Old Glory's Call. L: E.A. Rice; M: C.T. Sulcer, 1918

Old Glory's Calling. L: F.B. Pierce; M: Hermann M. Hahn, 1919

Old Glory's Calling Her Boys. L: J.A. Young; M: A.J. Tantis, 1918

Old Glory's Calling You (A Patriotic Song). L&M: M.D. Spencer, 1917

Old Glory's Sons. L: Camille Louis; M: Jerry Jerveld, 1918

Old Grand Army Man (March). L&M: Will Evans, 1917

Old Grand Army Man. L&M: Harry De-Costa, 1918

The Old Grey Mare (The Whiffle-Tree). L&M: Frank A. Panella, 1917

The Old Red, White and Blue. L: C. Dickson; M: Charles H. Driskell, 1916

The Old Red, White and Blue. L&M: Charles H. Gabriel, 1918

Old Satan Gets the Hun. L&M: C.L. Carrie, 1918

The Old Starry Flag. L: Granville Jones; M: E.M. Douthit, 1918

Old U.S.A. L: M.B. Long; M: P.B. Story, 1918

On a Battlefield in France When I'm Gone, Just Write to Mother. L&M: "Kissell and Howell" [Harry F. Kissell and E.M. Howell], 1918

On a Little Farm in Normandie. L: Ballard MacDonald; M: Nat Osborne, from stage production Atta Boy, 1919

On America's Calling Day (A Patriotic Song). L&M: J.J. Martin, 1917

On Boys, On to Berlin! L&M: Beatrice Baumgartner, 1919

On Business for My King. L: J.L. Frisbie; M: C.B. Gould, 1917

On Earth Good Will and Peace. L: F.W. Farrar; M: J.W. Lerman, 1915

On Earth—Peace. L: Florence Crawford; M: Edith Haines-Kuester, 1915

On Land and Sea (March). M: L.J. Oscar Fontaine, 1919

On, On, On, America! L&M: H.E. Cavanah, 1918

On, On to Berlin! L&M: J.H. Cryan, 1918

On, On to Victory! L&M: George Grether, 1918

On Our Way to Berlin. L: C. McNett; M: Carroll Day, 1918

On Our Way to Germany. L&M: William Henry Grumpelt, 1917

On Our Way, We're Going Somewhere. L: Cordelia Brooks Fenno; M: Francis Ames, 1918

On Patrol in No Man's Land. L&M: James Reese Europe, Noble Sissle, and Eubie Blake, 1919

On the Battlefield the Soldier Lay a-Sleeping. L: I. Dugger; M: Edward Wunderlich, 1918

On the Battlefield with the Red Cross. L: A. Moss; M: Maurice Levi, 1914

On the Broad Fields of Battle. L&M: C.M. Fersdahl, 1919

On the Day We Reach Old Berlin. L&M: H. Logan, 1918

On the Fields of France. L: George Morrow Mayo; M: J.S. Zamecnik, 1918

On the Fields of France. L&M: Minnie Lee Baker, 1919

On the Front Lines. L: Brown Rowland; M: Samuel W. Beazley, 1918

On the Good Ship U.S.A. L&M: Earl G. Cahoon, 1918

On the March. M: W.P. Armstrong, 1919

On the Old Gray Nag, I'll Follow the Flag. L&M: Frank Holland, 1918

On the Road That Leads Back Home (The Bells of Peace). L&M: Gitz Rice, 1918

On the Road to Calais. L: Al Bryan; M: Al Jolson and Jean Schwartz, from stage production *Sinbad*, 1918

On the Road to Home Sweet Home. L: Gus Kahn; M: Egbert Van Alstyne, 1917

On the Road to Victory. L: F.F. Fleischer; M: Oscar Williams, 1917

On the Shores of Italy. L: Jack Glogau; M: Al Piantadosi, 1918

*On the Sidewalks of Berlin. L&M: E. Clinton Keithley, 1918

*On the Somme Front. L: Joseph O'Connor; M: J. Tavender, 1918

On the Steps of the Great White Capitol (Stood Martha and George). L: Grant Clarke and Edgar Leslie; M: Maurice Abrahams, 1914

On the Trail of the Submarine. L: Mildred Harrington; M: Leo Friedman, 1918

On the Vimy Ridge of France. L: J.T. Smith; M: W.R. Flaskett, 1917

On the Way to Germany. L&M: J.B. Herbert, 1918

On the Way to the U.S.A. L&M: E.K. Thomas, 1918

On to Berlin. L&M: L.E. Cheeseman, 1917

On to Berlin. L: E.H. Jennings; M: Mildred Vivion Lowell, 1918

On to Berlin. L&M: Nellie M. Wright, 1918

*On to Berlin. L: J.C. Crisler; M: Lee Johnson, 1918

On to Berlin. L&M: F.S. Wanamaker, 1918

On to Berlin. L: F.L. Skinner; M: Leo Friedman, 1918

On to Berlin. L: J.S. McEwan; M: Leo Friedman, 1918

On to Berlin. L: J.L. Ripper; M: Jessie E. Brown, 1918

On to Berlin. L: A.H. Kitts; M: Leo Friedman, 1918

On to Berlin. L: S.M. Rice; M: J.M. Rice, 1918

On to Berlin. L&M: Mrs. C.J. Wallace, 1918

On to Berlin. L&M: Blanche Sherman, 1918

On to Berlin. L&M: G.S. Fitzgerald, 1918

On to Berlin. L: James M. Powers; M: Lillian R. Powers, 1918

On to Berlin. L&M: E.F. Stanton, 1919

On to Berlin. L: A.C. Lassiter; M: Leo Friedman, 1919

On to Berlin. L&M: H.G. Adams, 1919

On to Berlin. L&M: Jabez Whiting, 1919

On to Berlin and Victory. L&M: Jewell Ellison, 1918

On to France (March). M: H.J. Crosby, 1918

On to France. L&M: N. Louise Wright, 1918

On to France. L: J.F. Robinson; M: Leo Friedman, 1918

On to France (March). L&M: Philip Greely, 1918

On to the Battle. L&M: D.J. Evans, 1917

On to Victory. L&M: J.K. Roberts, 1917

On to Victory (March). M: Arling Schaeffer, 1917

On to Victory. L&M: Christine Burnham, 1918

On to Victory. L&M: Ida S. Cobb, 1918

On to Victory. M: M.J. Mulloy, 1918

On to Victory (March). L&M: John C. Zouboulakis, 1918

On to Victory (March). L: Frank B. Silverwood; M: Mary Newman, 1918

On to Victory (or, Americans All). L&M: Jessie Mead Rose, 1918

On to Victory (Song of Our Boys). L: V.A. Lewis; M: George Lowell Tracy, 1918

On to Victory, America. L&M: Kathryn Norris, 1917

On to Victory Over the Top. L&M: G.E. Malone, 1918

On to Victory: There Came a Call from O'er the Sea. L&M: Otto Palm, Jr., 1918

On to Victory We Go (March). L&M: James H. Underdue, 1917

On Wings of Victory (March). M: Edmond Lanier, 1918

On with the Flag, Boys! L&M: Isabella Fox, 1918

On with the Red Cross. L&M: J. Braswell, 1918

Once More the Liberty Bell Shall Chime Liberty to All. L: M. Wilson; M: Leo Friedman, 1919

One Day Nearer Going Home to the Dear Old U.S.A. L: E.M. Ganster; M: Amelia Clouch, 1918

One Flag, One Country. L: F.H. Baldwin; M: A.C. Mora, 1916

One for All and All for One. L: Neville Fleeson; M: Albert Von Tilzer, 1918

One for All and All for One (World Democracy). L&M: C.H. Hope, 1918

One God — One Flag — One Home. L&M: E.J. Mackay, 1917

101st Regiment, U.S.A. (March). M: Bert Potter, 1917

100 Per Cent American. L: Belle KaDell; M: Leo Friedman, 1919

102nd Regiment March. M: Fred G. Guilford, 1919

107th Field Artillery March. M: V.D. Nirella, 1918

136th U.S.A. Field Artillery (March). M: Henry Fillmore, 1919

124th Infantry. L&M: A.B. Pooley, 1918

127th Infantry Regiment (March). M: J. Prind, 1918

One Is the Call of Our Country. L: M.C. Waller; M: Leo Friedman, 1918

One Last Fond Look (The Soldier's Talisman). L&M: Herbert Owen Holderness, 1917

One Life to Give. L: Loza Jarrett; M: Leo Friedman, 1919

One Million Men Are Fighting. L: A.P. Schneider; M: Leo Friedman, 1919

One Mother to Uncle Sam. L&M: C.L. Claxton, 1919

One of the Boys Over There. L&M: Flossie Gorbet, 1919

*One, Two, Three, Boys (Over the Top We Go). L&M: Charles K. Harris, 1918

Only a Rag (A Patriotic War Song). L: Mrs. L.M. Dunn; M: John C. Ford, 1918

Only a Rose on No Man's Land. L: Arthur J. Lamb; M: Alex Marr, 1918

Only a Sammy. L&M: Margaret Price, 1918

Only a Soldier's Widow. L: Ward Morde Smith; M: Charles T. Edwards, 1918

Only One Flag to Lick the Kaiser. L: R. Culverwell; M: Leo Friedman, 1918

The Only Starry Banner in the World. L&M: Edwin L. Foster, 1917

The Only Way Yankee Doodle Do. L&M: Mrs. M. Hildebrant, 1919

Onward! (Song of World Freedom).L: William P. Taylor; M: Frederick Hall, 1918

Onward, America! L&M: Bessie Walker Knott, 1918

Onward Boys, Over the Top! L&M: J. Cutler-Wixom, 1918

Onward Christian Soldiers (Hymn). L: Sabine Baring Gould; M: H.J. Kurtz, 1918

Onward, Onward, We Are Marching! L: William O'Connell; M: Leo Friedman, 1917

Onward to Berlin. L: D. Bruff Johnson; M: Mrs. D. Bruff Johnson, 1918

Onward to Peace. L&M: Hattie Quigley, 1917

Onward to Victory. L&M: Julia Wingate Sherman, 1917

Onward to Victory (March). M: Mrs. J.H. O'Callaghan, 1918

Onward to Victory (March). L&M: Elliott H. Pendleton, 1918

Onward to Victory. L: Mrs. B. Bottini; M: Leo Friedman, 1918

Onward to Victory. L: H. Pattison; M: Leo Friedman, 1919

Ooh, La-La, I'm Having a Wonderful Time! L: Bud Green; M: Edward G. Nelson, 1918

*Oui Oui, Marie. L: Al Bryan and Joseph McCarthy; M: Fred Fisher, 1918

Our Airships Will Go Sailing O'er the Sea. L: J.W. Tenney; M: Leo Friedman, 1918

Our Allied Trio. L: A.R. Barber; M: Leo Friedman, 1918

Our Allies! Say, It's Grand! L&M: L.E. Schumacher, 1918

Our America (National Hymn). L: Alice Morgan Harrison; M: A.E. Stetson, 1916

Our America. L&M: Anna Case, 1917

Our America. L: Henry J. Zelley; M: Philip Wuest, 1918

Our America (Oh, America, We Love You So) (March). L: Laura L. Smith; M: John W. Keck, 1918

Our American Boys. L&M: G. Cabot Moore, 1917

Our American Bunch. L: Mrs. J.P. Richards; M: Frank W. Ford, 1919

Our American Flag. L: F.L. Price; M: Leo Friedman, 1919

Our American Soldier. L: C.J. Gardner; M: Leo Friedman, 1919

Our Answer to the Call. L&M: Elizabeth Garrett, 1917

Our Army. L: E. Wayne; M: Roy Hartzell, 1919

Our Banner. L: E.E. Hahn; M: Leo Friedman, 1918

Our Battle Cry. L: C.M. Himel; M: Mildred Forsyth, 1918

Our Battle Hymn. L&M: R.N. Saunders, 1917

Our Battle Song. L: Hugh Cameron; M: J.B. Overmyer, 1917

Our Blue Jackets (March). M: Frederick Bertram, 1917

Our Bonny Boys in Blue. L&M: Sabina Penrod, 1918

Our Boy in France. L&M: Gertrude L. Berg, 1918

Our Boy Is Coming Home. L&M: E. Hilden, 1919

Our Boys. L&M: G.E. Wolf, 1917

Our Boys. L&M: H.C. Williams, 1917

Our Boys (March). L: Katherine M. Fiorini; M: Mary L. LoCascio, 1917

Our Boys. L&M: Hermann M. Hahn, 1918

Our Boys. L: E. Torrence; M: Leo Friedman, 1918

Our Boys. L: William Burke; M: R.M. Silby, 1918

Our Boys. L: A.D. Gerds; M: Leo Friedman, 1918

Our Boys. L: I.D. Van Zandy; M: Leo Friedman, 1918

Our Boys. L: Theodor L. Clemens; M: Mary E. Clemens, 1918

Our Boys. L&M: Cora M. Lane, 1918

Our Boys. L: H.G. Randolph; M: Leo Friedman, 1919

Our Boys Across the Sea. L: R.N. Elwell; M: Herbert W. Rainie, 1918

Our Boys Across the Sea. L: F. Easterday; M: Leo Friedman, 1918

Our Boys Across the Sea. L&M: F.S. Colburn, 1918

Our Boys Across the Sea (March). M: Joe Hahn, 1919

Our Boys and Flag. L&M: Sallie Grant Gates, 1918

Our Boys and the Red, White and Blue. L&M: Samuel L. Peckham, 1918

Our Boys Are Coming Back. L&M: Caroline Irene Brittin, 1919

Our Boys Are Coming Home. L: Agatha Harrington; M: Leo Friedman, 1919

Our Boys Are Coming Home Again. L: C.O.

Bedford; M: Artie Bowers, 1919

Our Boys Are in the Trenches. L: S.A. Thayer; M: George W. Marton, 1918

Our Boys at the Front. L: H.L. Broughton; M: Robert H. Brennen, 1918

Our Boys at the Front (March). M: Jules Bolle, 1918

Our Boys at the Front. L&M: C.F. Hanson, 1919

Our Boys' Departure. L: Gertrude Littledale Roberts; M: Hattie Carter Renner, 1918

Our Boys (for Liberty We Are Fighting). L&M: Estelle M. Hurll, 1917

Our Boys from the U.S.A. L&M: Gertrude Baine, 1918

Our Boys Have Gone Over the Ocean. L: A.C. Slaby; M: Leo Friedman, 1918

Our Boys Have Hit the Trail. L: Mardis Gilmer; M: Leo Friedman, 1918

Our Boys in Blue. L: D. Nugent; M: Ben Stanley, 1918

Our Boys in France (Grand March). M: Louis Weber, 1917

Our Boys in France. L: Henry T. Thomas; M: Otto F. Bauman, 1918

Our Boys in France. L: Mrs. E. Hoffer; M: Leo Friedman, 1918

Our Boys in France. L: C.E. Henry; M: Leo Friedman, 1918

Our Boys in France. L: I.P. Bartlett; M: Grace Miner Weston, 1918

Our Boys in Khaki. L: M.S. Grady; M: Roy Hartzell, 1919

Our Boys in Khaki, the Pride of Our Land. L: G.W. Stormes; M: Leo Friedman, 1919

Our Boys in No Man's Land. L: H.J. Theis; M: George Graff, Jr., 1919

Our Boys' March. M: Hugo Frey, 1917

Our Boys of the Dare and Do. L: Rosalie Bockelman; M: Leo Friedman, 1919

Our Boys of the U.S.A. L&M: Lottie McCandless, 1917

Our Boys of Uncle Sam (March). L&M: Michael B. Rock, 1918

Our Boys on Their Way to France. L: Claire Hendrix; M: Leo Friedman, 1919

Our Boys Over There (March). M: Clayton C. Curwen, 1918

Our Boys Over There (Under Three Flags). L: J.C. and Mary Ferguson; M: Charles L. Johnson, 1918

Our Boys Overseas and the Red, White and Blue. L: A.E. Vassar; M: E.J. Stark, 1918

Our Boys, the Knights of Liberty. L: M. Emerson; M: Bernard Jewett, 1918

Our Boys, They'll Fight or Die. L&M: C.W. Crankshaw, 1918

Our Boys, They'll Fight or Die. L&M: J. Chambers, 1918

Our Boys Who Went Over to Stay. L: B. Case; M: Leo Friedman, 1919

Our Brave American Boys. L&M: Mrs. W.A. Freese, 1918

Our Brave Heroes. L&M: Mrs. S.J. Zerger, 1919

Our Brave Old Yankee Soldiers. L: J.R. Packard; M: Leo Friedman, 1918

Our Brave Sammies O'er the Sea. L: P.T. Kimball; M: Leo Friedman, 1918

Our Brave Soldiers of the Good Old U.S.A. L: W.J. Storz; M: Harry P. Guy, 1917

Our Brothers 'Cross the Sea. L: William DePaul; M: Nodrog Rednuht, 1918

Our Brother's Fighting for the U.S.A. L&M: S. Warren, 1918

Our Buddies. L: J.H. Forsythe; M: Leo Friedman, 1918

Our Bugles Never Sound Retreat. L&M: L.A. Orvis, 1918

Our Colors. L: C.R. Fuller; M: H.T. Fitz Simons, 1917

Our Colors. L&M: R.A. Hilton, 1918

Our Country (March). M: W.A. Barrington Sargent, 1915

Our Country. L&M: Charles F. Stayner, 1916

Our Country. M: Otto Anschuetz, 1917

Our Country. L&M: Frank Taft, 1917

Our Country. L&M: W.C. Piatt, 1917

Our Country. L: Edna Dean Proctor; M: David Proctor, 1917

Our Country (March). L&M: Constan Jensen, 1917

Our Country. L&M: G.W. Marton, 1918

Our Country First of All. L: A.C. Kufen; M: Leo Friedman, 1919

Our Country Forever (National March). M: George Bowen, 1916

Our Country Is Calling. L: B. Bordeaux; M: Leo Friedman, 1918

Our Country, Our Heroes, Our Flag. L&M: G.W. Wiswell, 1918

Our Country Right or Wrong. L&M: "San A. Tonio" [Robert Sturmberg], 1915

Our Country, the Land Beyond Compare. M: Theodore Henckels, 1918

Our Country, the Soldier Man and You. L: M. Lintz; M: Katharine R. McCoy, 1918

Our Country, 'Tis Our Love for Thee. L&M: H.B. Loeb, 1918

Our Country's Call. L: C.L. Smith; M: E.S.S. Huntington, 1917

Our Country's Call. L&M: Bertha Slater Smith, 1917

Our Country's Call. L: N. Ovitt; M: Don Sillaway, 1917

Our Country's Call. L: W. Blackshaw; M: Robert H. Brennen, 1917

Our Country's Call. L&M: George Bliss, 1917

Our Country's Call. L&M: E.M. Copeland, 1918

Our Country's Call. L: D.C. Tetzloff; M: Raymond A. Brown, 1918

Our Country's Call. L: L.H. Seymour; M: Leo Friedman, 1919

Our Country's Calling. L&M: S. Hanes, 1918

Our Country's Calling You. L: J. Wyatt; M: Leo Friedman, 1918

Our Country's Defense. L&M: E. Blorn, 1918

Our Country's Emblem. L: G.J. Brothers; M: Louise Hoffmeyer, 1918

Our Country's Flag. L: Florence L. Dresser; M: J. Truman Wolcott, 1915

Our Country's Flag. L&M: Anna Davis, 1916

Our Country's Flag. L: Edwin K. Hurlbut; M: F.M. Paine, 1917

Our Country's Flag. L&M: Alice Maxwell Chalmers, 1917

Our Country's Flag. L&M: Mary Sitz Parker, 1917

Our Country's Flag. L: J.C. Bramwell; M: Alfred Damm, 1917

Our Country's Flag. L: Gertrude L. Roberts; M: Hattie C. Renner, 1918

Our Country's in It Now (We've Got to Win It Now). L: Arthur Guy Empey; M: Charles R. McCarron and Carey Morgan, 1918

Our Country's Prayer. L: Carl Roppel; M: Arthur Farwell, 1919

Our Country's Voice Is Calling (March). L: O. Ebel and Luella Stewart; M: O. Ebel, 1917

Our Daddy Soldier Boy. L: Marjorie Hibbs; M: B. Alexander, 1918

Our Dear Old Flag Is Calling. L: Harriet Williams Barton; M: Arthur Hull Rigor de Eva, 1918

Our Dear Old U.S.A. L&M: Herman Struebing, 1919

Our Debt to France. L: Mrs. E.M. Babcock; M: Edouard Hesselberg, 1919

Our Defenders (March). M: R.F. Seitz, 1918

Our Emblem It Is True. L&M: Edmond Leischner, 1919

Our Emblem of Democracy. L: A.H. Baker; M: Leo Friedman, 1918

Our Emblem of Glory. L: H.S. Durand; M: Morton F. Mason, 1917

Our Faithful Watchman of the U.S.A. L&M: A. Bohlender, 1918

Our Fight for Right. L&M: C.P. Sherman, 1917

Our Fighting Chaplain (March). M: James E. Son, 1918

Our Fighting Heroes (March). M: George Barker, 1918

Our Fighting Sammies (March). M: J.J. Romaniello, 1918

Our Fighting Yankee Boy. L&M: J.L. Galloway, 1919

Our First Line of Defense (March). L: Tulley Shelley; M: Max Karasyk, 1917

Our Flag. L: Margaret Sangster; M: William D. Armstrong, 1915

Our Flag. L: Jeremiah A. O'Leary; M: Adalbert Schueler, 1916

Our Flag. L: William J. Dawson; M: C.F. Marks, 1916

Our Flag. L&M: J.T. Pope, 1916

Our Flag. L: Maude M. Grant; M: "Churchill-Grindell," 1917

Our Flag. L&M: Alva A. Shaw, 1917

Our Flag. L&M: Garna Vallah, 1917

Our Flag. L: C.W. Augustus; M: Reinhard Jugel, 1917

Our Flag. L: C.W. Augustus; M: Daniel Protheroe, 1917

Our Flag. L: Anonymous; M: C.T. Schubarth, 1917

Our Flag. L&M: C. Geerken, 1917

Our Flag. L&M: Kate E. Blake, 1918

Our Flag. L: Charles L.H. Wagner; M: Will Ellsworth Brown, 1918

Our Flag. L: Lucia Beck; M: Leo Friedman, 1918

Our Flag. L: L. Noeske; M: Leo Friedman, 1918

Our Flag. L: J.E. Nye; M. Olivia J. Thomas, 1918

Our Flag. L&M: D.H. Walmsley, 1918

Our Flag. L: Thomas W. Dunn; M: D.J. Michaud, 1918

Our Flag. L: L.G. Hanley; M: Collier Grounds, 1918

Our Flag. L: H.M. Hopewell; M: Abbie Norton Jamison, 1918

Our Flag. L: A. Whipple; M: Robert H. Brennen, 1918

Our Flag. L: V. Mengel; M: George Graff, Jr., 1919

Our Flag. L: Frank Laurence Jones; M: William J. Guard, 1919

Our Flag. L&M: J.A. Pickard, 1919

Our Flag and Freedom. L: J.F. Smith; M: Thomas F. Priest, 1917

Our Flag and Motherland. L&M: William Arms Fisher, 1917

Our Flag and Motto. L&M: Henri Plante, 1918

Our Flag and the Fleur-de-Lis. L: G.H. Marquis; M: Roy Hartzell, 1919

Our Flag (Freedom, Home and Liberty). L&M: Charles W. Cordrey, 1916

Our Flag Is There. L: C.K. Hammitt; M: Paul Ambrose, 1918

Our Flag Knows Only Victory. M: Myron May, 1918

Our Flag of Freedom. L&M: Joseph Robinson, 1917

Our Flag of Liberty. L&M: W.S. Stoner, 1917

Our Flag on the Rhine. L: Asa Baxter; M: Artie Bowers, 1919

Our Flag, Red, White and Blue. L: Mrs. L. Antaya; M: Tony A. Pailo, 1918

Our Flag Shall Conquer. L&M: R.M. Woods, 1917

Our Flag Shall Float Forever. L&M: M.E.P. Mitchell, 1917

Our Flag, the Red, White and Blue. L: W.T. LaForest; M: Leo Friedman, 1918

Our Flag to the Sea. L: J. Will Callahan; M: F. Henri Klickmann, 1914

Our Flag Was Never Made to Fall in Battle. L: Henry J. Schmieder; M: Carl Heil, 1915

Our Flag Was There. L: E.C. Monroe; M: Frank W. Ford, 1919

Our Flag's Great Emblem. L&M: H.F. Thomas, 1918

Our Gallant Hero Lads (the Boys in Brown). L&M: J.B. Wolff, 1918

Our Gallant Sammy Boys in That Sunny Land of France. L&M: William J. Faulkner, 1917

Our Gallant Soldier Boys (March). L&M: J.E. Burns, 1918

Our Gallant Yankee Tars. L&M: J.H. Alleman, 1917

Our General Over There. L: M. Isabella Osman; M: H. Lafayette Brooks, 1918

Our Glorious Land. L: Theophil Stauge; M: Frank van der Stucken, 1917

Our Glorious Sons of Today. L: H.F. Marath; M: Leo Friedman, 1918

*Our God, Our Country, and Our Flag. L&M: Edward Machugh, 1917

Our Goddess of Liberty, the Red Cross Nurse. L&M: H.C. Williams, 1918

Our Good Old U.S.A. L&M: L.L. Stowe, 1917

Our Great and Glorious Flag. L&M: Julie Bischoff, 1918

Our Great Land (A National Song). L: Helen Bagg and Jessie Bonstelle; M: Lulu Jones Downing, 1917

Our Great United States. L: M.E. Mooney; M: Nicholas Devereux, 1918

Our Hearts Go Out to You, Canada (Hats Off to You). L: J. Keirn Brennan; M: Ernest R. Ball, 1916

Our Hero. L&M: Fred W. Pearson, 1918

Our Heroes. L&M: Ayol Zinth, 1919

Our Heroes. L&M: H.E. Schmaus, 1919

Our Heroes Have Not Fought in Vain. L: Anna Rosendahl; M: Leo Friedman, 1919

Our Heroes Homeward Bound (Victory Song). L&M: Zetta Learmonth, 1918

Our Heroes Marching On. L&M: Mary Augusta Lee, 1918

Our Heroes Over There. L: Edith J. Perry; M: R.E. Smith, 1918

Our Heroes Over There. L&M: Mary Augusta Lee, 1918

Our Home in the U.S.A. L: K.M. Bowyer; M: F. Arlington Smith, 1918

Our Homeland, O, Our Homeland. L&M: Bessie S. Dexheimer, 1919

Our Honor Boys. L&M: C.B.V. Sturges, 1918

Our Khaki Boys for Freedom. L: Mrs. F. Walker; M: Leo Friedman, 1918

Our Laddies. L&M: Florine Bigbee, 1919

Our Lads Have Answered the Call. L: A. Henderson; M: Frank W. Ford, 1918

Our Lads in Olive Drab. L&M: M.H. Sweet, 1918

Our Land It Is America, the Home of the Free. L&M: May Worrell, 1918

Our Lanky Yankee Boys in Brown. L: Edward Madden and Robert F. Roden; M: Theodore Morse, 1917

Our Liberty. L&M: E.R. Kelm, 1918

Our Liberty Land. L&M: A.A. Gayne, 1918

Our Loyalty to Freedom (Now the Yanks Are Going Over). L&M: O.W. Perry, 1918

Our Marching Song of Liberty. L&M: C.W. Marsh, 1917

Our Message to the Boys Over There. L&M: Ida C. Young, 1918

Our Military Home. L&M: Howard Johnson, Alex Gerber, and Harry Jentes, 1916

Our Millions Did It. L: E.A. Roscoe; M: Leo Friedman, 1919

Our Motherland (Song of America). L&M: F. Nevin, 1917

Our Nation. L: B.B. Ussher; M: Mabel Tait Elliott, 1917

Our Nation. L&M: J. Lincoln Hall, 1918

Our Nation and the Allies Depend on You. L&M: E.G. Harper, 1918

Our Nation in Its Glory. L&M: M.J. Bayless, 1919

Our National Banner. L&M: C.S. Peregrine, 1917

Our National Flag (Old Glory). L&M: Elenor Raynor, 1917

Our National Honor (March). M: Grant Brooks, 1918

Our National President (March). M: Antonio Celfo, 1915

Our National Song. L&M: James G. Dailey, 1918

Our Nation's Flag. L: Carl Kunter and William Corteen; M: Edwin Klein, 1917

Our Nation's Prayer. L&M: W.A. Wood, 1918

Our Nation's Roused Again. L: Walter J. Coe; M: Paul Kellogg, 1918

Our Nation's Song of Glory. L&M: Adam Geibel, 1918

Our Native Land. L&M: William Lester, 1917

Our Native Shore (The New World War Song). L: A.L. Platte; M: R.T. Campbell, 1918

Our Navy (March). M: F.A. Haight, 1915

Our Navy Forever (March). M: Otto Anschuetz, 1918

Our New America. L&M: C.I. Ingerson, 1919

Our Old Glory. L&M: W.L. Gilpin, 1918

Our Old Red, White and Blue. L: S.R. Wallbaum; M: Leo Friedman, 1918

Our Own America (National Hymn). L&M: Ada M. Farr, 1917

Our Own America. L&M: B.E. Comey, 1918

Our Own America, Farewell. L&M: Marian Sargent, 1917

*Our Own American Boy. L&M: William C. Wilbert, Max Friedman, and George F. Olcott, 1917

Our Own Beloved America. L&M: Mary Smyth Davis, 1917

Our Own Red, White and Blue. L&M: Thomas Meekin, 1916

Our Own Red, White and Blue. M: F. Serre, 1917

Our Own Red, White and Blue (March). L: Eleanor Allen Schroll; M: Henry Fillmore, 1917

Our Own Red, White and Blue. L: James B. Sprague; M: F.E. Connelly, 1918

Our Own United States. L&M: Mrs. A. Willis, 1918

Our Own United States. L: Margaret Norton; M: Leo Friedman, 1919

Our Peppering Guns. L&M: Edison D. Stout, 1918

Our Peppering Guns. L&M: Henri Duval, 1918

Our Pledge to the U.S.A. (March). L&M: Gene Shirley, 1917

Our Ready Sammies, M: Unknown; arranged by James G. Ellis, 1916

Our Red Cross Patriots (the Nation's Life Savers). L: W.R. Thompson; M: E.H. Thompson, 1917

Our Right Place in the Sun. L&M: A. Estoclet, 1918

Our Sacred Dead. L: Thomas Gaffrey; M: Leo Friedman, 1919

Our Sailor Boys. L&M: May Murray, 1917

Our Sammee Boys (March). L&M: Willard Spencer, 1917

Our Sammie Boys. L: M.M. Duffee; M: Luther A. Clark, 1917

Our Sammies. L&M: W.P. and Alice M. Hershey, 1918

Our Sammies. L: R.M. Feeley; M: Leo Friedman, 1918

Our Sammies. L: J.R. Shannon; M: Carl D. Vandersloot, 1918

Our Sammies. L&M: Coralee Campbell, 1919

Our Sammies' Dreams. L&M: A.W. Judd, 1919

Our Sammies in the Trenches. L: J. Heaney; M: Andrew Dory, 1917

Our Sammies of the U.S.A. L&M: F.G. McCauley, 1918

Our Sammies Over There. L: J.M. Beavert; M: Leo Friedman, 1918

Our Sammies (Somewhere in France). L: Arthur J. Matthews; M: C.B. Gilliland, 1917

Our Sammies Will Hold Their Own. L&M: I.V. Hollenbeck, 1918

Our Sammy Boys. L: G. Allyn Rockwell; M: Guy Call, 1917

Our Sammy from the U.S.A. L&M: Mabel Todd, 1918

Our Sammy Goes a-Courtin'. L: Mrs. H.H. Embrey; M: Leo Friedman, 1918

Our Service Flag. L: Arthur M. Corwin; M: Daniel Protheroe, 1918

Our Service Flag Is No Red Rag (or, Will Bill Get His, Bill Will). L&M: "Dr. Smiles" [Nathan L. Teeple], 1919

Our Service Flag Star's Turned to Gold. L&M: J.E. Thomas, 1919

Our Slogan, U.S.A. (March). L&M: J. Lewis Browne, 1917

Our Soldier Boys (March). L&M: Charles E. Roat, 1918

Our Soldier Boys. L&M: John A. Goode, 1918

Our Soldier Boys. L: Mary McDonald; M: Joseph J. Fecher, 1918

Our Soldier Boys. L&M: Delmar Owens, 1919

Our Soldier Boys. L: Mrs. L.R. Churchill; M: Artie Bowers, 1919

Our Soldier Boys. L: D.E. Russ; M: Roy Hartzell, 1919

Our Soldier Boys (March). M: Bert R. Anthony, 1919

Our Soldier Boys in Blue. L&M: Jessie Perdue, 1919

Our Soldier Boys So True. L: M.P. Kellar; M: Se Deviner, 1918

Our Soldier (the Hope of the World). L&M: Gertrude Zimmer-Boyd, 1918

Our Soldiers (March). M: Kaetchen L. Hensel, 1916

Our Soldiers. L&M: W.C. Ames, 1918

Our Soldiers Depart. L&M: Fred Telfer, 1919

Our Soldier's Dream. M: Werde W. Oliver, 1918

Our Soldiers' Fighting Song. L&M: J.H. Richardson, 1918

Our Soldiers of '17 (March). L: Thomas D. Casale; M: Harry J. Lincoln, 1917

Our Soldiers, Welcome Home (March). L: Shapcott Wensley; M: Joseph L. Roeckel, 1918

Our Song of Liberty. L: A.T. Schulz; M: Harry L. Alford, 1917

Our Souls Are Thine, America. L: Frederic Manley; M: Francis Arnes, 1918

Our Star-Spangled Banner Now Is Floating in France. L: J. Craig; M: Luther A. Clark, 1917

Our Stars and Stripes Forever. L&M: Amil Holinger, 1918

Our Stars and Stripes of U.S.A. L: G.A.W. Boedecker; M: Genevieve Scott, 1914

Our States So Free (A Patriotic Hymn). L&M: Cordelia C. Muir, 1917

Our Statue of Liberty. L: F.J. Johnson; M: Carl Heil, 1915

Our Stripes and Stars (Camp Meade March). L: Llewella Pierce Churchill; M: E.R.R. Ort, 1918

Our Training Camps (or, Down with the Kaiser). L: T.J. Pettijohn; M: "Battle Hymn of the Republic," 1918

Our True Uncle Sam. L: Ethel Walker; M: Leo Friedman, 1918

Our Uncle Sam. L&M: Frederic W. Root, 1916

Our Uncle Sam. L&M: J.S. Ramey, 1917

Our Uncle Sam. L&M: Blanche Perkins Derry, 1918

Our Uncle Sam (March). M: June Bauer, 1918

Our Uncle Sammy. L&M: Erma M. Patterson, 1919

Our Uncle Sam's on His Way. L&M: Arch S. Hill, 1918

Our United States (A Patriotic Hymn). L&M: Blanche I. Bremner, 1917

Our U.S. Boys. L&M: Beulah Ward McCloud, 1917

Our U.S. Soldier Boy. L: Harry Sherwood; M: Leo Friedman, 1918

*Our U.S.A. Boys (Will Force All Nations to Respect Humanity). L&M: Richard F. Staley, 1917

Our Victors (March). M: Kate Vannah, 1918

Our Victory. L&M: Mrs. Otto Kuehn, 1919

Our Victory. L&M: D.A. Schermerhorn, 1919

Our Victory. L&M: Philo Davis, 1919

Our War Menu. L&M: L.E. Hansen, 1918

Our Washington (All Hail to Our Flag of the Free, United States, and God Bless Our Land Always—Always). L&M: W.K. Forbes, 1917

Our Wilson Is the Greatest Man This World Has Ever Seen. L: Adelbert Reynolds; M: Carl Demangate, 1919

Our Yankee Boy. L: D.H. Sutton; M: Roy Hartzell, 1919

Our Yankee Boys. L: K. Stine; M: Marie Everett, 1918

Our Yankee Boys. L: Mrs. G.H. McGowan; M: Leo Friedman, 1919

Our Yankee Boys Are Coming Home from Somewhere. L&M: Belle C. Stewart, 1918

Our Yankee Boys Are Winning Over There. L: M.A. Schenberger; M: Leo Friedman, 1919

Our Yankee Boys' Victory (March). M: Mrs. J.A. Flanders, 1917

Our Yankee Doodle Boys Are Back. L&M: Orville C. Seeley, 1918

Our Yankee Doodle Dandy (March). L: Irving R. Bacon; M: Carl Hauser, 1917

Our Yanks Are Sailing Home. L&M: Marie Annette, 1919

Out of No Man's Land Comes Heroes Day. L: G.H. McFarland; M: Frank W. Ford, 1919

*Out on the Bounding Billows. L: Walter S. Atus; M: Hector Richard, 1919

Out on the Sea (It's the Navy). L&M: John R. Rathom, 1918

Out There. L&M: Herman Hupfeld, 1917

Out to Old Germany. L&M: Nannie Craft, 1919

Over Field and Meadow. M: J. Lawrence Erb, 1915

Over Here. L&M: C. B. Weston, 1917

Over Here. L: Jack A. Gunn; M: Rogelio Rigau, 1918

Over Here. L&M: "Sisk and James," 1918

Over Here. L: Tanny Galloway; M: T.G. and James F. Topping, 1918

Over Here. L: F. Sanft; M: A. Kuehl, 1918

Over Here. L: C.W. Hoffman; M: Willard Hoffman, 1919

Over Here. L: C.J. German; M: Leo Friedman, 1919

Over Here. L: Mrs. A.B. Logsdon; M: Artie Bowers, 1919

Over Here from Over There. L&M: Abbie F. Gaskill, 1919

Over Here We Are Dreaming, Boys, of You. L: John W. Dick and William D. Howell; M: Jown W. Dick, 1918

Over Here When We Get Back from Over There. L&M: Mrs. George Barton, 1917

Over in France. L&M: Belle Weaver, 1919

Over in Hero-Land. L: Arthur Freed; M: Louis Silvers, 1918

Over the Hindenburg Line. L: L.M. Meredith; M: Leo Friedman, 1919

Over the Ocean to France. L: Mrs. O.C. Matheny; M: Leo Friedman, 1918

Over the Rhine. L: Jack Yellen; M: Albert Gumble, 1918

Over the River Rhine, on to Berlin. L&M: V.L. Lackey, 1917

Over the Sea to Black Jack. L: E.C. Smith; M: J.W. Buford, 1918

Over the Sea to Germanee. L: John F. Erb; M: Clarence Gridley, 1917

Over the Seas, Boys. L&M: Irving Berlin, 1917

Over the Seas for Liberty. L: Henry D. Axelby; M: William A. Stanley, 1917

Over the Seas to France (March). L&M: Gertrude E. Stevens, 1918

Over the Top. L: Harold Atteridge; M: Sigmund Romberg, from stage production *Over the Top*, 1916

*"Over the Top." L: Marion Phelps; M: Maxwell Goldman, 1917

Over the Top. L: Al Bryan; M: Pete Wendling and Jack Wells, 1917

*Over the Top. L: Herbert W. Rainie; M: George H. Perkins, 1917

Over the Top (March). M: Geoffrey O'Hara, 1917

Over the Top (March). M: Julius Fucik, 1918

Over the Top. L: Alice Birdsall; M: Leo Friedman, 1918

Over the Top. L&M: Bert E. Wendler, 1918

Over the Top. L: H.G. Bach; M: Leo Friedman, 1918

Over the Top. L: R. Jacoby; M: Leo Friedman, 1918

Over the Top. L: G.G. Currie; M: Robert H. Brennen, 1918

Over the Top. L: William M. Runyan; M: H.D. Loes, 1918

Over the Top. L&M: Will Edgar, 1918

Over the Top. L&M: W.R. Hartpence, 1918

Over the Top. L: B. Benson; M: Naome Stage, 1918

Over the Top. L: Wilbur J. Powell; M: William W. Bentley, 1918

Over the Top. L&M: G. McCollor, 1918

Over the Top. L: R. Hopper; M: Leo Friedman, 1919

Over the Top. L: E. Miller; M: Leo Friedman, 1919

Over the Top and Across the Rhine. L&M: D.W. Honn, 1918

Over the Top and at 'Em! L&M: J.A. Roscoe, 1918

Over the Top and at 'Em, Boys! L: M. Lawrence; M: Leo Friedman, 1918

Over the Top Boys! (March). M: S.M. Berg, 1918

Over the Top for Me. L: Herman J. Bryce; M: W.G. Jones, 1918

Over the Top for U.S.A. L: C.W. and R.B. Tharp; M: R.B. Tharp, 1918

Over the Top Goes Sammy. L&M: T.E. Rhodes, 1917

Over the Top, the Top We Go! L&M: J.G. Dewey, 1918

Over the Top to Somewhere on the Rhine. L&M: H. Higgins, 1918

Over the Top to Victory (March). M: Francis A. Myers, 1918

Over the Top We Go. L: J. Stokes; M: Leo Friedman, 1918

Over the Top We Go. L&M: F.A. Smith, 1918

Over the Top We Go. L&M: J.E. Wilson, 1918

Over the Top We'll Go. L: M.M. and F.P. Marks; M: J.C. Marks, 1918

Over the Top with Jesus. L: J.A. Hansen; M: Mary A. Havilland, 1918

Over the Top with Jesus. L&M: G.L. Johnson, 1918

Over the Top with Old Glory. L&M: Claire Cox Keith, 1918

Over the Top, with the Best of Luck and Give Them Hell! L: Jack Wensley; M: Will Carroll, 1918

Over the Top with Your Uncle Sam. L&M: E.J. Stolz, 1918

Over the Top, Ye Sammy Lads. L: Eva C. Reddish; M: M.L. Oglesbee, 1918

*Over There. L&M: George M. Cohan, 1917

Over There Old Glory's Waving. L: N. Blanche Phillips; M: Leo Friedman, 1919

Over Yonder Where the Lillies Grow. L&M: Geoffrey O'Hara, 1918

Overseas (March). M: Herbert W. Lowe, 1918

P

The Pacifist (A Patriotic Song). L&M: John B. McPhail, 1918

*Pack Up Your Troubles in Your Old Kit Bag and Smile, Smile, Smile. L: George Asaf; M: Felix Powell, from London stage production Her Soldier Boy, 1915

Palace of Peace (March). M: C.M. Vandersloot, 1915

The Parting Kiss from Your Sweetheart (Puts the Good in Goodbye). L: Howard Johnson and Artie Mehlinger; M: George W. Meyer, 1918

The Parting Sailor Boy's Vow. L: C.C. Ehrgott; M: A.F. Kahl, 1918

Passing in Review (March). M: N.M. Aldrich, 1919

Passing of the Grand Army. L&M: Charles H. Miller, 1916

Patria. L: George Graff, Jr.; M: Mrs. Vernon [Irene] Castle, from silent film serial Patria, 1917

The Patriot. L: J.E. Webb; M: Leo Friedman, 1918

The Patriot. L&M: G. Acres, 1918

Patriot Girl (March). L&M: F.J. O'Neill, 1918

Patriotic America. M: George Spencer, 1916

The Patriotic Duties of the Girl He Left Behind. L&M: H.C. Eldridge, 1918

Patriotic France. M: George Spencer, 1916

Patriotic Trot (the Jazz Craze of the U.S.A.). L: O.A. Ortell; M: Edward B. Ellison, 1918

Patriotic U.S.A. L&M: Homer Patton, 1919

Patriotism. L: W.H. Day; M: Geoffrey O'Hara, 1917

Patriotism (Why Are We Here Tonight, Boys?). L&M: J.J. Ridgway, 1918

Patriot's Call. L&M: Alice Tabitha Davis, 1917

Patriot's Song. L: R. Martin; M: Robert Stevens, 1917

*Paul Revere (Won't You Ride for Us Again?). L: Joe Goodwin; M: Halsey K. Mohr, 1918

Peace. L: Corinne B. Dodge; M: Gertrude Ross, 1915

Peace. L: George E. Woodberry; M: Louis Adolphe Coerne, 1915

Peace (Hymn of Propaganda for Worldwide, Everlasting Peace). L&M: A.V. Angelis, 1915

Peace. L: Mrs. W.M. Baugh; M: George C. Polini, 1915

Peace. L&M: Arthur F. Fuller, 1916

Peace. L&M: G.G. Gillespie, 1917

Peace. L&M: J.J. McDonald, 1918

Peace. L&M: Maude M. Price, 1919

Peace. L: B.L. Knight; M: Leo Friedman, 1919

Peace and Good Will. M: Ira B. Wilson, 1916

Peace and Honor (March). M: G.B. Snyder, 1916

Peace and Liberty (March). M: Charles L. Gordon, 1916

Peace and Liberty. L&M: D.G. Baltimore, 1917

Peace Be on Earth. L: K.H. Schmidt; M: Arthur Ryan, 1917

Peace Be Still. L&M: Arthur Bristow, 1918

Peace Chimes. L: L.E. Jobe; M: Artie Bowers, 1919

Peace Cry of the U.S.A. (or, Let Us All Be Soldiers of Honor). L: W.A. Larson; M: Robert Van Sickle, 1916

Peace Flag (March). M: Isaac G. Withers, 1915

Peace for Christ's Sake. L&M: W.R. Prime, 1918

Peace Forever (March). M: O. Nielsen, 1916

Peace Forever (March). M: W.L. Floyd, 1916

Peace Forever. L&M: B.J. Hoffacker, 1919

Peace Forever. L: Oliver Smith; M: Leo Friedman, 1919

Peace Forever (March). M: James Long, 1919

Peace Has Come. L&M: F.R. Howard, 1919

Peace Hymn. L&M: G.D. Rogers, 1915

Peace Hymn of the Republic. L: Henry Van Dyke; M: Lawrence Camilieri, 1916

Peace Immortal. L&M: C.B. Derr, 1919

Peace of All Nations (March). M: Giovanni DeCaro, 1915

Peace, Oh Star of Hope. L&M: Mrs. R.E. Slesnick, 1917

Peace on Earth. L&M: H. Bauer, 1915

Peace on Earth. M: Edward O. Schaaf, 1918

Peace on Earth and Good-Will Towards Men. L: Arthur Fields; M: Jack Glogau, 1916

Peace on Earth, Good Will to Men. L: Lulu Garretson Reynolds; M: Richard R. Trench, 1916

Peace Over Land and Sea. L: J.J. Lieberum; M: Frank W. Ford, 1919

Peace Patrol. M: Charles Spencer Chaplin, 1916

Peace, Peace. L. Mrs. L.M. Jeffrey, 1919

Peace, Peace, Be Still. L&M: "Madame Alvano," 1916

Peace, Peace, Reechoed Cheer. L: Julius Schmidt; M: F.L. Cabello, 1915

Peace, Perfect Peace. L: Edward H. Bickersteth; M: Irenee Berge, 1915

Peace, Perfect Peace. L: Henry Cressilen; M: William W. Meadows, 1915

Peace Reigns on Earth. L: Carolyn Lamberton and D. Kohn; M: Bert Keene and L. Ernest Walker, 1919

Peace Song. L: Thomas Ince; M: Victor Schertzinger, from silent film *Civilization*, 1916

Peace, Sweet Peace (A Meditation). M: Mary E. Cox and Archie E. Lloyd, 1916

Peace, Sweet Peace, That's Liberty. L&M: C.W. Argersinger, 1919

Peace Terms (March). M: J.N. DuPerè, 1919

Peace Through Victory. L&M: J.S. Park, 1917

Peace Through Victory (March). M: H.J. Crosby, 1919

Peace to Mankind (March). L&M: Amelia B. Clough-Ramar, 1915

Peace Triumphal. L: Samuel Platt; M: Grace Clough-Leighter, 1916

Peace Triumphal. L: Samuel Platt; M: Alexander MacFayden, 1918

Peace Universal. L&M: Will R. Wilson, 1917

Peace Walk. M: Harry Tierney, 1915

Peaceful Tomorrow. L: W.F. Hood; M: Eugene Lundgren, 1918

Pearl of Liberty. L&M: Ora Rossean, 1918

The Pep of the Yankee Boy. L&M: G.S. Morris, 1918

Perfect Peace. L&M: June Bauer, 1918

Perfect Peace. L: Fanny J. Crosby; M: Charles H. Gabriel, 1918

P-E-R-S-H-I-N-G. L&M: Eugene West, 1919

Pershing for President. L: Mark J. Samuels; M: Jean Havez, 1919

Pershing Invited Me. L&M: M.E. Whitney, 1918

Pershing, It's Up to You. L: W.J. Dougherty; M: A.F. Mengel, 1918

Pershing Patrol. M: Herbert Phillips, 1918

Pershing's Army Song. L: George G. Sherwood; M: William Brunsvold, 1918

Pershing's Boys. L&M: F.P. Wallis, 1918

Pershing's Brave Boys. L&M: Paul C. Biersach, 1918

Pershing's Guards Return. L&M: Anna M. Hoskin, 1919

Pershing's March. M: Mrs. A.S. Watt, 1918

Pershing's March. M: E.G. Kummer, 1918

Pershing's Men (March). M: G.K. Fredericks, 1918

Pershing's Requittal. L: J.P. Walker; M: Leo Friedman, 1919

Picardy (A Martial Hymn). L: J.A. Shoemaker; M: Dacia Custer-Shoemaker, 1918

*Pick a Little Four-Leaf Clover (and Send It Over to Me). L: C. Francis Reisner and Ed Rose; M: Abe Olman, 1918

Place a Candle in the Window (Till Your Laddie Boy Comes Home). L: Fern Glenn; M: Maxwell Goldman, 1918

Played by a Military Band. L: Ballard MacDonald; M: Halsey K. Mohr, from stage production *Ned Wayburn's Big Revue*, 1915

Playing Baseball on the Western Front. L&M: A.A. Westman, 1918

Please Bring Back My Daddy to Me. L: F.E. Hathaway; M: Leo Friedman, 1918

Please Don't Call Me Hun. L: W.R. Wright; M: G.A. Mortimer, 1918

Please, Mr. President, We Don't Want War. L&M: Alfred E. Williams, 1916

Please Touch My Daddy's Star Again and Change It Back to Blue. L: Marion Phelps; M: Clarence Brandon, 1918

Pledge for Freedom. L&M: E.M. Markham, 1918

Pledge of Allegiance to My Flag. L: Anonymous; M: M.K. Fowler, 1917

*Poor Butterfly. L: John L. Golden; M: Raymond Hubbell, from stage production *The Big Show*, 1916

Poor Old Kaiser. L&M: Eli Mounts, 1918

Poor Old Kaiser Bill (or, For the Red, White and Blue) (March). M: Waldo Reed, 1917

Pour la Gloire de Notre Drapeau. L&M: Gordon V. Thompson; French version by Armand LeClaire, 1918

Praise the Lord for Victory. L: Roger M. Hickman; M: H.A. Hammontree, 1915

Praise the Lord, O Jerusalem, for He Maketh the Wars to Cease. M: R. Spaulding Stoughton, 1919

Praise to the Soldier. L: Anonymous; M: F.A. Boieldieu, 1918

A Prayer. L&M: George Thornton Edwards, 1914

Prayer for Our Boys. L&M: A.F. Mason, 1918

Prayer for Our Boys. L: Frank C. Huston; M: L.I. Shrader, 1918

Prayer for Peace. L: P. Linkhart; M: Leo Friedman, 1918

Prayer of a Soldier in France. L: Joyce Kilmer; M: Camille W. Zeckwer, 1919

Prayer of the Boys Out There. L: Mayme Wakeford; M: Leo Friedman, 1919

The Prayer to Whip the Kaiser Is Our Dollar Bills. L&M: J.H. Phillips, 1919

Prepare the Eagle to Protect the Dove, That's the Battle Cry of Peace. L: Henry T. Bunce; M: William Donaldson, 1916

Preparedness. L&M: Fred J. Eddy, 1916

Preparedness. L&M: Jerome Don Conor, 1916

Preparedness. L&M: B.J. Moore, 1916

Preparedness. L: F.W. Flude; M: Lewis A. Michalowsky, 1916

Preparedness (March). M: G.F. Hammond, 1916

Preparedness (March). M: Theron Perkins, 1916

Preparedness (March). M: V. Spadea, 1916

Preparedness. L&M: C.E. Edwards, 1916

Preparedness (March). M: C.H. Jones, 1916

Preparedness (March). M: Guido Deira, 1917

Preparedness (March). M: Luther McGee, 1917

Preparedness March. M: Leo Bennett, 1917

Preparedness (Pacifist vs. Patriot). L: A.G. Murray; M: F.H. Murray, 1916

Preparedness (Your Country Needs Your Efforts in Time of Peace or War). M: Lillian Bush, 1916

President Wilson, Be Proud of Your Boys. L: B. Kermode; M: Leo Friedman, 1918

President Wilson March. M: Pasquale Fressola, 1917

*President Wilson U.S.A. L: J. Ellison; M: J. Ellison and Lee J. Kratz, 1918

President Wilson's Wedding March. M: George Fairman, 1915

Pride of a Nation. L: E.M. White; M: Artie Bowers, 1919

Pride of Our Country. L: G.H. McFarland; M: Frank W. Ford, 1919

Pride of Our Great Country (Red, White and Blue). L&M: A.A. Nelles, 1917

Pride of Our Nation. L: L.E. Jobe; M: Leo Friedman, 1919

Pride of the White House (March). M: Karl Lenox, 1916

Private Alexander. L&M: Lloyd Garrett, 1917

*Private Arkansaw Bill (Yip-I-Yip and a Too-Ra-Le-Ay!). L&M: Lloyd Garrett, 1917

Private Brown. L&M: Lud Worsham, 1918

Private Flynn. L&M: Lloyd Garrett, 1918

Private Jerry Jones. L&M: J.H. Briscoe, 1918

Private Mike M'Gee. L: Will D. Cobb; M: Gus Edwards, 1918

Private Percy Prim. L&M: Lloyd Garrett, 1917

Proctor's Military March. M: Walter Proctor, 1917

Protect Our Flag. L&M: Elsa M. Jacobs, 1917

Protect the U.S.A. L: T. Donnelly; M: Arthur A. Penn, 1917

Proud Flag of America. L: E.G. Blair; M: Frank A. Schoedler and Herbert D. Murphy, 1918

Pull Off Your Coat, Uncle Sam (A Motto for Every Man). L&M: Agnes W.L. Tracy, 1917

Pure Democracy. L: J. Marion Taylor; M: Rose J. O'Brien, 1918

Pushing On! L: Guy F. Lee; M: John Philip Sousa, 1918

Put a Light in the Window for the Boy That's Coming Home (March). L: Wellington Cross; M: Clarence Senna, 1919

Put a Star in the Service Flag for Me. L&M: P.S. Miller, 1918

Put It Across (to Send Across for Uncle Sam). L: H.A. Stedman; M: E.W. Stedman, 1918

Put on a Bonnet with a Red Cross on It. L: Howard Johnson and Harry Pease; M: Harry Jentes, 1917

Put on Your Khaki Suit, for Uncle Sammy Needs You. L: Mrs. H.L. Higgins; M: Leo Friedman, 1918

Put on Your Uniform of Blue for Your Country's Calling You. L: Mary Burns Bahr; M: Charles William Bahr, 1917

Put the Kaiser Down. L: J.S.C. Nicholls; M: F.L. McFarland, 1917

Put the Kaiser Wilhelm on the Run. L: Mrs. F.F. Kaiser; M: Leo Friedman, 1918

Put the Lid on Kaiser Bill. L&M: Marc Hanna, 1918

Put Your Hands in Your Pockets and Give, Give, Give. L: Gus Kahn; M: Egbert Van Alstyne, 1918

Putting "Am" in Uncle Sam to Stay (National Preparedness March). L&M: J.N. Stewart, Jr., 1917

R

Ragtime Drafted Man. L&M: Arthur E. Williams, 1918

Ragtime European War. L: Lizzie G. Rogers; M: Paul Shannon, 1915

Ragtime Fight. L: Rida Johnson Young; M: Sigmund Romberg, from stage production *Her Soldier Boy*, 1916

Ragtime Razor Brigade. L&M: Irving Berlin, from stage production *Yip, Yip, Yaphank*, 1918

Ragtime Soldier Man. L&M: Irving Berlin, 1917

*The Ragtime Volunteers Are Off to War. L: Ballard MacDonald; M: James F. Hanley, 1917

Rah! Rah! for the Old United States. L&M: J.J. Mahoney, 1917

The Rainbow Boys Had Something Up Their Sleeves. L&M: I.B. Geiger, 1919

The Rainbow Division. L&M: A.C. Russell, 1918

Rainbow Division March. M: V.D. Nirella, 1918

Rainbow from the U.S.A. L&M: Jack Mahoney, William Jerome, and Percy Wenrich, 1918

Raise the Flag (March). M: Mackie-Beyer, 1915

Raise the Stars and Stripes (Anthem). L: Marion Mills Miller; M: A.L. Baldwin, 1918

Rally Around Old Glory. L: Arthur Oberling; M: Leo Friedman, 1918

Rally Around Old Glory, Boys. L: W. Corbett; M: Edward Bergenholtz, 1917

Rally Around the Standard. L: H. Russell; M: Leo Friedman, 1918

Rally to the Colors. L&M: Mrs. J.A. Anderson, 1917

Rally to the Stars and Stripes, Boys. L&M: W.B. Glisson, 1917

The Ranks of Peace. L: "Yants"; M: Harry Stirling, 1915

Raus Mit der Kaiser (He's in Dutch). L: Andrew B. Sterling and Bartley Costello; M: Arthur Lange, 1917

Recrootin. L: Richard Fechheimer; M: W.B. Kernell, from stage production *Goodbye, Bill*, 1918

Red and White and Blue. L: Dona Rickard; M: Leo Friedman, 1919

The Red Cross (March). M: George O. Frey, 1917

The Red Cross. L: Betty Meyers; M: Meyer Frank Meyers, 1918

The Red Cross (March). M: C. Maffei, 1918

Red Cross Day. L&M: Arthur Bristow, 1918

The Red Cross Forever (March). M: George E. York, 1918

Red Cross Girl. L&M: E.O.B. Gilbert, 1917

Red Cross Girl. L: E.R. Greenlaw; M: Gilfillan Scott, 1918

Red Cross Girl. L&M: Harley E. Cash, 1918

The Red Cross Girl Is the Girl I Love. L&M: Leon Berg, 1918

The Red Cross Maids for Me. L: Jennie A. Perry; M: A.A. Wrightman, 1918

Red Cross March. M: D.H. Getchell, 1918

Red Cross March. M: Stuart James, 1918

Red Cross March. M: Mr. and Mrs. Hiram B. Browning, 1918

The Red Cross Message. L&M: Ella T. Crawford, 1917

Red Cross Nurse. L&M: H.G. Walsh, 1917

Red Cross Nurses. L: J.A. Meyer; M: Leo Friedman, 1918

Red Cross Rally Song. L: James Rowe; M: J.B. Herbert, 1918

Red Cross Song. L&M: Frank P. Cassidy, 1918

The Red Cross Spirit Speaks. L: John Finley; M: Horatio Parker, 1918

The Red Cross Story. L&M: I.A. Miller, 1918

Red-Haired Soldier Boy. L: F.J. Clemon; M: Fred G. Fuller, 1917

The Red, Red Cross. L&M: Albert Hayden Thacher, 1918

Red, White and Blue (March). L: George Arthur; M: Louis A. Hirsch, 1914

Red, White and Blue. L: I.W. Irving; M: L.W. Harriman, 1915

Red, White and Blue. L: Stephen Fay; M: Arthur Bergh, 1918

Red, White and Blue. L: L. Tolley; M: Leo Friedman, 1918

Red, White and Blue. L: W.E. Gilbert; M: Roy Hartzell, 1919

Red, White and Blue. L&M: B.T. Brown, 1919

Red, White and Blue. L: Eva Williams; M: Leo Friedman, 1919

Red, White and Blue, I Love You. L: B.O. Carpenter; M: Leo Friedman, 1919

Red, White and Blue, I'll Live and Die for You. L&M: F.E. Mathewson, 1918

The Red, White and Blue Is Calling. L: A. MacDonald; M: Leo Friedman, 1918

The Red, White and Blue Is Calling You. L&M: Billy Johnson, 1916

The Redemption of Alsace-Lorraine (March). M: Joseph Kiefer, 1918

The Regiment of the Sambre and the Meuse. L&M: Robert Planquette, 1917

Regretful Blues. L: Grant Clarke; M: Cliff Hess, from stage production *Cohan Revue of 1918*, 1918

The Regular Army Man. M: Jack Graham, 1918

Regular Soldiers Across. L: John Klebanski; M: Artie Bowers, 1919

Remember, Boys, Your Duty When You're on the Firing Line. L&M: Charles Bridge, 1917

Remember God and Fight. L: Henry J. Zelley; M: W. Philip [Philip Wuest], 1918

Remember the Lusitania. L&M: V. Johnsen, 1915

Remember the Lusitania. L&M: Jess Sechrist, 1917

Remember the Lusitania. L: Mrs. W.C. Cochran; M: Artie Bowers, 1919

Remember the Maine. L&M: George Thornton Edwards, 1914

Remember Your Girlie at Home. L: C. Irwin; M: Roy Hartzell, 1918

Republic Song—the Khaki Boys. L: S.B. Hacker; M: Leo Friedman, 1918

Response to Liberty's Call (March). L&M: W.D. Crews, 1917

Rest Ye in Peace, Ye Flanders Dead. L: R.W. Lillard; M: George B. Nevin, 1919

The Return Home of the Boys (Welcome Home). L: G.W. Tawzer; M: M.M. Tausig, 1918

Return of the Sammies. L&M: Ella Harris, 1919

Return of the U.S. Boys (March). M: G.W. McAdams, 1918

Return of the Victorious Legions (March). M: Francis A. Myers, 1919

Return of the Yanks (March). M: C.C. Haugh, 1919

The Returning Brave. L: T.R. Sturm; M: Leo Friedman, 1919

Reveille. L&M: William H. Figg, 1917

Reveille. L&M: Mana Zucca, 1918

Reveille. L: Laura Amsden Fowler; M: A. Griffith, 1918

Right and Justice Must Everywhere Prevail. L: D. Kohn; M: E.C. Penn, 1918

Right Hath Victory. L&M: E.J. Spence, 1918

Right on to France (March). L&M: George Byron Ulp, 1918

Right Over the Top. L: F.R. Thomas; M: Leo Friedman, 1918

Right Shall Triumph, Kaiser Bill. L: Irene Gates Moffet; M: Horton B. Green, 1918

Right Triumphant. L: A.R. Watson; M: T.C. Reynolds, 1917

The Right Will Win the War. L&M: George W. Bilbo, 1918

Righteous Victory. L&M: A. Esberger, 1918

Ring Out, Liberty Bell. L: Harold Atteridge; M: Sigmund Romberg, from stage production Passing Show of 1917, 1917

Ring Out, Liberty Bell! (March). L&M: Fred W. Hager, 1918

Ring Out! Sweet Bells of Peace L: William H. Gardner; M: Caro Roma, 1918

Ring Out the Glad Tidings, Oh Bells of Creation! L: W.L. Hemmingson; M: Clarence Kohlmann, 1918

Ring Out, Ye Bell of Liberty! L&M: Thomas Williams, 1918

The Road to Berlin's Getting Shorter. L: Eddie Cantor; M: Leon Flatow, 1918

The Road to France. L: Daniel M. Henderson; M: Signe Lund, 1917

The Road to France. L: Daniel M. Henderson; M: Ruth Nelson Butler, 1918

The Road to Paris. L: J.J. Cross; M: Leo Friedman, 1918

The Road to Victory. L&M: Francis C. Chantereau, 1918

Rocked in the Cradle of Liberty. L&M: Richard Howard, 1916

Rollin' de Bones at Coblenz on de Rhine. L: Bide Dudley; M: John Lou Nelson, 1919

Rookies (March). M: George Drumm, 1917

The Rookie's Lament. L&M: Lloyd Garrett, 1918

*Root for Uncle Sam. L: Jean C. Havez; M: Louis Silvers, 1917

Ropin' the Kaiser. L: M. Briscoe; M: Al Kloess, 1918

*Rose of No Man's Land. L: Jack Caddigan; M: James A. Brennan; French lyric by Louis Delamarre, 1918

Rose of Verdun. L: Raymond B. Egan; M: Richard A. Whiting, from stage production Toot Sweet, 1919

*Roses of Lorraine. L: Sidney Carter; M: Walter Smith, 1918

*Roses of Picardy. L: Fred E. Weatherly; M: Haydn Wood, 1916

*'Round Her Neck She Wears a Yeller Ribbon (for Her Lover Who Is Fur, Fur Away). L: George A. Norton; M (adapted): George A. Norton, 1917

Rouse Ye, America! L&M: E.W. Newton, 1917

Row on, Woodrow, Row on, L: M.V.B. Blood; M: George Barton, 1918

The Rube Soldier. L: G.M. Sattes; M: Leo Friedman, 1918

Run the Hun. L&M: D. Wescott, 1918

(The Russians Were Rushin') The Yanks Started Yankin'! L: Carey Morgan; M: Charles R. McCarron, 1918

S

S Stands for Sammy. L: J. MacNaughton; M: Jean MacNaughton, 1918

Sail on, Victorious, Unseen, Sail! L: J.H. Edwards; M: L.H. Hurlburt-Edwards, 1918

Sailing Around, L: Charles A. Bayha; M: Nat Vincent, 1917

Sailing for France. L: John Temple Groves, Jr.; M: John Lingard Tindale, 1918

Sailing Home. L: E.L. Dow; M: Frank W. Ford, 1919

Sailing to the Good Old U.S.A. L&M: Edward S. Payne, 1919

Sailor Boy. L: "Hersh & Gillette"; M: Cy Ullian, 1917

Sailor Boy. L&M: H.E. Cross, 1918

Sailor Boy, You Are My Hero. L&M: Lessing Alch, 1917

Sailor Boy's Dream (A Reverie). M: Louis Weber, 1917

The Sailor Lad Is the Lad for Me. L: R.R. Davidson; M: E.A. Lord, 1918

Sailor Song. L&M: Irving Berlin, from stage production Stop! Look! and Listen!, 1915

A Sailor's Dream. L: C.F. Holcomb; M: Frank W. Ford, 1918

Sailors of the U.S.A. L&M: M.A. Edwards, 1918

Sailor's Story (A Nautical Yarn). L&M: George L. Spaulding, 1915

Salute the Colors (March). M: A.E. Warren, 1918

Salute the Flag (March). M: Gustave Schumann, 1915

Salute the Flag (March). M: John A. Allen, 1917

Salute the Flag (New National Song). L: James MacRae; M: William Hewitt, 1917

Salute the Flag. L: Henry B. Tierney; M: W. Paul, 1918

Salute the Flag. L: Frances Savin Graef; M: Elizabeth Graef, 1918

Salute the Stars in That Old Flag (for They Symbolize True Blue). L: Fred R. Alexander; M: Lucy-Berry Kirkendall, 1916

Salute to America. L&M: Harry J. Lincoln, 1915

Salute to Old Glory. L: Mrs. D. Ray Campbell; M: A. Bohlender, 1917

Salute to the Flag. L&M: G.A. Sahlin, 1915

Salute to the Flag. L: Unknown; M: William J. Kraft, 1917

Salute to the Flag. L: Father Tierney; M: William Stein, 1917

Salute to the Flag. L&M: Frank Horace Wheeler, 1917

Salute to the Flag. L&M: Laura Sedgwick Collins, 1917

Salvation Lassie of Mine. L&M: Jack Caddington and Chick Story, 1919

Salvation Nell, We'll Not Forget What You Did for Us Over There. L: Hal L. Kiter; M: Winfield Peter DeLong, 1919

Salvation Rose. L: Robert Levenson; M: Jack Mendelsohn, 1919

Salvation Sal. L: Raymond B. Egan; M: Richard A. Whiting, from stage production *Toot Sweet*, 1919

Sam, Sam, Sammy of the U.S.A. L: B.M. Graybill; M: Dan Blanco, 1918

Sambo Sammies. L: William J. Hartley; M: John T. Hall, 1918

The Same Sun Shines on Flanders That Is Shining Over You. L: Jack O'Connor; M: Leo Friedman, 1919

Sammee. L&M: Willing Hitt, 1917

Sammee Boys (March). L&M: Willard Spencer, 1917

Sammie (A Yankee Trench Song). L&M: George Clinton Baker, 1918

Sammie [y] Boy (March). L&M: Paul A. Cunningham, 1917

Sammie on the Sea. L&M: Jessie Beattie Thomas, 1917

Sammie, Think of Your Mammy and You're Bound to Bring the Bacon Home. L&M: Dannie O'Neill, 1918

Sammies. L&M: Mrs. J.R. Dodd, 1919

Sammies. L&M: Ella Harris, 1919

Sammies. L: J.W. Trevethan; M: Leo Friedman, 1919

The Sammies' Aim. L&M: S.H. Judge, 1918

The Sammies Are Coming. L&M: Albert Allen Ketchum, 1917

The Sammies Are Coming. L: Walter S. Hunt; M: E.A. Powell, 1917

The Sammies Are Coming. L&M: S.C. Dunn, 1918

The Sammies Are Marching to Plant Our Flag in Old Berlin. L: Mrs. C.F. Walker; M: Leo Friedman, 1918

The Sammies Are Off to War. L: H. Lionel Brown; M: Eddie Elliott and W. Max Davis, 1917

The Sammies Aroused. L: J.D. English; M: Clifford Tasa Love, 1918

The Sammies' Ditty to the Kaiser. L: M.S. Robertson; M: "Burns," 1918

Sammies, Fighting Sammies. L&M: H.A. Drumm, 1918

Sammies from the U.S.A. L: G.D. Duncan; M: Roy Hartzell, 1919

Sammie's Lamentation of the Girl I Left Behind Me. L&M: W.F. Clay, 1918

Sammies Marching Song. L: L.M. Burchnall; M: Leo Friedman, 1918

Sammies of the U.S.A. L&M: C.P. Thompson, 1917

Sammies of the U.S.A. L&M: G.G. Dopp, 1918

Sammies on Parade (March). M: E. Earl Foster, 1918

Sammies' Own (March). M: E. Meinardus, 1917

Sammie's Saving Souvenirs for the Girl He Left Behind. L: Charles Parrott and James Adams; M: Chris Schomberg, 1918

The Sammies Will Go by Millions. L&M: Silvio Previtale, 1918

Sammy. L: C.A. Sweetland; M: Leo Friedman, 1917

Sammy. L: J. McCree; M: Edward Stembler, from stage production *Goodbye, Boys*, 1917

*Sammy (March). L: Richard Western; M: Arthur Olaf Andersen, 1918

Sammy Atkins. L&M: David Nyvall, 1918

Sammy Boy. L&M: Leora Kennedy, 1918

Sammy Boy. L&M: Bonia Dean, 1918

Sammy Boy, Your Father Deserves a Medal. L&M: James Kendis and James Brockman, 1918

Sammy Boys. L: H.F. Knorr; M: James Monk, 1918

Sammy, Get the Kaiser. L&M: G.F. Dring, 1918

Sammy, Give 'Em the Union Yell. L&M: Al E. Chamberlain, 1917

Sammy, Have a Smoke on Me. L&M: Margaret B. Wright, 1918

Sammy Lad. L&M: Gitz Rice, 1918

Sammy Lads. L: Caroline L. Dier; M: Marguerite Laurence, 1918

Sammy of the U.S.A. (Yankee Sammy). L: Milt Hagen; M: Dick Paris, 1918

Sammy's Going to Get You If You Don't. L: J.E. Ripper; M: J.E. Brown, 1918

Sammy's Goodbye. L: O.P. Hart; M: Leo Friedman, 1918

Sammy's Goodbye Message. L: S. and E. Kerr; M: Leo Friedman, 1918

Sammy's Got Wilhelm's Goat (A Patriotic Song). L&M: E.S. Raiford, 1918

Sammy's Message to Tommy. L: Evelyn Wylie; M: Leo Friedman, 1919

Sammy's Neutral Still. L&M: M. Dedos Vires, 1915

Sammy's Sentiment. L: O.B. Reed; M: Leo Friedman, 1918

Save All Your Kisses for Me Till I Come. L&M: L.E. Rudisill, 1918

Save All Your Lovin' Till I Come Back Home and Grin, Grin, Grin. L&M: Harold Dixon, 1918

Saving the World for Democracy. L: H.S. Whitney; M: C.S. Arnt, 1918

*Say a Prayer for the Boys "Out There." L: Bernie Grossman; M: Alex Marr, 1917

Say Au Revoir, but Not Goodbye. L&M: Harry Kennedy; arranged by E.T. Paull, 1918

Say I Died for My Country's Sake. L: Casper Nathan; M: F. Henri Klickmann, 1914

Say, You Haven't Sacrificed at All! (March). M: J. Fred Lawton and Will E. Dulmage, 1918

The Scrappin' Three-Tenth. L&M: Pvt. Harold J. Upright, 1918

See It Through! L&M: Sgt. George E. Battle and Max Weinstein, 1918

See Those Irish Volunteers March Away (Through Tears and Cheers). L: Sidney D. Mitchell; M: Willie White, 1917

Send a Lot of Jazz Bands Over There. L&M: Irving Berlin, from stage production *Yip, Yip, Yaphank*, 1918

*Send Back Dear Daddy to Me. L: Alex Sullivan and Harry Tenney; M: Irving Maslof, 1917

Send Back My Young American to Me. L: G.C. Rice; M: Leo Friedman, 1919

Send Him Back to Home Sweet Home. L: Mrs. M. Fujii; M: Leo Friedman, 1919

*Send Me a Curl. L&M: Geoffrey O'Hara, 1917

*Send Me a Line (When I'm Across the Ocean). L: Irving Crocker; M: George L. Cobb, 1917

Send Me Away with a Cheer, Dear. L: J.G. Fitzpatrick; M: Leo Friedman, 1918

Send Me Away with a Smile. L: Louis Weslyn; M: Al Piantadosi, 1917

Send Me My Girl from U.S.A. L&M: C.A. Pfeiffer, 1918

Send Me to the Kaiser. L: B.B. Mitchell; M: Leo Friedman, 1919

Send the Boys Something to Smoke. L: N.G. Monroe; M: Leo Friedman, 1918

Send Them Away With a Smile. L: A. Martin; M: Leo Friedman, 1918

Send Us Over There. L: Cavan Jones; M: Walter Wild, 1918

Sentinel of the Marne. L: M.C. Thornton; M: William Rehnor and Erma Lyons, 1919

Service Flag. L&M: Emma Hanson Bartmess, 1918

Service Flag. L&M: William Edwin Wims, 1918

Service Flag. L: William Herschell; M: Floyd J. St. Clair, 1918

Service Flag. L: Anonymous; M: Emma Hanson, 1918

Service Flag. L: Frances A. Huston; M: J.J. Riffle, 1918

Service Flag. L: J. Burns; M: B. Wall, 1918

Service Flag. L&M: E.H. Lokke, 1919

Service Flag. L&M: Pearl Linkhart, 1919

Service Flag. L: J.C. Rearick; M: Roy Hartzell, 1919

Service Flag Carol. L: Marjory L. Cooley; M: J. Truman Wolcott, 1918

Service Flag, Every Eye's on You. L: E.R. McCloskey; M: Mildred Meade, 1918

Service Flag March. M: Frank H. Losey, 1918

Service Flag (There's a Star Out for Him). L&M: Laura Frances Deem, 1918

Service Star (My Star of Liberty). L: Charles T. Edward; M: E.S.S. Huntington, 1918

Service Stars Are Shining. L: Cordelia Brooks Fenno; M: Frederick S. Converse, 1918

Set Aside Your Tears. L&M: L. Wolfe

Gilbert, Malvin Franklin, and Anatol Friedland, 1917

The 73rd Infantry. M: R.A. Quigley, 1918

She Gave One Star to Glory. L&M: J.F. Dougherty, 1918

She Is Going to Raise Her Boy to Be a Soldier. L&M: Charles F. Conrad, 1919

She Is Knitting, Knitting, Knitting, This Little Maiden Fair. L: J.L. Olp; M: Leo Friedman, 1918

She Is My U-Boat. L: C. St. Clair; M: H.F. Boyds, 1918

She Was a Soldier's Mother. L&M: Cassie Parker Robinson, 1919

She Was a Soldier's Sweetheart. L: Monroe H. Rosenfeld; M: Frank Church, 1918

She Wears a Cross Upon Her Sleeve (A Song of Tribute). L&M: H.C. Eldridge, 1917

She Wears a Red Cross on Her Sleeve. L: Mrs. J.H. Seifert; M: Leo Friedman, 1919

She Wears the Red Cross on Her Sleeve. L: M. Maxwell; M: Leo Friedman, 1918

She'll Be Waiting When You Come Back Home (March). L: Rega-Farran; M: Albert Chiaffarelli, 1917

*She'll Miss Me Most of All. L: Will J. Hart; M: Edward G. Nelson, 1918

Sherman Is Right. L&M: Victor G. and M. Vecki, 1918

Sherman Said War Is Hell. L&M: C.E. Sullivan, 1918

She's Going to Raise Her Boy to Be a Soldier. L: Charles F. Conrad; M: Dell Lampe, 1918

She's Just a Girl That's Serving Uncle Sam. L: Lon W. Babb; M: Nina Moon, 1917

She's Not in Tipperary. L&M: Frances Chapin, 1918

She's Teaching Me to Parlez Vous Francais (and I'm Learning More and More Each Day). L: Al Wilson; M: Ted Fiorito, 1918

She's Wond'ring If Her Boy's All Right. L: Marinda Lindley; M: Leo Friedman, 1918

Shield of Liberty. L: J.J. Enright; M: Leo Friedman, 1919

The Ship Named U.S.A. (or, Wilson's War Cry of Peace). L: J.F. Whitehorn and T.E. Ambrose; M: William Lorraine, 1915

Ship of Uncle Sam. L&M: Daisy M. Pratt Erd, 1917

A Short Farewell Is Best. L: Edward Clark; M: Silvio Hein, from stage production *Furs and Frills*, 1917

Should the Stars in Your Service Flag Turn to Gold. L: Dora F. Hendricks; M: Charles H. Gabriel, 1918

Shout Aloud in Triumph (Song of Victory). L&M: Charles Fonteyn Manney, 1919

Shout Hurrah for America, It's the Best Land of All! L&M: Harold Freeman, 1914

Shout Hurrah for Our Soldier Boy! L&M: John H. Bronson, 1918

Show Me That You Fought for the U.S.A. L: Moses E. Simpson; M: Frank C. Cullum, 1919

Show Me the Way to Ger-man-ee. L&M: R.E. Hall, 1917

Show the Kaiser. L: Chief Caupolican; M: Ernest Zeckiel, 1917

Show the World Just Where You Stand. L: Lizzie DeArmond; M: B.D. Ackley, 1915

Shrapnel (March). M: W.S. Pontin, 1917

Shrine of Liberty. L: J.A. Eaton; M: Barclay Walker, 1919

Since I Lost the Sunshine of Your Smile. L&M: W.R. Williams, 1918

Since It's Over, Over There. L: Mrs. E.F. Milligan; M: Al Farnham, 1919

Since Johnny Got His Gun. L: Lew Brown; M: Darl MacBoyle, 1917

Since Little Boy Blue Marched Away. L: Bernie Grossman; M: Ernie Erdman, 1918

Since the Boys Came Home from France. L: Charles A. Bayha; M: Harry Carroll, 1919

Since the Darkies Have Returned from France. L: Lester Beutel; M: George Graff, Jr., 1919

Since the Day You Said Goodbye. L&M: Lew Porter, 1919

Since the Yanks Sailed 'Cross the Sea. L: W.P. Armour; M: J.W. Rey, 1919

Since They Learned to Parley Vous Français. L: C.T. Wiese; M: James M. Abramowitz, 1919

Since They Took You Away from Me, Dear. L: Ralph Elton; M: Jack Brooks, 1917

Since This Cruel War Is Over. L: T.J. Thomas; M: Leo Friedman, 1919

Since You Marched Away. L&M: E.S. McNary, 1918

Sing for Freedom. L: M.K. Fuller; M: Leo Friedman, 1918

Sing! for the Dawn Has Broken (The Song of Victory Cantata). L: Edward M. Chapman; M: Louis Adolphe Coerne, 1919

Sing My Country 'Tis of Thee, and Let God's Will Be Done. L&M: Leo F.J. Murray, 1918

Singing As They Go (March). L&M: K.E. Elliott, 1918

*Sister Susie's Sewing Shirts for Soldiers. L:

R.P. Weston; M: Herman E. Darewski, 1914

Sky Fighting Boys. L: L.Y. Lenhart; M: Inez C. Hall, 1917

Slacker, Don't You Get My Girl. L&M: Glen D. Fleak, 1919

Slacker Man. L: J. McCree; M: Edward Stembler, from stage production *Goodbye, Boys* 1917

Sleep, Little Soldier. L: Dana Burnet; M: Ernest R. Ball, 1918

Sleep, My Son, in France. L: M.J. Doherty; M: Leo Friedman, 1919

Sleep on, Brave Boys, Sleep On. L: M.C. Robedeaux; M: R.A. Browne, 1915

Sleep, Soldier, Sleep. L&M: C.J. North, 1918

Sleep, Soldier, Sleep (Requiem). "Adapted from Schubert's Quartette in D Minor by Samuel Abbott," 1918

*Smile and Show Your Dimple. L&M: Irving Berlin, 1918

Smile as You Kiss Me Goodbye. L: Raymond B. Egan; M: Art Gillham, 1918

The Smile of the Red Cross Nurse. L: Edward Evatt; M: F.S. Chamberlain, 1919

Smile While I'm Leaving — Don't Cry When I'm Gone. L: Eugene West; M: Victor Hyde, 1918

*Smiles. L: J. Will Callahan; M: Lee S. Roberts, 1917

Smiling Sammy. M: Arthur M. Kraus, 1917

*So Dress Up Your Dollars in Khaki (and Help Win Democracy's Fight). L: Lister R. Alwood; M: Richard A. Whiting, 1918

So Long, France. L: M. Baratta; M: George Graff, Jr., 1919

So Long, Ki-Yi-Kaiser. L: C.J. Dobson; M: Leo Friedman, 1919

So Long, Mother. L: Alex Raffey; M: Will Corbin, 1917

So Long, Mother. L: Raymond B. Egan and Gus Kahn; M: Egbert Van Alstyne, 1917

So Long, Old Uncle Sammy. L: L.I. Skelton; M: Nona C. Arnold, 1918

*So Long, Sammy, L: Benny Davis and Jack Yellen; M: Albert Gumble, 1917

So Sammy's Off (The Good Luck Marching Song). L&M: Jean duRocher Macpherson, 1917

So the World Will Be Safe. L: C.J. German; M: Leo Friedman, 1919

So the World Will Have Liberty. L: J.L. Garitty; M: E.A. Garitty, 1918

Softly the Shadows Are Stealing (Over the Sunset Sky). L: H. Roe Goulding; M: Arthur C. Morse, 1918

The Soldier. L: Mrs. A.C. Ross; M: Carl Heil, 1915

The Soldier. L: Rupert Brooke; M: H.T. Burleigh, 1916

Soldier and Sailor Boy. L: Lt. Edwin Murphy, U.S.N.; M: A. Fred Phillips, 1918

The Soldier and the Sailor of the U.S.A. L: R.M. Niemyer; M: Leo Friedman, 1918

Soldier Bill (or, Oh, I Wish My Mother Had Raised Her Girl to Be a Soldier). L&M: Alma Bates, 1918

Soldier Blues. L: Admond Nivelles; M: Billy Smythe, 1919

*Soldier Boy. L: D.A. Esrom; M: Theodore Morse, 1915

Soldier Boy. L&M: L.F. Demarest, 1917

Soldier Boy. L&M: Mary E. Partridge, 1917

Soldier Boy. L&M: A.B. Crawley, 1917

Soldier Boy. L&M: M.V.E. Williams, 1917

Soldier Boy. L&M: Nora McGuire, 1918

Soldier Boy. L&M: C.N. Guttenberger, 1918

Soldier Boy. L: Pauline Sprague; M: Roy Hartzell, 1918

Soldier Boy. M: Vernon Lloyd, 1918

Soldier Boy. L: Fannie Campbell; M: Leo Friedman, 1918

Soldier Boy. L&M: A.T. Huntington, 1918

Soldier Boy. L: Johanna Wischoff; M: Leo Friedman, 1919

The Soldier Boy and Home. L: G.M. Taylor; M: Leo Friedman, 1918

Soldier Boy and Sailor Boy, We're Proud of You. L: Donald Ayer; M: A. Fisk, 1918

The Soldier Boy and the Girl at Home. L: W.E. Rose and M.C. Robbins; M: George L. Whiteman, 1916

Soldier Boy, Come Back to Me. L: Paul B. Armstrong; M: F. Henri Klickmann, 1918

Soldier Boy from Illinois. L: A. McFarlane; M: Leo Friedman, 1918

Soldier Boy, I'll Be Here to Welcome You. L&M: D. O'Rourke, 1919

Soldier Boy, I'm Waiting Ever and Only for You. L&M: Lyman Fordyce, 1919

Soldier Boy March. M: J.A. Schmidt, 1917

A Soldier Boy There. L: J.C. Fitzpatrick; M: Leo Friedman, 1919

Soldier Boy, We Are Backing You. L&M: Gayle Fisher, 1919

Soldier Boys. L: M.A. Harrold; M: Leo Friedman, 1918

Soldier Boys. L&M: Clara L. Baker, 1918

Soldier Boys. L: Arthur Guiterman; M: J.A. Parks, 1919

Soldier Boy's Farewell. L: C.A. Coats; M: Leo Friedman, 1918

Soldier Boy's Farewell. L: H.C. May; M: Leo Friedman, 1918

Soldier Boy's Farewell. L&M: Mollie Lillian Laughlin, 1918

Soldier Boy's Farewell. L: E.M. Smith; M: Everett J. Evans, 1918

Soldier Boy's Farewell. L: Mrs. H. Landsee; M: Leo Friedman, 1919

Soldier Boy's Farewell to Mother. L: J.P. Wright; M: R.W. Gebhardt, 1918

Soldier Boys of Uncle Sam. L&M: Hiram R. Lurvey, 1916

Soldier Boy's Return. L&M: G.A. Pfeiffer, 1918

The Soldier Brave and the Red Cross Maid. L: Elizabeth F. Guptill; M: T.B. Weaver, 1917

Soldier-Cap. M: Mabel W. Daniels, 1918

Soldier, Farewell. L: A.D. Noland; M: G.R. Mattheys, 1919

Soldier Girl. L: H.W. Crawford; M: Leo Friedman, 1918

Soldier, Goodbye. L&M: E.A. Hoover, 1918

Soldier Heroes. L: G.P. Smith; M: Harry Stirling, 1915

Soldier Lad. L: Jesse Morgan Stoughton; M: Jesse Morgan Stoughton and P. Merritt, 1917

Soldier Lad. L&M: M.M. Bailey, 1918

Soldier Lad, My Soldier Lad. L&M: E.G. Toothaker, 1917

Soldier Laddie. L: R. Stewart; M: Leo Friedman, 1919

Soldier Lad's Return. L&M: Mrs. J.A. McMaster, 1919

Soldier Lover. L: Elsie Janet French; M: H.W. Fairbanks, 1918

Soldier Lover's Farewell. L: G.G. Currie; M: Robert H. Brennen, 1918

Soldier Man, I'm Waiting Ever and Only for You. L&M: Lyman Fordyce, 1919

Soldier Mine. L&M: C.M. Schofield, 1918

Soldier of Our Allied Boys. L: C. Enright; M: Leo Friedman, 1919

Soldier of the Legion. L: A.M.D.A. Britten, 1917

Soldier of Uncle Sam (March). L&M: Alberto Himan and Thomas H. West, 1917

Soldier Rest. L: Ashby Wood; M: C.W. Waggoner, 1917

Soldier Rest. L: Sir Walter Scott; M: Charles P. Scott, 1919

The Soldier Safely Home. L: J. Busch; M: Charles Lewis, 1917

A Soldier Still. L&M: Florine Bigbee, 1919

Soldier, We Welcome You. L: J. McCauley; M: A. Stanley-Moore, 1919

Soldier's a Word That Means the World to U.S. L&M: Pearl Creighton, 1919

Soldier's Adieu. L&M: Mrs. A. Willis, 1918

Soldier's Benediction. L: J.R. Clements; M: Theodore E. Perkins, 1917

Soldier's Bride. L: Sarah Wykes; M: Harry Stirling, 1915

Soldier's Call. L: Ethie Bennett; M: Leo Friedman, 1919

Soldier's Caress. L: H.W. Prince; M: Leo Friedman, 1919

Soldiers Coming Home. L&M: E.W. Kruse, 1919

Soldier's Courage. L: M.C. Daseler; M: Artie Bowers, 1919

Soldier's Dream. L&M: Ion Arnold, 1915

Soldier's Dream. L&M: Byron Gay, 1918

Soldier's Dream. L: Henrietta Verheul; M: Leo Friedman, 1918

Soldier's Dream. L: Ella Nikisher; M: Leo Friedman, 1919

Soldier's Dream. L: Mrs. J. Murray; M: Leo Friedman, 1919

Soldier's Dream. L: Emma Doenges; M: Leo Friedman, 1919

Soldier's Dream of Home. L: Clarence Raymond Rungee; M: Benjamin Frederick Rungee, 1915

Soldier's Dream of Home (Reverie Pathetique). M: Louis Weber, 1917

Soldier's Dream of Home. L: Mrs. M.J. Tooze; M: Leo Friedman, 1918

Soldier's Dream of Home. M: Charles Kunkel, 1918

Soldier's Dream of Home. M: E.R. Metcalf, 1919

Soldier's Farewell. L&M: G.E. Smallwood, 1915

Soldier's Farewell. L: May M. Duffee; M: R.A. Browne, 1917

Soldier's Farewell. L: Daniel M. Kleist; M: Albert H. Gleich, 1917

Soldier's Farewell. L: Milo Keene; M: Roy Hartzell, 1918

Soldier's Farewell. L: Elmer Horlan; M: Leo Friedman, 1918

Soldier's Farewell. L: D.W. Potter; M: Leo Friedman, 1918

Soldier's Farewell. L: M. Breigel; M: Leo Friedman, 1918

Soldier's Farewell (Waltz). M: Bert R. Anthony, 1918

Soldier's Farewell. L&M: A. Edwards, 1918

Soldier's Farewell. L: R. Powers; M: H. Teuber, 1918

Soldier's Farewell. L&M: O.E. Schamu, 1918

Soldier's Farewell. L&M: Mrs. S.M. Scogin, 1919

Soldier's Farewell. L: Isadore Kehl; M: Leo Friedman, 1919

Soldier's Farewell to Mother. L: Carl Petersen; M: Leo Friedman, 1918

Soldier's Goodbye. L&M: Kate Ellis, 1917

Soldier's Goodbye. L: Zelinda E. Foley; M: Mario Hediger, 1918

Soldier's Goodbye. L: Mrs. Dave E. Nichols; M: Glen Snelgrove, 1918

Soldier's Goodbye. L&M: Ethel Bjorklund, 1919

A Soldier's Grave in Flanders. L: Thomas McGovern; M: Leo Friedman, 1918

Soldier's Homecoming. L: Mrs. J.W. Moore; M: Leo Friedman, 1918

Soldier's Honor. L: F. Ferguson; M: Glen Snelgrove, 1919

The Soldier's Idea of Heaven. L&M: D.T. Brabant, 1919

The Soldier's Job. L&M: L.W. Squier, 1918

Soldier's Last Dream. L&M: Herman Struebing, 1919

Soldier's Last Farewell. L: W.H. Wonn; M: Roy Hartzell, 1918

Soldier's Last Farewell. L: M. Mattingly; M: Roy Hartzell, 1919

Soldier's Last Farewell. L&M: Belle Wallower, 1919

Soldier's Last Prayer. L: Sophia Beck; M: Leo Friedman, 1918

Soldier's Last Words. L: Lillian Jansen; M: Leo Friedman, 1919

A Soldier's Letter Home. L&M: W.B. Clarke, 1918

Soldiers' March. M: Platon Brounoff, 1918

Soldiers' Marching Song. L&M: Annie A. Ferree, 1917

Soldier's Memories of Home. M: Mary L. Conway, 1918

Soldier's Message. L: Mrs. C. Langford; M: Roy Hartzell, 1919

Soldier's Molly. L&M: Emma J. Haney, 1919

Soldier's Mother. L&M: L. Trowbridge, 1918

A Soldier's Mother's Lullaby. L: J. Whalen; M: P.C. Caporossi, 1918

A Soldier's Mother's Request. L: C.L. Hayes; M: H. Fredrick, 1917

Soldiers of a New Day. L&M: Neva Deal Anderson, 1918

Soldiers of America. L: William H. McMasters; M: Lillian G. McMasters, 1918

Soldiers of Freedom. L: J.W. Williams; M: J.W. Tussing, 1918

Soldiers of Freedom (March). M: Herbert Forrest Odell, 1918

Soldiers of Freedom, the Bugles Are Calling. L: R.B. Pike; M: Edgar Belmont Smith, 1918

Soldiers of Glorious America. L&M: James H. Lockwood, 1917

Soldiers of the Sea (March). M: Fred K. Huffer, 1914

Soldiers of the Sea. L: William Cary Duncan; M: Winthrop Cortelyou, 1917

Soldiers of the Sea. L&M: Arthur Bowes, 1918

Soldiers of the U.S.A. L&M: Mrs. J. Kyle, 1918

Soldiers of Uncle Sam. L&M: A.B. Rasmussen, 1918

Soldiers of Uncle Sam. L&M: H.G. Phelps, 1918

Soldiers of Uncle Sam. L: Thomas Burke; M: Leo Friedman, 1918

Soldier's Prayer. L: M.A. Dunn; M: Leo Friedman, 1919

Soldier's Prayer. L: N.R. Howard; M: Leo Friedman, 1919

A Soldier's Prayer Over There — Our Answer Over Here. L: O.M. Dahl; M: Frank W. Ford, 1919

The Soldier's Reason. L: Mrs. A. Bowman; M: Leo Friedman, 1918

Soldier's Return. L: M.S. Snyder; M: Leo Friedman, 1919

Soldier's Reverie. L&M: Katherine T. Lawry, 1918

Soldier's Reverie. M: Eva Sundgren, 1918

Soldier's Rosary. L: James E. Dempsey; M: Joseph A. Burke, 1918

Soldier's Song. M: Sidney Steinheimer, 1915

Soldier's Song. L: George B. Harris, Jr.; M: Ivan S. Langstroth, 1915

Soldier's Song. L: Richard Butler Glaenzer; M: Giovanni Romilli, 1917

Soldiers' Song. L&M: E.C. Rogers, 1918

Soldier's Song. L: Alice Neumeister; M: L.B. Starkweather, 1919

Soldier's Thoughts. L&M: F.H. Fornfeist, 1919

Soldiers to the Front (March). M: Martin Greenwald, 1917

Soldier's Trinity. L: M.M. Duffee; M: Leo Friedman, 1919

Soldiers' Triumphant Return. L: F. Eustis; M: Artie Bowers, 1919

Soldiers True. M: Laurence Gardner, 1918

Soldier's Vision. L: R. Courtney; M: Leo Friedman, 1918

Soldier's Visions. L: E.W. Rooney; M: Leo Friedman, 1919

A Soldier's Word to Mother. L: Art Dooley; M: Dan Cavanaugh, 1918

A Soldier's Yester Year. L&M: Annie U. Johnson, 1918

Solid Men to the Front (March). M: John Philip Sousa, 1918

Some Boy's Mother. L: Laura Carmien; M: Leo Friedman, 1919

Some Day We're Back to Dear Old Glory. L&M: H. Carolyn, 1918

Some Mother's Boy Is Over There. L: Maggie Taylor; M: Leo Friedman, 1919

Some Mother's Son Will Not Return. L: W.B. Spagnola; M: Artie Bowers, 1919

Somebody's Boy. L: D.A. Esrom; M: Theodore Morse, 1917

*Somebody's Boy. L: James E. Dempsey; M: Joseph A. Burke, 1918

Someday I'll Come Back to You. L&M: Gitz Rice, 1919

Someday They're Coming Home Again. L&M: Harry Hilbert, 1917

Someone Else May Be There (While I'm Gone) L&M: Irving Berlin, 1917

Someone from This Home Is Somewhere in France. L: G.R. Fremont; M: Walter Matthews, 1918

*Someone Is Longing for Home Sweet Home (Thousands of Miles Away). L&M: David Berg, William Tracey, and Jack Stern, 1918

Someone Is Waiting Somewhere for a Letter from No Man's Land. L: Louis E. Thayer; M: Jacques Cole, 1918

Somewhere Across That Mighty Blue Sea, There's a Heart That Belongs to Me. L&M: Charles V. Gross, 1918

Somewhere for Freedom a Soldier Died. L: Clara Nelson; M: Leo Friedman, 1919

Somewhere He's Marching. L: C. Llewellyn Tarlton; M: Alice Brady Como, 1918

Somewhere in America. L: Richard Fechheimer; M: W.B. Kernell, from stage production Elsie Janis & Her Gang, 1919

Somewhere in France. L&M: Alfred A. Copping, 1915

Somewhere in France. L&M: Earl Carroll and Rubey Cowan, 1915

Somewhere in France. M: Herbert Ivey, 1916

Somewhere in France. L&M: Charles Henry and James C. Quinn, 1916

Somewhere in France. L: Mabel Gregg; M: J. Stafford Sumner, 1917

Somewhere in France. L: James P. Sinnott; M: May Hartmann, 1917

Somewhere in France. L: D. Ireland Thomas; M: James W. MacNeal, 1918

Somewhere in France. L: Mrs. J.R. Schroeter; M: Leo Friedman, 1918

Somewhere in France. L: Thomas Coxon; M: Leo Friedman, 1918

Somewhere in France. L: H.G. Lainhart; M: Leo Friedman, 1918

Somewhere in France. L: Lucy Vogel; M: Leo Friedman, 1918

Somewhere in France. L&M: Kitty Yarnall, 1918

Somewhere in France. L: Mrs. T.A. McClellan; M: Leo Friedman, 1918

Somewhere in France. L&M: Mary Carlisle Howe, 1918

Somewhere in France. L&M: N.M. Patty, 1918

Somewhere in France. L&M: Nathan L. Lewis, 1918

Somewhere in France. L: Mildred Hitchinson; M: Leo Friedman, 1919

Somewhere in France. L: Sally G. Shanks; M: Leo Friedman, 1919

Somewhere in France. L: K.P. Moul; M: Leo Friedman, 1919

Somewhere in France He Is Sleeping. L&M: Clark Hill, 1919

Somewhere in France Is a Soldier's Grave. L&M: H.G. Phelps, 1919

*Somewhere in France Is Daddy. L&M: "The Great Howard" [Howard Miller], 1917

Somewhere in France Is My Laddie. L&M: Laura Walker Colgrove, 1918

*Somewhere in France (Is the Lily). L: Philander Johnson; M: Joseph E. Howard, 1917

Somewhere in France Is Your Sweetheart. L&M: John James, Jr., 1918

Somewhere in France Lies My Laddie. L: A.L. James; M: W.M. Surdam, 1919

Somewhere in France the Sound of Bugle Calling. L&M: Bessie B. Law, 1918

Somewhere in France There's Someone You Know. L&M: I.L. Sachs and S. Leavey, 1918

Somewhere in France Tonight. L&M: Jewell Ellison, 1918

Somewhere in France with You. L: Sadie E. Watts; M: E.S.S. Huntington, 1918

Somewhere in Heaven There's a Boy of Mine. L: J. Lisson; M: Leo Friedman, 1919

Somewhere in the Trenches. L: Clarence Wood; M: Leo Friedman, 1919

Somewhere in the U.S.A. (Memorial Song). L&M: Thomas Long, 1919

Somewhere in the Valley of the Marne. L: George Oliver [G.G. Davis]; M: George P. Hulten, 1918

Somewhere on the Sea Twixt Here and Over There. L: E.K. Couty; M: Leo Friedman, 1918

Somewhere Our Stars Are Gleaming. L: M.C. Egan; M: Leo Friedman, 1919

Somewhere Out There. L&M: Leonore Sollender Hanby, 1918

Somewhere Over There. L&M: Rose Villar, 1917

Somewhere Over There. L: Medora Bowen Pulver; M: Ed O'Keefe, 1918

Somewhere Over There. L: Josephine C. Turner; M: Billy P. Augustin, 1918

Somewhere Over There. L: M.L. Busch and R. Harry; M: Leo Friedman, 1918

Somewhere Over There. L: N.R. Williams; M: Leo Friedman, 1919

Somewhere, Somewhere in France. L: William Vaughan Dunham; M: Shelton Brooks, 1917

Somewhere the Boys Are Fighting. L: C.H. Stump; M: Leo Friedman, 1918

Somewhere There's Thousands of Broken Hearts (March). L: Albert Rossi; M: Tobia Acciani, 1916

Somewhere Tonight. L: Harold G. Frost; M: E. Clinton Keithley, 1918

The Son of God Goes Forth to War. L: R. Heber; M: Harry F. Asbury, 1918

Son of My Heart. L: Adelaide V.K. Swift; M: Charles Gilbert Spross, 1918

Son of Uncle Sam. L&M: W. Walker, 1918

Song for Our Soldiers and Nurses. L&M: Della Rodefer, 1918

Song of America, L: C.R. Piety; M: Samuel W. Beazley, 1915

Song of America. L&M: Louise R. Waite, 1915

Song of France. L&M: Bryceson Treharne, 1917

Song of Freedom. L: Alex W. Grant; M: T.A. Simpson, 1916

Song of Freedom. L&M: Anna Benson, 1918

Song of Freedom. L: Mrs. Charles E. Brown and T.H. Weber; M: T.H. Weber, 1918

Song of Freedom. L&M: Brabazon Lowther, 1919

Song of Liberty. L: Franklin Crispin; M: Wassili Lips, 1918

Song of Liberty. L: W.J. Perman; M: Amy Perman, 1918

Song of Liberty. L: S. Gardner; M: M.G. Downs, 1918

Song of Liberty. L&M: G. Darlington Richards, 1918

Song of Liberty. L&M: W. Brown Leonard, 1918

Song of Liberty (or, Hail to the Flag, the New National Song). L&M: George Blodgett Johnson, 1918

Song of Peace. L&M: Thurland Chattaway, 1915

Song of Peace. L: William Hude Nelson; M: Elizabeth Bowen Foster, 1915

Song of Peace. L: Hannah Laura Stevens; M: D.P. Hughes, 1917

Song of Peace. L&M: Maude Horton, 1919

Song of Peace. L: Margaret Rabideau; M: Leo Friedman, 1919

Song of Service. L: Louise Ayres Garnett; M: Peter Christian Lutkin, 1919

Song of the A.E.F. L: G.W. Norris; M: George Graff, Jr., 1919

Song of the Allies (Go to It, Boys, the Hour Has Come!). L&M: M.D. Austin, 1918

Song of the Allies — Our God Alone Is King. L&M: Eliza Doyle Smith, 1918

Song of the Far-Off War. L: Maisie D. Green; M: Carl Heil, 1915

Song of the Fatherland. L: Rachel Reubelt; M: Claude Wellington, 1915

Song of the Flag. L: Frederick H. Martens; M: William Lester, 1917

Song of the Flag. L: George Morrow Mayo; M: I.H. Meredith, 1918

Song of the Free. L: A.F. Christy; M: Frank W. Ford, 1919

Song of the Freemen. L: F.F. Brumback; M: Roger William Duke Beecher, 1917

Song of the Liberty Bell. L&M: D. Erwin Force, 1915

Song of the Private. L&M: Jack Frost, 1919

Song of the Rookies (March). L&M: Ransom Judd Powell, 1918

Song of the Sammies. L&M: Horace Stroud, 1917

Song of the Slacker. L: Ada Hurst; M: Leo Friedman, 1918

Song of the War. L: Pearl McCracken; M: Leo Friedman, 1918

Song of Uncle Sam's Boys. L&M: James Arnott, 1917

Song of Victory. L&M: P.D. Bird, 1918

Song of Victory. L&M: May Jackson Carter, 1918

Song of Victory. L: Edward M. Chapman; M: Louis Adolphe Coerne, 1919

Song of Victory. L: Ellen M.H. Gates; M: Frank T. Hart, 1919

Song to Old Glory. L: C.E. Graves; M: Leo Friedman, 1918

Song to the Flag. L&M: William W. Sleeper, 1917

Sons of America (March). M: E.W. Davis, 1917

*Sons of America (America Needs You). L: Arthur F. Holt; M: William T. Pierson, 1917

Sons of England. L: A.W.J. Hemmings; M: Paul Shannon, 1915

Sons of Freedom. L: F.G. McCauley; M: C.C. Case, 1917

Sons of Italy (March). M: Joseph LoCascio, 1916

Sons of Liberty. L&M: Inez Juanita Carusi, 1918

Sons of Liberty. L&M: F.G. Teichman, 1919

Sons of the Blue and Gray. L&M: Clifton Edson, 1918

Sons of the Empire. L: F.A. Knott; M: Leo Friedman, 1919

Sons of the U.S.A. L: Albert J. Skinner; M: Henry Keefe, 1917

Sons of Uncle Sam (March). M: Earl McCoy, 1917

Sons of Uncle Sam. L: G. Mitchell; M: Leo Friedman, 1919

Sons of Uncle Sam Have Always Brought the Bacon Home. L&M: Chris Smith and Henry Troy, 1917

Sons of Victory. L&M: Edith May Gibbs, 1917

Soul of Freedom. L: Mrs. L.A. Morgan; M: Roy Hartzell, 1918

Soul of Old Glory. L: W.W. Woodbridge; M: Carl Eppert, 1917

The Sound of the Bugle Is Calling. L&M: M.D. Hall, 1918

Spare Our Homes, Spare Our Fire-Side and the Boys That We Love. L&M: Mrs. C.L. McClanahan, 1918

Speak a Word for Wilson, He's Been Mighty Good to You. L: Frank J. Clennan; M: Fred G. Fuller, 1919

Speed Up, America! (You're Going to Win). (March). L: R.J. Beckhard; M: Joseph Bradley, 1917

Spirit of America (March). M: John Hazel, 1916

Spirit of America (A Patriotic Patrol). L&M: J.S. Zamecnik, 1917

Spirit of America. L: J.B. Shanahan; M: Leo Bartosh, 1917

Spirit of America (March). M: G.M. Messina, 1919

Spirit of America, 1917. L&M: Andrew Miller, 1917

Spirit of Democracy (March). M: Z. Vebeit, 1919

Spirit of France (March). M: E.T. Paull, 1918

Spirit of Freedom. L: McLelland Read; M: Lillie Holland, 1918

Spirit of Freedom. L: D.L. Hill; M: Henry Jacobsen, 1919

Spirit of Heroes. L: Mary Sibley Evans; M: Roman Steiner, 1917

Spirit of Nineteen-Seventeen. L: C.R. Warren; M: Percy Burton Arant, 1918

Spirit of 1917 (March). M: Ivan Kennedy, 1917

Spirit of Our Boys (A Patriotic Song). L&M: F.F. Kells, 1918

Spirit of Our Boys. L: D.W. Jenkins, Sr.; M: Leo Friedman, 1919

The Spirit of Our Soldier Boys at the Front. L: C.E. Lewis; M: Leo Friedman, 1918

Spirit of Peace (March). M: W.H. Kiefer, 1915

Spirit of Peace (March). M: Joseph Perrone, 1916

Spirit of '17. L: J.M. Murray; M: Byron Morgan, 1917

Spirit of '17. L&M: L.J. Mackey, 1917

Spirit of '17 (March). M: C.D. Bethel, 1917

Spirit of '17 (Salute the Flag). L&M: G.A. Maloy, 1918

Spirit of '17 as America Enters the Great World War. L&M: Lora Townsend Dickinson, 1917

Spirit of '76. L&M: G. Frederick Bickford, 1917

Spirit of '76. L: A.G. Easton; M: Arthur Heft, 1917

Spirit of the Navy. M: A.E. Boroughf, 1918

Spirit of the U.S.A. (March). M: J.N. Burke, 1917

Spirit of the U.S.A. L&M: Emil Edouard; English lyric by Louis LaPierre, 1918

Spirit of the U.S.A. L&M: Paul Specht, 1918

Spirit of Victory (March). M: E.S. Phelps, 1919

Spread the News of Victory. L: William T. Pettengill; M: Duke M. Farson, Jr., 1918

Stainless Soldier on the Walls. L: Ralph Waldo Emerson; M: Clarence Dickinson, 1918

Stamps, Stamps, Stamps, They'll Help Our Boys! L&M: N.L. Mearns, 1918

Stand Behind the Man Behind the Gun. L&M: Jennie Boree Mikesell, 1918

Stand Behind the Man Behind the Gun. L: John Keevon; M: E. Fortunata, 1918

Stand by Old France to the End. L&M: Robert G. Claypoole, 1918

Stand by Old Glory. L&M: W.C. Steely, 1917

Stand by Old Glory. L&M: F.A. Wilson, 1918

Stand by Our Colors, Boys. L: S.J. Taylor; M: Leo Friedman, 1918

Stand by the Colors. L&M: A.L. Thompson, 1918

Stand by the Flag. L: Ida W. Bartlett; M: M. Loomis Bartlett, 1917

Stand by the Flag. L&M: Clarence E. Billings, 1918

Stand by the Flag. L&M: S.A. Frost, 1919

Stand by the Flag, Boys (March). L&M: Tessie de St. Croix Johnstone, 1917

Stand by the Flag, Boys. L&M: B.E. Ward, 1919

Stand by the President. L&M: H.E. Engle, 1915

Stand by the President. L&M: Blanche Evans Abrahams, 1917

Stand by the President. L: G.G. Currie; M: Robert H. Brennen, 1918

Stand by Uncle Sam. L&M: Vernon T. Stevens, 1918

Stand by Your President. L&M: Dick Kettlewell, 1918

Stand by Your Uncle Sam. L&M: Lucy Younger, 1917

Stand Fast, America. L&M: G.A. Hall, 1917

Stand Firm. L: John Grayson; M: Samuel W. Beazley, 1917

Stand, Stand Up America! L&M: Edward Horsman, 1917

*Stand Up and Fight Like H---. L&M: George M. Cohan, 1918

Stand Up for Old Glory. L&M: Guy A. Surber, 1918

Stand Up for the Soldier Boy. L&M: Zella Estelle Leighton, 1917

Stand Up for Your Uncle Sammy. L: Edwin W. Jones and Frank P. Hoyt; M: F.J. LeSeur, 1918

A Star in the Window Is Shining for a Soldier Boy in France. L: W.H. Burr; M: Leo Friedman, 1919

The Star in Their Window Has Turned to Gold. L&M: Myrtle Houghton, 1918

The Star of Blue Has Changed to Star of Gold. L&M: P.B. Story, 1918

Star of Gold. L: Herman A. Heydt and P.C. Warren; M: Mana-Zucca, 1918

Star of Gold. L&M: E.M. Patterson, 1919

Star of Hope. L: Esmeralda Scott; M: Leo Friedman, 1919

Star of Liberty. L: Aaron Powery; M: "R.B.," 1918

Star of Peace. M: Mary Earl, 1918

The Star-Spangled Banner for All. L: J.L. Perry; M: Robert H. Brennen, 1917

The Star-Spangled Banner for Mine. L: A.C. James; M: W.M. Surdam, 1916

The Star-Spangled Banner No. 2. L&M: W.J. Wilson, 1917

The Star-Spangled Banner of Democracy. L&M: Harry Six, 1918

The Star-Spangled Banner That Waves Far and Wide. L&M: J.M. Rowan, 1918

The Star-Spangled Banner's Ours. L: A.M. Castello; M: Laura Sedgwick Collins, 1917

The Star That Turned from Blue to Gold. L: Margeret Barnett; M: Leo Friedman, 1919

Starry Banner (A Patriotic Song). L&M: T.C. Clark, 1918

Starry Flag of Liberty. L&M: T.J. White, 1917

The Starry Flag We'll Raise. L: O.S. Matthews; M: Harry Weston, 1917

The Stars and Bars Are Waving. L&M: Mary E. Patton, 1918

Stars and Stripes. L: W.W. Gillette; M: Harry J. Lincoln, 1915

Stars and Stripes. L&M: T.J. White, 1917

Stars and Stripes. L: William Cullen Bryant; M: B.J. Hoffacker, 1919

Stars and Stripes. L: D.A. Merz; M: Leo Friedman, 1919

The Stars and Stripes and Union Jack. L: W.C. O'Neill; M: Alfred Wooler, 1918

The Stars and Stripes and You. L&M: Ethel B. Mowry, 1918

The Stars and Stripes Are Calling. L: Eleanor Gregston Thompson; M: N. Julius Kirsch, 1918

The Stars and Stripes Are Flying 'Round the World. L&M: E. Adelaide Ourat [E.A. Kroner], 1918

The Stars and Stripes Are Yours as Well as Mine. L&M: N.E. Walker, 1918

The Stars and Stripes Can Never Fall. L&M: Violet Savage, 1918

The Stars and Stripes for Me. L&M: J.H. Alleman, 1917

The Stars and Stripes Forever. L: J. Albertin; M: P.B. Story, 1918

The Stars and Stripes Forever. L: Goldie Norton; M: Leo Friedman, 1919

The Stars and Stripes Forever. L: C.E. Keith; M: Leo Friedman, 1919

The Stars and Stripes Have Joined the Fray. L: G.A. Anderson; M: Leo Friedman, 1918

Stars and Stripes Hymn. L&M: R.H. Locke, 1915

Stars and Stripes, I Pledge My Life to Thee. L: C. Aug; M: Charles Aug and Charles Howard, 1917

Stars and Stripes in France. L&M: John McKelvie, 1917

The Stars and Stripes Incentive. L: B.W. Young; M: Leo Friedman, 1919

The Stars and Stripes Is His Emblem. L&M: Wesley L. Silverwood, 1917

The Stars and Stripes Lead On (March). L&M: E.A. Leatzow, 1918

The Stars and Stripes of Old Glory. L&M: T.P. White, 1918

The Stars and Stripes Our Only Hope. L: F.W. Blaine; M: Leo Friedman, 1918

The Stars and Stripes Over Old Berlin. L: Ethel Parks; M: Leo Friedman, 1919

The Stars and Stripes Shall Never Trail the Dust. L&M: J.E. McGirt, 1917

The Stars and Stripes, Uncle Sam, and You (March). L: J.F. Murry; M: Fred W. Clement, 1917

The Stars and Stripes Shall Wave. L: Henry J. Zelley; M: J.W. Hughes, 1918

The Stars and Stripes Shall Win, Prevail. L: Salome Severn; M: P.B. Story, 1918

Stars and Stripes, We Love You. L&M: Edna Randolph Worrell, 1917

The Stars and Stripes Were Waving. L&M: C.B. Estes, 1917

Stars and Stripes, You Are the Flag for Me. L&M: Charles Aug and Charles Howard, 1914

The Stars in Old Glory. L&M: Herbert Miles, 1918

Stars in Old Glory and Stars in His Crown. L: L. Featherstone; M: Leo Friedman, 1919

Stars of Blue and Gold. L: F. Von Kapff; M: Leo Friedman, 1919

Stars of Gold. L: M.E. Smith; M: Leo Friedman, 1919

Stars—Red, White and Blue. L&M: W.J. Carter and Al Dotzler, 1917

The Stars Up in Heaven Are Gold. L: C.R. Barker; M: Leo Friedman, 1919

The Statue of Liberty Is Smiling on the

Hearts of the World Today. L: Jack Mahoney; M: Halsey K. Mohr, 1918

The Sterling Waltz (Victory). M: Boston White, 1919

Stick by Your Uncle Sammy. L: A.D. Minnick; M: Everett J. Evans, 1917

Stick to the Dear Old Flag. L&M: Harry Taylor, 1914

Still Guard the Land We Love. L: James Rowe; M: Anthony J. Showalter, 1918

Stop the War. L&M: Octavo Kossuth White, 1916

*The Story of Old Glory, the Flag We Love. L: J. Will Callahan; M: Ernest R. Ball, 1916

The Story of the Boy That Went Away. L: H.L. Doyle; M: William D. Hansen, 1919

The Story of Uncle Sam. L&M: Bobby Heath and Billy James, 1918

Strike! Sons of Liberty. L: G.B. Whitney; M: Harry L. Alford, 1918

Stripes and Stars. L: L.W. Mattox; M: Bessie Elmare, 1918

Strolling 'Round the Camp with Mary. L: Ballard MacDonald; M: Nat Osborne, from stage production Atta Boy, 1918

Strong and Steady, Rough and Ready, Sons of Uncle Sam. L&M: John N. Bloominger, 1918

The Submarine (March). M: Herman A. Hummel, 1915

The Submarine (Waltz). M: M.A. Bishop, 1916

The Submarine-Chaser with a Yankee Crew. L&M: Max Maxwell, 1917

Sunbeam Soldiers. L: Mrs. Elliott Ross; M: Charles H. Gabriel, 1917

Sunlit Hills of Picardy. L: D.J. Mitchell; M: Leo Friedman, 1918

Sunshine of the Army. L: E. Penney; M: Leo Friedman, 1919

Sunshine of Your Smile. L: Leonard Cooke; M: Lilian Ray, 1916

Sure, We Are Some Big America. L&M: Harry Wolfe, 1917

Surrender, Bill. L&M: M.F. Bradley, 1918

Sweet, Enduring Peace. L: F.S. Shepherd; M: William Hammond, 1918

Sweet Land of Freedom. L&M: "By an American Woman," 1917

Sweet Land of Liberty. L&M: Charles F. Stayner, 1917

Sweet Land of Liberty. L&M: H.C. Coates, 1918

Sweet Land of Liberty. L: Ida Holdmair; M: Leo Friedman, 1918

Sweet Liberty. L: C.F. Turkis; M: Leo Friedman, 1918

Sweet Peaches (I Hope This Letter Reaches You and Brings You Back to Me). L&M: Clarence Gaskill and Walter Donaldson, 1918

Sweet Salvation Lassie, May God Bless You. L&M: Agnes V. Denison, 1919

Sweetheart, I've Come Back to You. L: Pauline Huff; M: Artie Bowers, 1919

Sweetheart, 'Mid Battle I'm Dreaming. L: B.L. Henning; M: Leo Friedman, 1918

Sweetheart of Our Nation, Miss Liberty, We're All in Love With You. L: William A. Willander; M: Harry DeCosta, 1916

Swing in Line. L&M: H.H. and C.D. Byron, 1918

Swing on to Victory with the U.S.A. L: Fred K. Huffer; M: J.G. Bennett, 1918

T

*Take a Letter to My Daddy "Over There." L: Roger Lewis and Bobby Crawford; M: Billy Baskette, 1918

Take Care of My Sweetheart While I'm Away. L&M: W. Thomas, 1917

Take Care of the Man in a Uniform. L: Jimmie Conlin; M: Frank Westphal, 1919

Take Care of Yourself, My Boy. L&M: J.F. Chval, 1918

Take Good Care of Mother While I'm Gone. L&M: M.R. Callan, 1918

Take Me Back to New York Town. L: Andrew B. Sterling; M: Harry Von Tilzer, 1918

Take Off Your Hat, It's a Grand Old Flag. L&M: Duncan J. Muir, 1914

Take Off Your Hat to the Sammies. L&M: Earl G. Cahoon, 1918

Take Off Your Hat to the Stars and Stripes. L&M: E.H. Webb, 1917

Take Off Your Hat When the Flag Goes By. L&M: C.F. Weigle, 1918

Take Off Your Hats, Boys, and Cheer (March). L: E. Moran; M: Antonio Galvan, 1918

Take Out a Bond (March). L: P. Hunt; M: D.A. Summo, 1918

Take This Message of Love to My Mother. L&M: Fred C. Swan, 1917

Take This Uniform to My Dear Old Mother. L: J. Storey; M: Leo Friedman, 1918

Take Up Dear Old Glory. L: Marrie L. Paddock; M: Rolf Grant, 1917

*The Tale the Church Bell Told. L: Sam M. Lewis and Joe Young; M: Bert Grant, 1918

The Tank Fox Trot. M: Raoul Moretti, 1917

Taps Are Calling. L&M: Carl Albert Gray, 1919

Tars' Song. L&M: J.L. Hatton, 1917

Teach Me to Be a Brave Soldier (One Like Daddy Is Now). L&M: Kerry Mills, 1918

*Tell Me (Why Nights Are Lonesome). L: J. Will Callahan; M: Max D. Kortlander, 1919

Tell Mother Not to Weep for Me. L&M: George Fluckey, 1919

Tell Pershing I'll Be There. L: E. Gwin; M: A.B. Condo, 1918

Tell That to the Marines! L: Harold Atteridge and Al Jolson; M: Jean Schwartz, from stage production Sinbad, 1918

Tell the East the West Is Coming. L: Frank A. Gause; M: Charles H. White, 1918

Tell the Kaiser We Are Coming. L: M.T. Ready; M: Arthur J. Ready, 1918

Tell the Last Rose of Summer, Goodbye. L&M: Bartley Costello and Al Piantadosi, 1917

Tell Uncle Sam Here I Am. L: J. Strothers, Jr.; M: Leo Friedman, 1918

Tenting One Night on the Rhine. L&M: Cyril Mee, 1919

Thank God for Liberty. L: C.F. Bedell; M: Henry Philip Noll, 1918

Thank God for Victory. L: Edward M. Chapman; M: Louis Adolphe Coerne, 1919

Thank God I Am an American. L&M: Rollin C. Ward, 1917

Thank God the War Is Over. L: Clyde Monroe; M: Arnulf Cintura, 1919

Thank God the World's at Peace. L: G. Hart; M: George Graff, Jr., 1919

Thank God They Come (The Song of Our Allies) (March). L&M: W.J. Millard, 1918

Thanks from Our Allies. L: J. Powels; M: Leo Friedman, 1919

Thanksgiving, or Peace, Anthem. L: 117th Psalm; M: Robert Elder, 1918

That Banner Still Waves. L: E. Thompson; M: Artie Bowers, 1919

That Grand Old Gentleman (Uncle Sam). L: Will D. Cobb; M: Gus Edwards, 1917

That Happy Day, When the Boys Come Home Again. L&M: Mrs. Edward M. Bush, 1919

That Liberty Bond. L&M: O.E. Henry, 1918

That Long, Long Trail Is Getting Shorter Now. L&M: Jack Mahoney, 1919

That Neutrality Rag. L: L.H. Meares, Jr.; M: Edward Wunderlich, 1915

That Old Flag So True. L: C.H. Randolph; M: John Menown, 1918

That Old Glory May Still Wave. L: J.R. Wasley; M: Leo Friedman, 1918

That Pershing Lullaby. L: Annelu Burns; M: Madelyn Sheppard, from stage production *Hooray for the Girls*, 1918

*That Red Cross Girl of Mine. L&M: Ed C. Cannon, 1917

That Smile of Victory (or, Welcome Home). L&M: E.E. Hanyen, 1919

That Soldier Boy of Mine. L: Marybe A. Stoll; M: Frank W. Ford, 1919

That Starry Spangled Banner. L: Henry Hughson; M: Jacques Mustert, 1918

That Strictly Neutral Jag. L: Joseph Noel; M: Joseph E. Howard and Herbert P. Stothart, from stage production *Girl of Tomorrow*, 1915

That Syncopated Sailor Band. L&M: Herman Hupfeld, 1918

*That's a Mother's Liberty Loan. L&M: Mayo C. Tally and Clarence Gaskill, 1917

That's All One Mother Can Do. L: Ivan Reid; M: Peter DeRose, 1917

That's the American Plan. L: Nelson Irwin; M: Ernest Breuer, 1916

*That's the Feeling That Came Over Me. L&M: Herbert H. Power, 1919

That's the Flag of Flags for Me. L: Edward T. Gahan; M: E.A. Jackson, 1917

That's the Meaning of Uncle Sam. L: Frank Dairs; M: Win Brookhouse, 1916

That's the Way That I've Missed You. L: Gus Kahn; M: Egbert Van Alstyne, 1919

That's What God Made Mothers For. L&M: Leo Wood, 1918

That's What the Red, White and Blue Means to Ev'ry True Heart in the U.S.A. L: Robert Levenson; M: E.E. Bagley, 1918

That's What We'll Raise with Germany. L: Carroll Higbey; M: Frank Cook, 1917

That's What We're Fighting For. L: Morris M. Einson; M: James Kendis, 1917

*That's What We're Fighting For. L&M: Sgt. Clifton S. Anthony, 1918

That's Why I Want to Be a Soldier. L&M: M. DeDominicis, 1917

That's Why Mother-Love Was Made. L: Louis Weslyn; M: Frederick W. Vanderpool, 1917

That's Why They Call Us Yanks. L: A.C. Heimbach; M: Leo Friedman, 1919

That's Why We Love You, Betsy Ross. L&M: Ivan Reid and Peter DeRose, 1917

That's Why You're Called United States. L: Howard Johnson; M: Fred Fisher, 1917

*Their Hearts Are Over Here. L&M: George M. Cohan, 1918

Then, America, We'll Come Back Again. L: Anthony Szpak; M: Leo Friedman, 1919

Then Fight, Fight, Fight! L&M: Mrs. Walter Cook, 1918

Then Germany Shall Be Free. L: R.R. Davidson; M: Emma A. Lord, 1918

Then I'll Be Home Again. L&M: Phil Uphardt, 1917

Then I'll Come Back to You. L&M: John W. Bratton, 1917

Then I'll March Right Back to You. L&M: Paul Estabrook, 1918

Then Our Debt to France Is Square. L: V.W. Knutsen; M: Leo Friedman, 1918

Then Our Soldiers Will Come Back to Yankee Land. L&M: W.H. Bernrath, 1918

Then the Yankee Boys Will Slide for Home. L&M: Jack Mahoney, 1918

Then We Went Marching Toward Berlin. L: J. Lord; M: Leo Friedman, 1919

Then We'll Come Back Home Again. L: Lou Winer; M: Leo Friedman, 1918

Then You'll Know the World Is Free. L&M: S.R. Harcourt, 1918

Then Your Daddy's Coming Home. L: Leland Yerdon; M: Harold Dixon, 1918

There Ain't Goin-a-Be No Rhine. L&M: Victor Young, 1918

There Are a Lot of Things We'll Do When We Get Over There. L&M: Harry Galanter, 1918

There Are Smiling Faces Everywhere Since the Boys Came Home from Over There. L&M: Tom Delaney and Eleanor Harris, 1919

There Is a Nation That Is Nicknamed Uncle Sam. L: A.A. Scaletta; M: Kathryn I. White, 1918

There Is a Star in Old Glory. L: Josephine Keizer Littlejohn; M: Helen Pendleton Jones, 1917

There Is No Death—They All Survive. L: Frederick W. Bentley; M: F. Henri Klickmann, 1919

There Is Only One Flag for Me (A Patriotic Song). L&M: H.C. Washburn, 1917

There Is Only One Flag in This World for Me. L: Sadie Murphy; M: Clarence Clark, 1918

There Is Pep in the American Soldier. L&M: Mrs. F. Speckman, 1919

There Once Was a War. L: Edward Anthony; M: Louis G. Merrill, from stage production *Good Luck, Sam*, 1918

There Was a Hohenzollern Kid, Wilhelm by Name Was He. L&M: G.W. Sheppard, 1918

There Waves the Flag. L: Charles Horwitz; M: Gaston Borch, 1917

There Will Be a Jubilee When Our Brave Boys Come Home. L: Scott R. Dively; M: Charles J. Kiewicz, 1918

There Will Be a New Star in Old Glory. L: G.A. Miles and R. Fringer; M: Leo Friedman, 1919

There Will Be a Yankee Movement in the Watch on the Rhine. L: R.M. Erwin; M: Frank W. Ford, 1919

There Won't Be Any Kaiser Any More. L: H.J. Hancock; M: Leo Friedman, 1918

There'll Be a Great Time When All the Boys Come Home. L&M: P.J. Dixon, 1918

There'll Be a Hot Time for the Kaiser. L: P.H. Sommers; M: R.A. Browne and F.O. Boos, 1917

*There'll Be a Hot Time for the Old Men (While the Young Men Are Away). L: Grant Clarke; M: George W. Meyer, 1917

There'll Be a Hot Time When the Boys Get Mustered Out. L: Leland Yerdon; M: Harold Dixon, 1918

There'll Be No German Kaiser. L: W.C. Freeland; M: G.D. Barnard, 1918

There'll Be No Kaiser When We Get Through. L&M: The Rev. J.B. Bair, 1918

There'll Be Nothing Too Good for the Boys. L&M: George L. Boyden, 1918

There'll Be Something Doing When the War Is Over. L: Harry Tenney and Irving Maslof; M: Abner Silver, 1918

There'll Be Sunshine for You and for Someone You Are Waiting For. L: Al Dubin; M: James V. Monaco, 1918

There'll Never Be a Stain on Old Glory. L: Oliver T. Lenz; M: J. Edward Woolley, 1917

*There's a Battlefield in Ev'ry Mother's Heart. L: Howard E. Rogers; M: M.K. Jerome, 1918

There's a Call for You and Me, Carry On (March). L: Philander C. Johnson; M: William T. Pierson, 1918

There's a Colonel Missing in the Ranks. L&M: Saza M. Spearin, 1918

There's a Cross in My Window Tonight. L: C. Davis; M: Otto Merz, 1918

There's a Cross in the Window. L&M: J.W. Whealton, 1918

There's a Cross on the Arm of the Girl I Love (A Tribute). L&M: Coletta Power Livingstone, 1918

There's a Flag Calling Me. L: P.M. Bennett; M: George Hansford, 1918

There's a Flag That Each Yankee Will Fight For (the Flag That Is Red, White and Blue). L&M: R.W. Manning, 1917

There's a Garden of Crosses in No Man's Land. L: William Robinson; M: Gus Wackrow, 1919

There's a Girl for Every Soldier. L&M: J.P. Long and Maurice Scott, 1917

There's a Girl in Chateau Thierry. L: E. Ray Goetz; M: Melville Gideon, 1919

There's a Girl Who Is Knitting for You. L: George Hopkins; M: F.M. Nixson, 1918

There's a Good Time a-Coming (March). L&M: Erle Threlkeld, 1919

There's a Gray-Haired Mother Waiting. L&M: Edward S. Spora, 1918

There's a Green Hill Out in Flanders (There's a Green Hill Up in Maine). L&M: Allan J. Flynn, 1917

There's a Happy Heart in Maryland (and a Broken Heart in Brittany). L: Al Bryan; M: Jean Schwartz, 1919

There's a Light Shining Bright in the Window Tonight. L&M: C.A. Pfeiffer, 1918

*There's a Little Blue Star in the Window (and It Means All the World to Me). L: Paul B. Armstrong; M: F. Henri Klickmann, 1918

There's a Little Butterfly in Normandy. L&M: Harold Shaw, 1918

There's a Little Gold Star in the Service Flag. L: Joe Cronson; M: Harold B. Freeman, 1918

There's a Little Spark of Love Still Burning. L: Joseph McCarthy; M: Fred Fisher, 1915

*There's a Long, Long Trail. L: Stoddard King; M: Zo Elliott, 1913

There's a Lot of Lovin' Comin' to You When You Come Home. L: Bud Green; M: Edward G. Nelson, 1918

There's a Lump of Sugar Down in Dixie. L: Al Bryan and Jack Yellen; M: Albert Gumble, 1918

(There's a Maid in America) Made in America (a Maid for Every Boy). L&M: Glenn C. Leap, 1914

There's a Million Heroes in Each Corner of the U.S.A. L: Sam M. Lewis and Joe Young; M: Maurice Abrahams, 1917

There's a Mother Sitting in Sadness. L&M: Gust Miller, 1919

There's a Mother Waiting. M: John Dengler and William P. Zimmer, 1918

There's a Motherland for Every Yankee Man. L&M: Jesse Marion Worley, 1918

There's a New Flag Flying in Berlin. L: C.B. Snell; M: Leo Friedman, 1919

There's a New Watch on the Rhine. L&M: J.B. Foster, 1918

There's a No Man's Land Over Here. L: Max Cohn; M: Leo Friedman, 1919

*There's a Picture in My Old Kit Bag. L&M: Al Sweet, 1918

There's a Pretty Brown-Eyed Girlie and a Soldier Boy in Blue. L: A.M. Gilpatrick; M: Everett J. Evans, 1918

There's a Raggin' Tune, Democracy. L: J.G. Alexander; M: Bert Crossland and J.G. Alexander, 1918

*There's a Red-Bordered Flag in the Window. L: Fred Ziemer; M: J.R. Shannon, 1918

*There's a Service Flag Flying at Our House. L: Thomas Hoier and Bernie Grossman; M: Al W. Brown, 1917

There's a Service Flag in the Window. L&M: James A. Dillon, 1918

There's a Service Flag in the Window. L&M: C. Young, 1918

There's a Service Star Shining from Heaven (Some Are Red, White, and Blue and Gold). L: F. Guest; M: Artie Bowers, 1919

There's a Silver Star in Heaven for Every Star of Gold. L: Walter Gregory; M: Harold Dixon, 1919

There's a Soldier Boy Somewhere in France. L: J.L. Ripper; M: Carle M. Gibson, 1918

There's a Soldier Lad in Khaki Over There. L&M: Katherine Call Simonds, 1918

There's a Star for You in the Service Flag. L: A.W. Owen; M: E.D. Palmer, 1918

There's a Star in Blue in the Window for You. L: Ellen Reiff; M: Roy Hartzell, 1919

There's a Star in My Window for You. L: Mrs. W.W. Cox; M: Leo Friedman, 1919

There's a Star in Our Parish Flag for You. L: James Spaulding; M: A.H. Weber, 1918

There's a Star in Our Window. L: Max Dill; M: Leo Flanders, from stage production *As You Were*, 1919

There's a Star in the Service Flag for Me. L: M.H. Cox; M: Leo Friedman, 1918

There's a Sweet Little Girl (and She's Waiting for Me). L: Paul Wilson; M: R.A. Browne, 1918

There's a Tender Spot in This Heart of Mine

for the Boy Who Sailed Away. L: Al Parker; M: George L. Robertson, 1918

There's a Trace of the War in Everyone's Home. L: Edward Anthony; M: Louis G. Merrill, from stage production *Good Luck, Sam*, 1918

There's a Transport in the Harbor That Brought Me Back to You. L&M: Zella Mosher, 1919

*There's a Vacant Chair in Ev'ry Home To-night. L: Al Bryan; M: Ernest Breuer, 1917

There's a Vacant Chair in My Old Southern Home. L: Jack Yellen; M: Al Piantadosi, 1917

There's a Welcome Waiting for Them. L&M: Frank Swanson, 1919

There's a Winding Road Through Flanders. L: David M. Allan, Jr.; M: S. Harden Church, Jr., 1918

*There's an Angel Missing from Heaven (She'll Be Found Somewhere Over There). L: Paul B. Armstrong; M: Robert Speroy, 1918

There's Glory in Old Glory. L: Mrs. L.M. Sligh; M: Jack Gardner, 1917

There's Going to Be a Hot Time Someday in Berlin. L&M: Fanna Simmerman, 1918

There's Going to Be Another Independence Day. L&M: Jesse M. Winne, 1918

There's Going to Be Hell in Kaiserland, Kaiser Bill. L&M: H.G. Dunn, 1918

There's Going to Be Some Doin's While We're Flying Over There. L: C. Davis; M: Nellie Risher Roberts, 1918

There's No Friends Like the Friends from Way Back Home. L&M: F.C. Swan, 1918

There's No One Home to Miss Me When I Go Over There. L&M: H.C. Hardley, 1918

*There's Nobody Home but Me. L: Sam Ehrlich; M: Con Conrad, 1918

There's Not a Girl in France Like Mine. L&M: W.E. Healey, 1919

There's Not a Place Like the U.S.A. L&M: C.E. Braun, 1918

There's Nothing Left for Us to Do But Fight, Fight, Fight. L&M: Carlton Hughes, 1918

There's Nothing Too Good for Our Boys. L: Ethel Brunson; M: Leo Friedman, 1919

There's One More River That We're Going to Cross and That's the River Rhine. L: Ole Olson; M: Isham Jones, 1918

There's Room in the Ranks. L: Elsie Duncan Yale; M: Adam Geibel, 1917

There's Someone from This House Some-where in France. L: G.A. Mullen; M: R. Rech, 1918

There's Someone More Lonesome Than You.
L: Lou Klein; M: Harry Von Tilzer, 1917

There's Something 'Bout a Uniform That
Makes the Ladies Fall. L: Henry Fink; M:
Abner Silver, 1918

There's Ten Million Feathers in the Eagle
Over There. L&M: J.G. Fox, 1918

There's Victory in Your Eyes, Uncle Sammy.
L: Mrs. E.H. Smith; M: Leo Friedman,
1918

These Colors Will Not Run. L: Joseph Mc-
Carthy; M: Harry Carroll, from *Oh, Look*,
1918

These Soldier Boys of Dear Old Yankee
Land. L&M: Frank I. Hubin, 1919

These to the Front. L&M: M. A. DeWolfe
Howe; M: George W. Chadwick, 1918

They All Sang "Annie Laurie" (the Song
That Reaches Ev'ry Heart). L: J. Will
Callahan; M: F. Henri Klickmann, 1915

They Answered the Call. L: A.D. Orcutt; M:
Leo Friedman, 1919

They Are Fighting for Liberty. L: Augustus
F. Dannic; M: Marie Dannic, 1918

They Are Going to Win the Victory. L: William Sonders; M: Leo Friedman, 1918

They Are on Their Way. L: G.R. Stubing;
M: Frank W. Ford, 1918

They Are Tenting Tonight in Far-Off France.
L: J. Will Callahan; M: J. Will Callahan
and Blanche M. Tice, 1918

They Are Waiting Their Returning. L&M:
H.B. Tremain, 1919

They Are Yankee Doodle True. L: L. Baxter;
M: Robert H. Brennen, 1918

*They Can't Down the Red, White and Blue.
L&M: G.A. Pfeiffer, 1918

They Did Their Share, Now I'll Do Mine.
L&M: Harry Tobias, 1917

They Fought for Ev'ry One of Us. L: Bessie
Perry; M: Leo Friedman, 1919

They Fought for the Stars and Stripes. L&M:
Andrew Mack, 1917

They Go to End War. L: C.B. Galbreath;
M: A.J. Gantvoort, 1918

They Got the Kaiser's Goat. L: Pearl A.
McCoy; M: Artie Bowers, 1919

They Have Called Us to the Colors. L: John
R. Clemens; M: Charles H. Gabriel, 1917

They Have to Thank America. L&M: Mrs.
A.H. Frazer, 1918

They Have Won, Our Boys on the Western
Front. L&M: J.B. Chilcote, 1918

They Kept the Stars in Old Glory. L: T.J.
Sheehan; M: Leo Friedman, 1919

They Know It Now in Kaiserland. L: E.J.
Murphy; M: Leo Friedman, 1919

They Needed Us Over Here. L: V.L. Furse;
M: Frank W. Ford, 1919

They Shall Not Pass (Battle of the Marne
War Song). L: Henry E. Muchmore; M:
Otto C. Schasberger, 1918

They Shall Not Pass (March). L: A.W.
Osborn; M: Frank W. Ford, 1919

They Shall Return. L: J. Lewis Milligan; M:
John W. Worth, 1918

They Sleep in Fields of Battle. L&M: Duncan J. Muir, 1919

They Sleep, Sleep, Sleep (Memorial Quartet).
L&M: The Rev. J.B. Blair, 1918

They Took a Slice of Paradise and Made the
U.S.A. L: Harry Dexter; M: Harry Dexter
and Luther A. Clark, 1917

They Took Down the Kaiser Bill. L&M:
C.W. Welsh, 1918

They Were All Out of Step but Jim. L&M:
Irving Berlin, 1918

They Will Come Back to Me from Across
the Sea. L&M: Eleanor M. Biddle, 1919

They Will Get Him Over There. L: F.L.
Schifler; M: Leo Friedman, 1918

They'll Be Mighty Proud in Dixie of Their
Old Black Joe. L&M: Harry Carroll, 1918

They'll Come Back to the Land of the Free.
L&M: William Hurley, 1919

They'll Make the Kaiser Go. L: Francis
Marion; M: Z.M. Parvin, 1918

They'll Never Give Up the Fight Till the
Kaiser's Out of Sight. L: J. Acott; M: Leo
Friedman, 1918

They'll Never Lick the Infantry (in a Hundred Thousand Years). L&M: Sinclair
Randall, 1918

They'll Whip the Kaiser Yet. L&M: Marie
Leighton, 1918

They're All True Blue. L&M: Frank R.
Deuell, 1918

They're Camped Beneath the Stars and
Stripes to Fight for Uncle Sam. L&M: Earl
S. Rogers, 1917

*They're Coming Back. L&M: Sam Habelow,
1919

They're Coming Back to the U.S.A. (Tramp,
Tramp, Tramp). L&M: Tom Page, 1918

They're Coming Home. L&M: R.J. Powers,
1918

They're Coming Home, All but One. L: Gertrude McCollor; M: Leo Friedman, 1919

They're Going to Fight for You and Me. L:
Mrs. C.A. Shine; M: Leo Friedman, 1918

They're in the Trenches. L&M: Jule J. Levy, 1918

They're Knitting Everywhere I Go. L: E.H. Nagel; M: Leo Friedman, 1918

They're Off to Gain the Victory and Fight for Uncle Sam. L&M: Gertrude E. Stevens, 1917

*They're on Their Way to Germany. L&M: Halsey K. Mohr, 1917

They're on Their Way to Kan the Kaiser. L: Harry C. Pyle, Jr.; M: Louis Thomas, 1918

They're on Their Way to the U.S.A. L: Philip Shapiro; M: Sam Chefitz, 1919

They're Over There, They're Over There! L: William Eiff; M: Leo Friedman, 1918

They're the Stars in Our Service Flag. L: Jack Mason and Al Piantadosi; M: Jack Glogau, from stage production *Who Stole the Hat?*, 1918

They've Camped Beneath the Stars and Stripes to Fight for Uncle Sam. L&M: Earl S. Rogers, 1917

They've Gone to Fight Old Kaiser Bill. L: V. Callaghan; M: Roy Hartzell, 1919

They've Never Beaten Old Glory and They Never, Never Will! L: A.J. Tucker; M: George Graff, Jr., 1919

They've Taken My Laddie Away from Me. L: Gail Allenbaugh; M: Leo Friedman, 1918

They've Troubled Our Uncle Sammy, Tried to Tramp on the Red, White and Blue. L: J. Ulrich; M: Theodore M. Kratt, 1918

Think of the Boys from Home Sweet Home. L&M: Harry F. Kissell, 1919

Think of the Boys Over There (March). L&M: J.W. Stewart, 1918

Think of the Joy When the Boys Come Home. L&M: H. Roe Goulding, 1918

Thirtieth Division. L: C. Robertson; M: Artie Bowers, 1919

This Present Trouble Will Not Long Endure. L: Maria Malmquist; M: Roy Hartzell, 1918

Those Draftin' Blues. L&M: Maceo Pinkard, 1917

Those Victory Bells. L&M: Lillian May Skuce, 1919

*(Though Duty Calls) It's Hard to Say Goodbye. L&M: W.R. Williams, 1917

Though I Shared My Love with Uncle Sam (I Gave My Heart to You). L&M: Leo T. Corcoran, 1917

Though I'm a Long, Long Way from Tipperary, My Love Lies Where the Hills Are Green. L: Jack Gartland; M: Charles

James, 1914

Thoughts of Peace. L: D. Swanberg; M: Leo Friedman, 1918

Three Cheers for Liberty. L&M: Marie A. Miller, 1918

Three Cheers for Little Belgium. L: Charles Wilmott; M: Herman E. Darewski, 1915

Three Cheers for Old U.S.A. L&M: Maud J. Howe, 1918

Three Cheers for Our Boys. L: A.D. Baker; M: Robert H. Brennen, 1917

Three Cheers for Our Country, the U.S.A.! L: J. Forbym; M: Eugene Platzmann, 1918

Three Cheers for the Army & Navy. L&M: Gordon V. Thompson, 1917

Three Cheers for the Boys. L: Lyman Whitney Allen; M: Grant Colfax Tullar, 1915

Three Cheers for the Flags of the Allies. L: J.B. McAulay; M: Leo Friedman, 1919

Three Cheers for the Grand Old Flag. L&M: Edmund M. Capen, 1917

Three Cheers for the Land of the Free. L&M: Adam Preston [Henry S. Sawyer], 1918

Three Cheers for the Red Cross. L: M. Latremoille-Wells; M: George Lowell Tracy, 1917

Three Cheers for the Soldier Boys. L: M. Boyd; M: Artie Bowers, 1919

Three Cheers for the U.S.A. L&M: Josephine C. Nolan, 1918

Three Cheers for the U.S.A. L&M: A.A. Kuester, 1918

Three Cheers for the U.S.A. L: Babelle Reinhardt; M: Henry deSola Mendes, 1918

Three Cheers for Uncle Sam. L: J. Scott Junkin; M: M.K. Legler, 1917

Three Cheers for Uncle Sam. L&M: Anita L. Weidemann, 1918

Three Cheers for Uncle Sammy, Hip, Hip, Hooray! L&M: E.F. Knapp, 1918

Three Cheers for Yankee Doodle and Dixie Land! L&M: Nell Marshall, 1918

Three Cheers for You, Uncle Sam (March). L: Nixon Waterman; M: Leo Rich Lewis, 1917

Three Colors, Red, White and Blue. L: J. Frank Davis; M: H.W.B. Barnes, 1917

Three Great Big Cheers for Uncle Sam! L&M: Victor Courville, 1918

The 362nd Infantry March. M: F. Destabelle, 1918

Three Wonderful Letters from Home. L: Ballard MacDonald and Joe Goodwin; M: James F. Hanley, 1917

Through Germany We Will Go. L: George W. Bilbo; M: B. Wise, 1917

Through the Gates of Old Berlin. L&M:
G.M. Blaine, 1919

Through the Straits (March). M: P.F. Brady,
1918

*Throw Me a Kiss (from Over the Sea). L:
Raymond B. Egan; M: Richard A. Whiting, 1917

*Throw No Stones in the Well That Gives
You Water. L: Arthur Fields; M: Theodore
Morse, 1917

Tidings of Peace. L&M: Minnie Roberts
Smith, 1915

Till All Be Free. L&M: A.S. Crockett, 1918

Till Germany Is Beaten to Her Knees. L&M:
T.J. Honaker, 1918

Till I Come Home to You. L: Richard Fechheimer; M: W.B. Kernell, from stage production *Goodbye, Bill*, 1918

Till Over the Top We Go. L&M: Roy L.
Burtch, 1918

Till the Liberty Bell Rings Out Once More
(As It Did in the Days Gone By). L: Percival Knight; M: Gitz Rice, 1918

Till the Stars and Stripes Are Flying in Berlin. L: M.J. MacNeill; M: J.M. Smith, Jr.,
1918

*Till the Work of the Yanks Is Done. L&M:
Leon DeCosta, 1917

Till Victory Is Won. L&M: R.B. Dugan, 1919

Till We Conquer on Land and Sea. L: M.A.
Hanscom; M: Leo Friedman, 1918

Till We Have Pushed Them Out of France.
L&M: G.W. Richie, 1918

*Till We Meet Again. L: Raymond B. Egan;
M: Richard A. Whiting, 1918

Till We Meet Again. L&M: Erle Threlkeld,
1918

Till You Come Home Again. L: Edward
Lockton; M: Brenda Gayne, 1916

Tim Rooney's at the Fightin'. L&M: Norah
Flynn, 1915

Time Will Bring Peace and You, Dear. L:
Kate Gibson; M: Vincent Shaw, 1918

Tip-Top Tipperary Mary. L: Ballard Mac-
Donald; M: Harry Carroll, 1914

'Tis Not the Uniform That Makes the
Soldier. L: Sam M. Lewis; M: Monroe H.
Rosenfeld, 1917

'Tis the Same Star-Spangled Banner. L: J.R.
Lintelman; M: Roy Hartzell, 1918

'Tis the Trumpet of Duty Sounding for Me.
L&M: Eben Francis Thompson, 1918

'Tis Your Country Calling You. L: S.A. Mc-
Elhinny; M: G. Burg, 1917

To a Lonesome Heart (The Soldier's Ode).
L&M: Paul L. Specht, 1917

To a Soldier's Sweetheart. L: A.G. Wilson;
M: Leo Friedman, 1918

To All America: Come, Let's Arise! L:
E.Z.G. Walter; M: Roy Hartzell, 1919

To America and You. L&M: Orville C.
Seeley, 1918

To Arms (March). L: R.B. Eastman; M:
Walt S.H. Jones, 1917

To Arms. L: E.B. Jackson; M: Leo Friedman, 1918

To Arms. L: Mrs. William Martin; M: Leo
Friedman, 1918

To Arms, All Ye Americans! L: F.D. Smith;
M: Leo Friedman, 1918

To Arms! Canadians! L: W.T. Sleeman; M:
Leo Friedman, 1918

To Arms, to Arms, 'Tis Your Country's Call!
L&M: M.H. Hansen, 1917

To Arms, Ye Loyal Sons! L&M: J.H. Alleman, 1917

To Arms, Ye Sons of Victory! L&M: J.W.
Lambert, 1918

To Berlin (or, The Victory March). L: C.O.
Lind; M: Artie Bowers, 1919

To Berlin We Will Go (March). M: George
Henry Lloyd, 1917

To Conquer Germany. L: Ralph Butterfield;
M: William Pegg, Jr., 1917

To Democracy's Call. L&M: L. Birkhead,
1918

To France. L: Daniel M. Henderson; M: R.
Huntington Woodman, 1918

To France (March). L&M: Giacomo Quintano, 1918

To France for France and Old Glory. L:
John Suarez; M: Leo Friedman, 1918

To Get the Kaiser. L: E. Landrus; M: Artie
Bowers, 1919

To Hell Mit Kaiser Bill. L&M: J.W. Speer,
1919

To Help Our Uncle Sam. L: Mrs. I.L.
Decker; M: Leo Friedman, 1918

To Keep Old Glory Waving. L&M: Pearl
Connor Riggs, 1918

To My Lonely Girl Back Home. L: A.F.
Shinhearl; M: Leo Friedman, 1918

To Our Colors. L: G.W. Pangburn; M:
William C. Radtke, 1918

To Our Comrades O'er the Sea. L: J.F.
Weybright; M: Leo Friedman, 1918

To Save the World for Freedom. L: Frederick H. Martens; M: Arthur Leonard, 1917

To the Blue and the Gray on the Fields of
France. L: George Morrow Mayo; M:
Charles H. Gabriel, 1918

To the Boys Over There. L: W. Zschunke; M: Leo Friedman, 1918

To the Foe. L: P.J. O'Reilly; M: Raymond Loughborough, 1914

To the Front (March). M: S.B. Stambaugh, 1915

To the Front. L: W.C. Poole; M: B.D. Ackley, 1918

To the German Son. L: L.C. Pierce; M: Frank W. Ford, 1918

To the Goal. L: A. Bateman; M: Leo Friedman, 1919

To the Mothers. L: Mrs. W.H. Blanton; M: Leo Friedman, 1918

To the Nations. L: J.C. Stewart; M: Leo Friedman, 1918

To the Sons of the Blue and Gray. L: George Morrow Mayo; M: H.W. Fairbanks, 1918

To the Youth of Our Land. L&M: Mollie [Julia M. Moore], 1918

To Victory. L&M: Haldor Lillenas, 1918

To Victory. L: M.M. Byrne; M: Leo Friedman, 1918

To Victory (March). L: Ethel Watts Munford; M: Henry Hadley, 1918

To Victory (March). L&M: Alrick G. Spencer, 1918

To Victory (March). M: Theodora Dutton, 1919

To Victory and Berlin. L: R. Richardson; M: Leo Friedman, 1918

To Victory and to Glory. L&M: E.V.Z. Mallaby, 1917

To Victory! To Victory! with Wilson, Our President, as Guide. L: J.J. Carney; M: P.B. Story, 1918

Toast to Our Flag. L: Thomas McElligott; M: John McKenzie, 1917

Together We Go to the Front Today. L: Elizabeth F. Guptill; M: Leon Berg, 1918

Tom, Dick, and Harry and Jack (Hurry Back). L: Howard Johnson; M: Milton Ager, 1917

Tommie Atkins (International March Song). L: E.T. Luckie; M: Ella R. Luckie, 1917

Tommy and Frenchy and Sammy, That's Me. L: C. Thompson; M: C.H. Jensen, 1918

Tommy's Army. L: Fred E. Weatherly; M: Arthur W. Marchant, 1915

Too Proud to Fight Beneath the Spangled Banner. L: K.H. Schmidt; M: George Schleiffarth, 1917

Toot Sweet. L: Raymond B. Egan; M: Richard A. Whiting, from stage production *Toot Sweet*, 1919

Torpedo Jim. L: Roger Lewis; M: James V. Monaco, 1917

Torpedo Rag. M: Oscar Young, 1917

Tramp, Tramp, Tramp (March). L: Edna Schluraff; M: Walter Webb, 1918

Tramp. Tramp, Tramp, Boys (March Song of the Allies). L&M: Robert T. Baxter, 1917

Tramp, Tramp, Tramp to Battlefields of France. L: John Whaley; M: Leo Friedman, 1918

Trench, Trench, Trench, Our Boys Are Trenching. L: W. Dillen; M: May Hill, 1918

Trench Trot. L: Jack Frost; M: F. Henri Klickmann, 1918

Tribute to Our Flag. L: E.F. Pigg; M: Leo Friedman, 1919

Tribute to Our Soldiers. L: F. McGuire; M: Luther A. Clark, 1918

Tribute to the National Guards, Army and Navy. L&M: B.A. Koellhoffer, 1917

Triumph for Old Glory. L: E.C. Mason; M: Leo Friedman, 1919

Triumph of Democracy (March). L: G. Attenborough; M: E.R.U. Civita, 1918

Triumph of Freedom (March). L&M: Clara B. Groves, 1918

Triumph of Old Glory. L&M: J.E. Wells, 1918

Triumphant Mourning. L: Gertrude Knevels; M: Louis Victor Saar, 1919

Triumphant Troops (March). M: Lillian M. Cory and P. Corte Dalbey, 1919

Trooper Flynn. L&M: Jack Mahoney, 1917

True Blue America (March). M: Ed Pharion, 1917

True Born Soldier Man. L&M: Irving Berlin, 1917

True Stars of Blue. L: Damian Lavery; M: Andrew Green, 1918

True to My Soldier Boy. L&M: O.R. Gable, 1918

True to the Old Red, White and Blue. L: N.M. Vallier; M: Roy Hartzell, 1918

Trusting Uncle Sam. L&M: W.J. Hales, 1918

Try to Be a Hero, Serve the Old Red, White and Blue. L: W.C. Beaver; M: S. Montroy, 1918

The Tune of the Stars and Stripes. L&M: Willie White, 1918

Tune Your Bugles (or, The Allies' Jollification) (A Patriotic Song). M: Hazel O'Neall, 1918

'Twas Only the Kaiser's Dream. L&M: Harold Rubin, 1918

The 26th [Division]. L&M: Mrs. L.B. Bent, 1919

Twilight in Lorraine. L&M: Arthur A. Penn, 1918

Two Little Eyes Are Watching for a Daddy Far Away. L&M: H.C. Weasner, 1918

U

U — and the Red, White and Blue. L: J. Calvert; M: Leo Friedman, 1919

U-Boat Deutschland (March). M: Joseph Thome, 1916

Uncle Sam. L&M: Elizabeth Ayres Kidd, 1917

Uncle Sam. L&M: James Cooper Madden, Jr., 1917

Uncle Sam. L&M: J. William Pope, 1917

Uncle Sam. L&M: E. Niedringhaus, 1918

Uncle Sam. L&M: M.C. Guitteau, 1919

Uncle Sam. L: Anna Galligan; M: Leo Friedman, 1919

Uncle Sam. L: H. Wilcox; M: Arthur Stanley, 1919

Uncle Sam and Aunt Columbia. L&M: C.W. Freeman, 1917

Uncle Sam and His Battering Ram. L: R.P. Hall; M: Ida K. Mervine, 1918

Uncle Sam and His Family (March). L: C. Roth; M: Will N. Rogers, 1918

Uncle Sam and the Boys. L&M: Irene M. Chavannes, 1918

Uncle Sam and William. L&M: J.W. Van DeVenter, 1917

Uncle Sam and You. L: L.M. Johnston; M: Leo Friedman, 1919

Uncle Sam, Are You Prepared? (Patriotic Reverie). L: Jacob E. Meeker; M: E. Van Loock, 1916

Uncle Sam Can Lick Them All. L&M: Gus Schaffer, 1918

Uncle Sam, Do You Need Any of My Help? L: Joseph Perrone; M: Leo Friedman, 1919

Uncle Sam, Don't Take My Man Away. L&M: Harold Shaw, 1918

Uncle Sam, Every Man Will See You Through. L&M: J.C. Spray, 1918

Uncle Sam Fighting the German Kaiser, Old Fritz, and the Prussian Huns. L&M: Thomas J. Northey, 1919

Uncle Sam Has Called His Boys. L: C. Calcote; M: Leo Friedman, 1919

Uncle Sam Has His Arms Around the World. L: Roa A. Robbins; M: H. Gunn, 1918

Uncle Sam Has Hit the Trail. L: Margaret Wallace; M: Charles A. Sheldon, Jr., 1917

Uncle Sam Has No Chip on His Shoulder. L: G.W. Steele; M: Anna J. Reheiser, 1916

Uncle Sam, Here I Am. L: Bertha S. Tiffany; M: Bernie K. Wiseman, 1917

Uncle Sam, Here's My Hand. L&M: S.J. Chamberlain, 1917

Uncle Sam, Hold Our Flag Up High. L&M: Anna Yogg, 1918

Uncle Sam, I Am Sure Sorry for You. L: R.H. Perrett; M: Leo Friedman, 1917

Uncle Sam Is a Grand Old Man (War Song). L&M: John Christian, 1917

Uncle Sam Is Asking for Your Hand Today. L: E. Lippert; M: Leo Friedman, 1918

Uncle Sam Is Calling. L: Helen Keller; M: P.B. Story, 1917

Uncle Sam Is Calling. L&M: Joseph D. Nirella, 1917

Uncle Sam Is Calling. L: Lura M. Emerson; M: C. Philip Goewey, 1918

Uncle Sam Is Calling Me. L&M: Pauline M. Vanderburg, 1918

Uncle Sam Is Calling Me. L: A. Livingston; M: John G. Zabriskie, 1918

Uncle Sam Is Calling Now. L: Robert Odgers; M: Leo Friedman, 1918

Uncle Sam Is Calling You. L: M. Batson; M: Glennie Clark, 1917

Uncle Sam Is Calling You. L&M: Nadine C. Waltner, 1917

Uncle Sam Is Calling You. L: B.B. Bromley; M: Leo Friedman, 1919

Uncle Sam Is Calling You, Wilson. L&M: Charles C. Miles, 1916

Uncle Sam Is Hot. L: G.H. Dorton; M: Leo Friedman, 1918

Uncle Sam Is in the Game. L: W.W. Campbell; M: John LaMalfa, 1918

Uncle Sam Is Now Calling You (or, The Spirit of 1917). L&M: Vincenzina Colosimo, 1917

Uncle Sam Is Over There. L&M: H.E. Evans, 1918

Uncle Sam Is Praying for the Stars and Stripes and You. L: F. Toutloff; M: Arthur Stanley, 1919

Uncle Sam Marching Through Germany. L&M: W.A. Mott, 1918

Uncle Sam Needs You. L: W.J. MacDonald; M: Minerva G. Trumble, 1917

Uncle Sam Needs You. L: D.M. Thompson; M: John Krewson, 1917

Uncle Sam Over There. L: W.B. James; M: W.H. Banks, 1919

Uncle Sam, Please Keep Your Eye on That Gal of Mine. L: Charles A. Snyder; M: Oscar Doctor and Charles A. Snyder, 1917

Uncle Sam, the Peaceful Fighting Man. L:
F.J. Hohnhorst; M: Leo Friedman, 1918

Uncle Sam to the Front (March of Liberty).
M: Jack Roberts, 1918

Uncle Sam, Uncle Sam, I'll Fight and Die for
You. L: J.J. Gallagher; M: G.H. Madin,
1917

Uncle Sam, We Hear You Calling. L&M:
Joe Jordan, 1917

Uncle Sam, We Love You. L&M: George K.
Wenig, 1917

Uncle Sam, We'll Help You Win the War. L:
"Fennwood"; M: Lenna Wood, 1918

Uncle Sam, We're Ready. L&M: William M.
Wright, 1917

Uncle Sam, We're Strong for You. L&M:
T.H. Dempsey, 1917

Uncle Sam, We're with You. L&M: B.E.
Savage and "Winkle and Dean," 1917

Uncle Sam Will Be Right There. L: O.
Jenne; M: O.H. Wood, 1917

Uncle Sam Will Fight (A Patriotic Song).
L&M: John B. McPhail, 1918

Uncle Sam Will Strike the Kaiser Out. L&M:
Robert Dixon, 1918

Uncle Sam, You're a Grand Old Man. L:
Joseph King; M: Orlando Jones, 1915

Uncle Sam, You're the Man! L&M: A.J.
Collison, 1918

Uncle Sammie's Boys. L&M: L.C. Ross, 1917

Uncle Sammie's Boys in Khaki. L: E.D.
Hamilton; M: Leo Friedman, 1919

Uncle Sammies of the Red, White and Blue.
L&M: Lillian Copeland, 1918

Uncle Sammie's Sam (A Patriotic Song).
L&M: Alice Mathews, 1918

Uncle Sammy. L: C. Davis; M: Nellie Risher
Roberts, 1918

Uncle Sammy. L&M: Mr. and Mrs. Hiram
B. Browning, 1918

Uncle Sammy (March). L&M: Abe Holz-
mann, 1918

Uncle Sammy and the Kaiser. L&M: A.L.
Purdy, 1917

Uncle Sammy, Here's My Boy. L&M: Richard Cox and Francis Wright, 1917

Uncle Sammy Is a-Calling You. L&M: Jimmie N. Hall, 1917

Uncle Sammy Keeps the Family Collar Full.
L&M: Harry D. Kerr, Anna Chandler, and
Dave Dreyer, 1917

Uncle Sammy Loves the Stars and Stripes.
L&M: H.A. Shambaugh, 1917

Uncle Sammy! Oh, Uncle Sam! L: A.R.
Koller; M: Leo Friedman, 1918

*Uncle Sammy, Take Care of My Girl. L:
Betty Morgan; M: Jimmie Morgan, 1918

Uncle Sammy Wants Me. L: H. O'Connor;
M: Leo Friedman, 1918

Uncle Sammy Wants You Now. L&M: J.H.
Saxton, 1918

Uncle Sammy, We'll Be There. L&M: R.S.
Freese, 1917

Uncle Sammy, We'll Fight for You. L&M:
Lew Morgan, 1917

Uncle Sammy's Army. L: M.H. Morse; M:
H.M. Dolph, 1916

Uncle Sammy's at Bat. L&M: "The Great
Howard" [Howard Miller], 1918

Uncle Sammy's Boys. L&M: Clara L. Baker,
1918

Uncle Sammy's Boys (March). L&M: L.A.
Jouanneau, 1918

Uncle Sammy's Calling You. L&M: John
Heron, 1917

Uncle Sammy's Goin' to Win This War. L:
J.T. Cover; M: Leo Friedman, 1919

Uncle Sammy's in This Fight. L&M: Frank
E. Nugent, 1917

Uncle Sammy's Little Rookies. L&M: Effie
Louise Koogle, 1918

Uncle Sammy's Sammee. L: Harold R. Parsons; M: Edward Gage, 1917

Uncle Sam's a Father. L: W.E. McCasland;
M: Leo Friedman, 1918

Uncle Sam's Army. L: H. Reich; M: Roy
Hartzell, 1919

Uncle Sam's Army. L: M.H. Morse; M:
H.M. Dolph, 1916

Uncle Sam's Awake. L&M: Charles B. Weston, 1917

Uncle Sam's Boys. L: H.B.S. Short; M:
Carlo Carleton, 1917

Uncle Sam's Boys. L: Mrs. H. Barnes; M:
Roy Hartzell, 1918

Uncle Sam's Boys. L: M. Adams; M: Leo
Friedman, 1918

Uncle Sam's Boys. L: I.M. Hooper; M: Leo
Friedman, 1919

Uncle Sam's Call. L&M: Anthony J. Showalter, 1918

Uncle Sam's Call to Arms. L&M: Pearl M.
Matthews, 1918

Uncle Sam's Crusaders (American Boys Over
the Sea). L: O.F. Conlon; M: Fay Foster,
1918

Uncle Sam's Glories. L&M: Lu B. Cake, 1918

Uncle Sam's Gone a-Gunning. L: Charlotte
Butz; M: Edna Pennington, 1917

Uncle Sam's Justice for All. L: Mrs. C.A.
Morgan; M: Artie Bowers, 1919

Uncle Sam's Laddies. L: W.H. Slingerland; M: C.H. Congdon, 1918

Uncle Sam's on the War Path (Kaiser Bill Is Feeling Blue). L: J.C. Oakes; M: Leo Friedman, 1918

Uncle Sam's Prayer. L: S.J.N. Brock; M: Leo Friedman, 1918

Uncle Sam's Roundup. L: Wallace D. Coburn; M: Homer Tourjée, 1918

Uncle Sam's Sons. L: G.M. Marshall; M: Leo Friedman, 1919

Uncle Sam's Warning. L&M: W.R. Prime, 1916

Uncle Samuel's Men. L&M: W.L. Armstrong, 1918

Unconditional Surrender Is Our Plea. L&M: M.S. Goldner, 1919

Und Yah, der Kaiser, Too. L&M: H.W. Copeland, 1917

Under Liberty's Banner (March). M: Harold Otto Piatti, 1917

Under Old Glory. L&M: Frederick Wilson, 1918

Under Our Old Flag. L: G.M. Beiriger; M: Leo Friedman, 1918

*Under the American Flag. L: Andrew B. Sterling; M: Harry Von Tilzer, 1915

Under the Banner of Victory (March). M: Franz Von Blon, 1919

Under the Blue Skies of France. L: Arthur J. Lamb; M: Alfred Solman, 1918

Under the Flag of Peace (March). M: Alfred Palumbo, 1915

Under the Red Cross (March). M: T.H. Rollinson, 1919

Under the Red, White and Blue. L&M: C.C. Case, 1918

Under the Skies of France. L: E.M. Stevens; M: Leo Friedman, 1919

Under the Starry Flag (March). M: F.E. Cook, 1917

Under the Stars and Stripes (March). L&M: Edward J. Grant, 1916

Under the Stars and Stripes (March). L: Madison Cawein; M: Frederick S. Converse, 1918

Under the Stars and Stripes. L&M: L.B. Lane, 1918

Under Victory's Flag (March). M: H.H. Kortemeyer, 1919

The Undesirable Hun. L&M: S. Wilson, 1918

Unfurl the Flag. L&M: S.L. Harkey, 1917

Unfurl the Flag. L: M.M. Parker; M: W.W. Wright, 1917

Unfurl the Flag (March). M: Alberto Himan. 1917

Unfurl the Flag of Freedom (A Patriotic Hymn). L&M: E.J. Adams, 1917

Unfurling of the Flag. L: Clara Endicott Sears; M: John Hopkins Densmore, 1917

Union and Liberty. L: Oliver Wendell Holmes; M: Frederick A. Stock, 1918

Union and Liberty. L: Oliver Wendell Holmes; M: J.C. Donovan, 1918

The Union Boys Are Coming. L: Mary P. Sayers; M: W.E. Potter, 1918

United America (March). M: Ernest Weber, 1916

United Hearts in the United States. L: F. DeRahhal; M: Leo Friedman, 1918

United Nations' Banner. L&M: G.F. Jefferson, 1918

United States. L: Philip C. Walters; M: Taliesin Griffith, 1917

United States (the People's National Hymn). L&M: William Leander Sheets, 1917

United States. L&M: A.H. Powell, 1918

United States. L&M: Henry Gamble, 1919

United States, America. L: H.A. Pooch; M: Leo Friedman, 1918

United States, America. L: W. Boughton; M: Carl G. Schmidt, 1918

The United States Army (March). M: H.J. Crosby, 1916

United States Democracy March. L&M: Eliza Doyle Smith, 1918

United States Field Artillery March ("The Caissons Go Rolling Along"). Arranged by John Philip Sousa, 1918

United States Girls. L: Gertrude E. Merrifield; M: Leo Friedman, 1919

United States Navy (March). M: H.J. Crosby, 1917

United States of America (New National Song). L&M: Marie Paapke, 1915

United States of America. L&M: J. Austin Springer, 1917

United States of America. L: L. Rodrigue; M: Harry Weston, 1917

United States Song (A New National Anthem). L&M: Jessie Beattie Thomas, 1914

United States, the Country We Love (March). L&M: A. Tallman, 1918

United We Should Stand. L: C.G.V. Sjöström; M: O. Sjöström, 1917

United We Stand. L&M: Fred E. Holly, 1917

United We Stand (March). L&M: Rubin Rudolfe, 1917

United We Stand (for Country, Honor, Home, Love and Liberty). L&M: R. Clark, 1918

Universal Democracy (or, The World Must Be Free). L&M: Brayton Vanderwater, 1918

Universal Peace (March). L&M: Jack Mahoney, 1914

Universal Peace. L&M: Ted S. Barron, 1917

Universal Peace Jubilee (March). M: H.F. Neilsson, 1914

*Universal Peace Song (God Save Us All). L: Al Bryan; M: Harry Tierney, 1917

Unknown, Alone, Somewhere Over There He Sleeps. L&M: Louise A. Biechner, 1919

Until You Went Away. L: Ed Pottle; M: Floyd E. Whitmore, 1919

Up and At 'Em (A Patriotic Military One-Step). L: H.A. Stedman; M: E.W. Stedman, 1918

Up! Up! America! L&M: Herbert Gould, 1917

Up with the Flag. L: Julia H. Johnson; M: C.C. Case, 1917

Up with the Flag, Old Glory. L&M: G.E. Smith, 1917

Up with the Stars and Stripes. L: G.L. Battersby; M: Leo Friedman, 1918

Upon the Battlefield. L: Victor Machet; M: Arthur Angel and Goebel Reeves, 1917

The Urge of the Liberty Loan. L: Mrs. F. Wilder; M: Jeanette Wilder, 1918

U.S. L: A.M. Hard; M: Roy Hartzell, 1918

U.S. and England. L: J.J. Azbill; M: George C. Polini, 1915

U.S. Army (March). L&M: A. Staeger, 1918

U.S. Aviation Blues. M: Clyde Divers, 1918

U.S. Aviators March. M: Lester Emerson, 1918

U.S. Battle Cry. L&M: D.T. Heide, 1918

U.S. Boys (March). L&M: V. Rogers-Griffin, 1917

U.S. Boys in France. L: H.D. Thompson; M: Leo Friedman, 1919

U.S. Call to Arms (March). M.O. Ruch, 1916

U.S. First. L: E.A. Perkins; M: Clifton Keith, 1915

U.S. Flag. L&M: M.A. Rader, 1918

U.S. Forward Forever! (March). M: A.E. Norma, 1918

The U.S. Is with You. L&M: A.J. Leisner, 1918

U.S. Khaki Song. L&M: Alma Bates, 1918

U.S. Lads. L: Jennie Ellis; M: Leo Friedman, 1918

U.S. Loyalty. L: W. Cheney Beckwith; M: Alfred Henry Beckwith, 1915

U.S. Marines (March). L&M: M.J.C. Macauley, 1915

U.S. Marines — You're Three-in-One. L&M: J. Sullivan, 1918

U.S. National Spirit (March). M: Elizabeth McFadden, 1917

U.S. Navy League. L&M: A.J. Denis, 1917

U.S. Neutrality March. M: Eva Joy Shadday, 1916

The U.S. of the World. L: K. Oliver-McCoy; M: John F. Thomas, 1917

U.S. Patriots. L: M. Cramer; M: Eddie Williams and Arthur Jahnke, 1917

U.S. Patrol (March). M: W.A. Crocker, 1918

U.S. Rainbow Division (March). M: Otto C. Schasberger, 1918

U.S. Soldiers' March Song. L&M: Viola C. Snider McManis, 1917

U.S. Spells Us. L&M: Hazel M. Bell, 1918

U.S. Spells Us. L: William Coleman Wilson; M: Harold Johnston, 1918

U.S. Starry Emblem March. M: W.L. Skaggs, 1918

The U.S., Us, All for Us. L&M: A.B. Lenz, 1918

U.S. Victory (March). M: F.J. LoSciuto, 1918

U.S.A. L: L.C. Eddy, Jr.; M: Dorothy Eddy, 1917

U.S.A. L. Watt Reber; M. Alfred Holzworth, 1917

U.S.A. L: E.M. Fish; M: Leo Friedman, 1919

U.S.A. Did Win the Day. L: Mrs. F.M. Waggener; M: Leo Friedman, 1919

U.S.A. Doing Her Bit. L: Irene C. Simmons; M: Leo Friedman, 1918

U.S.A. for Me. L&M: L.L. Picket, 1919

The U.S.A. for Mine. L: Mrs. C.H. Kemper; M: Leo Friedman, 1918

U.S.A. Forever. L: Edmund Vance Cooke; M: "Dixie," 1918

U.S.A. Grand March. M: H.G. Schuette, 1918

The U.S.A. Is Calling Me. L&M: Donie Gray, 1917

The U.S.A. Is Here to Stay. L: Ella Campbell; M: Ruby Miller, 1918

U.S.A. Liberty Waltz. M: Mrs. L.E. Schroeder, 1917

U.S.A. March to Victory. L: Marion Vedder; M: G.F. Rodrock, 1918

The U.S.A. Must Win. L: L.L. Sackinger; M: D.H. Hawthorne, 1918

U.S.A. 1917 (March). M: Charles C. Heath, 1917

The U.S.A. Soldier Boys Are Off for Germanee. L: G. Brothers; M: P.B. Story, 1918

U.S.A. Victory. L: T.A. Regan; M: Leo Friedman, 1918

U.S.A. Victory (March). M: D.M. Gittelson, 1918

U.S.A. Victory March (Our Own America). L: William E. Cornwell; M: William E. Cornwell and A. Jackson Bloom, 1918

The U.S.A. Was in the Game to Stay. L: E.H. Clifton; M: Leo Friedman, 1919

The U.S.A. Was Never Defeated, Kaiser Bill. L: C.E. Handshoe; M: Leo Friedman, 1919

U.S.A., We Love You. L&M: E.G. Bauman, 1917

The U.S.A. Will Find a Way (A Patriotic Song of Faith). L&M: H.C. Eldridge, 1917

*The U.S.A. Will Lay the Kaiser Away. L: Jacob Dettling; M: Charles Roy Cox, 1917

The U.S.A.'s the Place for Me. L&M: H.T. McCormick, 1918

Usona's Liberty Song. L&M: Irene deS. Willis, 1918

V

Vanguard of Democracy (March). M: K.L. King, 1918

Vanguard of Freedom (Floating Ever the Red, White and Blue). L&M: J.M. Day, 1918

Verdun. L: Harold Begbie; M: D.W. Rowley, 1918

The Verdun Front. L&M: Helen Despard, 1918

Verdun Shivers. M: G.T. McDowell, 1918

The Veteran and His Flag. L: E.M. Giffin; M: Leo Friedman, 1919

Veterans of the Great World War. L: Tom Twohig; M: Sam Habelow, 1919

Victorious America (March). L&M: Clarence M. Jones, 1918

Victorious Democracy. M: Gaston Borch, 1919

Victorious Return. M: William E. Haesche, 1919

Victorious Sons of America. L&M: Grace Hamilton Morrey, 1919

Victorious 26th Yankee Division (March). M: Barrington Seargent, 1918

Victory. L: W.L. Lauher; M: Juna B. Lauher, 1917

Victory. L: Jack Wilson and Ben Bard; M: M.K. Jerome, 1918

Victory. L&M: J.C. Fish, 1918

Victory. L&M: J.N. King, 1918

Victory (March). L&M: John C. Zouboulakis, 1918

Victory (March). M: Adeline Shepherd, 1918

Victory (March). L&M: G.A. Hastreiter, 1918

Victory (March). M: Carl Wilhelm Kern, 1918

Victory. L&M: S.A. Meek, 1918

Victory. L&M: J.E. Bailey, 1918

Victory. L&M: H.A. Haeckler, 1918

Victory (or, The Fight You Have Won). L&M: Stanley Scott Jenkins, 1918

*Victory. L&M: Nicholas Colangelo, 1918

Victory. L: Margaret L. Allen; M: H.M. Arthur, 1918

Victory. L&M: Mrs. M.A. Williamson, 1918

Victory. L: Ellen Barbour Glines; M: F. Porrata-Doria, 1918

Victory. L&M: A.F.M. Custance, 1918

Victory (A Soldier Boy's Last Request). L&M: C.B. Weston, 1918

Victory. L&M: C. Haisler, 1919

Victory. L&M: Ella Jost, 1919

Victory. L&M: Fentom R. Mathews, 1919

Victory. L&M: Sina E. Weber, 1919

Victory. L: F. Grem; M: Frank W. Ford, 1919

Victory. L: J.L. Lyshon; M: Frank W. Ford, 1919

Victory. L: Harry A. Munn; M: Max Dolin, 1919

Victory. L&M: A. Drott, 1919

Victory. L: F. Farley; M: Leo Friedman, 1919

Victory. L: K.P. Gore; M: Leo Friedman, 1919

Victory. L: Mary Delva; M: Leo Friedman, 1919

Victory. L: Mrs. J. Hayes; M: Leo Friedman, 1919

Victory. L: Della V. Opdycke; M: Leo Friedman, 1919

Victory (or, Heroes of Liberty). M: Edward I. Pfeiffer, 1919

Victory Bell (March). M: Paul O. Schaeffer, 1919

Victory Bells. L&M: Frances Bedford Chapin, 1919

Victory Boys. L: Walter O'Keefe; M: George Graff, Jr., 1919

Victory Call. L&M: B.J. Hoffacker, 1919

Victory Day (March). M: Herman Bellstedt, 1919

Victory First and Then Our Peace. L&M: E. Reinke, 1918

Victory for the U.S.A. L: Mrs. C. Foerstner; M: Leo Friedman, 1918

Victory Forever. L&M: B.D. Westfall, 1919

Victory Is Calling. L: Mrs. E. Nelson; M: Leo Friedman, 1919

Victory Is Won. L: Mrs. M.G. Mulkins; M: Leo Friedman, 1919

Victory Liberty Loan March. M: Foster A. Beck, 1919

Victory March. L: Ella L. Smith; M: G. Vernon Strout, 1917

Victory March. M: Lonnie A. Bailey, 1918

Victory March. L&M: Rudolph Aronson, 1919

Victory of the Red, White and Blue. L&M: E.C. Gregory, 1918

Victory or Death. L&M: Dick Kettlewell, 1918

Victory! Praise God! L&M: Jay Davison Townsend and R. Blamquist, 1918

Victory Prayer. L&M: Clarence Gustlin, 1918

Victory Song. L&M: Martha A. Entwistle, 1918

Victory Song for the U.S. Boys. L&M: E.S. Harper, 1919

Victory Through the Blood. L&M: Minnie Hurlburt, 1918

Victory, Triumph, Peace (March). L: L.S. Ristine; M: Frank W. Ford, 1918

Victory Waltz. M: J.F. Jacobson, 1918

Victory Waltz. "By a presentation nun," 1919

Victory Waltz. M: M.B. Anderson, 1919

Victory Will Be Ours. L: Alice Birdsall; M: Leo Friedman, 1918

Victory Won! The Boys Are Coming Home. L&M: William B. Hartley, 1918

Victory, Yes We Got It! L: R. Joles; M: George Graff, Jr., 1919

Violets of Picardy. L: Amy Sherman Bridgman; M: Lillian B. Hughes, 1917

Virginia from Virginia (Wait for Me). L: David S. Jacobs; M: David S. Jacobs and Charles Roy Cox, 1917

Viva La France and Liberty! L: Fred Lennon; M: Leo Friedman, 1919

Voice from France. L&M: W.J. Schnetter, 1918

Voice of Belgium. L&M: Irving Berlin, 1916

Voice of France. L&M: Hal E. Goodwin, 1918

Voice of Liberty. L: E. Biddle; M: Maurice Stretch, 1917

Voice of Liberty. L&M: E. A. Powell, 1918

Voice of the Starry Flag. L&M: A.T.S. Hoag, 1918

Volunteer Battle Song and March. L: A.T. Hitchcock; M: Mary R. Smith, 1917

Volunteer Boys, the Navy Needs You! L: Freda Hager; M: Justin Ring, 1918

The Volunteers. L&M: S. Terranova, 1917

The Volunteer's Goodbye. L: Mayme Thompson; M: Leo Friedman, 1918

The Volunteers' Goodbye to Their Sweethearts. L&M: Ella Rebecca Miller, 1918

W

Wait for Me, Virginia. L: Arthur J. Lamb; M: Alex Marr, 1918

Wait for Us at the Rhine. L: H.E. Gess; M: Leo Friedman, 1919

Wait for Your Honey Boy. L&M: C.A. Pfeiffer, 1917

Wait Till I Come Home from France. L: H.M. Morton; M: Leo Friedman, 1918

Wait Till the Great Day Comes. L: Edward Teschemacher and Sidney D. Mitchell; M: Ivor Novello, 1918

Wait Till We Get There (A Patriotic Song). L&M: Henry Morse, 1918

Waiting. L: Annelu Burns; M: Madelyn Sheppard, 1918

*Wake Me Early, Mother Dear. L: Alex Sullivan; M: Arthur Lamont, 1918

Wake Up, America. L: George Graff, Jr.; M: Jack Glogau, 1916

Wake Up, America (The New York Hippodrome March). L&M: John Philip Sousa, 1916

Wake Up, America, Wake Up! L: Charlotte Ratcliff; M: Leo Friedman, 1918

Wake Up and Do Your Share. L: D.V. Menges; M: Leo Friedman, 1918

Wake Up the Kaiser. L&M: Mrs. T. Roberts, 1918

Wake Up, Uncle Sam. L: Matylda Laura Schroeder; M: B.F. Waeber, 1915

War. L: Dana Burnet; M: James H. Rogers, 1915

War. L: Corinne B. Dodge; M: Gertrude Ross, 1915

War. L: Judah A. Joffe; M: Cesar Cui, 1917

War and the Prince of Peace. L: Florida Howard; M: Florida Howard and Jessie Pedrick, 1915

*War Babies. L: Ballard MacDonald and Edward Madden; M: James F. Hanley, 1916

War Baby's Lullaby. L&M: Adele Farrington, 1918

War Baby's Lullaby. L&M: Matilda deBartoky, 1918

War Bells. L: A. Rescord; M: Leo Friedman, 1919

War Brides. L: Ballard MacDonald; M: James F. Hanley, from silent film *War Brides*, 1916

War Cloud. M: D.J. LaRocca and Larry Shields, 1918

War Correspondent March. M: G.E. Holmes, 1919

War Garden. L: Harry B. Smith; M: A. Baldwin Sloane, from stage production *Look Who's Here*, 1918

The War in Snider's Grocery Store. L&M: Hank Hancock, Ballard MacDonald, and Harry Carroll, 1914

The War Is Over and They're Coming Home. L&M: Isabelle Ritter, 1918

The War Is Over, Mother. L: Donal Hurley; M: Leo Friedman, 1919

War March of Our Soldier Boys. L&M: Edmund West, 1918

War Message. L: D.H.M. Wolslayer; M: Leo Friedman, 1918

War Mother. L: Maude Zeitz; M: Leo Friedman, 1918

War Never Again. L&M: E.A. Burke, 1919

The War of European Nations. L: J. Wilson; M: Carl Heil, 1915

The War of 1914-1915. L&M: F. Gaertner, 1915

The War Pill of Kaiser Bill. L: Mrs. E.G. Wray; M: Aubert D. Murphy, 1918

War Song About the Steamer of True Love. L&M: E.J. Johannis, 1917

The War Wife. L: Avery Gaul; M: Harvey B. Gaul, 1916

The War Will Soon Be Over, Then I'm Coming Back to You. L: L.A. Marshall; M: Leo Friedman, 1918

The War's Three Thousand Miles Away. L: J.N. Stotelmeyer; M: Leo Friedman, 1918

Wartime. L: Jean A. Doucette; M: John Francis, 1915

Wartime Lullaby (Cradle Song). L&M: Mildred E. Mabie, 1917

Wartime Lullaby. L&M: Orste Vessella, 1918

Wartime Lullaby. L: L. Purcell; M: Robert H. Brennen, 1918

Wartime Song. L&M: W.H. Pettibone, 1918

Washington (March). L&M: C.H. LaTourette, 1917

Washington and You (A Patriotic Marching Song). L: Wilbur W. Hadley; M: Ned Douglass, 1917

*(Watch, Hope and Wait) Little Girl ("I'm Coming Back to You"). L: Lew Brown; M: Will Clayton, 1918

Watch O'er My Boy Over There. L: Maria Evans; M: Leo Friedman, 1919

Watch on the Rhine. L&M: Carl Wilhelm, 1916

Watch Out for Uncle Sam and the Red,

White and Blue. L: C.W. Huels; M: J. Marion Taylor, 1918

Watch the Bee Go Get the Hun. L&M: Walter Hawley, 1918

Watch Your Step, America. L&M: William C. Pierpont, 1918

Watching the Soldiers. M: Arthur G. Colborn, 1917

Wave Old Glory, We'll Come to You. L: F.M. Brown; M: Paul Allyn, 1916

Wave on, Wave on in Peace, Star-Spangled Banner. L: Julia Stevenson; M: Walter Wolff, 1916

Wave the Flag of Victory. L: A.R. Buff; M: Raymond A. Brown, 1919

Wave the Flags, Boys, Wave the Flag! L: George Ridley; M: G.F. McKeown, 1918

Waving Our Colors. L: E.E. Hewitt; M: B.D. Ackley, 1917

*'Way Back Home in Dear America. L&M: Laura H. Rathbone, 1918

Way Back Home, Someone Back Home Is Thinking of You. L&M: Herbert MacKenzie, 1918

'Way Down There (a Dixie Boy Is Missing). L: Stanley Murphy; M: Harry Tierney, 1917

Way O'er in France. L: Lloyd M. Holmes; M: Leo Friedman, 1918

The Way of Peace. L: "N.B.T."; M: B.D. Ackley, 1916

We All Love the Flag. L: F.D. Budlong; M: William H. Sprague, 1917

We Also Serve Who Watch and Wait. L: Jessie Gammill; M: P.B. Story, 1917

We Americans. L&M: E.W. Wright, 1918

We Answer the Call (March). L: O.H. Olson; M: T.C. Ford, 1919

We Are a Peaceful Nation. L&M: C.E. Little, 1915

We Are a Peaceful Nation. L: Darl MacBoyle; M: R. Kenneth Dawson, 1916

We Are After Kaiser Bill. L: E. Schick; M: Leo Friedman, 1919

We Are All Americans. L&M: W.K. Allen, 1917

We Are All Americans (Allegiance). L: Fanny Hodge Newman; M: Carrie Jacobs-Bond, 1918

We Are Coming. L&M: Beecher Winckler, 1917

We Are Coming. L: James H. Blount; M: M.R. Wragg, 1918

We Are Coming (Marching-Song of America). L: Edith Willis Linn; M: John Philip Sousa, 1918

We Are Coming Back to You, America. L&M: C.P. Pursley, 1919

We Are Coming, France. L&M: George Kilpatrick, 1918

We Are Coming Home Again to Greet You, Mother. L: Alphonsus F. Joseph; M: Anthony Joseph, 1919

We Are Coming, Kaiser Bill. L: Mary E. Patton; M: N.B. Ransome, 1918

We Are Coming, Mr. Kaiser. L: E. Grimes; M: Frank W. Ford, 1918

We Are Coming Over There (March). L&M: Charles Washington Hunt, 1918

We Are Coming Tommy Atkins (A Patriotic Song). L: Clara Griffith Gazzam; M: Orste Vessella, 1917

We Are Coming, Uncle Sammy. L: John Stark; M: E.J. Stark, 1917

We Are Fighting for Old Glory. L&M: Henry Morse, 1917

We Are Fighting for the Honor of the Good Old U.S.A. L: Mrs. J.H. Swofford; M: Leo Friedman, 1918

We Are Going Over, Over. L&M: W.H. Wruck, 1918

We Are Going to Crush the Kaiser (March). L&M: G.W. Thomas, 1918

We Are Going to Give Woodrow the Chance. L&M: Jennie Allstoff, 1918

We Are Going to Help the Allies Win the War. L: Laura B. Crosby; M: Roy Hartzell, 1919

We Are Going to Whip the Kaiser. L: E.A. Chapman; M: Frank W. Ford, 1918

We Are Going to Win This War. L&M: Bessie Miller, 1918

We Are Here, Lafayette. L: W.P.J. Murray; M: Robert H. Brennen, 1918

We Are Here to Catch Big Willie and Little Willie, Too. L: Marianne McNelly; M: Leo Friedman, 1918

We Are Here to Get Your Scalp, Bill, and Nothing Else Will Do. L&M: Ira R. Windall, 1918

*We Are Hitting the Trail Through No Man's Land (and We'll Soon Be Coming Home). L&M: Corp. Leon Britton and Pvt. Walter B. Cooper, 1918

We Are Off to the War. L: Robert Reed; M: Leo Friedman, 1918

We Are Off to the War, Boys (March). L&M: Clara and Grace Carroll, 1917

We Are Out for the Scalp of Mister Kaiser Man. L: Charles Summers; M: Harry Schwartz, 1917

We Are Proud of You, Boys in Khaki, Boys in Blue. L&M: O.W.L. Buss, 1918

We Are Proud of You, Yankee Soldier Boy. L&M: Robert G. Claypoole, 1918

We Are Ready, Brother Woodrow. L: G. Willard Bonte; M: R.A. Browne, 1918

We Are Ready to Follow Old Glory. L&M: T.J. Quigley, 1917

We Are Ready When You Need Us, Uncle Sammy. L: John C. Dykema; M. Everett J. Evans, 1917

We Are Soldiers of the U.S.A. L&M: I.M. Briggs, 1917

We Are Sons of Old Columbia. L: G.B. Whitney; M: Harry L. Alford, 1918

We Are the Boys of the U.S.A. L: Max J. Gleissner; M: R.J. Gleissner, 1918

We Are the Lads, Just Like Our Dads. L: L.Y. Lenhart; M: Inez C. Hall, 1917

We Are the Only Happy Huns in All the World Today (March). L: Franklin Clark Sawhill; M: Kathryn I. White, 1918

We Are the Sammies of the U.S.A. L&M: E.H. Temple [Eva Williams Best], 1918

We Are the Sons of Yankeeland. L: Z. Dziurkieqicz; M: Leo Friedman, 1919

We Are Uncle Sammy's Little Nephews. L: Sgt. Bernard Satz; M: Lt. W.E. Sheaffer, 1918

We Are with You, General Pershing. L&M: E.S. Gushee, 1917

We Are with You, Mr. President. L: N.A. Jennings; M: Laura Sedgwick Collins, 1917

We Are with You, Tommy Atkins. L: Darl MacBoyle; M: Albert Von Tilzer, 1917

We Are Yankees, We Are Sammies. L&M: W.J. Hunt, 1918

We Are Yanks, Of Course We're Yanks! L&M: W.O. Easton, 1918

We Belong to Uncle Sam. L: L.J. Leavens; M: Katharonza Clarvoe, 1918

We Boys Are Coming Home. L: M.J. Henry; M: Leo Friedman, 1919

We Can Muster, Uncle Sammy, Ten Million Men or More. L: Frederick H. Green; M: Martin Greenwald, 1917

We Can't Forget Old Glory. L: Olga Marohn; M: Leo Friedman, 1918

We Carried the Star-Spangled Banner Through the Trenches. L&M: Daisy M. Pratt Erd, 1917

We Come (March). L&M: F.M. Whitehall, 1918

We Couldn't Have Heroes Over There If It Wasn't for Those Heroes Over Here. L:

Grant Clarke and Howard Johnson; M: Harry Jentes, 1919

We Did It, Of Course We Did (Victory Song). L&M: James G. Dailey, 1919

We Didn't Want to Fight, but by Golly Now We Do. L: John Kirby; M: "Grossman and [John] Kirby," 1918

*We Don't Know Where We're Going (but We're on Our Way). L&M: W.R. Williams, 1917

We Don't Like the Name of Sammie (Call Us the Yanks from the Land of the Free). L&M: C.A. Reynolds, 1918

*We Don't Want the Bacon (What We Want Is a Piece of the Rhine). L&M: "Kid" Howard Carr, Harry Russell, and Jimmie Havens, 1918

We Dwell in Peace, Old U.S.A. L: Fred W. Miller; M: Carl Heil, 1915

We Fought for the Sake of Liberty. L: S. Guzy; M: Artie Bowers, 1919

We Gave Them What They Wanted When They Tackled Uncle Sam. L: C.E. Braim; M: Kathryn I. White, 1918

We Give You All a Welcome Home. L&M: Hugh V. Coyle, 1919

We Got the Kaiser's Bacon Before We Reached the Rhine (Rind). L: Eva A. Ball; M: Amber G. Lasley, 1919

We Have Another Lincoln, and Wilson Is His Name. L&M: F.J. Lowe, 1917

We Have Heard Our Country's Call. L: Glenn E. Fales; M: Edward Wunderlich, 1917

We Have Heard the Boches. L: C.W. Cromer; M: Leo Friedman, 1919

We Have Pershing. L: M.M. Nelson; M: Leo Friedman, 1919

We Have to Hand It to the Marines. L: W.E. Bryant; M: Leo Friedman, 1919

We Hear You, Uncle Sam (Song of Loyalty). L&M: W.G. Brown, 1917

We Knew We'd Meet in America Again. L: Mrs. M.E. Donnelly; M: Leo Friedman, 1919

We Know They Did Their Share Over There. L: E. Lederer; M: Leo Friedman, 1919

We Love America. L&M: D.E. Bennett, 1918

We Love Our Flag. L&M: M.M. Whittlesey, 1917

We Love Thee, America. L&M: Ruby Barrett Carson, 1918

We Love You, 'Deed We Do, Uncle Samuel. L&M: Dora Olive Cunningham, 1917

We Made the Kaiser Rally to the Red, White and Blue. L: E.M. Patterson; M: Leo Friedman, 1919

We March to Victory. L: Gerald Moultrie; M: E.S. Hosmer, 1916

We March to Victory. L: Francis C. Young; M: Hugo Bach, 1917

We March to Victory. L: J. Howe; M: Charles E. Peel, 1918

We March! We March for the Dear Homeland. L: Emily M. Hills; M: Edward J. Smith, 1915

We Must All Fight for Uncle Sam, America. L: M. Zavodnik; M: Henry A. Russotto, 1918

We Must Back the Right (A Song for Fighting Men). L&M: Alexander Throckmorton, 1918

We Must Press the Battle On. L&M: Haldor Lillenas, 1917

We Need You, God Speed You, Sam (A Patriotic Song). L: Albert Kennedy; M: Walter Wolff, 1918

We Never Did That Before. L&M: Edward Laska, 1918

We Never Will Surrender Old Glory. L: M.A. Funk; M: Forest Cook Castle, 1918

We Said Hello to Sunny France but Now We Say Goodbye. L: E.M. Cunningham; M: Leo Friedman, 1919

We Sailed Away. L: E.E. Sherk; M: Leo Friedman, 1918

We Sent Our Boys to France. L: A. Neumeister; M: L.B. Starkweather, 1919

We Should Worry, Uncle Sam. L: Henry Blossom; M: A. Baldwin Sloane, from stage production We Should Worry, 1917

We Shouldered Our Guns. L&M: J.M. O'Dear, 1919

We Stand (A Song of Devotion to the United States). L: C.D. Platt; M: L.R. Lewis, 1918

We Stand for Peace While Others War. L&M: W.R. Williams, 1914

We Stopped Them at the Marne (It's to ---- with Germany). L&M: Gitz Rice, 1918

We Take Our Hats Off to You. L: J.E. Corcoran; M: Leo Friedman, 1919

We Take Our Hats Off to You, Mr. Wilson. L&M: Blanche Merrill, 1914

We Thank That Mother for Her Boy Who Will Never Return. L&M: Edith Nelson, 1919

We Want a Mighty Navy! L: Howard Wesley; M: Charles Elbert, from stage production Passing Show of 1915, 1915

We Want Our Daddy Dear Back Home (Hello

Central, Give Me France). L: James M. Reilly; M: Harry DeCosta, 1918

We Want the Kaiser's Helmet Now. L&M: C.W. Foster, 1917

We Want the Right to Triumph. L: A. Raywinkle; M: Leo Friedman, 1919

We Want Wilson in the White House Four Years More. L&M: James Kendis, 1916

We Were Bound to Win. L: A. Christen; M: Artie Bowers, 1919

We Were Bound to Win with the Yanks Behind the Guns. L: M.C. DuBois; M: H.F. DeVol, 1919

We Will All Stand by You, Uncle Sammy. L&M: E.F. Buckmeyer, 1918

We Will Always Stand Up and Fight. L: Joseph Affront; M: Bert V. Peters, 1916

We Will Bring Our Yanks Back Home. L: D.M. Wheaton; M: Artie Bowers, 1919

We Will Can the Kaiser, Submarines and All. L&M: Alfred E. Williams, 1918

We Will Defend Our Land. L&M: N.C. Christiansen, 1917

We Will Fight and Fight and Fight! L&M: Gertrude Nash Locke, 1918

We Will Fight for Our Freedom and Old Glory We'll Uphold. L&M: William Jolly, 1918

We Will Fight for the U.S.A. L&M: Adeline Ivey, 1918

We Will Follow Our Flag. L&M: Clara L. Baker, 1918

We Will Follow the Red, White and Blue. L: J.W. O'Connell; M: Charles L. Johnson, 1917

We Will Honor You Forever. L: M.C. Fekete; M: Joseph Psota, 1919

We Will Keep Old Glory Flying. L: J.J. Gill; M: Roy Hartzell, 1918

We Will Leave Old Glory Waving There. L: James Cameron; M: Leo Friedman, 1919

We Will Make the Kaiser Wiser. L: C.J. Baer; M: "John Brown's Body," 1917

We Will Never Say Goodbye Again. L: Joseph McCarthy; M: Fred Fisher, 1919

We Will Never Surrender Old Glory. L: A. Funk; M: Forest Cook Castle, 1918

We Will Show Them What America Can Do (March). L&M: S.B. Wright, 1917

We Will Stand by Our President. L&M: A.B. Waggoner, 1919

We Will Stand by the Stars and Stripes Forever. L&M: George Goldsmith, 1916

We Will Stand by the Stars and Stripes Forever. L&M: Oscar A. Hill, 1917

We Will Stick to Our Flag. L&M: M. Aldridge, 1919

We Will Then Have Liberty. L&M: Emil Podhola, 1918

We Will Win It Bye and Bye. L: A. Kirchem; M: Terry C. Miller, 1918

*We Will Win the War of '17. L&M: George B. Pitman, 1917

We Won! (Victory Song). L: D. Strong; M: Fred Mohr, 1919

We Won. L: J.E. Licence; M: Leo Friedland, 1919

We Won't Come Back Till Then. L&M: Lundberg Goddard, 1918

We Won't Come Back Until the Vict'ry's Won. L&M: S.A.H. Baldwin, 1918

We Won't Stop for Nothing. L: E. Stengel; M: Leo Friedman, 1918

We Would Rather Be Over There Fighting Than in Cantonments Over Here. L: C.A. Foster; M: Robert H. Brennen, 1918

We Yanked the Kaiser's Moustache Down. L&M: Edward Moray and Antonio Galvan, 1918

We Yankee Boys, Our Aim Is World Democracy. L: W.H. Dalrymple; M: W.B. Clarke, 1918

Wearing the Red Cross. L: T.B. Smith; M: A.D. McCampbell, 1918

Welcome Back Home. L&M: O. Clingan, 1919

Welcome, Brave Boys. L: Marie M. Wolfrath; M: B.J. Hoffacker, 1919

Welcome, Heroes. L&M: D.A. Martak, 1919

*Welcome Home. L: Bud Green; M: Edward G. Nelson, 1918

*Welcome Home. L&M: Daisy M. Pratt Erd, 1919

Welcome Home. L: E.L. Correll; M: Leo Friedman, 1919

Welcome Home. L: J. Gibson; M: Artie Bowers, 1919

Welcome Home Again. L&M: J. Rosamond Johnson, 1919

Welcome Home, Boys. L&M: Charles Montresor Brown, 1919

Welcome Home, Boys. L: Connie Max; M: Leo Friedman, 1919

Welcome Home, Boys. L&M: A.N. Wagner and Leroy Scheingold, 1919

Welcome Home, Boys, Welcome Home. L: J.B. Engell; M: Artie Bowers, 1919

Welcome Home, Laddie Boy. L&M: A.V. Stark, 1919

*Welcome Home, Laddie Boy, Welcome

Home. L: Will D. Cobb; M: Gus Edwards, 1919

Welcome Home, My Soldier Hero, Now It's Ended Over There. L: O.F. Ballou; M: Theodore Metz, 1919

Welcome Home, My Soldier Sammy Boy. L: Marvin Oreck; M: Samuel J. Segal, 1919

Welcome Home (Our Boys of the U.S.A.). L&M: Sarah L. Gardner, 1919

Welcome Home, Soldier Boy. L&M: I.T. Cartwright, 1919

Welcome Home, Soldier Boy, Welcome Home. L&M: Harry R. Hamburg, 1919

Welcome Home, Soldier Boys. L&M: Ruby Hooper, 1919

Welcome Home, Soldiers. L&M: J.R. Hammonds, 1919

Welcome Home to Our Soldier Boys. L&M: Jennie D. Kane, 1918

Welcome Home to Pennsylvania. L: Benjamin D. Anton; M: J. Carlton Podolyn and Rebecca Hornstine, 1919

Welcome Home, Yanks. L&M: Alva N. Setser, 1919

Welcome, Mr. Soldier, There's a Job for You to Do. L&M: H.C. Eldridge, 1918

Welcome Our Heroes. L: N.J. Neeb; M: Leo Friedman, 1919

The Welcome That's Awaiting in the Homeland. L: E.B. Pendleton; M: Leo Friedman, 1919

Welcome to Our Heroes. L: L.H. Trail; M: Leo Friedman, 1919

Welcome to Wilson. L: Katharine Lee Bates; M: Robert Armstrong, 1919

Welcome 26th! Welcome Conquerors! L&M: J.F. Finley, 1919

Welcome, Welcome Our Lads. L&M: J.E.P. Thomas, 1919

We'll All Be After You, Jack Pershing. L&M: Helena Hartzhorne, 1918

*We'll All Be Glad to See You When It's Over. L: Clyde N. Kramer; M: R.G. Gradi, 1918

We'll All Befriend Old Glory. L: A. Clement; M: Earle Hopkins, 1917

We'll All Cheer the Flag (March). L: A.E. Gebhardt; M: Dudley Huntington McCosh, 1918

We'll All Help to Win This War. L&M: Helen M. Cody, 1918

We'll All Make Billy Pay the Bill He Owes (March). L: W.J. Jansen; M: William P. Jansen, 1918

We'll Be a Big Brother to All Nations. L&M: Kate Beirne O'Rourke, 1915

We'll Be Back to Dixie or Give Out Lives for You. L: J.F. Oates; M: William J. Oates, 1917

We'll Be Glad to See the Boys Return Again. L: G.C. Sherman; M: Leo Friedman, 1918

We'll Be Happy When You Come Back Home. L&M: Nathan L. Lewis, 1918

We'll Be Home. L&M: Harry Heisler, 1918

We'll Be Playing Yankee Doodle in the Streets of Berlin. L&M: C. and M. McCafferty, 1918

We'll Be There on the Land, on the Sea, in the Air. L: Ballard MacDonald; M: James F. Hanley, 1917

We'll Be There to Meet You, Uncle Sammy. L: H.W. Hart; M: W.A.S. Parker, 1918

We'll Be There, Uncle Sammy (March). L: William K. Devereux; M: Arthur Pryor, 1917

We'll Be There with the Red, White and Blue. L&M: E.A. Keith, 1917

We'll Be True to the Red, White and Blue. L&M: Elizabeth F. Ebling, 1918

We'll Be Waiting When You Come Back Home. L: Charles H. Gabriel; M: Homer A. Rodeheaver, 1918

We'll Be with You Over There. L: N.H. Cross; M: Charles H. Gabriel, 1918

We'll Be with You, Uncle Sam. L: E.F. Swan; M: Nonie E. Swan, 1917

We'll Blaze the Way to Victory. L: D. Alexander; M: Leo Friedman, 1918

We'll Break the Line of Hindenburg. L: Jasper Laird; M: Leo Friedman, 1918

We'll Bring Him Back to Tipperary. L&M: Billy Beecher [Roger William Duke Beecher], 1917

We'll Bring Our Heroes Home. L&M: Elizabeth Clayton Bacon, 1919

We'll Can the Kaiser. L: H.P. Christy; M: Leo Friedman, 1918

We'll Carry Old Glory to Berlin. L: L.E. Gilgenbach; M: Leo Friedman, 1918

We'll Carry Old Glory to Victory. L: F.D. Smith; M: Leo Friedman, 1919

We'll Carry the Star-Spangled Banner Through the Trenches. L&M: Daisy M. Pratt Erd, 1917

We'll Come Back. L&M: E.G. Tarantino and Theodore Metz, 1917

We'll Come Back. L: A. Fagan; M: Henry Long, 1919

We'll Conquer Germany. L: A.G. Brooks; M: E.S.S. Huntington, 1918

We'll Conquer in the End. L: L.A. Barry; M: B. Hassett, 1918

We'll Defend the Name of Old Glory. L&M: Mrs. T.H. McDonough, 1918

We'll Defend the World 'Gainst Tyrants. L: J.L. Bell; M: Leo Friedman, 1918

*We'll Do Our Share (While You're Over There). L: Lew Brown and Al Harriman; M: Jack Egan, 1918

We'll Fight and We'll Die for America. L: Douglas E. Donaldson; M: Mabelle Louise, 1917

We'll Fight, Fight, Fight! L: M.E. Ralston; M: Leo Friedman, 1918

We'll Fight for Dear Old Glory. L&M: E.L. Derenzy, 1917

*We'll Fight for Each Star in the Flag. L&M: Thomas H. McDonald, 1917

We'll Fight for the Red, White and Blue. L: A.L. Amend; M: Carl Heil, 1915

We'll Fight for Uncle Sam. L: Forrest S. Rutherford; M: A.J. Rutherford, 1917

We'll Fight for Uncle Sam. L: T.B. Peacock; M: Anthony S. Lohman, 1918

We'll Fight for Yankee Doodle. L&M: Jack Graham, 1917

We'll Fight for You, Old Glory (March). L&M: Sam J. Fox, 1917

We'll Fight, O Land, for Thee. L&M: George Warren Hayford, 1917

We'll Follow Great Old Glory. L&M: D.D. Carpenter, 1918

We'll Follow Pershing Into Old Berlin. L: R.C. Young; M: Will Carroll, 1917

We'll Follow the Flag. L: C.W. Allen; M: Leo Friedman, 1919

We'll Follow the Stars and Stripes to H-E-Double-L to Win for Uncle Sam (A Real War Whoop). L&M: Waldo Reed, 1918

We'll Get Kaiser's Goat. L: F.J. Jancsar; M: Leo Friedman, 1918

We'll Get the Kaiser. L&M: The Rev. J.B. Bair, 1917

We'll Get the Kaiser. L: F.J. Gibson; M: Anonymous, 1918

We'll Get the Kaiser's G-O-A-T. L: Mebel R. Nelson; M: Leo Friedman, 1918

We'll Get There Though Many Fall. L: N.H. Pease; M: E.S.S. Huntington, 1918

We'll Get You, You Hun! L&M: Elizabeth McLean, 1918

We'll Give Our Support to Good Old Uncle Sam. L: L.D. Nourse; M: Roy Hartzell, 1918

We'll Go a-Whirlin' to Berlin. L: T.A. Thomas; M: Leo Friedman, 1918

We'll Go Into Battle, Mother. L: Mary L. Word; M: W.H. Craig, 1918

*We'll Have Peace on Earth and Even in Berlin. L: James A. Flanagan; M: Thomas J. Flanagan, 1917

We'll Help to Win the War. L&M: T. Vanderhoof, 1919

We'll Hold the Line for France. L: M.Y. Faulkner; M: Leo Friedman, 1918

We'll Join Pershing. L: G.E. Schiffler; M: Roy Hartzell, 1919

We'll Keep Old Glory Flying. L: Carleton S. Montanye; M: A. Louis Scarmolin, 1917

*We'll Keep Things Going Till the Boys Come Home (Won't We, Girls?). L: Andrew B. Sterling; M: Alfred Solman, 1917

*We'll Knock the Heligo—Into Heligo—Out of Heligoland! (March). L: John J. O'Brien; M: Theodore Morse, 1918

*We'll Lick the Kaiser If It Takes Us Twenty Years. L&M: Ralph L. Grosvenor, 1918

We'll Make Old Kaiser Bill Kiss the Red, White and Blue. L: A.W. Hille; M: E.W. Hille, 1918

*We'll Make the Germans All Sing "Yankee Doodle Doo." L: David M. Kinnear; M: Gerrit B. Fisher, 1918

We'll March to Victory. L: Gerald Moultrie; M: Harry F. Asbury, 1918

We'll Meet Them Over in France. L&M: H.A. Beasley, 1918

We'll Nail the Stars and Stripes to the Kaiser's Door. L&M: F.L. and R.T. Moreland, from stage production *Somewhere in America*, 1918

We'll Never Let the Kaiser Win. L: Mrs. W.F. Lintt; M: W.F. Lintt, 1918

We'll Never Let the Old Flag Fall (March). L&M: Henry Kenning, 1917

We'll Pay Our Debt to Lafayette. L&M: F.B. Teeling, 1918

We'll Plant Our Flag in Old Berlin. L: Mrs. F.M. Waggener; M: Leo Friedman, 1918

We'll Put Another Star in the Star-Spangled Banner (the Golden Star of Peace). L: Arthur J. Lamb; M: James G. Ellis, 1916

We'll Put It Over Kaiser Bill. L: Barney Goldstein; M: Glen Holly, 1919

We'll Rag Our Way Through Germany, We Will Fox Trot Over the Rhine. L: E.J. Tompkins; M: C.C. Miller, 1918

We'll Raise Helena When I Get Back to You. L: Charles Jordan; M: Gus Winkler, 1918

We'll See Them Through (March). L&M: J.H. Wigmore, 1917

We'll Send Our Boys to France. L: A. Neumeister; M: L.B. Starkweather, 1918

We'll Send Our Yankee Dollars. L: T.D. Oakley; M: Charles S. Brown, 1917

We'll Show Them the Yankee Way. L: Leona Lloyd; M: Leo Friedman, 1918

We'll Show You the Way to Germany (March). L: Walker B. Coats; M: R. Roy Coats, 1917

(We'll Sing for) Sammy Land. L&M: Albert E. Man, 1918

We'll Sing It Back to Home Sweet Home (March). L&M: Edwin L. Taylor, 1918

We'll Sing of the Stripes and Stars (March). L: Laura Roundtree Smith; M: Irving Gingrich, 1917

We'll Soon Be Sailing Away. L&M: Mary Carrlin, 1918

We'll Stand by Our Country. L: John L. Golden; M: Raymond Hubbell, from stage production *The Big Show*, 1916

We'll Stand by Our Flag. L&M: V.E. Mac-Allister, 1918

We'll Stand by this Flag and Be True (A Patriotic Song). L: D.L. Cushman; M: Martha Green, 1917

We'll Stand by Uncle Sam. L: J. Eugene Trabacco; M: H.G. Ridgway, 1917

We'll Stand Up for Our Country (A Patriotic Song). L&M: R.L. Noel, 1918

We'll Stick Till America Comes Through. L: T. Hesdon; M: Still Harcourt, 1917

We'll Swat the Kaiser for Uncle Sam. L&M: Alfred Danieux, 1918

We'll Take Care of You All. L: Harry B. Smith; M: Jerome Kern, from stage production *The Girl from Utah*, 1915

We'll Take Old Berlin or Bust. L&M: H.D. Murray, 1917

We'll Win the Fight for You. L&M: S.B. Weaver, 1918

We'll Win the Victory. L&M: A.B.P. Adams, 1918

We'll Win This War. L: Mrs. H. Wolever; M: Leo Friedman, 1918

We're a Part of Uncle Sam. L&M: D.A. Beckwith, 1918

We're After the Kaiser. L: Hazel Piersall; M: Leo Friedman, 1918

We're After You. L: Jeff Branen; M: Evans Lloyd, 1917

We're After You, Heinie. L&M: M.S. Grupp, 1918

We're All Alike in Khaki (March). L&M: Henry Montgomery Campbell, 1918

We're All Americans Under One Flag. L: Charles M. Johnston; M: E.S.S. Huntington, 1917

We're All Behind You, Uncle Sammy. L&M: C. Otis, 1918

We're All Coming Back. L: Bertha Siedler; M: Leo Friedman, 1919

We're All for the U.S.A. L: J.L. Allabough; M: Jack Rich, 1917

We're All for Uncle Sam. L: James Wells; M: Walter J. Pond, 1916

We're All Going Calling on the Kaiser. L: Jack Caddigan; M: James A. Brennan, 1918

We're All in It, in It to Win It for All. L&M: H.E. Weiner, 1918

We're All True Americans. L&M: C.S. Conant, 1918

We're All Uncle Sam's Boys Now. L&M: J.B. Herbert, 1917

*We're All with You, Dear America. L&M: Lew Schaeffer and Phil Leventhal, 1917

We're All with You, Mr. Wilson *see* Mr. Wilson, We're All with You

We're All with You, Uncle Sam. L: W.C. Keene; M: Bessie L. Cox, 1918

We're Behind You, Lads. L&M: C.W. Arthur, 1919

We're Bound to Get the Kaiser. L&M: William Hogan, 1917

We're Bound to Win the Day (March). L: A.F. Peelman; M: Henry Snyder, 1918

*We're Bound to Win with Boys Like You. L&M: James Kendis, James Brockman, and Nat Vincent, 1918

We're Building a Bridge to Berlin (The Mastersingers' War Song). L: C.K. Gordon; M: Bart E. Grady, 1918

We're Coming! L&M: E.B. Cahn, 1918

We're Coming Back. L: C.T. Smithers; M: Leo Friedman, 1918

We're Coming Back. L&M: Arthur Gaetka, 1919

We're Coming Back Again. L&M: Mrs. T.R. Anderson, 1919

We're Coming Back to California. L: Ralph Hogan; M: Frank Walterstein, 1918

We're Coming Back to You and U.S.A. L&M: O.D. Hopkins, 1918

We're Coming Back to You When the Fighting Days Are Through. L: Monty C. Brice; M: Walter Donaldson, 1917

We're Coming, Bill, to Get You. L&M: C.W. Noble, 1917

We're Coming, Boys. L&M: E.F. Dahlaine, 1918

We're Coming, Fellows. L: J. Debenham; M: Leo Friedman, 1919

We're Coming, France, We're Coming.
L: E.T. Ellis; M: Bessie T. Comas,
1918

We're Coming, Fritz! L&M: F.G. Vivian,
1918

We're Coming, Sister France! L&M: Norman
Meadows, 1917

We're Coming, Uncle Sam, to You (March).
L&M: F.E. Hathaway, 1917

We're Coming, We Are Coming to Fight for
Liberty. L: M.R. MacCulloch; M: Thomas
H. Chilvers, 1918

We're Doing Our Bit. L&M: F.E. Payne,
1918

We're Fighting. L&M: L.E. Spencer, 1918

We're Fighting for Liberty. L&M: Benjamin
Bronfin, 1918

*We're Fighting for Liberty. L&M: C.W.
Wallace, 1918

We're Fighting for Our Colors, the Red,
White and Blue. L: J.E. Williams; M: Leo
Friedman, 1919

We're Fighting for You, Uncle Sam. L&M:
C.E. Wright, 1918

We're Fighting Over There 'Neath Old
Glory. L: T. Naismyth; M: Jack Burdette,
1919

We're from the U.S.A. L&M: J. Braswell,
1918

We're Glad to Be in the Service. L&M: H.
Breeden, 1919

We're Goin', Daddy Woodrow. L&M: C.A.
and H.D. Herman, 1918

We're Goin' ter Get th' Kaiser—We Yankee
Doodle Yankees. L: Mary Elizabeth Oakley; M: Charles H. Gabriel, 1917

We're Goin' to Fight to the Bitter End. L:
E.T. Doran; M: Leo Friedman, 1919

We're Goin' to Knock the Hel Out of Wilhelm and It Won't Take Us Long. L&M:
Paul Stewart, 1918

We're Going Across. L: Joe Fields; M: William Schroeder, from stage production *Biff
Bang*, 1918

We're Going Across for You, Stand Back of
Us. L&M: Howard J. Gee, 1918

We're Going Across the Pond, Boys. L&M:
M. DuFrerre, 1918

We're Going Across the Pond, Boys. L&M:
M.D. McKinnon, 1918

We're Going Home. L&M: Jessie Sage Robertson, 1918

We're Going Over and Do Our Share. L&M:
Edgar J. Dowell, 1918

We're Going Over Somewhere in France.
L&M: C.A. Pfeiffer, 1917

*We're Going Over the Top (and We'll Be
Marching Through Berlin in the Morning).
L: Andrew B. Sterling and Bernie Gross-
man; M: Arthur Lange, 1917

We're Going Over the Top. L: Arnold Lam-
bertz; M: Leo Friedman, 1918

We're Going Over There. L&M: Harry L.
Reed, 1917

We're Going Over There. L&M: The Rev.
J.B. Bair, 1918

We're Going Over to Yank the Kaiser Over
to Yankee Land. L: R.A. O'Brien; M: Leo
Friedman, 1918

We're Going There (March). L: L.A. Tibbs;
M: Adam Zant, 1918

We're Going Through to Berlin (March). L:
J.S. Arnold; M: William Thomas Pierson,
1918

*We're Going to Celebrate the End of War
in Ragtime (Be Sure That Woodrow Wilson Leads the Band). L&M: Coleman
Goetz and Jack Stern, 1915

We're Going to Fight for U.S.A. L: Stella
Metzger; M: Leo Friedman, 1918

We're Going to Get Along Without the
Kaiser. L&M: Charles Durham, 1918

We're Going to Get the Kaiser. L&M: F.P.
Mitchell, 1918

We're Going to Get to Berlin Through the
Air. L&M: Harold Dixon, 1918

*We're Going to Hang the Kaiser (Under the
Linden Tree). L&M: James Kendis and
James Brockman, 1917

We're Going to Keep Old Glory Floating
from on High. L&M: Grace Lee Slayback,
1918

We're Going to Kick the Hell Out of Will-
Hell-Em. L&M: L.M. Long, 1918

We're Going to Protect the American Flag.
L: P.S. Brooks; M: Gertrude H. Shaw,
1917

We're Going to Pull Together to the Finish.
L: C.P. Gow; M: Leo Friedman, 1919

We're Going to Show the Kaiser the Way to
Cut Up Sauerkraut (and Serve It Delicate).
L: J. Calvin Stewart; M: Charles A.
Meyers, 1918

*We're Going to Take the Germ Out of Ger-
many. L: Arthur J. Lamb; M: Frederick
V. Bowers, 1917

We're Going to Take the Germ Out of Germany. L&M: C.E. Bailey, 1918

We're Going to Take the Sword Away from
William. L&M: Willie Weston, 1917

We're Going to Whip the Kaiser. L&M: Jennie E. Reed, 1917

We're Going to Win for Old Glory. L: Edward P. Womack; M: Harry P. Guy, 1918

We're Going to Win the War. L: Frederick M. Davis; M: Leo Friedman, 1918

We're Going to Win This War. L: Katherine Pyke; M: Leo Friedman, 1919

We're Here, Lads, We're Here. L&M: Edward Auten, Jr., and A.A. Dart, 1918

We're Here, Lafayette, We're Here. L&M: Edward Auten, Jr., and A.A. Dart, 1918

We're in It and We'll Win It. L: James McLaren; M: Jacques Perrin, 1918

We're in It to Win It. L: Henry J. Zelley; M: W. Philip [Philip Wuest], 1918

We're in the Army Now. L&M: Tell Taylor, Ole Olsen, and Isham Jones, 1917

We're in the War to See It Through (March). L&M: H.F. Andrews, 1917

We're in the War to Stay. L&M: J.F. Mayfield, 1917

We're in to See It Through. L&M: R.C. Lafferty, 1917

We're in to Win. L&M: Mrs. H.B. Sargent, 1919

We're Just a Bunch of Sammies. L&M: H.G. Dunn, 1918

We're Landin' in London, We'll Land in the Land of the Hun. L: Max C. Freedman; M: Louis Herscher, 1918

We're Marching on to Berlin. L: K. Walstrum; M: A. Traxler, 1919

We're Marching on to Freedom's Call. L&M: Clarence H. Reed, 1918

We're Marching on to Victory. L&M: John H. Taylor, 1918

We're Marching on, We're Marching on to Victory. L: Carl F. Wilson; M: Carl F. Wilson and Frank G. Wilson, 1918

We're Not Coming Back Till the Kaiser Plays Square. L&M: Samuel A. Nielson, 1917

We're Off for the U.S.A. L&M: I. Witter, 1918

We're Off Today for the Mighty Fray. L: J.E. Wall; M: Mae Trescher Brady, 1917

We're on Our Way to Berlin. L: Eva A. Ball; M: Amber G. Lasley, 1918

We're on Our Way to France. L&M: Irving Berlin, from stage production *Yip, Yip, Yaphank*, 1918

We're on Our Way to France (to Fight for Liberty). L: D.M. Buchanan; M: Ned Clay, 1917

We're on Our Way to Germany. L: W.A. Sweet; M: Leo Friedman, 1918

We're on Our Way to Helgoland (the Kaiser's Gibraltar). L: Elsa Gregori; M: Leo Friedman, 1918

We're on Our Way to Meet You, General Pershing. L&M: G. Merle, 1917

We're on Our Way to the U.S.A. L: A. Meise; M: Leo Friedman, 1919

We're on the Road to France. L: C. Davis; M: Nellie Risher Roberts, 1918

We're on the Way to France. L&M: Paul Holbrook, 1918

We're One for Uncle Sam (March). L: Robert Freeman; M: Antonette Ruth Sabel, 1918

We're Out to Get the Kaiser. L&M: J.E. Fisher, 1918

We're Over. L&M: James Anderson, 1918

We're Proud of You Soldier Boys. L&M: Oscar Harrison, 1918

We're Proud That We're Americans. L&M: Edna Iona Tyler, 1918

We're Soldiers of the U.S.A. L: E. Bushway; M: Leo Friedman, 1918

We're Sons of Uncle Sam. L: Zillah Eden; M: Webb Long, 1916

We're the Boys from U.S.A. L&M: J.R. Laverick, 1918

We're the Boys of the U.S.A. L&M: L.S. Whitaker, 1918

We're the Boys of Uncle Sam. L: C.O. McDonnell; M: Leo Friedman, 1918

We're the Girls You Left Behind. L: Jennie S. Ennis; M: C.P. Solomon, 1919

We're the Sammies from Across the Ocean. L&M: Joe Seiler, 1918

We're the Sammies of the U.S.A. L: A.L. Sweeney; M: Leo Friedman, 1918

We're the Sons of the Stars and Stripes. L&M: A. Christopher, 1918

We're the Yanks. L: Mrs. C.B. Horner; M: Leo Friedman, 1919

We're Truly on Our Way to Can the Kaiser (Sammy March Song). L&M: J.S. Ramey, 1917

We're Uncle Sammy's Soldier Boys. L: Bertha Baird; M: Leo Friedman, 1919

We're Uncle Sam's Children. L: A.M. Silknitter; M: Leo Friedman, 1918

We're Waiting for the Call, Mr. Wilson. L: J.W. Metrie and S.W. Cloutman; M: George Gerber, 1917

We're with Mr. Wilson (That's All). L&M: Joseph F. Brennan, 1918

*We're with You, Boys, We're with You! L: L.M. Townsend; M: J.B. Walter, 1918

We're with You, Tommy Atkins! L: Darl MacBoyle; M: Albert Von Tilzer, 1917

We're with You, U.S.A.! L: A.G. Damhorst; M: Carl R. Zerse, 1918

We're Yours, Uncle Sam (March). L: Lora Kelly; M: James H. Rogers, 1917

We've Backed Up Our Brave Army, and They Have Done the Rest. L: S.L. Moore; M: Artie Bowers, 1919

We've Called the Kaiser's Bluff. L: L.C. Lewis; M: Edgar Allyn Cole, 1917

We've Got the Boches on the Run. L&M: Jack Downey, 1919

We've Got the Hun on the Run. L&M: C.B. Elderkin, 1918

We've Got the Kaiser on the Run (A Patriotic Song). L: DeWolfe Pineo [Queen A. McNutt]; M: A.J. Logan, 1918

We've Got to Get the Kaiser (Uncle Sam Will Lead the Way). L&M: Norman C. Morgan, 1918

We've Had 'Em on the Run. L&M: V. Micari, 1918

We've Knocked the 'El Out of Wilhelm. L: J. Logan; M: E. Krinn, 1918

We've Paid Our Debt to You. L: H.I. Gilbert; M: F. Slocum, 1919

We've Turned His Moustache Down. L: E.S. Thornton; M: B. Kessler, 1918

What a Meeting That Will Be. L&M: Charles B. Weston, 1918

*What a Wonderful Dream (It Would Be). L&M: Charles K. Harris, 1918

What a Wonderful Message from Home. L: Ivan Reid; M: P.L. Eugene, 1918

*What an Army of Men We'd Have (If They Ever Drafted the Girls). L&M: Al Piantadosi and Jack Glogau, 1918

What Are We Doing for Our Boys? L: R.C. Bondy; M: C.S. Brown, 1918

*What Are You Going to Do to Help the Boys? L: Gus Kahn; M: Egbert Van Alstyne, 1918

*What Are You Going to Do When Our Boys Come Home? L: Ivan Reid; M: Peter DeRose, 1918

What Does a Soldier Care? L: A.J. Mills; M: Bennett Scott, 1917

What Fight You For? Freedom and Liberty. L: W.E. Brown; M: W.R. Wilson, 1917

What General Pershing Will Do to Germany Is Just What Dewey Did at Manila Bay. L&M: H. Lyon Smith, 1918

What Have You Done for Your Country? L: M. Moore; M: Angelus Stuart, 1918

What Have You Done to Help Your Uncle Sam? L: F.R. Farron; M: Clarence Kohlmann, 1917

What If George Washington's Mother Had Said, "I Didn't Raise My Boy to Be a Soldier"? L: Grant Clarke; M: James V. Monaco, 1915

What Is Your Opinion, Kaiser Bill? L&M: A.A. Westman, 1918

What Kind of an American Are You? L: Lew Brown and Charles R. McCarron; M: Albert Von Tilzer, 1917

What Matter the Name (A Patriotic Song). L&M: H.F. Dye, 1918

What Our Sammies Can Do. L: T.J. Matthews; M: R.A. Brown, 1918

What Our Yankee Boys Can Do. L&M: Jennie Collins, 1918

What Peace Has Meant to Me. L: H.I. Murry; M: Leo Friedman, 1919

What Shall We Do When the Boys Come Home? L&M: Edna Randolph Worrell, 1918

What Sherman Said Was Right, War Is Hell. L: Mabel Beck and M. Westerman; M: Charles L. Johnson, 1918

What the Gold Service Star Means. L: Irene Severson; M: Edouard Hesselberg, 1919

What the Little Blue Star Means to Me. L: F.M. Davis; M: A.F. Heckle, 1918

What the U.S.A. Stands For. L: Mrs. L.A. Morgan; M: Frank W. Ford, 1919

What the Yankee Boys Can Do. L: Louise Fenderson; M: Paul Jones, 1918

What the Yankee Doodle Boy Will Do. L: Mr. and Mrs. M.L. Lewis; M: Leo Friedman, 1919

What the Yankee Doodle Do. L: John Jackson; M: John N. Brown, 1918

What the Yankee Doodle Do. L: O.Q. Beckworth; M: Katharine Beckworth, 1918

What the Yankees Will Do Over There. L&M: M. Read, 1918

What Uncle Sammy Said. L: J.E. Carney; M: Leo Friedman, 1919

What We Do When We Know We're Right. L: W.D. Ashley; M: Leo Friedman, 1918

What We'll Do to Kaiser Bill. L&M: F.H. Mitchell, 1918

What Will We Do for Our Uncle Sam? L: C.L. Austin; M: Leo Friedman, 1918

What Will You Do to Help Your Uncle Sam? L: F.J. Twyman; M: Hazel Bee Hurd, 1918

What'll We Do with Him, Boys? (The Yanks Made a Monkey Out of You). L: Andrew B. Sterling; M: Arthur Lange, 1918

What's a Poor Little Soldier Going to Do? L&M: James F. Hanley, 1919

Wheatless Day. L: P.G. Wodehouse; M:

Jerome Kern, from stage production *Oh, Lady! Lady!!* 1918

When a Blue Service Star Turns to Gold. L: Caspar Nathan; M: Theodore Morse, 1918

When a Blue Star Turns to Gold. L: F.E. Smith; M: George Graff, Jr., 1919

*When a Boy Says Goodbye to His Mother (and She Gives Him to Uncle Sam). L&M: Jack Frost, 1917

When a Yankee Doodle Band Plays Yankee Doodle. L: John Mogan; M: Newton B. Heims, 1916

*When a Yankee Gets His Eye Down the Barrel of a Gun. L&M: Fred S. Campbell, 1918

*When Alexander Takes His Ragtime Band to France. L&M: Al Bryan, Cliff Hess, and Edgar Leslie, 1918

When Alexander's Ragtime Band Hits France. L: L.K. Alexander; M: Artie Bowers, 1919

When Alexander's Ragtime Band Plays Over There. L&M: G.W. Graham, 1918

When All the World's at Peace. L: Fleta Jan Brown; M: Charles N. Grant, 1914

When America Crosses the Rhine. L&M: John E. Hays, 1918

When America Wins the War. L&M: E.C. Wilson, 1918

*When Angels Weep (Waltz of Peace). L&M: Charles K. Harris, 1914

When Billy Boy Comes Home. L: Earl Welshimer; M: Leo Friedman, 1919

When Blue Star Turned to Gold. L: John P. Gibbons; M: Catherine Merrick, 1919

When Blue Stars Have Been Turned Into Gold. L&M: C.M. Freel, 1919

When Blue Stars Turned to Gold. L&M: Nellie Olds-Haight, 1918

When Cometh Peace. L&M: Charlotte Looney, 1918

When Cometh the End of the War? L: E.E. Hewitt; M: Carl V. Price, 1917

When Company B and Company C Goes Over. L&M: J. McLaughlin, 1918

When Daddy Came Back from France. L: Nettie Endicott; M: Leo Friedman, 1919

When Daddy Comes Back O'er the Sea. L&M: M.C. Smith, 1918

When Daddy Comes Home. L: Stella Simpson; M: Leo Friedman, 1919

When Did You Write to Mother Last? L&M: Charles K. Harris, 1914

When Duty Calls (A Patriotic Song). L: F.R. Ball; M: Ivan Kennedy, 1918

When E'er Your Star of Blue Takes on a Golden Hue. L: C.S. Corrigan; M: W.T. Porter, 1918

When Ephraim's Band from No Man's Land Starts Playing a Dixie Melody. L: Carl F. Wilson: M: Carl F. and Frank G. Wilson, 1919

When Fritzie Saw Our Yankee Lads Go Over. L: W.L. Schroeder; M: Leo Friedman, 1919

When General Pershing Comes Home. L: W.R. Meyers and J.A. Martin; M: Frank J. Gillen, 1919

When Germany's Had Her Fall. L&M: R.H. Lefavour, 1918

When God Turns the Trenches to Gardens Again. L&M: Gilbert C. Tennant, 1918

When He Comes Back to Me. L: Gene Buck; M: Dave Stamper, from stage production Ziegfeld Midnight Frolic, 1916

*When He Fought for the Flag of the Free. L&M: L.P. Lemire, Jr., 1918

When He Returns. L: L.F. Wolbert; M: George Graff, Jr., 1919

When He Returns to Mother Over Here (A Patriotic Waltz Song). L&M: L.M. Ballowe, 1918

When Her Boy Returns. L&M: J. Hargreaves, 1919

When Her Sweetheart in Khaki Returns to His Home. L: Mrs. H. Anderson; M: Leo Friedman, 1919

When Hindenburg Reaches Paris. L: James Hinch; M: Leo Friedman, 1918

When I Come Back. L&M: Teddy Fields, 1919

When I Come Back to You (A Military Ballad). L: Arthur J. Lamb; M: J. Anton Dailey, 1915

When I Come Back to You. L&M: H.J. Mikkelson, 1918

When I Come Back to You. L: A.D. Campbell; M: Walter E. Kalinowski. 1919

*When I Come Back to You (We'll Have a Yankee-Doodle Wedding). L&M: William Tracey and Jack Stern, 1918

When I Come Home to You. L: J. Will Callahan; M: Frank H. Grey, 1918

When I Dream of Old Glory, I Dream Also of You. L: W. Eberle; M: Leo Friedman, 1919

When I Get Back. L&M: Zilpha Sheets Ricard, 1919

When I Get Back (from Over There). L: DeWitt H. Morse; M: William H. Farrell, 1918

When I Get Back Home to You. L&M: Anita Owen, 1919

When I Get Back to America and You (March). L&M: Joseph Newman, 1918

When I Get Back to My American Blighty. L: Arthur Fields; M: Theodore Morse, 1918

When I Get Back to the U.S.A. L&M: Irving Berlin, from stage production *Stop! Look! and Listen!*, 1915

When I Get Back to the U.S.A. L&M: Harry G. DeVaux, 1919

When I Get You, Kaiser Wilhelm. L&M: Antone Frias, 1919

When I Gets Out on No Man's Land, I Can't Be Bothered with No Mule. L&M: W.E. Skidmore and Marshall Walker, 1918

When I Grow Up, I'm Going to Be a Soldier. L: Jean Havez; M: Gus Edwards, from stage production *Band-Box Revue*, 1917

When I Grow Up to Be a Soldier Man. L&M: Florence Lugren, 1917

When I Make the Kaiser Kiss the Stars and Stripes, Then I'm Coming Back to You. L: J. Bellanton; M: Harry E. Rodgers, 1918

When I Return. L&M: C.P. Taylor and Leon R. Kennedy, 1918

When I Return to the U.S.A. L: T.J. Alford; M: Emil Peter Barth, 1918

*When I Send You a Picture of Berlin (You'll Know It's Over, "Over There," I'm Coming Home). L&M: Frank Fay, Ben Ryan, and Dave Dreyer, 1918

When I Was a Soldier in France. L: J.B. Hill; M: Leo Friedman, 1919

When I'm a Soldier Boy. L: O.C. Hogue; M: Leo Friedman, 1918

*When I'm Through with the Arms of the Army (I'll Come Back to the Arms of You). L&M: Earl Carroll, 1917

When Ireland Takes Her Place Among the Nations of the Earth. L: Harry F. Henry; M: Austin Walsh, 1919

(When It Comes to a) Lovingless Day. L&M: Jack Frost, 1917

When It Strikes Home. L&M: Charles K. Harris, from silent film *When It Strikes Home*, 1915

When It's All Over (Then It's Home Sweet Home for Me). L&M: C.A. Pfeiffer, 1918

When It's Christmas Time on the Battlefield. L&M: J.N. Burke, 1917

*When It's Over, Over There, Molly Darlin'. L&M: Benjamin Purrington and Neil Morét, 1918

When Jack Comes Sailing Home Again. L&M: Nora Bayes, 1918

When Jerry Flynn Gets to Old Berlin. L: E. Ray McCloskey; M: Mildred Meade, 1918

When Johnnie Comes Marching Home Again. L&M: C.B. Weston, 1918

When Johnny Comes Marching Home. L&M: Unverified, 1863/1918

When Kaiser Bill Wakes Up. L: F.B. Padgett; M: Leo Friedman, 1919

When Kaiser Wilhelm Falls. L: J.J. Cross; M: Leo Friedman, 1918

When Laddie Boy Comes Sailing Back to Me. L: E. Makeever; M: Leo Friedman, 1919

When Liberty Is King. L&M: Mrs. Tyler Miller, 1919

When My Boy Meets the Kaiser. L&M: H.E. Gifford, 1918

When My Daddy Bid Goodbye. L&M: Maude L. Neale, 1919

When My Honey Comes Home. L: Mrs. W. Offer; M: Leo Friedman, 1919

When My Red Cross Girl Comes Home. L&M: J.P. Gilroy, 1917

When My Sailor Boy Comes Back. L&M: Minnie I. Dowling, 1918

When My Sammie Comes Back to Me. L: C.W. Hamilton; M: Leo Friedman, 1918

When Old Glory Floats Over the Rhine. L&M: Leone Driscol, 1918

When Old Glory Goes Over the Top. L: James Sharp; M: Leo Friedman, 1919

When Old Glory Sails the Rhine. L: H. DeBrose; M: L. Fox, 1918

When Old Glory Stands in Danger. L: F. O'Brien; M: Leo Friedman, 1918

When Old Glory Unfurls on Berlin (March). L&M: E.S. and H.L. Hodges, 1918

When Orders Come to Go (March). L: F.W. Regá and E. Farran; M: Fred W. Hager, 1917

When Our Boys All Get Across. L&M: G.W. Garwood, Jr., 1918

When Our Boys Are Homeward Bound. L: M.C. Egan; M: Leo Friedman, 1919

When Our Boys Arrive in France. L: H.D. Shaiffer; M: Clarence Kohlmann, 1917

When Our Boys Come Back. L: E.C. Bachman; M: Leo Friedman, 1919

When Our Boys Come Home. L&M: Valeria Maye Rutter, 1919

When Our Boys Come Home Again. L: Clara C. Pasel; M: Anson Calvin Jacobs, 1918

When Our Boys Come Home Again. L&M: Frank C. Huston, 1918

When Our Boys Come Marching Back. L: H.V. Shimp; M: Zona Shimp, 1919

When Our Boys Come Marching Home. L&M: H. Klebanoff, 1918

When Our Boys Come Marching Home. L&M: A.D. Bowman, 1918

When Our Boys Come Marching Home. L: Tillie Knuth; M: Leo Friedman, 1918

When Our Boys Come Marching Home. L: G.A. Skeen; M: Frank W. Ford, 1918

When Our Boys Come Marching Home. L&M: Lizzie Lautz, 1919

When Our Boys Come Marching Home Again. L: Mattie H. Browne; M: Mattie H. Browne and Herman Berl, 1918

When Our Boys Come Marching Home from Berlin. L: J.M. Bartlett; M: George Graff, Jr., 1919

When Our Boys Come Sailing Home. L: F.A. Giannini; M: Victor Giannini, 1919

When Our Boys Come Sailing Home from Overseas. L: Harry Taggart; M: Artie Bowers, 1919

When Our Boys Get Over There. L&M: J.A. Mercer, 1918

When Our Boys Go Over the Top. L&M: Frank F. Moore, 1918

When Our Boys Make It Safe Across the Sea. L: J. Becktel; M: Walter A. Goodell, 1919

When Our Boys Return. L&M: Dixie Scott Pace, 1918

When Our Boys Return. L&M: Hattie Carter Renner, 1918

When Our Boys Went Over the Sea. L: H.A. Fish; M: Leo Friedman, 1919

When Our Fighting Blood Is Up, See What We'll Do! L&M: Mrs. M.L. Spangler, 1916

When Our Five Million Soldiers Are in France. L: Joseph Hill and A. Hoffman; M: Robert C. Horwood, 1918

When Our Heroes Wore Khaki. L: A. Fritz; M: Edouard Hesselberg, 1919

When Our Mothers Rule the World. L: Al Bryan; M: Jack Wells, 1915

*When Our Service Star Was Turned to Golden Hue. L&M: Allen R. Richmond, 1919

When Our Soldier Boys Come Home. L: M.D. Ingalls; M: Flavil Hall, 1918

When Our Soldier Boys Come Home from France. L&M: E. Dickey, 1918

When Our War Work Is Done. L: Thomas Harris; M: Leo Friedman, 1918

When Our Yankee Boys Go Marching. L&M: M.B. Benson, 1918

When Pat O'Brien Goes Over the Line with His Irish Volunteers. L: Jean McLane and Daniel McGeehan; M: Eugene Platzmann, 1918

When Peace Sounds the Trumpet, I Will Come Back to You. L&M: Isabelle Sasse, 1919

When Pershing Gets Hello from Kitty Reilly. L: John O'Keefe; M: J.A. Parks, 1918

When Pershing Hoists Old Glory in Berlin. L: T.C. Adamson; M: O.B. Rogers, 1918

When Pershing Leads Them Over (March). L: Ruth Thorbourn; M: Ramon Corpus, 1917

When Pershing Says "Let's Go." L: Walter J. Coe; M: Paul Kellogg, 1918

When Pershing Takes Berlin. L: Jimmie Brennan; M: Leo Friedman, 1918

When Pershing's Band Plays Dixieland in Berlin, Germany. L: Thomas O. Mountain; M: Lon Sloop, 1918

When Pershing's Men Go Marching Into Picardy. L: Dana Burnet; M: James H. Rogers, 1918

When Rastus Johnson Cakewalks Through Berlin. L&M: John Atkinson, 1918

When Sammie Comes Marching Home. L&M: M.J. Heck, 1918

When Sammie Crosses O'er the Rhine. L&M: E. Stacy, 1918

When Sammie Gets to Berlin. L: Alleen Riggins; M: Leo Friedman, 1918

When Sammy Comes Home. L: W.H. Rogers; M: Leo Friedman, 1918

When Sammy Comes Marching Home. L: C.C. Gruber; M: Leo Friedman, 1919

When Sammy Comes Marching Home Again. L&M: M. Spear, 1919

When Sammy Comes Sailing In. L: F.M. Farwell; M: Leo Friedman, 1919

When Sammy Gets a-Going. L: Tom Slick [Otto I. Salick]; M: Don Sillaway, 1917

When Sammy Gets a Letter from His Home Sweet Home. L: Herbert E. Marsh; M: Noble Coucheron, 1918

When Sammy Goes Over the Top. L: "Hyland"; M: "Tillman," 1918

When Sammy Goes Over the Top. L: T.A. Snook; M: Leo Friedman, 1919

When Shall We Return from France, Boys? (March). L&M: J.C. Brindmore, 1918

When Taps Are Softly Blowing, We Are Dreaming All of You. L&M: Harry L. Watson, 1918

When Teddy [Theodore Roosevelt] Leads the Boys Across the Water. L&M: Samuel Bullock, 1917

When That Flag of Peace Is Raised, I'll Come Back to You Only. L&M: Hannah Menke, 1918

When That Glorious Message Came Flashing Through the Land. L: Calvin P. Crawford; M: Artie Bowers, 1919

When the Allies Parade the Streets of Berlin. L&M: Z.F. Gorbett, 1917

When the American Army Gets the Kaiser's Goat. L&M: E.H. James, 1917

*When the Apple Blossoms Bloom in France. L: Harold Freeman; M: Harry C. Elsesser and J. Edwin Allemong, 1918

When the Band from Dixieland Plays La Marseillaise. L: Charles Howard Shaw; M: A.J. Gibson, 1918

When the Band Plays "Indiana," Then I'm Humming "Home Sweet Home." L&M: Billy Gaston, 1918

When the Band Plays Old Dixie in Berlin. L&M: N.L. Atkins, 1918

When the Band Plays the Star-Spangled Banner. L: Sara G. Trott; M: George C. Polini, 1915

When the Band Plays Yankee Doodle. L: Daniel A. Lord; M: John F. Quinn, from stage production *Over and Back*, 1919

When the Band Plays Yankee Doodle Doo. L&M: W.L. Strickland, 1918

When the Battle Is Over. L: Doris Dabbs; M: Leo Friedman, 1918

When the Battle of the Brave Is Over (I'll Come Marching Home to You). L&M: John T. Graham, 1917

When the Bell for Freedom Rings. L: M.A. Black; M: E. Inez Wilcox, 1918

When the Bells of Belgium Ring Again. L: Howard Johnson; M: Joseph H. Santly, 1918

When the Blue Star Turns to Gold. L&M: Mrs. W.J. Foster, 1919

When the Blue Star Turns to Silver and the Silver Turns to Gold. L&M: N.E. Davis, 1918

When the Blue Stars Turn to Gold. L&M: Alice Sherwood, 1918

When the Blue Stars Turn to Gold. L: James Fitzpatrick; M: Leo Friedman, 1919

*When the Boat Arrives (That Brings My Lovin' Daddy Home). L&M: George Fairman, 1918

When the Bonnie, Bonnie Heather Is Blooming (I'll Return, Annie Laurie, to You).

L&M: James G. Ellis, 1915

When the Boy Comes Back to His Mother. L&M: W. Finley, 1919

When the Boys at the Front Are Fighting. L&M: E. Holt, 1918

*When the Boys Come Back Again. L&M: Ernest B. Orne, 1918

When the Boys Come Back Again. L: Charles W. Vaughan; M: Adger M. Pace, 1918

When the Boys Come Back from Berlin. L: May Dawson Jordan; M: Jessie Crosby Osborne, 1918

When the Boys Come Back from Over the Sea. L&M: I.G. Eagon, 1918

*When the Boys Come Home. L: John Hay; M: Oley Speaks, 1915

When the Boys Come Home. L: E. Sheldon Darling; M: J.A. Parks, 1918

When the Boys Come Home. L&M: Charles H. Gabriel, 1918

When the Boys Come Home. L: John May; M: W.T. Porter, 1918

When the Boys Come Home. L: John Hay; M: Calvin W. Laufer, 1918

When the Boys Come Home. L: Ora A. Newlin; M: Roy Gourley, 1918

When the Boys Come Home. L: L.G. Monroe; M: Leo Friedman, 1919

When the Boys Come Home. L&M: W.A. Turberville, 1919

When the Boys Come Home. L&M: J. Filer, 1919

When the Boys Come Home from Europe. L&M: Bert and Emily Van Allen, 1918

When the Boys Come Home with Glory. L: W.L. Lauher; M: Juna B. Lauher, 1918

*When the Boys Come Marching Home. L: Jamie Kelly; M: William Cahill, 1916

When the Boys Come Marching Home (March). M: Leo Friedman, 1916

When the Boys Come Marching Home. L&M: Joseph E. Howard, 1917

When the Boys Come Marching Home (March). L&M: W.E. Davis and H. Bossert, 1917

When the Boys Come Marching Home. L&M: Plunkett Dillon, 1918

When the Boys Come Marching Home. L&M: J. Ferdon, 1918

When the Boys Come Marching Home. L&M: W.L. Ridenour, 1918

When the Boys Come Marching Home. L&M: J. Ernest Reels, D. Rosenwein, and H. Rosenthal, 1919

When the Boys Come Marching Home.
  L&M: F. Hite, 1919
When the Boys Come Marching Home
  Again. L: Mattie Hughes Browne; M:
  Mattie Hughes Browne and H. Berl, 1918
When the Boys Come Sailing Home. L&M:
  J.G. Eddowes, 1918
When the Boys Come Sailing Home. L: Rob-
  ert N. Lister; M: Elise Salisbury Lister,
  1918
When the Boys Come Sailing Home. L&M:
  C.J. Novak, 1918
When the Boys Come Sailing Home. L: J.W.
  Mantica; M: P. Emma, 1918
*When the Boys Come Sailing Home
  (March). L&M: Floyd Delker, 1918
When the Boys Come Sailing Home. L&M:
  Charles Govone, 1918
When the Boys Come Sailing Home. L&M:
  M.F. Schram, 1918
When the Boys Come Sailing Home (March).
  L: Helen Albert; M: John Philip Sousa,
  1918
When the Boys Come Sailing Home, What a
  Wonderful Time There'll Be. L: Charles
  Gesele; M: Edward Huether, 1918
When the Boys from Dixie Eat the Melon on
  the Rhine. L: Al Bryan; M: Ernest Breuer,
  1918
When the Boys Get Back to Dixie. L: W.M.
  Locher; M: Leo Friedman, 1919
When the Boys Have All Returned. L&M:
  J.P. Lawrence, 1919
When the Boys in Khaki Sail Away. L: Ar-
  thur Snow; M: Fred J. Richardson, 1917
When the Boys Return. L&M: The Rev. J.B.
  Bair, 1918
When the Bugle Calls. L&M: Lillie A.
  Renken, 1918
When the Bugle Calls. L&M: R.M. Heath,
  1918
When the Bugle Calls (The Great March
  Song). L&M: Roy L. Burtch, 1918
When the Bugle Calls for Peace. L&M:
  Amelia M. Gerle, 1917
*When the Clouds Have Passed Away. L:
  William Jerome; M: Seymour Furth, 1918
*When the Clouds of War Roll By. L: Nat
  Binns; M: Earl Haubrich, 1917
When the Colored Regiment Goes Off to
  War. L: Harold Atteridge; M: Sigmund
  Romberg, from stage production *Ruggles
  of Red Gap*, 1915
When the Cruel War Is Over (and the Boys
  Come Marching Home). L&M: John
  Chapman, 1918

When the Decks Are Cleared for Action.
  L&M: H.B. Edwards, 1918
When the Devil Gets the Kaiser, Won't He
  Jump! L&M: J.F. Drennen, 1918
When the Drums Are Drumming and the
  Bugle Calls. L: M. Eller; M: S.J. Stocco,
  1919
*When the Eagle Flaps His Wings (and Calls
  on the Kaiser). L: C. Francis Riesner; M:
  Thomas L. McCarey, Jr., 1918
When the Eagle Screams. L&M: J.J. Pope,
  1915
*When the Eagle Screams Hurrah! L&M:
  Edmond Dallas [Annie E. Hicks], 1917
When the Fightin' Irish Come Home. L:
  John W. Bratton; M: Joseph H. Santly,
  1919
When the Fighting Yankees Come Back
  Home. L&M: William P. Chase, 1918
*When the Flag Goes By. L: Marian Dear-
  born Merry; M: George B. Nevin, 1917
When the Flag of Peace Is Waving. L: A.
  Bartelme; M: Harry L. Alford, 1918
When the Flag of Peace Is Waving, I'll Re-
  turn. L: M.R. Meyer; M: Barnie G.
  Young, 1917
When the Flag Waves in Berlin. L: Lenora
  Henley; M: Leo Friedman, 1919
When the Flags of All Nations Unite. L&M:
  Adelaide S. Davis, 1916
When the Flags of Freedom Wave. L&M:
  H.A. Kiernan, 1917
When the Fleet Comes Sailing Home. L: Carl
  M. Legg; M: T. Jay Flanagan, 1918
*When the Flowers Bloom on No Man's
  Land (What a Wonderful Day That Will
  Be). L: Howard E. Rogers; M: Archie
  Gottler, 1918
When the Girls Come Back from Over There.
  L: Mrs. F. Bockhorst; M: Leo Friedman,
  1919
When the Indian Goes to Paris to Fight the
  Huns in France. L&M: Luke S. Murdock,
  1918
When the Irish Go Over the Top. L: Arthur
  Denvir; M: Edwin F. Kendall, 1918
When the Kaiser Crosses the Rhine to the
  Yankee Doodle Time. L: F.K. Tomer; M:
  Leo Friedman, 1918
When the Kaiser Does the Goose-Step to a
  Good Old American Rag. L: Jack Frost;
  M: Harold Neander, 1917
When the Kaiser Heard of the Colored
  Soldiers, He Packed Up and Left for
  Holland. L: T.J. Morris; M: Artie Bowers,
  1919

When the Kaiser Is in Hock (March). L&M: J.P. Gilroy, 1917

When the Kaiser Left Germany. L&M: Clara M. Wiles, 1919

When the Kaiser Pays the Yankee Jeweler to Fix the Watch on the Rhine. L: C.E. Mathias; M: C.E. Mathias and F.J. Fortier, 1918

When the Kaiser Was Stumped. L: Earl Richardson; M: Leo Friedman, 1919

When the Kaiser Whips the Allies, Old Ireland Will Be Free. L&M: Michael Mulcahy, 1915

When the Khaki and the Blue Come Home. L: R. Friere; M: Edouard Hesselberg, 1919

When the Khaki Boys Come Home. L: Virginia Knauer; M: Leo Friedman, 1919

When the Khaki-Clad Sammies Got There. L: B. Brewster; M: Roy Hartzell, 1919

When the Khaki Lad Comes Home (March). L: A.M.L. Hawes; M: Willard Mayberry, 1919

When the Last Reveille Has Sounded. L&M: H.H. Sangston, 1918

When the Lights Go Out on Broadway. L&M: Al Selden, Max Friedman, and Sam H. Stept, 1917

*When the Lilies Bloom in France Again. L: Robert Levenson; M: George L. Cobb, 1918

When the Lord Makes a Record of a Hero's Deeds, He Draws No Color Line. L: Val Trainor; M: Harry DeCosta, 1918

When the Lusitania Went Down. L: Charles R. McCarron; M: Nat Vincent, 1915

When the Moon Is Shining (Somewhere in France). L&M: Pvt. Frederick Rath, 1917

When the Odor of the Lilacs Fill the Lane. L: Dora R. Croft; M: Z.M. Parvin, 1917

*When the Old Boat Heads for Home. L&M: Earl Fuller, 1918

When the Right Shall Triumph Over Wrong. L: Maggie Burke; M: Leo Friedman, 1919

When the Robert E. Lee Arrives in Old Tennessee, All the Way from Gay Paree. L&M: Paul Cunningham and James V. Monaco, 1919

When the Roll Is Called in Berlin, We'll Be There (March). L: N.M.B. Marshall; M: James Hume, 1917

When the Roses Bloom in Avalon. L: Al Bryan; M: Jack Wells, 1914

When the Sammie Boys Come Home. L: M. Webster; M: J.W. Reams, 1918

When the Sammies Cross the Rhine (March). L&M: Thomas H. West, 1918

When the Sammies Get the Kaiser by the Crown. L: J. Chason; M: T.A. Dunster, 1918

When the Service Star of Blue Turned to Gold. L: M.E. Hofer; M: Leo Friedman, 1919

When the Sixty-Ninth Comes Back. L: Joyce Kilmer; M: Victor Herbert, 1919

When the Soldier Boys Come Marching Home. L&M: F.D. Hall, 1918

When the Spirit of Seventy-Six Made the U.S.A. (A Patriotic Song). L&M: Henry E. Champness, 1917

When the Stars and Stripes Are Planted Everywhere. L: J.A.T. Wood; M: D. Baxter, 1918

When the Stars and Stripes Are Waving in Berlin. L: Anna D. and Raymond B. Egan; M: Roy Cossar, 1918

When the Stars and Stripes Are Waving O'er the Rhine. L&M: M.E. Herbert, 1918

When the Stars and Stripes Set the World Right. L&M: Frances E. Hinderman, 1918

When the Stars in Old Glory Shine Over Berlin. L: Thomas J. Sheehan; M: John F. Wiltjer, 1918

When the Stars in Our Flag Turn to Gold. L&M: R.C. Fuehrer, 1918

When the Strife Is Over, I'll Come Back to You. L: Lulu Williams; M: Leo Friedman, 1919

When the Sun Goes Down in Flanders. L: Neville Fleeson; M: Albert Von Tilzer, 1918

When the Sun Goes Down in France. L&M: Gilbert C. Tennant, 1917

When the Sun Goes Down in France, My Heart Will Be with You. L: H. Vogel; M: Thorval Shevland, 1917

When the Sun Goes Down in Normandie (Then Is When I Sit and Dream of You). L: Jeff Branen; M: Evans Lloyd, 1918

When the Uniform We Don. L: G.H. Burton; M: Leo Friedman, 1918

When the U.S. Band Plays Dixie in Berlin. L: H. Martin Snow; M: D. Durgin Lash, 1918

When the U.S.A. Gets Through. L: M. Barr; M: Leo Friedman, 1918

When the War Is Over. L: Mabel B. McKee; M: Frank W. McKee, 1915

When the War Is Over. L: Robert Spencer; M: Charles L. Johnson, 1915

When the War Is Over. L: S. Barrett; M: Henry Stirling, 1915

When the War Is Over. L: G.B. Gerke; M: Leo Friedman, 1918

When the War Is Over. L&M: Anthony J. Showalter, 1918

When the War Is Over. L: J. Sharpnack; M: Leo Friedman, 1918

When the War Is Over and the Boys March Home Again. L&M: Mattie W. Hancock, 1915

When the War Is Over, Darling. L: Mrs. Ernest Toole; M: Leo Friedman, 1918

When the War Is Over Darling (I'll Return to You). L: Bide Dudley; M: Frederic Watson, 1918

When the War Is Over, Eileen Dear. L: L.E. Lee; M: Everett J. Evans, 1915

When the War Is Over, I'll Return. L: A.M. Dunn; M: Leo Friedman, 1918

When the War Is Over, I'm Coming Back to You. L: R.S. Taylor; M: Leo Friedman, 1918

When the War Is Over, Marjorie. L: E. McCarthy; M: Edward Wunderlich, 1917

When the War Is Over Over There (I'll Come Marching Back to You). L: Billy Mason; M: Joseph Landes Mann, 1918

When the World Is Made Safe for Democracy. L: R.R. Davidson; M: E.A. Lord, 1918

When the Yankee Boys Go Marching Through France. L&M: W.J. Cormay, 1918

When the Yankee Boys Go Marching Up Broadway. L: Jimmie Shea; M: Sam H. Stept, 1918

When the Yankee Boys Meet Kaiser Bill. L: Mrs. W.C. Russell; M: Leo Friedman, 1919

When the Yankee Eagle Screams (March). L: W.B. Davy; M: Arthur Barts, 1918

When the Yankees Cross the Rhine. L&M: J.L. Galloway, 1918

When the Yankees Go Into Battle. L: A. Rossi; M: Christian A. Praetorius, 1917

When the Yankees Yank the Germ from Germany. L: M.T. Willey; M: Leo Friedman, 1918

When the Yanks at the Marne Went Over the Top. L: P.J. Gallagher; M: George Graff, Jr., 1919

When the "Yanks" Come Marching Home. L: William Jerome; M: Seymour Furth, 1917

When the Yanks Come Marching Home. L: L. Fields; M: Leo Friedman, 1919

When the Yanks Come Marching, Marching Home. L: William Charles Buser; M: Milton E. Tyner, 1918

When the Yanks Get Into Berlin. L: G.H. Sheffield; M: Frank W. Ford, 1919

When the Yanks March Through Berlin. L&M: O.B. Brown, 1918

When the Yanks Started Out for the Rhine. L&M: M. Knuckey, 1919

When the Yanks Yank the Germ Out of Germany. L: Alex Rogers and Lester A. Walton; M: Luckey Roberts, 1918

When There's a Home Sweet Home on Every Shore. L&M: Joe Guinan, 1918

*When There's Peace on Earth Again. L&M: Roger Lewis, Bobby Crawford, and Joseph Santly, 1917

When They Called Us Up on the Hindenburg Line. L: A.I. Foster; M: Leo Friedman, 1919

When They Give Me Back My Boy. L: D.L. Woods; M: Leo Friedman, 1919

When They Heard the Call to Colors. L&M: J.H. Kennedy, 1918

When They Listed Colored Soldiers in the U.S.A. L: G. and I. McNorwood; M: Leo Friedman, 1918

When They See the Light from Our Miss Liberty. L&M: Herbert H. Power, 1918

When They Tackle Your Uncle Sam. L&M: J.P. Doyle, 1917

When They're Fighting for Their Country's Call. L: R. Hendrix; M: Leo Friedman, 1918

When They're Saying Au Revoir to Sammie Over There. L&M: L. Lee, 1919

When This Cruel War Is Over. L: Lillias Tucker Whitlock; M: Henry Tucker, 1915

When Those Yankee Boys Went Gunning Over There. L: Malcolm Violette; M: Nell Marshall, 1918

When Tommy Atkins Comes Marching Home. L&M: E.V. Holden, 1915

When Tommy Comes Back to Me. L&M: Thomas A.Y. Hodgson, 1918

*When Tony Goes Over the Top. L&M: Alex Marr, Billy Frisch, and Archie Fletcher, 1918

When Trooper Dan Plays His Banjo Over There. L&M: Charles R. McCarron and Carey Morgan, 1918

When Twilight Shadows Are Falling. L&M: Lew Berk, 1917

When Uncle Joe Steps Into France. L: Bernie Grossman; M: Billy Winkle, from stage production Ziegfeld Follies of 1918, 1918

When Uncle Sam Calls His Boys to the Front. L: Ervin Long; M: Leo Friedman, 1918

When Uncle Sam Gets Down to Bizz. L:
Mrs. W.H. States; M: Leo Friedman, 1918

When Uncle Sam Gets Fighting Mad. L: A.J.
Stevens; M: Merlin L. Dappert, 1917

When Uncle Sam Gets Ready. L: B.D. Coulter; M: Robert H. Brennen, 1917

When Uncle Sam Gets Ready. L&M: O.W.
Lane, 1917

When Uncle Sam Gets Riled. L&M: H.R.
Cole, 1918

When Uncle Sam Is Ruler of the Sea. L:
Henry Blossom; M: Victor Herbert, from
stage production *Century Girl*, 1916

When Uncle Sam Makes the German Band
Play Yankee Doodle. L: J.W. Williams;
M: J.W. Tussing, 1917

When Uncle Sam Plays Yankee Doodle in
Berlin. L: W.D. Pitt; M: Leo Friedman,
1918

When Uncle Sam Says Forward. L: C.E.
Broyles; M: Barclay Walker, 1917

When Uncle Sam Stepped Into France. L:
S.W. Woodson; M: H. Richard, 1919

When Uncle Sam Will Clear the Sea. L: L.
Davis and D.D. Barrett; M: Jean Walz,
1919

When Uncle Sammy Calls Come. L: J.T.
Sullivan; M: Samuel L. Studley, 1918

When Uncle Sammy Fires My Soldier Boy.
L: Mrs. J.P. Boyd; M: Leo Friedman, 1919

When Uncle Sammy Is Through with Me. L:
G. Graybill; M: Leo Friedman, 1918

When Uncle Sammy Leads the Band. L: Lou
Klein; M: Harry Von Tilzer, 1916

When Uncle Sammy's Boys Come Marching
Home. L&M: Helen O. Diamond, 1919

When Uncle Sam's Brave Boys Arrive in
Germany. L&M: Beryl H. Gundy, 1917

When Victory Has Been Won. L: W.C.
Brookshire; M: Leo Friedman, 1918

When Victory Is Won Over There. L: A.M.
Sutter; M: Leo Friedman, 1919

When War Is O'er. M: J. Lawrence Erb, 1915

When We All Go Down to Germany. L&M:
Harry Rapoport, 1918

When We All Go Over the Top. L: J.B.
Morrison; M: Leo Friedman, 1918

When We Are Called to France. L: T.C.
Banks; M: Leo Friedman, 1918

When We Boys Get Back on Broadway,
We'll Bring the Kaiser's Goat Along. L:
L.M.V. Rech; M: Leo Friedman, 1918

When We Come Back. L&M: J.H. and O.L.
Cook, 1918

When We Come Home Again. L&M: W.
Wilson, 1917

When We Come Home Again. L: F.C.
Sagendorf; M: Leo Friedman, 1918

When We Come Marching Home. L&M:
P.F. Bowe, 1918

When We Come Marching Home. L&M:
Richard E. Lippincott, 1918

When We Come Marching Home. L&M:
M.L. Christian, 1919

When We Cross the Rhine River. L&M:
T.A. Buskirk, 1919

When We Crossed That Hindenburg Line. L:
Anna Luke; M: Leo Friedman, 1919

When We Crossed the Rhine. L: F.E. Mastin; M: Leo Friedman, 1919

When We Follow Woodrow Wilson in the
Morning. L&M: William W. Hinshaw, 1917

When We Get Into Germany. L&M: S.E.
Johnson, 1918

When We Get Over There. L&M: A.P. Trubey, 1918

When We Get Over Yonder. L: Mrs. R.L.
Nicholas; M: Roy Hartzell, 1918

When We Get Ready, Willie. L: C.W.
Torgensen; M: Leo Friedman, 1918

When We Get the Kaiser's Goat. L: Hattie
E. Green; M: Leo Friedman, 1918

When We Get There. L: Billy Frisch and
Lew Fagan; M: Alex Marr, 1917

When We Get There. L: F.H. Eckfeld; M:
Leo Friedman, 1918

When We Go Marching Through Kaiserland.
L: Walter Blake; M: E.S.S. Huntington,
1918

When We Go Over the Rhine Line. L&M:
Margaret Flor Thomas, 1918

When We Go Over the Top. L&M: S.B.
Wright, 1917

When We Go Over the Top. L&M: Frank
Templeton, 1918

When We Go Through Berlin. L&M: W.F.
Sill, 1918

When We Go to Conquer Germany, L: Mrs.
J. Jersey; M: Leo Friedman, 1918

When We Have Paid Our Debt. L: B.W.
Young; M: Leo Friedman, 1919

When We Have Peace Once More. L&M:
Charles L. Johnson, 1916

When We Hear No More the Cannon's Roar.
L: A.W. Camp; M: Leo Friedman, 1918

When We Leave Our Trenches, Mother. L:
B.L. Henning; M: Leo Friedman, 1918

When We Lick the Kaiser and His Huns. L:
Edward Outwater; M: Robert H. Brennen,
1918

When We Make the Kaiser See Stars, Then

He Will Respect the Stripes. L: A.T. Rubin; M: Charles L. Johnson, 1917

When We March Down Through the Streets of Old Berlin. L&M: Charles W. Barrett, 1917

When We March Into Old Berlin. L: A.C. Holland; M: Nathan Lord [Frank A. Remick], 1918

When We March Through Germany. L&M: J.H. Oberdorf, 1918

When We Meet Down by the Rhine. L: Ida Scafe; M: Harry Smyth, 1919

*When We Meet in the Sweet Bye and Bye. L&M: Stanley Murphy, 1918

When We Meet You Over Here. L: J.E. Finn; M: Leo Friedman, 1919

When We Paid Our Debt to Lafayette. L: M. Anderson; M: Leo Friedman, 1919

*(When We Reach That Old Port) Somewhere in France. L: Al Selden; M: Sam H. Stept, 1917

When We Welcome Our Boys Back Home (Victory March Song). L: Ralph Abell; M: Leon Rundell, 1919

When We Welcome Our Heroes Home. L&M: Norrie Bernard, 1919

When We Whirl Into Berlin Through the Air. L&M: James Kendis, James Brockman, and Nat Vincent, 1918

*When We Wind Up the Watch on the Rhine (March). L: Gordon V. Thompson; M: Gordon V. Thompson and William Davis, 1917

When We Wind Up the Watch on the Rhine. L: George Sawyer; M: William Ganse, 1918

When We're Going Over. L: John Irwin; M: Everett J. Evans, 1917

When We're Marching Down the Main Street of Berlin (War Song of the Squadrons). L: H.E. Negley; M: John Henri Sugden, 1917

When Will the War Be Over? (March). L&M: W.A. Freese, 1917

When Wilson Sailed Away. L&M: O.E. Britain, 1919

When Woodrow Wilson Takes a Hand. L&M: Shirley E. Cox, 1918

When Yankee Doodle Goes to France. L: Will B. Johnstone; M: Bruce F. Bundy, 1917

When Yankee Doodle Lands in France. L&M: F. Tucker, 1918

*When Yankee Doodle Learns to "Parlez Vous Francais." L: Will J. Hart; M: Edward G. Nelson, 1917

*(When Yankee Doodle Marches Through Berlin) There'll Be a Hot Time in the U.S.A. L: Andrew B. Sterling; M: Arthur Lange, 1917

*When Yankee Doodle Sails Upon the Good Ship "Home Sweet Home." L: Addison Burkhardt; M: Fred Fisher, 1918

When Yankee Soldiers Keep the Watch on the Rhine. L: W.D. Pitt; M: Roy Hartzell, 1918

When Yankee Troops March in Berlin. L: Mrs. James Murray; M: Leo Friedman, 1919

When Yankees Go a-Fightin'. L&M: A.V. Fiske, 1918

When Yo' Comin' Back to Me? (or, I Jes' Know I Can't Behave). L&M: Jim Lockhart, 1918

When You Answer the Call. L: "Jack"; M: "Gill," 1917

When You Bid Your Sweetheart Goodbye. L: Harry B. Smith; M: Victor Jacobi, 1917

When You Break the News to Mother, Tell Her Our Side Is on the Top. L&M: Marie Robinson, 1919

When You Come Back. L: Olivette Harrison; M: Benella Harrison, 1919

*When You Come Back (and You Will Come Back, There's a Whole World Waiting for You). L&M: George M. Cohan, from stage production *Cohan Revue of 1918*, 1918

When You Come Back, My Soldier Boy. L&M: Karl R. Goetze, 1918

When You Come Back to Me. L: Harry Williams; M: Neil Morét, 1919

When You Come Back to Oregon. L: F.J. Schniederjost; M: Leo Friedman, 1919

When You Come Back to the U.S.A. L&M: J.H. Briscoe, 1918

When You Get Back to Illinois. L&M: Coleman Goetz, Frank Fay, and Dave Dreyer, 1918

When You Hear Pershing's Band Play Hip, Hip, Hooray! L&M: R.W. Nicol, 1918

When You Hear the Bugle Call. L&M: George Byrd Dougherty, 1916

When You Hear Your Country Call "Soldier Boy." L&M: Martie B. Bergen, 1916

When You Hear Your Uncle Sammy Call for Soldiers. L&M: Mary Stanholtzer, 1918

When You Kiss Your Dear Old Mother Goodbye. L: Joseph Laverick; M: M. Cammarata, 1918

*When You Kiss Your Soldier Boy Goodbye. L&M: M. Russell Brown, 1917

When You Leave the Dear Old U.S.A. (You

Leave the World Behind). L: O. Harter; M: Leo Friedman, 1919

When You Return. L: F. Potts; M: Leo Friedman, 1919

When You Rile Your Uncle Sam. L&M: J. Zimmermann, 1918

When You See Old Glory Far Away from Home. L: C. Warren Landon; M: S. Snowden Cassard, 1915

When You See Old Glory Waving, Think of Mother. L: B.M. Walters; M: Leo Friedman, 1918

When You Struck at Old Glory, You Made a Mistake. L&M: Harry Beecher Stowe, 1917

When You Write, Send a Letter of Cheer. L&M: Charles A. Ford, 1917

When Your Boy Comes Back to You. L&M: Gordon V. Thompson, 1917

When Your Boys Come Home to You. L&M: S.E. Atkinson, 1918

When Your Country Is in Danger. L: H. Zistel and J. Grady; M: H. Ziztel, 1917

*When Your Sailor Boy in Blue Comes Sailing Home to You. L: Annelu Burns; M: Madelyn Sheppard, 1918

When Your Uncle Gets the Kaiser. L: O.C. Hogue; M: Leo Friedman, 1918

When You're a Long, Long Way from Home. L: Sam M. Lewis; M: George W. Meyer, 1914

When You're Nobody's Soldier Boy. L: H. Bernardo; M: Harry E. Webb, 1918

When You've Proved Yourself a Real Live Yank. L: G. Neibaur; M: Frank W. Ford, 1919

Whene'er Your Star of Blue Takes on a Golden Hue. L: C.S. Corrigan; M: W.T. Porter, 1918

Where Are the Boys? L&M: K. Brunson, 1918

Where Are the Brave Boys Marchin'? L&M: D.R. Enness, 1918

Where Are the Heroes of Today? L&M: J.W. Woller, 1917

Where Do We Go from Here? L: Howard Johnson; M: Percy Wenrich, 1917

Where E'er Our Banner Waves. L: Jack Smith; M: Will Morrison, 1914

Where Is My Daddy Gone? L: J.L. Benoit; M: Leo Friedman, 1919

Where Is My Soldier Boy Tonight? L&M: L.A. Starr, 1918

Where Is the Boy Who Went Over the Sea? L&M: Marie Rich, 1918

Where Is the Girl I Left Behind? L&M: George M. Cohan, 1919

Where Is There Peace? L&M: M.O. Burford, 1918

Where Is Your Boy Tonight? L&M: George C. Stebbins, 1918

Where It's Peace-Jam Makin' Time. L&M: James Kendis, James Brockman, and Nat Vincent, 1915

Where Our Wilson Shines — Democracy (March). L&M: Michael Perna, 1918

Where Poppies Bloom. L: Alex Sullivan; M: Lynn Cowan, 1918

Where the Stars and Stripes Are to Wave 'Way 'Cross in Those Germany Towns. L&M: W.G. Hall, 1917

*(Whether Friend or Foe, They're Brothers) When They're Dreaming of Home Sweet Home. L: Darl MacBoyle; M: S. Roughsedge, 1916

While Coming Home. L&M: Charles Bade, 1919

While Fighting for Liberty. L: T.W. Harris; M: H.A. Hummer, 1918

While Fighting for Uncle Sam, My Thoughts Come Back to You. L: M.E. Coffin; M: M.E. Coffin and Charles T. Edwards, 1918

While I Am Somewhere in France (She Is Waiting in the U.S.A.). L&M: Ethel Myers, 1918

While Onward Marching Through France, Boys. L: G.H.W. Cloud; M: Walter Lewis, 1918

While Our Banner Floats Above. L&M: M.D. Neville, 1918

While Our Guns Back the Flag on the Sea. L&M: J.H. Alleman, 1917

While the Bells of Freedom Ring Onward to Victory. L: M.C. Fekete; M: Joseph Psota, 1919

While the British Bull-Dog's Watching the Door. L&M: Harry Lauder, 1915

While the Fearful Storm of Shot and Shell Is Raging. L: John Boe; M: Clifton Keith, 1917

While the War Rages Over the Sea. L: E.P. French; M: Dorothy W. Barrows, 1918

While Uncle Sam Sings Yankee Doodle to the Kaiser. L&M: F.D. Lamb, 1917

While We Are Marching to Berlin. L: Leslie Borton; M: Leo Friedman, 1918

While We Are on Our Way to Europe (A Patriotic Song). L: W.E. Walter; M: Henry Clay Work, 1917

While We Go Marching to Victory. L: Mrs. M.B. Shannon; M: Leo Friedman, 1918

While We're Marching to Berlin. L: S.E. Kysor; M: Leo Friedman, 1918

While You Are Away, Boys. L: E.E. Johnson; M: Leo Friedman, 1919

While You're Away. L&M: L. Wolfe Gilbert and Anatol Friedland, 1918

While You're Over the Sea. L: Sanders Reynolds; M: L.B. Shook, 1918

*While You're Over There in No Man's Land (I'm Over Here in Lonesome Land). L: Jessie Spiess; M: Jack Stanley, 1918

Whistling Soldier Boys. M: George L. Spaulding, 1917

The White House Is the Light House of the World. L&M: Isador [Irving] Caesar and Al Bryan, 1918

The White House Is the Light House of the World. L: Daniel Unger and Augustus F. Dannic; M: Marie R. Dannic, 1918

The White House Melody of Peace. M: William L. Needham, 1914

Who Gave You the Name of Old Glory? L&M: E.L. Young, 1917

Who Is Wiser Than the Kaiser? Ans: Uncle Sam, Why, Uncle Sam. L&M: Howard Griffith, 1918

*Who Put the "Germ" in Germany? L: Thomas R. Rees; M: Lawrence E. Eberly, 1917

Who Said America Would Not Fight? L: Mrs. J.A. McCombs; M: Leo Friedman, 1919

Who Said Yankees Couldn't Fight? L&M: Maxine Rideout, 1918

Who Shall Prepare for the Battle? L: Walter S. Percy; M: H. LeRoy Goodwin, 1917

Who Stopped the Hun? L&M: A.I. Foster, 1919

Who Will Love Poor Me If Papa Falls on the Battlefield? L&M: Ralph W. Leisher, 1917

The Whole World Is Calling You. L&M: Clifton S. Anthony, 1917

Who'll Take Care of the Harem (When the Sultan Goes to War). L: Jimmie Kaufmann and Archie Mayer; M: William J. Lewis, 1915

Who's Afraid of the Kaiser? L&M: L. Wolfe Gilbert and Anatol Friedland, 1918

Who's Who in Berlin. L&M: Jewell Ellison, 1918

Who's Who? U.S.! Not You! L&M: Florence Thayer, 1918

Why Can't We Have a Little Bit of Green in the Old Red, White, and Blue? L&M: Howard Johnson and E. Ray Goetz, 1917

Why Did They Stop the War? L: Jean Havez; M: Edward Laska, 1919

Why Don't Daddy Come Home? L&M: C.R. Tennant, 1919

Why Hasn't Daddy Come Home from the War? L: E. Shaw; M: George Graff, Jr., 1919

Why I'm a U.S. Soldier Boy. L&M: J.M.B. Stapleford, 1917

Why I'se Fighting. L: Mrs. W.T. Burt; M: Leo Friedman, 1919

Why Walk to Berlin When We Can Ride in a Tank? L&M: Mrs. N.E. Coan, 1919

Why We Want to Lick Germany. L: Raymond Lee Roy Blymyer; M: George H. Klary, 1918

Why Winnie Went to War to Be a Nurse. L&M: Joseph McManus, Jr., 1915

The Widow of a German Threw Him Down. L: Jeff Branen; M: Evans Lloyd, 1918

Will He Come Home (or, World Democracy). L&M: D.P. Sims, 1918

Will the Angels Guard My Daddy Over There? L: Paul B. Armstrong; M: F. Henri Klickmann, 1917

Will You Be One of the Soldier Boys? L: C.A. Gifford; M: H.C. Weasner, 1916

Will You Be True to a Sammy Boy? L: E. Gilchrist; M: Leo Friedman, 1918

Will You Love Me When the War Is Over, Dear? L&M: G. Gregory, 1919

Will You Wait, Little Girl, for Me? L&M: Max Clay, 1916

William Didn't. L: A.B. Craig; M: Artie Bowers, 1919

William the Vanquished. L: Mrs. Walker Murray; M: Leo Friedman, 1919

Wilson. L: B.R. Mintus; M: Leo Friedman, 1918

W-I-L-S-O-N. L: C. Kennedy; M: Leo Friedman, 1918

Wilson Against Wilhelm. L: Norma Fewings; M: Leo Friedman, 1918

*Wilson, Democracy, and the Red, White and Blue. L&M: Pvt. William H. Hollingsworth, 1918

The Wilson-Lincoln Reign. L: R.B. Grey; M: Charles J.W. Jerreld, 1915

Wilson the Wise. L: Beatrice Ponsonby; M: Paul Shannon, 1915

Wilson, You're the Man Behind the Man Behind the Gun (March). L&M: Lee Johnson, 1919

Wilsonian March. M: Einar Sorensen, 1918

Win We Must. L: E.H. Condon; M: Leo Friedman, 1919

Winds from Dixie. L: Emily Melvin; M: Leo Friedman, 1919

Wings of Liberty. L&M: D.W. Matthie, 1918

Wings of the U.S.A. L: W.H. Blanchard; M: Caroline H. Blanchard, 1917

Winning the War. L: Lorenza Brunet; M: Leo Friedman, 1919

Wise Uncle Sam. L: F. Alley; M: James M. Bisset, 1918

With a Yankee Noose Around the Kaiser's Neck. L: T. Patrick Henry; M: C.S. Mills, 1918

With Colors Waving (March). M: Matilee Loeb-Evans, 1919

With Drum and Fife (March). L: Leopold Jacobson and Leo Stein; M: Oscar Straus, from stage production *Beautiful Unknown*, 1917

With Ev'ry Thought I Breathe a Pray'r for You. L: J. Will Callahan; M: Blanche M. Tice, 1918

With Flying Banners. M: Carl Wilhelm Kern, 1918

With Liberty Bonds. L&M: J.O. Frank, 1918

With Our Comrades O'er the Sea. L&M: J.W. Van DeVenter, 1917

With the Colors. L: C.R. Boucher; M: Einar V. Sorensen, 1918

With Waving Colors. M: Ludwig Renk, 1917

Women of the Homeland (God Bless You, Every One). M: Bernard Hamblen, 1918

Wonderful Emblem of Freedom (A Patriotic Song). L&M: William Gram, 1917

Wonderful Letters Spell Home. L: Harold Slater; M: Leo Friedman, 1919

Wonderland (American National Hymn). L&M: Bertha F. Gordon, 1917

Won't You Buy a War Stamp? L: Harold Atteridge; M: Ray Perkins, from stage production Passing Show of 1918, 1918

Won't You Come Back to Me? L&M: Leo Wood, 1915

Woodrow at the Wheel. L&M: Fanny Powell, 1917

Woodrow Wilson. L: M. Isabella Osmun; M: Roy Hartzell, 1918

Woodrow Wilson and the Red, White and Blue. L&M: George Hansford and George Wollow, 1917

Woodrow Wilson and U.S.A. L: C.E. Hull; M: E.S.S. Huntington, 1918

Woodrow Wilson Four Years More. L&M: W.M. Treloar, 1916

Woodrow Wilson Is the Man. L&M: T.A. Buskirk, 1919

Woodrow Wilson, Leader of the U.S.A. L: Henry Rupprecht; M: Waldemar Maass, 1918

Woodrow Wilson, May God Be with You. L&M: P.J. Paul, 1918

The Woodrow Wilson Military March. M: J. Lambremont, 1917

Woodrow Wilson of the U.S.A. L: Jack Taylor; M: Adam Carroll, 1919

Woodrow Wilson, the Whole World's Proud of You. L&M: Charles T. Keating, 1918

Woodrow Wilson, You're the Man! L: L. Crumpacker; M: Henry Mather, 1915

Working for the Government Now. L&M: Theodore Tinnette, 1918

The World Calls to America. L: M. Oliver; M: Leo Friedman, 1918

World Democracy Versus Autocracy. L: G.W. Simmons, Jr.; M: J.L. White, 1918

The World for Democracy (President Wilson's Call). L: M. Probasco; M: Metta J. Shoemaker, 1917

The World for Democracy (March). M: M.E. DeGraff, 1919

World Freedom (March). M: F.M. Paine, 1919

World Peace. L&M: W.H. Wilgus, 1918

World War Blues. L&M: George B. Harris, Jr., 1918

The World War Ended. L: E. McLaughlin; M: Frank W. Ford, 1919

The World's Assassin-Kaiser (A Patriotic Song). L&M: H.F. Spalding, 1918

The World's at Peace Once More. L&M: Frieda Schmidt, 1919

The World's Battle-Cry. L: Mrs. J.T. Ricker; M: W.H. Aiken, 1918

The World's Freedom. L: E. Wright; M: W. Steffe, 1918

The World's Greatest War Is Over. L&M: Albert Schmid, 1919

The World's Jubilee. L: John F. Howard; M: Harvey B. Gaul, 1919

The World's Peace Anthem. L&M: W.W. Chapple, 1916

The World's Peace Anthem (Let the House of Ho-hen-zollern Fall). L&M: A.P. Fuquay, 1918

The World's Victory (March). M: F.P. Barnitz, 1918

The World's War Song. L&M: G.B. Freeman, Jr., 1917

Worldwide Democracy. L&M: W.S. Spradling, 1919

Worldwide Liberty (March). M: H.C. Miller, 1918

The Worldwide War Is Over. L&M: H.S. Cohen, 1919

*The Worst Is Yet to Come. L: Sam M. Lewis and Joe Young; M: Bert Grant, 1918

Would That Bring You Back Again? L: Ivan Reid; M: Peter DeRose, 1918

*Would You Rather Be a Colonel with an Eagle on Your Shoulder (or a Private with a Chicken on Your Knee)? L: Sidney D. Mitchell; M: Archie Gottler, from stage production Ziegfeld Follies of 1918, 1918

Wounded Soldier. L: Mrs. G. Booth; M: Ed Wills, 1915

A Wounded Soldier Lied. L: Wendell Thompson; M: Leo Friedman, 1919

Wrap Me in the Colors of the Red, White and Blue (It's the Emblem of Uncle Sam). L: M.A. Sabin; M: Thorma Ruff, 1918

Write a Letter Home to Mother. L: J. Will Callahan; M: Frank C. Huston, 1917

Write to Me, My Soldier Boy. L&M: H.D. Neides, 1918

Write to Some Lonesome Sailor Boy. L: Julia Pence; M: Leo Friedman, 1919

*Write to Your Dear Sweet Mother (If It's Only Just a Line). L: Ernest S. Stafford; M: Charles Haller, 1917

Write, Write, Write. L&M: J.J. Haviside, 1918

Y

Y Stands for Yankee. L: John MacNaughton; M: Jean MacNaughton, 1918

The Yank Across the Sea. L&M: J.P. James, 1918

A Yank in the Ranks of America. L&M: G.H. Johnson, 1919

Yank of the U.S.A. L: Pearl McMillan; M: Leo Friedman, 1919

Yankee. L&M: Arnold Thomas, 1919

Yankee Boy. L: Fred Ziemer; M: J.R. Shannon, 1918

Yankee Boy (The Great War-Drive Song). L&M: C.E. Henry, 1918

Yankee Boy, We're All for You. L&M: Jessie Oliver Cook, 1918

Yankee Boy, You're Welcome Back to the U.S.A. L&M: J.C. Palmer, 1919

Yankee Boys. L: D. Stewart; M: Leo Friedman, 1918

Yankee Boys. L: R.H. Charnock; M: Leo Friedman, 1918

The Yankee Boys Are Coming. L: J.D. Alexander; M: Leo Friedman, 1919

The Yankee Boys Came Home. L: Flossie Jessup; M: Leo Friedman, 1919

The Yankee Boys for Me. L: W. Douglas; M: Arnulf Cintura, 1918

Yankee Boys from Yankee Land Are on Their Way to France. L: Joseph Ferguson; M: Thomas E. Evans, 1917

Yankee Boys in Italy (March). L: F.A. Giannini; M: Victor Giannini, 1918

Yankee Boys March. M: Grace R. Spellacy, 1919

The Yankee Boys Today. L&M: E.L. Reed, 1918

Yankee Dear. L: Pearl Browning; M: Leo Friedman, 1919

Yankee Division March. M: Oliver E. Story, 1919

Yankee Doodle. L&M: E.K. Heyser, 1914

A Yankee Doodle Boy Is Good Enough for Me. L&M: W.L. Livernash, 1916

Yankee Doodle Dandies, Come Along! L: M.T. Jeffrey; M: Leo Friedman, 1918

Yankee Doodle Dixie. L&M: J.W. Jervey, 1917

Yankee—Doodle Do. L&M: Agnes G. Bacon, 1918

Yankee Doodle Dude. L&M: Clara H. Rees, 1918

Yankee Doodle Is in France to Save Democracy (Help the Victory Over Here). L&M: Morris Silnutzer, 1918

Yankee Doodle Lads. L&M: William D. Rich, 1917

Yankee Doodle Land. L: M. Robinson; M: Leo Friedman, 1918

Yankee Doodle on the Rhine. L: J.B. Woods; M: Marvin Radnor, 1917

Yankee Doodle Sammies. L&M: E.C. Converse, 1918

Yankee Doodle's Going to Berlin. L&M: Kent Perkins, 1918

Yankee Girl (March). L: Paul M. Tebault; M: Clifford E. Slider, 1918

Yankee Girl and Yankee Land. L&M: B.E.P. Matthews, 1919

Yankee Girl, I'm Coming Back to You. L: Jack O'Brien; M: Billy Timmins, 1919

Yankee Girls. L: David A. Carson; M: Vincent J. Nery, 1918

Yankee Grit (March). M: H.A. Vandercook, 1919

Yankee Gunner in the Navy. L&M: J.A. Hurley, 1918

Yankee Heroes. L: H. Thompson; M: Leo Friedman, 1918

*Yankee (He's There, All There). L&M: Charles K. Harris, 1917

Yankee Lad. L&M: Alonzo Newton Benn, 1918

Yankee Lads. L: Sarah Lawrence; M: Leo Friedman, 1918

Yankee Land. L&M: Harry E. Reardon, 1918

*Yankee Land, Fairest Land. L&M: Rudolph Schiller, 1918

Yankee Land Is Good Enough for Me. L: K. Leaver; M: J.E. Smyth, 1919

Yankee Land, My Yankee Land. L&M: M.G. Patrick, 1919

The Yankee Lanky Boys So True. L: Millie Bibbs; M: Leo Friedman, 1919

Yankee—McAdoo-dle. L&M: S.O. Hawkins and J.S. Hall, 1918

A Yankee Message to France (March). L&M: G.W. Burton, 1918

Yankee Mother's Pray'r. L: L.J. Juliano; M: Leo Friedman, 1919

Yankee Noodle. L&M: E.K. Myers, 1917

Yankee of 1918. L&M: Cassie Hall, 1918

Yankee on the Kaiser's Track. L: W.H. Smith; M: Leo Friedman, 1918

Yankee Pep. L&M: O.D. Hopkins, 1918

Yankee Punch. L&M: Phil Ramsey, 1917

Yankee Punch. L&M: W.T. Stevens, 1918

Yankee Sammies. L&M: Lorene M. Decker, 1918

Yankee Sammy. L: Bill Stinger [Richard H. Mouser]; M: Maud B. Bonnell, 1918

Yankee Ships Are Going Over There. L&M: C.J. Potter, 1918

Yankee Soldier Boy. L&M: H.L. Smith, 1918

Yankee Spirit (Democracy Forever). L&M: Anna Frada, 1918

Yankee Tank. L: W.H. Shirley; M: Louis Panella, 1918

Yankee Tars (March). M: John Boulton, 1919

Yankee Time. L: A.A. Craig; M: Jack Berger, 1918

Yankee Triumphal March. M: Jessie Crosby Osborne, 1918

Yankeeland (March). M: C.D. Henninger, 1917

Yankeeland. L&M: Clint R. Carpenter, 1918

Yankeeland to Frenchland (March). L&M: J.W. Hanley, 1918

The Yankees Are Coming. L: E.E. Seammen; M: Leo Friedman, 1918

The Yankees Are Coming (March). L&M: Margaret McClure-Stitt, 1918

The Yankees Are Coming. L: James W. Tavenner; M: Robert H. Brennan, 1919

The Yankees Are Whis'ling Now. L: I.J.A. Miller; M: Jack Berger, 1918

Yankees from the U.S.A. (March). L&M: Carlotta Lake, 1919

Yankee's Jubilee. L: M.E. Thompson and Helen Gerhart; M: Adapted from the melody of "Kingdom's Coming," 1918

Yankees on the Rhine. L: F.N. Graves; M: John A. O'Shea, 1917

Yankees on the Rhine, Yankees on the Brine (March). L: F.N. Graves; M: C.W. Bennett, 1918

Yankees' Pride. L: R.E. Broderic; M: Leo Friedman, 1919

Yankees, Tommies, Poilus! L: J. Jefferson; M: Leo Friedman, 1919

Yanko-Franco Drive (March). L: P. Hunt; M: D.A. Summo, 1918

The Yanks Are Coming! L: Clara Cooper; M: Leo Friedman, 1919

The Yanks Are Coming, Hooray! Horray! L: Eva Allen Ball; M: Amber G. Lasley, 1918

The Yanks at Last Are in Berlin. L: Nellie Thomas; M: Ed Smith, 1919

The Yanks Belong to Uncle Sam. L: W.L. Ross; M: Artie Bowers, 1919

Yanks, Go to It Over There! L&M: L. Moore, 1918

Yanks of the U.S.A. L&M: Leona Volkmar, 1919

Yanks on the Rhine. L&M: Clara Long, 1919

The Yank's Returning. L: Mrs. L. Craft; M: Edouard Hesselberg, 1919

The Yanks' Victory. L&M: C. Regnier Davis, 1918

The Yanks Will Take Care of You. L: I.J. Rigdon; M: Leo Friedman, 1919

The Yanks with the Tanks Will Go Through the German Ranks (and Roll Right Through Berlin). L&M: Corporal Jimmie Shea, 1918

The Yaphank Yank. L: Junior Willud; M: George Longstaff, 1917

Ye Gallant Sons of America. L&M: James W. Johnson, 1918

Yes, I'll Help Bring Peace Again. L: Chauncey Long; M: C.E. Keller, 1917

Yiddisha Army Blues. L&M: J. Cooper, 1918

You Are Children of the U.S.A. L: Edward Van Every; M: James W. Conrad, 1917

You Are Full of the Bull from ze Boulevard. L: Howard Johnson; M: Howard Johnson and George W. Meyer, 1919

You Are Welcome Home Again, Soldier Boy. L&M: W.H. Peel, 1919

You Buy and I'll Buy More War Savings Stamps. L&M: E.K. Mallory, 1918

You Call Me Old Glory. L&M: R.D. Bagley, 1918

You Can Have Our Boy, America. L: Mrs. H.F. Alber; M: Leo Friedman, 1918

You Can Tell That He's an American. L: Howard Johnson; M: Percy Wenrich, from stage production Ziegfeld Follies of 1918, 1918

You Can Trust Me, Mother Dear (with Old Uncle Sam). L: R.M. Botter; M: G.C. Snyder, 1917

You Can't Beat Us for We've Never Lost a War. L: J. Keirn Brennan; M: Ernest R. Ball, 1918

You Can't Blame the Girlies at All, They All Want to Marry a Soldier. L: Alex Gerber; M: Abner Silver, 1919

You Can't Down the American Flag (March). L&M: Levi Clark, 1917

You Can't Hold the Yankees Back. L&M: Rose Kimmel Kaufman, 1918

*You Can't Stop the Yanks (Till They Go Right Through). L&M: Jack Caddigan and Chick Story, 1918

You Can't Tread on Uncle Samuel's Toes. L: S.E. Van Eman; M: Leo Friedman, 1919

You Can't Whip Old Uncle Sammy. L: Roger Rickey; M: Leo Friedman, 1918

You Cooked the Goose of the Kaiser. L&M: Marjorie Rodger, 1918

You Great Big Handsome Marine. L&M: Harold Dixon, 1918

You Great Big Soldier Man. L: Sarah Evelyn Claxton; M: William Busé, 1918

*You Keep Sending 'Em Over and We'll Keep Knocking 'Em Down. L: Sidney D. Mitchell; M: Harry Ruby, 1917

You Kissed Me (and Said Goodbye). L: Eleanor Alverson; M: Charles K. Harris, 1917

You Krazy Kaiser. L&M: N. Haywood [W.J. Brown], 1918

You Man in Khaki, You Man in Blue. L&M: Charles Torgensen, 1919

You Must Honor the Banner That's Mine. L: R.L. Small; M: Leo Friedman, 1918

You Must Shoot the Way You Shout. L: Lulu Kellar; M: Leo Friedman, 1918

You Needn't Try to Bluff Your Uncle Sammy. L&M: M.G. Hill, 1919

You Never Found a Partner to Conquer Uncle Sam. L&M: L.E. Miller, 1919

You Owe It to the Brave Boys Over There. L: Louis E. Thayer; M: Victor M. Paulson, 1918

You Raised a Noble Hero for the Good Old U.S.A. L: James Sunderland and John J.

McGlinchy; M: William T. Gilmore, 1917

You 21 and You 53, You Both Stand for Liberty. L: Andrew B. Sterling; M: Arthur Lange, 1917

You Were the Kind of Son, Dear, That I Hoped You'd Be. L: Rose E. Nelson; M: Leo Friedman, 1918

You Would Fight for Your Mother, How About Your Country? L: V.L. Roussell; M: Leo Friedman, 1919

You'd Better Be Nice to Them Now! L&M: William Tracey and Jack Stern, 1918

You'd Better Get a Girl Before the Boys Come Home. L&M: Sidney D. Mitchell, Joseph H. Santly, and Cliff Hess, 1918

You'd Better Hang Up Your Flag. L&M: J.L. Cook, 1917

You'd Better Raise Your Boy to Be a Soldier. L: John McA. Stirling; M: Robert B. Stirling, 1916

You'll Be Proud to Be a Soldier Boy. L: J.J. Clark; M: Pat Paderewsky, 1918

You'll Be Sadder But Wiser, Mr. Kaiser, When Uncle Sam Gets Over There. L&M: Joe McKiernan, 1918

You'll Be Welcome as Flowers in the Maytime. L: Raymond B. Egan; M: Richard A. Whiting, 1918

You'll Find Old Dixieland in France. L: Grant Clarke; M: George W. Meyer, from stage production Ziegfeld Follies of 1918, 1918

You'll Have to Put Him to Sleep with the Marseillaise and Wake Him Up with a Oo-La-La. L: Andrew B. Sterling; M: Harry Von Tilzer, 1918

You'll Have to Take Your Hat Off to the Old Red, White and Blue. L&M: Emory C. O'Hara, 1916

You'll Know Uncle Sam Went Some. L&M: W.O. Miller, 1918

You'll Sing, I'll Sing, We'll All Sing Together When the Boys Come Home. L&M: Samuel Brecker, 1918

Young America (We're Strong for You). L&M: William McKenna, 1915

Young Democracy. L&M: Jay Ess [Julius Schmidt], 1917

Your Boy and My Boy. L: Minnie L. Upton; M: Jack Doran, 1917

Your Boy and My Boy. L&M: W.R. Garbutt, 1918

Your Comrades from the U.S.A. L&M: Richard E. Lippincott, 1918

Your Country Calls. L&M: C.T. Greenawald, 1917

Your Country Calls You. L&M: Viola B. Lewis, 1917

Your Country Is Calling. L: F.P. Patterson; M: Mae Betts, 1917

Your Country Needs You. L&M: Edgar Allyn Cole, 1917

Your Country Needs You. L: Edith Waite Colson; M: Emily Wood Bower, 1917

Your Country Needs You. L&M: W.J. Kennedy, 1918

Your Country Needs You. L&M: Roy M. Evans, 1918

Your Country Needs You Now. L: Al Dubin; M: Rennie Cormack and George B. McConnell, 1917

Your Cross and My Cross (A Patriotic Song). L: Anonymous; M: J.T. Kerker, 1918

*Your Daddy Will Be Proud of You. L: J. Will Callahan; M: Paul C. Pratt, 1918

Your Daddy's a Soldier Man. L&M: Bob Harvey, 1918

Your Daddy's Gone to Heaven (from Somewhere in France). L: Dick Riley; M: Leo Friedman, 1919

Your Father Was a Soldier. L: Harry Williams; M: Egbert Van Alstyne, 1917

Your Flag and Country Want You (We Don't Want to Lose You). L: Paul A. Rubens and Frank North; M: Paul A. Rubens, 1915

Your Flag and Mine. L: Harriet H. Pierson; M: Ira B. Wilson, 1918

Your Flag and My Flag. L: Wilbur D. Nesbit; M: H.W.B. Barnes, 1917

Your Flag and My Flag. L: Wilbur D. Nesbit; M: R.M. Frandsen, 1917

Your Flag and My Flag. L: George Orlia Webster; M: I.H. Meredith, 1917

Your Flag and My Flag. L: Wilbur D. Nesbit; M: Miss C. Buchanan, 1917

Your Flag and My Flag. M: Harley Joseph Wood, 1917

Your Flag and My Flag. L: Wilbur D. Nesbit; M: F.R. Rix, 1918

Your Flag—My Flag. L&M: May E. Hollingsworth, 1918

Your King and Country Want You (March). M: Paul A. Rubens, 1914

Your Lad and My Lad. L: Randall Parrish; M: Rossetter G. Cole, 1918

Your Lad and My Lad. L: Gerald Grey; M: J.A. Parks, 1918

Your Land and Mine. L: Ada Simpson Sherwood; M: David Nyvall, Jr., 1918

Your Lips Are No Man's Land but Mine. L&M: Arthur Guy Empey, Charles R. Mc-

Carron, and Carey Morgan, from silent film *Over the Top*, 1918

Your Little Girl Is Waiting in the Good Old U.S.A. L&M: Albert S. Mills, 1918

Your Mother Is Waiting for You, Lad. L: S.C. Stocking; M: Leo Friedman, 1919

Your Mother's a Soldier, Too (March). L: Mell Faris; M: Ed East, 1917

Your Papa Will Never Come Home, Dear. L: J.N. Albert and Harry N. Bradford; M: J.E. Andino, 1918

Your Sailor Boy. L: J.T. Dunnington; M: Leo Friedman, 1919

Your Soldier Boy Will Come Again to You. L&M: Edson D. Stout, 1918

Your Soldier's Last Goodbye. L&M: Francis C. Chantereau, 1918

Your Sweetheart Is Waiting for You. L: M.J. Hertlein; M: Leo Friedman, 1918

Your Uncle Sam Is Mighty Proud of Sammy. L: C. Price; M: C. Botefuhr, 1919

Your Uncle Sam Will Get a Square Meal When the Kaiser Gets a Lunch. L: E. Popplewell; M: Harry J. Lincoln, 1917

Your Uncle Sammy Now Is Calling for the Boys of the U.S.A. (March). L&M: B. Frank Dennis, 1917

Your Uncle Sam's Sammy. L&M: W.M. Shields, 1918

Your Uncle Samuel's Hat Is in the Ring (or, The Scream of the War Eagle). L&M: C.C. Kirk, 1918

You're a Better Man Than I Am, Mr. Wilson. L: John W. Bratton; M: Joseph H. Santly, 1918

You're Coming Back. L&M: F. Stanton, 1919

You're Coming Back Some Day. L&M: Roy Atwell, 1918

You're Either for the U.S.—or You're Not. L&M: H. Conover, 1918

You're in the Army Now. L&M: Unknown

You're Missing Down in Dixie But You're Serving Over There. L&M: Mabel Noland, 1918

*You're My Beautiful American Rose. L&M: Charles A. Ford, 1917

You're So Cute, Soldier Boy. L: Edgar Allan Woolf; M: Anatol Friedland, from stage production *Toot Toot*, 1918

*You're the Greatest Little Mothers in the World (Mothers of America). L: Sam M. Lewis and Joe Young; M: Archie Gottler, 1918

You're the Leader of Them All, My U.S.A. L&M: Joe Cronson, 1917

You're the Son of the U.S.A. L&M: Bert Haft and Jack Altman, 1917

You're Your Mama's Little Daddy Now! L: Will D. Cobb; M: Gus Edwards, 1918

Yours Truly, Uncle Sam. L&M: H.C. Hardley, 1918

You've Gone Too Far with Uncle Sam (March). L&M: W.C. Archer, 1917

You've Got to Be in Khaki. L: Will D. Cobb; M: Gus Edwards, 1918

You've Got to Do Something for Uncle Sam. L: G.R. Chins; M: Alevia R. Chins, 1918

*You've Got to Go In or Go Under. L: Percival Knight; M: Gitz Rice, from stage production *Getting Together*, 1918

You've Won the Victory. L: Mrs. A.A. Stacy; M: Leo Friedman, 1919

Z

Ze Yankee Boys Have Made a Wild French Baby Out of Me. L: Eugene West; M: Joe Gold, 1919

Part III
Complete Lyrics of Selected Songs

The following are complete lyrics to a collection of 321 representative songs, including most of those discussed at length in Part I. Their arrangement is alphabetical by title, treating parenthesized words as a regular part of a title. Lyricist, composer, and copyright information are provided for each. Photographs of many original sheet music covers are included.

(After the Battle Is Over) Then You Can Come Back to Me. L&M: L. Wolfe Gilbert and Anatol Friedland. Copyright 1918 by Gilbert & Friedland, Inc., New York.

1st Verse:
Wonderful boy, wonderful girl,
So hard to part, he is leaving.
Her heart is strong, 'tis not for long,
He, strange to say, does the grieving.
"When shall I come back to you, dear?
When will the old love renew, dear?"
Girlie replies, "Save all your sighs,
Here's when I'll want you":

Chorus:
"After the battle is over
And you've fought as you ought to have
    done.
After you've served for your country
And the struggle for freedom is won.
When you've revenged little Belgium
And when peace on earth there shall be,
After you've covered yourself with glory,
Then you can come back to me."

2nd Verse:
Wonderful girl proud of her boy,
Somewhere in France he is fighting;
Stories are told, deeds brave and bold,
Each message reads more exciting.
What she had said when they parted
Filled him with cheer when he started.
On to the fray to win the day,
He could hear her say:

After the War Is Over. L&M: James W. Casey. Copyright 1917 by Echo Music Publishing Co., Seattle, Wash.

1st Verse:
A soldier boy in a foreign land
Was lonely as he could be;
Though danger lurked on ev'ry hand,
His thoughts were across the sea.
Then in the din of the cannon's roar
(Back to the one he was longing for),
Quickly he pencilled a little note,
This is the message he wrote:

Chorus:
"After the war is over,
After the world's at rest,
I'm coming back to you, dear,
The one I love the best.
Then there will be no sorrow,
Sunshine will come once more;
We'll have a happy tomorrow,
After the war is o'er."

2nd Verse:
The weary days slowly dragged along,
Yet his heart knew no fear;
His regiment kept fighting on,
With victory seeming near.
Back in the village someone doth yearn,
Praying each day for his safe return;
Pressed to her heart is his tender note,
She loves each word that he wrote:

After the War Is Over (Will There Be Any "Home Sweet Home"). L: E.J. Pourmon and Joseph Woodruff; M: Harry Andrieu. Copyright 1917 by Broad & Market Music Co., Newark, N.J.

1st Verse:
Angels they are weeping o'er the foreign war,
Transports are sailing from shore to shore;
Brave heroes are falling to arise no more,
But still the bugle's calling ev'ry man to war:

Chorus:
After the war is over and the world's at
    peace,
Many a heart will be aching after the war
    has ceased.
Many a home will be vacant,
Many a child alone;
But I hope they'll all be happy
In a place called "Home Sweet Home."

2nd Verse:
Changed will be the picture of the foreign
    lands,
Maps will change entirely to diff'rent hands;
Kings and Queens may ever rule their fellow
    man,
But pray they'll be united like our own free
    land:

All Aboard for Home Sweet Home. L: Addison Burkhardt; M: Al Piantadosi and Jack Glogau. Copyright 1918 by Al Piantadosi & Co., Inc., New York.

1st Verse:
Cheer up, mothers, dry your eyes,
He's coming back to you.
Sweethearts, you'll soon hear the cheers
For your hero true.
Battles' roar he'll hear no more,
Soon he'll sail from France's shore
When he's paid the debt
He owes to Lafayette,
He will say goodbye and cry:

Chorus:
"All aboard for home sweet home;
Again to the girl I left behind
I'll go sailing 'cross the foam again,
What a welcome there I'll find.
And the day that I return to her
I will make that girl my own;
Hello, dear home town, I'm homeward
    bound;
All aboard for home sweet home."

2nd Verse:
When our boys sail up the bay
A great day that will be;
They'll be more than proud to say,
"Hello, Liberty."
With joy our hearts will be filled,
Soon our France we will rebuild,
For you've been true blue;
So now we say to you,
"Au revoir" but not "Goodbye":

All for America! L&M: Josie Bleuler. Copyright 1917 by Josie Bleuler, New York.

1st Verse:
Old Glory is the emblem of the land that
    gave me birth;
To me it is the dearest, brightest spot on all
    the earth.
I'd gladly give my service to defend it near or
    far:
All for America!

Chorus:
All for America,
What devotion such a motto would
    command.
All for America,
Many are the nations in our land.

All for America,
For humanity and freedom it shall stand;
Let the slogan none debar,
Let us show them that we are
All for America.

2nd Verse:
Stand by our country first and last whate'er
    the struggle be;
If fight we must, our cause is just, we'll win
    the victory.
United with each land in strongest friendship
    we will be
All for America!

All Together ("We're Out to Beat the Hun"). L: E. Paul Hamilton; M: M.L. Lake. Copyright 1918 by Jerome H. Remick & Co., New York.

1st Verse:
One night in sleep the Kaiser thought
The whole world he could rule;
And when he woke he started in
To plan, the poor old fool.
His spies he sent
On mischief bent in all lands to prepare
The fateful day without delay
When he could spring his snare.
He found a chance to hit at France through
    Russian faith to Serb;
His robber bands in Belgian lands,
The world's peace did disturb;
The Belgian braves,
The British Tars,
The mighty French Creusot
Soon proved to Bill a bitter pill,
He could not beat the lot:

Chorus:
All together! Ev'ry mother's son;
All together! We're out to beat the Hun!
All together! We'll stick to see it through;
We won't give in until we win and "Win we
    must!" say you.
All together! We'll make them rue the day!
All together! We'll make the Germans pay!
Yes, all together! We'll stand together!
We're right, we'll fight with all our might for
    liberty!

2nd Verse:
On women then and children, too,
The Hun waged war on seas,
Then did we try to reason why
Such horrors sure must cease.

But German ways in our days are treach'rous
    and unfair,
They keep no word,
That German horde,
And treaties they just tear.
So Uncle Sam quick told them straight,
"We'll join the others, too."
And now we're in, we're bound to win,
We'll see this darn thing through;
The Belgian braves,
The British Tars,
The heroes of great France, brave Italy,
They soon will see America advance:

A-M-E-R-I-C-A. L&M: May Greene and
Billy Lang. Copyright 1917 by D.W.
Cooper, Boston.

1st Verse:
We're proud of the stars in Old Glory!
We're proud of our great history!
It's been told by both song and by story
Why they call us the "Land of the Free."
So we know why our glorious country
In all our hearts stands alone;
For you and for me
It always will be
America, our home.

Chorus:
America!
From coast of Maine to California,
All our hearts are true
And beat with loyalty for dear old inde-
    pendence.
Our U.S.A. has given us our liberty,
All our hats are off to you
And the Red, White and Blue,
A-m-e-r-i-c-a! A-m-e-r-i-c-a!

2nd Verse:
Ev'ryone has a love for his country,
We are true to the land of our birth.
But America first and forever,
For we know it's the finest on earth.
Although far from its shores we may wander,
Through other lands we may roam,
Still we all agree
It's the best place to be,
America, our home.

America, I Love You. L: Edgar Leslie;
M: Archie Gottler. Copyright 1915 by Kalmar & Puck Music Co., Inc., New York.

One of the great patriotic songs, "America, I Love You" (1915) praised the nation "of wond'rous population,/ And free from ev'ry King," proudly reminding all Americans that it's "your land and my land,/ A great do or die land."

1st Verse:
Amid fields of clover,
'Twas just a little over a hundred years ago,
A handful of strangers,
They faced many dangers to make their
    country grow;
It's now quite a nation
Of wond'rous population and free from ev'ry
    King;
It's your land, it's my land,
A great do or die land,
And that's just why I sing:

Chorus:
"America, I love you,
You're like a sweetheart of mine;
From ocean to ocean,
For you my devotion
Is touching each bound'ry line;
Just like a little baby
Climbing its mother's knee,
America, I love you,
And there's a hundred million others like me!"

2nd Verse:
From all sorts of places,
They welcomed all the races to settle on their
    shore;

They didn't care which one,
The poor or the rich one, they still had room
   for more;
To give them protection
By popular election, a set of laws they chose;
They're your laws and my laws,
For your cause and my cause,
That's why this country rose:

A-M-E-R-I-C-A (Means "I Love You, My Yankee Land"). L&M: Jack Frost. Copyright 1917 by Frank K. Root & Co., Chicago.

1st Verse:
I've spelled a name called mother,
'Twas dearest to my heart;
But now I'll spell another,
For she and I must part.
I'd love to live and love her
Beneath her smiling skies;
They mean much more than dad or brother,
And spell a Yankee's paradise:

Chorus:
"A" means you're "anybody's country,"
"M" means you're "meant for me";
"E" means you're "everybody's sweetheart,"
And "R" for the "right of liberty."
"I" stands for "independence first and all,"
"C" for your "colors so grand";
"A-M-E-R-I-C-A," America,
Means "I love you, my Yankee land."

2nd Verse:
Our hist'ry tells the story,
How heroes fought and fell;
Our children love Old Glory
And learn that name to spell.
We're proud of all our splendor,
And ev'ry heart today
Should rise and worship to defend her,
And learn to spell her name this way:

America Needs You Like a Mother (Would You Turn Your Mother Down?). L: Grant Clarke; M: Jean Schwartz. Copyright 1917 by Kalmar, Puck & Abrahams Consolidated Music Publishers, Inc., New York.

1st Verse:
I seem to see a picture of a mother
With her children by her side;
Some her own and some that she's adopted,
Still she looks at all with pride.

Now it seems the mother is in trouble
And she needs her children's aid;
Some are coming forth to help her,
But there's some who seem afraid:

Chorus:
America has been a mother
To the children of the world;
She has taken to her bosom
Ev'ry homeless boy and girl.
Now we find she's in trouble,
Danger's lurking all around.
America needs you like a mother,
Would you turn your mother down?

2nd Verse:
We know that there are diff'rent kinds of
   children,
There are some who love to roam;
Then again there's some who love their
   mother,
They would rather stay at home.
Still, with all our many faults and failings,
She remains our only friend.
Just like many loyal children,
We should help her to the end:

America Today. L: Herbert Moore; M: W.R. Williams. Copyright 1917 by Will Rossiter, Chicago.

1st Verse:
The hist'ry of America is wonderful,
Its chapters tell of men with hearts of gold;
Their names we'll always cherish,
Their fame will never perish,
Their splendid deeds will live for years
   untold;
But if we dwell on bygone days, there's
   danger
That we'll forget the qualities that last;
Place laurel on each great man's brow,
But don't forget the men of now,
Don't think that all the good lies in the past:

Chorus:
Don't say that all the statesmen died with
   Lincoln,
Don't think that all the heroes died with
   Grant;
You'll find we've still the power
To produce men of the hour;
Because they've had no call, don't say they
   can't,
Remember we've a heritage of glory,
And Liberty's still standing in the bay;

As in his former days of might,
Don't worry, Uncle Sam's all right!
We'll fight for America today.

2nd Verse:
We have the mem'ry of the Revolution,
And we've the memory of Sixty-One,
We tell in song and story
They battled for Old Glory,
And we'll protect the victories they won;
We're strong for peace, if it is peace with
    honor,
But don't forget we're stronger still for Right;
Whatever the future days may bring,
Our country first, that's *the* big thing;
United to a man we still can fight:

America, We're Proud of You. L&M: Eva
C. Hardy. Copyright 1919 by L.S. Florence
Music Publishing Co., Haverhill, Mass.

1st Verse:
Now the fight for Right is over
And the boys are coming home.
We must be there with a cheer but no tear
To greet them from across the foam.
They offered up their lives to free a nation
Plunged in war and moaning in pain.
Our land in mercy heard their cry
And gave them liberty again:

Chorus:
The Stars and Stripes will lead in all that's
    right,
Hurrah for Uncle Sam!
No bluff nor sham, but proud and grand,
Our flag led onward through the fight!
When the boys were under fire, each one
Firmly backed up the Red, White and Blue!
'Twas then the Yanks victorious marched into
    Germany.
America, we're proud of you!

2nd Verse:
Homeward bound the ships come sailing
With the boys whose hearts have yearned
For mother's kiss, sweetheart's bliss, baby's
    lisp,
The home their fight for freedom earned.
So ev'ry loving heart must hide its sorrow
Just for the dear ones all in vain;
They fought a noble victory,
They died to end the tyrant's reign:

American Beauty. L: Al Bryan and Edgar
Leslie; M: M.K. Jerome. Copyright 1918

by Waterson, Berlin & Snyder Co., New
York.

1st Verse:
It was in a garden fair,
'Mid the roses rich and rare,
An American beauty hung her head in
    despair;
Then a soldier boy drew nigh,
He had come to say goodbye,
And he lovingly told her
As he gazed into her eyes:

Chorus:
"American Beauty,
Red rose of my heart,
American Beauty,
Oh, why should we part?
I'd love to hold you and gently fold you
Right against my breast;
But the fleur-de-lys
Far across the sea,
I hear her calling me.
American Beauty,
The way may be long,
American Beauty,
But my love is strong.
And I will fight my way
To mother and you some day;
My American Beauty,
Come kiss me goodbye."

2nd Verse:
To that garden ev'ry night
Comes a maiden all in white
Just to dream of her hero in the moon's
    tender light.
She is dreaming of the day
When he took her heart away;
As the stars kiss the roses,
Ev'ry breeze seems to say:

The American Boy for Me. L&M: Bessie
Westphal. Copyright 1916 by Bessie Westphal, Los Angeles.

1st Verse:
The American boy for me,
He's the lad to keep in mind,
Who wins the love of the world
And the praises of mankind.
All rejoice in the strength of him,
Whose heart of such manly grace
And brave soul will forever be
The stay and honor of his race:

Chorus:
The American boy for me,
The pride of the U.S.A.,
He's the dream of all the maids
And the hopes of the world today.
While my heart responds to love,
My most fervent prayer will be:
May heaven bless and spare him,
This American boy, for me.

2nd Verse:
The American boy for me,
He's the first to sing the strain
Of a song with peace and love,
And good will for the refrain.
Let the world now hear his voice,
With its note of hope and joy;
May his song teach all to sing
That they love this American boy:

Anchors Aweigh. L: Capt. Alfred H.
Miles; M: Charles A. Zimmerman. Copyright 1907, The United States Naval Academy, Annapolis, Md.

Original Football Chorus:
Stand, Navy, down the field,
Sail set to the sky!
We'll never change our course,
So, Army, you steer shy-y-y-y!
Roll up the score, Navy,
Anchors aweigh!
Sail, Navy, down the field
And sink the Army,
Sink the Army gray!

Later 1st Chorus
(Revised lyric by George D. Lottman):
Stand, Navy, out to sea,
Fight our battle cry!
We'll never change our course,
So, vicious foe, steer shy-y-y-y!
Roll out the T.N.T.,
Anchors aweigh!
Sail on to victory
And sink their bones to Davy Jones, hooray!
Yo-ho there, shipmate,
Take the fighting to the far-off seas;
Yo-ho there, messmate,
Hear the wailing of the wild banshees.
All hands, firebrands,
Let's blast them as we go!
So stand, Navy, out to sea,
Fight our battle cry!
We'll never change our course,
So, vicious foe, steer shy-y-y-y!

Roll out the T.N.T.,
Anchors aweigh!
Sail on to victory
And sink their bones to Davy Jones, hooray!

Later 2nd Chorus
(Revised lyric by George D. Lottman):
Anchors aweigh, my boy,
Anchors aweigh!
Farewell to college joys,
We sail at break of day-day-day-day!
Through our last night on shore
Drink to the foam;
Until we meet once more,
Here's wishing you a happy voyage home.
Heave a-ho there, sailor,
Ev'rybody drink up while you may;
Heave a-ho there, sailor,
For you're gonna sail at break of day;
Drink away, drink away,
For you sail at break of day, hey!
Anchors aweigh, my boys,
Anchors aweigh!
Farewell to college joys,
We sail at break of day-day-day-day!
Through our last night on shore,
Drink to the foam;
Until we meet once more,
Here's wishing you a happy voyage home.

And He'd Say "Oo-La-La! Wee-Wee!" L&M: George Jessel and Harry Ruby. Copyright 1919 by Waterson, Berlin & Snyder Co., New York.

1st Verse:
Willie Earl met a sweet young girl one day in
  France,
Her naughty little glance
Put Willie in a trance;
Willie Earl couldn't understand her talk, you
  see,
He only knew two words in French
That he learned in the trench,
They were "oo-la-la!" and "wee wee."
They would spoon beneath the moon above;
It was fun to hear them making love:

1st Chorus:
She'd say, "Compronay voo, papa?"
And he'd say, "Oo-la-la! wee-wee";
She'd smile and whisper, "Mercy bacoo,"
He'd answer, "I don't mind if I do."
She'd say, "If you be my papa,
Then I will be your ma cherie."

Hoping to win the love of a charming French girl, soldier Willie Earl is handicapped by knowing only two French words, which he would repeat over and over again whenever the couple met in postwar Paris. But, according to George Jessell and Harry Ruby's "And He'd Say 'Oo-La-La! Wee-Wee'," the soldier's limited vocabulary failed to hinder his courtship.

She'd pinch his cheek and say, "You keska-
    say,"
He'd say, "Not now, dear, but later I may."
Then she'd say, "Compronay voo, papa,"
And he'd say, "Oo-la-la! wee-wee."

2nd Verse:
Willie Earl said, "This little girl is meant for
    me,
No more I'll cross the sea,
I'll stay in Gay Paree."
Ev'ry day you would hear him say to his
    babee,
"Your talk I do not know but I
Will manage to get by
With my oo-la-la! and wee-wee."
Ev'ry evening Willie would rehearse;
Instead of getting better, he got worse:

2nd Chorus:
She'd say, "Compronay voo, papa?"
And he'd say, "Oo-la-la! wee-wee."
She'd say, "Come see" and then roll her eyes,
He'd answer, "Baby, you'd be surprised."
Each evening they would promenade

Upon ze boulevarde, you see.
One day at lunch she said, "Cafe voo la,"
He'd say, "My dear, don't forget where you
    are."
Then she'd say, "Compronay voo, papa?"
And he'd say, "Oo-la-la! wee-wee."

(And Then She'd) Knit, Knit, Knit. L: Eddie Moran; M: Harry Von Tilzer. Copyright 1917 by Harry Von Tilzer Music
Publishing Co., New York.

1st Verse:
Pretty little Kitty's got the patriotic craze,
Knitting scarfs for soldiers day and night;
Silly little Billy now is spending all his days
Watching Kitty knit with all her might.
She even knits when out in his canoe,
She knits while Billy tries to bill and coo:

1st Chorus:
He'd take a hug, then he'd hug her some
    more,
While she'd knit, knit, knit, knit, knit;
He'd steal a kiss, then he'd take an encore,
And she'd knit, knit, knit, knit, knit.
Under a tree he would rest with a smile,
She'd lay her knitting down for just a while;
A bird in a nest said, "Oh, give us a rest,
Go on and knit, knit, knit."

2nd Verse:
Pretty little Kitty said, "Now, Willie, do your
    bit;
Here's some yarn and needles, you can start.
Come sit beside me and I'll teach you how to
    knit,
That's the way that you can win my heart."
He'd knit a while and then he'd want to woo,
He'd look at her and drop a stitch or two:

2nd Chorus:
He'd take a hug, then he'd hug her some
    more,
She'd say, "Knit, knit, knit, knit, knit."
He'd steal a kiss, then he'd take an encore;
She'd say, "Knit, knit, knit, knit, knit."
One day a tug passed them by in a squall,
Looking through glasses was captain and all;
They both heard a yelp, "Do you need any
    help?"
And she said, "Knit, knit, knit."

Angel of No Man's Land. L: H. Mac-
Donald Barr; M: Grant Colfax Tullar.

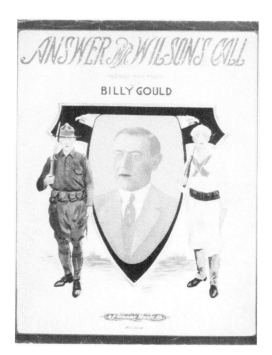

A typical call to arms was issued by Billy Gould in his stirring "Answer Mr. Wilson's Call," published shortly after the president's declaration of war against Germany.

Copyright 1918 by Tullar-Meredith Co., New York.

1st Verse:
O, a soldier may strike with a zeal untold
Ev'ry foe on the battlefield,
And he may with a courage deep and bold
Bravely perish before he yield.
Though fearless he may be in war
And laugh at the cannon's roar,
Let's not forget there is one thing yet
That can help us to win this war:

Chorus:
Then here's to the girl,
The Red Cross girl,
And to all of her noble band!
To the girl you know,
One who said "I'll go,"
To the angel of No Man's Land.
Then here's to the girl,
The Red Cross girl
And to all of her noble band!
To the little girl you know,
To the one who said "I'll go,"
To the angel of No Man's Land.

2nd Verse:
O, a soldier may walk with a martial tread
In the midst of a crimson stream;
He may leap from the trench and plunge ahead
Where the battle may deadly seem.
Though foes are near, he knows no fear,
He's fighting to win or die;
Nor, if he fall, does he vainly call,
For the angel is passing by:

Answer Mr. Wilson's Call. L&M: Billy Gould. Copyright 1917 by A.J. Stasny Music Co., New York.

1st Verse:
Dear Old Glory is in danger,
Our own dear Red, White and Blue;
So Yankee Doodle Dandies,
It's clearly up to you.
Let's remember George Washington,
Dear old "Honest Abe" and Lee,
And show our might, preserve our right
To sail upon the sea:

Chorus:
Your Uncle Sam is calling you,
Calling you and I;
Let's all be real Americans,
Ready to do or die;
For our country must be free
Though every man must fall;
We've suffered abuses,
So now don't make excuses,
But answer Mr. Wilson's call.

2nd Verse:
Now our Eagle's loudly screaming
With its wings spread to the sky;
So Yankee Doodle Dandies,
It's up to you and I.
Let's remember dear old Bunker Hill,
Sherman's march down to the sea,
Each lad be glad this chance he's had
To fight for humanity:

Any Old Place the Gang Goes (I'll Be There). L&M: William J. McKenna. Copyright 1918 by Broadway Music Corp., New York.

1st Verse:
Mickey Fay, he marched away to the sound of beating drums,
A sergeant he, his company were all his pals and chums;

His sweetheart, Kate, stood by the gate with
tear-dimmed eyes of blue,
As Mike went by he heard her cry, "Good-
bye, good luck to you."
"Where shall I write?" she cried,
And smiling Mike replied:

Chorus:
"Any old place the gang goes, I'll be there,
Nobody knows where we'll go,
Devil a one of us cares.
Give us a kiss for luck, dear,
I'm off to do me share,
[All of the sharks are hungry,
At swimmin' I'm just fair],
[We're on our way to Berlin,
And we won't pay our fare],
And [But] ['Cause] any old place the gang
goes,
I'll be there."

2nd Verse:
Sergeant Fay one summer's day with his
comrades brave and true
Got on a ship to make the trip across the
ocean blue,
A lad named Ford fell overboard and a cry
for help he gave;
Mike's company dove in the sea, their com-
rade's life to save.
"Don't jump," the captain cried,
Saluting, Mike replied:

3rd Verse:
In a trench upon a bench stood Mike beside
the guns,
When suddenly his company began to charge
the Huns;
Mike held his breath, he knew 'twas death to
jump into the fray.
But with a shout he started out to help them
win the day.
"Go back," he heard them yell;
Mike said "I will like ---," well!:

Are You Lending a Hand to Yankeeland?
L: J. Will Callahan; M: Blanche M. Tice.
Copyright 1918 by Blanche M. Tice Music
Publishing Co., Sioux City, Ia.

1st Verse:
Far away across the ocean
Heroes fight for you and me,
Braving all with true devotion,
Dying for liberty.
While the flag they are defending,
Let me ask of you,

If a helping hand you're lending
And doing what you can:

Chorus:
Are you lending a helping hand to Yankee-
land,
The country that gave you birth?
Are you showing that you are staunch and
true
And proving your honest worth?
Are you standing the test and doing your best
Just like all the rest from east to west?
Are you lending a hand to Yankeeland,
The greatest of lands on earth?

2nd Verse:
Ev'rything we love and cherish,
Ev'ry blessing great or small,
Ev'ry home itself would perish,
If once the flag should fall.
Ask yourself each night and morning
When you kneel to pray,
"Have I heard my country's warning
And heeded in ev'ry way?"

**Are You the O'Reilly? ("Blime Me,
O'Reilly — You Are Lookin' Well").** Original Version, 1890, by Pat Rooney; New
version, 1915, by P. Emmett. Copyright
1915 by Leo Feist, Inc., New York.

1st Verse:
I'm Terrence O'Reilly, I'm a man of renown,
I'm a thoroughbred to the backbone;
I'm related to O'Connor,
My mother was Queen
Of China, ten miles from Athlone.
But if they'd let me be,
I'd have Ireland free.
On the railroads you would pay no fare.
I'd have the United States under my thumb,
And I'd sleep in the President's chair:

Chorus:
Are you the O'Reilly who [tha'] keeps this
hotel?
Are you the O'Reilly they speak of so well?
Are you the O'Reilly they speak of so highly?
Gor blime me, O'Reilly,
You are lookin' well.

2nd Verse:
There's Shamus O'Reilly, who kept the hotel,
He's assigned to the Commissary;
Back home in old Dublin
He did very well,
But he's now working for the army.

He once served us at the "Pub,"
But he's now serving grub,
And it's flavored with powder and lead.
He took the King's shilling to go do his kill-
ing,
But he's cooking for sojers instead:

3rd Verse:
Young Ludwig O'Reilly, that may be his
name,
In the trench on the enemy's side;
I glimpsed his big helmet
And potted the same,
And to "helmit" went Ludwig's right eye.
Then his brother named Fritz
Nearly gave us all fits,
We were laughing at what he had done,
When up rose the blighter, a bally good
fighter,
And he started us all on the run:

As Her Soldier Boy Marched By. L&M:
Lena Leonard Fisher. Copyright 1917 by
Lena Leonard Fisher, Cleveland. (*Note:*
The back cover of this sheet music carried
the following message: "Every penny of
profit from this little song will go on a
glad, sad journey to France to help save
the lives of wan-faced children whose
fathers have fallen, and whose mothers
have died in the cause of world freedom.")

1st Verse:
O'er all the land the call to arms is sounding,
Once more the bugle call is in the air;
Is threatened that fair freedom God had
founded,
Unless in its defense strong men shall dare.
Speaks a mother to her boy with eyes that
glisten,
For the drumbeat she had heard with throb-
bing heart:
"Go, my boy, your country calls and you
will listen;
I have raised you so you'll long to do your
part":

Chorus:
And the red of the sunset glory
And the blue of the summer sky,
And the white of the stainless story
Of men who for freedom die.
They blended a garland for her,
Lit the fire flash in her eye;
And God's angels hovered o'er her
As her soldier boy marched by.

2nd Verse:
Marched away her darling boy to be a
soldier,
Marched for glorious freedom as his sires
had done,
And the trusty musket on his stalwart
shoulder,
It would speak ere sweetest liberty were won.
So back she forced her tears, that loyal
mother,
And firm she grasped her soldier boy's strong
hand;
"I'll prove," she told him, "and there's many
another
That a woman's heart beats true for native
land":

Back Home I'll Come. L&M: Edmund M.
Capen. Copyright 1917 by Edmund M.
Capen, Marlboro, Mass.

1st Verse:
One day the ships went sailing aross the deep
blue sea,
A soldier boy was leaving
To fight for liberty.
His mother she was grieving, her heart was
filled with pain,
Her soldier boy was singing
A song with this refrain:

Chorus:
"O! do not weep, dear, it makes me sad;
When I return, dear,
You will feel so glad.
No more I'll leave you,
I'll stay at home.
Back home I'll come, dear, back home I'll
come."

2nd Verse:
Bravely her boy was fighting upon that
foreign shore;
He saw their flag was falling, he heard the
cannon's roar.
His comrades they were calling,
He heeded not their cry;
Round him his mates were falling,
That flag he nailed on high:

2nd Chorus:
Your soldier boy will come home again,
He's always singing
This same refrain:
"No more I'll leave you,
I'll stay at home.

Back home I'll come, dear, back home I'll
come."

Battle-Call of Alliance. L: Percy Mackaye; M: Reginald DeKoven. Copyright
1917 by G. Schirmer, New York.

1st Verse:
Awake! Awake! The winds of dawn
Blow fire across the world;
The ships go forth where dangers spawn
And coils of death are curled;
And souls of men go forth with them
And hearts of men aspire,
New kindled by the ancient flame
Of man's immortal fire:

Chorus:
To arms! to arms for freedom
And end the reign of czars!
America, America
Unfurls her flaming stars!
To arms! To arms for freedom,
And end the reign of czars!
America, America
Unfurls her flaming stars!

2nd Verse:
Arise! Renew with nobler dreams,
The faith we name our own;
The bugle calls to vaster schemes
Which God hath dreamed alone.
To save a planet's liberties
He joineth now our hands
With brothers fighting overseas
Among the ruined lands:

Because You're Here. L: Harold Robè;
M: Gitz Rice. Copyright 1919 by G. Ricordi
& Co., Inc., New York.

1st Verse:
Ever since we've parted
I've prayed for you each day,
I've been most broken-hearted
To have you, dear, away.
But cares can't last forever,
For sun must follow rain,
And now that we're together
The world is bright again:

Chorus:
Home now is Home Sweet Home because
you're here,
Life fills with gladness while I hold you near;
God brought you through

And turned the grey skies blue, my loved
one.
Home now is Home Sweet Home because
you're here.

2nd Verse:
How I missed your laughter,
And at our parting place,
All lovely every after,
I seemed to see your face.
But gone are cares and gloom, dear,
And now that you've returned,
The flowers of love will bloom, dear,
For happiness we've learned:

Belgium, Dry Your Tears. L: Arthur
Freed; M: Al Piantadosi. Copyright 1918
by Al Piantadosi & Co., Inc., New York.

1st Verse:
Belgium, we can hear you calling,
Belgium dear, your tears are falling;
Still, you've kept a brave heart true blue,
We are filled with love for you.
Clouds of fear soon pass away,
Love's golden sun will come to stay:

Chorus:
Belgium, Belgium, dry your tears,
We will be at your side.
Into our hearts with a message you came,
Ev'ry American loves your dear name.
Mothers, sweethearts, brothers of war,
It's you we're fighting for,
And we'll never stop
Till we're "over the top."
Belgium, dry your tears.

2nd Verse:
Belgium, though you're worn and tired,
You have left us all inspired,
For you've shown us grit and brav'ry,
Spurred us on to victory;
Land of heroes staunch and true,
We'll soon be marching side of you:

**Betty's Basting Belly Bands for Belgians
(Susie's Sister's Song).** L: Charles Roy
Cox; M: E. Dick Lerch. Copyright 1915 by
Buckeye Music Publishing Co., New York-
Cincinnati-Cleveland-Columbus, Ohio.

1st Verse:
"Now ev'rybody's heard about the war across
the sea,

But now there's war at our house 'cause the folks don't notice me;
I know you've heard about my sister Susie sewing shirts,
But now that Betty's started,
Why, I tell you, boys, it hurts":

Chorus:
For Betty's basting belly bands for Belgians,
Running Sister Susie some close race,
Burning blisters on her busy fingers,
Ripping, tearing, sewing ev'ry place.
Betty's basting belly bands for Belgians,
Big ones, small ones, long ones, short ones, too;
She's working day and night
For the victims of the fight,
For Betty's basting belly bands for Begians!

2nd Verse:
"The girls in high society are working ev'ry day,
Instead of balls they're knitting shawls, so all the papers say.
Now 'Bet' and Susie had to have some brand new sort of fad,
And that's how things got started;
Gee, it surely makes me mad":

The Biggest Thing in a Soldier's Life (Is the Letter That Comes from Home). L: Robert F. Roden; M: Edward G. Nelson. Copyright 1918 by F.B. Haviland Publishing Co., New York.

1st Verse:
They brought him back from the firing line,
A hero wounded he lies;
He won a cross for his bravery,
But he turns with eager eyes
To a letter just from home
From his dear ones o'er the foam:

Chorus:
For the biggest thing in a soldier's life
Is the letter that comes from home;
Far away from battle honors
When he hears from the ones left alone.
In his dream he's back with mother
And his sweetheart o'er the foam;
For the biggest thing in a soldier's life
Is the letter that comes from home.

2nd Verse:
The cross he won is forgotten now,
His thoughts are across the sea,
With those he loves in his dear old home,

Those who wait so hopefully.
He forgets all thoughts of fame,
As he breathes each tender name:

Billy Boy. L: Lester A. Walton; M: Luckey Roberts. Copyright 1917 by Walton Publishing Co., New York.

1st Verse:
Tommy Atkins is a warrior bold,
Merrie England loves him more than gold,
And to France the hero of today
Is fighting in the trenches miles away.
Now Billy Boy has gone across the sea
To help them in their fight for liberty:

Chorus:
Billy Boy, Billy Boy, you're a soldier of renown,
Billy Boy, Billy Boy, in a uniform of brown.
What a grand old sight
As you battle for the Right;
Billy Boy, Billy Boy, with a heart so fond and true
For the Red, White and Blue.
You are loyal through and through,
You put the "brave" in bravery,
You are my pride and joy.
Now let the bugle blow,
Come on, come on, let's go,
Atta boy, my Billy Boy!

2nd Verse:
There is Russia with a mighty host,
Of her sturdy cossacks she can boast,
And for valor no one can forget
Those fearless Belgian lads who're fighting yet.
Now Billy Boy, it's put right up to you
To help them win, so show what you can do!:

Bing! Bang! Bing 'Em on the Rhine! L&M: Jack Mahoney and Allan J. Flynn. Copyright 1918 by Jerome H. Remick & Co., New York.

1st Verse:
I stood upon the corner as the boys went marching by,
I saw that "do or die" in ev'ry soldier's eye;
At first they started humming,
Then they burst into a song,
Each one singing, swinging right along.
They kept in step with ev'ry note and word,
And as I listened this is what I heard:

Chorus:
"We'll bing! bang! bing 'em on the Rhine,
   boys,
We'll show the Kaiser, too,
What a Yankee bunch can do.
When we swing, swing, swing right through
   their line, boys,
We'll shake 'em as we'll make 'em yelp
Help!
When they hear those guns go bingaling,
This will be the Yankee countersign;
They will soon know all about it,
Get together now and shout it,
[They won't take a drink of Pilsen,
They'll get Haig and Haig and Wilson],
[We'll hit Berlin like a rocket,
Get the "Watch am Rhine" and hock it],
'Bing! Bang! Bing! Bang! Bing 'em on the
   Rhine!'"

2nd Verse:
They sang, "We'll make the Kaiser whistle
   Yankee Doodle Do,
We'll crown the Crown Prince, too,
As we have crowned a few;
We'll make the world safe for democracy,
   you bet we will,
But it won't be safe for Kaiser Bill.
And when we all go swimming in the Rhine,
We'll hang our clothes on Hindenburg's old
   line":

3rd Verse:
"We'll put some Yankee pot roast on the
   Kaiser's bill of fare,
With English roast beef rare,
'Twill be his last meal there.
If he wants Russian caviar on his Vienna roll,
We will toss his Turkey for a goal;
And for dessert he'll get French pastry, then
We'll help the French to paste him once
   again":

**Blighty (The Soldier's "Home Sweet
Home").** L&M: R.P. Weston and Bert
Lee. Copyright 1916 by Francis, Day &
Hunter, New York.

1st Verse:
What's the song the boys are singing out in
   France?
It isn't "Tennessee," that's not the melody.
You don't hear them sighing now for Dixie-
   land,
They've a diff'rent tune upon the Army band.

Listen and you'll hear each gallant khaki boy
Singing this song of joy:

Chorus:
"Blighty! Blighty! That is where we're going
   back to,
Blighty! Blighty!
Mother, put my nightie
By the fire to air,
I'll soon be there.
When the job is over,
All aboard for Dover
And for Blighty! Blighty!
Hear those big propellers making music in
   the foam,
See that transport ready to start,
Bound for Blighty, glad to depart.
Don't you know where Blighty is?
Why, bless your heart!
It's the soldier's 'Home Sweet Home'."

2nd Verse:
When we get the happy news they're home-
   ward bound,
There'll be some joy once more upon the
   Blighty shore.
Hear the people on the quay, all shout
   Hooray!
When they see that steamer coming down the
   bay.
Listen and you'll hear the merry khaki throng
Singing their homeland song:

Boy of Mine. L: Brenta F. Wallace; M:
Mercy P. Graham. Copyright 1918 by
French & Lloyd, New York.

1st Verse:
"While I am sleeping,
Perhaps, dear, you are creeping
Out in the dark and treacherous night
Into No Man's Land, with your trusty gun in
   hand,
Fighting with all your might
Through the wire entanglements.
And midst the falling shell,
Come, the foeman to expel"!:

Chorus:
"Boy of mine, boy of mine,
Do you know our hearts they glow as you
   sow
The harvesting of peace for humanity,
The blessings of a lasting victory?
Boy of mine, boy of mine,
Let your courage prove so true

That the whole [world] shall be heaven on
  earth.
Oh, boy of mine, I'll pray for you."

2nd Verse:
"Here at home we're keeping
The dear old hearthfire leaping
Brightly in flaming crimson and gold,
So that you, returning, may gladden at its
  burning,
Sharing its warmth as of old.
Though you're seared and worn, my dear,
We want you with a will,
Come, your vacant place to fill!":

The Boys Who Fight for You. L&M:
Ralph Hyatt. Copyright 1918 by Fisk Publishing Co., San Francisco.

1st Verse:
Many hearts are saddened now
Because they've lost their joys in California.
There are griefs well mixed with pride
In their soldier boys
Who've left their native homes.
They are all such handsome lads,
Never know a care,
Never have a fear,
Never take a dare.
When their country calls on them,
They gladly do their share
To serve the land they love:

Chorus:
If you can't fight
Just do what's right
To support the boys who go to fight for you.
Remember that freedom for us all
May stand behind the bugle call.
So have a heart
And do your part,
Give your money,
Save your food in ev'ry way.
Make ev'ry boy who fights for you
Proud of the old U.S.A.

2nd Verse:
There is courage and new hope
In many soldiers' hearts over in Flanders,
Just because we're in the fight
And going to do our part
To save their homes for them.
Just across the trenches
All the Huns are in a stew,
Don't know what to do,
Know that they are through;

Don't forget to honor "The Boys Who Won't
Come Home" was the heartfelt message of one
grieving mother in Harry Hamilton and Ed
Thomas's 1919 elegy to the battlefield dead.

And our soldier boys will teach them
Things they thought they knew
In a way they won't forget:

The Boys Who Won't Come Home. L:
Harry Hamilton; M: Ed Thomas. Copy-
right 1919 by Broadway Music Corp., New
York.

1st Verse:
The flags were waving gaily all along the
  village street,
The air was filled with music and the sound
  of marching feet;
The boys had come back home again,
Their fighting days were done,
And ev'ry heart was filled with pride
For the glory they had won.
A gray-haired mother tried to smile
Amid the cheers and cries,
She murmured softly as she gazed
With sad and tear-dimmed eyes:

Chorus:
"My boy was one of those who went away;
He was my pride and joy,

I loved him just as ev'ry other mother loves
    her boy;
He gave his life to Uncle Sam,
He's sleeping o'er the foam.
So while you're cheering,
Don't forget the boys who won't come
    home."

2nd Verse:
"He heard his country calling and he
    answered to the call,
He went like all of Pershing's men prepared
    to give his all;
He took my blessing with him
When he sailed across the sea,
And since he went, I've prayed for him
And waited patiently.
But greater glory claimed him
And I'm proud that he could go;
He's sleeping now in Flander's field,
Where crimson poppies grow":

The Bravest Heart of All. L: Raymond B.
Egan; M: Richard A. Whiting. Copyright
1917 by Jerome H. Remick & Co., New
York.

1st Verse:
I saw a mother and a baby on an ocean pier
    today,
I heard the baby cry for daddy when the big
    ship sailed away.
As the steamer slowly vanished,
Bound for France across the sea,
The mother clasped the baby,
And she whispered tenderly:

Chorus:
"My little laddie boy,
Oh, my laddie boy,
You're only five years old today.
You have your daddy's eyes, bluer than the
    skies,
And they sparkle when you play.
Mother loves her little shaver,
He's the sunshine heaven gave her,
Just to cheer away all the tears that stray
Since your daddy sailed away.
My little laddie dear,
There's a day I fear,
When you will be so brave and tall.
Someday you'll be a man, sir, and then you'll
    answer
To dear Old Glory's call;
Like your dad you'll sail away
With a heart so brave and gay.

But when you depart,
Then your mother's heart
Will be the bravest heart of all."

2nd Verse:
Today there's many, many daddies who will
    sail across the foam,
And there are many, many mothers who will
    wait and pray at home.
There are many, many teardrops
That are only born to stray
Down cheeks of little laddies
As they hear their mothers say:

Bring Back a Belgian Baby to Me. L&M:
Ben Black. Copyright 1918 by Sherman,
Clay & Co., San Francisco.

1st Verse:
"It's very diff'rent, daddy, ever since you
    went away;
Mother seems so lonely and I get so tired of
    play.
I hope you win the war real soon,
It sure would make me glad,
For there is something that I want,
And, gee, I want it bad!
Please do this favor, daddy dear, for me,
When you come back from far across the
    sea":

Chorus:
"Bring back a Belgian baby to me,
I think they're just as sweet as can be;
One who's lost a father or mother,
A sister or brother,
I'm sure that we could love each other.
They don't know what the war's all about,
They're just as innocent as they can be.
So bring back, bring back a Belgian baby to
    me."

2nd Verse:
"I know you're busy, daddy, 'cause you're
    fighting day and night,
Mother says it's awfully hard to teach the
    Hun what's right.
She says that there are lots of babies
Who have no place to sleep,
And ev'ry time I think of it,
Why, I just want to weep.
Now, daddy, we have lots of room to spare,
And ev'rything I've got I'll gladly share":

Bring Back My Daddy to Me. L: William
Tracey and Howard Johnson; M: George

This prayer of an anguished little girl for the safe return of her soldier father in "Bring Back My Daddy to Me" (1917) featured a cover photograph of film actress Madge Evans, then an eight-year-old child star of such 1917 films as *The Volunteer* and *The Little Patriot*.

W. Meyer. Copyright 1917 by Leo Feist, Inc., New York.

1st Verse:
A sweet little girl with bright golden curls
Sat playing with toys on the floor;
Her dad went away to enter the fray
At the start of this long, bitter war.
Her mother said, "Dear, your birthday is near,
Tomorrow your presents I'll buy."
The dear little child
Quickly looked up and smiled,
And said with a tear in her eye:

Chorus:
"I don't want a dress or a dolly,
'Cause dollies get broken 'round here.
I don't want the skates,
The books or the slates,
You bought for my birthday last year.
If you'll bring the present I ask for,
Dear mother, how happy I'll be;
You can give all my toys
To some poor girls and boys,
But bring back my daddy to me!"

2nd Verse:
Her ma softly sighs and tears fill her eyes
As she hears her dear baby's plea;
She answers, "My dear, if daddy were here
What a wonderful present 'twould be."
How many homes yearn for someone's return
With Honor and Justice and Right?
There are more little girls
In this grief-stricken world,
All saying the same thing tonight:

Bring Back My Soldier Boy to Me. L: Walter Hirsch; M: Frank Magine. Copyright 1918 by Al Piantadosi & Co., Inc., New York.

1st Verse:
"Soldier boy, you've gone away,
In my heart I hope and pray
That you will return some day.
My soldier boy,
While you're over there,
This will be my prayer":

Chorus:
"Oh! bring back,
Oh! bring back my soldier boy to me;
Watch him, protect him while he's across the sea.
I'm lonesome,
Each night I'm longing and praying constantly
That God will bring back my soldier boy to me".

2nd Verse:
"Though you go, I know it's best,
You must go with all the rest,
Put your courage to the test.
My soldier boy,
Ev'ry night and day
I will always pray":

Bring Me a Letter from My Old Home Town. L: A.G. Delamater; M: Will R. Anderson. Copyright 1918 by M. Witmark & Sons, New York.

1st Verse:
A nurse was passing by a cot where a wounded Sammy lay,
Lay dreaming night and day
Of his old home far away.
She asked him, "Won't you tell me what would drive away that frown?"

The boy replied, as he softly sighed,
"To hear from my old home town":

Chorus:
"Bring me a letter from my old home town,
One with jokes from my old pal, Jim Brown.
Bring me a letter from that girl of mine,
Saying that she's longing for me all the time.
Bring me a letter from my proud old dad,
Who knows that we are winning, and I'll bet
    he's glad.
But more than any other,
A line from my old mother;
Bring me a letter from my home town."

2nd Verse:
"I've had a lot of comforts, nurse, from my
    little comfort kit
And things that women knit,
They have always done their bit.
The only thing that cheers me when my
    spirits are 'way down,
And I've the blues,
Is to get good news from those in my old
    town":

The Caissons Go Rolling Along. L:
Robert M. Danford, William Bryden, and
Edmund L. Gruber; M: Edmund L.
Gruber. Copyright 1908.

1st Verse:
Over hill, over dale,
We have hit the dusty trail,
And those caissons go rolling along.
"Counter march! Right about!"
Hear those wagon soldiers shout,
While those caissons go rolling along:

Chorus:
For it's hi! hi! hee! in the Field Artillery,
Call off your numbers loud and strong;
And where e'er we go
You will always know
That those caissons are rolling along,
That those caissons are rolling along.

2nd Verse:
To the front, day and night,
Where the doughboys dig and fight
And those caissons go rolling along.
Our barrage will be there
Fired on the rocket's glare,
While those caissons go rolling along:

Call of a Nation. L&M: Edward J. Boyle.
Copyright 1918 by Edward J. Boyle and
Arthur L. Ward, Worchester, Mass.

1st Verse:
Down the street a group of new recruits
    came marching,
They had pledged themselves to Uncle Sam
    that day.
Ev'ryone in town turned out to cheer them,
They cried, "Boys, don't forget the U.S.A.!"
A vet'ran of the Civil War stood waiting,
And they halted ere they passed his humble
    door;
Then the old man raised his head,
And with trembling voice he said
As he proudly waved on high the flag he bore:

Chorus:
"'Tis the voice of your nation that calls you,
And I'm glad to see you ready to obey.
What matter if death befalls you,
Who would not die to serve the flag today?
When old Uncle Sammy cries, 'Boys, your
    country needs you,'
That's the time for you to show that you are
    there.
'Tis an honor, lads, to die
For the flag that waves on high,
O'er the proudest and grandest of all na-
    tions."

2nd Verse:
"In the days of Sixty-One our country called
    us,
And with buoyant hearts we hastened to obey;
Down this little street we marched together,
The most of us have long since passed away.
But thank God I am spared to see you
    leaving,
To wave the banner Lincoln loved to see.
When the Yankee emblem flies
Then the Yankee heart replies:
'For America, for love and liberty'":

Camouflage. L&M: L. Wolfe Gilbert and
Anatol Friedland. Copyright 1917 by
Joseph W. Stern & Co., New York.

Verse:
This war has brought us trouble,
And lots of humor, too,
For life is just a bubble,
I'll prove that fact to you.
Our friends abroad have coined a word
That probably we've never heard;

It sounds so funny and absurd,
It surely is a bird.
Oh, Dan! Oh, Dan! You dictionary man:

Chorus:
Camouflage, camouflage, that's the latest
    dodge;
Camouflage, camouflage, it's not a cheese or
    lodge.
We'll say a Yankee trench is here,
The artist paints a keg of beer
That's bound to bring the Germans near,
[You buy a Ford that's second-hand,
You paint it red, it looks so grand,
And near a "Stutz" you let it stand],
[Now Missus Cohn is fifty-six,
With all young boys she likes to mix,
She dyes her hair and paints her cheeks],
[Now LaFollette he talks too much,
To me he's funny as a crutch,
They say he got himself in dutch],
That's camouflage!

Cheer Up, Father, Cheer Up, Mother. L:
Al Bryan; M: Herman Paley. Copyright
1918 by Jerome H. Remick & Co., New
York.

1st Verse:
You have a boy over there,
Your heart is filled with despair;
But could you only see him tonight,
He wears a smile that's cheery and bright.
Though he's very far away,
Don't you seem to hear him say:

Chorus:
"Cheer up, father, cheer up, mother,
Cheer up, sister, cheer up, brother,
I'll be coming back to you some day.
And when the bands are playing,
You'll be "hip-hooraying."
Keep on smiling,
All your cares beguiling,
Dry your tears away;
For the more you miss me,
All the more you'll kiss me,
When your boy comes home some day."

2nd Verse:
Each night he's there in your dreams,
Back home again—or so it seems.
I can just picture him in your arms,
Telling of war and victory's charms.
Some day you will wake up, too,
Find your dreams have all come true:

Cheer Up, Mother. L&M: Mary Earl.
Copyright 1918 by Shapiro, Bernstein &
Co., Inc., New York.

1st Verse:
"Goodbye, mother mine, time to fall in line,"
Said a soldier unafraid.
"When they march away you'd not have me
    stay
While my country needs my aid.
Other mothers' sons bravely shoulder guns,
They are going, why not I?
Let me see you smile,
For a smile's worthwhile,
When it's time to say goodbye":

Chorus:
"Cheer up, mother, smile and don't be sigh-
    ing,
Dry the teardrop in your eye;
We'll come back with colors flying
After the war clouds roll by,
Homeward bound then
We'll come sailing, mother.
We will win out, never fear;
Dad came home from fields of glory,
Maybe I'll repeat his story,
So cheer up, mother dear."

2nd Verse:
"Mother, don't you know how long ago
Dad would sit me on his knees,
Point to his old gun, tell me how they'd won
Many hard-earned victories?
Maybe years from now I'll tell my son how
I helped keep our country free;
Maybe, mother, you
Will be telling, too,
What my daddy told to me":

**Cheer Up, Mother, It's All Right Now and
Everything Is All O.K.** L&M: Tod Wein-
hold. Copyright 1918 by Meyer Cohen
Publishing Co., Inc., New York.

1st Verse:
"Oh, mother dear, this letter here
I'm writing you today
Will be read by Mister Censor
Just to see what I've to say.
I can't tell where I'm at just now,
Or what we're going to do;
But you can read between the lines;
Just this I'll say to you":

Chorus:
"Cheer up, mother, it's all right now

And ev'rything is all O.K.
Say, no need to worry, we are doing fine,
I'm buying you a bungalow beside the Rhine.
Uncle Sam is in a hurry now,
The Kaiser has no more to say.
Tell dad to meet me with the Henry flivver;
Lordy, what a hug and kiss I'm going to give
    you.
Cheer up, mother, it's all right now
And ev'rything is all O.K."

2nd Verse:
"The Crown Prince lost one hundred pounds
Since Pershing had arrived,
And when those two million Yanks
Came over, Kaiser Bill near died.
Von Hindenburg looks hungry,
And in fact he's getting thin.
If Censor lets this news go by
I'm much obliged to him":

Cheer Up, Tommy Atkins. L: Will J.
Hart; M: Edward G. Nelson. Copyright
1918 by F.B. Havilland Publishing Co.,
Inc., New York.

1st Verse:
Somewhere afloat aboard a boat
There is a Yankee bunch,
They're full of pep to make a rep',
And they all have a hunch
That they will kill old Kaiser Bill.
Their minds made up to win,
Once o'er the top they'll never stop
Till they reach old Berlin.
To cheer their pals and get the Kaiser's goat,
By wireless they sent this cheery note:

Chorus:
"Cheer up, Tommy Atkins,
You needn't worry or sigh,
Just keep up your scrapping
When you capture Kaiser Willie.
There's a place in Piccadilly
With home-fires burning,
They'll welcome you, ev'ry one.
Though they're shooting at your noodle,
With the aid of Yankee Doodle,
You can capture the son of a Hun."

2nd Verse:
Mary Jane from Portland, Maine,
She loved an English lad;
Though far away, she'd write each day
To cheer him up when sad.
She wrote one line, it sounded fine,

"We're with you in the fray;
My brother and another lad
Have volunteered today.
Although I can't do much to help along,
To cheer you up I wrote this little song":

Cheers to Our Khaki Lads. L&M: H.
Marie Cass. Copyright 1919 by H. Marie
Cass, Peterboro, N.H.

1st Verse:
When the khaki boys appeared
Upon the battlefield;
That's when the Allies cheered and cheered,
They knew they would win the shield.
Yes, our khaki lads are best of all,
Oh, they are so strong and brave!
When they answered to the call,
Many shouts to them we raised:

Chorus:
Oh, khaki, khaki, it's a color grand,
Come, let us give the dear old khaki boys a
    hand;
Come, show some pep, stand up and sing,
Make the echoes ring;
Cheers to our brave lads we raise.
It was a wonderful, a wonderful sight
When our khaki boys began to fight.

2nd Verse:
They are on their homeward way,
Let's sing and make them glad,
The heroes staunch in battle fray;
Uncle Sam sure was proud of each lad.
We can never do too much for them,
And we'll prove ourselves most true
To our men who fought for us
And saved the dear Red, White and Blue!

**Clap Your Hands, My Baby (for Your
Daddy's Coming Home).** L: Frankie
Williams; M: Edward G. Nelson. Copy-
right 1918 by F.B. Haviland Publishing
Co., Inc., New York.

1st Verse:
Baby is learning to talk,
Mamma says, "Soon he will walk";
Baby says "dada" in a baby way—
Looks up and smiles when he hears his
    mamma say:

Chorus:
"Clap your hands, my baby,
For your daddy's coming home;

It was a happy, not doleful, infant who appeared on the 1919 cover of "Clap Your Hands, My Baby (for Your Daddy's Coming Home)," which expressed one mother's joyful advice to her little son.

Let your mamma see you smile,
No more we'll be alone.
Oh! how happy you will be
When your daddy bounces you on his knee;
So clap your hands, my baby,
For your daddy's coming home."

2nd Verse:
Sister is smiling with joy
'Cause mamma brought her a boy;
They play together the whole day long —
She tries to teach him to sing this little song:

The Colors That Will Not Run. L: Dora F. Hendricks; M: Charles H. Gabriel. Copyright 1918 by Homer A. Rodeheaver Co., Philadelphia.

1st Verse:
They said we never could do it, boys,
The dyestuff never was made
In this old blessed U.S.A.
That would not run or fade!
But turn back the pages of history
And in words that shine as the sun

Is the tale so old of our colors bold,
The colors that will not run:

Chorus:
Listen and hear the bugle blow!
See how they glow in the sun,
The royal colors we love so well,
The colors that will not run!
They've been baptized with fire, boys,
Been slandered by the Hun,
But the blessing of God is on them, boys,
The colors that will not run!

2nd Verse:
The colors, boys, they were set with tears
Shed in the struggle gone by;
They'll never fade but brighter shine
Against the blue, blue sky!
Turn forward the pages of history,
And in words that shine like the sun
Will the tale be told of our colors bold,
The colors that will not run:

3rd Verse:
No tyrant ever has unfurled them, boys,
Unstained they ripple on high.
They'll never be touched by hand profane
While one man's left to die!
Then stand with us high on the mount of
    faith,
And let hope and courage beat true,
And a-down the years you will see with tears
The glorious Red, White and Blue!:

Come On, America! L: Edward Vance Cooke; M: Kenneth M. Murchison. Copyright 1918 by Oliver Ditson Co., Boston.

1st Verse:
America! America!
Your friends are standing guard,
The gallant French die in the trench,
And the British line holds hard!
America! America!
Italia's cry is strong,
The land of art, the land of heart,
Shall welcome you with song:

Chorus:
Come on, America,
For now the bugles call!
And by your aid, no longer stayed,
The world may stand or fall.
Come on, America,
America, stand by!
For we'll push the line across the Rhine
Or know the reason why;

So, come on, America!
Come on, America!
Come on and do or die!

2nd Verse:
America! America!
The Anzac host is here;
The bold Canuck has proved his pluck
Forever and a year!
America! America!
Your guns shall cast their vote
Against the horde which lays the sword
Upon the Belgian throat!:

Daddy's Land. L&M: J. Francis Kiely.
Copyright 1915 by Empress Publishing
Co., St. Louis.

1st Verse:
It's night in the trenches, the fighting is done,
The battle is stopped for the day.
There 'mongst the wounded is somebody's
    son
Whose life blood is ebbing away.
The captain's surprise as he knelt by his side
Was a story he heard from the lad:
How he came away from his dear U.S.A.
To fight for the land of his dad:

Chorus:
"I've fought for the land of my daddy,
For daddy fought for mine.
When Lincoln called for volunteers,
Why, he was there in line.
I've just one wish," he whispered,
"Before the last command:
May God help my United States
Bring peace to daddy's land."

2nd Verse:
"My dad left his birthplace when only a boy
To fight for the land of the free;
He fought with Grant," said the lad with a
    sigh,
"With Sherman he marched to the sea.
Now I've done the same for his country and
    name,
And it's all that he'd wish me to do;
Please tell them at home how I died here
    alone
And prayed for the Red, White and Blue":

A Daddy's Prayer. L&M: Harold B. Freeman. Copyright 1918 by Harold Freeman
Publishing Co., Providence, R.I.

1st Verse:
A little girl sat on her father's knee
Just at the close of day.
She looked up and said, "When I go to bed
Have I got to kneel and pray?"
And then daddy kissed her and held her near,
And a tear was in his eye;
He said, "Don't forget brother is far, far
    away,
And you'll pray the same as I":

Chorus:
"Bring back my wand'ring boy tonight,
My soldier so dear to me,
The boy who was once my joy and light,
The pride of my life to be.
Now somewhere in France 'mid shot and shell
He's fighting over there;
I'm here all alone,
Dear God bring him home."
That was a daddy's prayer.

2nd Verse:
The little girl thought for a time and then
Looked in her father's eyes;
She said, "I'll pray, too, just the same as you,
And then p'raps God will get wise!
I want to see brother come home again,
'Cause I know you're awfully sad."
Then they knelt there alone in that cheerless
    home,
And she prayed beside her dad:

The Dixie Volunteers. L&M: Edgar Leslie
and Harry Ruby. Copyright 1917 by
Waterson, Berlin & Snyder, New York.

1st Verse:
See the folks all arrayed?
They're dressed up for the parade,
The Dixie boys are on their way,
They're goin' to sail this very day.
You can tell at a glance
They're anxious to get to France;
And you can bet they'll do their share
When they get "over there":

Chorus:
Let's all give three cheers
For the Dixie volunteers;
See those great big Southern laddies,
Just like their dear old daddies,
They are proud to go.
And they want the world to know
They're coming! they're coming
From the land of Old Black Joe.

Peaceful sons have shouldered guns,
And now they're going to be
Fighting men like Stonewall Jackson and like
   Robert E. Lee;
When they hit that line,
And they cross the River Rhine,
You'll wish you came from Dixie
With the Dixie volunteers!

2nd Verse:
They are all full of pep,
Just see those boys keep in step.
Behind their regimental band
They're playing tunes from Dixieland,
See the smile on each face?
They'll give the Kaiser a chase,
They'll hand the enemy a scare,
When they get "over there!":

Don't Be Anybody's Soldier Boy but Mine.
L: Joe Lyons; M: Frank Magine. Copyright 1918 by Ted Browne Music Co., Chicago.

1st Verse:
There are many ways we can say goodbye
When a soldier goes away;
Smiles and words of praise, or perhaps a
   sigh,
But I heard a little maid say:

Chorus:
"Don't be anybody's soldier boy but mine,
Keep a little thought for me each day,
Each weary day.
I'll be lonely for you, dearie, all the time,
Days will seem like years with you away,
Mind what I say.
If a little longing creeps into your heart,
Write and say it's then you dream of me,
That true you'll be;
And then my kisses sweet and new,
Dear, I'll save them all for you;
So don't be anybody's soldier boy but mine."

2nd Verse:
Let a little song send him on his way,
Fill his heart with sunshine bright;
Through the whole day long, then his
   thought will stray
Where he knows you're burning love's light:

Don't Bite the Hand That's Feeding You.
L: Thomas Hoier; M: Jimmie Morgan. Copyright 1915 by Leo Feist, Inc., New York.

1st Verse:
Last night as I lay a-sleeping
A wonderful dream came to me;
I saw Uncle Sammy weeping
For his children from over the sea;
They had come to him friendless and starving
When from tyrant's oppression they fled,
But now they abuse and revile him,
Till at last in just anger he said:

Chorus:
"If you don't like Uncle Sammy,
Then go back to your home o'er the sea,
To the land from where you came,
Whatever be its name,
But don't be ungrateful to me.
If you don't like the stars in Old Glory,
If you don't like the Red, White and Blue,
Then don't act like the cur in the story,
Don't bite the hand that's feeding you."

2nd Verse:
"You recall the day you landed
How I welcomed you to my shore;
When you came here empty-handed
And allegiance forever you swore,
I gathered you close to my bosom,
Of food and clothes you got both;
So when in trouble I need you,
You will have to remember your oath":

Don't Cry, Frenchy, Don't Cry. L: Sam
M. Lewis and Joe Young; M: Walter Donaldson. Copyright 1919 by Waterson, Berlin & Snyder Co., New York.

1st Verse:
They met while clouds were hanging over
   Flanders,
A soldier's glance, a war romance;
But now he's leaving her alone in Flanders,
And he softly whispers to his maid of France:

Chorus:
"Don't cry, Frenchy, don't cry
When you kiss me goodbye;
I will always keep the fleur-de-lis, dear
You gave to me, dear,
So dry your eye.
Sometime, Frenchy, sometime
We'll hear wedding bells chime.
Oh! please don't cry, Frenchy, don't cry,
   don't cry;
Until we meet again, goodbye, goodbye."

2nd Verse:
"The peaceful stars will heal the scars of

Flanders,
One tiny spark will light the dark;
For it will bring a message back to Flanders,
Just a word of love to you, my Joan of Arc":

Don't Forget the Red Cross Nurse. L&M:
Lew Orth. Copyright 1917 by Orth & Coleman, Publishers, Boston.

1st Verse:
Ev'ry man is on his toes 'cause ev'rybody
    knows
That Uncle Sam's been forced into this fight.
Since the day our flag unfurled we have
    always led the world,
And just because we fought for what was
    right.
Our soldiers and marines they have proved
    the best, it seems,
Our gen'rals and commanders they are first;
But there is still another,
To the soldiers she's a mother,
And she is the Red Cross nurse. So:

Chorus:
Don't forget the Red Cross nurse,
Don't forget the Red Cross nurse,
On the field of battle 'mid cannon's roar and
    rattle,
She will think of your life first.
She may be someone's wife,
Still she's willing to give up her life;
To the wounded she brings joys,
Our hats off to her, boys!
So don't forget the Red Cross nurse.

2nd Verse:
She is dainty and demure, still all hardships
    she'll endure,
She's always in the thickest of the fray;
While the battle rages on she will hum to
    you a song,
And tell you that we're bound to win the day.
She has loved ones of her own, but she never
    thinks of home,
Her thoughts are always of the wounded first.
She's American through and through,
And now it's up to you,
So don't forget the Red Cross nurse. So:

**Don't Let Us Sing Anymore About War,
Just Let Us Sing of Love.** L&M: Harry
Lauder. Copyright 1918 by T.B. Harms
and Francis, Day & Hunter, New York.

1st Verse:
When the cry of peace went ringing
Through the ranks of the English-speaking
    race,
There were shouts of joy
From ev'ry soldier boy,
And a big smile on his face.
Then they all gathered 'round the old dugout,
Where their home has been for long,
Then cried, "Hurray, we've won the day,
Let us sing this song!":

Chorus:
"Hurray, the war is over!
Hurray, the fight is won!
Back from the life of a rover,
Back from the roar of the gun.
Back to the dear old homeland,
Home with the peaceful dove;
Don't let us sing anymore about war,
Just let us sing of love."

2nd Verse:
When the cry of peace went ringing
Through the ships, and the crowds began to
    throng,
There were shouts of joy
From ev'ry sailor boy,
And their cheers were loud and long.
Then they all gathered 'round the old canteen,
Where they sometimes all get wet,
Then cried, "Hurray, we've won the day,
We'll be home by Christmas yet!":

**Don't Try to Steal the Sweetheart of a
Soldier.** L: Al Bryan; M: [Gus] Van and
[Joe] Schenck. Copyright 1917 by Jerome
H. Remick & Co., New York.

1st Verse:
He marched off and left his girl behind him,
On the battlefield of France you'll find him.
Are you on the square with his sweetheart
    fair
While he's over there?
"All is fair in love and war," they say,
But would you steal his girl away?:

Chorus:
Don't try to steal the sweetheart of a soldier,
It's up to you to play a manly part;
Though he's over there and she's over here,
Still she's always in his heart;
They may not meet again to love each other,
Still he prays that he'll come back some day.

While he fights for you and me
To protect our liberty,
Don't try to steal his girl away.

2nd Verse:
Night and day of her he's always dreaming,
On the field or by the campfire gleaming.
In his dreams at night, in the battle fight,
She's his heart's delight;
Would you steal her kisses while you knew
That he was fighting for you, too?:

Down in the U-17. L: Roger Lewis; M:
Ernie Erdman. Copyright 1915 by Forster,
Music Publisher, Chicago.

1st Verse:
The U-Seventeen was a big submarine
With a jolly old musical crew;
On the ocean they'd float
In their funny old boat,
And none of them ever felt blue.
They all loved the life on the billowy sea
And dangers the ocean would bring;
So out there each night when there wasn't a
    fight,
They'd lock up the hatches and sing:

Chorus:
"Oh, we'll glide like a fish
And then we'll rock like a bear;
We sleep on the ocean bed
But what do we care?
We're built like a whale,
So we'll dance on our tail;
We'll wobble like a jelly fish and crawl like a
    snail;
Oh, we'll rock and we'll reel and then we'll
    twist like an eel,
Dancing in that old submarine.
On the seas we're a wonder,
Go up or go under,
When we're down on the U-Seventeen."

2nd Verse:
To all foreign ports went these jolly old
    sports
And torpedoed their way to the bar;
As their engines were cool,
They drank plenty of fuel,
It burned mighty good in the tar.
They'd stay till the lights in the lighthouse
    went out,
Till they were all light in the head,
And hurry away to the boat in the bay
And sing as they jumped into bed:

Each Stitch Is a Thought of You, Dear.
L: Al Sweet; M: Billy Baskette. Copyright
1918 by Leo Feist, Inc., New York.

1st Verse:
By the lamplight's glow in the evening
Sits a mother old and gray,
Silently knitting with fingers worn
For her boys so far away.
Though her heart is heavy with sorrow
And her brow all wrinkled with care,
With ev'ry stitch that is fashioned,
She breathes a gentle prayer:

Chorus:
"Each stitch is a thought of you, dear,
Woven with loving care.
I'm knitting my heart in each garment, dear,
To send to you somewhere.
My hands are old and worn, dear,
The stitches may not be true,
But there's love in each one,
A mother's love for her son,
Each stitch is a thought of you."

2nd Verse:
"There's a scarf for Jimmie of woollen
And a cap for Bobbie dear;
God keep them always safe from all harm
And forgive a mother's tear.
I have knitted their baby stockings,
And I'm proud to do it again,
And though the cradle stopped rocking
For my four brave men":

Enlist! for the Red, White and Blue.
L&M: W.T. Holmes. Copyright 1917 by
W.T. Holmes, Lewiston, Me.

1st Verse:
In the days of old, so the story is told,
Your forefathers so brave and true
Arose in their might to fight for the Right,
Their freedom, their country, and you.
Let the spirit of old return to you tenfold,
Their courage be your cue;
So hustle the while, join in the rank and file,
Enlist for the Red, White and Blue!

Chorus:
From Washington to Sixty-One
Our forefathers fought so true;
In Ninety-Eight they knew their slate,
So you see it's up to you.
So while you may, join in the fray
Before the battle's through,

Just don't be late, it's simply great
To enlist for the Red, White and Blue!

2nd Verse:
In the times at hand throughout all the land
There's oppression far and near,
In church and state, in empires great,
Where there is much to fear.
Fight for the Right with all your might,
Trust in God, He will see you through;
With armor bright, go to, go through it right,
Enlist for the Red, White and Blue!

Every Mother's Son. L&M: Calla Gowdy
Gregg. Copyright 1917 by Calla Gowdy
Gregg [Publishing Co.], Indianapolis, Ind.

1st Verse:
"Mother dear, your tears are falling,
But over land and sea
I can hear my country calling
To fight for liberty.
Oh, hold me close, dear mother,
Just as we used to be;
And dream I am a boy again
And kneeling at your knee":

Chorus:
"We are coming, Uncle Sammy,
Yes, coming ev'ry one.
We are ready, Uncle Sammy,
Yes, ev'ry mother's son.
Long wave Old Glory,
And for her we would die;
Then kiss me, mother, once again
Before we say goodbye."

2nd Verse:
"Oh, think of this, dear mother,
When I am far away,
Your boy is not a coward,
And you would not have me stay.
I am going now, dear mother,
And soon I'll cross the sea,
But when you say your ev'ning prayer,
O, then remember me":

**Every Mother's Son Must Be a Soldier (A
Patriotic Song on Preparedness).** L: William H. Pease; M: Leola E. Pease. Copyright 1915 by Pease & Pease [Eastern
Music Co., Mt. Vernon, N.Y.].

1st Verse:
The old Red, White and Blue should mean a
    lot to you,

My boy, if you're a true American,
For the U.S.A. must stand for justice in our
    land,
For progress due alike to ev'ry man.
Old Uncle Sam has stood for everything
    that's good,
And equal right we'll give to every one.
We still have in our bones the spirit of Paul
    Jones,
The courage and the grit of Washington:

Chorus:
Every mother's son must be a soldier,
Ever ready for the nation's call,
And then we'll never need a great big navy,
Just a few to lead us, that is all.
Our flag has ever stood for peace and
    progress,
For Right with Might we'll fight until we fall.
We're unprepared today to make ready for
    the fray,
So every mother's son must be a soldier.

2nd Verse:
America the free has stood for liberty,
For progress that has ever made us true;
For our boys will never fight unless the cause
    is right,
And to uphold the old Red, White and Blue.
The Minute Men that won the day at Lexing-
ton,
Their spirit is still leading us today.
And when the rolling drum declares the time
    has come,
Prepared we'll win the victr'y in the fray:

**Everybody Welcome — Everything Free
(That Is the Slogan of the K of C).** L:
Alex Sullivan; M: Thomas Egan. Copy-
right 1918 by E & S Publishing Co., New
York.

1st Verse:
There is a well-known Order
Whose service at the border
Caused our boys to praise its name.
It lends a helping hand
To our lads in ev'ry land;
That's how the K of C is winning fame:

Chorus:
Ev'rybody welcome, ev'rything free,
That is the slogan of the K of C.
For all the boys here and "over there"
The K of C is doing its share.
No matter their color, their race, or creed,

For ev'ry Yankee's welfare
K of C takes heed.
So don't forget the slogan of the K of C:
"Ev'rybody welcome, ev'rything free!"

2nd Verse:
Where'er our flag is flying,
All shot and shell defying,
K of C boys will be found.
They're half a million strong
To speed victory along,
They'll never let our dear flag touch the
    ground:

**E-Yip-Yow! Yankee Boys, Welcome
Home Again!** L&M: Bob F. Sear and Al
W. Brown. Copyright 1918 by Frank K.
Root & Co., Chicago.

1st Verse:
Welcome! Welcome! Welcome's ringing
    ev'rywhere!
Boys are coming back again from over there,
Hang a flag from ev'ry window, staff, and
    dome.
Here's a song to sing when they come march-
    ing home:

Chorus:
"E-Yip-Yow! Yankee boys, welcome home
    again!
Proudly does Old Glory wave;
We're strong for you, we've waited long for
    you,
You stood the tide of battle so brave.
There's nothing too good for our heroes,
We'll have a jubilee so grand.
E-Yip-Yow! Yankee boys, welcome home
    again!
Welcome back to Yankeeland!"

2nd Verse:
Ev'ry mother's son who has enrolled his
    name
Soon will see it hung in ev'ry hall of fame.
At the bugle call he proved to be so brave,
Crossed the sea for you and me the world to
    save:

**Fight for the Flag, Boys, Red, White and
Blue.** L&M: Theodore A. Metz. Copyright
1917 by Mets Music Co., Stamford, Conn.

1st Verse:
We know that in the U.S.A.
The boys are smart and bright,

And that they're always first in ev'rything.
When war broke out in Sixty-One,
They were right there to fight,
"My country 'tis of thee," you'd hear them
    sing.
It's war again, so rally 'round the flag, boys,
Staunch and true be ready, boys, and mind
    the bugle call;
And when you hear those bells
That mean come one, come all,
Fight for the flag Red, White and Blue:

Chorus:
Fight for the flag, boys, Red, White and
    Blue,
Do as your dads did in Sixty-Two;
And when the bullets fly
You will hear the battle cry:
"Fight for the flag, boys, Red, White and
    Blue,
Come on! Fight for the Red, White and
    Blue!"

2nd Verse:
We know that ev'ry mother's son
Will soldier be or scout in ev'ry corner of the
    U.S.A.
The old men they will grab a gun,
The Home Guard will turn out,
They'll be right in the thickest of the fray.
America, you glorious land,
We're with you to a man,
And we will fight for you and die for you,
And when they ring those bells,
Throughout our land so grand,
We'll be on hand our bit to do:

For a Girl Like You. L: Sgt. Dave M.
Allan, Jr.; M: Sgt. C. Truman Collins.
Copyright 1918 by Will Rossiter, Chicago.

1st Verse:
Sweetheart, the music is calling,
Calling to you and to me;
Tears from your dear eyes are falling,
Clouds in our sky I see.
But ere I answer war's alarms
Once more I'll hold you in my arms, darling:

Chorus:
Tenderly pressed to my breast
While the dreamy waltz is playing;
Melody rare, dreams fill the air,
Set my heart with love a-swaying.
If I could hold you forever like this,
Heart to heart beating,

Our souls in a kiss,
All I would give, forever to live
For a girl like you

2nd Verse:
Far o'er the sea I'll be going
Just for humanity's sake,
But in my heart I'll be knowing
All of your love I'll take.
And there beneath the starlight gleams,
Again you'll be with me in dreams, darling:

For God, America, and You. L&M: Lewis
J. Fay and Bennie McLaughlin. Copyright
1917 by Lewis J. Fay, Boston.

1st Verse:
Our President had called for a million volun-
    teers,
Our flag had been insulted as it had not been
    in years;
A mother old with heart of gold which can-
    not be denied
Gave up her son, her only one,
Then said with Yankee pride:

Chorus:
"Your [My] grand-granddaddy was at Valley
    Forge,
Your [My] granddad was with Scott,
And your [my] own dear dad, when but a
    lad,
At Fred'ricksburg was shot.
In the fight with Spain
We were right there again,
With hearts from fear so free.
[With hearts that fear ne'er knew].
So go, my dear boy, give battle to the foe
[And now I must go to battle with the foe]
For God, for America, and you."

2nd Verse:
How all the people cheered as this lad of
    tender years
Walked up to the recruiting stand, his eyes
    bedimmed with tears;
The tears were for the mother who was giv-
    ing all she had,
He loved her well, then like a bell,
These words came from the lad:

For the Freedom of All Nations. L&M:
Eleanor Everest Freer. Copyright 1917 by
Will Rossiter, Chicago.

1st Chorus:
For the freedom of all nations
We are on our way to France,
And to fight against oppression
God has given us this chance.
Who can e'er forget the anguish
Of the women in the waves,
As the Lusitania's masthead
Sank to please the Prussian knaves.

2nd Chorus:
To attack our fellow beings
On pursuits of peaceful aim
Did a foe arise in anger,
And without a lawful claim
Rob the freedom of all nations.
Belgium, Italy, and France,
To avenge them is our duty,
And Old Glory must advance.

3rd Chorus:
Shall we see our homes demolished
As in Belgium and in France,
Women taken into slavery,
For their children not a chance?
Not a moment must we tarry,
Shoulder knapsack, gun, or lance;
Victory must be our watchword
As we're marching on through France.

**For Your Boy and My Boy (Buy Bonds!
Buy Bonds!).** L: Gus Kahn; M: Egbert
Van Alstyne. Copyright 1918 by Jerome
H. Remick & Co., New York.

1st Verse:
Hear the bugle call,
The call to arms for liberty;
See them one and all,
They go to fight for you and me;
Heroes we will find them,
Ev'ry mother's son,
We must get behind them
Till their work is done:

1st Chorus:
For your boy and my boy
And all of the boys out there,
Let's lend our money to the U.S.A.
And do our share;
Ev'ry bond we are buying
Will help to hold the fighting line;
Buy bonds, buy bonds
For your boy and mine!

2nd Verse:
Hear the bugle call,

The call to those who stay at home;
You are soldiers all,
Though you may never cross the foam.
Keep Old Glory waving
Proudly up above,
Praying, working, saving
For the ones you love:

2nd Chorus:
For your boy and my boy
And all of the boys out there,
Let's get together till they come back home
And do our share;
Ev'ry bond that we are buying
Will help the boys to cross the Rhine;
Buy bonds, buy bonds
For your boy and mine!

Frenchy, Come to Yankee Land. L: Sam
Ehrlich; M: Con Conrad. Copyright 1919
by Broadway Music Corp., New York.

1st Verse:
You remember Rosie Green, who went across
  the sea
And fell in love with soldier Jean, a chap
  from gay Paree;
She just returned so angry and they say she's
  feeling blue
Because her "Frenchy" taught another girl to
  parley-vous;
But Rosie got a lonesome spell today,
Then quickly sent this cablegram away:

Chorus:
"Frenchy, come over, Frenchy,
I'm sorry, dearie, I made you cry,
But when you smiled at K-K-K-K-Katy,
I was angry and said goodbye;
Bring all the kissing that you promised
Your little Rose in No Man's Land,
And pack up your la-la's in your old kit bag
And, Frenchy, come to Yankee Land."

2nd Verse:
Rosie waited for a day but Jean had not
  replied,
She quickly figured out a way to bring him
  to her side;
Beneath the kitchen window she prepared a
  lovely trench,
And furnished it completely, then she took a
  course in French;
Into the cable office Rosie flew
And wired, "I've dug a little home for you":

**(Gee, What a Wonderful Time We'll Have)
When the Boys Come Home.** L&M: Mary
Earl. Copyright 1917 by Shapiro, Bernstein
& Co., Inc., New York.

1st Verse:
The East, the West have days they love best,
And so have the South and the North;
A certain date they all celebrate,
And that is the glorious Fourth.
But there is a day soon to come
When America'll make things hum:

Chorus:
Gee, what a wonderful time we'll have
When the boys come home.
The girls will be dressed in their Sunday best
When the boys come home.
The flags will fly and the bands will play,
We'll all turn out with a smile so gay,
And ev'ryone shouting "hip-hip-hooray!"
When the boys come home.

2nd Verse:
The sun will surely shine on that day
To welcome our soldier boys home;
As stiff as starch we'll watch them all march,
Our heroes from over the foam.
A welcome they're going to get
That America won't forget!:

General Pershing (March). L: J.R. Shannon; M: Carl D. Vandersloot. Copyright
1918 by Vandersloot Music Publishing
Co., Williamsport, Pa.

Verse:
Hear the bugles sounding o'er the sea
Like heart throbs of the free,
The pulse of liberty.
Uncle Sammy's boys are on their way,
With Pershing's mighty band
Proclaiming freedom's hand.
All the world's eyes are upon you and your
  boys, Gen'ral John,
Victorious we know you'll be
As you march bravely on;
'Neath the starry Spangled Banner you are
  sure to win the day,
So, onward Christian Soldiers!
We're with you in the fray!:

Chorus:
There's no mother on this side of the great
  ocean
Who would not gladly give her cherished sons
  to you,

And you can count upon a hundred million
people
All for you, brave and true, who'll die or do.
When the dawn of peace again shall hover
o'er us,
And true democracy shall be an endless
chain,
"Black Jack" Pershing will be honored by all
nations,
And Old Glory will still wave without a stain.

General Pershing's March to Berlin.
L&M: Daniel LaGrove. Copyright 1918 by
Daniel LaGrove.

Hoora, hoora, the battle is on and we are
going to win!
Hoora, hoora, the battle is on, all men and
women join in!
Hoora, hoora, the battle is on and we are
sure to win!
Hoora, hoora, all men and women join in!
We're going to get there, sure, you bet we
are,
We're going to get there, don't you cry.
We're going to get there, Uncle Sam he
knows the way.
The world is so large and the dream of the
Kaiser is the devil in command,
And the Kaiser will lose just as sure as the
world,
And the demon that possessed him
Is the curse of the Kaiser forever more.
Now boys, come on, we must be there,
Don't be too long delaying,
Let us be there, doing our share,
Then we'll be home again.

**The Girl He Left Behind Him (Has the
Hardest Fight of All).** L: Al Bryan and
Edgar Leslie; M: Harry Ruby. Copyright
1918 by Waterson, Berlin & Snyder Co.,
New York.

1st Verse:
I saw him kiss his girl goodbye,
Then proudly march away;
I saw her dry her tear-stained eyes,
She hadn't much to say.
They'll speak about his bravery,
But she's just as brave as he:

Chorus:
For the girl he left behind him
Has the hardest fight of all;

The waiting, the worry, and the loneliness borne
by sweethearts and wives of soldiers were celebrated by lyricists Al Bryan and Edgar Leslie in
the 1918 ballad "The Girl He Left Behind (Has the
Hardest Fight of All)."

She may not have to face the foe over there,
But in her heart she has a sorrow to bear.
When she sits alone at twilight,
Then her tears begin to fall;
She's waiting for a word from her soldier
lad,
Maybe it's good,
Maybe it's bad;
The girl he left behind him has the hardest
fight of all.

2nd Verse:
I saw the postman call one day,
A letter in his hand;
He heard her sigh, then turn away,
He couldn't understand.
I watched to see that smile appear,
But I only saw a tear:

**The Girl Who Wears a Red Cross on Her
Sleeve.** L&M: Will Mahoney. Copyright
1915 by P.J. Howley Music Co., New
York.

1st Verse:
There's a gray-haired mother in a far-off
town,

"She works with the heart of an angel/ 'Mid the sound of the cannon's roar," wrote Will Mahoney in his 1915 salute to the International Red Cross, "The Girl Who Wears a Red Cross on Her Sleeve."

And her thoughts are on the field of war;
She is thinking of the million broken hearts
There will be when the battle is o'er.
She says "I would be glad
If I had a lad
To fight for his country like a man;
And though I had no boy,
It just filled me with joy
To give my darling girl when war began":

Chorus:
There's a girl at the front among the
   soldiers —
She is one of a thousand girls or more —
Who works with the heart of an angel
'Mid the sound of the cannon's roar.
She is caring with love so sweet and tender
For the sons of the mothers who grieve,
And many are the hearts that are grateful
   tonight
To the girl who wears a red cross on her
   sleeve.

2nd Verse:
There's another mother in that far-off town
And her eyes are filled with joyous tears,
For she got a letter from her soldier boy

And it made her forget all her fears;
Here's the message he sent
That filled her with content:
"I went through the battle without harm,
But just whisper a prayer
For the brave girls who wear
A little cross of red upon their arm":

Girls of France. L&M: Al Bryan, Edgar Leslie, and Harry Ruby. Copyright 1918 by Waterson, Berlin & Snyder Co., New York.

1st Verse:
We always thought you a fickle coquette,
Girl of France, girl of France;
Something to fondle and then to forget,
Just made for love and romance.
Now we point with pride to you,
And we love you, too:

Chorus:
Girls of France, girls of France,
We're mighty proud of you;
When shadows fell and all was dark
You led your sons like Joan of Arc.
We know our brothers will never feel blue,
They'll find a sister in each of you.
Brave and true,
Beautiful, too,
Wonderful girls of France.

2nd Verse:
There came a foe to the land of your birth,
Girl of France, girl of France.
You met his thrust like an angel on earth,
Victory shone in your glance.
Sisters all of Lafayette,
We shall not forget:

Give a Job to the Gob and the Doughboy. L: Lew Porter and Alex Sullivan; M: Max Friedman. Copyright 1919 by Jerome H. Remick & Co., New York.

1st Verse:
There is more to be done than say
   "Welcome,"
There are more things to do than to cheer;
What good is all the noise
If we can't protect the boys
When they get back over here:

Chorus:
Are you ready with a job that's steady

Give a Job to the Gob and the Doughboy

Song

Lyric by
LEW PORTER
& ALEX SULLIVAN

Music by
MAX FRIEDMAN

A plea to employers to let lame-duck servicemen "have the jobs they held before," "Give a Job to the Gob and the Doughboy" respectfully reflected concern over the growing postwar unemployment crisis developing throughout American industry.

Now that they are coming back once more?
Don't forget them and be proud to let them
Have the jobs they held before.
They were glad to fight for us both night and
    day,
Show them that you're willing to repay;
Give a job to the gob and the doughboy,
For they helped to make the whole world
    free.

2nd Verse:
They have all risked their lives for their
    country,
And the boys gave their all with a will;
They've made good while away,
Now that they are back to stay,
Our pledges we must fulfill:

Give Me a Kiss, Mirandy ('Cause I'm Going Over There). L: Forrest S. Rutherford; M: Althea J. Rutherford. Copyright 1917 by A.J. Rutherford, assigned to M. Witmark & Sons, New York.

1st Verse:
A raw recruit from old Mizoo enlisted in the
    ranks,
They slipped some khaki breeches upon his
    spindle shanks;
Then all dressed up he went to woo Mirandy
    down the way,
And when she cut the little curl,
This raw recruit did say:

Chorus:
"Aw, gimme a kiss, Mirandy, 'cause I'm
    goin' over there,
I need a little bracer now besides a lock of hair.
I know you're not the slacker kind,
You've got the goods for fair!
So gimme a kiss, Mirandy, 'cause I'm goin'
    over there."

2nd Verse:
Mirandy hung her pretty head and gave a lit-
    tle sigh,
Her boy was goin' to fight in France and
    mebbe for to die.
She puckered up her lips and said, "I'll do my
    little bit,"
And when she let him have a kiss,
He didn't want to quit:

**Give Three Cheers for "Unc' Sam's" Sol-
diers.** L&M: Maurice G. Attree. Copyright 1918 by M.G. Attree.

1st Verse:
"Darling dear, I'm going now to fight for the
    U.S.A.,
To help old 'Uncle Sam' to stand and have
    his flag fly free;
So don't you cry and don't you sigh
For I must go away.
I hear the bugle calling me,
It's calling me today.
When you see us marching by,
Just cheer us as we go,
With our dear flag on high
We march against the foe.
Then":

Chorus:
"Give three cheers for 'Unc' Sam's' soldiers
With their guns upon their shoulders,
Onward 'gainst the foe.
As they march they're bravely cheering,
Never shot nor shell are fearing, cheering as
    they go.
Oh! hear the bugle calling,

While in line they're falling;
Stripes float high
As we're proudly marching by,
On to victory!
Let us see you dry your tears,
And give three good hearty cheers for 'Unc'
    Sammies' boys,
Then give three hearty cheers
For the boys of the U.S.A.!"

2nd Verse:
As the lassie stood by with tears in her blue
    eyes,
She saw the soldiers passing and she heard
    their cheerful cries;
She saw the face of her dear boy
As off to war he went,
He bore a smile of happiness,
And to her kisses sent.
She then remembered his last word
As she saw him go;
Let us also cheer them on
Forward against the foe.
And:

Go Lad, and May God Bless You. L:
Haven Gillespie; M: Henry I. Marshall.
Copyright 1917 by Jerome H. Remick &
Co., New York.

1st Verse:
The bugle called to the boys to march away,
In the throng stood a mother old and gray;
Her thoughts went back to a bygone day,
Sixty-One, the blue and the gray.
The beat of the drums was sounding down
    the way,
As she kissed her boy farewell,
He heard her say:

Chorus:
"Go, lad, and let them know, lad,
That they're your foe, lad,
And, sonny, fight all your might.
I'm grieving to see you leaving,
But freedom's way calls today, sonny,
That's why I say—
Fight for the rights that your daddy died for,
His was a cause true blue.
So go, lad, the rest you know, lad,
And may God bless you."

2nd Verse:
The last faint ray of the sun has died away,
All alone sits a mother old and gray;
Her thoughts all stray back to a child at play

And to one who had marched away.
And in her prayers we hear his mother say:
"May heaven guide
And keep him on his way":

God Spare Our Boys Over There. L&M:
William Jerome and J.F. Mahoney. Copyright 1918 by Leo Feist, Inc., New York.

1st Verse:
The voice of the country called forth ev'ry
    son,
And nobly they echoed the answer as one;
The flame in their hearts dried the nation's
    sad tears,
Let us pray night and day through our hopes
    and fears:

Chorus:
God spare our boys over there,
Keep them in Your tender care.
Mothers are kneeling, loved ones appealing,
Angels, protect them somewhere.
Hear our fervent prayer,
On bended knee hear our hearts' rosary
And spare the boys over there.

2nd Verse:
The heart of the nation is throbbing today,
In one cause united her sons march away.
O, mothers of heroes, O, mothers of men,
May your boys share the joys of the home-
    fires again:

Good Luck to the U.S.A. L: Arthur J.
Lamb; M: Frederick V. Bowers. Copyright
1917 by Frederick V. Bowers, Inc., New
York.

1st Verse:
A maiden away down in Dixie
To her sweetheart said "Goodbye,
I love my country, too,
Go forth to do or die.
I'll think of you ev'ry night,
And you think of me.
There's a little girl in Dixie who waits for
    you,
Go fight for liberty!":

Chorus:
"Good luck to the boys of the U.S.A.
And the fairest flag that flies,
For it ne'er has been defeated,
It is the emblem we prize.

The Army and Navy forever
Are bound to win the day
By land or sea.
Go fight, my love, for me;
Good luck to the U.S.A."

2nd Verse:
A soldier was longing for Dixie
When he heard his gen'ral cry:
"Who'll take this message forth
And bring back a reply?"
Then forward the soldier speeds,
A shot lays him low.
"There's a little girl in Dixie," they hear him
    say,
"Tell her I had to go":

Good Morning, Mr. Zip-Zip-Zip! L&M:
Robert Lloyd. Copyright 1918 by Leo
Feist, Inc., New York.

1st Verse:
We come from ev'ry quarter,
From north, south, east and west,
To clear the way to freedom
For the land we love the best;
We've left our occupations
And homes so far and dear,
But when the going's rather rough,
We raise this song of cheer:

Chorus:
Good morning, Mister Zip-Zip-Zip,
With your hair cut just as short as mine;
Good morning, Mister Zip-Zip-Zip,
You're surely looking fine!
Ashes to ashes, and dust to dust,
If the camels don't get you,
The Fatimas must;
Good morning, Mister Zip-Zip-Zip,
With your hair cut just as short as,
Your hair cut just as short as,
Your hair cut just as short as mine.

2nd Verse:
You see them on the highway,
You meet them down the pike,
In olive drab and khaki
Are soldiers on the hike;
And as our column passes,
The word goes down the line,
"Good morning, Mister Zip-Zip-Zip,
You're surely looking fine":

(Goodbye and Luck Be with You) Laddie

GOOD MORNING MR. ZIP-ZIP-ZIP!

By Robert Lloyd
Army Song Leader

One of the few comic songs dealing with the war,
"Good Morning, Mr. Zip-Zip-Zip!", poked a little
harmless fun at the freshly inducted army recruit
forced to undergo a close-to-the-scalp haircut.

Boy. L: Will D. Cobb; M: Gus Edwards.
Copyright 1917 by Gus Edwards Music
House, New York.

1st Verse:
War in the air,
Blare, bugles, blare!
Drums beat the loud roll call!
Hark! down the street,
Tramp, tramp of feet,
Up go the windows all!
North and south, east and west
Forth come the country's best.
Never mind that parting tear,
Let there be one parting cheer:

Chorus:
Goodbye and luck be with you, laddie boy,
    laddie boy,
Whatever your name may be,
There's a look in your eye
As you go marching by
Tells me you will dare and do and die;
And when you hear those shells begin to sing,
There'll be someone somewhere will murmur
    this prayer:
"May you win your share of glory
And come back to tell the story."
Goodbye and good luck, laddie boy.

2nd Verse:
Somewhere in France
There waits the chance,
One fighting chance, that's all.
May you return
To hearts that yearn,
Or like a soldier fall.
As in granddaddy's day,
Though today no blue nor gray,
Clad in khaki fine and fit,
Marching on to do your bit:

Goodbye Broadway, Hello France. L: C.
Francis Reisner and Benny Davis; M: Billy
Baskette. Copyright 1917 by Leo Feist,
Inc., New York.

1st Verse:
Goodbye, New York town, goodbye, Miss
    Liberty,
Your lights of freedom will guide us across
    the sea;
Ev'ry soldier's sweetheart bidding goodbye,
Ev'ry soldier's mother drying her eye;
Cheer up, we'll soon be there,
Singing this Yankee air:

Chorus:
Goodbye Broadway, hello France,
We're ten million strong;
Goodbye sweethearts, wives, and mothers,
It won't take us long;
Don't you worry while we're there,
It's for you we're fighting, too;
So goodbye Broadway, hello France,
We're going to square our debt to you.
[We're going to help you win this war].

2nd Verse:
"Vive Pershing!" is the cry across the sea,
We're united in this fight for liberty;
France sent us a soldier, brave Lafayette,
Whose deeds and fame we cannot forget;
Now that we have the chance,
We'll pay our debt to France:

Goodbye, Dear Old Girl, Goodbye. L&M:
E.J. Pourmon. Copyright 1917 by Broad &
Market Music Co., Newark, N.J.

1st Verse:
Sweetheart, I must leave you,
I must go away;
Pray don't let it grieve you,
Love cannot bid me stay.

Hear the bugle calling,
Goodbye, sweet sweetheart.
Though your tears are falling,
Dear old girl, we two must part.
Goodbye, darling:

Chorus:
When the Blue and Gray united
Are fighting far across the sea,
Victory soon will be sighted
In the name of humanity.
While I'm gone, may God above protect you,
And caress you when you weep and sigh.
Ev'ry night, dear, say a prayer,
God speed our heroes over there;
Goodbye, dear old girl,
Goodbye.

2nd Verse:
While campfires are gleaming
Far away in France,
Poor old girl, I'm dreaming
Of love's departing glance.
Keep the lovelight burning
In your heart so true
For me when returning
To my home sweet home and you.
Goodbye, darling:

Goodbye, France. L&M: Irving Berlin.
Copyright 1918 by Waterson, Berlin &
Snyder Co., New York.

1st Verse:
I can picture the boys "over there,"
Making plenty of noise "over there,"
And if I'm not wrong,
It won't be long,
Ere a certain song will fill the air;
It's all very clear,
The time's drawing near
When they'll be marching down to the pier,
    singing:

Chorus:
"Goodbye, France,
We'd love to linger longer,
But we must go home.
Folks are waiting to welcome us
Across the foam;
We were glad to stand side by side with you,
Mightily proud to have died with you.
So goodbye, France,
You'll never be forgotten by the U.S.A."

2nd Verse:
They are waiting for one happy day,

When the word comes to start on their way;
With a tear-dimmed eye
They'll say goodbye,
But their hearts will cry hip-hip hooray!
The friends that they made
Will wish that they stayed,
As they start on their homeward parade,
    singing:

Goodbye, Germany. L: J. Edwin and Lincoln McConnell; M: J. Edwin McConnell. Copyright 1918 by Ted Browne Music Co., Chicago.

1st Verse:
Uncle Sam is now fixed up for war,
Uncle Sam is angry to the core,
For that war-mad bully o'er the sea
Dares to murder people of the U.S.A.
My country is a land
Of the noble true and brave,
And though your submarine sharks
May fill the whole wide ocean,
Germany, you'll have to pay:

Chorus:
Goodbye, Germany, so long, Germany,
You've brought the Eagle down on your
    head,
For you've riled old Uncle Sam
And the people of his land.
From east to west you'll find your foes,
And 'way down yonder where the cotton
    grows,
The people are shouting for war,
And they're counting time on you.
When Uncle Sam goes after you,
The whole big world knows you are through,
So goodbye, Germany.
[When Sammy's boys go out to war,
The whole big world knows what they're for,
So goodbye, Germany].

2nd Verse:
We have watched you make your dirty fight,
Watched as you trampled ev'ry Right,
Trampled helpless people 'neath your heel,
Now the hand of power you shall surely feel.
My country is a land
Where the hearts of men beat true,
And when you murder the people
Of this grand old nation,
You'll get what's coming to you:

Goodbye, My Hero. L&M: Ernest R. Heck. Copyright 1917 by Ernest R. Heck [Whitmore Music Publishing Co., Scranton, Pa. and New York].

1st Verse:
"Sweetheart, I soon must leave you,
The soldiers are falling in line.
Sweetheart, don't let it grieve you,
I will return some time.
Don't let your heart grow weary.
Come little girl, don't sigh,
Hark, now the bugle's calling,
Sweetheart of mine, goodbye":

Chorus:
"Goodbye, my hero, soldier of mine,
God will protect you on the firing line.
You'll find me waiting
[Fight for Old Glory]
With heart true blue.
Goodbye, my hero,
Farewell to you."

2nd Verse:
A mother's sad heart was aching,
Her son he must now go to war.
News that war clouds were breaking
Sounded at ev'ry door.
One parting kiss he gave her,
Knelt at her side to pray.
Then as he rose to leave her,
I heard his mother say:

Goodbye, My Soldier Boy. L&M: Calla Gowdy Gregg. Copyright 1918 by Calla Gowdy Gregg [Publishing Co.], Indianapolis, Ind.

1st Verse:
"Hear the war drums beat, and the marching
    feet,
I must say goodbye, sweet Mary.
Though I leave you now,
Hear my parting vow,
I will come back, my girl, to you.
In our country's need, for our help she
    pleads,
We must answer duty's call!"
Mary's voice came, soft and low,
"Though I hate to see you go,
I will wait, soldier boy, for you":

Chorus:
"Here they come, those fighting Sammies,
They are heroes ev'ry one!

From those of the snowy Northland
To the boys 'neath the Southern sun!
Go and fight for God and freedom,
And we'll wait for you with joy;
'Till you come back with victory,
Goodbye, my soldier boy!"

2nd Verse:
"Though tonight I go from your side,
I know you will not forget me, Mary.
Though your tears may fall,
We must one and all
To the Stars and Stripes be true!"
Mary says, "Dear lad, please do not be sad,
I will not stay home and pine.
For I have a duty, too!
There'll be work for me to do
At the front, on the firing line":

Goodbye, My Soldier Boy (March). L&M:
June Bauer. Copyright 1918 by June Bauer
Co., Inc., Judsonia, Ark.

1st Verse:
"It breaks my heart, dear, to leave you,
Sweetheart, you must not cry.
Our Uncle Sammy needs me,
And we must say goodbye.
Hear how the bugle is calling,
It calls me to the flag;
I know you will not lag
With your little knitting bag.
Kaiser Bill, we will sure get you (the Crown
   prince, too)":

Chorus:
"Goodbye, my soldier boy,
Must I say farewell?
When you are far away,
In my prayers I'll always say,
Take care of him wherever he may be.
Goodbye, good luck to you,
Don't forget the little girl who's always true;
Although I'll be very lonely,
I'll be waiting for you only,
My own soldier boy."

2nd Verse:
"A ship is out in the harbor,
It sails away today.
I've come to say goodbye, dear,
Before you sail away.
Hear how the bugle is calling,
I know it calls for you.
Now when you are far away
In the thickest of the fray,

Just remember that I'm true blue (and strong
   for you)":

Goodbye, Sally (Good Luck to You).
L&M: Sam Habelow. Copyright 1919 by
George Jeffrey and Samuel Habelow, Bos-
ton.

1st Verse:
Johnny Doughboy was no slow boy "over
   there" in France.
He never missed a chance
To catch ze pretty maiden's glance.
He'd "oo-la-la" and "parlez vous"
With ev'ry girl he'd meet.
But when it came the day
He had to sail away,
To an "Army Lassie" I heard Johnny say:

Chorus:
"Goodbye, Sally, I'm leaving today,
So long, Sally, I'm sailing away
To the land that gave me birth,
To the grandest place on earth.
I'll tell the folks back home
About the good you've done,
We owe a lot to you.
Though the others used me fine,
Sally, you're the one for mine,
[Many times when things looked blue,
You stood by and helped us through],
Goodbye, Sally, good luck to you."

2nd Verse:
"The Army Lassie sure is classie,
Ev'ry bit true blue,
And I will say to you
That she's the one my hat's off to.
The war is won, my work is done
And now I'm glad I'm through.
Before I sail away back to the U.S.A.,
To you 'Army Lassies' once more I want to
   say":

**Goodbye, Sammie! (Gee, I'm Glad to See
You Go!).** L: Samuel L. Gassel; M:
Albert Tusso. Copyright 1918 by Samuel
L. Gassel and Albert Tusso, Publishers,
Vineland, N.J.

1st Verse:
Our country's calling, calling, calling,
You can hear it all o'er the land,
A call to arms across the sea, boys,
We must lend a helping hand.

America, the land of freedom,
Hear our call to you:
We need you, we need you, need you,
What are you going to do?:

Chorus:
"Goodbye, Sammie, gee, I'm glad to see you
  go,
Keep up the spirit, boys, of many days ago.
Hark, I hear the bugle calling
In the battle for liberty;
Many a man is going over,
We won't come back till it's over!
Oh say, can you see,
It's the song that makes it gripping;
We feel the Kaiser slipping
In this battle for democracy."

2nd Verse:
We've got another Abie Lincoln,
Another Thomas Jefferson,
We've got another Grant or Jackson,
Men whose fame lives on and on.
Men who are loyal to their country,
Ones whose work when done
Will be loved by all the people,
As they loved George Washington:

**The Greatest Day the World Will Ever
Know.** L: Ed Morton and James E.
Dempsey; M: Joseph A. Burke. Copyright
1918 by Joe Morris Music Co., New York.

1st Verse:
The eyes of all the nations are turned toward
  the east,
To where the clouds of battle hide the light,
A thrill of expectation is felt in ev'ry heart;
We are watching for the dawning
Of a morning fair and bright,
When vict'ry's sun shall rise above the sea,
Oh, what a wond'rous day that will be:

Chorus:
When the soldier returns to his sweetheart,
When he lays away his uniform and gun,
When daddy comes back to his baby,
When mother's arms are wrapped around her
  son;
When the stars that we love in Old Glory
With the light of victory are all aglow,
When we've made all nations free,
We'll thank God, for it will be
The greatest day the world will ever know.

2nd Verse:
When sweethearts gave their soldiers, when

mothers gave their sons,
It broke their hearts to see them march away.
Their grief will change to gladness, their tears
  will turn to smiles,
For the boys across the foam
Will all come sailing home some day.
We'll all be singing songs of victory,
Imagine what a day that will be!:

Hail! Hail! The Gang's All Here. L: D.A.
Esrom; M: Theodore Morse and Arthur
Sullivan. Copyright 1917 by Leo Feist,
Inc., New York.

1st Verse:
A gang of good fellows are we, are we, are
  we,
With never a worry, you see, you see, you
  see;
We laugh and joke, we sing and smoke,
And live life merrily;
No matter the weather when we get together,
We have a jubilee:

Chorus:
Hail! Hail! the gang's all here,
What the deuce do we care,
What the deuce do we care;
Hail! Hail! we're full of cheer,
What the deuce do we care, Bill!

2nd Verse:
We love one another, we do, we do, we do,
With brotherly love and it's true, it's true, it's
  true;
It's one for all, the big and small,
It's always me for you;
No matter the weather when we get together,
We drink a toast or two:

3rd Verse:
When out for a good time we go, we go, we
  go,
There's nothing we do that is slow, is slow, is
  slow;
Of joy we get our share, you bet,
The gang will tell you so;
No matter the weather when we get together,
We sing this song you know:

Hand in Hand Again. L: Raymond B.
Egan; M: Richard A. Whiting. Copyright
1919 by Jerome H. Remick & Co., New
York.

1st Verse:
There were tears in the hour that was
   darkest,
The hour that came just before dawn;
But a smile lurks today
Where a tear used to stray,
And the curtain of darkness is drawn:

Chorus:
Ev'ry heart is lighter,
Ev'ry smile is brighter,
Sad "Adieu" is changing to "Hello" again.
Sorrow walked before us
But a prayer watched o'er us;
We strayed far but here we are,
Hand in hand again.

2nd Verse:
Not a sparrow may fall from the treetop
Unknown to the angels above;
So then why should our fears
Turn our smiles into tears;
Heaven watches o'er all hearts that love:

Hello Central! Give Me No Man's Land.
L: Sam M. Lewis and Joe Young; M: Jean
Schwartz. Copyright 1918 by Waterson,
Berlin & Snyder Co., New York.

1st Verse:
When the gray shadows creep
And the world is asleep,
In the still of the night
Baby creeps down a flight;
First she looks all around
Without making a sound,
Then baby toddles up to the telephone
And whispers in a baby tone:

Chorus:
"Hello Central, give me No Man's Land,
My daddy's there,
My mamma told me;
She tip-toed off to bed after my pray'rs were
   said.
Don't ring when you get my number
Or you'll disturb mamma's slumber.
I'm afraid to stand here at the phone
'Cause I'm alone,
So won't you hurry;
I want to know why mamma starts to weep
When I say, 'Now I lay me down to sleep';
Hello Central, give me No Man's Land."

2nd Verse:
Through the curtains of night
Comes a beautiful light,

And the sunshine that beams
Finds a baby in dreams;
Mamma looks in to see
Where her darling can be;
She finds her baby still in her slumber deep,
A-whisp'ring while she's fast asleep:

**(He's Got Those Big Blue Eyes Like You)
Daddy Mine.** L&M: Lew Wilson and Al
Dubin. Copyright 1918 by M. Witmark &
Sons, New York.

1st Verse:
Our soldiers in the trenches received their
   mail today
From sweethearts and mothers
In the good old U.S.A.
There's one who's heart is dancing,
His eyes light up with joy,
He reads the letter over, and he shouts
   "Boys, it's a boy!":

Chorus:
"He's got those big blue eyes like you,
   daddy,
The kind of eyes that seem to speak,
And when he smiles he looks like you,
   daddy,
Yes, even to the dimple in his cheek.
I've named him after you,
For I knew you'd want me to,
He reminds me of you all the time.
When he grows to be a man,
I'll give him up to Uncle Sam,
Just like I did with you, daddy mine!"

2nd Verse:
The soldier boy's a reader, he's read Shake-
   speare and the rest,
And he knows Kipling backwards,
If you put him to the test.
But now he claims the greatest of poets never
   wrote
A poem half so pretty
As this welcome little note:

He's Well Worth Waiting For. L: Garfield
Kilgour; M: Harry Von Tilzer. Copyright
1918 by Harry Von Tilzer Music Publishing Co., New York.

1st Verse:
'Mid the roses' twining stands a dear, sweet
   lonesome lass
Dreaming of her boy across the foam.

Sunshine calls the songbirds
As the fleeting moments pass,
And they seem to tell her "He'll come home."
Her soldier boy has left her,
And they'll meet she knows not when,
But 'till he comes back again:

Chorus:
She's going to wait and watch for his return-
    ing
From over there, from over there.
He's gone to fight for Right
And bravely do his part,
And all the while a smile of hope
Is in her heart.
She's going to keep the lovelight burning,
Each night her prayer will reach that foreign
    shore;
She's going to wait, wait,
Although her heart may ache;
She's going to wait, wait,
Although her heart may break;
She's going to wait and watch for his return,
For he's well worth waiting for.

2nd Verse:
As the fading shadows tell her of the setting
    sun,
Night time brings her thoughts of him alone.
Though he's far away
She can't forget her dearest one,
And she dreams of "when he'll be her own."
Although she longs to hold him,
And she's very lonesome, too,
There is just one thing to do:

The Home Road. L&M: John Alden Carpenter. Copyright 1918 by G. Schirmer,
New York.

Verse:
Sing a hymn of freedom,
Fling the banner high!
Sing the songs of liberty,
Songs that shall not die.
For the long, long road to Tipperary
Is the road that leads me home,
O'er hills and plains
By lakes and lanes,
My woodlands! My cornfields!
My country! My home!

Chorus:
In the quiet hours
Of the starry night,

Dream the dreams of far away,
Homefires burning bright.
For the long, long road to Tipperary
Is the road that leads me home,
O'er hills and plains
By lakes and lanes,
My woodlands! My cornfields!
My country! My home!

Homeland (I Can Hear You Calling Me).
L: James E. Dempsey; M: Joseph A.
Burke. Copyright 1918 by A.J. Stasny
Music Co., New York.

1st Verse:
"Where the breezes sweet with new-mown
    hay
Play all the day,
In dreams I stray;
America, I hear you calling me from far
    away,
Where fond hearts pray,
My U.S.A.
It's a long, long way from sunny France
To my own native land;
Yet ev'ry word you say I understand":

Chorus:
"Oh! homeland, I hear you calling me,
Home of the free,
Across the sea;
My land of liberty,
Telling me not to forget
Our old-time debt to Lafayette,
For it was France who helped to break our
    chains
And set us free,
The Stars and Stripes must dry the tears of
    Normandy.
All through the rush and the rattle,
The roar of the battle,
Dear old homeland, I can hear you calling
    me."

2nd Verse:
"Little Belgian children once so gay
Along the way
No longer play;
Oh, Germany, you'll have a mighty heavy
    debt to pay!
What will you say on Judgment Day?
And I guess that's why
I hear my homeland
Calling out for me
To fight and bring back "Peace with victory":

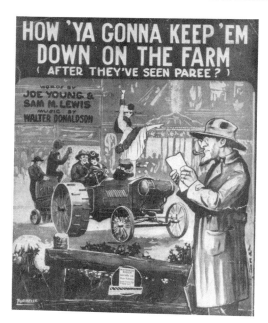

One of the all-time classic comic songs, "How 'Ya Gonna Keep 'Em Down on the Farm (After They've Seen Paree)?" related the worries of the parents of ex-doughboy Reuben. Their chief fear is that his happy off-duty hours spent in Paris have corrupted him beyond repair, making him unfit for farm work.

How 'Ya Gonna Keep 'Em Down on the Farm (After They've Seen Paree)?
L: Sam M. Lewis and Joe Young; M: Walter Donaldson. Copyright 1919 by Waterson, Berlin & Snyder Co., New York.

1st Verse:
"Reuben, Reuben, I've been thinking,"
Said his wifey dear;
"Now that all is peaceful and calm,
The boys will soon be back on the farm."
Mister Reuben started winking,
And slowly he rubbed his chin;
He pulled his chair up close to mother,
And he asked her with a grin:

Chorus:
"How 'ya gonna keep 'em down on the farm
After they've seen Paree?
How 'ya gonna keep 'em away from Broadway,
Jazzin' aroun' and paintin' the town?
How 'ya gonna keep 'em away from harm?
That's a mystery;
They'll never want to see a rake or a plow,
And who the deuce can parley vous a cow?

[Imagine Reuben when he meets his pa,
He'll kiss his cheek and holler 'oo-la-la!'].
How 'ya gonna keep 'em down on the farm
After they've seen Paree?"

2nd Verse:
"Reuben, Reuben, you're mistaken,"
Said his wifey dear;
"Once a farmer, always a jay,
And farmers always stick to the hay";
"Mother Reuben, I'm not fakin',
Though you may think it strange,
But wine and women play the mischief
With a boy who's loose with change":

Hunting the Hun.
L: Howard E. Rogers; M: Archie Gottler. Copyright 1918 by Kalmar, Puck & Abrahams Consolidated, Inc., Music Publishers, New York.

1st Verse:
Over in France there's a game that's played
By all the soldier boys in each brigade;
It's called Hunting the Hun,
This is how it is done:

Chorus:
First you go get a gun,
Then you look for a Hun,
Then you start on a run
For the son-of-a-gun.
You can capture them with ease,
All you need is just a little limburger cheese;
Give 'em one little smell,
They come out with a yell,
Then your work is done.
When they start to advance,
Shoot 'em in the pants,
That's the game called Hunting the Hun.

2nd Verse:
I met a soldier and he told me
It's just the latest thing across the sea.
It's a game that is new,
They're all doing it, too:

I Can't Stay Here While You're Over There.
L: Lew Brown and Al Harriman; M: Jack Egan. Copyright 1918 by Broadway Music Corp., New York.

1st Verse:
All alone in a little home
A mother old and gray
Would sit and write to her boy each night,

Who was many miles away.
Her heart was sad,
He was all she had,
He was her pride and joy.
And ev'ry word with tears was blurred,
As she'd write "My darling boy":

Chorus:
"I'm over here, you're over there,
And ev'ry night I say this prayer:
'I wish that I could share
All of your troubles and care;
I know you need me there
Just to comfort you now.
You'll always be my baby to me,
In dreams I seem to see
You back on my knee.
You know you are my pride and joy
And my place is by your side.
I can't stay here while you're over there.'"

2nd Verse:
Ev'ry day she would watch and pray
For some good word of cheer;
Her heart was sad but the hope she had
Always drove away each fear.
And ev'ry night by a candlelight,
A boy who's far away
Just dreams and dreams;
To him it seems
He can hear his mother say:

I Didn't Raise My Boy to Be a Soldier. L:
Al Bryan; M: Al Piantadosi. Copyright
1915 by Leo Feist, Inc., New York.

1st Verse:
Ten million soldiers to the war have gone
Who may never return again;
Ten million mothers' hearts must break
For the ones who died in vain.
Head bowed down in sorrow
In her lonely years,
I heard a mother murmur through her tears:

Chorus:
"I didn't raise my boy to be a soldier,
I brought him up to be my pride and joy;
Who dares to place a musket on his shoulder
To shoot some other mother's darling boy?
Let nations arbitrate their future troubles,
It's time to lay the sword and gun away;
There'd be no war today,
If mothers all would say,
'I didn't raise my boy to be a soldier.'"

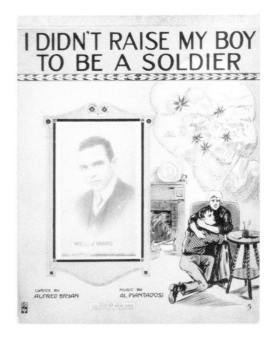

One of the greatest of all anti-war songs written by
Americans was "I Didn't Raise My Boy to Be a
Soldier," which in 1915 became the rallying cry of
the non-interventionist movement.

2nd Verse:
What victory can cheer a mother's heart
When she looks at her blighted home?
What victory can bring her back
All she cared to call her own?
Let each mother answer
In the years to be,
"Remember that my boy belongs to me!":

**I Don't Know Where I'm Going but I'm
on My Way.** L&M: George Fairman.
Copyright 1917 by Harry Von Tilzer Music
Publishing Co., New York.

1st Verse:
Goodbye everybody, I'm off to fight the foe,
Uncle Sammy is calling me so I must go.
Gee, I'm feeling fine,
Don't you wish that you were me?
For I'm sailing tomorrow
Over the deep blue sea:

Chorus:
And I don't know where I'm going
But I'm on my way,
For I belong to the Regulars, I'm proud to say.

And I'll do my duty night or day.
I don't know where I'm going
But I'm on my way.

2nd Verse:
Take a look at me,
I'm a Yankee through and through;
I was born on July fourth in Ninety-Two;
And I'll march away with a feather in my
    hat,
For I'm joining the Army,
What do you think of that?:

I Don't Want to Get Well. L: Harry Pease
and Howard Johnson; M: Harry Jentes.
Copyright 1917 by Leo Feist, Inc., New
York.

1st Verse:
I just received an answer to a letter that I
    wrote,
From a pal who marched away,
He was wounded in the trenches somewhere
    in France
And I worried about him night and day;
"Are you getting well" was what I wrote;
This is what he answered in his note:

1st Chorus:
"I don't want to get well,
I don't want to get well,
I'm in love with a beautiful nurse.
Early ev'ry morning, night, and noon,
The cutest little girlie comes and feeds me
    with a spoon.
I don't want to get well,
I don't want to get well,
I'm glad they shot me on the fighting line,
    fine!
The doctor says that I'm in bad condition,
But oh, oh, oh, I've got so much ambition;
I don't want to get well,
I don't want to get well,
For I'm having a wonderful time."

2nd Verse:
I showed this letter to a friend who lives next
    door to me,
And I heard him quickly say:
"Goodbye, pal, I must be going, I'm off to
    war,
And I hope I'm wounded right away;
If what's in this letter here is true,
I'll get shot and then I'll write to you":

2nd Chorus:
"I don't want to get well,

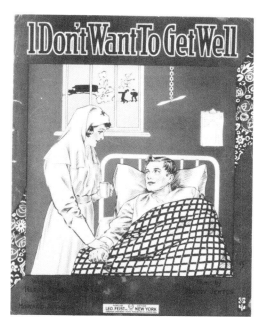

Verifying that the horrors of war had not stifled
America's sense of humor was "I Don't Want to
Get Well" (1917) in which one young man hopes to
get wounded so he can fall in love with a nurse.

I don't want to get well,
I'm in love with a beautiful nurse.
Though the doctor's treatments show results,
I always get a bad relapse each time she feels
my pulse;
I don't want to get well,
I don't want to get well,
I'm glad they shot me on the fighting line,
fine!
She holds my hand and begs me not to leave
her,
Then all at once I get so full of fever,
I don't want to get well,
I don't want to get well,
For I'm having a wonderful time."

I Miss Daddy's Goodnight Kiss. L&M:
James Kendis and James Brockman. Copy-
right 1918 by Kendis-Brockman Music Co.,
Inc., New York.

1st Verse:
Shades of night are falling,
Hear a mother calling,
"Sweet baby, come to bed and rest your
    sleepy head;
Service flag is flying,

Your daddy had to go,
He'll come back, maybe";
Then the little baby whispered soft and low:

Chorus:
"Oh, how I miss daddy's goodnight kiss,"
Sweet baby sighs, little tear-dimmed eyes;
She can't forget he said,
"Soon I'll be returning,"
She's daddy's pet and her little head is yearning.
In mother's arms, see her baby charms,
She held her tight,
Kissed her goodnight,
Behind her smile there was a tear;
While baby whispered, "Mama dear,
Oh, how I miss daddy's goodnight kiss."

2nd Verse:
Mother tells a story, fills her head with glory,
And soon in slumber deep
She's fallen fast asleep,
Just another picture that brings tears to your
    eyes.
She sighs in sorrow,
"He'll come tomorrow,"
Baby wakes and cries:

I Wouldn't Steal the Sweetheart of a Soldier Boy. L: Al Bryan; M: Herman Paley. Copyright 1916 by Jerome H. Remick & Co., New York.

1st Verse:
By the campfire gleaming
Soldier boy is dreaming;
Little girl is blue,
Someone else is telling tales of love compelling,
But her heart is true.
"Tell me, who's your sweetheart," he sighs,
    "pretty maid?"
"Just a soldier boy," she murmurs low.
Stranger gently answers, "Don't you be afraid,"
Tells her as he turns to go:

Chorus:
"I wouldn't steal the sweetheart of a soldier
    boy
While he is fighting far away;
They say that all is fair in love and war,
But I don't see it just that way.
I seem to hear him saying, 'Love, be true,
Wait till I come back home to you.'
I wouldn't steal the sweetheart of a soldier boy
And break a soldier's heart in two."

2nd Verse:
On the field of battle,

Where the cannons rattle,
'Mid the victory
While drums are beating, his heart keeps
    repeating,
"Does she think of me?"
See that you respect him, you who stay at
    home,
Just remember that he fights for you;
Treat him like a brother, leave his girl alone,
Be a man and tell her, too:

(If He Can Fight Like He Can Love) Goodnight, Germany! L: Grant Clarke and Howard E. Rogers; M: George W. Meyer. Copyright 1918 by Leo Feist, Inc., New York.

1st Verse:
Little Mary's beau said "I've got to go,
I must fight for Uncle Sam."
Standing in the crowd,
Mary called aloud
"Fare thee well, my lovin' man."
All the girls said, "Ain't he nice and tall";
Mary answered, "Yes, and that's not all":

Chorus:
"If he can fight like he can love,
Oh, what a soldier boy he'll be!
If he's just half as good in a trench
As he was in the park on a bench,
Then ev'ry Hun had better run
And find a great big linden tree.
I know he'll be a hero over there,
'Cause he's a bear in any Morris chair,
[I never saw him in a real good scrap,
But you're a goner when you're in his lap],
And if he fights like he can love,
Why, then, it's goodnight, Germany!"

2nd Verse:
Ev'ry single day all the papers say
Mary's beau is, oh, so brave,
With his little gun,
Chasing ev'ry Hun,
He has taught them to behave.
Little Mary proudly shakes her head
And says "Do you remember what I said?":

I'll Come Back to You When It's All Over. L: Lew Brown; M: Kerry Mills. Copyright 1917 by Leo Feist, Inc., New York.

1st Verse:
See that lonesome lassie kiss her soldier boy
    goodbye,

Containing humorous references to rationing was "I'll Do Without Meat, I'll Do Without Wheat, but I Can't Do Without Love," written in 1918 by Arthur J. Lamb and composer-entertainer-music publisher Frederick V. Bowers.

Her poor heart is breaking fast,
This one kiss may be their last.
"Don't you worry, dearie, let me try and dry
    your tears,
I may be gone for many days,
Perhaps for many years, but":

Chorus:
"I'll come back to you when it's all over, all
    over,
Back to you and fields of clover,
We'll start our sweetheart days all over
If your heart still beats as true.
There is a duty that ev'ry man should do,
My life defends it, but my heart belongs to
    you.
So pray for the day when it's all over,
'Cause I'm coming back to you."

2nd Verse:
See that lonesome lassie watch those soldier
    boys return,
She is looking ev'rywhere,
Something tells her he is there.
Soon her sweetheart threw a kiss and proudly
    marched ahead;
With joy and pride she marched beside
Her soldier boy, who said:

I'll Do Without Meat, I'll Do Without Wheat, but I Can't Do Without Love. L: Arthur J. Lamb; M: Frederick V. Bowers. Copyright 1918 by Frederick V. Bowers, New York.

1st Verse:
Said Mary to John, "Without any doubt
There's lots of things we must do without;
To go on like this has got me vexed,
Now, what will they ask us to give up next":

Chorus:
"I can do without this,
I can do without that,
Do without sugar,
Do without fat,
Do without sleep and do without light,
Do without heat and that is all right.
I'll keep ev'ry rule
And try to keep cool
While prices are soaring above;
I'll do without meat
And I'll do without wheat,
But I can't do without love."

2nd Verse:
Said Mary to John, "I tell all the folks
I don't eat candy, you cut out smokes,
We do without heat in our small flat,
But I won't cut out my new spring hat":

In Flanders Fields. L: Lt. Col. John Mc-Crae; M: Frank E. Tours. Copyright 1919 by M. Witmark & Sons, New York. (*Note:* This poem, or variations on it, was set to music by more than 20 other American composers between 1918 and 1919.)

In Flanders fields the poppies blow
Between the crosses row on row
That mark our place, and in the sky
The larks, still bravely singing, fly,
Scarce heard amid the guns below.
We are the dead.
Short days ago
We lived, felt dawn, saw sunset glow;
Loved and were loved,
And now we lie in Flanders Fields.
Take up our quarrel with the foe;
To you from failing hands we throw the Torch,
The Torch be yours to hold it high!
If ye break faith with us who die,
We shall not sleep,
Though poppies grow
In Flanders Fields.

Iron Men. L&M: J. Harley Coyle.
Copyright 1919 by J. Harley Coyle.

1st Verse:
From city streets and quiet country lanes,
They do their bit and take their chance;
Gallant men from the State of Penn,
You stood in line until the end;
In France you made the Fritzies dance
To the tune of Yankee Doodle.
Oh!:

Chorus:
Iron men, iron men, we're mighty proud of
    you,
You laughed at danger ev'ry chance,
When you were over there in France.
Brave and manly, frank and free,
First to fight for liberty,
You showed what you could do
For the old Red, White and Blue.
Oh! Iron men, iron men, we're mighty proud
    of you!

2nd Verse:
The old Home Guards are back with us again,
They just marched in from old Berlin.
Line in line from across the Rhine,
With red and blue you're warriors true;
And no more are you tin soldiers,
Now you're fearless, peerless, iron men.
Oh!:

It Isn't Any Fun to Be a Soldier (A Nation's Plea for Peace). L&M: Charles E.
Wood. Copyright 1915 by Charles E.
Wood Music Publishers, New York.

1st Verse:
Years ago our fathers fought to set this
    country free,
Each man was found right there,
Willing to do and dare
Just for home and liberty.
But today a diff'rent question's at our door
Since the foreign nations went to war.
They seem to be hanging around our shore,
They want to get us going once more;
But hold on, Uncle Sam,
Don't bring bloodshed on our land:

Chorus:
For it isn't any fun to be a soldier,
It isn't any fun to go to war.
There isn't any honor in a battle,
When you don't know what you're fighting
    for.

It isn't fun to be a soldier's mother
When they break the news her boy is dead.
There isn't any fun in battle 'mid the cannon's rattle,
It isn't any fun to be a soldier boy.

2nd Verse:
Mothers cry and each one pleads to lands
    across the sea,
God send us peace, they pray,
Help stop this war, they say,
Just for love and decency.
What a blow these foreign children all must
    bear
Just because their fathers didn't care.
This war is sure an outrage to think Kings
    dare
To scatter woe and pain ev'rywhere.
But Yankee boys in blue
Don't want any war, 'tis true:

It Won't Be Long (Till the Boys Come Marching Home). L&M: Frankie
Williams. Copyright 1918 by Krey
Publishing Co., New York.

1st Verse:
"Cheer up, cheer up, the war will soon be
    over,
Cheer up, cheer up, ev'rything will soon be
    clover.
Mothers and sweethearts, don't you cry,
Just wear a smile and dry your eyes,
They'll soon be from the fray;
Just listen to what I have to say":

Chorus:
"It won't be long, it won't be long
Till the boys come marching home;
Each mother's son, with vict'ry won,
For they soon will cross the foam.
Let's all prepare,
Yes, ev'rywhere,
For one big jubilee;
And when they get back,
They'll have an awful pack:
The Kaiser and his whole darn family."

2nd Verse:
"Just imagine the sight you're going to view,
To see the boys marching down Fifth Avenue;
So mothers and sweethearts, be prepared,
There'll be a hot time ev'rywhere;
They'll soon be over here
With victory, have no fear":

"It's a Long, Long Way to the U.S.A. (and the Girl I Left Behind)," a 1917 success, was only one of the 22 war-inspired songs composed by the prolific Harry Von Tilzer, whose non-war credits included "I Want a Girl Just Like the Girl That Married Dear Old Dad."

It's a Long, Long Way to the U.S.A. (and the Girl I Left Behind). L: Val Trainor; M: Harry Von Tilzer. Copyright 1917 by Harry Von Tilzer Music Publishing Co., New York.

1st Verse:
While the cannon shells were screaming
'Mid the battle's loudest roar,
[A] wounded Yankee boy was dreaming
Of his childhood home once more;
To his pal he's softly saying,
"Tell the little girl for me,
Night and day how I was praying
Her dear face once more to see":

Chorus:
"It's a long, long way to the U.S.A.
And the girl I left behind;
And if you get back some day,
Give my love to her and say
That her boy was true;
Tell dear mother, too,
Just to always treat her kind.
It's a long, long way to the U.S.A.
And the girl I left behind."

2nd Verse:
To his lips he fondly presses
One gray strand of mother's hair,
And a golden curl caresses
From his little sweetheart fair;
Sighing to his pal, "You'll meet them
Over on the other shore,
Tell them both I soon will greet them,
I'll be coming home once more":

It's a Long, Long Way to Tipperary. L: Jack Judge; M: Harry Williams. Copyright 1912 by B. Feldman & Co., London.

1st Verse:
Up to mighty London came an Irishman one day,
As the streets are paved with gold, sure ev'ryone was gay,
Singing songs of Piccadilly, Strand and Leicester Square,
Till Paddy got excited,
Then he shouted to them there:

Chorus:
"It's a long way to Tipperary,
It's a long way to go;
It's a long way to Tipperary,
To the sweetest girl I know!
Goodbye, Piccadilly,
Farewell, Leicester Square,
It's a long, long way to Tipperary,
But my heart's right there!"

2nd Verse:
Paddy wrote a letter to his Irish Molly O',
Saying, "Should you not receive it, write and let me know!
If I make mistakes in spelling, Molly dear," said he,
"Remember it's the pen that's bad,
Don't lay the blame on me":

3rd Verse:
Molly wrote a neat reply to Irish Paddy O',
Saying, "Mike Maloney wants to marry me, and so
Leave the Strand and Piccadilly or you'll be to blame,
For love has fairly drove me silly,
Hoping you're the same!":

It's a Long Way from Here to "Over There." L&M: Lew Peyton. Copyright 1918 by Jerome H. Remick & Co., New York.

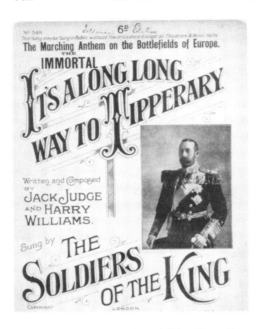

The reprinted British version of "It's a Long, Long Way to Tipperary" linked the 1912 song directly to World War I in the publisher's description, "The Marching Anthem on the Battlefields of Europe."

1st Verse:
Hear that band, ain't it grand,
See those soldiers leaving here for No-Man's
    Land?
Going over, happy and gay,
They won't stop 'till they put Kaiser away.
Drafted men, drafted men,
Now do your best to help the rest
And make us win.
Ev'ry man on land and sea fight for free
    democracy,
And save Old Glory's name!:

Chorus:
It's a long way from here to "over there,"
But we'll get there just the same.
In No Man's Land we will take our stand,
Show the Kaiser how to one-step to our Dixie
    band.
We'll make ev'ry Hun
Lay down his gun and run away;
And Home Sweet Home will welcome us
In the U.S.A.

2nd Verse:
Get your gun, don't you run,
Work or fight for Uncle Sammy must be
    done.
Do your duty, fall right in line.

Shoulder arms, forward march, over the
    Rhine!
Step with pep, don't forget,
The band is playing "Dixie";
We must do our bit.
Ev'ry hero brave and bold down in hist'ry
    will be told
Of our fighting soldier boys:

**It's a Long Way to Dear Old Broad-
way.** L&M: Ernest Breuer and George
Fairman. Copyright 1918 by Leo Feist,
Inc., New York.

1st Verse:
Yankee Doodle took his boys and sailed
    across the sea;
He said, "There is some work to do,
It's for democracy";
And when our boys got in the fray,
The boys from ev'rywhere,
They greeted Yankee Doodle with this
    familiar air:

Chorus:
It's a long way to dear old Broadway,
And the Statue of Liberty;
In God we're trusting,
He is adjusting
All the wrong done to the U.S.A.
Please stop your yearning,
We'll be returning
Just as soon as our work is through;
It's a long, long way to dear old Broadway,
But we're coming back to you.

2nd Verse:
Anything that Yankee Doodle starts he sees
    it through;
To win a battle on the square
To him is nothing new.
We'll give our men our ships, our food,
And ev'rything as well,
And to our enemies we'll give some Yankee
    shot and shell:

It's Time for Every Boy to Be a Soldier.
L: Alfred Bryan; M: Harry Tierney.
Copyright 1917 by Jerome H. Remick &
Co., New York.

1st Verse:
Most ev'ry fellow has a sweetheart,
Some little girl with eyes of blue;
My daddy also had a sweetheart,

Sketches of two wartime presidents, Lincoln and Wilson, adorned the first edition cover of "It's Time for Every Boy to Be a Soldier," a popular 1917 recruitment song.

And he fought to win her, too;
There'll come a day when we must pay
The price of love and duty;
Be there staunch and true:

Chorus:
It's time for ev'ry boy to be a soldier,
To put his strength and courage to the test;
It's time to place a musket on his shoulder
And wrap the Stars and Stripes around his breast.
It's time to shout those noble words of Lincoln,
And stand up for the land that gave you birth —
"That the nation of the people, by the people,
For the people
Shall not perish from the earth."

2nd Verse:
Boys of America, get ready,
Your motherland is calling you;
Boys of America, be steady
For the Old Red, White and Blue;
When Yankee Doodle comes to town
Upon his little pony,
Be there staunch and true:

I've Got My Captain Working for Me Now. L&M: Irving Berlin. Copyright 1919 by Irving Berlin, Inc., New York.

1st Verse:
Johnny Jones was a first-class private
In the Army last year,
Now he's back to bus'ness in his father's place.
Sunday night I saw him with a smiling face,
When I asked why he felt so happy,
Johnny chuckled with glee.
He winked his eye and made this reply,
"Something wonderful has happened to me":

Chorus:
"I've got the guy who used to be my captain working for me.
He wanted work
So I made him a clerk in my father's factory.
And bye and bye
I'm gonna have him wrapped in work up to his brow;
I make him open the office ev'ry morning at eight,
I come around about four hours late.
Ev'rything comes to those who wait:
I've got my captain working for me now."

2nd Verse:
"He's not worth what I have to pay him,
But I'll never complain;
I've agreed to give him fifty dollars per,
It's worth twice as much to hear him call me Sir."
While I sit in my cozy office,
He's outside working hard,
Out in the hall at my beck and call,
With a feather duster standing on guard":

Joan of Arc, They Are Calling You. L: Al Bryan and Willie Weston; M: Jack Wells. Copyright 1918 Waterson, Berlin & Snyder Co., New York.

1st Verse:
While you are sleeping,
Your France is weeping;
Wake from your dreams, Maid of France.
Her heart is bleeding,
Are you unheeding?
Come with the flame in your glance;
Through the Gates of Heaven with your sword in hand
Come your legions to command:

Chorus:
Joan of Arc, Joan of Arc,
Do your eyes, from the skies, see the foe?
Don't you see the drooping fleur-de-lis?
Can't you hear the tears of Normandy?
Joan of Arc, Joan of Arc,
Let your spirit guide us through.
Come lead your France to victory;
Joan of Arc, they are calling you.

2nd Verse:
Alsace is sighing,
Lorraine is crying,
Their mother, France, looks to you.
Her sons at Verdun,
Bearing the burden,
Pray for your coming anew;
At the Gates of Heaven, do they bar your
    way?
Souls that passed through yesterday:

Just a Baby's Prayer at Twilight. L: Sam
M. Lewis and Joe Young; M: M.K.
Jerome. Copyright 1918 by Waterson,
Berlin & Snyder Co., New York.

1st Verse:
I've heard the pray'rs of mothers,
Some of them old and gray;
I've heard the pray'rs of others
For those who went away.
Oft times a pray'r will teach one
The meaning of goodbye.
I felt the pain of each one,
But this one made me cry:

Chorus:
Just a baby's pray'r at twilight,
When lights are low.
Poor baby's years are filled with tears;
There's mother there at twilight,
Who's proud to know
Her precious little tot
Is dad's forget-me-not.
After saying "Goodnight, mama,"
She climbs upstairs,
Quite unawares,
And says her pray'rs:
"Oh! kindly tell my daddy that he must take
    care."
That's a baby's pray'r at twilight,
For her daddy "over there."

2nd Verse:
The gold that some folks pray for
Brings nothing but regrets;

Some day this gold won't pay for
Their many life-long debts.
Some pray'rs may be neglected
Beyond the Golden Gate;
But when they're all collected,
Here's one that never waits:

Just as the Sun Went Down. L&M: Lyn
Udall. Copyright 1918 by M. Witmark &
Sons, New York.

1st Verse:
After the din of the battle's roar,
Just at the close of day,
Wounded and bleeding upon the field
Two dying soldiers lay.
One held a ringlet of thin gray hair,
One held a lock of brown;
They closed their eyes to the earth and skies,
Just as the sun went down:

Chorus:
One thought of mother at home alone,
Feeble and old and gray;
One of the sweetheart he left in town,
Happy and young and gay.
One kissed a ringlet of thin gray hair,
One kissed a lock of brown,
Bidding farewell to the Stars and Stripes,
Just as the sun went down.

2nd Verse:
One knew the joys of a mother's love,
One of a sweetheart fair;
Thinking of home, they lay side by side,
Breathing a farewell prayer,
One for his mother so old and gray,
One for his love in town.
They closed their eyes to the earth and skies,
Just as the sun went down:

**Just Like Washington Crossed the Dela-
ware (General Pershing Will Cross the
Rhine).** L: Howard Johnson; M: George
W. Meyer. Copyright 1918 by Leo Feist,
Inc., New York.

1st Verse:
Looking backward through the ages,
We can read on hist'ry's pages
Deeds that famous men have done;
We are told of great commanders
Wellington and Alexanders,
And the battles they have won.
Take our own great Revolution

JUST LIKE WASHINGTON CROSSED THE DELAWARE. GENERAL PERSHING WILL CROSS THE RHINE

WORDS BY HOWARD JOHNSON

MUSIC BY GEO. W. MEYER

THEME SUGGESTED BY ELINORE & WILLIAMS

LEO. FEIST,— NEW YORK

Playing the dual role of a threat to the Germans and a vow to Americans, "Just Like Washington Crossed the Delaware (General Pershing Will Cross the Rhine)" was matched by few other 1918 songs in contempt for the enemy and optimism in the invincibility of the soldiers of democracy.

That began our evolution,
Washington then won his fame;
Today across the sea
They're making history,
The Yankee spirit still remains the same:

Chorus:
Just like Washington crossed the Delaware,
So will Pershing cross the Rhine;
As they followed after George
At dear old Valley Forge,
Our boys will break that line.
It's for your land and my land
And the sake of Auld Lang Syne;
Just like Washington crossed the Delaware,
Gen'ral Pershing will cross the Rhine.

2nd Verse:
There upon the roll of honor,
Ev'ryone the soul of honor,
We find heroes of the past;
Like the ones who've gone before them,
To our native land that bore them,
They were faithful to the last.
As they fought for Independence,
You and I and our descendants
Must preserve democracy.

In God we'll trust,
Our sword shall never rust,
We'll tell the world it simply has to be:

Keep the Home-Fires Burning (Till the Boys Come Home). L: Lena Guilbert Ford; M: Ivor Novello. Copyright 1914 by Ascherberg, Hopwood & Crew Ltd., London.

1st Verse:
They were summoned from the hillside,
They were called in from the glen,
And the country found them ready
At the stirring call for men.
Let no tears add to their hardship
As the soldiers pass along,
And although your heart is breaking,
Make it sing this cheery song:

Chorus:
Keep the home-fires burning
While your hearts are yearning,
Though your lads are far away,
They dream of home.
There's a silver lining
Through the dark cloud shining;
Turn the dark cloud inside out,
'Till the boys come home.

2nd Verse:
Overseas there came a pleading,
"Help a nation in distress!"
And we gave our glorious laddies,
Honour bade us do no less;
For no gallant son of freedom
To a tyrant's yoke should bend,
And a noble heart must answer
To the sacred call of "Friend":

Keep the Trench Fires Going (for the Boys Out There). L: Ed Moran; M: Harry Von Tilzer. Copyright 1918 by Harry Von Tilzer Music Publishing Co., New York.

1st Verse:
Uncle Sammy's boys are somewhere over
 there in France,
Someone's going to know they're in a fight;
Uncle Sammy's boys are not afraid to take a
 chance
When they're fighting for a cause that's right.
But while Uncle Sammy's boys are fighting
 brave and true,
There is something, too, that we have got to
 do:

KEEP THE HOME-FIRES BURNING

('TILL THE BOYS COME HOME)

SONG

WORDS BY

LENA GUILBERT FORD

MUSIC BY

IVOR NOVELLO

CHAPPELL & Co LTD.
41, EAST THIRTY-FOURTH STREET.
NEW YORK.

The original 1915 plain-cover American edition of "Keep the Home-Fires Burning (Till the Boys Come Home)," by Britishers Lena Guilbert Ford and the 21-year-old composer Ivor Novello.

Chorus:
Keep the trench fires going for the boys out
    there,
Let's play fair, do our share,
Our boys are fighting for you and me, can't
    you see?
For you and me and liberty.
Let's make a showing while they're over the
    foam,
Do you bit and bring them home.
Keep the trench fires going for the boys out
    there,
Let ev'ry son of Uncle Sammy do his share.

2nd Verse:
Uncle Sammy's boys are going over there to
    win,
Someone will be wiser when they're through.
Uncle Sammy's boys are going right into
    Berlin,
Then they'll tell the Kaiser what to do.
But if we want Uncle Sammy's boys to finish
    strong,
It's up to us to help the boys along:

K-K-K-Katy. L&M: Geoffrey O'Hara.
Copyright 1918 by Leo Feist, Inc., New
York.

1st Verse:
Jimmy was a soldier brave and bold,
Katy was a maid with hair of gold;
Like an act of fate
Kate was standing at the gate,
Watching all the boys on dress parade.
Jimmy with the girls was just a gawk,
Stuttered ev'ry time he tried to talk;
Still that night at eight
He was there at Katy's gate,
Stuttering to her this love-sick cry:

Chorus:
K-K-K-Katy,
Beautiful Katy,
You're the only g-g-g-girl that I adore;
When the m-m-m-moon shines
Over the cow shed,
I'll be waiting at the k-k-k-kitchen door!

2nd Verse:
No one ever looked so nice and neat,
No one could be just as cute and sweet,
That's what Jimmy thought
When the wedding ring he bought,
Now he's off to France the foe to meet.
Jimmy thought he'd like to take a chance,
See if he could make the Kaiser dance,
Stepping to a tune
All about the silv'ry moon,
This is what they hear in far-off France:

Lafayette (We Hear You Calling). L&M:
Mary Earl. Copyright 1918 by Shapiro,
Bernstein & Co., Inc., New York.

1st Verse:
Out of the ages from hist'ry's pages
There comes a silent plea;
Yet we can hear it,
Lafayette's spirit,
Calling from over the sea.
For there's a debt unpaid
To France, who needs our aid:

Chorus:
Lafayette, we hear you calling,
Lafayette, 'tis not in vain
That the tears of France are falling.
We will help her to smile again,
For a friend in need is a friend in deed;
Do not think we shall ever forget,
Lafayette, we hear you calling,
And we're coming, Lafayette.

2nd Verse:
When war clouds darkened our skies, you hearkened,
Your sword for us was drawn.
Now we are needed,
France we have heeded;
We'll meet our debt, we have sworn.
And ev'ry mother's son
Will fight till Right has won:

Let's All Be Americans Now. L&M: Irving Berlin, Edgar Leslie, and George W. Meyer. Copyright 1917 by Waterson, Berlin & Snyder Co., New York.

1st Verse:
Peace has always been our prayer,
Now there's trouble in the air;
War is talked of ev'rywhere,
Still in God we trust.
Now that war's declared,
We'll show we're prepared,
And if fight we must:

Chorus:
It's up to you!
What will you do?
England or France may have your sympathy
Over the sea,
But you'll agree
That now is the time to fall in line.
You swore that you would,
So be true to your vow,
Let's all be Americans now!

2nd Verse:
Lincoln, Grant, and Washington,
They were peaceful men, each one;
Still they took the sword and gun
When real trouble came,
And I feel somehow
They are wond'ring now
If we'll do the same:

Let's All Do Something (Uncle Sammy Wants Us Now). L: Andrew B. Sterling; M: Arthur Lange. Copyright 1917 by Joe Morris Music Co., New York.

1st Verse:
The bars are down, the die is cast,
And now it's up to us,
U.S., United States, us.
Now's the time to show what we are worth
And do something for the land that gave us

birth.
What are you goin' to do,
And what am I goin' to do
For the greatest little country on earth?:

Chorus:
Let's all do something,
We can all do something,
Ev'ry little bit helps,
So do it now.
We want the man with the sword,
The man with the gun,
The man with the hoe and the plow.
Girls, you don't need rehearsing
To go Red Cross nursing,
Your hand can soothe a soldier's brow;
Ev'ry boy can be a Scout,
Ev'rybody must turn out
And do his little bit of something;
Let's all do something,
Uncle Sammy wants us now.

2nd Verse:
We want the world to turn around
And take a look at us,
U.S., United States, us.
Sammy will surprise 'em over there;
And when Sammy rolls his sleeves up to prepare,
What are you goin' to do,
And what am I goin' to do?
We must, all of us, be doing our share!:

Let's Bury the Hatchet (in the Kaiser's Head). L&M: Addison Burkhardt. Copyright 1918 by Burkhardt-Horwitz Music Co., New York.

1st Verse:
While Yankee Doodle sails away
To fight the German foe,
The pacifists are shouting "Peace"
And say they shouldn't go;
They claim the hatchet must be buried by the Allies now;
Perhaps they're right,
We must have peace,
And so I'll tell them how:

Chorus:
Let's bury the hatchet,
Let's bury the hatchet,
Let's bury the hatchet in the Kaiser's head!;
We'll crown him on the noodle,
Make him whistle Yankee Doodle,
[When Berlin is in ashes,

We'll burn up his big moustaches],
Shouting the Battle Cry of Wilson!

2nd Verse:
We'll chain his brutal dogs of war
And then we'll get his goat,
We'll chop them into frankfurters
And stuff them down his throat.
We'll chase him out of Russia,
Then we'll try another stunt:
We'll punch him in the Belgium
And we'll smash his Western front:

Let's Help the Red Cross Now. L&M: Ted
S. Barron. Copyright 1917 by Metropolis
Music Co., New York.

1st Verse:
A soldier boy lay dying
'Neath the flag he fought to shield,
So far away from home and mother dear,
When suddenly a vision fair
Came cross the battlefield
And knelt beside him calmly without fear.
She took him in her arms so tenderly,
For she was just a Red Cross nurse, you see:

Chorus:
Let's help the Red Cross now,
Let's help the Red Cross now.
When shot and shell are flying,
They help the sick and dying,
Cooling each fevered brow,
So why not help the Red Cross now?
We all can help somehow,
When the fight starts they'll be in it,
Do your share and help them win it;
Come on, let's help the Red Cross now.

2nd Verse:
On ev'ry field of battle
They are always to be found;
To do their duty bravely without fear,
They carry off the wounded
While the shells are bursting 'round.
It is their prayers our dying soldiers hear;
Were Washington and Lincoln here today,
To ev'ry real American they'd say:

Liberty Bell (It's Time to Ring Again). L:
Joe Goodwin; M: Halsey K. Mohr. Copy-
right 1917 by Shapiro, Bernstein & Co.,
Inc., New York.

1st Verse:
You have rested, Liberty Bell,

For a hundred years and more;
End your slumber, Liberty Bell,
Ring as you did before.
It's time to wake 'em up,
It's time to shake 'em up,
It's a cause worth ringing for:

Chorus:
Liberty Bell,
It's time to ring again;
Liberty Bell,
It's time to swing again.
So ring all over this earth,
And ring for all you are worth,
The sweetest music on earth to all the people,
Like you did before, oh!
[We're in the same sort of fix
We were in Seventy-Six,
And we are ready to mix and rally 'round you
Like we did before, oh!]
Liberty Bell,
Your voice is needed now;
Liberty Bell,
We'll hear your call one and all;
Though you're old and there's a crack in you,
Don't forget Old Glory's backin' you.
Oh! Liberty Bell,
It's time to ring again.

2nd Verse:
Once you rang out, Liberty Bell,
As we watched Old Glory wave;
You have made us, Liberty Bell,
Land of the free and brave.
It's time to sing again,
It's time to ring again,
And your voice once more we crave:

Liberty Bell, Ring On! L: Haven Gillespie; M: Albert William Brown. Copyright
1918 by Frank K. Root & Co., Chicago.

1st Verse:
Liberty Bell! In a voice resounding,
Ringing your message clear and strong,
Telling of justice, truth, and freedom,
And that Right ever conquers wrong.
Liberty Bell! Liberty Bell!
Sing your song we love so well!:

Chorus:
Swing! Ring! Liberty Bell!
Ringing for freedom, let your message swell!
Where our flag's unfurled,
Let it echo 'round the world,
And ring out liberty's magic spell!

Swing! Ring! Liberty Bell!
Echoing strong and clear your message tell!
Swing! Ring forever!
Oh, Liberty Bell!
Ring on!

2nd Verse:
Liberty Bell! Destiny is calling,
Calling all free men to the fray,
Bidding them onward, never falt'ring
Till the dawning of freedom's day.
Liberty Bell! Liberty Bell!
To the world your message tell!:

A Little Bit of Sunshine (from Home). L:
Ballard MacDonald and Joe Goodwin; M:
James F. Hanley. Copyright 1918 by
Shapiro, Bernstein & Co., New York.

1st Verse:
Say, neighbor, did you write to say "Hello"
To Frank and Jim and Joe,
The boys who had to go?
Well, neighbor, don't you think it's time you
    did?
For a long, long way from home today
There's some poor lonesome kid (Remember):

Chorus:
Just a bit of sunshine,
A little bit of sunshine,
Will drive the clouds away;
You've got lots of time, so spend it,
Write a cheery note and send it,
It may help some fellow on his way.
There is pen and paper handy,
Send 'em cigarettes and candy,
Help those Yankee Doodle Dandies o'er the
    foam;
For a friendly sort of letter
Makes a fellow feel much better,
It's a little bit of sunshine from home.

2nd Verse:
Say, neighbor, put yourself in Johnny's shoes,
I'll bet you'd have the blues
If you received no news;
Well, neighbor, you can see it's mighty hard
In that lonesome camp, so stick a stamp
Upon a postal card (Remember):

A Long Fight, A Strong Fight. L: Leona
Upton; M: Robert Armstrong. Copyright
1918 by Oliver Ditson Co., Boston.

1st Verse:
We're in the fight, we know we're right!
We never will fall back!
Old Kaiser Bill shall have his fill!
We'll put him on the rack!
We're in to stay till Judgment Day,
If it should take that long (You bet)!
We'll lick the Hun, it must be done!
And here's our fighting song:

Chorus:
A long fight, a strong fight,
A fight all together;
A long fight, a strong fight
Till war is done forever.
So shoulder to shoulder
We'll break the Hunnish line;
We'll push them and drive them
Till they're beyond the Rhine.

2nd Verse:
We're side by side with soldiers tried
Who bore the battle's brunt;
They had the stuff to call the bluff
Of Fritzie at the front!
With Yankee grit we'll do our bit
To push the scrap along (You bet)!
For home and Right we'll fight the fight
And shout our sturdy song:

**Loyalty Is the Word Today (Loyalty to
the U.S.A.).** L: Dee Dooling Cahill; M:
J.E. Andino. Copyright 1917 by Dee Dooling Cahill; published by Great Aim Society, New York.

1st Verse:
North, South, East, and West, your country
    calls you,
To swear you'll be true to the Red, White
    and Blue.
United we stand, divided we fall,
A free sea and land means freedom for all.
Then show your colors bravely, each maid
    and man,
A true united nation, proud American;
With loyalty, with courage and pride we say:
"We stand by our flag and our country
    today!":

Chorus:
Loyalty is the word today,
Loyalty to the U.S.A.;
"Peace with honor," the nation cries,
Peace without, the nation dies!
Now's the time for hearty action,

Without fear and without faction.
Loyalty is the word today,
Loyalty to the U.S.A.!

2nd Verse:
'Tis no time for doubt, 'tis no time to pause,
With love and with faith we'll be true to our
    cause;
Defending our land, protecting our trust,
For freedom we'll fight, and die if we must.
Then show your colors bravely, each maid
    and man,
A true united nation, proud American;
With loyalty, with courage and pride we say:
"We stand by our flag and our country
    today!":

Madelon. L: Louis Bousquet; M: Camille
Robert; English lyric by Al Bryan. Copyright by L. Bousquet, Paris; copyright 1918
by Jerome H. Remick & Co., New York.

1st Verse:
There is a tavern way down in Brittany
Where weary soldiers take their liberty.
The keeper's daughter,
Whose name is Madelon,
Pours out the wine while they laugh and
    "carry on."
And when the wine goes to their senses,
Her sparkling glance goes to their hearts;
Their admiration so intense is,
Each one his tale of love imparts.
She coquettes with them all,
But favors none at all;
And here's the way they banter ev'ry time
    they call:

Chorus:
"O Madelon, you are my only one;
O Madelon, now that the foe is gone,
Let the wedding bells ring sweet and gay,
Let this be our wedding day.
O Madelon, sweet maid of Normandy,
Like Joan of Arc
You'll always be to me.
All through life for you I'll carry on,
Madelon, Madelon, Madelon."

2nd Verse:
He was a fair-haired boy from Brittany,
She was a blue-eyed maid from Normandy,
He said goodbye
To this pretty Madelon,
He went his way with the boys who "carry
    on."

And when his noble work was ended,
He said farewell to his command;
Back to his Madelon he wended
To claim her little heart and hand.
With lovelight in his glance,
This gallant son of France,
He murmurs as she listens with her heart en-
    tranced:

**The Makin's of the U.S.A. (A Plea for
Tobacco for the Boys Over There).** L:
Vincent Bryan; M: Harry Von Tilzer.
Copyright 1918 by Harry Von Tilzer Music
Publishing Co., New York.

1st Verse:
The boys in Yankee regiments have sox on
    every leg,
But they have no tobacco,
Nor tobacco can they beg;
The other allied soldiers are as cunning as a
    fox,
They've always got tobacco
In their old tobacco box.
A soldier cannot smoke a pair of sox,
So help to fill the old tobacco box:

Chorus:
If you are not a slacker,
Get a sack of good tobacco
And send it to your Yankee soldier right
    away;
Send on the old Bull Durham
And then he'll know you're for him,
Because it is the makin's of the U.S.A.

2nd Verse:
Italian smokes are strong enough to cause a
    mule to sneeze,
The smokes they capture from the Huns
Are like limburger cheese;
You have to wear a gas mask using smokes
    made by the French,
And English cigarettes
Will clear out any German trench.
A soldier cannot smoke a powder rag,
He'd rather have the makin's in a bag:

Mammy's Dixie Soldier Boy. L&M: Norman H. Landman. Copyright 1918 by Will
Rossiter, Chicago.

1st Verse:
One day a bugle blew in Dixieland
To call the Southern braves away,

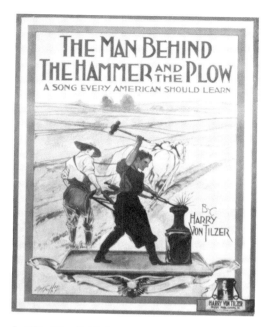

In "The Man Behind the Hammer and the Plow" (1917), Harry Von Tilzer echoed President Wilson's praise of mechanics and farmers as of equal importance with soldiers in helping to "win the battle now" by producing the matériel and foodstuffs needed to sustain the military and civilian populations.

And as the boys were sayin' their last fare-
  wells,
I saw a mammy bent and gray.
Her arms around a boy in khaki,
She was cryin' as though her heart would
  break.
I'm sure there's never been a more pathetic
  scene,
With ev'ry word her heart just seemed to
  ache:

Chorus:
"Honey, don't forget your dear old mammy
Back in Dixieland,
Though you're goin' to fight for Uncle
  Sammy
In a suit of khaki grand.
I've loved you like you were my own.
But now that you have grown,
They're taking you away from your mammy
  old and gray,
And from your dear old Southern home.
I can hear the bugle blowing,
It is time you all must go;
But if love and prayers will help you,
You'll return some day, I know.

Though they say a bugle call is music to a
  soldier's ear,
To your poor old mammy ev'ry single note's
  a tear.
Oh, honey, how i'se goin' to miss you,
'Cause you're mammy's Dixie soldier boy."

2nd Verse:
And so the Dixie boy off to the front
Soon proved himself a hero grand,
And when the good news came, "The battle's
  won,"
His thoughts went back to Dixieland.
He saw his sweetheart waving to him
As to war he'd proudly marched away;
He saw his mammy cry as he had said good-
  bye,
And in fancy seemed to hear old mammy say:

**The Man Behind the Hammer and the
Plow.** L&M: Harry Von Tilzer. Copyright
1917 by Harry Von Tilzer Music Publishing Co., New York.

1st Verse:
America, the world is calling you,
America, it needs you badly, too.
The nations o'er the sea
Cry out for liberty,
The Stars and Stripes can save and make you
  free;
The sons of Uncle Sam can win the fray,
And here's the man that has to save the day:

Chorus:
It's the man behind the hammer and the plow
Who made this county what it is today;
It's the man behind the hammer and the
  plow,
The gift of God's creation,
The builders of the nation,
Mechanic and the engineer,
All honest sons of toil,
The backbone of the world today,
The man who tills the soil,
It's up to him to win the battle now,
The man behind the hammer and the plow.

2nd Verse:
America, we know you'll do what's right,
America, you've never lost a fight;
You're bound to do your share
And do it on the square,
And when there's peace at least you will be
  square;
Now, working man, today you have the pow'r
To win for Uncle Sam, this is your hour:

The Marines' Hymn. Lyricists/Melody Adapter[s] unverified. Copyright 1919 by The United States Marine Corps.

1st Chorus:
From the halls of Montezuma
To the shores of Tripoli,
We fought our country's battles
In the air, on land and sea.
First to fight for Right and freedom,
And to keep our honor clean,
We are proud to claim the title
Of United States Marine.

2nd Chorus:
Our flag's unfurled to ev'ry breeze
From dawn to setting sun;
We have fought in ev'ry clime and place
Where we could take a gun.
In the snow of far-off northern lands,
And in sunny tropic scenes,
You will find us always on the job,
The United States Marines!

3rd Chorus:
Here's health to you and to our Corps,
Which we are proud to serve;
In many a strife we've fought for life,
And never lost our nerve.
If the Army and the Navy
Ever gaze on heaven's scenes,
They will find the streets are guarded by
The United States Marines.

Merrily We'll Roll Along. L: Andrew B. Sterling; M: Abner Silver. Copyright 1918 by Joe Morris Music Co., New York.

1st Verse:
Two sailor boys went rolling 'round the town
    to get some air,
They went rolling everywhere,
For they had a roll to spare;
And as they went a-rolling,
Soon they spied a rolling chair,
And said Jack to Jim,
"We'll do our rolling there,
For we know that Uncle Sam will pay the
    fare";
And as they rolled along,
They sang a rolling song:

Chorus:
Merrily we'll roll along, roll along, roll
    along,
We'll roll across the sea,
Roll to gay Paree,

Keep the ball a-rolling
'Till we roll to Germany.
And merrily we'll roll along
Far across the foam;
And when ev'rything's all over,
We'll roll the Kaiser over,
Then we'll all come rolling home.

2nd Verse:
Each time they'd sing the chorus, they would
    roll a cigarette,
And they'd both be rolling yet,
But they got their roll all wet;
They met a boatswain rolling,
But they didn't seem to fret,
For said Jack to Jim,
"He isn't in our set,
'Cause there's not another rolling chair to
    let";
And as they rolled away,
They rolled out hip-hoo-ray:

A Ministering Angel. L: Charles Dunlop; M: William Leigh. Copyright 1916 by Francis, Day & Hunter, London.

Gentle and sweet and ever kind,
Ready to serve and bear;
There is no richer gift to earth
Than woman's patient care.
A minist'ring angel, thou,
To work, to watch, to pray,
The troubled spirit prompt to calm
And smile its grief away.
Gentle and sweet and ever kind,
Instant to meet each call,
Thine to soothe the bed of pain
With tender thought for all.
Thy presence, like a sunny beam
That's cast upon the night,
O'er stricken men still softly shines
In purity and light.

Most Beautiful Flag in the World. L: Charles H. Newman; M: Jack Glogau. Copyright 1917 by Lew Berk Music Co., Rochester, N.Y.

1st Verse:
Old Glory, when I look at you,
It fills my heart with pride,
I see it is no wonder
That for you our fathers died.
You stand for all that's noble,

For liberty and love;
You are an inspiration
Direct from Him above:

Chorus:
The brightest stars from heaven
Are in your field of blue,
Your stripes are from the rainbow,
Taken out of heaven, too.
They made you with the greatest care,
And when you were unfurled,
God gave as His gift to America
The most beautiful flag in the world.

2nd Verse:
I swear to always honor you
At home and far away,
To fight for your protection
Even as I am today.
A hundred million people
Will proudly do the same;
And that is why, Old Glory,
You bear an honored name:

Mother. L: Rida Johnson Young; M: Sigmund Romberg. Copyright 1916 by G. Schirmer, New York.

Verse:
"Little tender mother song
From childhood's days remembered.
The night is dark and I am lonely,
I've strayed so far from home.
There's a haven that I long for only,
There would I rest, no more to roam.
Mother, take me to your arms and hold me,
Singing softly as your arms enfold me":

Chorus:
"Mother, mother, as of yore,
Take me in your arms once more,
Let the voice that I adore
Waft me to dreams as you hold me.
Mother, mother, you alone
Perfect love for me have shown,
For I've strayed so sad and lonely;
Mother, mother,
Grasp me close now and hold me,
Mother, sing now as your arms now enfold
    me;
Mother, mother,
Grasp me close now and hold me,
Mother, sing now as your arms now enfold
    me."

Mother, I'm Dreaming of You. L: Jack Caddigan; M: Chick Story. Copyright 1918 by Jack Mendelsohn Music Co., Boston.

1st Verse:
"The day now is ending,
The twilight is blending
The gold with the blue;
And with the gloaming
My thoughts go roaming
Homeward, dear mother, to you":

Chorus:
"Mother, I'm dreaming of you, dear,
Here in the campfire's glow,
And in all my dreams
I'm seeing, it seems,
That home I used to know.
I feel your arms twine about me,
I feel you kissing me, too,
And I know I've been blessed,
For at night when I rest,
Mother, I'm dreaming of you."

2nd Verse:
"Whenever I'm weary
Through nights long and dreary,
Then I think of you.
Then life seems brighter,
The burden much lighter,
Sweet thoughts come back to me, too":

Mothers of America (You Have Done Your Share!). L: Harry Ellis; M: Lew Porter. Copyright 1918 by Joseph W. Stern & Co., New York.

1st Verse:
When all is said and done,
When ev'rything is won,
Who paid the price to win the war?
Who sacrificed her all
And answered to the call,
M-O-T-H-E-R:

Chorus:
Mothers of America,
You have done your share;
You have given ev'ry son
So our battles could be won,
And with a smile you sent them over there.
When he wins upon the battlefield of glory,
For his safe return you say a pray'r;
You have given to the strife
Your heart, your soul, your life;
Mothers of America,
You have done your share.

A tribute to "Mothers of America (You Have Done Your Share)" was popularized beginning in late 1918 by Eva Tanguay, whose picture and facsimile signature appeared on the cover.

2nd Verse:
Then when all the boys return,
Each mother's heart will yearn
To meet their loved ones from afar;
While standing by her side,
Another smiles in pride,
M-O-T-H-E-R:

Mothers of France. L&M: Leo Wood.
Copyright 1918 by Meyer Cohen Music
Publishing Co., New York.

1st Verse:
Kneeling in sorrow I see you there,
Heartbroken mothers of France,
Patiently offering up your prayers,
Heartbroken mothers of France.
You've borne the burden for many a day,
Now other mothers' sons enter the fray:

Chorus:
Mothers of France,
Heartbroken mothers of France,
God bless your sons, ev'ry one,
For the fighting they have done.
They fought as never before,

They kept the Hun from our door,
And gave the world a fighting chance.
Oh, mothers of France,
You sonless mothers of France,
The world will never forget the debt it owes
    to you;
And ev'ry mother now is praying
And to ev'ry son they're saying,
"Go out and fight for the Right
And the mothers of France."

2nd Verse:
Don't think your praying has been in vain,
Heartbroken mothers of France;
All that was yours will be yours again,
Heartbroken mothers of France.
We'll never stop, let it cost what it may,
Yours is a debt we can never repay:

A Mother's Prayer for Her Boy Out There.
L: Andrew B. Sterling; M: Arthur Lange.
Copyright 1918 by Joe Morris Music Co.,
New York.

1st Verse:
Beside a vacant chair she's kneeling
When the lights are burning low,
'Way down in her heart the feeling
That only a mother can know.
And in her peaceful silence
By the vacant chair,
She softly says her evening prayer:

Chorus:
Just a little prayer
When shadows are stealing,
Just a little prayer,
A voice appealing;
To a baby shoe she's clinging
While the Angelus is ringing,
Come the words that start
From an aching heart:
"May angels guard him tenderly
Tonight and send my baby back to me."
That's a mother's prayer
For her boy "out there."

2nd Verse:
"My country needs me now," he told her,
"Mother darling, I must go."
Though he's fighting like a soldier,
He's only "her baby," you know.
And while her tears are falling
By the vacant chair,
She softly says her evening prayer:

A Mother's Prayer (for Her Boy "Over There"). L: Harold L. Cool; M: Arthur J. Daly. Copyright 1918 by Daly Music Co., New York.

1st Verse:
A mother sitting down to rest
At the close of day
Thinks of one she loves the best,
One who went away.
And to the fire's glow
She sobs in accents low:

Chorus:
"By your light his face I see,
Sitting on daddy's knee,
My only son, life just begun,
Always a baby to me.
A vacant chair, his baby stare,
Asking not why or where;
When war is done, send back my son,
Back to me,
O'er the sea."
That's a mother's prayer
For her boy over there.

2nd Verse:
But soon there came a happy day
As a golden sun
Pushed the clouds of war away,
Bringing back her son.
Now there's a brighter light
Shines from the hearth tonight:

My Alsace Lorraine (On to Paris or Berlin). L: L. Wolfe Gilbert; M: Lewis F. Muir. Copyright 1914 by F.A. Mills, New York.

1st Verse:
There's a big bound'ry line in my heart,
What to do I am puzzled to know.
There's my daddy, my ma and sweetheart,
They're apart and it's grieving me so;
Alsace Lorraine holds my sweetheart,
I don't know which way to go:

Chorus:
Alsace Lorraine, on to Paris or Berlin,
Come back again,
There are hearts that call within.
Berlin, my father's land,
Paris, my mother's land,
Oh, what a plight I am in!
Alsace Lorraine, 'on to Paris or Berlin.

2nd Verse:
If I could, then I'd please them all,
That's a thing that is so hard to do.
If I should go and pay someone a call,
I'd be grieving the dear other two.
Alsace and Berlin and Paris,
I'll bring them all over here:

My Angel of the Flaming Cross. L&M: Byron Gay. Copyright 1918 by Sunset Publishing Co., New York.

1st Verse:
On a home-bound transport,
As the sun was sinking low,
Stood a wounded soldier
Dreaming in the twilight's glow.
Visions of an angel,
Golden hair and eyes of blue;
Said a sailor lad, "Why are you so sad?"
Said the soldier, "I'll tell you":

Chorus:
"There's an angel over there,
An angel from I know not where;
Smiling sweetly through her tears,
She drove my fears away.
Little girl who nursed me through,
I owe my life to you;
Oh, come back,
Love that I found and lost,
My angel of the flaming cross."

2nd Verse:
When the war is over,
Many stories will be told,
Tales of war and romance,
Tales that never can grow old,
Tales of heroes fighting,
Tales of love and mercy, too.
But the best of all is the solider's call,
"Sweet Red Cross girl, to you":

My Daddy's Star. L: Ivan Reid; M: Peter DeRose. Copyright 1918 by F.B. Haviland Publishing Co., Inc., New York.

1st Verse:
A little tot had heard a lot
About the war in France;
Her daddy, too, "out there,"
Had gone to do his share.
Someone had told her that the "stars"
Were soldiers in the fray,
To show how many heroes went away;

And one night as she climbed on mother's
knee,
She looked up at the sky and made this plea:

Chorus:
"Please tell me which one is daddy's star
Shining somewhere up above,
I'm sure it knows just where we are
And that we're missing his love.
It must be brighter than all the rest
That watch over us from afar,
And each night when I pray,
I can look up and say
'I know which one is my daddy's star.'"

2nd Verse:
There are a million heroes now
Who stand for liberty,
And far across the foam
They've left someone alone.
They won't come back until they know
Their great work has been done,
Until they're sure the victory is won.
And while they're marching forward on their
way,
Back home some other little tot will say:

My Doughnut Girl. L: Elmore Leffingwell;
M: Robert Bertrand Brown. Copyright 1919
by The Salvation Army, New York.

1st Verse:
In the glory of light
That comes after the fight
To hallow a nation's brave,
There stands forth just a girl,
Who in war's bloody whirl,
Helped the fighter this country to save!:

Chorus:
Lassie, my Doughnut Girl!
There in the battle's mad swirl,
Oh! how your smiles helped us through,
As you toiled in the trenches
For the Red, White and Blue!
Mother, sister, and friend,
You stuck 'til the war's bitter end!
We lift our helmets to you,
My little Doughnut Girl!

2nd Verse:
When the shrapnel flew fast,
And our fellows were gassed,
You sang and baked and prayed;
As we bent back the line
Of the Hun toward the Rhine,
Cheered on by the doughnuts you made!:

**My Life Belongs to Uncle Sam (but My
Heart Belongs to You).** L: Schuyler
Greene; M: Otto Motzan. Copyright 1914
by Joe Morris Music Co., New York.

1st Verse:
Mollie darling, I have come to say goodbye,
And I must be leaving
For the front to help the soldier boys in blue,
Fight for the flag and you.
Mollie darling, when I'm far away,
Think of what I say:

Chorus:
My life belongs to Uncle Sam
But my heart still belongs to you.
When I hear the bugles calling,
There is nothing else to do
But join the boys as they rally 'round
Old Red, White and Blue;
For my life belongs to Uncle Sam
But my heart still belongs to you.

2nd Verse:
Down the street I hear the tramp of march-
ing feet
And the bugle calling,
Calling me away to war to fight the foe.
Goodbye, for I must go;
Mollie darling, dry those eyes of blue,
I'll come back to you:

**My Red Cross Girlie (the Wound Is
Somewhere in My Heart).** L: Harry
Bewley; M: Theodore Morse. Copyright
1917 by Leo Feist, Inc., New York.

1st Verse:
Ev'ry Red Cross girlie's like a soldier,
There's a feeling in her heart akin to love;
Some laddie with a gun upon his shoulder
Very often is the one she's thinking of.
Ev'ry soldier laddie has a yearning
For some noble girlie all in white;
In his heart the light of love is always burning
For a little Red Cross girlie day and night:

Chorus:
"My Red Cross girlie, for you I'm calling,
Though you're many miles away.
My Red Cross girlie, for you I'm falling,
Longing for you night and day.
I need you, sweetheart, for I am wounded
By a cunning fellow's dart;
But don't swoon, dear,
For the wound, dear,
Is only somewhere in my heart."

2nd Verse:
Ev'ry girlie loves a soldier laddie,
And ev'ry girlie loves a boy sincere;
She loves him better sometimes than her
    daddy,
Proud of one who doesn't know the thing
    called fear.
A soldier who goes into battle tireless
Doesn't mind the cannon's shot and shell,
If this message he can only send by wireless
To a Red Cross girlie whom he loves so well:

Never Forget to Write Home. L: Ballard
MacDonald; M: James F. Hanley. Copy-
right 1917 by Shapiro, Bernstein & Co.,
Inc., New York.

1st Verse:
The golden sun was sinking with its splendor
    in the west,
As a mother bade her son a fond farewell;
And her loving eyes were tender as she drew
    him to her breast,
For her heart held more than any tongue can
    tell.
The teardrops from her eyes began to steal,
As to her boy she made this last appeal:

Chorus:
"Never forget to write home,
Even if only a line,
Just try to make your mother [sweetheart]
    feel you've commenced to
Make good although you have the whole
    world against you.
Send us your love and a kiss,
Those are the things that we miss;
No matter where you may roam,
Never forget to write home."

2nd Verse:
You've often heard the proverb, "Out of
    sight is out of mind,"
Don't forget the little girl you left behind;
She is always thinking of you and her heart
    will ever yearn,
For she'll always be the same sweet girl,
    you'll find;
So one kind word from you is like a star
That sends its cheerful message from afar:

**No Matter What Flag He Fought Under
(He Was Some Mother's Boy, After All).**
L: J. Will Callahan; M: F. Henri Klick-
mann. Copyright 1915 by Frank K. Root &
Co., Chicago.

1st Verse:
Two Red Cross nurses searching upon the
    battlefield
Beheld a fair-haired soldier boy
Whose lips in death were sealed.
"What colors did he fight for?",
The younger maiden sighed;
"He fought for home and those he loved,"
The other nurse replied:

Chorus:
"No matter what flag he fought under,
No matter who's right in the strife,
'Mid war's awful rattle and thunder
He gave all he had—'twas his life.
Remember that someone will miss him
When he fails to answer her call;
No matter what flag he fought under,
He was some mother's boy, after all."

2nd Verse:
Amid the twilight shadows the Red Cross
    nurses there,
With tender hands smoothed back the curls
Of tangled golden hair,
And breathed a prayer to heaven
For her who'd wait and yearn
To greet again her soldier boy
Who never would return:

No One Said Goodbye to Me. L: L.B. Arthur; M: B.S. Edwards. Copyright 1914 by
Himan Music Co., New York.

1st Verse:
Hear the bugle's ringing blast loud and clear.
See the soldiers singing past, hear the cheer;
Ev'ry mother's son is there,
Brave of heart to do and dare.
Rank and file must bear their share without
    fear,
Sad farewells and fond goodbyes have been
    said,
Drums are beating time to quicken martial
    tread.
But one soldier boy alone
Sadly cries in mournful tone,
As he steps into the ranks and bows his head:

Chorus:
"No one said goodbye to me,
No one kissed a fond farewell,
No one's heart for me was aching,
No fond mother's teardrops fell.

Ev'ryone the flag was cheering,
I was lonely as could be;
Fond ones there with tear-dimmed eyes
Bid their soldier boy goodbye,
But no one said goodbye to me."

2nd Verse:
Hear the drummer's beating taps: vict'ry's
   won,
Hear the captain saying, "Chaps, nobly
   done."
But there's one sad duty yet,
Just a goodbye with regret
To the boys we can't forget, ev'ry one.
Some of them gave up their lives for our
   own,
Some have left sweethearts and wives all
   alone;
But a boy lay far away
Who had fallen in the fray,
And once again he cried in mournful tone:

Oh! How I Hate to Get Up in the Morning. L&M: Irving Berlin. Copyright 1918 by Waterson, Berlin & Snyder Co., New York.

1st Verse:
The other day I chanced to meet a soldier
   friend of mine;
He'd been in camp for sev'ral weeks and he
   was looking fine;
His muscles had developed and his cheeks
   were rosy red;
I asked him how he liked the life,
And this is what he said:

Chorus:
"Oh! how I hate to get up in the morning,
Oh! how I'd love to remain in bed;
For the hardest blow of all is to hear the
   bugler call:
You've got to get up, you've got to get up,
You've got to get up this morning!
Someday I'm going to murder the bugler,
Someday they're going to find him dead;
I'll amputate his reveille, and step upon it
   heavily,
[Oh boy! The minute the battle is over,
Oh boy! The minute the foe is dead;
I'll put my uniform away and move to
   Philadelphia],
And spend the rest of my life in bed."

2nd Verse:
A bugler in the Army is the luckiest of men,

One of the biggest of all World War I tunes, serious or comic, "Oh! How I Hate to Get Up in the Morning" was sung by Irving Berlin himself in his 1918 Army show *Yip, Yip, Yaphank.* He would sing it again in his World War II followup military musical *This Is the Army,* both stage (1942) and film (1943) versions.

He wakes the boys at five and then goes back
   to bed again;
He doesn't have to blow again until the
   afternoon,
If everything goes well with me,
I'll be a bugler soon:

Oh, Moon of the Summer Night (Tell My Mother Her Boy's All Right). L&M: Allan J. Flynn. Copyright 1918 by Al Piantadosi & Co., Inc., New York.

1st Verse:
Over there
The silv'ry moon was shining;
Over there
A soldier boy while pining
To the moon pleaded.
And if it heeded,
This is what it heard him, say:

Chorus:
"Oh! moon of the summer night,
Your silv'ry beams bring me dreams
Of the loved ones 'way back home.

Could you only tell them all
That I'm safe tonight,
How it would cheer up the loved ones
Far across the foam.
Over yonder in the golden West,
My mother's praying,
And the little girl I love the best
Is praying, too.
So I'm asking you, oh, moon!
Won't you send your light
And tell my mother for me, 'cross the sea,
Her boy's all right."

2nd Verse:
Over here
The night was dark and dreary,
Over here
Two loving hearts were weary,
Sweetheart and mother,
Asking each other,
"Will our soldier boy return?":

Oh! What a Time for the Girlies (When the Boys Come Marching Home). L: Sam M. Lewis and Joe Young; M: Harry Ruby. Copyright 1918 by Waterson, Berlin & Snyder Co., New York.

1st Verse:
Why are all the girlies feeling great?
Something's in the air;
They don't even want to make a date
With a poor old millionaire;
They're fixing up the Morris chair
And pulling down the blinds;
Soon there'll be somebody there,
And here's what's on their minds:

Chorus:
Oh! what a time for the girlies
When the boys come marching home;
They'll get the kissing that they've been missing
While they were over the foam;
Mary and Jane will explain to her soldier
How she spent her nights alone;
Think of all the loving they will get,
Two long years they've been without a pet;
[Every cutie waiting at the pier
Wants to do her duty over here],
[When a soldier squeezes you too hard,
Raise your hand and holler "Kamerad!"];
Oh! what a time for the girlies
When the boys come marching home.

2nd Verse:
Have you noticed any girlie who

Has a boy in France?
She was always feeling sad and blue,
You could tell it at a glance;
But now upon her face you'll see
A look of joy and pride;
It's because she knows that he
Will soon be by her side:

On the Sidewalks of Berlin. L&M: E. Clinton Keithley. Copyright 1918 by Frank K. Root & Co., Chicago.

1st Verse:
Now we all know that the Kaiser each day is getting wiser,
That some day soon he'll lose his little crown,
For he's hikin' to the border
To get his crew in order
To keep the Yankees out of Berlin town;
But he'll get all that's coming some fine day,
For this is what I heard a soldier say:

Chorus:
"We're drivin' 'em back, boys, we're drivin' 'em back,
We're gettin' nearer ev'ry day!
We're goin' to *smash* that Hindenburg Line,
And then we'll cross the River Rhine!
And when we are done, boys, we'll have some fun,
We're goin' to tan the Kaiser's skin!
And we'll sing 'Hail, Hail, the Gang's All Here!'
On the sidewalks of Berlin!"

2nd Verse:
There'll come a time when Willie will see how awf'ly silly
That he was when he tried to rule the world,
For although he whipped the Russians,
What a diff'rence when his Prussians
Against the men of Uncle Sam were hurled!
There'll be a change in Germany some day,
You feel it when you hear the soldiers say:

On the Somme Front. L: Joseph O'Connor; M: Pvt. J. Tavender. Copyright 1918 by Joseph O'Connor, published by P.B. Story, New York.

1st Verse:
The U.S.A. gave up her very best sons
To take those Germans, trenches, and guns,
While sisters and brothers so fond and true
Sent them smokes to help them through.

Sweethearts send them some cheer
In a letter so dear,
And don't forget to say,
"How proud are we of our boys o'er the sea,
On the Somme front so far away":

Chorus:
Somme front, so far away,
Where our boys are fighting night and day,
Where the bullets they tear the stars from the
    skies,
And bombs are bursting while the gases rise.
When the war is won
What will the Motherland say
For the boys that fought for you and me
On the Somme front, the Somme front
So far away.

2nd Verse:
Oh, Canada gave up their finest men to fight,
To teach those Prussians that Right is might,
While mothers and wives so dear,
So fond and true,
Sit knitting stockings to help them through;
Sweethearts send joy divine to them on the
    fighting line,
They want to hear you say
How proud are we of our boys o'er the sea
On the Somme front so far away:

On to Berlin. L: J.C. Crisler; M: Lee
Johnson. Copyright 1918 by J.C. Crisler,
assigned to Sherman, Clay & Co., San
Francisco.

1st Verse:
On to Berlin is the Allied cry,
On to Berlin or see freedom die;
Our fighting men will win, we know,
They've got the pep and on they'll go.
We'll open up the Hindenburg Line,
We can see the Allied vict'ry sign,
And the dove of peace is bound to win.
Hosts of freedom marching in,
And their shouts will drown the din,
We'll dictate terms to old Berlin!:

Chorus:
On to Berlin, boys, with your tank and plane,
Over the top, boys, and we'll at them again!
Over the trenches and over the Rhine,
Nobody home on the Hindenburger Line.
We'll hang a sign upon the Kaiser's tent
To point out the way that old Bill went.
Then we'll oust the Kaiser and his kin,
We can see his finish he's almost in,
And we'll dictate terms to old Berlin!

2nd Verse:
On to Berlin and the world's release,
On to Berlin and a lasting peace;
The stars of freedom brightly shine,
As over the top and over the Rhine,
We'll over the sea and over the Alps,
And our boys will get the Kaiser's scalp!
There'll be doings in old Fritzy's town,
With a jobless German crown,
He must pay for his nameless sin;
We'll make out terms in old Berlin!:

**One, Two, Three, Boys (Over the Top We
Go).** L&M: Charles K. Harris. Copyright
1918 by Chas. K. Harris, New York.

1st Verse:
What care we when bullets are a-whistling
    o'er our heads,
What care we for shrapnel or for shell;
They have tried their gases and their great
    big "Berthas," too,
Now you watch us make those fellows yell:

Chorus:
Now, all together,
Don't mind the weather,
One, two, three, boys,
And over the top we go!
Show them we're ready,
Keep cool and steady,
Think of only how they treat you
If they beat you.
Show them no quarter,
Don't think you oughta
Hold tight, just fight,
America's watching you!
Think of Belgium, fight and show her,
Think of France and all we owe her.
One, two, three, boys,
Over the top we go!

2nd Verse:
Nothing ever worries us and nothing ever will,
Nothing is too hard for us to try;
We go singing into battle 'cause we know
    we're right,
And we're over here to do or die:

Oui Oui, Marie. L: Al Bryan and Joseph
McCarthy; M: Fred Fisher. Copyright 1918
by McCarthy and Fisher, Inc., New York.

1st Verse:
Poor Johnny's heart went pitty, pitty pat

Somewhere in sunny France.
He met a girl by chance with ze naughty,
     naughty glance.
She looked just like a kitty, kitty cat,
She loved to dance and play;
Though he learned no French when he left
     the trench,
He knew well enough to say:

Chorus:
"Oui oui, Marie, will you do zis for me?
Oui oui, Marie, then I'll do zat for you.
I love your eyes,
They make me feel so spoony;
You'll drive me loony,
You're teasing me,
Why can't we parley-vous
Like other sweethearts do?
I want a kiss or two
From ma cherie.
Oui oui, Marie,
If you'll do zis for me,
Then I'll do zat for you,
Oui oui, Marie."

2nd Verse:
They walked along the boule, boulevard,
He whispered "You for me,
Some day in Gay Paree
I will make you marry me."
Just then a bunch of bully, bully boys threw
     kisses on the sly;
Marie got wise when they rolled their eyes,
They sang as they passed her by:

Our God, Our Country, and Our Flag.
L&M: Edward Machugh. Copyright 1917
by White-Smith Publishing Co., Boston.

Verse:
A land of peace and love have we,
Columbia fair and free;
Our hearts, our love, our lives we give
In loyalty to thee.
For us no wanton princely line,
Nor ruthless pow'r to stay;
America, our blessed land!
Thy name our shield for aye!

Chorus:
Dear motherland, dear hallowed land,
Our homeland e'er shall be;
Dear native land, dear freeman's land,
We pledge on bended knee
To live for thee, to cherish thee,
If need be to die for thee.

The welkin rings o'er plain and crag:
"Our God, our country, and our flag!"

Our Own American Boy. L&M: William
C. Wilbert, Max Friedman, and George F.
Olcott. Copyright 1917 by Max Friedman
Music Co., Pittsburgh.

1st Verse:
America, our country, the land of the free,
You're forced into a mighty war with lands
     across the sea.
You're there to fight for freedom,
The old Red, White and Blue,
And prove to all the world
Your sons are loyal, staunch, and true:

Chorus:
When the war is over and all is said and
     done,
When our boys are homeward bound
And vict'ry they have won,
They will always find a welcome in the land
     across the sea,
And they'll never be forgotten in our land of
     liberty.
They will find a sweetheart with a love that's
     fond and true,
And a mother dear a-waiting for them, too.
We'll greet them with sadness,
With gladness and joy,
Our own American boy.

2nd Verse:
We'll fight for Old Glory, for forever she'll
     wave,
We'll fight for our dear native land, our
     country we will save.
We'll show them we're no plaything
If they think we're a toy,
We'll show them just what constitutes
A plain American boy:

**Our U.S.A. Boys (Will Force All Nations
to Respect Humanity).** L&M: Richard F.
Staley. Copyright 1917 by Richard F. Staley, Rochester, N.Y.

1st Verse:
Many mothers' hearts are sore in our land
     today,
For our nation's now at war and her boy's
     going away.
For the freedom of the seas your boy's going
     to fight

And force the autocratic nations to treat
neutrals right.
Many mothers' hears are breaking,
Homes destroyed and fathers taken,
Children starving and forsaken just through
brutal might:

Chorus:
Our U.S.A. boys will march to the front
And will fight for universal liberty.
In the land where their forefathers sprang
from,
Who emigrated here just to be free,
Our U.S.A. boys will show their bravery,
Midst showers of shells you'll hear U.S.A.
yells!
They're not fighting for plunder,
But they'll make the whole world wonder,
With their pow'r to force all nations to
respect humanity.

2nd Verse:
Foreign mothers' hearts will beat with joy
and happiness
When your loving boys they greet and cheer
on to success.
The pow'r of love, the noble cause your sons
are fighting for,
Will send a chill of terror through inhuman
men at war.
Our Savior taught us to be meek,
When smitten, turn the other cheek;
For doing this we were called weak, and they
murdered all the more:

Out on the Bounding Billows. L: Walter
S. Atus; M: Hector Richard. Copyright
1919 by Walter S. Atus; published by
Legters Music Co., Chicago.

1st Verse:
Out on the bounding billows,
Somewhere out in the dark blue sea,
My sweetheart is joyfully sailing
Back to his home and to me.
How I long to look into his eyes of brown
And to know he comes back with a crown:

Chorus:
Out on the bounding billows,
Out on the dark blue sea,
Sailing is the ship that is bringing
My sweetheart back to me.

2nd Verse:
Now the ship's in, heaving,
And my sweetheart's back from the fight;

Now in our home we will be settling,
We'll happy be, day and night,
And our home will be full of joy and cheer,
For the one that I love will be here:

Over the Top. L: Herbert W. Rainie; M:
George H. Perkins. Copyright 1917 by
Perkins and Rainie, Concord, N.H.

1st Verse:
With a merry tune on the fifth of June
Johnny Smith marched down the street,
With ten million more he marked down the
score
That spelled Germany's defeat.
And on that fateful day,
Through the whole grand U.S.A.,
Rang the sound of marching hosts
That drove the Kaiser's dream away:

Chorus:
Over the top they'll go to fight for Uncle
Sam,
Flow'r of our youth, the best you'll find in
any land.
America's awake, her own part she'll surely
take,
These boys so strong will show ere long
That they can win for liberty's sake!
O, Mister Wilson, we are with you strong,
And you can count on us right to the end.
Now you watch us fight,
For we know we're right;
Tell the folks at home to just sit tight,
Over the top we'll go for dear old Uncle Sam!

2nd Verse:
As the months went by, Johnny Smith's reply
To the call that came to him
Was to take his stand for his own dear land
As a soldier straight and trim.
His mother smiled with pride
Even though she might have cried,
And she breathed a prayer he'd do his share
And come back to her side:

"Over the Top." L: Marion Phelps; M:
Maxwell Goldman. Copyright 1917 by
Buck and Lowney, St. Louis.

1st Verse:
From the trenches boldly ringing
Sounds a battle cry today,
'Tis the call to freedom
Springing from the ranks of U.S.A.

"Over the top" and all the way,
"Over the top" into the fray,
Out of the trenches, every one,
Into the lines of cruel Hun!:

Chorus:
"Over the top" to victory,
"Over the top" for liberty;
Follow the flag, ye Frenchmen all,
Italians and Britons will answer the call.
"Over the top's" our battle cry,
For future peace we'll win or die.
Our Sammies over there
Have gone to do their share,
[Our brave boys over there
Will free the world from care],
So "over the top," boys,
"Over the top!"

2nd Verse:
To the colors proudly leaping,
With a will to win or die,
You can see their brown ranks sweeping,
Don't you hear their battle cry?
"Over the top" and all the way,
"Over the top" into the fray,
Out of the trenches, on they go
Into the lines of the charging foe!":

Over There. L&M: George M. Cohan.
Copyright 1917 by William Jerome Publishing Corp., New York.

1st Verse:
Johnnie get your gun,
Get your gun, get your gun,
Take it on the run,
On the run, on the run,
Hear them calling you and me,
Ev'ry son of liberty;
Hurry right away,
No delay, go today,
Make your daddy glad to have had such a
   lad,
Tell your sweetheart not to pine,
To be proud her boy's in line:

Chorus:
Over there,
Over there,
Send the word,
Send the word over there,
That the Yanks are coming,
The Yanks are coming,
The drum rum-tum-tumming ev'rywhere!
So prepare,

Say a pray'r,
Send the word,
Send the word to beware,
We'll be over,
We're coming over,
And we won't come back
Till it's over, over there!

2nd Verse:
Johnnie get your gun,
Get your gun, get your gun,
Johnnie show the Hun
You're a son of a gun;
Hoist the flag and let her fly,
Yankee Doodle do or die;
Pack your little kit,
Show your grit, do your bit;
Yankees to the ranks from the towns and the
   tanks,
Make your mother proud of you
And the old Red, White and Blue:

**Pack Up Your Troubles in Your Old Kit
Bag and Smile, Smile, Smile.** L: George
Asaf; M: Felix Powell. Copyright 1915 by
Francis, Day & Hunter, New York.

1st Verse:
Private Perks is a funny little codger
With a smile, a funny smile;
Five feet none, he's an artful little dodger
With a smile, a funny smile;
Flush or broke, he'll have his little joke;
He can't be suppressed.
All the other fellows have to grin
When he gets this off his chest,
Hi!:

Chorus:
"Pack up your troubles in your old kit bag,
And smile, smile, smile;
While you've a lucifer to light your fag,
Smile, boys, that's the style.
What's the use of worrying?
It never was worthwhile, so
Pack up your troubles in your old kit bag,
And smile, smile, smile."

2nd Verse:
Private Perks went a-marching into Flanders
With his smile, his funny smile;
He was loved by the privates and com-
   manders
For his smile, his funny smile;
When a throng of Bosches came along,
With a mighty swing,

Tuneful and carefree, "Pack Up Your Troubles in Your Old Kit-Bag and Smile, Smile, Smile" was introduced in 1915 by Adele Rowland in the London stage production of *Her Soldier Boy*. (An American version of the musical, with music, by Sigmund Romberg, opened on Broadway the following year.)

Perks yelled out, "This little bunch is mine!
Keep your heads down, boys, and sing,
Hi!":

3rd Verse:
Private Perks he came back from Boche
   shooting
With his smile, his funny smile;
Round his home he then set about recruiting
With his smile, his funny smile;
He told all his pals, the short, the tall,
What a time he'd had;
And as each enlisted like a man,
Private Perks said, "Now, my lad,
Hi!":

Paul Revere (Won't You Ride for Us Again?). L: Joe Goodwin; M: Halsey K. Mohr. Copyright 1918 by Shapiro, Bernstein & Co., Inc., New York.

1st Verse:
With your lantern, Paul Revere,
You rode miles around;

"One if by land,
Two if by sea,"
Spreading alarm through ev'ry town.
You warned us then of danger that was near,
We need another warning, Paul Revere:

Chorus:
Paul Revere, Paul Revere,
Won't you ride for us again?
Won't you ride through each hamlet, village,
   and farm?
Ride, Paul Revere, and spread the alarm!
Paul Revere, Paul Revere,
You're a mem'ry we all hold dear;
Though you've rested for ages on history's
   pages,
Ride for us now, Paul Revere!

2nd Verse:
You were answered, Paul Revere,
On your midnight ride;
They heard you then,
Those Minute Men,
Liberty's call was not denied.
Today your country needs you, can't you
   hear?
So ride once more to help us, Paul Revere:

Pick a Little Four-Leaf Clover (and Send It Over to Me). L: C. Francis Reisner and Ed Rose; M: Abe Olman. Copyright 1918 by Forster Music Publisher, Inc., Chicago.

1st Verse:
Somewhere out there over in France
Came a note from a soldier boy,
A world of love each word contained,
And it brought his sweetheart joy.
"Remember me," she read through a tear,
"And next time you write to me, dear":

Chorus:
"Pick a little four-leaf clover
And send it over to me
Out on the battlefield.
Just like an armour shield,
It will help me to win the victory.
For the four-leaf clover
Makes wishes come true,
And my heart's yearning
And wishing for you.
So won't you pick a little four-leaf clover
And send it over to me?"

2nd Verse:
"Here boy, dear boy over the sea,
Is the clover I've picked for you;

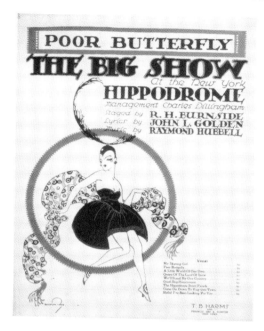

Written one year before the United States entered the war, "Poor Butterfly" (1916) reflected the sadness of war in its tale of one Japanese girl whose American sailor boyfriend had presumedly been lost at sea. The sympathetic reception accorded the song prompted William Jerome and Arthur N. Green late in 1916 to write the satirical sequel, "If I Catch the Guy Who Wrote 'Poor Butterfly,'" promising to "paint and decorate his eye and make him cry,/ 'Poor Butterfly, for you I'm falling,'" and then give him a good scolding as well. Written, apparently, for the fun of it, the spoof was dedicated to the original writers, Raymond Hubbell and John Golden.

That it may bring you back to me
Is the prayer of a sweetheart true.
When other hearts their love stories plead,
Then I'll be content just to read":

Poor Butterfly. L: John L. Golden; M: Raymond Hubbell. Copyright 1916 by T.B. Harms and Francis, Day & Hunter, New York.

1st Verse:
There's a story told of a little Japanese
Sitting demurely 'neath the cherry blossom
   trees,
Miss Butterfly her name;
A sweet little innocent child was she
Till a fine young American from the sea
To her garden came.

They met 'neath the cherry blossoms ev'ry day
And he taught her how to love in the
   'Merican way,
To love with her soul!
'Twas easy to learn,
Then he sailed away with a promise to return:

Chorus:
Poor Butterfly,
'Neath the blossoms waiting,
Poor Butterfly,
For she loved him so.
The moments pass into hours,
The hours pass into years.
And as she smiles through her tears,
She murmurs low:
"The moon and I know that he be faithful,
I'm sure he come to me bye and bye.
But if he don't come back,
Then I never sigh or cry,
I just mus' die,
Poor Butterfly."

2nd Verse:
"Won't you tell my love," she would whisper
   to the breeze;
"Tell him I'm waiting 'neath the cherry
   blossom trees
My sailor man to see;
The bees and the humming birds say they
   guess
Ev'ry day that passes makes one day less
'Till you'll come to me."
For once Butterfly she gives her heart away,
She can never love again, she is his for aye,
Through all of this world,
For ages to come;
So her face just smiles though her heart is
   growing numb:

President Wilson, U.S.A. L: Jewell Ellison; M: Lee G. Kratz. Copyright 1918 by Jewell Ellison, Publisher, Lucas, S.D.

1st Verse:
We are with you, Woodrow Wilson,
We are freedom's noble band.
We'll defend your lofty actions
With a loyal heart and hand.
With the aid of gallant heroes
From beneath the skies of fate,
Into freedom's placid harbor
You will guide the ship of state:

Chorus:
Yes, we're with you, Woodrow Wilson,

We are freedom's noble band.
We'll defend your lofty actions
With a loyal heart and hand.
Yes, we're with you, Woodrow Wilson,
We are freedom's noble band;
We'll defend your lofty actions
With a loyal heart and hand.

2nd Verse:
'Mid the joyful shouts of vict'ry,
With the flag of peace unfurled,
And with Justice, Love and Honor,
You will triumph o'er the world.
Then your deeds will be immortal,
Noble Captain of the free.
Through the golden trend of hist'ry,
Wilson's name will burnished be:

3rd Verse:
You'll be unexcelled by Lincoln
And by Washington of yore.
In the halls of fame your praises
Will resound forever more.
Yes, we're with you, Woodrow Wilson,
We are freedom's noble band;
We'll defend your lofty actions
With a loyal heart and hand:

Private Arkansaw Bill (Yip-I-Yip and a Too-Ra-Le-Ay!). L&M: Lloyd Garrett. Copyright 1918 by Frank K. Root & Co., Chicago.

1st Verse:
Arkansaw Bill came to camp one day
And brought his old fiddle along;
The only tune he was known to play
Was a little old Arkansaw song;
And now ev'rywhere that song's in the air,
You hear it all night and all day,
That foolish refrain gets into your brain,
It's "Yip-I-Yip and a Too-Ra-Le-Ay!":

Chorus:
Yip-I-Yip and a Too-Ra-Le-Lay!
Yip-I-Yip, you can hear it all day.
When that haunting strain gets in your weary brain,
Ev'ry now and then you start to sing it again.
Yip-I-Yip and a Too-Ra-Le-Ay!
No use, you can't drive it away;
So what's the use of tryin'
And what's the use cryin',
It's Yip-I-Yip and a Too-Ra-Le-Ay!

2nd Verse:
Arkansaw Bill went to church one day,
And as he walked down the main aisle,
He hummed his little old Yip-I-Ay
Till he made ev'rybody there smile.
The organist soon memorized the tune,
The choir then joined in the lay;
The preacher, perplexed, said "Brethren, my text
Is 'Yip-I-Yip and a Too-Ra-Le-Ay!'":

3rd Verse:
Ev'ryone's looking for poor old Bill
For starting that song all around;
A hundred fellows have said they'd kill
The poor devil as soon as he's found.
Why, only last night his dog took a bite,
Bill got hydrophobia, they say,
And poor old dog Tray broke out the next day
With "Yip-I-Yip and a Too-Ra-Le-Ay!":

The Ragtime Volunteers Are Off to War. L: Ballard MacDonald; M: James F. Hanley. Copyright 1917 by Shapiro, Bernstein & Co., New York.

1st Verse:
All the gals have got the blues
Since they heard the latest news,
That the ragtime volunteers,
Who haven't fought in nearly twenty years,
Will march away and leave their folks in tears.
They're gonna leave today,
That's what the papers say;
Here comes the band,
Come take your stand,
And watch them march away:

Chorus:
Just see those ragtime soldiers,
Left, right, left, right!
Knapsacks upon their shoulders,
Left, right, left, right!
Just watch that leader man
Control that "Jas-bo" band,
Ain't that some demonstration?
Oh! what syncopation!
Old Colonel Jones look like a pouter pigeon
As they go swinging by his door;
Each high brown turtle dove says:
"Farewell, my lady love,
The ragtime volunteers are off to war!"

2nd Verse:
See them coming down the street,

Watch those darkies lift their feet
To the music of that band;
Those melodies they play are simply grand,
They take you back to dear old Dixieland.
That drummer's full of pep,
He has a worldwide "rep";
He's ragging some
Upon his drum
To keep the boys in step:

Root for Uncle Sam. L: Jean C. Havez;
M: Louis Silvers. Copyright 1917 by Havez
& Silvers, New York.

1st Verse:
Come on, you Yankee boys and girls,
It's time to show your nerve,
We're out to give the enemy
The licking they deserve.
Although at peace they've sunk our ships,
As friends could never do,
They've turned their guns upon our flag,
I won't stand that, will you?:

Chorus:
"Ev'rybody,
Root for Uncle Sam!
I'm for Wilson,
You bet your life I am!
'Bring on your sneaky submarines
And lick us if you can.'
['We'll give those foreign autocrats
A good old Yankee slam'].
Ev'rybody,
Root for Uncle Sam!"

2nd Verse:
Give up your peaceful notions now,
The time has come to fight!
We might be wrong in some things, boys,
But this time we are right!
We've got the boats to get their goats,
We've got the gunners, too,
We've got the nerve we need to save
The old Red, White and Blue!:

The Rose of No Man's Land. L: Jack
Caddigan; M: James A. Brennan. Copyright 1918 by Leo Feist, Inc., New York.

1st Verse:
I've seen some beautiful flowers
Grow in life's garden fair,
I've spent some wonderful hours
Lost in their fragrance rare.

One of the last of the war's musical tributes to the
American Red Cross, "The Rose of No Man's
Land" (1918) characterized the battlefield nurse as
the "one red rose the soldier knows ... the work
of the Master's hand."

But I have found another,
Wondrous beyond compare:

Chorus:
There's a rose that grows on "No Man's
   Land,"
And it's wonderful to see;
Though it's sprayed with tears,
It will live for years
In my garden of memory.
It's the one red rose the soldier knows,
It's the work of the Master's hand;
'Mid the war's great curse
Stands the Red Cross nurse,
She's the rose of "No Man's Land."

2nd Verse:
Out of the heavenly splendor,
Down to the trail of woe,
God in His mercy has sent her,
Cheering the world below.
We call her "Rose of Heaven,"
We've learned to love her so:

Roses of Lorraine. L: Sidney Carter; M: Walter Smith. Copyright 1918 by Daniels & Wilson, Inc., San Francisco.

1st Verse:
"Dearie, I was happy when you wrote
That tender note
Saying that you're longing ev'ry day,
And always pray
That I'll soon return to you.
You must know I'm longing, too,
But there's work for us to do;
Listen, dearie, while I say":

Chorus:
"When the roses of Lorraine
Scent the air in ev'ry lane,
When the gold is on the grain,
I'll come back to you again.
When the poppies' flaming red
Are a-bloom where heroes bled,
I'll be returning to you,
With a heart that's beating true.
When the happy larks arise
Into bright and sunny skies,
Then the bells of vict'ry ring
Over ev'ry tyrant king.
And I know that you will pray
For the coming of that day;
I shall bring a greeting then
From the roses of Lorraine."

2nd Verse:
"Dearie, keep your courage and your cheer,
And never fear;
When the boys at last are homeward bound,
And bugles sound,
Smiles will drive your tears away
On that welcome, happy day.
Then I'm coming home to stay,
Coming back to home and you":

Roses of Picardy. L: Fred E. Weatherly; M: Haydn Wood. Copyright 1916 by Chappell & Co. Ltd., London.

1st Verse:
She is watching by the poplars,
Colinette with the sea-blue eyes;
She is watching and longing and waiting
Where the long white roadway lies.
And a song stirs in the silence,
As the wind in the boughs above;
She listens and starts and trembles,
'Tis the first little song of love:

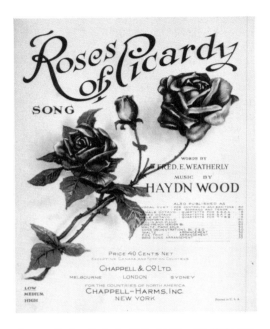

Among the loveliest of all World War I ballads was the British threnody "Roses of Picardy" (1916), in which a sweetheart laments the battlefield death of her lover while promising to remember him forever.

Chorus:
"Roses are shining in Picardy
In the hush of the silver dew,
Roses are flow'ring in Picardy,
But there's never a rose like you.
And the roses will die with the summertime,
And our roads may be far apart;
But there's one rose that dies not in Picardy,
'Tis the rose that I keep in my heart."

2nd Verse:
And the years fly on forever,
Till the shadows veil their skies;
But he loves to hold her little hands
And look in her sea-blue eyes.
And she sees the road by the poplars,
Where they met in the bygone years,
For the first little song of the roses
Is the last little song she hears:

'Round Her Neck She Wears a Yeller Ribbon (for Her Lover Who Is Fur, Fur Away). L&M (revised): George A. Norton. Copyright 1917 by Leo Feist, Inc., New York.

1st Verse:
Susie Simpkins in the village papers

Read about the soldiers' manly capers,
And made up her mind
That a soldier's bonnie bride she'd be.
Volunteers were called a little later;
Big Si Hubbard stopped a-hoeing 'taters,
Fell right into line
And mustered with a company.
She cried and kissed him when he marched
    away,
And she vowed to keep him in her mind each
    day:

Chorus:
'Round her neck she wears a yeller ribbon,
She wears it in the winter and the summer,
    so they say;
If you ask her "Why the decoration?",
She'll say "It's fur my lover who is fur, fur
    away,
Fur away (fur away),
Fur away (fur away)."
If she is milkin' cows or mowin' hay,
'Round her neck she wears a yeller ribbon,
She wears it fur her lover who is fur, fur
    away.

2nd Verse:
Months rolled by and patiently she waited,
Read the war news, greatly agitated;
No word from her boy
'Till a letter from his captain said,
"Your beau, Silas, he went out a-gunnin',
Soon he had the enemy a-runnin'."
Susie wept for joy,
Though further on the letter read,
"The enemy can run some, you can bet,
But they couldn't capture Si, he's runnin'
    yet":

Sammy (March). L: Richard Western; M:
Arthur Olaf Andersen. Copyright 1918 by
Richard Western and A.O. Andersen,
published by The Music Press, Chicago.

1st Verse:
They're calling him from near and far,
From office, forge, and plow,
Defender of the nation
For his country needs him now.
From Maryland to Oregon,
From Nome to Tampa Bay
Comes a marching host in khaki,
Fighting Sammy, U.S.A.!:

Chorus:
Oh, the nation's calling, Sammy,

There's a job for you to do!
On the battlefields of freedom
There's a fight ahead for you!
And we love and trust you, Sammy,
You're a soldier to the bone;
We'll be waiting for you, Sammy,
Waiting 'till you come back home!

2nd Verse:
When thund'ring gun and screaming shell
Crash out the battle hour,
With manly grit just do your bit,
Uphold Old Glory's pow'r.
When war is done, the vict'ry won,
Oh, Sammy boy, they'll say,
"Stand up, salute the hero!
Fighting Sammy, U.S.A.!":

Say a Prayer for the Boys "Out There." L:
Bernie Grossman; M: Alex Marr. Copy-
right 1917 by Joe Morris Music Co., New
York.

1st Verse:
A mighty nation hears a ringing call to arms,
A call that draws her sons from city, vale,
    and farm;
A nation sends the best of us across the sea,
That the rest of us forever may be free;
And while a mighty nation's heart will yearn,
Let's pray that they soon will return:

Chorus:
Won't you say a prayer for the boys out
    there,
For our heroes o'er the sea,
In that raging fray by night and day
They're fighting for you and me;
When they take their stand in No Man's
    Land,
We know they'll do their share;
So that we may live,
Their lives they give;
Say a prayer for the boys out there.

2nd Verse:
A mighty nation's voice will reach across the
    sea,
And cheer the hearts of those who fight for
    liberty;
A nation's prayers will help the weaker ones
    along,
And will strengthen them when everything
    goes wrong;
And while a nation's sons will do or die,
Let's call to the One upon high:

Send Back Dear Daddy to Me. L: Alex Sullivan and Harry Tenny; M: Irving Maslof. Copyright 1918 by Joseph W. Stern & Co., New York.

1st Verse:
In a quaint old country schoolroom,
The teacher asked each little girl and boy
To tell her in a simple note
What would give them greatest joy.
One girlie's note brought tears to the
    teacher's eyes
When she read with great surprise:

Chorus:
"I don't want any more dollies,
Brother don't want any pollies,
Sister don't want any fancy things,
Mother don't want any diamond rings.
There's but one gift that we pray for,
One thing we long night and day for:
Stop all this war and give us victory,
And send back dear daddy to me."

2nd Verse:
Now the holidays are over,
The kiddies have once more returned to
    school;
Though all seem glad and full of cheer,
There's one exception to the rule;
One little girl is sad, just as sad as can be,
For no one heard her plea:

Send Me a Curl. L&M: Geoffrey O'Hara. Copyright 1917 by Huntzinger & Dilworth, New York.

1st Verse:
Soldiers ev'rywhere,
See the people stare!
All the boys are on their way.
Goodbye, here we go,
Step out, don't be slow,
We will leave for France today.
But though we go
To fight across the foam,
We won't forget the folks at "Home Sweet
    Home":

Chorus:
There's a corner in my heart
That I'm keeping all apart
For the little girl I left behind.
I can see her waiting there
With the flowers in her hair,
And the roses in her cheeks entwined;

So when you're thinking of me over yonder,
When you wonder what I'd like to wear,
Send a pretty little curl
From the sweetest little girl
In my home town.

2nd Verse:
While we're fighting here
I see mother dear,
Good old dad and sister May;
Just that lonesome three,
Making things for me,
Thinking of me night and day.
And then I see
A little wedding ring;
I know there's "Someone" hears me when I
    sing:

Send Me a Line (When I'm Across the Ocean). L: Irving Crocker; M: George L. Cobb. Copyright 1917 by Walter Jacobs, Boston.

1st Verse:
Just a line to let you know that I've been
    called away,
I'm leaving home today,
And here's what I must say:
You're the one to cheer me up whenever I
    am blue,
So this is what I'd like to have you do:

Chorus:
Send me a line when I'm across the ocean,
Send me a line to show me your devotion,
A letter nice and long,
As sweet as any song,
To tell me that you'll remember ev'ry prom-
    ise while I'm gone.
Write me a word about my dear old mother,
I know I'll miss her more than I can say;
So while I'm o'er the sea,
Just show your love for me
By sending a line to me each day.

2nd Verse:
Things will happen ev'ry day that you can
    write about,
If you should be in doubt,
Now I will help you out.
Just say that you love me true and no one
    else will do,
For you know I'll be coming back to you:

She'll Miss Me Most of All. L: Will J. Hart; M: Edward G. Nelson. Copyright

1918 by A.J. Stasny Music Co., New York. (Referring to Will J. Hart, a note on the second page of the sheet music reads: "The author of the lyrics of this song was called away for military duty and was unable to complete the second verse, as he is now 'Somewhere in France.'")

1st Verse:
Last night I joined the Regulars,
I'm glad I volunteered,
Soon I'll leave my friends so dear
'Mid a Yankee Doodle cheer.
Now most of you, with hearts so true,
You'll wish the best for me,
But those at home I leave alone,
They'll need your sympathy:

Chorus:
My sweetheart, when we part,
She will sigh and cry;
My old dad, he'll feel bad
As the troops march by.
Little sister Jane,
She will cry in vain,
When I'm away she'll pray each day
That I'll come back again.
Brother Joe when I go,
He'll be proud, I know,
For I've answered my country's call.
But my dear gray-haired mother,
She'll sigh like no other,
[But that dear gray-haired lady
Who still calls me baby],
For [Why] she'll miss me most of all.

Sister Susie's Sewing Shirts for Soldiers. L: R.P. Weston; M: Herman E. Dareweski. Copyright 1914 by Francis, Day & Hunter, New York.

1st Verse:
Sister Susie's sewing in the kitchen on a "Singer,"
There's miles and miles of flannel on the floor and up the stairs,
And father says it's rotten getting mixed up with the cotton
And sitting on the needles that she leaves upon the chairs;
And should you knock at our street door,
Ma whispers, "Come inside,"
Then when you ask where Susie is,
She says with loving pride:

Chorus:
"Sister Susie's sewing shirts for soldiers,
Such skill at sewing shirts our shy young sister Susie shows!
Some soldiers send epistles,
Say they'd sooner sleep in thistles
Than the saucy, soft, short shirts for soldiers sister Susie sews."

2nd Verse:
Piles and piles and piles of shirts she sends out to the soldiers,
And sailors won't be jealous when they see them, not at all.
And when we say her stitching will set all the soldiers itching,
She says our soldiers fight best when their back's against the wall.
And little brother Gussie,
He who lisps when he says "yes,"
Says, "Where's the cotton gone from off my kite?
Oh, I can gueth!":

3rd Verse:
I forgot to tell you that our sister Susie's married,
And when she isn't sewing shirts, she's sewing other things,
Then little sister Molly says, "Oh, sister's bought a dolly,
She's making all the clothes for it with pretty bows and strings."
Says Susie, "Don't be silly,"
As she blushes and she sighs;
Then mother smiles and whispers
With a twinkle in her eye:

Smile and Show Your Dimple. L&M: Irving Berlin. Copyright 1917 by Waterson, Berlin & Snyder Co., New York.

1st Verse:
Little girlie, you look sad,
I'm afraid you're feeling bad,
Because he's leaving;
But stop your grieving (little girl).
He don't want you to feel blue,
For it's not the thing to do;
It will soon be over,
Then he'll come marching back to you:

Chorus:
Smile and show your dimple,
You'll find it's very simple;
You can think of something comical

In a very little while.
Chase away the wrinkles,
Sprinkle just a twinkle,
Light your face up,
Just brace up and smile.

2nd Verse:
Little girlie, don't you know
That your pearly teeth will show
If you start smiling;
So keep on smiling (little girl).
You can cut your cares in half
If you only try to laugh;
Look into my cam'ra,
I'm goin' to take your photograph:

Smiles. L: J. Will Callahan; M: Lee S.
Roberts. Copyright 1917 by Lee S. Roberts;
assigned 1918 to Jerome H. Remick & Co.,
New York.

1st Verse:
Dearie, now I know
Just what makes me love you so,
Just what holds me and enfolds me
In its magic glow;
Dearie, now I see
'Tis each smile so bright and free,
For life's sadness turns to gladness
When you smile on me:

Chorus:
There are smiles that make us happy,
There are smiles that make us blue;
There are smiles that steal away the teardrops
As the sunbeams steal away the dew;
There are smiles that have a tender meaning
That the eyes of love alone may see,
And the smiles that fill my life with sunshine
Are the smiles that you give to me.

2nd Verse:
Dearie, when you smile
Ev'rything in life's worthwhile;
Love grows fonder as we wander
Down each magic mile;
Cheery melodies
Seem to float upon the breeze;
Doves are cooing while they're wooing
In the leafy trees:

**So Dress Up Your Dollars in Khaki (and
Help Win Democracy's Fight).** L: Lister
R. Alwood; M: Richard A. Whiting.
Copyright 1918 by Jerome H. Remick &

Only mildly popular in 1917, Irving Berlin's "farewell" song, "Smile and Show Your Dimple," was
later reconstituted by the songwriter and renamed
"Easter Parade" (1933).

Co., New York.

1st Verse:
From lowland to highland,
In your land and my land,
Our warriors are marching away
To join their commanders
In France and Flanders
To help the world win in this fray.
But Uncle Sam is calling stay-at-homes, too,
For the pathway to freedom is rocky.
So prove you're a soldier by saying "Yes,"
    you!,
And dress up your dollars in khaki:

Chorus:
Oh! dress up your dollars in khaki a spell
And help in Democracy's fight.
With your nickels and dimes and quarters as
    well
You can set the whole question aright,
For the lender is freedom's defender,
But the spender's the worst of them all.
Let a War Savings Stamp send your money
    to camp
And answer the President's call.
[Ev'ry Thrift Stamp's a sign that the "Watch
    on the Rhine"
Will be wound up fore'er by fall].

[If we're there with the dough, sure the war
bread will go,
And Uncle Sam's baker can't call].
[So let's all put the "pay" into patriot today,
And turn William's Hunny to gall].

2nd Verse:
You're America's friend
When you're willing to send
All your savings to serve at the front.
But the spender sits tight
And lets his comrades fight,
He could play the game right but he won't.
It's all my little bills and it's all your bills,
too,
That will lick this "Big Bill" over there, boys;
So let's dress up our dollars in khaki, let's do!
And lick the old Kaiser for fair, boys!:

So Long, Sammy. L: Benny Davis and
Jack Yellen; M: Albert Gumble. Copy-
right 1917 by Jerome H. Remick & Co.,
New York.

1st Verse:
We're mighty proud of you, Sammy boy,
You proved that you are true, Sammy boy.
Though the time has come to part,
There's something in my heart
That seems to turn the sadness into joy.
We're sorry that you have to go,
But you won't be gone for long, I know:

Chorus:
So long, Sammy!
May good luck be your guide,
You've filled your dear old mammy's heart
with pride.
Keep smiling, Sammy,
Go and show what you can do.
We love you, Sammy boy,
Goodbye and good luck to you!

2nd Verse:
While you are over there, Sammy boy,
We know you'll do your share, Sammy boy.
There are many wrongs to right,
That's why we're in the fight,
So fight with all your might, Sammy boy!
A hundred million hearts will pray
For our faithful Sammy ev'ry day:

Soldier Boy. L: D.A. Esrom; M: Theodore Morse. Copyright 1915 by Leo Feist,
Inc., New York.

1st Verse:
You're a man that's brave and true, soldier
boy,
And I'm mighty proud of you, soldier boy;
When the bugle call, so clear,
Called for men, you answered "Here,"
With a voice so full of cheer, soldier boy!:

Chorus:
Soldier boy,
One kiss before you go, soldier boy,
I'll miss you, that you know,
Ev'ry night I'll pray for you far away,
And trust to Him above
To send you back some day.
In my heart
A love will always yearn,
And I'll wait for your return.
So go and fight for the cause you know is
right,
God bless you, my soldier boy.

2nd Verse:
Though a teardrop dims my eye, soldier boy,
With a smile I'll say goodbye, soldier boy.
For a cause so great and grand,
Side by side we all must stand;
Give our best to our homeland, soldier boy!:

Somebody's Boy. L: James E. Dempsey;
M: Joseph A. Burke. Copyright 1918 by
Jerome H. Remick & Co., New York.

1st Verse:
I watched a transport yesterday,
And as the soldiers sailed away,
I heard their sweethearts bravely cry,
"Au revoir but not goodbye."
I heard a mother murmur low,
"When duty calls, somebody's boy must go":

Chorus:
Somebody's boy
Will take a million hearts with him over
there,
Breathing a prayer.
Somebody's boy
Will add a few more threads of gray to the
hair
Of someone who'll care.
Somebody's boy
Will thrill the nation with joy;
When peace is signed,
We'll write below it,
"We owe it
To somebody's boy."

2nd Verse:
Somebody's eyes will watch in vain,
Somebody's heart will ache with pain,
Somebody's lips can only pray:
"He'll come back again some day."
Somebody's arms would thrill with joy
If they were wrapped around somebody's
  boy:

Someone Is Longing for Home Sweet Home (Thousands of Miles Away). L&M: David Berg, William Tracey, and Jack Stern. Copyright 1918 by Douglas & Newman Music Co., Inc., New York.

1st Verse:
Only a letter to Home Sweet Home
From somebody far away,
Only a boy across the foam
Dreaming of yesterday.
There's a picture that comes to his mind,
Of someone he left behind:

Chorus:
Someone is longing for Home Sweet Home
Thousands of miles away,
But he's proud to fight
For a cause that is right,
He'll battle on till the end's in sight.
And while he is sighing,
He sees someone trying
To smile through clouds of gray;
Someone is longing for Home Sweet Home
Thousands of miles away.

2nd Verse:
Only an answer from Home Sweet Home
To someone o'er the sea,
Telling a boy to keep right on
Fighting for liberty.
There's a mother who's proud of her son,
And she'll wait till the fight is won:

Somewhere in France Is Daddy. L&M: "The Great Howard" [Howard Miller]. Copyright 1917 by William J. Moran, published by Howard and LaVar Music Co., New York.

1st Verse:
A little boy was sitting on his mother's knee
  one day,
And as he nestled close to her these words
  she heard him say:
"Oh, mama dear! please tell me why our

daddy don't come home,
I miss him so and you do, too,
Why are we left alone?"
She tried hard not to cry
As she answered with a sigh:

Chorus:
"Somewhere in France is daddy,
Somewhere in France is he,
Fighting for home and country,
Fighting, my lad, for liberty.
I pray ev'ry night for the Allies,
And ask God to help them win.
For our daddy won't come back
Till the Stars and Stripes they'll tack
On Kaiser Wilhelm's flag staff in Berlin."

2nd Verse:
He put his arms around her neck and kissed
  away a tear,
And whispered to her gently, "Gee! I'm proud
  of daddy dear,
He's fighting for the U.S.A to uphold Old
  Glory's fame,
And show the world when our flag's unfurled
We fight in freedom's name."
Then she greatly gave a sigh
And made him this reply:

Somewhere in France (Is the Lily). L: Philander Johnson; M: Joseph E. Howard. Copyright 1917 by M. Witmark & Sons, New York.

1st Verse:
One day as morning shed its glow
Across the Eastern sky,
A boy and girl in accents low
In a garden said "Goodbye."
She said "Remember as you stray,
When each must do his share,
The flowers blooming here today
Are emblems over there!":

Chorus:
"Somewhere in France is the lily,
Close by the English rose,
A thistle so keen
And a shamrock green,
And each loyal flow'r that grows.
Somewhere in France is a sweetheart
Facing the battle's chance;
For the flow'r of our youth
Fights for freedom and truth
Somewhere in France."

2nd Verse:
Each morning in that garden fair,
Where sweetest perfumes dwell,
The lassie whispers low a pray'r
For the flow'rs she loves so well.
And over there as night draws near,
Amid the shot and flame,
Unto the flag he holds so dear,
A soldier breathes her name:

Sons of America (America Needs You). L:
Arthur F. Holt; M: William T. Pierson.
Copyright 1917 by W.T. Pierson & Co.,
Washington, D.C.

1st Verse:
Hark to the call, high over all!
Hark to grim war's alarms!
Our Uncle Sam, as perils befall,
Sounds the loud call, "To Arms!"
Rally, brave sons, your land to defend;
Stand to your guns and nobly contend;
You are the ones on whom we depend;
Valorous sons, "To Arms!":

Chorus:
Sons of America,
America needs you.
Protect your country's flag,
The old Red, White and Blue.
Fight for America,
Home of the free.
United stand to guard the land of liberty!

2nd Verse:
Fight for the flag, glorious flag,
Banner of stripe and star.
When it's assailed, what coward will lag?
Come with a loud hurrah,
Boldly to fight, the foeman defy,
"Freedom and Right" your rallying cry;
You are our might, on you we rely,
Sons of America!:

Stand Up and Fight Like H---. L&M:
George M. Cohan. Copyright 1918 by
Maurice Richmond Music Publishing Co.,
New York.

1st Verse:
My father was a soldier as brave as he could
    be,
But father never used to boast about his
    bravery,
But of my famous father the neighbors used

Few World War I battle songs equalled the
muscular tone of George M. Cohan's "Stand Up
and Fight Like H---," written by the acknowledged
monarch of Broadway in 1918.

    to brag
Of how he went with a regiment
And how he saved the flag.
One day says I to father, says I,
"I'm going away;
Before I go
I'd like to know if you've a word to say."
"Goodbye, my son," he murmured,
His voice was soft and low,
"Remember, son, my only one,
No matter where you go":

Chorus:
"Stand up and fight,
Fight for the Right,
Don't give the foe a chance;
Just grab a gun
And shoot the Hun,
And drive him out of France.
Show Kaiser Bill you're out to kill,
Fill him with shot and shell,
And see that he gets what's coming to him,
Stand up and fight like h---!"

2nd Verse:
There never was a Prussian or any other man
Who'd ever stand a chance to whip one good
    American;
We'll beat them with the bay'net, we'll beat
    them with the gun,

We'll beat them right if they stand and fight,
We'll catch them if they run;
We'll chase them out of Belgium,
We'll smash their fighting line;
We'll chase them helter skelter
Till they cross the River Rhine,
For once we get them going,
They'll see we're out to win,
We'll never stop until we cop
The Kaiser in Berlin!:

The Story of Old Glory, the Flag We Love.
L: J. Will Callahan; M: Ernest R. Ball.
Copyright 1916 by M. Witmark & Sons,
New York.

1st Verse:
You have read about the birth of this great
    nation,
Of how our heroes fought and bled and died,
But have you e'er been told the tale that
    ne'er grows old,
The hist'ry of our flag so glorified?
Then listen and I'll tell it now to you,
The story of the old Red, White and Blue:

Chorus:
The angels up in heaven took a fleecy cloud
    of white
And fashioned it into a banner fair,
Then striped it with the crimson of the dawn's
    eternal light,
With just a bit of sky to hold the stars a-
    gleaming there;
Then with their wings they fanned it till its
    spangled folds unfurled
In radiant splendor o'er the throne above,
Then God Almighty blessed it as He gave it
    to the world;
That's the story of Old Glory, the flag we
    love.

2nd Verse:
There's no other flag with such a holy
    mission,
No other banner given work so grand,
To wave o'er land and sea, proclaiming
    liberty,
The starry emblem of God's chosen land!
The banner of the loyal tried and true,
The flag we love, the old Red, White and
    Blue.:

Take a Letter to My Daddy "Over There."
L: Roger Lewis and Bobby Crawford; M:

Billy Baskette. Copyright 1918 by Leo
Feist, Inc., New York.

1st Verse:
He was just a youngster,
Only seven, that was all,
His daddy was a soldier who had heard his
    country's call;
This boy was mighty lonesome
Since his dad had gone away,
He whispered to the mailman when he called
    the other day:

Chorus:
"Take a letter to my daddy over there,
Tell him that each night for him I say a
    pray'r;
He's a soldier brave and true.
Tell him God will bless him, too,
'Cause he's fighting for his country
Like a hero ought to do.
Tell him that I miss him
While he's far away,
And I'm praying he'll return to me some day;
He means all the world to me,
And how happy I will be
If you only take a letter to my daddy."

2nd Verse:
"I don't know the address,
But it's out in France somewhere,
My mammy never tells me, all she says is
    'over there';
I know that you can find him
Over there across the sea,
He always wears a locket with a photograph
    of me":

The Tale the Church Bell Told. L: Sam
M. Lewis and Joe Young; M: Bert Grant.
Copyright 1918 by Waterson, Berlin &
Snyder Co., New York.

1st Verse:
In the shattered part of France,
In the very heart of France,
A soldier from a Yankee shore
Lay dreaming by an old church door;
From the belfry in the sky
He thought he heard the old bell sigh:

Chorus:
"I was lonely in my steeple,
How I missed the birds of spring;
Looking down upon my people,
It just broke my heart to ring.
Through the din of cannon thunder

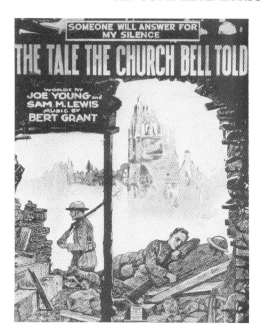

The destructiveness of war was graphically described on the cover and in this elegy to a ruined country churchyard, "The Tale the Church Bell Told" (1918).

I could hear the cries of young and old;
Someone will answer for this vi'lence,
Answer for my silence";
That's the tale the church bell tolled.

2nd Verse:
"Now the clouds have all rolled by,
Up here in a peaceful sky,
I'll ring again and then I'll see
My people coming back to me;
Ev'ry time they kneel to pray,
I'll dry their tears of yesterday":

Tell Me (Why Nights Are Lonesome). L: J. Will Callahan; M: Max Kortlander. Copyright 1919 by Lee S. Roberts; assigned to Jerome H. Remick & Co., New York.

1st Verse:
I've some questions, dear,
You can make them clear;
For your answers I am yearning
Like a schoolboy seeking learning;
Although I've searched in vain
With my might and main,
All the knowledge learned at college,
Still that don't explain:

Chorus:
Tell me why nights are lonesome,
Tell me why days are blue,
Tell me why all the sunshine
Comes just at one time
When I'm with you;
Why do I hate to go, dear,
And hate to say goodbye?
Now somehow it's always so, dear,
And if you know, dear,
Please tell me why.

2nd Verse:
Ev'ry time we meet
My heart starts to beat,
Sorrows vanish, cares go winging,
All around me birds are singing;
And when we say goodbye,
Something makes me sigh,
Life grows weary, days grow dreary,
Can you tell me why?:

That Red Cross Girl of Mine. L&M: Ed C. Cannon. Copyright 1917 by Buckeye Music Publishing Co., Columbus, Ohio.

1st Verse:
There are Sue and Jane in their uniforms
With a band around their arm;
There are girls next door and across the street
Who will keep our courage warm.
It's a sacrifice, little girl, we know,
It has won our true esteem;
On the field of service while the dark draws
    o'er us,
Our hearts just seem to sing:

Chorus:
I'll go to sleep tonight and dream
Of that Red Cross girl of mine;
She's just the kind of girl to dream of,
She's lovely, she's divine.
What chance has Kaiser Bill to win
When we have a million men in line
Who have plucky little girls to keep them
    well,
Like that Red Cross girl of mine.

2nd Verse:
Ev'ryone is called now to do their part
For the good old U.S.A.
And the girls you'll find over all the land,
They are ready, boys, today.
And we'll fight and win for we'll always
    know
They'll save those who might be lost;

For our Red Cross beauties will perform
their duties
No matter what the cost:

That's a Mother's Liberty Loan. L&M:
Mayo & Tally and Clarence Gaskill. Copy-
right 1917 by M. Witmark & Sons, New
York.

1st Verse:
There's a lonely little mother
In a lonely home tonight,
She's thinking of her soldier boy
Who marched away to fight.
Though she's only one in millions,
And she has no gold to spare,
Her tear-dimmed eyes just seem to say:
"I think I've done my share!":

Chorus:
"I gave my boy to Uncle Sam
To fight for you and me,
Just like his dad at Gettysburg
In Eighteen Sixty-Three.
If life must pay for liberty,
I'm giving all I own,
And when the battle's won
I'll then take back my son.
That's a mother's liberty loan!"

2nd Verse:
Ev'ry night this lonely mother
Has a dream that makes her sad;
She seems to see her soldier boy
When he was but a lad.
He is playing with his soldier toys,
They're scattered o'er the floor;
She never thought that some day he
Would hear the call of war:

That's the Feeling That Came Over Me.
L&M: Herbert H. Power. Copyright 1919
by Herbert H. Power, published by Cutter
Stock Co., New York.

1st Verse:
Did you ever have a feeling
That made you feel like kneeling,
To kiss the hand of ev'ry Yankee soldier
Who went away to fight
For what he knew was right
With heart of steel and gun upon his
shoulder?
Did you ever have a yearning
To see them soon returning,

So you could help to cheer when they pass
by?
That feeling surely must have come
To ev'ry mother's son,
For this is the reason why:

Chorus:
On November eleven in the morning,
It was early before the break of day,
The bells had started ringing,
The people soon were singing,
Parades were forming up and down the way.
Ev'ry step I took that day,
Something in me seemed to say,
"This world's a decent place to live in, gee!"
I wanted to shake the hand
Of ev'ry Yankee boy in the land,
For that's the feeling that came over me.

2nd Verse:
Soon the flags of ev'ry nation
Who fought for their salvation
Sprang into view to join the celebration.
Then ringing through the air
Came cries from ev'rywhere,
Democracy is safe for all creation.
Then we listened to the story
Of why our own Old Glory
Was carried to the front and there to stay.
It was to save humanity
On land and on the sea,
And that's why we're glad today:

That's What We're Fighting For. L&M:
Sgt. Clifton S. Anthony. Copyright 1918
by Clifton S. Anthony.

1st Verse:
The time has come for ev'ryone
To help to win this fight,
So do your share and send your son
For honor, liberty, and Right.
Don't listen to the traitor's words
We have no right to war,
Just tell to all who do not know
What we are fighting for:

Chorus:
To sheathe the sword that's drawn in shame,
To hold aloft our country's name,
To end the dream that Might is Right,
To flash the ray of freedom's light,
For he that bled ten million hearts
Must never have his say.
So with Old Glory unfurled,
We'll show him he can't rule the world;
That's what we're fighting for.

2nd Verse:
The years have gone and men have passed
That liberty might reign;
For those who died lift up your hearts,
For you who live will have the gain.
The time has come to end this war
And war forever more.
So tell to him who dares to ask
What are we fighting for?:

Their Hearts Are Over Here. L&M:
George M. Cohan. Copyright 1918 by
Waterson, Berlin & Snyder Co., New
York.

1st Verse:
I hear an echo clear
From over there 'way over here.
A song is in the air
'Way over there, and yet it's near.
I can hear that old melody
Like a message over the sea.
Listen, you will hear it, too,
If your fancy carries with me:
"Give my regards to Broadway,"
I can hear it plain as can be:

Chorus:
The boys are over there,
But their hearts are over here;
For they left them behind
When they softly whispered, "Goodbye,
   dear."
A song is in the air
Like a pray'r that has a tear:
"Give my regards to Broadway,"
I can hear them singing over here.

2nd Verse:
Again I hear a strain,
An old refrain, it's very plain.
I hear the echo clear
From over there 'way over here.
Just another old melody
That they're singing over the sea.
Listen, you will hear it, too,
If your fancy carries with me:
"Give my regards to Broadway,"
I can hear it plain as can be:

**There'll Be a Hot Time for the Old Men
(While the Young Men Are Away).** L:
Grant Clarke; M: George W. Meyer.
Copyright 1918 by Leo Feist, Inc., New
York.

1st Verse:
All the girls are grieving
'Cause the boys are leaving.
Gone to face the foe;
But the men of fifty,
They feel mighty nifty,
They don't have to go.
Young men are sailing ev'ry day,
Who will love the girlies while they're away?:

Chorus:
There'll be a hot time for the old men
While the young men are away.
When the young men go to France,
Oh, won't the old men have a wonderful
   chance
To raise the dickens with all the chickens,
They'll have ev'rything their way.
Now that the young men have all disap-
   peared,
Ev'ry young girl grabs a man with a beard;
[All the old men read the papers and laughed
When all the young men were caught in the
   draft];
There'll be a hot time for the old men
While the young men are away.

2nd Verse:
While the young men stayed here
They had ev'ry maid here,
Things have changed somehow.
And the real old fellow
Never was as mellow
As he is right now.
It's not very hard to figure them,
All the old men think they're young again:

**There's a Battlefield in Ev'ry Mother's
Heart.** L: Howard E. Rogers; M: M.K.
Jerome. Copyright 1918 by Waterson,
Berlin & Snyder Co., New York.

1st Verse:
I watched a mother old and gray
Read a letter from her lad,
One of the first to sail away
And leave her poor heart sad.
When I saw the tears in her dear eyes,
They made me realize:

Chorus:
There's a battle raging down in each mother's
   heart,
There's a struggle tearing it apart,
Mem'ries so tender of her boy "out there"
She won't surrender, but fights her despair.

Ev'ry message from him brings the tears to
    her eyes,
But she has to play a soldier's part;
Her head is bowed in a prayer ev'ry night,
But she is proud he is there in the fight.
Though she's far, far away
From the scene of the fray,
There's a battlefield in ev'ry mother's heart.

2nd Verse:
Each mother played a noble part
When they heard their country's call;
Although it made the teardrops start,
They gladly gave their all.
Now they wait alone and only pray
That he'll come back some day:

**There's a Little Blue Star in the Window
(and It Means All the World to Me).** L:
Paul B. Armstrong; M: F. Henri Klickmann. Copyright 1918 by Frank K. Root &
Co., Chicago.

1st Verse:
There's a little blue star in the window,
And it means all the world to me;
There is a lad who is true
To the Red, White and Blue,
And he's serving his flag o'er the sea.
But it does not reflect golden sunshine,
Never gleams in the dead of night;
In the brightness of day,
As the night wears away,
It shines with its own holy light:

Chorus:
There are stars in the high heavens shining
With a promise of hope in their light;
There are stars in the field of Old Glory,
The emblem of honor and Right.
But no star ever shone with more brightness,
    I know,
Than the one for my boy o'er the sea.
There's a little blue star in the window,
And it means all the world to me.

2nd Verse:
When the sun sinks to rest in the evening,
And the stars in the dark'ning sky
Shine with soft, tender light
Till the heavens are bright,
Then a glorious sight greets the eye;
But the brightest of stars in the heavens
Does not shine with the brilliancy
As the little one there

In the window — my prayer
For my laddie over the sea:

There's a Long, Long Trail. L: Stoddard
King; M: Zo Elliott. Copyright 1913 by
West & Co.; assigned 1915 to M. Witmark
& Sons, New York.

1st Verse:
Nights are growing very lonely,
Days are very long;
I'm a-growing weary only list'ning for your
    song;
Old remembrances are thronging through my
    memory,
Till it seems the world is full of dreams
Just to call you back to me:

Chorus:
There's a long, long trail a-winding
Into the land of my dreams,
Where the nightingales are singing
And a white moon beams;
There's a long, long night of waiting
Until my dreams all come true,
Till the day when I'll be going down
That long, long trail with you.

2nd Verse:
All night long I hear you calling,
Calling sweet and low,
Seem to hear your footsteps falling ev'ry-
    where I go,
Though the road between us stretches many
    a weary mile.
I forget that you're not with me yet,
When I think I see you smile:

There's a Picture in My Old Kit Bag.
L&M: Al Sweet. Copyright 1918 by Ted
Browne Music Co., Chicago.

1st Verse:
A soldier boy was writing home
To his mother o'er the sea,
Telling of the strange and awful sights
In this war for humanity.
He told his love for ones so dear,
How he missed them all at home,
And through her tears a mother read
These words for her alone:

Chorus:
"There's a picture in my kit bag
In a worn old leather frame,

It's as dear to me as our grand old flag
And I'll cherish it just the same.
On the long, long trail to No Man's Land,
When my weary footsteps lag,
There's a cheer all the while in my mother's
   smile
In that picture in my old kit bag."

2nd Verse:
A soldier wounded, near to death,
In the heart of No Man's Land,
There's a white-robed nurse, knelt by his side,
On his head gently laid her hand.
She raised him up into her arms
As he brushed a tear away;
His lips moved slowly as he smiled,
These words she heard him say:

There's a Red-Bordered Flag in the Window. L: Fred Ziemer; M: J.R. Shannon. Copyright 1918 by Vandersloot Music Publishing Co., Williamsport, Pa.

1st Verse:
Why are you sad, little mother,
Why do your eyes fill with tears?
Surely, some sorrow or other
Has happened to darken your years!
Is it the flag in the window,
The flag with its star of blue,
Telling a wartime story,
Breaking the heart of you?:

Chorus:
There's a red-bordered flag in our window
Hung with a tear and a prayer,
Telling of love and devotion
For the boy who is now over there.
He is fighting for our Uncle Sammy,
He is safeguarding you and me;
'Tis the emblem of a mother's love
For the land of liberty.

2nd Verse:
Just dry your tears, little mother,
Think of the others like you,
Bearing some burden or other
And serving the Red, White and Blue.
Sometime when the war is over,
Someday when our dreams come true,
You'll share a soldier's glory,
Like mothers always do:

There's a Service Flag Flying at Our House. L: Thomas Hoier and Bernie

Grossman; M: Al W. Brown. Copyright 1917 by Joe Morris Music Co., New York.

1st Verse:
See the people running,
Hear the rum-tum-tumming,
Military music fills the air;
Ev'ryone is waiting,
Hearts are palpitating,
Flags are flying ev'rywhere.
Of ev'ry allied nation
From nearly all creation,
Their banners wave from ev'ry staff and
   dome;
But the one I love to see,
That means so much to me,
Is the flag that's flying at home:

Chorus:
There's a service flag flying at our house,
A blue star in a field of red and white;
Father is so proud of what his boy has done,
There's a tear in mother's smile and she mur-
   murs, "My son";
Perhaps he may return with fame and glory,
But if by chance we lose him in the fight,
There'll be a service flag flying at our house
And a new star in heaven that night.

2nd Verse:
There beside Old Glory,
Telling all our story,
Until the end that flag is going to fly;
We are proud to show it,
Want the world to know it,
We will do or we will die.
There's a million others
Giving sons and brothers,
And proudly watch them as they march away,
And although their hearts may ache,
Although their hearts may break,
There's a million glad they can say:

There's a Vacant Chair in Ev'ry Home To-night. L: Al Bryan; M: Ernest Breuer. Copyright 1917 by Maurice Richmond Music Co., Inc., New York.

1st Verse:
In ev'ry mansion, ev'ry cottage all throughout
   the land
There's a mother's heart that's feeling blue;
Her darling boy is missing;
He has gone with sword in hand
To make the country safe for me and you.
In ev'ry mother's eye there is a tear
And on her lips a prayer, could you but hear:

Chorus:
There's a vacant chair that's waiting there
In ev'ry home tonight,
And a lonesome mother's dreaming
By the fireside burning bright.
She is thinking of her gallant boy
Who is fighting for the Right;
There's a vacant chair in ev'ry home,
In ev'ry home tonight.

2nd Verse:
She fondly gazes at his picture hanging on
   the wall;
Seems but yesterday he went away.
Her dear lips keep repeating,
"He's the bravest boy of all,
I'm lonely but I'm proud of him today."
And oft she murmurs to herself alone,
"I hope that I'll be here when he comes
   home":

**There's an Angel Missing in Heaven (She'll
Be Found Somewhere Over There).** L:
Paul B. Armstrong; M: Robert Speroy.
Copyright 1918 by Frank K. Root & Co.,
Chicago.

1st Verse:
Picture a beautiful country,
Picture a fam'ly at prayer;
Picture a crimson sun sinking low,
Contentment and peace ev'rywhere.
Then picture grim war's devastation,
The cry of a child on the air,
No sister, no brother, no father, no mother,
Desolation and grief ev'rywhere:

Chorus:
There's a Cross
And it stands for atonement,
Bringing hope to both you and to me;
There's a Cross
At the end of a string of pearls—
My Rosary, my Rosary.
There's a Cross,
A Red Cross that means mercy,
Devotion and tenderest care.
There's an angel who's missing from heaven,
She'll be found somewhere over there.

2nd Verse:
Picture the maimed and the dying,
Picture the crushing of youth;
Picture the blackness of fear, the doubt
Of virtue and Right and of truth.
Then picture this angel of mercy,

Like Bethlehem's Star in the night;
She brings us the message that God is still
   living,
And that Might will be conquered by Right:

There's Nobody Home but Me. L: Sam
Ehrlich; M: Con Conrad. Copyright 1918
by Broadway Music Corp., New York.

1st Verse:
A garden gate, a lad of eight
Dressed in a uniform of brown;
Across the way a troop that day
Were getting volunteers in town.
"Who's home with you, my boy?", they cried.
The child saluted and replied:

Chorus:
"My brother's over in the trenches,
And sister's gone to nurse out there;
While daddy's making ammunition
My mama also does her share.
I've got my uniform all ready,
A soldier boy I'd like to be.
So if you're over here for a brave volunteer,
There's nobody home but me."

2nd Verse:
A snow white bed, a curly head,
A mother kisses baby dear.
Her sleepy boy awakes with joy
And cries, "The soldier boys were here,
They came to take us all away.
And, mama, I was proud to say":

**They Can't Down the Red, White and
Blue.** L&M: G.A. Pfeiffer. Copyright 1918
by G.A. Pfeiffer, published by Academy
of Music, Middleton, Mass.

1st Verse:
By the campfire tonight I am thinking tonight
Of my mother home all alone,
And I think of the day that I started away
For the battlefield far from home.
And in fancy I see her sweet face once again,
When I kissed her goodbye, she sang this
   sweet refrain:

Chorus:
"Go fight for your own Uncle Sammy,
Stand up for the Red, White and Blue.
Remember, my boy, whate'er befalls
Your country is loyal and true.
On brave boys like you we're depending

To conquer the foe, now that's true.
So up with Old Glory,
And remember this story,
They can't down the Red, White and Blue."

2nd Verse:
Now a fight has begun, so I shoulder my gun
Midst the shrieking of shot all around,
Overhead burst a shell, first I reeled, then I fell
On my knees, then sank to the ground.
As I lay on the field with a wound in my head
I can see mother dear by my side as she said:

They're Coming Back. L&M: Sam Habelow. Copyright 1919 by Habelow & Jeffrey, Boston and New York.

Verse:
It's time for us to brag
And rave about our flag
That floats o'er Yankee land so grand;
Our boys in blue and khaki
Showed that they were plucky
When they took their stand in that foreign land;
We'll welcome them, each one,
Yes, ev'ry mother's son:

Chorus:
They're coming back,
They're coming back,
We'll go to meet them,
We'll go to greet them;
Then we'll cheer loud and clear,
For they did the job, all right!;
You can bet that Bill the Kaiser
Will be sad but wiser —
Hip, hooray! Hip, hip, hooray!
For they're the boys who won the day.
Raise your voices,
Let the echoes ring,
Ev'rybody join in and sing,
They're coming back,
They're coming back,
To their homes in the good old U.S.A.!

They're on Their Way to Germany. L&M: Halsey K. Mohr. Copyright 1917 by Shapiro, Bernstein & Co., Inc., New York.

1st Verse:
Ten million Yankee Doodle hearts have answered to the call,

Ten million hands will lift the flag and never let it fall;
A gun on ev'ry shoulder and the Stars and Stripes unfurled,
They'll follow Uncle Sammy though he lead them 'round the world;
From North and South
And East and West,
America has given of her best:

Chorus:
For they're on their way to Germany
And victory across the sea,
With a message in ev'ry gun they're coming,
Yankee Doodle is the tune that they are humming.
'Neath the Stars and Stripes they'll pave the way
To a world democracy;
And there'll be a vacant chair
In the palace over there,
For they're on their way to Germany.

2nd Verse:
The deeds of brave America all hist'ry's pages fill,
For when our flag's in danger, we have answered with a will;
The old Star-Spangled Banner and the Yankee Doodle strain
Will lead our boys to victory and bring them back again;
Our cause will be
For liberty,
And freedom of the world on land and sea:

(Though Duty Calls) It's Hard to Say Goodbye. L&M: W.R. Williams. Copyright 1917 by Will Rossiter, Chicago.

1st Verse:
There's something in the air,
You feel it everywhere;
Our country's wide awake and full of pep.
We know we're at war
And what we're fighting for.
And though the battle's hard, we'll get 'em yet;
And when our boys must go away,
We'll take 'em by the hand and say:

Chorus:
Ev'rybody knows you'll do your duty,
Ev'rybody knows your heart is true,
While you're here today
Or when you're far away.

Ev'rybody loves you through and through.
Ev'rybody knows you're making history,
Ev'rybody knows you'll do or die,
But when we come to part,
We know in ev'ry heart,
Though duty calls, it's hard to say goodbye.

2nd Verse:
There's honor for us all
To answer duty's call,
The day has come to show our real worth.
Your sense of right is clear
Or you would not be here
To represent the greatest land on earth;
And if temptation comes your way,
Just think of home and what we say:

Throw Me a Kiss (from Over the Sea). L:
Raymond B. Egan; M: Richard A. Whit-
ing. Copyright 1917 by Jerome H. Remick
& Co., New York.

1st Verse:
There's miles and miles of deep blue sea
Between your lips and mine,
And when you write a note to me,
The Censor reads each line;
He'll cross out all the crosses, dear,
That mean a loving kiss,
But we can fool the Censor yet
If you will just do this:

Chorus:
Throw me a kiss from over the sea,
Send it tonight, the Censor won't see;
Press it, caress it, address it to me, dear,
Throw me your kisses from over the sea.

2nd Verse:
The goodbye kiss you gave to me
Was my last happiness,
But love will drift across the sea
On Cupid's wireless.
Each sweet caress will seek me out
And cheer my dreams of you;
And, dear, for ev'ry kiss you throw,
I'll gladly send back two:

**Throw No Stones in the Well That Gives
You Water.** L: Arthur Fields; M: Theo-
dore Morse. Copyright 1917 by Leo Feist,
Inc., New York.

1st Verse:
Harm should be done to no man,

"Throw Me a Kiss (from Over the Sea)" was written in 1917 by frequent collaborators Raymond B.
Egan and Richard A. Whiting, who specialized in
soldier-to-sweetheart ballads.

But if harm should be done to you,
Stand up and fight,
Fight for what's right,
Then all are behind anything you do — or
    might.
And now that we're forced into battle
And liberty cries out for help,
Don't stand in the way, don't try to betray
The land that made you what you are today:

Chorus:
"Throw no stones in the well that gives you
    water"
Is a saying that's old but true;
Remember the story about the cur:
"Don't bite the hand that's feeding you."
There's a hat in the ring and if it fits you,
Put it on, there's a gun goes with it, too;
Throw no stones in the well that gives you
    water,
Come through, show us what you mean to
    do.

2nd Verse:
All lands forever united,
Democracy on ev'ry shore;
Freedom for all, answer the call,

Humanity's at stake,
Will you stand to see it fall?
So come show the world that you're ready,
Give your life for the cause that is best,
It's now up to you, but whatever you do,
Be fair and prove that you can stand the test:

Till the Work of the Yanks Is Done.

L&M: Leon DeCosta. Copyright 1917 by
International Edition Publishing Co., New
York.

1st Verse:
Do you hear that noise?
Do you hear those boys
Who are coming down the street?
And their looks so bold
Tell a story old
To the sound of marching feet.
They are volunteers,
And the ringing of cheers
Tell the world they will be "there."
There's a debt to pay,
They are on their way,
Ev'ry Yankee will do his share:

Chorus:
Keep your eyes on the boys from the U.S.A.,
Watch the Yanks do their bit in this fight;
We'll follow the flag like our fathers did,
And no longer will "Might be Right."
Let them know that the bird of America
Is a dove and an eagle in one;
We'll tramp, tramp, tramp,
Till the work of the Yanks is done.

2nd Verse:
When across the sea,
There will always be
Just one thought within our mind:
When we're through out there,
We'll come back and care
For the ones we left behind.
There's no sign of gloom,
There's no fear of doom,
There's no chance that we refuse;
And like all the rest,
We will do our best,
There is no such a word as "lose":

Till We Meet Again.

L: Raymond B.
Egan; M: Richard A. Whiting. Copyright
1918 by Jerome H. Remick & Co., New
York.

1st Verse:
There's a song in the land of the lily
Each sweetheart has heard with a sigh;
Over high garden walls
This sweet echo falls
As a soldier boy whispers goodbye:

Chorus:
"Smile the while you kiss me sad adieu,
When the clouds roll by I'll come to you;
Then the skies will seem more blue
Down in lover's lane, my dearie.
Wedding bells will ring so merrily,
Ev'ry tear will be a memory;
So wait and pray
Each night for me,
Till we meet again."

2nd Verse:
Though goodbye means the birth of a tear-
    drop,
Hello means the birth of a smile,
And the smile will erase
The tear-blighting trace
When we meet in the after-a-while:

Uncle Sammy, Take Care of My Girl.

L: Betty Morgan; M: Jimmie Morgan. Copyright 1918 by Forster Music Publisher, Inc.,
Chicago.

1st Verse:
I just saw a letter from a soldier boy
Who was sailing across the sea;
It was addressed to his Uncle Sam
And it was a soldier's plea.
I remember ev'ry word he wrote,
This is what was in his little note:

Chorus:
"Uncle Sammy, take care of my girl
While I'm over there,
Please treat her fair;
I'll do my bit and I won't mind
As long as you are kind
To the girl I left behind,
I'll be thinking of her ev'ry day.
She's more precious to me than a pearl,
And it may be some time
Before we get to the Rhine;
So, Uncle Sammy, take care of my girl."

2nd Verse:
As I sit and wonder 'bout the soldier boys
Who went sailing across the foam,
They're going over to do their best
And protect the folks back home.

Ev'ry note that comes from over there,
It reminds me of that soldier's pray'r:

Under the American Flag. L: Andrew B.
Sterling; M: Harry Von Tilzer. Copyright
1915 by Harry Von Tilzer Music Publishing
Co., New York.

1st Verse:
I've trotted all around the globe,
I've been in ev'ry clime,
I've had a thousand sweethearts
And I've had a lovely time.
And then the war broke out
And I came sailing 'cross the foam
To meet my Waterloo right here,
A girl I know down home;
My first attack met with repulse,
Then pierced by Cupid's dart,
With my two arms around her,
She surrendered me her heart:

Chorus:
No more I'll roam,
I'll build a home,
Under the American flag;
The land of honey, Honey,
Don't you hear me, Sonny?
Now I've got the girlie and I'm goin' to get
    the money,
Under the American flag.
We'll hug and kiss and also chew the rag.
A little Yankee country home with chickens
    by the score,
A little Yankee sweetheart
That I've loved since days of yore;
We'll raise a lot of vegetables and maybe
    something more,
[To sing a Yankee Doodle tune I've often
    tried before,
But since the twins have come
It seems I'm singing more and more;
And ev'ry morning they call me to rehearse
    at half-past four],
Under the American flag.

2nd Verse:
I've gazed with admiration
At the castles on the Rhine,
But there's the grand old Hudson
With its Palisades so fine;
For I'm in love with Mary,
That's my Yankee sweetheart's name.
So while they do the fighting,
We'll just sit and watch the game;
For married life's a battlefield,

And if we two must fight,
I'll not throw bombs but kisses
At the enemy each night:

Universal Peace Song (God Save Us All).
L: Al Bryan; M: Harry Tierney. Copyright
1917 by Jerome H. Remick & Co., New
York.

1st Verse:
The tramp of armies marching
Now shakes the earth again,
Two years they have been fighting all in vain.
Ten million men have fallen,
Ten thousand more each day,
For ev'ry one a mother kneels to pray.
The burden of her prayer just seems to say:

Chorus:
When England, France, and Germany
Will advance in peace and harmony;
Friends on the land,
Friends on the sea,
Noble and grand,
And contented and free;
When love will rule this whole creation,
And the world will be one happy nation,
Singing heart to heart and hand to hand,
United to stand or to fall,
Then we'll all get together and loudly sing,
"God save us all."

2nd Verse:
What matters now who caused it,
What matters who's to blame,
The burden of each prayer should be the
    same.
It's time to stop the slaughter
And lay their swords away;
Let's hope and pray that God will speed the
    day
When love will come to rule the world for
    aye:

The U.S.A. Will Lay the Kaiser Away.
L&M: Jacob Dettling and Charles Roy
Cox. Copyright 1918 by Buckeye Music
Publishing Co., Columbus, Ohio.

1st Verse:
The Kaiser had a big idea that he could lick
    the world
And be a mighty ruler over all;
Some forty years preparing never did the
    Kaiser dream

That someday he would take a mighty fall;
He struck at Belgium, England, Russia,
    France, and Italy,
And forced into the war the U.S.A.
Now America will use her mighty strength
    across the sea,
I know that you are with me when I say:

1st Chorus:
Old Kaiser Bill will have to swallow some pill
And bury with him autocracy;
It's up to Yankee Doodle, so they say,
To make the world safe for democracy.
Kaiser Bill has gone just a little too far,
That's all Uncle Sam has to say,
For the U.S.A. is in the war to stay,
'Till the Kaiser is laid away.

2nd Verse:
The great U.S. conscription and the Liberty
    Loan bond
Was one almighty blow to Kaiser Bill,
And when he heard about the Red Cross
    millions for defense,
He got right busy making out his will.
He sees his monarchy is getting weaker every
    day,
The handwriting he reads upon the wall;
And he knows unless he gives himself up to
    the U.S.A.,
He'll have to take his medicine, that's all:

2nd Chorus:
Our guns will roar and our great airplanes
    will soar,
We'll march to Berlin in the spring;
We'll win our way and you'll soon see the
    day
When everlasting peace on earth we'll bring.
We will take the germ out of old Germany,
Old Glory will soon lead the way,
For the U.S.A. is in the war to stay,
'Till the Kaiser is laid away.

Victory. L&M: Nicholas Colangelo. Copyright 1918 by Nicholas Colangelo, Providence, R.I.

1st Verse:
I hear the bugles calling the boys of all the
    nations
To fight across the ocean, give us peace and
    freedom's right;
The Allies fought great battles to beat the
    Huns so hated,
But now it's up to Uncle Sam to fight.

Cheer up, dear boys, great sons of God,
The Yankee boys are coming
To help you 'long to win this war
And send the Kaiser home.
Nations so great are fighting,
Heroes brave are crying,
"When shall we see our peaceful Home
    Sweet Home?":

Chorus:
There's a new star in heaven called Victory,
It's the emblem of Red, White and Blue;
Uncle Sam sent across Yankee boys to fight,
To beat Kaiser, the devil, some day.
Fly, dear Old Glory, far up in the sky,
Lead us to final victory;
There's a new star in heaven called Victory,
The whole world will bless you, U.S.A.

2nd Verse:
The war is on in Europe, they fight to do all
    justice,
United States, Great Britain, France, and
    Italy fight there.
Some thousands now are dying while millions
    more are starving,
That's what the Allies fight for ev'rywhere.
Wake up, O slaves, you'll soon be free,
We'll strike the vital blow now,
Let's all be proud, the war'll be won
When we send the Kaiser home.
Then we can see peace coming
When Kaiser Bill's defeated;
Keep all the home-fires lit 'till we come home:

Wake Me Early, Mother Dear. L: Alex Sullivan; M: Arthur Lamont. Copyright 1918 by Al Piantadosi & Co., Inc., New York.

1st Verse:
In the twilight's soft glow
A little tot, three or so,
Said, "Mother dear, I am ready to go";
And when she asked her darling, "Where?"
He proudly answered, "Over there";
And as she stroked his curly head,
Her little soldier said:

Chorus:
"Wake me early, won't you, mother dear,
Tomorrow I must say goodbye;
Last night I dreamt dear daddy called me
Far across the sea,
And I must go
'Cause he can't come home to me.

I'll bring a kiss from you to daddy dear,
So mother, don't you cry;
Just pack the things I'll take,
And if I'm gone before you wake,
Mother dear, goodbye."

2nd Verse:
As the sandman's dream ship
Went from its white pillow slip,
Goldenlocks sailed on a wonderful trip;
And what he saw across the sea
Is all a dreamland mystery;
But when next morn the clock struck ten,
He came back home again:

War Babies. L: Ballard MacDonald and
Edward Madden; M: James F. Hanley.
Copyright 1916 by Shapiro, Bernstein &
Co., Inc., New York.

1st Verse:
Forsaken, alone, amid tumbled-down stone
In the dust of what once was a home,
Two little tots lay as the close of the day
Cast its shadow o'er heaven's blue dome.
From afar in the gloom
Came the cannon's dull boom,
The roar of its shells filled the air,
And it lulled them to rest,
Tightly held to the breast
Of the mother who died for them there:

Chorus:
Little war babies, our hearts ache for you,
Where will you go to, and what will you do?
Into a world full of sorrow you came,
Homeless and helpless, no one knows your
   name.
Gone is the mother love tender and true,
Gone is your dear daddy, too;
But you'll share in the joys
Of our own girls and boys,
War babies, we'll take care of you.

2nd Verse:
While sitting some night by your fireside
   bright,
With the children you love and adore,
Just let your thoughts roam to that tumbled-
   down home,
That once stood in the pathway of war;
As the vision appears,
You can see through your tears
The two little tots all alone;
Will you wait till they plead
For the things that they need?
Just suppose those two babes were your own:

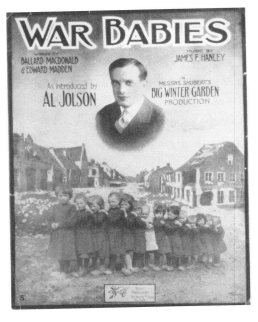

Another Al Jolson hit song, "War Babies" (1916),
promised that Belgian children orphaned by the
war would be cared for by sympathetic Americans.

**(Watch, Hope and Wait) Little Girl ("I'm
Coming Back to You").** L: Lew Brown;
M: Will Clayton. Copyright 1918 by Broad-
way Music Corp., New York.

1st Verse:
Dearie, I can hardly write,
I'm so overjoyed tonight;
Oh! what wondrous news,
No more cause for blues;
All the world looks bright,
In my dreams I now can see
Happy days for you and me;
Though I'm here, have no fear,
For it's all over, dear:

Chorus:
Watch, little girl, and hope, little girl,
And wait, little girl, for me;
Smile, little girl, all the while, little girl,
Though I'm across the sea.
Give my love to ma,
Say "hello" to pa;
I'm not there but, dear, I know
How overjoyed you are.
It means, little girl, that our dreams, little
   girl,
Are surely coming true;
We have won, little girl,

Our duty's done, little girl,
I'm coming back to you.

2nd Verse:
We'll stroll down the lane once more
As we did in days of yore,
And we'll climb the hill
Leading to the mill
Like we did before.
There's a little cottage there,
Roses blooming ev'rywhere,
In the spring birds will sing,
And wedding bells will ring:

'Way Back Home in Dear America. L&M:
Laura H. Rathbone. Copyright 1918 by
Laura Harney Rathbone, Kenilworth, Ill.

1st Verse:
It's a long way back to old America,
To the only girl I long to see,
To that little old home town
And a girl with eyes of brown
Who is waiting there for me.
Though 'tis many miles away,
I am going back some day
To the girl who is all the world to me,
To that country o'er the sea,
Sweetest land of liberty,
For she is waiting there for me:

Chorus:
'Way back home in dear America
There's a girl I long to see,
'Way back home in dear America,
There my heart would be.
'Way back home in dear America,
Far across the stormy sea,
'Way back home in dear America
She is waiting there for me.

2nd Verse:
It's a long way back to old America,
But my longing heart is oft'times there;
For no matter where I roam,
There is no place like home,
Where I never knew a care.
With the girl you love the best,
In that little old home nest —
Oh, she's the only girl I long to see,
For she's loyal and she's true
To our flag red, white and blue,
And to our boys on land and sea:

**We Are Hitting the Trail Through No
Man's Land (and We'll Soon Be Coming**

Home). L&M: Corp. Leon Britton and
Pvt. Walter B. Cooper. Copyright 1918 by
Holmes Music House, Inc., Middletown,
N.Y.

1st Verse:
We leave our dear homes to fight for liberty
And land of the brave and free;
We will win this war like those who have
    before,
Hurrah for democracy!
We will fight for the Right and conquer,
Lead on till the dawn of that day!
We'll be faithful to the man,
We must, we will, we can!
We will win, that's why we say:

Chorus:
We are hitting the trail through No Man's
    Land,
And we'll soon be coming home,
When we've conquered the Hun and the
    vict'ry is won,
We will no longer roam.
We will carry our flag through the streets of
    Berlin
And hang it on the Kaiser's dome.
We're hitting the trail through No Man's
    Land,
And we'll soon be coming home.

2nd Verse:
Our vict'ry is near, may God give us cheer
To lead till that one great day,
When the battles won shall honor ev'ry son
Of the dear old U.S.A.
For it's peace unto all till Judgment
Calls us to that unknown land;
With our hands across the sea,
Firmly held with all that's free,
Then united we will stand:

**We Don't Know Where We're Going (but
We're on Our Way).** L&M: W.R. Wil-
liams. Copyright 1917 by Will Rossiter,
Chicago.

1st Verse:
Goodbye, ev'rybody,
My country's calling me,
The time has come when ev'ryone
Must fight for liberty;
Our Uncle Sam's in trouble,
Today I got a hunch,
That I'm all fit
To do my bit,
And so I joined the bunch:

Chorus:
We don't know where we're going,
But we're on our way;
We're out to make a showing for the U.S.A.;
There's goin' to be a hot time for us some
 fine day,
We don't know where we're going,
But we're on our way.

2nd Verse:
Goodbye, ev'rybody,
My duty's calling me,
The cause is just and fight we must
For all humanity;
We'll follow dear Old Glory,
We're with you to a man;
When we begin,
We're out to win,
It's up to Uncle Sam:

We Don't Want the Bacon (What We Want Is a Piece of the Rhine). L&M: "Kid" Howard Carr, Harry Russell, and Jimmie Havens. Copyright 1918 by Harry Russell, Chicago, Ill.; assigned 1918 to Shapiro, Bernstein & Co., Inc.

1st Verse:
If you have read your hist'ry,
Then you're bound to know
That we have always held our own with any
 foe;
We've always brought the bacon home,
No matter what they've done.
But we don't want the bacon now,
We're out to get the Hun:

Chorus:
We don't want the bacon,
We don't want the bacon,.
What we want is a piece of the Rhine;
We'll crown Bill the Kaiser with a bottle of
 Budweiser,
We'll have a wonderful time.
Old Wilhelm the Gross will shout, "Vas iss
 los,"
When we hit that Hindenberg line,
FINE!
We don't want the bacon,
We don't want the bacon,
What we want is a piece of the Rhine.

2nd Verse:
When first this war began,
They said we had no chance;
They couldn't figure how we'd get our men

to France.
But they will soon discover
Uncle Sam is out to win;
We've got the Fritzies on the run,
We're headed for Berlin:

We Will Win the War of '17. L&M: George B. Pitman. Copyright 1917 by Innella-Pitman Music Publishing Co., Boston.

1st Verse:
Battles were lost and battles won
In other years gone by.
In our country's wars
Many a mother's son
Went fighting to win or die;
And hist'ry tells us today
Of vict'ries won by the U.S.A.:

Chorus:
We were at war in the year Seventy-Six,
Fighting for liberty.
Amid shot and shell many brave heroes fell,
But we won a great victory.
In the war of Ninety-Eight,
Now I'm proud to relate,
We were the victor and all was serene.
And our grandfathers won in the war of
 Sixty-One,
And we will win in the war of Seventeen.

2nd Verse:
Just look up hist'ry any day
And you will surely see
That in all the wars
Of the U.S.A.
They have won a victory.
And all of us know right now
That we will win in this war somehow:

Welcome Home. L: Bud Green; M: Edward G. Nelson. Copyright 1918 by A.J. Stasny Music Co., New York.

1st Verse:
Skies of gray have given way to brightness,
Hearts that once were sad are feeling gay;
The news has flashed around,
Our boys are homeward bound,
And we'll be there to meet them just to say:

Chorus:
Welcome home,
The day of peace on earth is here;
Welcome home,

What words of cheer!
We've kept our home-fires a-burning while
  yearning for you;
Your vacant chair is waiting, too, you know.
Welcome home,
Each mother's heart sings out with joy;
Welcome home,
My soldier boy!
And now that all the war clouds safely have
  passed,
And God has brought me sunshine at last,
Oh! welcome, welcome,
You are welcome home!

2nd Verse:
Ev'ry mother's waiting for her loved one,
Ev'ry sweetheart's waiting at the pier;
Each baby will be glad
To see her fighting dad,
And this whole nation's proud to see you
  here:

Welcome Home. L&M: Daisy M. Pratt
Erd. Copyright 1919 by Daisy M. Erd, New
York.

1st Verse:
Sound the bugle, they're coming home,
The boys of the U.S.A.!
To foreign shore we sent them,
With pride they sailed away;
They met the foe and conquered,
Humanity set free.
We welcome to our shores today
Our boys of victory:

Chorus:
Welcome, welcome to your own home town,
Welcome to the U.S.A.!
With tears we sent you from our side,
With tears we welcome you today.
Ev'rybody's here to celebrate
Your coming from afar,
Welcome Blue and Khaki!
Welcome from the war!

2nd Verse:
From the trenches across the foam
The boys return today,
With colors flying proudly
They come back from the fray.
Attention! See Old Glory
Has set the whole world free
And waves a welcome to our boys,
Brave lads of liberty!:

**Welcome Home, Laddie Boy, Welcome
Home.** L: Will D. Cobb; M: Gus Ed-
wards. Copyright 1918 by M. Witmark &
Sons, New York.

1st Verse:
What's that noise? That's our boys
A-marching up the street;
Grab your bonnet, Kate,
Hurry, don't be late,
You must be there your boys to greet.
Oh, goodbye and luck be with you, laddie
  boy,
That's what we sang as they marched away,
But now they've won their share of glory,
And come back to tell the story;
Let this be our song today:

Chorus:
Welcome home, laddie boy, welcome home,
To the arms you left for arms across the
  foam,
To the one you loved the strongest on that
  parting day,
To the one you kissed the longest when you
  marched away.
But now you're home again, home again,
Never more to roam again;
Here's the way I feel about it,
From the roof I want to shout it,
Welcome home, laddie boy, welcome home!

2nd Verse:
How's it feel when your heel
Hits your own hometown street;
Kinda good, I guess,
Well, I should say yes;
It's Uncle Sammy's turn to treat,
And the best he's got he'll give you, laddie
  boy!
But that's not any too good for you,
For you've upheld his starry banner;
In the well-known Yankee manner,
You've shown all the world who's who:

**We'll All Be Glad to See You When It's
Over.** L: Clyde N. Kramer; M: R.G.
Gradi. Copyright 1918 by Kramer and
Gradi; published by Knickerbocker Music
Co., Dayton, Ohio.

Verse:
I got a letter yesterday,
It must have lingered on the way,
For it was written sometime in early fall;
It was from a distant shore

Where folks are all in war,
And from a pal to whom I'd give my all.
Of all the good things he relates
He says the boys all miss the States,
And says they speak of us by night and day;
Today I took my pen in hand
And I have sent to No Man's Land
A word of good cheer which reads this way:

Chorus:
"We'll all be glad to see you when it's over,
You'll be welcome back to Yankeeland,
'Cause ev'rybody loves you,
Even Rover cries each day to lick your loving
    hand.
Just do your best and soon you'll be in
    clover,
Don't forget to write whene'er you can,
May we very soon expect you,
And the good Lord protect you;
We'll all be glad to see you when it's over."

**We'll Do Our Share (While You're Over
There).** L: Lew Brown and Al Harriman;
M: Jack Egan. Copyright 1918 by Broad-
way Music Corp., New York.

1st Verse:
Ev'ryone wants a little sunshine,
And we can make it come to stay,
If we all help at one time,
We'll drive the clouds away;
Mothers are smiling though they're longing
For those who are away,
I know of one who wrote to her son,
Hear what she had to say:

Chorus:
"I'm over here, you're over there,
And ev'ry night I say this prayer:
Though I cannot be there
To bear your troubles and care,
I hope you'll do your share,
It will comfort me so.
You'll always be
My baby to me.
In dreams I seem to see
You back on my knee.
You know the vict'ry must be won,
And it's up to you, my son,
We'll do our share
While you're over there."

2nd Verse:
Picture the boy who gets the letter,
He starts to read, "My darling boy,"

Then he feels so much better.
His heart just fills with joy,
Knowing his mother doesn't worry,
Knowing we're with him, too;
By candlelight he reads each night
Her letters through and through:

We'll Fight for Each Star in the Flag.
L&M: Thomas H. McDonald. Copyright
1917 by F.B. Haviland Publishing Co.,
Inc., New York.

1st Verse:
There's a flag that we love, it's the Red,
    White and Blue,
As it waves o'er the land and the sea,
For each star and each bar in Old Glory so
    fair
Has a meaning for you and for me.
Its color of white stands for all that is right,
Protecting the weak 'gainst the strong,
And the red is a signal of danger to all
Who would dare offer insult or wrong:

Chorus:
There's a star in the flag for each state that
    we have,
And we all love the Red, White and Blue;
For each stripe of the white has a meaning to
    me,
And its blue has a meaning to you.
Its color of red means the blood that we shed
That we might be free, and we proudly brag
That each stripe there was fixed back in
    Seventy-Six,
And we'll fight for each star in the flag.

2nd Verse:
Now the Stars and the Stripes with its colors
    so bright
We will follow where e'er it may guide,
For its color of blue means a purpose that's
    true
In a cause for which thousands have died.
Where e'er it may be on the land or the sea
It must be respected by all,
For no yellow is found in the flag that we
    love,
Ev'ry bluff we'll be ready to call:

**We'll Have Peace on Earth and Even in
Berlin.** L: James A. Flanagan; M: Thomas
J. Flanagan. Copyright 1917 by Thomas J.
Flanagan Music Publishing Co., Syracuse,
N.Y.

1st Verse:
Hark! hear the bugle calling,
Calling for you and for me
To uphold the honor and glory of our homes
In the land of the free.
We'll do the same as our forefathers did
A hundred years ago,
And just like the rest,
We'll try and do our best,
And march upon the foe:

Chorus:
Just a million strong, we're going to march
   along
To fight for liberty;
We'll play "Yankee Doodle" on the Kaiser's
   noodle
When we reach old Germany,
For the sons of dear Old Glory have never
   failed to win.
When our boys begin to shout,
"Kaiser Wilhelm, this way out!",
We'll have peace on earth and even in Berlin.
[When the German folks get wise,
They'll take Wilson's good advice
And they'll drive Kaiser Wilhelm from
   Berlin].

2nd Verse:
And when the battle's over
And we have peace over there,
All nations then can be thankful
That our old Uncle Sam did his share.
He's there to fight for a cause that is right
And freedom through the land;
Our cause we've attained,
And liberty we've gained,
We'll remember this refrain:

**We'll Keep Things Going Till the Boys
Come Home (Won't We, Girls?).** L: Andrew B. Sterling; M: Alfred Solman. Copyright 1917 by Joe Morris Music Co., New York.

1st Verse:
Listen, girls, it's up to us,
We've got a lot to do,
The boys are going over
And they'll stay till they get through.
And now's the time for ev'ry girl
To show her Yankee grit,
For ev'ry girl must do her little bit;
They'll tell us that we can't, we know we can,
And a girl will take the place of ev'ry man:

1st Chorus:
We'll keep things going till the boys come,
Won't we, girls?
Bet your life ev'ry sweetheart and wife
Will do her bit for Yankee Doodle;
We'll take care of all the boodle,
Won't we, girls?
You bet your life.
Mother's taking father's job,
He was a steeplejack,
She wears a pair of overalls
That button up the back;
And she'll have a ripping time some day
When she climbs up a stack!
But we'll keep things going till the boys come
   home.

2nd Verse:
Listen girls, we'll cast aside
The paint and powder puff,
The girl behind the plow's the thing,
Although the work is rough.
We'll keep the fact'ries running,
We'll make ammunition, too,
And ev'ry boat will have a lady crew.
There'll be a girl conductress on each car,
And, by jingos!, there'll be ladies tending
   bar:

2nd Chorus:
We'll keep things going till the boys come
   home,
Won't we girls?
Bet your life ev'ry sweetheart and wife
Will do her bit for Yankee Doodle,
Show the world we've got some noodle,
Won't we, girls?
You bet your life.
Aunt Priscilla, just to show
She couldn't hold aloof,
Now runs an elevator,
Isn't that sufficient proof?
And the other night she got mixed up
And ran it through the roof!
But we'll keep things going till the boys come
   home.

**We'll Knock the Heligo — Into Heligo —
Out of Heligoland! (March).** L: John O'Brien; M: Theodore Morse. Copyright 1917 by Leo Feist, Inc., New York.

1st Verse:
The bos'n blew and a Yankee crew
Had stopped to hear him say,
"My Lads, get under way,

We're leaving port today, hooray!
We're going to meet the German fleet
And blow them inside out."
Each sailor boy was filled with joy,
And all began to shout:

Chorus:
"We're on our way to Heligoland
To get the Kaiser's goat,
In a good old Yankee boat
Up the Kiel Canal we'll float;
I'm a son-of-a-gun, if I see a Hun
I'll make him understand.
We'll knock the Heligo into Heligo,
Out of Heligoland, Yip!"

2nd Verse:
The anchor's hauled as the captain called,
The crew are standing by;
Each man to do or die,
When shells begin to fly, goodbye!
"We're going to go and let them know
We hit with all our might;
I'd like to bet when we have met
They'll know they had a fight!":

We'll Lick the Kaiser If It Takes Us Twenty Years. L&M: Ralph L. Grosvenor. Copyright 1918 by Ralph L. Grosvenor, published by Minute Men, New York.

1st Verse:
We're in the fight, we're in the right,
We will back up our flag in the world!
And the day has come when we'll show the Hun
We're made of stuff he cannot put his feet upon!
We all, both great and small,
Will fight for liberty!
Sing the Kaiser's knell with our shot and shell,
That all men may be free:

Chorus:
We'll lick the Kaiser if it takes us twenty years,
We'll lick the Kaiser though it be through pain and fears.
There's a call for us to fight,
And we know we're in the right;
There is nothing that can stop us now we're in.
We'll get you, William, if it takes us to Berlin,
Your bloomin' propaganda! It can never win.

We will treat our captives well,
But we'll fight like fiends in hell,
And we'll lick him if it takes ten thousand years!

2nd Verse:
We've got to win! We've got to win!
If we die we will die in the fight!
Ev'ry man of us knows the cause is just,
We'll strike, we'll fight,
We'll stand by what we know is right!
We're in this world to live,
With freedom it must be!
We will stand no rule from that Potsdam fool,
This world is for the free:

We'll Make the Germans All Sing "Yankee Doodle Doo." L: David M. Kinnear; M: Gerrit B. Fisher. Copyright 1918 by David M. Kinnear, published by Capital City Music Bureau, Albany, N.Y.

1st Verse:
Now then, go forward, boys, so strong and brave and true,
And we are sure you'll win the fight,
For you are in the fray
And France and England say
That they both know that you're all right.
So march along, heads high, and shoulder arms so proud,
And do your bit with all your might.
Just give the Kaiser, Bill, a good old lively time,
And show him how the Yankees fight!:

Chorus:
We're going over there, we're going through the air,
We're going to fight for the Red, White and Blue.
We'll make that bloomin' Kaiser pack up and run,
And we will teach a Yankee song to ev'ry Hun.
For when we reach Berlin and Old Bill's let us in,
And all the Teutons stand in line,
They've got to learn it,
They've got to sing it, too,
We'll make the Germans all sing "Yankee Doodle Doo"!

2nd Verse:
We know there's just one thing that you will surely do

When on Old Bill you get the drop;
You'll make that butcher Hun pick up his
   tools and run,
For you will chase him o'er the top.
Go right on to Berlin,
You're surely going to win,
And make the Kaiser hock his crown;
And when you come back home, your
   welcome will be great
In ev'ry good old U.S.A. town:

We're All with You, Dear America. L&M:
Lew Schaeffer and Phil Leventhal. Copy-
right 1917 by Lew Schaeffer Music Co.,
New York.

1st Verse:
We're with you, strong for you, Uncle
   Sammy,
With that spirit of do or die;
We are surely with you, dear Sammy,
We'll be there with a steady eye.
We're with you, right or wrong,
One hundred million strong:

Chorus:
We're all with you, dear America,
And we'll do just as you say;
We're all with you, dear America,
Now that you are in this fray.
O'er the top we will go for you,
Even if what Sherman said was true.
We're all with you, dear America,
Three cheers for the Red, White and Blue!

2nd Verse:
We will fight for our right, Uncle Sammy,
With that spirit of Sevn'ty-Six;
We'll go over for you, dear Sammy,
With the foe we will gladly mix.
Been with you, right or wrong,
And for you we are strong:

We're Bound to Win with Boys Like You.
L&M: James Kendis, James Brockman,
and Nat Vincent. Copyright 1918 by
Kendis-Brockman Music Co., Inc., New
York.

1st Verse:
I saw a gray-haired mother
Kiss her soldier boy goodbye,
Though in her heart a sigh,
Not a teardrop dimmed her eye;
He'd just received his orders,

It was time to march away,
And in that last fond moment
I heard her proudly say:

1st Chorus:
"It was boys like you at Valley Forge with
   Washington,
And boys like you were Minute Men at Lex-
   ington;
You built up this wonderful nation and then,
When Lincoln called for volunteers, you
   answered again.
It was boys like you who fought with Grant
   and Sherman,
And with Lee 'way down in Dixie, too;
And this will always be
A land of liberty,
For we're bound to win with boys like you!"

2nd Verse:
"We've read on hist'ry's pages
Of the deeds our sons have done,
So it's up to ev'ryone now
To go and get the Hun.
You're in the fight for freedom,
And your cause is just and right;
When you return from vict'ry,
We'll cheer with all our might":

2nd Chorus:
"It was boys like you with Farragut's flotilla,
It was boys like you with Dewey at Manilla,
And with boys rough and ready you took
   San Juan Hill,
Whenever you were needed you have shown
   Yankee skill.
It was boys like you who answered Woodrow
   Wilson,
And are fighting now with Pershing, too.
We've never known defeat,
And hist'ry will repeat,
For we're bound to win with boys like you!"

We're Fighting for Liberty. L&M: C.
Walter Wallace. Copyright 1918 by C.
Walter Wallace, Williamsport, Pa.

1st Verse:
Now our khaki boys are 'cross the ocean,
Soon they'll have the Germans in commotion.
Ev'ry Kaiser's son will soon be on the run
From break of day until the set of sun;
And they will be sorry they are in it,
For we'll keep them jumping ev'ry minute,
For our Yankee boys are not a set of toys,
Just watch them spoil the Kaiser's joys:

1st Chorus:
Oh, we are going, yes, we are going
To fight for our democracy,
From Alabama, Louisiana and Carolinas and
    Kentucky,
From the New Englands and Pennsylvania,
New York, New Jersey, Tennessee.
Oh, we are fighting by the millions,
And their submarines can't stop us,
For we'll fight for liberty!

2nd Verse:
Old Bill Kaiser says we have tin soldiers,
He don't know about our iron moulders
And our foundry men and all our mining
    men
That number by the millions in our land.
And he says we have a wooden navy.
And our aviators are but babies.
In the months that's few our khaki boys so
    true,
Will show him a thing or two:

2nd Chorus:
Oh, we are going, yes, we are going
To fight for our democracy,
From California and Minnesota and from
    Montana and Mississippi,
From Indiana and the Dakotas,
From ev'ry state from sea to sea.
Oh, we are going to fight the Hohenzollerns
Until they are conquered
And we have our liberty.

**We're Going Over the Top (and We'll Be
Marching Through Berlin in the Morning).**
L&M: Andrew B. Sterling, Bernie Grossman, and Arthur Lange. Copyright 1918
by Joe Morris Music Co., New York.

1st Verse:
The boys out in the trenches have a song you
    never heard,
They wrote it going over, ev'ry man put in a
    word;
The colonel sent a copy just to give us all a
    chance
To see just how it goes.
The melody just flows,
And here's the song they sing all over France:

Chorus:
"We're going over the top,
We're going over the top,
We're going O-V-E-R the top!
When they hear that Yankee cheer,

Then they'll know that the gang's all here.
And we'll never stop (I'll bet you),
We'll never stop
Until we all go over the top!
While the boys back home are waltzing
With the girls we left behind,
We'll be marching through Berlin in the
    morning.
[While the folks back home are hanging
Out their weekly wash to dry,
We'll be hanging the Kaiser in the morning].
[While they're canning corn and sending
Comfort kits to keep us cute,
We'll be kaning the Kaiser in the morning]."

2nd Verse:
The colonel wrote and asked me if I'd sing it
    high and low,
And teach the boys the chorus over here
    before they go.
Just picture Bill the Kaiser when he hears ten
    million strong
Out there in No Man's Land,
Led by a Yankee band,
Rise up and sing the chorus of this song:

**We're Going to Celebrate the End of War
in Ragtime (Be Sure That Woodrow Wilson Leads the Band).** L&M: Coleman
Goetz and Jack Stern. Copyright 1915 by
Shapiro, Bernstein & Co., Inc., New York.

1st Verse:
Ev'rybody's asking when
We will be at peace again,
Ev'rybody wants prosperity;
I hear many people say
"Lay the sword and gun away,"
But they're still fighting 'cross the sea;
The end must come, it's true,
That's why I say to you:

Chorus:
We're going to celebrate the end of war in
    ragtime,
Ev'ry nation soon will sing in ragtime,
England, France and Germany,
Even folks from Italy.
The aristocrats and the diplomats,
Marching arm in arm,
See them tip their hats
To a raggy melody so pretty;
Ev'rywhere there's harmony.
So when we celebrate the end of war in
    ragtime,
Be sure that Woodrow Wilson leads the band.

2nd Verse:
Ev'ryone will feel so gay,
There'll be one long holiday,
When each nation claims neutrality;
There'll be lots of waving flags,
Waving to the raggy rags,
Each one will have their liberty.
With peace in ev'ry land,
I trust you'll understand:

We're Going to Hang the Kaiser (Under the Linden Tree). L&M: James Kendis and James Brockman. Copyright 1917 by Kendis-Brockman Music Co., Inc., New York.

1st Verse:
Have you heard the news? Have you heard the news?
The news that's going all around
Chase away the blues,
The weary, weary blues;
Our Yankee boys are Berlin bound.
Somebody has been fooling with the deck,
Somebody's goin' to get it in the neck:

Chorus:
We're going to hang the Kaiser under the linden tree,
Under the linden tree over in Germany;
We'll take along a clever little bumble bee
To sting him, to sting him upon the helmet,
The helmet, the Kaiser!
Tramp, tramp, tramp, the boys are marching
To fight for peace and for democracy;
We'll trim his moustache nice and neat
And then we'll cut off his retreat,
[We've never lost a battle yet
And we won't lose this one, you bet],
And [We'll] hang him under the linden tree.

2nd Verse:
If the rope should break, if the rope should break,
We won't send him very far.
He will take a trip,
A lovely little trip,
Where he can play with Nick, the Czar.
Somebody has been bragging much too much,
Somebody we know surely is in dutch:

We're Going to Take the Germ Out of Germany. L: Arthur J. Lamb; M: Frederick V. Bowers. Copyright 1917 by Frederick V. Bowers, Inc., Music Publishers, New York.

1st Verse:
There's a song the boys are singing ev'rywhere,
You can hear the echoes ringing over there;
It must be right for it can't be wrong,
They sing this song as they march along:

Chorus:
"We're going to take the germ out of Germany,
And a happy land 'twill be;
We're going to take the germ out of Germany,
As all the world will see.
Sweet flowers will bloom when the cannons boom,
Eternal peace will be planned,
And when we take the germ out of Germany,
They'll all love the Fatherland."

2nd Verse:
Though they think we may blunder, we don't care,
You can bet the Germans wonder over there;
But they'll find out, as they will see,
We're fighting the cause of liberty:

We're with You, Boys, We're with You! L: L.M. Townsend; M: J.B. Walter. Copyright 1918 by Oliver Ditson Co., Boston.

1st Verse:
All of us are in this war,
At home and "over there,"
And all of us are fighting
For the thing that's fair and square.
Over here we pledge again
That we will faithful be
To all our gallant fighting men
So far across the sea:

Chorus:
We're with you, boys, we're with you
When far away you fight!
We're mighty blue for lack of you,
But don't forget we're back of you.
We're with you, boys, we're with you
To prove the might of Right;
So don't forget we're back of you
With heart and mind and might!

2nd Verse:
All of us are in this war,
And in this war to stay!

And all of us are fighting
For the things for which we pray!
Over here we'll wage our fight
With hearts across the foam,
Till flying Vict'ry's banner bright
Our boys come sailing home!:

What a Wonderful Dream (It Would Be).
L&M: Charles K. Harris. Copyright 1918
by Chas. K. Harris, New York.

1st Verse:
Ev'ry home in the nation,
No matter what station,
Some brave boy has answered the call.
While their mothers have blessed them,
Have kissed and caressed them,
Yet smilingly gave up their all:

Chorus:
What a wonderful, wonderful dream it
    would be
If our laddie boys came sailing home,
With their bright, smiling faces,
No scars and no traces of dark, weary nights
    spent alone.
What a wonderful, wonderful dream it would
    be
If the mothers could live just to see
Their boys safe at home sleeping,
No heartaches or weeping,
What a wonderful, wonderful dream.

2nd Verse:
'Cross the sea men are slaying,
Back home mothers are praying
The good angels guard her brave boy,
While she reads of the battle
Where shot and shell rattle,
The battle which may end her joy:

**What an Army of Men We'd Have (If
They Ever Drafted the Girls).** L&M: Al
Piantadosi and Jack Glogau. Copyright
1918 by Al Piantadosi & Co., Inc., New
York.

1st Verse:
"We're not prepared" was all we heard a year
    ago or so,
But you don't feel that way today, and that
    of course I know,
So when you consider, then,
That we've raised two million men,
Tell me, did you ever stop to think:

1st Chorus:
What an army of men we'd have
If they ever drafted the girls;
There'd be no work laws in sight,
Each old man would insist that he'd fight,
They'd all flock to enlist as one,
No recruiting would need be done.
Why, they'd be swimming out to get to that
    war zone,
You'd have to shoot him dead to keep a man
    at home.
What an army of men we'd have
If they ever drafted the girls.

2nd Verse:
The grit our Yankee girls possess would whip
    the enemy,
Offensives would become a joke, that plainly
    you can see,
All the headlines would read then
"Surrender of a million men";
Now picture in your mind and try to think:

2nd Chorus:
What an army of men we'd have
If they ever drafted the girls,
Each time they'd make an attack
They would bring the whole regiment back,
All the foe then would just retreat,
Girls would never stand for defeat.
The man was never born could make a girl
    say "Quit,"
The enemy would waste their time, now
    you'll admit.
What an army of men we'd have
If they ever drafted the girls.

**What Are You Going to Do to Help the
Boys?** L: Gus Kahn; M: Egbert Van
Alstyne. Copyright 1918 by Jerome H.
Remick & Co., New York.

1st Verse:
Your Uncle Sam is calling now
On ev'ry one of you,
If you're too old or young to fight,
There's something else to do.
If you have done a bit before,
Don't let the matter rest,
For Uncle Sam expects that ev'ry man
Will do his best:

Chorus:
What are you going to do for Uncle Sammy,
What are you going to do to help the boys?
If you mean to stay at home,

While they're fighting o'er the foam,
The least that you can do
Is buy a Liberty Bond or two.
If you're going to be a sympathetic miser,
The kind that only lends a lot of noise,
You're no better than the one who loves the
 Kaiser;
So what are you going to do to help the
 boys?

2nd Verse:
It makes no diff'rence who you are
Or whence you came or how,
Your Uncle Sammy helped you then
And you must help him now.
Your brothers will be fighting
For your freedom over there,
And if you love the Stars and Stripes,
Then you must do your share:

**What Are You Going to Do When Our
Boys Come Home?** L: Ivan Reid; M:
Peter DeRose. Copyright 1918 by F.B.
Haviland Publishing Co., Inc., New York.

1st Verse:
We've got a bunch of lanky lads
Fighting over the sea,
Ready to give up ev'rything
Just for democracy,
Don't you think they deserve a lot,
All the dollars and cents we've got?
If you refuse to help them when you can,
Please tell me:

Chorus:
What are you going to do when our boys
 come home?
What are you going to say to make them
 glad?
Will you tell them that you've tried to do
 your share
While they were fighting for your freedom
 over there?
Now, neighbor, will you come out
And greet them with a cheery smile,
Ready to prove that you've been tried and
 true?
When they march back with a Yankee Doo-
dle band,
Will you be the first to take them by the
 hand?
[Ev'ry dollar that is sent across the sea
Helps to make the world safe for democracy].
Oh, what are you going to do when our boys
 come home,

When they bring the Kaiser back from old
 Berlin?

2nd Verse:
All of our lanky Yankee boys,
Many miles o'er the foam,
Dream of the great old times they'll have
When they come marching home.
When our boys hear the bugle sound
And they know that they're homeward
 bound,
What sort of welcome will our fighters find?:

**When a Boy Says Goodbye to His Mother
(and She Gives Him to Uncle Sam).** L&M:
Jack Frost. Copyright 1917 by Frank K.
Root & Co., Chicago.

1st Verse:
Ev'ry time I see a suit of khaki,
I am proud though my heart is sad;
I think each time I see a Yankee Jackie,
He is some Yankee mother's lad;
Just think of how she watched and loved him
Since he was knee high,
Then think how her old heart must sigh:

Chorus:
When a boy says goodbye to his mother
And the sound of the bugle is heard,
He knows that tear in her eyes means
"Come back bye and bye,"
Though her fond lips breathe never a word.
All the angels are praying above her
That he'll come back to Yankee land,
When a boy says goodbye to his mother
And she gives him to Uncle Sam.

2nd Verse:
No one knows just how her soul is aching
When she whispers, "Come back again,"
And no one knows her heart is nearly
 breaking.
Still he knows she will not complain,
For she's a Yankee mother true,
And when it's time to start,
She's ready to do all her part:

**When a Yankee Gets His Eye Down the
Barrel of a Gun.** L&M: Fred S. Campbell.
Copyright 1918 by Fred S. Campbell,
Lynn, Mass.

1st Verse:
The Germans called the Yankees dudes,
All right, if that is true,

Those dudes have shown Bill Kaiser
What the Yankee Dude'll do!
For we are there, and if they call us,
Millions more will come,
And at the Marne they found
That we were there more ways than one!:

1st Chorus:
For when a Yankee gets his eye down the
   barrel of a gun,
There's something doing, Mister Hun, you
   needn't try to run!
You're going to see your finish,
You'll be added to the list!
If the Yankee's out of ammunition,
He'll just use his fist!
He wades right through the Boches
Like he would an apple pie,
A song upon his lips, determination in his
   eye!
For when a Yankee gets his eye down the
   barrel of a gun,
It's Smash! Whang! Crash! Bang!
Bing!, Another Hun!

2nd Verse:
The Yankees don't know what fear means,
They'll always take a chance!
Retreat, they don't know that at all,
Their middle name's Advance!
And with Old Glory flying
Into Berlin they'll go!
They never quit a fight
Until they land the knockout blow!:

2nd Chorus:
For when a Yankee got his eye down the
   barrel of a gun,
Things moved in good old Yankee style and
   paralyzed the Huns!
They dropped their arms,
Threw up their hands,
And "Kamrad!" they cried,
But the Yankees kept on shooting fast at
   ev'ry Hun they spied.
They didn't want the war to end
Until all lies had ceased;
The thing the Yanks were fighting for was
   everlasting peace.
So when a Yankee got his eye down the bar-
   rel of a gun,
It was Smash! Whang! Crash! Bang!
Bing! Another Hun!

3rd Chorus:
For when a Yankee got his eye down the
   barrel of a gun,

It meant the fight would soon be over—home
   again they'd come!
So get your kisses ready, girls, for Billy, Jim,
   and Jack,
You can bet your life they'll make up
For lost time when they get back!
They've seen Italian, English, Belgian,
Pretty French girls, too,
But the girls that they were fighting for
Were Yankee girls like you.
For when a Yankee got his eye down the
   barrel of a gun,
It was Smash! Whang! Crash! Bang!
Bing! Another Hun!

4th Chorus:
For when a Yankee got his eye down the
   barrel of a gun,
A German always bit the dust! His fighting
   days were done!
They used to think that baseball was the
   great American game,
But they changed their sport to chasing
   Huns,
And got there just the same!
And ev'ry Boche they'd come across
They'd forced him to his knees,
They'd make him sing "America,"
Then spank his BVDs!
For when a Yankee got his eye down the
   barrel of a gun,
It was Smash! Whang! Crash! Bang!
Bing! Another Hun!

**When Alexander Takes His Ragtime Band
to France.** L&M: Al Bryan, Cliff Hess,
and Edgar Leslie. Copyright 1918 by
Waterson, Berlin & Snyder Co., New
York.

1st Verse:
What's that tune I hear
A-ringing in my ear?
Come on along,
Come on along,
It's a wonderful idea.
It's Alexander's band
From down in Dixieland;
He's going over there
To do his share:

Chorus:
When Alexander takes his ragtime band to
   France,
He'll capture ev'ry Hun
And take them one by one.

Those ragtime tunes will put the Germans in
  a trance,
They'll throw their guns away—
Hip-hooray!
And start right in to dance.
They'll get so excited
They'll come over the top,
Two-step back to Berlin with a skip and a
  hop;
Old Hindenburg will know he has no chance,
When Alexander takes his ragtime band to
  France.

2nd Verse:
There's no time to lose,
They'll put on dancing shoes,
They'll glide away
And slide away,
When they hear those weary blues.
The goosestep's on the wane,
The two-step's in again;
Like they advanced at first,
They've just reversed:

When Angels Weep (Waltz of Peace).
L&M: Charles K. Harris. Copyright 1914
by Chas. K. Harris, New York.

Glory to the highest,
Peace on earth,
Good will to men.
Glory to the highest,
Hear our prayers ascending above.
Grant us sweet peace,
Oh, Angel of love;
Bless all the nations on earth,
We are brothers all.
Glory to the highest,
Peace on earth,
Good will to men.
Glory to the highest,
Hear our prayers ascending above;
Grant us sweet peace,
Oh, angel of love,
We are all pleading
This war to cease,
Let us dwell in love and peace.

When He Fought for the Flag of the Free.
L&M: L.P. Lemire, Jr. Copyright 1918 by
L.P. Lemire, Music Publisher, Worcester,
Mass.

1st Verse:
A faithful soldier of Uncle Sam,

Sad but brave of heart, stands, gun in
  hand;
Says with a sigh his last goodbye
To his gray old mother standing by.
To fight for the flag of the brave and the
  free,
And honor its fairly won liberty,
He falls in line with his comrades all,
And proudly he marches away:

Chorus:
On the battlefield stands our brave soldier,
A loyal son of the U.S.A.
While slowly 'round him one by one
His comrades fall in the fray.
Now gather dim the shades of night,
Crimson-dyed in the field of fight,
For 'twas splashed with the blood of might
When he fought for the flag of the free.

2nd Verse:
Far from his home he is now engaged,
Brave in victory, brave in defeat.
'Round him his comrades are falling fast,
But are bravely fighting to the last.
Now through the dark comes the fierce fatal
  dart,
At last it has pierced our brave soldier's
  heart;
Just at the moment of victory,
He died for the flag of the free:

**When I Come Back to You (We'll Have a
Yankee-Doodle Wedding).** L&M: William
Tracey and Jack Stern. Copyright 1918 by
Douglas & Newman Music Co., New
York.

1st Verse:
Duty calls and I must leave you, sweetheart
  mine,
By tomorrow I'll be on my way;
Though the great big ocean blue divides us,
I'll be with you night and day;
Uncle Sam has work for me to do,
And when it's over
I'll come back to you:

Chorus:
Save all your love and I'll save all of mine
Till I come back to you;
Though we must part while I'm o'er the sea,
Down in your heart you'll be proud of me;
So light up your face with a smile, little girl,
You have no cause to feel blue,

One of many 1918 love songs looking forward to a peaceful future rather than at the dismal present was "When I Come Back to You (We'll Have a Yankee-Doodle Wedding)."

For we'll have a Yankee-Doodle wedding
When I come back to you.

2nd Verse:
Even though you're lonesome for your
    soldier boy
While I'm fighting far across the foam,
Just imagine what a rousing welcome
We'll get when we come back home;
Don't you worry, dearie, I'll be true,
Because I'll leave my heart
Back here with you:

When I Send You a Picture of Berlin (You'll Know It's Over "Over There," I'm Coming Home). L&M: Frank Fay, Ben Ryan, and Dave Dreyer. Copyright 1918 by Harry Von Tilzer Music Publishing Co., New York.

1st Verse:
Johnny Johnson's feeling fit,
Uniform and army kit;
Johnny was a cam'ra fiend,
Of that trip had often dreamed;
Sweetheart crying at the pier,
Said, "I'm proud of you, my dear,
Now you'll realize your dreams

Taking pictures of those scenes."
Said John, "That's what I'll do,
And I'll send them home to you":

Chorus:
When I send you a picture of London,
Then you'll know I've landed safely "over
    there";
When I send you a snapshot of Paris,
You'll know I'm ready to do and dare
(I'll do my share).
You'll know I'm thinking about you
When I send you my photo all alone;
But when I send you a picture of Berlin,
You'll know it's over "over there,"
I'm coming home.

2nd Verse:
Sweetheart waving at the pier,
Saw the transport disappear,
Dried her tears and heaved a sigh,
Said he'll come back "bye and bye";
There are millions more like him,
Full of vim in fighting trim,
Smiling when they sail away,
Our debt to France they're glad to pay;
We'll miss them all at home,
But there's truth in Johnny's poem:

When I'm Through with the Arms of the Army (I'll Come Back to the Arms of You). L&M: Earl Carroll. Copyright 1918 by Leo Feist, Inc., New York.

1st Verse:
When a boy tells a girlie his love,
That's the sweetest story ever told;
But when you hear him say
That he must go away,
No sweetness does that story hold.
You'll see him wave goodbye,
You'll see her bravely try to dry
The tiny teardrops in her eye,
When she hears her sweetheart cry:

Chorus:
"When I'm through with the arms of the
    Army,
I'll come back to the arms of you;
When the lines of the foe we are taking,
My arms will be aching,
For you they'll be breaking.
Oh, you know I love you,
But that old flag above,
You know I love it, too.

So when I'm through with the arms of the
   Army,
I'll come back to the arms of you."

2nd Verse:
"Lift your head and be brave, little girl,
Ev'ry boy has got his work to do.
And though you cry, I know
You'd rather have me go
Than try to stay behind with you.
Who knows how long I'll be
When I have sailed across the sea?
So when you hear this melody,
Will you sometimes think of me?":

When It's Over Over There, Molly Darlin'.
L&M: Benjamin Purrington and Neil
Morét. Copyright 1918 by Daniels & Wilson, Inc., San Francisco.

1st Verse:
Hear them trampin',
Hear them stampin',
See the boys in khaki gray.
There's an argument in Flanders,
And we leave for there today.
Come and kiss me,
Will you miss me,
Will you promise to be true?
We'll chase von Hindenburg clear into
   Heidelberg
Before I see the smile of you:

Chorus:
When it's over over there, Molly darlin',
When it's over over there, Molly dear,
When we've made the Kaiser wise,
Your smiling eyes
Will shine more safely here.
When we've Yankee Doodled under the
   Linden,
When we've wound up the watch on the
   Rhine,
When we give Alsace Lorraine to France
   again,
[When we've wound up the watch on the
   Rhine,
When there's liberty in view for Belgium,
   too],
I'll come sailing home to you.

2nd Verse:
Don't be sighin',
Don't be cryin',
For I love to see you smile.
Don't be grievin' that we're leavin',

We'll be gone a little while.
Out in France, dear,
There's a chance, dear,
For each son of liberty;
And for the glory of the dear old land we
   love,
We'll chase the U-boats from the sea:

**When Our Service Star Was Turned to
Golden Hue.** L&M: Allen R. Richmond.
Copyright 1919 by Richmond Publishing
Co., Washington, D.C.

1st Verse:
I am dreaming of that day not long ago, laddie boy,
When you buckled on your sword and
   marched away;
From your home and loved ones true our
   America called you,
Oh, how bravely you went forth, my laddie
   boy.
I was standing in the doorway when you left
   us
With my hand upon your dear old daddy's
   arm,
Though a tear dimmed his eye
When he told his boy goodbye,
Smilingly he bade you godspeed on your way:

Chorus:
When our service star was turned to one of
   golden,
All the sunshine seemed to leave the dear old
   home;
You were called from life's young dream
To that sacrifice supreme
That forever freedom's banner o'er the brave
   might wave.
As the long days come and go and time rolls
   onward,
We shall miss your footstep and your cheerful voice;
Though our hearts ached for our son,
Yet God's will, not ours, be done
When our service star was turned to golden
   hue.

2nd Verse:
Far away in foreign lands you fought and
   died, laddie boy,
For the liberty that we all love so well,
For your flag and country dear you went forward without fear,
Yes, we knew that you'd be true, my laddie
   boy.

On our service flag a lone blue star was
   shining,
Proudly speaking of a boy gone forth to war,
When an angel from on high
Touched it with a golden dye,
Telling us that you had answered your last
   call:

**When the Apple Blossoms Bloom in
France.** L: Harold Freeman; M: Harry C.
Elsesser and J. Edwin Allemong. Copy-
right 1918 by Imperial Music Co.,
Roanoke, Va.

1st Verse:
'Tis the land of beautiful roses,
France, my own.
As the day so softly closes, I'm alone,
Dreaming of you, my fairest rose,
You and your eyes of blue;
And when the war is over,
I'll be coming back to you:

Chorus:
When the apple blossoms bloom in France,
   dear,
And the skies are blue once more,
In that dreamy land of old romance, dear,
After the war is o'er.
My love for France shall never die,
I long for her sunny shore,
When the apple blossoms bloom in France,
   dear,
And the skies are blue once more.

2nd Verse:
'Twas the land of sunshine and laughter
Long ago;
Now the land is bowed in sorrow.
We all know horror of war and the death of
   men,
God grant it soon may cease,
And we shall see the rainbow
Of everlasting peace:

**When the Boat Arrives (That Brings My
Lovin' Daddy Home).** L&M: George Fair-
man. Copyright 1918 by George Fairman,
Music Publisher, New York.

1st Verse:
I just received a cablegram
From my ever-lovin' man.
He's on a transport headed west,
Bound for the land he loves the best,

I'm just as happy as can be.
We'll have a great big jubilee,
I've saved all my lovin' since he's been away,
And believe me when I say:

Chorus:
When I hear that whistle of the transport
   blowin',
Bringin' my honey boy from over there,
Down to the levee you will find me goin',
Yes indeed, I'll be there;
I'll Eagle Rock [Ball the Jack] when the band
   starts playin',
Funny little tunes that make you sigh and
   moan,
And when I see his smilin' face,
I'm goin' a-shimmie all over the place,
When the boat arrives that brings my lovin'
   daddy home.

2nd Verse:
I bought a brand new yellow gown
And the swellest hat in town.
When I go walkin' down the street,
You'll hear the folks say, "Ain't she neat";
They'll wonder where I got the dress.
They'll never know, but I'll confess
To just hug and kiss that lovin' man of mine,
I'm excited all the time:

When the Boys Come Back Again. L&M:
Ernest B. Orne. Copyright 1918 by Orne
Publishing Co., Portland, Me.

1st Verse:
Mother, wives, and sweethearts,
Now all o'er the land,
Are thinking of their dear ones
Over there for Uncle Sam.
No wonder they are lonely
And their thoughts are far away,
For they are waiting for the time,
For that grand old day:

Chorus:
When the boys come back again,
When the boys come back again,
You'll hear the bands all playing
Some old-time sweet refrain.
Smiles will drive away the pain
Like the sunshine after rain;
Hearts that are sad
Then will be glad,
When the boys come back again.

2nd Verse:
Many chairs now vacant

Wait our soldier boys,
And manly hearts now aching
Soon will feel a thrill of joy.
With vict'ry on their banners
And their duty nobly done,
Dear Yankeeland will welcome them
When freedom's cause is won:

When the Boys Come Home. L: John
Hay; M: Oley Speaks. Copyright 1917 by
G. Schirmer, New York.

There's a happy time coming when the boys
    come home,
There's a glorious day coming when the boys
    come home;
We will end the dreadful story
Of the battle dark and gory
In a sunburst of glory
When the boys come home.
The day will seem brighter when the boys
    come home,
And our hearts will be lighter when the boys
    come home;
Wives and sweethearts will press them
In their arms and caress them
And pray God to bless them,
When the boys come home.
The thin ranks will be proudest when the
    boys come home,
And our cheer will ring the loudest when the
    boys come home.
The full ranks will be shattered
And the bright arms will be battered,
And the battle standards tattered
When the boys come home.
Their bayonets may be rusty when the boys
    come home,
And their uniforms be dusty when the boys
    come home.
But all shall see the traces
Of battle's royal graces
In the brown and bearded faces,
When the boys come home.
Our love shall go to meet them when the
    boys come home,
To bless them and to greet them when the
    boys come home.
And the fame of their endeavor
Time and change shall not dissever
From the nation's heart forever,
From the nation's heart forever,
From the nation's heart forever,
When the boys come home.

When the Boys Come Marching Home. L:
Jamie Kelly; M: William Cahill. Copyright
1916 by Shapiro, Bernstein & Co., Inc.,
New York.

1st Verse:
"Mother, don't sigh,
Brush that tear from your eye,
Soon this cruel war will be over.
Dad will come home,
No more to roam,
Then we'll be living in clover.
Keep that light burning bright
In the window each night,
'Twill guide daddy dear on his way."
Then he climbed on her knee,
Saying, "Still you have me,"
As she kissed him, then she heard him say:

Chorus:
"When the boys come marching home,
Back from the fields of battle,
When the boys come marching home
Far from the roar and rattle;
Tramp, tramp, tramp, the boys are marching
Back to their home sweet home.
There'll be many a tear and many a sigh,
The bands will play and the flags will fly
When the boys come marching home."

2nd Verse:
"One summer's day
Daddy dear marched away,
Seems I can hear him sighing;
His last goodbye
Brought a tear to my eye,
He said 'Cheer up, don't be crying.'
I am glad that my dad
Told me not to be sad;
He'd proved when he went far away
He was ready to fight
For what he thought was right.
And we surely will welcome the day":

**When the Boys Come Sailing Home
(March).** L&M: Floyd Delker. Copyright
1919 by Floyd Delker.

1st Verse:
Far across the deep blue ocean in the khaki
    uniform,
Our brave lads are waiting, they have faced
    the battle's storm,
To meet the friends and dear ones here
    across the briny foam,
They turned the tide of battle and they'll
    soon be sailing home:

Chorus:
And when the boys comes home
From "Over There" across the sea,
A joyous greeting waits for them,
Like none other there can be.
A wife, a sweetheart true,
Or a mother waits alone,
But we'll all be by their side
When the boys come sailing home.

2nd Verse:
We stood by our soldiers fighting far across
    the ocean blue,
We loaned our money freely, we did all that
    we could do;
They entered with war clouds dark and all
    seemed in dismay,
They swiftly pushed the war clouds back and
    turned night into day:

3rd Verse:
Words cannot express our feelings, well, we
    know it is quite true,
We've kept the home-fires burning while their
    duty they did do;
We're proud that we may meet them and
    we're proud that they can say,
We've done our duty, so have you, world's
    freedom's here to stay:

When the Clouds Have Passed Away. L:
William Jerome; M: Seymour Furth. Copy-
right 1918 by A.J. Stasny Music Co., New
York.

1st Verse:
There seems to be a message in the air
From those we really care for over there;
From each mother's joy and pride
Over on the other side,
In Yankeeland it's ringing ev'rywhere:

Chorus:
When the clouds have passed away,
As they surely will some day;
When the birds in lover's lane
Croon again love's sweet refrain
Over hill and over plain;
When the sunshine fades away
Ev'ry little speck of gray
Under peaceful skies of blue;
I'll come sailing back to you,
When the clouds have passed away.

2nd Verse:
When ev'ry boy has laid away his gun,
And liberty forever has been won,

Ev'ry mother old and gray,
She will kneel and bless the day
When she can welcome back her loving son:

When the Clouds of War Roll By. L&M:
Nat Binns and Earl Haubrich. Copyright
1917 by Ted Browne Music Co., Chicago.

1st Verse:
Ev'ryone's excited,
Let us get united,
Shoulder arms to crush the foe.
Bugle call is sounding,
Boys in blue are rounding,
To France they soon will go.
Sweetheart, have no fears,
Come, let me dry your tears:

Chorus:
When the clouds of war roll by,
I'll come marching home to you.
Until then I'll bid goodbye,
Just say that you will be true blue.
Marching to victory
For true democracy;
Back, back to you I'll come,
When the clouds of war roll by.

2nd Verse:
When the dawn was breaking,
My poor heart was aching,
Just to be back that day.
Cannons they were roaring,
Boys in blue were scoring
In the thickest of the fray.
At last we broke their line,
To this tune we're keeping time:

**When the Eagle Flaps His Wings (and
Calls on the Kaiser).** L: C. Francis Riesner; M: Thomas L. McCarey, Jr. Copyright 1918 by Daniels & Wilson, Inc., San
Francisco.

1st Verse:
Remember old Bill Bailey,
Well, he just sailed away;
He took his ukulele,
Always plays it night and day.
He entertains the khaki boys,
He plays just what they please,
And while they're dozing
Bill's composing wartime melodies.
Well, here's a song he wrote
That'll get the Kaiser's goat:

Chorus:
"We can, we will,
We can, we will, we must,
We know we can,
We'll show we can
Get Kaiser Bill or bust!
In Berlin there is a bum on the throne,
There'll soon be a throne on the bum,
[The bullets are flying, our flag is unfurled;
He'll think it's the end of the world],
When the Eagle flaps his wings and calls on
    the Kaiser!"

2nd Verse:
One day poor Bill got wounded,
The nurses were so kind;
The way he'd swear and tear his hair,
They thought he'd lose his mind.
The Sammies came from near and far
When they heard Bill was sick,
They found him raving and behaving
Like a lunatic.
It seemed he would get worse
Until they sang this verse:

When the Eagle Screams Hurrah! L&M:
Edmund Dallas. Copyright 1917 by Edmond Dallas, Providence, R.I.

1st Verse:
Somewhere in France her heroes are falling,
Somewhere in France people are calling,
"America, we need you,
America, God speed you!
Send to us your gallant sons so loyal, brave,
    and true
To fight for the Right with all their might!
Let your starry banners wave with ours in
    battle!
Lafayette was Washington's best friend,
He was ever faithful to the cause of freedom,
He would fight unto the end":

Chorus:
Uncle Sam has called for boys, we'll be there;
When the gen'ral roll is called, we'll be there.
With a rah-rah, hip hurrah
We will sail away to France.
When the Eagle screams hurrah,
It will make the Kaiser dance,
And we'll fight for liberty
When we sail across the sea;
We'll be over there, we'll be there!

2nd Verse:
Somewhere in France Old Glory is waving,

Somewhere in France our Gen'ral is saying,
"We'll rally 'round the flag, boys,
We'll rally once again, boys.
Let them see that Yankee lads are not afraid
    to fight,
To fight for the Right with all their might!
Forward into battle, follow now your leader
As your grandsires did in days of yore.
When they see Old Glory, that will tell the
    story;
It will spread from shore to shore":

When the Flag Goes By. L: Marian Dear-
born Merry; M: George B. Nevin. Copyright 1917 by Oliver Ditson Co., Boston.

1st Verse:
Does your heart beat faster
Or your eyes grow dim
When the flag goes by?
Is there something—just the sight of it—
That rouses all your vim
When the flag goes by?
All its colors are so clear,
All it stands for is so dear,
Don't you want to shout and cheer
When the flag goes by?:

Chorus:
When the flag goes by,
When the flag goes by,
Is there something—just the sight of it,
That rouses all your vim,
When the flag goes by?
All its colors are so clear,
All it stands for is so dear,
Don't you want to shout and cheer
When the flag goes by?

2nd Verse:
There's a sad and somber side
And another view to take
When the flag goes by,
Of the many, many hearts
That in anguish throb and ache
When the flag goes by.
Mother, sister, sweetheart, friend,
Who their dear ones bravely send
Right and country to defend
When the flag goes by:

3rd Verse:
Rouse, then, comrades ev'rywhere!
And let each one do his part
When the flag goes by.
With a wisdom born of courage

And a truly loyal heart
When the flag goes by.
Not for dollars, self, or gain,
Nor for mean ends to attain,
But ideals to retain
When the flag goes by:

When the Flowers Bloom on No Man's Land (What a Wonderful Day That Will Be). L: Howard E. Rogers; M: Archie Gottler. Copyright 1918 by Kalmar, Puck & Abrahams Consolidated, Inc., Music Publishers, New York.

1st Verse:
There's a vision always haunts me
Of a day I long to see,
When hearts that are sad all will be glad
On this wonderful day to be;
When joys take the place of fears
And smiles take the place of tears:

Chorus:
When the flowers bloom on No Man's Land,
Bringing a message of peace and love,
And the cannon's roar is heard no more,
What a blessing from above!
When the sun shines through the clouds of war,
When peace covers all of the earth and sea,
And when each mother's son has laid down his gun,
What a wonderful day that will be.

2nd Verse:
Ev'rywhere a heart is longing,
Praying that the day is done
When far from alarms, safe from all harms,
Ev'ry mother will hold her son;
When good will to ev'ry man
Will be ev'ry nation's plan:

When the Lilies Bloom in France Again. L: Robert Levenson; M: George L. Cobb. Copyright 1918 by Walter Jacobs, New York.

1st Verse:
There's a field over there where the lilies grew
And the birds sang on ev'ry bough;
It was not long ago when the skies were blue,
But there is nothing left there now.
Oh, they have not died in vain,
For these flow'rs will bloom again,
That's a part of ev'ry soldier's vow:

Chorus:
When the lilies bloom in France again
And the fields are white as snow,
Then our work will be done
And I'll come back to the one
Who'll be waiting for me, I know.
Then we'll all see the silver lining
That will soon pierce the dark clouds through;
When the lilies bloom in France again,
I'll come back, sweetheart, to you.

2nd Verse:
When the skies turn to gray and the sunshine's gone,
And you find that you're feeling blue,
Bear in mind after darkness must come the blue,
And with it lots of gladness, too.
When the lilies bloom once more,
Then our troubles will be o'er,
And I'll soon be coming back to you:

When the Old Boat Heads for Home. L&M: Earl Fuller. Copyright 1918 by Broadway Music Corp., New York.

1st Verse:
Mothers and sweethearts and dads
Waiting for news from your lads,
You have no reason to feel blue,
For soon they'll be back home with you!
Bravely our sons have all fought,
Vict'ry and peace they have brought,
And when the good ship starts to sail o'er the sea,
We know what a time there will be:

Chorus:
When the old boat heads for home,
Ploughing her way through the foam,
Ev'ryone happy and ev'ryone gay,
Hats in the air,
Yelling hip-hip-hooray!
Oh! what a crowd at the pier,
Watching the boat drawing near;
Throughout the nation,
Some celebration,
When the old boat heads for home!

2nd Verse:
Won't ev'rybody feel proud,
Can you imagine the crowd?
'Twill be the greatest ever known
To welcome all the boys back home.
We've never lost in a fight,

We never fight till we're right;
Our boys don't know defeat and they never
    will,
We've proved that to old Kaiser Bill:

When There's Peace on Earth Again.
L&M: Roger Lewis, Bobby Crawford, and
Joseph Santly. Copyright 1917 by Leo
Feist, Inc., New York.

1st Verse:
Before us lies a mighty task,
With all this world at war;
A thousand times the question's asked,
"What are we fighting for?"
We're fighting now for wars to cease
So all the world again may live in peace:

Chorus:
When there is peace on earth again,
The world will be a garden fair;
The battlefields like clouds will fade away
And turn to meadowlands where children
    can play.
Between each land a tie there'll be
Of friendship, love, and sympathy,
And ev'ry nation, whether large or small,
Will know there must be equal rights for all;
'Twill be like sunshine after rain,
When there is peace on earth again.

2nd Verse:
When battles have been fought and won,
No conquest will we seek;
We'll have a "Brotherhood of Man,"
With justice for the meek.
No more will hearts be bowed in pain,
For happiness will rule the world again:

When Tony Goes Over the Top. L&M:
Alex Marr, Billy Frisch, and Archie
Fletcher. Copyright 1918 by Joe Morris
Music Co., New York.

1st Verse:
Hey! You know Tony the barber,
Who shaves and cuts-a the hair?
He said skabooch to his Mariooch,
He's gonna fight over there.
Hey! You know how Tony could shave you,
He'd cut you from ear to ear;
I just got a letter from Tony,
And this is what I hear:

Chorus:
"When Tony goes over the top,

He no think of the barber shop;
He grab-a da gun and chase-a da Hun
And make 'em all run like a son-of-a-gun!
You can bet your life he'll never stop,
When Tony goes over the top;
Keep your eyes on that fighting wop;
With a fire in his eyes
He'll capture the Kais';
He don't care if he dies,
[With a rope of spagett
And a big-a stilette,
He'll make-a the Germans sweat],
When Tony goes over the top!"

2nd Verse:
"Hey! What-a you call them-a fellow
What fly away up in the air,
Dey hum and a-hum and drop-a da bomb
Then fly away like he don't care?
Well, Tony he fight that-a fellow,
He bring-a down five in one place;
Now Tony's a regular hero,
They call him 'Italian Ace'":

When We Meet in the Sweet Bye and Bye.
L&M: Stanley Murphy. Copyright 1918 by
Jerome H. Remick & Co., New York.

1st Verse:
He was true, so would you be, too,
If you loved a girl like Sally.
She was sad when her soldier lad
Left her all alone in the valley,
Till her sweetheart wrote her
"I'll be coming home some day,
Be cheery till the war clouds roll away":

Chorus:
"In the sweet bye and bye,
When the skies are clear and blue,
We shall meet, you and I,
And I'll tell you of the battles I've been
    through.
And then we'll dream down by the stream,
Beneath the silv'ry moon in the summer sky;
So save your kisses, and so will I,
Till we meet in the sweet bye and bye."

2nd Verse:
Colonel said "In the fight you led,
You're a credit to your nation;
Make your bow, you're a sergeant now,
And you've earned a long vacation."
Soon another letter
That came to her in June said:
"Our sweet bye and bye is coming soon":

(When We Reach That Old Port) Somewhere in France. L: Al Selden; M: Sam H. Stept. Copyright 1917 by A.J. Stasny Music Co., New York.

1st Verse:
See this little letter in my hand,
It's a summons to serve my native land;
Though it grieves me, dearie, to my heart,
There is nothing left to do,
So, sweetheart, we must part:

1st Chorus:
I'm off today on a ship that sails away,
And it's bound for some port somewhere in
    France;
Dearie, don't cry,
I will be back bye and bye,
When it's all over there
And with France our debt is squared,
When with Germany we're through,
We'll hoist the old Red, White and Blue;
So, goodbye, old pal,
I'll be thinking of you, gal,
When we reach that old port somewhere in
    France.

2nd Verse:
Though they double-crossed us, you'll agree,
Still you know we have waited patiently;
They all know how strong we are today;
Time has come when Uncle Sam
Will make the Kaiser pay:

2nd Chorus:
I'm off today on a ship that sails away,
And it's bound for some port somewhere in
    France;
Cheer up, dear girl,
Yankee boys are loyal all;
If the Germans get gay,
We'll make them hail U.S.A.;
We'll make Kaiser Bill shed tears
For what he's done these past few years,
For we'll call their bluff
And we'll make them yell "Enough!",
When we reach that old port somewhere in
    France.

When We Wind Up the Watch on the Rhine (March). L: Gordon V. Thompson; M: Gordon V. Thompson and William Davis. Copyright 1917 by Leo Feist, Inc., New York.

1st Verse:
Now we must part, heart of my heart,

In one of the first of the American "farewell" songs, the soldier protagonist of "(When We Reach That Old Port) Somewhere in France" (1917) promised his lady love that "I will be back bye-and-bye/ When it's all over there,/ And with France our debt is squared,/ When with Germany we're through." (The frequent American war-song references to repaying the debt the nation owed to France — and especially to the Marquis de Lafayette — referred to France's support of the colonists in the Revolutionary War.)

I can hear the bugle sounding with a call so
    clear!
Till I return, my heart will yearn
For the girl I leave behind me
In the homeland, dear:

Chorus:
When we wind up the watch on the Rhine
And we grind up the Kaiser's last line,
When the war is done and the victory won,
I'll come back to the girl that I call mine!
When we wind up the watch on the Rhine,
We will bind up two hearts that entwine,
Wedding bells will be ringing,
"Home Sweet Home" we'll be singing,
When we wind up the watch on the Rhine!

2nd Verse:
Just one short line, sweetheart of mine,
I am battling for my country far from home
    tonight.
Though foes assail, Right must prevail,

So keep knitting still and smiling
Till we win our fight!:

When Yankee Doodle Learns to "Parlez Vous Francais." L: Will J. Hart; M: Edward G. Nelson. Copyright 1917 by A.J. Stasny Music Co., New York.

1st Verse:
When Yankee Doodle came to Paris town,
Upon his face he wore a little frown;
To those he'd meet upon the street
He couldn't speak a word,
To find a miss that he could kiss
It seemed to be absurd,
But if this Yankee should stay there a while,
Upon his face you're bound to see a smile:

Chorus:
When Yankee Doodle learns to "Parlez Vous
    Francais,
Parlez Vous Francais" in the proper way,
He will call each girlie "Ma cherie."
To ev'ry miss that wants a kiss
He'll say, "Wee, wee, On ze Be, On ze Bou,
On ze Boule, Boulevard."
With a girl with a curl
You can see him promenade;
When Yankee Doodle learns to "Parlez Vous
    Francais,"
"Oo la, la, Sweet Papa,"
He will teach them all to say.

2nd Verse:
Soon Yankee Doodle left old Paris town,
Upon his face there was a coat of brown,
For ev'ry man of Uncle Sam
Was fighting in a trench.
Between each shell, they learned quite well
To speak a little French;
When Yankee Doodle gets back to Paree,
He'll break a million hearts, take it from me:

(When Yankee Doodle Marches Through Berlin) There'll Be a Hot Time in the U.S.A. L: Andrew B. Sterling; M: Arthur Lange. Copyright 1917 by Joe Morris Music Co., New York.

1st Verse:
The whole population of the big French
    nation
Were lined up on the street one day,
Ev'ry flag was flying, ev'ry heart was sighing,

As early as the late spring of 1917, only a few months after America entered the conflict, such tunes as "(When Yankee Doodle Marches Through Berlin) There'll Be a Hot Time in the U.S.A." confidently predicted quick victory over Kaiser Wilhelm II.

For the Yankee boys were coming down that
    way;
When suddenly a Yankee voice cried out,
They could tell it was a Yankee when they
    heard him shout:

Chorus:
"Here they come, here they come,
And the drums are beating,
There'll be no retreating,
They'll be there,
They'll be there,
For there's vict'ry in the air!
And they'll win, yes, they'll win,
Then they'll flash the news to old Broadway;
And when Yankee Doodle marches through
    Berlin,
There'll be a hot time in the U.S.A."

2nd Verse:
Just picture them dashing when the news
    comes flashing,
"We've hauled the Kaiser's black flag down!"
To set bonfires burning for the boy returning
From the trenches to his little home town.
"Just take a look," they heard that Yankee
    cry,

"Then go tell the Kaiser he can kiss himself
    goodbye":

**When Yankee Doodle Sails Upon the Good
Ship "Home Sweet Home."** L: Addison
Burkhardt; M: Fred Fisher. Copyright 1918
by McCarthy & Fisher, Inc., New York.

1st Verse:
Fathers, mothers, sisters, brothers,
Listen, sweethearts, too,
Our loving sons who chased the Huns
Are coming back to you;
Ev'rybody makes a lot of noise
And shakes the hands of our fighting boys:

Chorus:
There's goin' to be a great big holiday,
A raising Hail Columbia jolly day,
Like Christmas, New Year's, and Thanks-
    giving
All rolled into one.
There'll be a great big smile on ev'ry face,
There'll be a great big welcome ev'ry place,
All the bands will play,
'Twill be the wildest day
That the whole world ever knew.
There'll be a million mothers meeting them,
There'll be a million sweethearts greeting
    them;
There'll be a hot time in the old town
When they come across the foam;
There'll be a scrap to see each chap again
Who put Belgium on the map again,
When Yankee Doodle sails upon the good
    ship "Home Sweet Home."

2nd Verse:
How we love our Yankee heroes,
And our allies, too;
You proved your worth, the best on earth
Is none too good for you;
Ev'rybody wants to shout and laugh,
And we'll soon kill the fatted calf:

**When You Come Back (and You Will
Come Back, There's the Whole World
Waiting for You).** L&M: George M.
Cohan. Copyright 1918 by M. Witmark &
Sons, New York.

1st Verse:
From Frisco Bay to old Broadway,
Today all over the U.S.A.,
We know we're fighting the foe.

So we all stand steady and ready to go,
We know no fear, we know no tear,
And all we hear is the Yankee cheer.
I heard a girlie say
To her boy as he marched away:

Chorus:
"When you come back, if you do come back,
You'll hear the Yankee cry, 'Atta boy, Jack!'
And when you return, remember to bring
Some little thing that you get from the King,
And drop me a line from Germany,
Do, Yankee Doodle, do!
When you come back, and you will come
    back,
There's the whole world waiting for you!"

2nd Verse:
It's rum, tum, tum, the fife and drum,
So march in time for the time has come
To smash right through with a bang,
With the same old spirit when liberty rang!
To win, begin to rush right in
And fly our flag over old Berlin!
Let's let our message be
To the Yankee across the sea:

**When You Kiss Your Soldier Boy Good-
bye.** L&M: M. Russell Brown. Copyright
1917 by M. Russell Brown.

1st Verse:
Our boys are off for France
With but a fighting chance
To ever be with dear ones here again;
With hearts so brave and true,
'Neath the Red, White and Blue,
We know their going cannot be in vain:

Chorus:
Then smile, smile, smile
All the while, while, while
You kiss your soldier boy goodbye;
Even if your heart must break,
Give him a smile to take,
When you kiss your soldier boy goodbye.

2nd Verse:
And when the war shall cease,
May universal peace
Reign over all this broad and mighty land;
God guide our men aright
When in the awful fight
For justice and sweet liberty they stand:

When Your Sailor Boy in Blue Comes Sailing Home to You. L: Annelu Burns; M: Madelyn Sheppard. Copyright 1918 by Waterson, Berlin & Snyder Co., New York.

1st Verse:
Many hearts are aching now as fond farewells
   are said,
Hands are reaching out in love across the sea.
Many eyes with tears are wet
For the boys they can't forget,
Many lips are praying now so tenderly:

Chorus:
When your sailor boy in blue
Comes sailing home to you,
When the dreary hours of parting shall be
   o'er,
Then will care and sorrow flee,
And you will so happy be
When the dear old days of love return once
   more.
What if skies seem lined with gray,
Sunbeams chase the clouds away,
And tomorrow's dawn shall be of rainbow
   hue;
Then, no matter if it's long,
Let your heart still hold a song
Till your sailor boy comes sailing home to
   you.

2nd Verse:
Then, be full of hope and courage like your
   sailor boy,
There's no time for bitterness and tears today.
You must heed our country's call,
Never let her standard fall,
You must smile if you would help her win
   the fray:

(Whether Friend or Foe, They're Brothers) When They're Dreaming of Home Sweet Home. L&M: Darl MacBoyle and S. Roughsedge. Copyright 1916 by Franklyn Wallace, Music Publisher, New York.

1st Verse:
There's an ivy-covered cottage in old England
With the roses blooming 'round the door;
There's a weary soldier in the trenches
Where the never-tiring cannon roar;
There's a mighty foe before him strong and
   daring,
And they fight the battle through,
But in the silent night they both are sharing
The sweetest dream a soldier ever knew:

Chorus:
The soldier boys dream not of glory
That will be theirs in the battles won,
Nor do they care if song or story
Will tell the world how it was done.
Back to their sweethearts, wives, and
   mothers,
That's where their mem'ries always roam;
And whether friend or foe they're brothers
When they're dreaming of home sweet home.

2nd Verse:
All around the cottage still the flowers are
   smiling,
Hearts within are trying to be brave,
While they're wond'ring if there's still a
   soldier
Or there's just "Somewhere in France" a
   grave.
Through the day behind the guns they keep
   a-thundering
Songs of hate to fellow men;
But with the battle through they all are won-
   dering
If they will ever see their homes again:

While You're Over There in No Man's Land (I'm Over Here in Lonesome Land). L: Jessie Spiess; M: Jack Stanley. Copyright 1918 by Will Rossiter, Chicago.

1st Verse:
I knew that you would do it, sweetheart,
Now go right to it,
You play your part in this fight,
And I'll keep the home fires bright:

Chorus:
While you're over there in No Man's Land,
I'm over here in Lonesome Land,
But I'm proud that you are mine,
Proud to know that you're in line;
And while you do your share,
I'll send this little prayer
To our Maker up above —
To dry the tears of Belgium and Lorraine,
To send you safely to my arms again,
And bring you home once more,
Back to the open door
To Lonesome Land and me.

2nd Verse:
Daytime, my heart is calling;
Night time, my tears are falling.
If smiles will help you go through,
Then I'll dry my tears just for you:

Who Put the "Germ" in Germany? L: Thomas R. Rees; M: Lawrence E. Eberly. Copyright 1917 by Hansen & Nathan Co., Salt Lake City, Utah.

1st Verse:
Professor Spindle was buggy 'bout bugs,
So he went to Germany (heck with Germany!).
He would inspect
Ev'ry little insect
And each germ that he could see.
He got all his dope
With a microscope
And was doing fine until
He found the unexpected,
For the land was all infected
With a germ called Kaiser Bill.
Then he paused and scratched his head,
And this is what he said:

Chorus:
"Who put the 'Germ' in Germany,
That's what puzzles me.
Oh, Mr. Edison,
Please make some medicine
To knock the Kaiser into Eternity.
This germ is sure a fright,
It haunts me day and night.
I know the guy who put 'It' in Italy,
But I'm darned if I know who it can be
Who put the 'Germ' in Germany;
That's the thing that puzzles me."

2nd Verse:
Now this old vermin became very wild
In this land across the sea (heck with Germany!).
Nations at stake,
All decided to break
With the germ of Germany.
They found it no joke,
This old pest to choke,
So the Kaiser Bill was free
To put a "P" in Russia,
And then mark it off as Prussia,
Just a part of Germany.
Now this germ pervades the land,
But the world can't understand:

Wilson, Democracy, and the Red, White and Blue. L&M: Pvt. William H. Hollingsworth. Copyright 1918 by Pvt. William H. Hollingsworth, published by Haward Publishing Co., Kansas City, Mo.

1st Verse:
The war in France now is over,
The boys will soon come sailing home,
To live in America's clover,
For peace lies over the foam.
'Cause victory rests on their shoulders,
Along with the Red, White and Blue,
America's proud of her soldiers,
And, Wilson, we're proud of you:

Chorus:
Wilson, democracy, the Red, White and Blue,
We owe our victory all to you.
Kultur is done, democracy won,
Hip, hip, hurrah for the U.S.A.!
So let's give three cheers for Old Glory,
For she's been tried and true,
And the Army and Navy forever,
With Wilson, democracy, the Red, White and Blue!

2nd Verse:
The boys on their way to Berlin
Were ready to do or to die,
O, and democracy they did win,
Shouting the old battle cry!
President Wilson behind them,
Fighting with allied King and Lord,
For Wilson's the man who can show them
The pen's mightier than the sword:

The Worst Is Yet to Come. L: Sam M. Lewis and Joe Young; M: Bert Grant. Copyright 1918 by Waterson, Berlin & Snyder Co., New York.

1st Verse:
In childhood day we'd sing and play
A game we loved so well:
"I oh! the cherry oh!,
The farmer in the dell";
But since the war, the days of yore
Have changed to fit the times,
The melody is the same to me
But the kids have changed the rhymes;
The Kaiser has the measles,
The Crown Prince had the croup;
And ev'ry one of his other sons
Will soon be in the soup:

Chorus:
But the worst is yet to come,
The worst is yet to come,
You won't know what it's all about
Or where it's coming from.
You said you'd plaster Paris

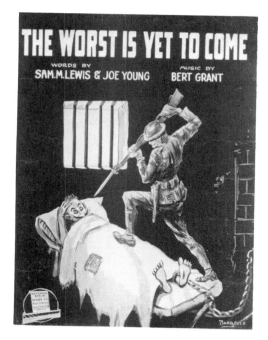

Threatening that "The Worst Is Yet to Come" this 1918 Kaiser-baiting song featured one of the more hair-raising covers designed by the gifted sheet music illustrator Albert Barbelle.

With your Hindenburg machine,
But now it looks as if you're
On the road to Paris Green.
But the worst is yet to come,
The worst is yet to come.
You tried to put the whole world on the bum;
Now, you crazy Kaiser, you've gotta give up,
You've gotta give up,
You've gotta give up;
But don't let it worry you,
The worst is yet to come!

2nd Verse:
Old Kaiser Bill went up the hill,
But soon came tumbling down;
Oh! Chateau Thierry, oh!,
That's where he lost his crown.
He thought a bit and tried to quit,
'Cause ev'rything looked black;
A note he sent to the President,
And he got this answer back:
"Oh! Willie, Willie, wild fellow,
Growing up so high,
You'd better order your coffin now
Because you're gonna die!":

Would You Rather Be a Colonel with an Eagle on Your Shoulder (or a Private with a Chicken on Your Knee)? L: Sidney D. Mitchell; M: Archie Gottler. Copyright 1918 by Leo Feist, Inc., New York.

1st Verse:
Once I heard a father ask his soldier son,
"Why can't you advance like other boys have done?
You've been a private mighty long,
Won't you tell me what is wrong?"
And then the soldier lad
Said, "Listen to me, Dad":

1st Chorus:
"I'd rather be a private than a colonel in the Army,
A private has more fun,
When his day's work is done;
And when he goes on hikes,
In ev'ry town he strikes
Girls discover him
And just smother him
With things he likes.
But girlies act so shy
When colonel passes by,
He holds his head so high with dignity;
So would you rather be a colonel with an eagle on your shoulder
Or a private with a chicken on your knee?"

2nd Verse:
Ev'ry night you find some private in the park,
Spooning on a bench where it is nice and dark;
He's just as happy as can be
With his girlie on his knee,
But colonel never dares
To mix in such affairs:

2nd Chorus:
"I'd rather be a private than a colonel in the Army,
A colonel out in France
Can never take a chance,
For though his job is great,
He dare not make a date;
All that he can do
Is just parley-voo
Then hesitate;
But privates meet the ma,
And then they treat the pa,
And then they 'oo-la-la' with 'wee Marie';
So would you rather be a colonel with an eagle on your shoulder
Or a private with a chicken on your knee?"

Write to Your Dear Sweet Mother (If It's Only Just a Line). L&M: Ernest S. Stafford and Charles Haller. Copyright 1917 by Haller & Stafford, New York.

1st Verse:
"Farewell, dear lad," said my dear dad,
"Go be a man, my son.
Well do I know you want to go
As I did when twenty-one.
When far from home,
Where e'er you roam,
Write to your mother, my boy,
If just to tell
That you are well;
Her heart will beat with joy":

Chorus:
"Write to your dear sweet mother,
If it is only a line;
She's always there a-waiting;
Her love is sublime.
Your sweetheart, your sister and brother,
Remember them all in time;
Write to your dear sweet mother,
If it's only just a line."

2nd Verse:
"Some future day when you're away,
When things go wrong, you're blue,
Don't ever quit, you have the grit,
My lad, just you see it through.
Son, bear in mind,
Hardships you'll find,
Roads to success are not clear.
You have the pluck,
Goodbye and good luck,
Write to your mother dear":

Yankee (He's There, All There). L&M: Charles K. Harris. Copyright 1918 by Chas. K. Harris, New York.

1st Verse:
Gather 'round me, Scots and Celts,
And I'll tell you a story,
How the laddies from 'cross the sea
Fought for us and the glory.
When they landed so slick and clean,
Called for soda and plain ice cream,
We offered them porter,
They drank just plain water,
But oh! how those Yankees could fight,
(Good night!):

Chorus:
Yankee, he's a soldier,

There's no laddie bolder;
Yankee, he's a fighter
From his head down to his toes.
He can dance the Fandango,
Fox trot, waltz, or the tango;
But when there's fighting in the air,
He's there, all there.

2nd Verse:
Soon he landed in the trench,
His blue eyes all a-smiling,
Smoked his little cigarette,
Calm and so beguiling.
Through the air came a screamin' shell,
He just looked up and sail, "O, well!
Don't be in a hurry, you'll get yours!"
Don't worry, believe me,
He got them all right,
(You bet!):

Yankee Land, Fairest Land. L&M: Rudolph Schiller. Copyright 1918 by Rudolph Schiller; published by Charles W. Homeyer & Co., Boston.

1st Verse:
Yankee Land, fairest land,
Democracy enshrined.
A struggling world calls for your aid,
You've never lagged behind;
Your sons and daughters are not serfs,
Proud of their freedom they.
With faithfulness and unafraid,
They bravely point the way:

Chorus:
Righteousness shall still prevail,
Truth and honor must avail.
Let your slogan ever be
"Onward, forward, victory;
They shall not pass,
They shall not pass."

2nd Verse:
Yankee Land, fairest land,
Columbia calls to you!
Unfurl your banners, close the ranks,
Your boys are brave and true.
Then sound the trumpets, beat the drums,
And stir the sleeping mass!
It is for liberty we fight;
It is for honor and for Right:

You Can't Stop the Yanks (Till They Go Right Through). L&M: Jack Caddigan and

Chick Story. Copyright 1918 by Land
Music Publishing Co., Boston.

1st Verse:
Ev'rywhere, Americans hearts are feeling gay,
Just because America's started on her way.
Yankees long and thin
Hiking to Berlin,
Stopping the slaughter
Over the water,
There's the dickens to pay:

Chorus:
Oh, you can't stop the Yankees till they go
  right through,
What a job they'll do when they do go
  through.
They'll make the Kaiser look like thirty dirty
  cents,
They can stop a million of his rotten regi-
  ments.
[They'll take the lily that the Frenchmen tried
  to save,
You'll find it blooming on the blooming
  Kaiser's grave].
[They'll give the Germans what they tried to
  give to France,
They'll kick the bottom out of little Willie's
  pants].
Oh, you can't stop the Yankees till they go
  right through,
And for them that's nothing new.
They're a bunch of business-makers,
For the Germans undertakers.
[Though the Germans may be tricky,
They are full of Bullsheviki].
[And that baby-killing sinner
Will stand up to eat his dinner].
Oh, you [And they] never can stop the
  Yankees until they're through.

2nd Verse:
Ev'rywhere, America's sons are going strong,
They are only helping the French to right a
  wrong,
Having lots of fun
Picking off the Hun,
Driving the cattle
Out of the battle,
Poor old Germany's done:

**You Keep Sending 'Em Over and We'll
Keep Knocking 'Em Down.** L: Sidney D.
Mitchell; M: Harry Ruby. Copyright 1918
by Waterson, Berlin & Snyder Co., New
York.

YOU KEEP SENDING 'EM OVER
AND WE'LL KEEP KNOCKING 'EM DOWN

words by
Sidney D. Mitchell
music by
Harry Ruby

**With a cover illustration as searing as the lyric,
"You Keep Sending 'Em Over and We'll Keep
Knocking 'Em Down" (1918) dared the Kaiser to
"send on ev'ry Hun,/ No matter how tall," fol-
lowed by the warning, "The bigger they come,/
The harder they fall."**

1st Verse:
Our Yankee soldiers fighting in the trenches
  over there
All sing a little air
That makes the Germans swear;
The Huns attack and then our boys go at
  'em with a swing,
It drives the Germans crazy to hear the
  Yankees sing:

Chorus:
"You keep sending 'em over
And we'll keep knocking 'em down,
We'll plant 'em under the clover
Six feet under ground.
Send on ev'ry Hun
No matter how tall;
The bigger they come,
The harder they fall;
[Send on ev'ry Hun,
Don't overlook one;
The faster they come,
The sooner we're done;]
So, you keep sending 'em over,
And we'll keep knocking 'em down."

2nd Verse:
The Kaiser told the Germans that the
    Yankees were a bluff,
But they learned soon enough
That fighting Yanks are tough,
And even though the Huns don't know our
    language very well,
They quickly make for cover each time the
    Yankees sing:

Your Daddy Will Be Proud of You. L: J.
Will Callahan; M: Paul C. Pratt. Copy-
right 1918 by Buckeye Music Publishing
Co., Columbus, Ohio.

1st Verse:
I just read a letter to a soldier at the front
Written by his daddy, and 'twas mighty brief
    and blunt;
It began, "Dear Jimmy, I hope you're feeling
    fine,"
And wound up with this good advice,
With a punch in ev'ry line:

Chorus:
"Your great granddaddy was a soldier
In the days of Washington,
And your old grandpap had a hand in the
    scrap
In Eighteen Sixty-One.
I followed Teddy up the San Juan Hill,
Now you know what you're to do.
Just write me that you're well,
Then wade in and give 'em hell,
[Just put the map of France
On the seat of William's pants],
And your daddy will be proud of you."

2nd Verse:
I'd just like to see him when he reads the old
    man's note,
Vowing to his comrades that he'll get old
    William's goat;
That's the kind of letters the boys are long-
    ing for,
'Twill cheer them up in their lonely hours
And will help to win the war:

You're My Beautiful American Rose.
L&M: Charles A. Ford. Copyright 1917 by
Charles A. Ford, Newark, N.J.

1st Verse:
You've been writing, dearie,
Have I lost the hope in my heart?

Described by the writer-publisher as a "song gem,"
1917's "You're My Beautiful American Rose" expressed the confidence of one young man that he
and his lover will soon be reunited.

Ev'ry day I'm weary,
I thought, as you, we'd never part.
We have been sweethearts together,
Why not always be the same?
Don't think I am the thorn, dear,
You're my rose, I love the name:

Chorus:
Rose, Rose, my beautiful Rose,
You're like the finest of flowers that grow;
My heart does settle when I kiss a petal
Of that sweet scented rose.
When I stroll in the garden,
All I can see
Is the one little flower that's dear to me;
Ev'ryone knows that I love you, Rose,
You're my pretty American Rose.

2nd Verse:
You have waited, dearie,
And I will soon be back to you;
Even now I'm thinking
You're my love and rose so true.
For all the days are so lonely,
And the night shades never fall;
When the rose, dear, sends its fragrance,
It's my rose that sends the call:

You're the Greatest Little Mothers in the World (Mothers of America). L: Sam M. Lewis and Joe Young; M: Archie Gottler. Copyright 1918 by Waterson, Berlin & Snyder, New York.

1st Verse:
Who gives our nation its heroes?
Who bears the burden alone?
Who gives and gives
As long as she lives?
There's a Joan of Arc in ev'ry home:

Chorus:
Mothers of America,
The eyes of the world are on you.
When you gave your lad,
You gave all you had, your courage will
  guide us through.
There's a tear behind your smile
Ev'ry time that our flag is unfurled.
Mothers of America,
You're the greatest little mothers in the
  world!

2nd Verse:
Who makes the coward a hero?
Who feels each wound and each blow?
Who knows the pain
Of waiting in vain?
You who rocked their cradles long ago:

You've Got to Go in or Go Under. L: Percival Knight; M: Gitz Rice. Copyright 1918 by G. Ricordi & Co., Inc., New York.

1st Verse:
There is a call resounding,

Now you hear it everywhere,
In ev'ry town and square,
It comes from "over there."
The U.S.A. is in the fight and you know
  what that means;
That ev'ry lad is joining from the north to
  New Orleans.
If you can't wear a uniform, there's one
  thing left to do,
Don't ever quit, just "Do your bit,"
You know it's up to you:

Chorus:
You've got to go in or go under,
You've got to be going all day;
We know you're not in khaki or in blue,
But you're as big a man and you've got a job
  to do.
In Flanders they're calling for soldiers,
They're calling for you and for me.
If you can't come along,
Back us up good and strong,
[If you can't cross the pond,
Buy a Liberty Bond],
And we'll drive them back to Germany.

2nd Verse:
Ev'ry day some thousand soldiers
Sail across the sea
To fight for you and me,
To save "Democracy."
The men who can't go over can do some-
  thing, never fear,
They all can volunteer to lick the Germans
  here.
Pro-Germans are a danger,
They are lurking at your door;
So wake up! Now, America, we've got to
  win this war:

Bibliography

Arnold-Forster, Mark. *The World at War*. New York: Stein and Day, 1983.

ASCAP Biographical Dictionary (4th Edition). New York: Bowker, 1980.

Atkinson, Brooks. *Broadway*. New York: Macmillan, 1970.

Bach, Steven. *Marlene Dietrich: Life and Legend*. New York: William Morrow, 1992.

Bailey, Thomas A., and Paul B. Ryan. *Hitler vs. Roosevelt*. New York: Free Press, 1979.

Barnouw, Erik. *The Golden Web: A History of Broadcasting in the United States, 1933–1953*. New York: Oxford University Press, 1968.

Black, Shirley Temple. *Child Star*. New York: McGraw-Hill, 1988.

Brooks, John. *Once in Golconda: A True Drama of Wall Street, 1920–1938*. New York: Norton, 1969.

Burns, James MacGregor. *Roosevelt: The Soldier of Freedom, 1940–1945*. New York: Harcourt Brace Jovanovich, 1970.

Burrows, William E. *Richthofen: A True History of the Red Baron*. New York: Harcourt, Brace & World, 1969.

Catalog of Copyright Entries, 1914–19. Library of Congress. Washington, D.C.: Government Printing Office.

Dalleck, Robert. *Franklin D. Roosevelt and American Foreign Policy, 1932–1945*. New York: Oxford University Press, 1979.

Eisenhower, John D. *Intervention!: The United States and the Mexican Revolution, 1913–1917*. New York: Norton, 1993.

Ewen, David. *Great Men of Popular Song*. Englewood Cliffs, N.J.: Prentice-Hall, 1970.

Farago, Ladislas. *The Game of the Foxes*. New York: David McKay Co., Inc., 1971.

Farnsworth, Marjorie. *The Ziegfeld Follies*. London: Peter Davies, 1956.

Fuld, James J. *The Book of World-Famous Music: Classical, Popular and Folk* (2nd Edition). New York: Dover, 1985.

Garraty, J.A. *Henry Cabot Lodge, a Biography*. New York: Knopf, 1953.

Gilbert, Martin. *The First World War: A Complete History*. New York: Henry Holt, 1994.

Goodwin, Doris Kearns. *No Ordinary Time. Franklin and Eleanor Roosevelt: The Home Front in World War II*. New York: Simon & Shuster, 1994.

Henig, Robin Marante. "Flu Pandemic." *The New York Times Magazine*, Nov. 29, 1992, p. 28ff.

Iriye, Akira. *Power and Culture: The Japanese-American War, 1941–1945*. Cambridge, Mass.: Harvard University Press, 1981.

Karl, Barry D. *The Uneasy State: The United States from 1915 to 1945*. Chicago: University of Chicago Press, 1983.

Kimball, Warren F. *The Most Unsordid Act: Lend-Lease, 1939–1941*. Baltimore: Johns Hopkins University Press, 1969.

Langer, W.L., and S.E. Gleason. *The Undeclared War: 1940–1941*. New York: Harper & Brothers, 1953.

Le Tissier, Tony. "Horst Wessel." *After the Battle* (Number 75). London, England: Battle of Britain Prints International Ltd., 1992.

Lex, Roger, and Frederick Smith. *The Great Song Thesaurus* (2nd edition). New York: Oxford University Press, 1989.

Link, A.S. *Woodrow Wilson and the Progressive Era, 1910–1917*. New York: Harper & Brothers, 1954.

Lissauer, Robert. *Lissauer's Encyclopedia of Popular Music in America: 1888 to the Present*. New York: Paragon House, 1991.

Manchester, William. *The Glory and the Dream* (Volume I). Boston: Little, Brown, 1973.

Mattfeld, Julius. *Variety Music Cavalcade, 1920–1969* (3rd edition). Englewood Cliffs, N.J.: Prentice-Hall, Inc., 1971.

Mau, Hermann, and Helmut Krausnick. *German History, 1933–45*. New York: Frederick Ungar Publishing Co., 1963.

McCabe, John. *George M. Cohan: The Man Who Owned Broadway*. Garden City, N.Y.: Doubleday, 1982.

McKinley, Silas Bent. *Woodrow Wilson: A Biography*. New York: Frederick A. Praeger, 1957.

Middleton, Drew. *Crossroads of Modern Warfare*. Garden City, N.Y.: Doubleday, 1983.

Mitchell, Otis C. *Hitler Over Germany: The Establishment of the Nazi Dictatorship (1918–1934)*. Philadelphia: Institute for the Study of Human Issues, 1983.

Morehouse, Ward. *Matinee Tomorrow: Fifty Years of Our Theater*. New York: Whittlesey House, 1949.

Osgood, R.E. *Ideals and Self-Interest in American Foreign Relations, II*. Chicago: University of Chicago Press, 1953.

Raph, Theodore. *The Songs We Sang: A Treasury of American Popular Music*. New York: A.S. Barnes, 1964.

Sacks, Howard L., and Judith Rose Sacks. *Way Up North in Dixie: A Black Family's Claim to the Confederate Anthem*. Washington, D.C.: Smithsonian Institution Press, 1993.

Shachtman, Tom. *The Phony War, 1939–1940*. New York: Harper & Row, 1982.

Shapiro, Nat, ed. *Popular Music: An Annotated Index of Popular Songs* (Volume II). New York: Adrian Press, 1965.

Shapiro, Nat, and Bruce Pollock, eds. *Popular Music, 1920–1979*. Detroit: Gale Research Co., 1985.

Shirer, William L. *The Nightmare Years, 1930–1940*. Boston: Little, Brown, 1984.

Spencer, Samuel R., Jr. *Decision for War, 1917*. Rindge, N.H.: Richard R. Smith Publisher, Inc., 1953.

Tansill, C.C. *America Goes to War*. Boston: Little, Brown, 1938.

Truman, Harry S. *Memoirs by Harry S. Truman, Volume I: Year of Decisions*. Garden City, N.Y.: Doubleday, 1955.

Turner, E.S. *The Phony War, Britain's Home Front 1939–1940*. New York: St. Martin's, 1961.

Waters, Edward N. *Victor Herbert: A Life in Music*. New York: Macmillan, 1955.

Williams, John R. *This Was Your Hit Parade*. Rockland, Me.: Courier Gazette, Inc., 1972.

Index

The following index comprehensively lists not only song titles, composers, lyricists, publishers, and textual subjects but also (in quotation marks) keywords-in-context of the song lyrics that appear in this book. Superscript numbers follow citations to pages in parts II and III to indicate the column in which a given item appears. Song titles are not enclosed in quotation marks; thus they are distinguished from keywords-in-context. Subjects appear in small capital letters, except when they must be italicized (as in the case of books, films and plays). The occasional enclosure of a part of a lyricist's or composer's name in parentheses indicates that the songwriter copyrighted songs under more than one form of his or her name, as for example by substituting initials for the first and or middle names or by omitting the middle initial.